D X

CAST A LONG SHADOW

CAST A LONG SHADOW

FRANK BONHAM

THORNDIKE
CHIVERS

LIBRARY OF CONGRESS CATALOGING-IN-PUBLICATION DATA

Bonham, Frank.
    Cast a long shadow / by Frank Bonham.
        p. cm. — (Thorndike Press large print western)
    ISBN-13: 978-1-4104-1137-2 (alk. paper)
    ISBN-10: 1-4104-1137-0 (alk. paper)
    1. Large type books. I. Title.
PS3503.O4315C3 2008
813'.54—dc22   2008036541

BRITISH LIBRARY CATALOGUING-IN-PUBLICATION DATA AVAILABLE

Published in 2008 in the U.S. by arrangement with Golden West Literary Agency.
Published in 2009 in the U.K. by arrangement with The Golden West Literary Agency.

U.K. Hardcover: 978 1 408 42167 3 (Chivers Large Print)
U.K. Softcover: 978 1 408 42168 0 (Camden Large Print)

Printed in the United States of America
1 2 3 4 5 6 7 12 11 10 09 08

CAST A LONG SHADOW

CHAPTER ONE

Vallecito was a swing stop on the stage line from the West Texas border to the Panhandle. In ten minutes teams were changed, passengers and mail dealt with, and the stage sent rolling on across the flinty range land. The dust of the northbound's arrival had hardly settled that October day when the shotgun guard blew his copper bugle and the coach swung from the depot and on up the shallow canyon of dun-colored buildings into the prairie . . .

The passenger who had arrived from Kingbolt with no luggage, and a Colt on his hip, came from the washroom behind the station. His name was Artie Judd. He was big, somnolent and slow-moving, not a cowboy by his look, not a businessman — a hard type to peg. He wore a shirt of striped material, like a barber's apron, lavender sleeve-garters, and black trousers stuffed into his boots — on the inner side, Texas style. He looked neither lean enough nor stove-up enough to be a cowpuncher, nor did he appear sufficiently harried to be a rancher in that corner of Texas, where it took a section of grass to fatten a couple of dozen cows.

He walked up to the stationmaster, who was talking to a paunchy, middle-aged man, put his boot on the hub of a wagon, and looked at them. The heavy-set man, who wore a star, glanced at him with cautious interest. He had a yellowish, jaded and somehow sad face.

"Something?" asked the stationmaster.

"What time does the Kingbolt stage come through?" Judd asked.

The stationmaster smiled. "Kingbolt? You just came from there, mister."

The sheriff punched the stage man lightly on the shoulder. "See you later, Howie. Got to feed the animals." He strolled down the boardwalk toward a blocklike building sitting by itself at the front of a large lot.

Judd said to the stationmaster, "All right. I just came from there. In an hour I'll finish my business and head back. When's the stage?"

The other man looked at a silver pocket-watch. "Hour and a half. Do you want a ticket?"

"I've got a ticket — traveling round-trip. What about the westbound stage?"

"To El Paso?"

"To Arizona."

"Same stage. Comes through about five o'clock tonight."

"How much is the fare to Tucson?"

"I'd have to look it up."

Judd waved a hand toward the station. The stage man, with a frown of irritation, went into the building. Judd followed. At his desk, the agent donned spectacles and consulted a schedule.

"Sixty dollars," he said, glancing up.

"Gimme a ticket. One way."

"From here?"

Judd sighed and placed both hands on the man's desk. "If you'd been born any slower, you'd'a been a desert turtle! One ticket *from here.* That is correct. Reckon you can get it written up before five o'clock?"

For a moment the stationmaster's eyes grew tart; then, after a better look into Judd's hard, fleshy features, he muttered and began writing up the ticket.

Artie Judd paid the fare with three gold double-eagles. He folded the ticket and slipped it into the pocket of his striped shirt. But as the other man turned away, Judd caught his arm.

"Oh, uh-know a man named McCool?"

The stationmaster, his face frozen with dislike, said, "I know three men named McCool. Two are in the cemetery and one's in jail."

"The one I want is named Rian."

"You're in luck. That's the live one."

"Live as ever?" Judd said, with a grin.

"Hard to say. Tell better when he hits the street. He was live enough when he went in a year ago. Lord knows the McCools were always live enough for three men, once they'd put away a couple of whiskies. You a friend of Rian's?"

Frowning faintly, Artie Judd pursed his lips. "You might say so. I want to do him a favor. I reckon that makes me a friend, don't it?"

The agent shrugged, and Judd went to the door. For some reason, the agent looked at the gun on Judd's hip. It had the prettiest grips he had ever seen: tortoise shell, with a silver design countersunk into them. The sun glowed amber through the tortoise shell as the man from Kingbolt walked into the light. Artie Judd tucked his hands under his belt and strolled up the street.

In the jail office, as he entered, Sheriff Charlie Crump was just sitting down with a heavy china cup of coffee. A fragrance of chili beans hung in the air, but no food was in sight; Judd supposed he had just fed his prisoners — "the animals," as he called them. The sheriff glanced at him.

"Hello," he said, with dry disinterest.

"George Hughson wrote you about me, sheriff. I'm Artie Judd."

"Allowed you were."

"You can turn McCool loose any time now," Judd said.

"I can, eh?" said the sheriff ironically, looking again at Judd. "You tell Hughson something for me when you go back. I don't like his way of doing things. I've held Mc-Cool a week beyond his sentence on your boss man's say. If he wanted a welcome-home committee on hand when McCool got out, why couldn't he send somebody up on time?"

"Somebody?" Judd smiled. "That would be me. I was busy. First chance I've had to get up here. You'll get your campaign contribution, so what's eating on you?"

"Superintendent!" snorted the sheriff. "You don't look like no stage man to me. What do you know about horses and rolling stock?"

Judd rubbed his chin. "I work more with people," he said. "Mr. Hughson takes care

11

of the other details."

The sheriff drank some coffee and set the cup down. "What kind of shenanigans are you planning?"

"The boss man said to bring McCool his regards."

"Why couldn't the boss man bring them himself?"

"He's busy with his new stage line."

Crump snorted. "Busy running it into the ground, I hear."

Judd regarded him for a moment, then touched the brim of his hat. "Take care, Sheriff. Ready any time you are. Oh — keep his gun. You can send it to him in Arizona."

"Why Arizona?"

"Because that's where he's going from here."

CHAPTER TWO

Rian McCool lay on the jail cot, smoking the cigar he had found on his lunch tray. One arm kinked under his head, he gazed thoughtfully at the ceiling, luxuriously blowing smoke at the beams. He half expected the cigar to explode. On the other hand, he took the gift of a cigar to be significant. Maybe he was going to be turned loose today. In the week since he figured he should have been released, Sheriff Crump had surprised him with a number of little favors, despite their running argument about when his sentence ended. Hard man to figure out.

McCool's finger traced a series of penciled marks on the wall above his bed. It had pleased him to defile public property in this way; also, it had enabled him to count the days. McCool was twenty-three, an inch under six feet and large-boned. He had a snub nose and a wide mouth, with reddish-brown hair that needed cutting. Though his color was pasty from long confinement, he was in good physical condition. He had seen men dissolve into wheezy fatness when they suddenly gave over heavy work to which they were accustomed. Twice a day he had chinned himself on the bars and managed what exercise he could in such tight quarters.

McCool suddenly raised his voice. "Hey, Sheriff!"

A barred door opened and the sheriff came plodding to his cell. "What's the problem?"

With the cigar, the prisoner pointed at the marks on the wall. "I just counted them again, I'm seven days overtime already!"

Crump smiled. "How much ciphering did you have in school, Rian?"

"Enough to learn to count the days in a year."

"Maybe this was leap year."

Knocking ash on the floor, McCool said, "I'll sue you for every extra day you hold me."

"That's fair enough. How much do you figure your valuable time is worth?"

"Fifty dollars a day."

"Is that what George Hughson paid you to break horses for his stage line?" the

14

sheriff asked.

"Don't forget, I had a ranch, too, when I came here."

Crump laughed. "So you did. A ranch that lost so much money you had to close up and break horses to pay your taxes! How's the stogey?" he asked.

Rian looked at it thoughtfully. "I keep wondering how I'll look with powder burns on my face."

"It's a two-bit cigar, son. A going-away present."

Rian rolled to his feet and hastened to the barred door. "Am I getting out?"

With a sad smile, the sheriff nodded. "Any minute now. Rian, I'm sorry — I did hold you past your time. But I was afraid to let you out till your attitude improved."

"My *what?*" Rian stared at him.

"The way you felt about things. Take it from me — if you hit the sidewalk looking for George Hughson to square with him for testifying against you, you'll be back before the horned toads hibernate. Don't do it, Rian. You lost a little time. But you're young. You can make a new start."

McCool took a deep breath. Already his lungs seemed to expand more freely. "My sentence didn't include listening to advice from you," he said. "That would be what they called 'cruel and unusual punishment,' wouldn't it?"

Crump's jaundiced eyes blinked slowly. "Well, you're kind of an unusual prisoner. Got it from your father, I reckon. Or your older brother — may his brawler's soul rest in peace. Unusualness kind of runs in your family, seems like. Every time your father got tanked up, he'd get so unusual it took a dozen men to subdue him so I could arrest him."

Rian turned away to start collecting the few small possessions he had been allowed to keep with him. Pulling a box from under his cot, he threw a frowning glance at the lawman.

"Why didn't you jug some of the men that put him up to his foolishness? Like Tom Baker. Baker got bounced out of Cloverleaf for taking liberties with a bar girl in the sight of the whole saloon. He couldn't make an issue of it, him being a bank manager, or it would have gotten back to his wife. So he told my Old Man the bouncer had been saying he could whip any McCool, including him, with one hand."

Crump frowned. "Is that the way it happened?" he said, seemingly surprised and disturbed.

"That's the way it happened," Rian said

doggedly. "The Old Man couldn't let a slur like that pass, so he came charging into the Cloverleaf and the bouncer belted him with a pool cue. Self-defense."

Crump massaged his flabby cheeks with his fingertips. "It *was* self-defense. Everybody saw your father start the fight."

"A bouncer ought to be able to subdue a sixty-year-old man without a club. Without killing him, at least. Ah, hell — forget it," McCool sighed. "I had some money when I came here. Do I get it back?"

"You'll get it," Sheriff Crump said with a sigh. "About twenty bucks. Pack your stuff while I unlock my safe."

"Wait a minute," McCool said. He walked to the door and gazed earnestly into the lawman's face. "Can I ask you something, off the record?"

"Why not?"

"You don't really think I made that stage team bolt, do you?"

"What's the difference? At the trial you didn't seem to know yourself what you'd done. You were too drunk that night to hit the ground with your hat. It's done and past. Forget it."

Packing, Rian tried to penetrate the black fog of that night which had changed his life.

He remembered clearly the start of it and the end. The end was right here. The start was in a restaurant where he and Abby Burland had had dinner.

Abby was a pretty, gray-eyed widow who was trying to operate a ranch and showing no talent for ranching whatever. Rian soon found the troubles he'd acquired since his father's death augmented by one more complication: he was in love.

At first it had seemed like wonderful good fortune. He and Abby talked about marriage, and a house near town. Rian was breaking horses for George Hughson at the time, while waiting for some of his beef cattle to mature so that he could raise cash for his new year's operations. About all he'd been left at his father's death was a big silver watch and a hatful of delinquent bills.

Though neither he nor Abby had much in the way of land, together they would have had something to build on. He'd reached the point of wondering whether the tiny diamond ring his mother had left on her death ten years ago was a suitable engagement ring.

So that night at the restaurant he produced the ring — duly polished with baking soda — and tried to slip it on her finger. Abby rejected it, startled, then angry. She

18

glanced around, hoping no one had seen. Then she went outside.

He followed her, dazed. "What's wrong, Abby?"

"Well, if you don't know — ! Good heavens! I don't mind, being *friends* with you but —"

Ice began to form in Rian McCool's belly. "What do you mean?"

The idea, it appeared, was that roughhousing and violent death seemed to be occupational hazards of the McCool clan; that it had been rather embarrassing to keep company with him, but she had been lonesome since her husband's death. And that she had been seeing George Hughson lately and —

Shaking with rage and hurt, Rian turned his back and walked off.

At eleven o'clock that night, Rian had traded his mother's engagement ring for the last round of drinks at the saloon, and staggered off to the stage station to find his cot in the harness room, where he was bunking while he broke horses.

Something was going on at the stage depot that night; something he had not been able to cipher out in a year of puzzling.

He recalled seeing the night mail-stage to Alamos, a little four-horse Troy coach, waiting in the yard. There were seldom any passengers for the run. Biff Shackley, the driver, stood beside it in the darkness, apparently ready to travel.

What stopped Rian was the strange light in the stage office — an eerie, flickering blue glow. Even in his drunken state, he was puzzled. There was something peculiar in Shackley's silence, too. He'd never hit it off with Shackley, a glowering bull of a man who doubled as superintendent and once-a-week night driver. But, full of whiskey, Rian forgave him all his failings.

He pulled a pint bottle from his pocket and shook it. The bottle gurgled, so he knew there was some liquor left. He raised it, toastlike, toward Shackley.

"Biff," he called, starting forward. "Hey, Biff — hair of the dog, ole buddy?"

Then he saw the light in the stage station flare higher, and he stopped and stared at it. "Holy cow, Biff — is that a fire in there?" he croaked.

There was an earsplitting explosion beside his head. Orange light blinded him. He heard the horses squeal and stampede out of the yard, with Shackley yelling, "Ho, fools — ho, there!"

An instant later, something landed heavily on Rian's head and that was the end of his evening.

The charge was tampering with U. S. mails, firing a gun in the city limits, being drunk and disorderly. One of the horses had to be destroyed when it stumbled and broke a leg. He could have gotten ten years in Leavenworth. Because he was drunk, he got off with a year.

But what had been going on at the station that night? He had blundered into something. When, on the witness stand, he tried to explain his impressions — the blue light and all — the jury smiled. Alcoholic hallucinations. Nevertheless, he'd like about an hour with George Hughson or Biff Shackley to talk about it.

For Hughson, too, it had been quite a year: taking over the old McCool place at a delinquent tax sale; marrying Abby Burland and acquiring her ranch; selling both of them, and his stage line, and moving to a booming new area on the border, of which Kingbolt was the heart. A big — suspiciously big — year.

You couldn't argue with success, they said. But you could sit down quietly with a man and ask him some questions about how he got successful so fast. This was the first order of business on McCool's calendar — the *only* order, for a man with no money and few talents.

"I'll have to keep your gun, Rian," the sheriff explained as he returned Rian's money and possessions.

"Why?"

"It's the law. You'll get it back in a week. If you should leave town, drop me a card from where you're going."

McCool shrugged. Maybe just as well, he thought. After all, the name's still McCool. "So long, Sheriff," he said.

"So long, Rian. Luck, son."

CHAPTER THREE

Rian stepped into the sunlight and looked at the world. It was beautiful — a clear sky as blue as Indian turquoise; a warm breeze blowing against his face, and miles and miles of open prairie beyond the town. He felt tears fill his eyes. Turning his face up, he let the warm sky pour down on him like a waterfall.

After a moment, carrying his belongings in a roll under his arm, he started toward the stage station. He knew the schedule — it was nearly all he did know about the world, these days — and he wanted to see how far his twenty dollars would take him.

"Well, what do you know?" a man said. "So that's the great McCool."

Rian halted. The man lounged in a recessed window of an adobe building. He was big, bluntly made, with a buttoned collarband shirt of striped material, but no necktie. At his hip was a Colt with striking

23

tortoiseshell grips. The gun made Rian think of the empty holster he carried rolled under his arm. Bullnecked and solid, the stranger had eyebrows thickened with scar tissue like a pug's. He stood up and grinned at Rian.

"It *is* McCool, ain't it?"

"That's right. Who are you?"

"Name of Judd. I work for Frontier Stage Lines. George Hughson sent me. I've got something for you."

Rian's principal emotion was one of disappointment. So that was why Charlie Crump had held him past the day of his release! The sheriff was not exactly a clear-eyed fighting lawman, but Rian had not believed him capable of setting up something like this. He knew now why his gun had not been returned.

Artie Judd handed him a slip of paper, and he took it. It was a printed ticket, with *Tucson, A.T.,* written on it in violet ink. He tucked it into his shirt pocket.

"Thanks," he said, starting on.

Judd put himself in his path. "Not so fast. Are you going?"

"Sure, I'm going."

Again Judd had to block his way. The burly straw boss seemed perplexed that he had not had more trouble with him.

"The stage is at five o'clock," he said sullenly.

"Not my stage," Rian said. "It'll be along in about an hour. I'm going to Kingbolt. I'll turn this one in on it and have about thirty dollars left, I should reckon."

Judd's eyes whetted. On the rim of his vision, Rian could see a few townsmen across the street watching him. He wondered about the sheriff. Had he locked up and ridden away in order not to be dragged into whatever was coming?

Judd caught a thumb in his cartridge belt and rested his hand above his Colt. "Mr. Hughson told me to explain that if you ever come back to Texas, he'll take it to mean you're armed. Because hell-raisers like you ain't needed here. You savvy?"

Rian nodded. "You bet. Thanks, Judd. Nice talking to you."

Again he started toward the stage station. This time Judd's thick fingers closed on his arm and yanked him back.

"Wait a minute, McCool!"

Rian started his swing as he pivoted. His fist came around like a rock whirled at the end of a cord. It smacked into the gunman's mouth with a meaty sound. Judd floundered back into the wall, his mouth loose, eyes out of focus. Blood smeared his wide-spaced front teeth.

Rian did not wait for him to recover. Judd was there to provoke a fight; he carried a gun and had seen to it that Rian did not. As the gunman shook his head to clear it, Rian yanked the gun from its holster and tossed it into the street.

Across the way, a man bawled hoarsely, "McCool's out!" A horse stamped nervously at a hitchrack. A child screeched and ran down a boardwalk.

Big and indestructible, Artie Judd suddenly collected himself and lunged from the wall. Sliding away, Rian smashed a blow to the side of his head and followed it with a fist dug into his kidney. Judd whirled to follow him. He threw a backhand smash at Rian which collided with the side of his head.

Rian's vision blurred. His knees started to give way.

Judd was upon him savagely, ripping short, hard blows at his head. Rian fell, but instantly rolled under a hitchrack and into the street as Judd tried to kick him. He could see the legs of the man who had collected to watch the brawl. He scrambled up, breathless and dazed, the objects around him touched with a soap-bubble shimmer. He saw the gunman duck under the rail to follow him.

Stepping in quickly, Rian drove his knee into Judd's face while he was bent over. Judd sprawled back onto the walk. A pain in Rian's chest stabbed him every time he breathed, making him gasp. One way or another, he knew, this fight was about over.

He ducked under the rack and was set in a wide stance when Judd floundered up, his bloody mouth cursing. Rage shook his judgment. He drove in wildly. Rian ducked under his flailing arms and brought a fist up under his jaw to turn Judd's face up to the sun. The big man's whole body loosened. While he seemed to hang there, McCool sank his fist into his belly, straightened him again with a looping uppercut, then hammered a right with all he had into the massive jaw.

Judd fell back, his arms dropping. His heel caught and he sprawled backward on the walk. He rolled over, hunched up as if to rise, then groaned and relaxed.

Rian slumped against the wall of a building and closed his eyes while the world revolved about him.

When he boarded the stage that afternoon, a handsome Colt gleamed in his holster — Artie Judd's. He had washed up, rested on his old cot, and by stage time was functioning again. He did not see Judd, though he had expected to. A realist, McCool told himself: *I'll see him in Kingbolt.* No doubt about that. Judd, who obviously made his living with a gun, would have to clean up this unfinished business before he could conscientiously resume his trade of journeyman gunman.

All Rian hoped was to see George Hughson and Biff Shackley first.

The afternoon passed in a series of dusty crossroads towns, the sun burning in from the west as the coach traveled toward the border. Rian dozed, awakening when they made a meal stop at sundown.

Ahead, the gullied scenery was breaking up into mountains. Somewhere beyond the mountains was the Big River, and Mexico. He had never been to Kingbolt, but he knew it was on the north bank of the river, and did a prosperous trade with the mines and the ranch communities across the border.

During the night the coach slowed as the road roughened and began to climb. He slept fitfully. Once, it seemed to him that Abby Burland — Abby *Hughson,* rather — sat beside him. She was weeping quietly. "I'm sorry I hurt you, Rian. I shouldn't have led you on —" Another time she was laughing. He had seldom heard her laugh, for she was usually grave, almost shy. And her lips were as red as a saloon girl's when she laughed in harsh mockery.

"You thought I'd marry *you?* You idiot, Rian! You're just as crazy as all the others of your family, aren't you? Oh, excuse me — there aren't any others in your family now, are there? Your face, Rian! It's a scream. You're puckered up to cry, like a little boy."

The curious thing was that there were tears in his eyes when he awoke.

He had the strangest feeling that while he slept he had been given the vision to see her as she truly was; that she had seen the moment coming when he would give her a ring, and had relished it.

Lots to settle in Kingbolt, he thought.

CHAPTER FOUR

In a cool, windy dawn, the stagecoach halted at a small town high in the mountains. Beyond the buildings, Rian glimpsed small cedars and piñons bathed in pink light. There was a pleasant taste of wood smoke in the air. Stiff and tired, he trudged into the station with the other passengers and had a breakfast of flinty corn bread and fried fat-pork. A baggage counter spanned one wall, with a hog-wire partition forming an office at one end of it. Two men stood behind the partition. Rian could hear them talking.

"Now, your petty cash should *never* be counted with the rest," one man was saying. "Otherwise you're counting it twice, don't you see? And this — this item here —"

The speaker was a small man wearing a bowler hat and a suit as black and shiny as a blackbird's wing. He looked energetic and compact, with the wiriness of a man who

30

might have swung a double-bitted axe in his younger years. He seemed to be showing his companion, an older man, how to keep his post-office accounts straight. Probably a postal inspector, Rian conjectured.

When the conductor said, "Five minutes, folks!" the man in the black suit said quickly, "That's it, Henry. You're doing fine. Don't let my nit-picking upset you." He laughed and slapped the postmaster on the back.

Several passengers boarded for Kingbolt. Since it was going to be crowded inside, McCool climbed to the hurricane deck, taking the seat behind the driver. Soon the postal inspector joined him.

"Man alive! Too crowded down there to breathe without jostlin' somebody." He smiled at Rian and offered his hand. "Sylvester Morton." Two gold teeth gleamed when he smiled.

"Rian McCool."

The stage ran on. "Where to?" Morton asked Rian.

"Kingbolt."

"Locating there?"

"Hard to say."

Morton drew a flat bottle of liquor from his coat pocket. He uncorked it, started to drink, then offered it to Rian. "Have a drink?"

Remembering his last drink, Rian shook his head. Morton again started to drink, realized the coach was jouncing so hard he would probably chip a tooth, and frowned. He leaned forward to tap the driver on the shoulder.

"Matt — hand 'em in a bit, eh?"

"Yes, sir. You bet, Mr. Morton," the driver said. He pulled the horses in to a walk.

Rian was pleasantly startled. Ask a stage driver to slow his team for your comfort? Not if you valued your health. At best, you would probably be put off the stage. It gave Rian insight into the power of a postal inspector to bestow or take away mail franchises.

"All right. Thanks," the little man said, and the horses hit the collars again.

"What kind of work do you do?" he asked Rian.

For an instant, Rian was irritated by the man's inquisitiveness. Yet it seemed to grow from genuine interest in him, perhaps a liking. He relaxed.

"I'm a rancher. That is — I was a rancher. My last job was breaking horses for a stage line."

"You're a shade pale for a man who works outdoors."

Rian set his jaw and stared down the road.

32

It swept into a high, rocky pass beyond which he knew there would be a valley. "It's a long story, friend."

"Say no more," said Morton. "I was prying — can't help it sometimes. Reckon I just like people. I was thinking, though," he added, "that if you'd just come out of the hospital, say, I might be able to speak to one of my business acquaintances about you, help you get lined up with a job."

"Thanks anyway. I'm only going to be around a week or so. Collect some money a man owes me, and take off."

Morton leaned toward him, his breath spiced with liquor. "The man wouldn't be Arthur Judd, would he?" At Rian's astounded expression, Morton slapped his thigh and laughed.

Then Rian remembered the gun in his holster. He glanced down at it.

Morton chuckled. "I know George Hughson well, and I've met Artie Judd. What in the world are you doing with his gun?"

In the end, Rian told him most of the story.

"So you're going to Kingbolt to kill Hughson," Morton said gravely.

"No, that's not the idea at all. I'm going to demand some of the money he owes me. He bought my ranch for back taxes, after scaring off all the other possible buyers who might have paid me a fair price, I figure that if he's nervous enough, he might pay me a thousand dollars to go away. He must be nervous, or he wouldn't have sent Judd to flag me off."

"Bosh. You're going there in the hope that Hughson will provoke a fight and you can kill him. You're thinking with your hands, not your head, McCool," he sighed.

"Maybe that's the best way, for a man with a fourth grade education."

Morton was silent. At last he said, "You've come to a fork in the trail, McCool. I came to a fork once, myself . . ." Rian did not prod him; he did not have to. Morton was merely pondering it carefully. "Well, that's neither here nor there. The fact is, you strike me as a man of ability and determination. I hate to see you point your compass in the wrong direction and lose your way."

"It points to Kingbolt, Mr. Morton."

"All right! Agreed. But use your wits. You want your money — you want to square with a man. That's fine. But don't kill him. Break him!"

Rian studied him, frowning. "How?"

"Well . . . for example — you might take a job with Hughson's competitor. Hughson doesn't have a mail contract, you know. But he's trying hard for one, and if he doesn't get it, he'll probably go under."

"Who does have it?"

"Man named Reese — Dan Reese. Churchly old citizen. Not geared for running a stage line in a growing country. His daughter's the businessman of the family, I suspect. But he was there first, and he's had the franchise for years. Then Hughson came. He offered to buy Reese out, but the old man refused. So Hughson went in competition. He's already taken over most of the business. Whatever else you can say about George Hughson, he gets the job done — which is more than the Reeses are doing, unfortunately."

Rian smiled wryly. "So I take a job breaking horses for Dan Reese. How does that hurt Hughson?"

Morton sighed. Lowering his voice, he said, "I can't take sides in the awarding of a mail contract, you understand. In fact, when Reese's franchise comes up for renewal, I may have to recommend termination in favor of Hughson's line. *But —*" he raised his forefinger portentously — "suppose you took a job with the Reeses and got their line moving again. Then I'd be justified in approving their renewal."

Rian rubbed his jaw, a warm interest

spreading through him. "I see . . ."

With a dry chuckle, the postal inspector said, "Hughson *might* be able to sell out before his creditors pounced. But I doubt it. Just between you and me, he and his lovely young wife are up to their eyeballs in debt."

The stage topped a divide. Below them spread a wide and golden plain. In the heart of it, a river glinted in a haze of greenery. A few miles south of the mountains lay a town, its environs patterned with irrigated fields. Smoke hung above the area.

Excitement began to pound in McCool. *Hughson and his lovely wife.* A chance to hang the man's hide on a fence — to show Abby that the name McCool did not necessarily imply stupidity and impoverishment.

Morton was saying, "Of course, you'd have to make a deal with the Reeses. Can't expect to break horses or drive for them and make any money. Insist on a partnership."

Rian bit his lip. The rub, always the rub. But a partnership with what? "I've got fifty-one-dollars, Mr. Morton," he sighed.

"And Artie Judd's gun. The Reeses need that more than they need money. They've had a lot of hard luck with their rolling stock: coaches running off the grade, horses getting lost. Maybe it's just coincidence. But a young man able to disarm Artie Judd might be able to pull them through. Like to see you try," he said.

Rian drew the gun and looked at it. When he cocked it, the hammer would not stay back; the sear had been filed off for fast firing. He reholstered the gun.

Morton removed his black bowler hat. From the lining he drew a little leather packet of business cards. He extracted one and returned the rest. "I'll write a few words on this when the stage stops," he said. "Show it to Dan Reese — no, to his daughter. She's the brains of the outfit. Maybe it'll help."

As Rian looked at the little white pasteboard which could make a total change in his life, a warmth of gratitude spilled through him. He gripped Morton's hand.

"Mr. Morton, I — I don't know how —"

Morton drew his hand away, embarrassed. "Tut, tut! Just pointing out things you're too close to to see for yourself. Will you take one more word of advice?"

Rian nodded, his eyes eager.

Morton's chin tilted up a little, his voice grew sonorous. "Be true to yourself — decide what you're going to do, *then don't let anything stop you.* Nothing! Nobody in this world really gives a damn whether you sink or swim; that's the big lesson. So see to it that faint-heartedness doesn't betray you when the chips are down."

It was a little bewildering. Rian was not sure he got the message. But the words, *Be true to yourself,* burned in his mind like the after-image of a strong light stared at too long.

By God! he thought. *I never have been true to myself. I've let them discount me — even in my own eyes.* He seemed to glimpse success like a candle at the end of a long corridor lined by a hundred dark and sinister doors. He felt absolutely sure of reaching the end of the corridor.

At the first swing-stop, Morton scribbled on the back of the card and handed it to Rian.

This will introduce Mr. Rian McCool, a personal friend. Any favor extended to him will be a favor to me . . .

At last the stage road hit the valley and they rushed through golden, stirrup-high grass toward a town a couple of miles ahead. Morton leaned toward him.

"After you get lined up with a job, tear up the card. Wouldn't make me look good if anybody asked *why* I gave it to you. You and I know it's an act of friendship, right?"

"Of course," Rian said, nodding.

Morton pulled a buckskin purse from his pocket, glanced into it and gave an embarrassed laugh. "Pshaw! How do you like that? Two dollars in my pocket! I've got a rather large check in my valise, but I hate to hit a postmaster with it. And the bank will be closed." He closed the purse with a snap.

"Say! As long as we'll both be around town until I leave on the eleven o'clock stage, maybe you'd loan me fifty dollars for the evening? I'll meet you at the Pastime Bar at ten-thirty and pay you back. By that time I'll run into somebody who'll cash it without any embarrassment to me."

Fifty dollars! Rian knew he had only fifty-one dollars in his pocket. He hesitated. Either this little man was a liar and a fraud, or he was a magician who had touched his future with gold. For fifty dollars he could find out.

"What the hell!" he said. "For a friend?" He dug the coins from his pocket, finding he had nearly two dollars left after giving Morton the fifty.

The postal inspector slapped Rian's knee as he pocketed the money. "Good boy," he said.

Now the stage was rolling into the heart of a booming adobe metropolis. It slowed for the traffic of buggies, pedestrians, and dogs. Many Mexicans were on the street in their huge *jipi*-straw sombreros and white pajamalike clothing. Freight wagons rumbled along the scarred dirt streets, while cowboys jogged aside and a dray loaded with beer barrels pulled over to let the coach rattle past. On the walks were well-dressed ladies and businessmen in dark suits.

Rian cringed. This was a prosperous town, with many irons in the fire. And Rian Mc-Cool, jailbird and horse-breaker, was going to try to bluff it! He had nothing to sell but nerve. Inwardly, he quaked.

The stage rocked to a halt in a stage yard. Rian glanced at Morton, needing reassurance. The little man smiled and whispered:

" 'This above all — to thine own self be true — !' "

They gripped hands. "Ten-thirty — Pastime Bar!" said Morton.

Rian breathed deeply. Then, with no baggage but Artie Judd's six-gun, he dropped down and set his feet in the earth of his new life.

CHAPTER FIVE

Waiting nervously in their town buggy, the Hughsons saw the stagecoach coming down the street. "There it is!" Abby Hughson exclaimed. She was a small, beautifully formed girl with creamy skin and lustrous black hair. Her skin was naturally tawny, her teeth very white.

At her side, her husband glanced impatiently at her. "For God's sake, don't sound so eager," he said. "We're here to ask Morton to dinner. He isn't the President, you know."

Abby looked at him reproachfully. "Perhaps I'm eager because it's my money we stand to lose if we go under."

George Hughson smiled. He was tall and muscular in a gray suit, with a dove-gray Stetson placed on the side of his head. He wore a neat dark mustache. There was a look of solidness to George Hughson, an air of importance and reliability. But Abby had seen the mask come off. In the bedroom, that first night, and every time he toted up profits and losses and realized that with all his solidness and deep-voiced bluff, he was losing ground in this too-fast-paced gamble.

Hughson said in a pleasant, almost affectionate voice, "Oh, come now, Abby. You know better than that. 'Your' money? Not according to the laws of the great State of Texas. It's *our* money, ever since the first night I took you to bed."

His language embarrassed her; for an instant her eyes fell. Looking at her hands clenched in her lap, she said, "I'm glad you've said it, at last. That was the only reason you married me, wasn't it? For a grubstake."

Hughson chuckled. "Let's just say that if *two* girls like you had thrown themselves at me — equally pretty — I'd have married the one with the ranch. In other words, I didn't hold your ranch against you."

Tears filled her eyes as she looked up. "I suppose you think you could divorce me now and leave me with nothing but a settlement. Well, you can't!"

Hughson sighed. "Don't be silly. And for God's sake, don't get your eyes and nose red, or you'll tout Morton off coming to dinner. You're going to feed him and laugh

42

at his backwoods jokes — that's your department. Then he's going to have brandy and cigars and play a little poker — that's mine. And when he leaves, we can practically list a mail contract among our assets."

Abby sniffed. "You said that six months ago. But the Reeses are still in business. An old man and a girl — are they too much for you, George?"

Hughson, smiling, rested his hand on her leg. Abby caught her breath as his fingers dug into the nerves above her knee.

"I can handle the Reeses if you do your part. I handled McCool, didn't I? Now, are you going to dry your eyes and charm Mr. Morton?"

Abby's mouth had dropped open as she stared at the coach swinging into the yard in a nutmeg fog of dust. *"George!"* she whispered.

Hughson twisted to stare at the coach. Then he saw Rian McCool standing up as he prepared to dismount.

"That idiot, Judd!" he groaned. He bit his lip, thinking quickly. "All right — nothing's changed. I'll deal with McCool. Morton's coming to dinner. That's all that concerns you. Ready?"

She looked at him for strength. Some of her shock dissipated as she saw his cool-

43

ness. He stepped down and reached a hand up to help her.

As she stepped onto the boardwalk, an elderly man and a young woman hurried by them into the stage yard. Daniel Reese and Justina — there on the same business that brought the Hughsons. Hughson chuckled as he gazed after them.

"God help Morton! They're probably going to rope him and drag him off like a steer! Why don't you wait here?" he suggested. "There's no use in our looking too eager."

For a moment there was confusion in the stage yard, the tired team being unlatched from the tugs, baggage being unearthed from the rear luggage boot, the express box tossed down by the conductor. A dozen townsmen had gathered to meet travelers or to watch the excitement. In this crowd, Hughson found it easy to take a place beside Justina Reese, out of Abby's view. When the girl glanced at him, he smiled and tipped his hat.

"Meeting someone, Miss Justina?"

"Oh, not really. Just looking for a package." The girl smiled. She hated him, he knew, but she wouldn't let her feelings show. She was a girl who knew how to play her cards.

Hughson liked that about her. She was really quite lovely, too: a reddish blonde with braids arranged like plaited gold wire, and the golden look of healthy girls who spend much time in the sun. She looked somewhat flushed with excitement. He saw her father glaring at him, a tough-looking little man with ram's-horn mustaches, shaggy brows, and the amber eyes of a mountain lion. The look meant nothing. He was stupid and completely inept. He actually sang hymns in the back room when he was worried!

"I wish you people would think about retiring and enjoying the good things," Hughson said. "My offer to buy you out still stands."

"Havin' troubles, are you?" old Daniel Reese leered.

Before Hughson could answer, Sylvester Morton was coming toward them. Hughson quickly stepped forward and offered his hand. At the same moment, Justina put herself in Morton's path. The postal inspector looked surprised and bewildered, glancing from one to the other. Then he smiled, shook hands with Hughson, nodded pleasantly to the girl.

"I have my turnout," Hughson said quickly. "Mrs. Hughson will be heartbroken if you don't dine with us —"

Justina laughed, a musical sound with throatiness in it. "Don't listen to him, Mr. Morton! Father and I regard your visits as the high points of our year. We'd be *so* pleased —"

Morton said, "Folks, you're all too kind, but I have a previous engagement. Besides, I leave at eleven o'clock."

"Brandy and cigars then, before you leave —" Hughson pressed him.

Morton bit his lip. "Well . . . all right. Ten o'clock?"

"Fine — at my office. I'll have you on the stage when it leaves."

Morton hurried into the stage office. The Reeses, disappointed, moved off.

Bracing himself, Hughson turned to look at the young fellow who had stood in the background all the while. Rian McCool was gazing steadily at him. He looked pallid but fit. Beside his mouth were two deep, bitter lines he did not remember. There was a change in the way he looked at a man, too — a cold intensification of a certain natural bluntness.

"Artie Judd sent his best," McCool remarked easily.

"His best," said Hughson calmly, "is none too good."

"Neither is mine," McCool replied. "Be sure you don't bring out the worst in me."

Hughson saw the gun in his holster. He could only speculate on what had taken place in Vallecito. Dead or alive, Judd had come off second best. What he knew, as surely as he knew anything, was that Mc-Cool had to be killed or bought off.

As McCool started to pass, Hughson spoke.

"What's your hurry? We'll only have to hunt each other up later and say what's on our minds."

He turned and walked into the stage station without a backward glance, and Mc-Cool started to follow. Then he halted, with a dark look of anger. The way men like Hughson — the takers of this world — made their moves with such high-chinned confidence. It galled him almost as much as the way his own kind, the natural-born givers, frisked along after them like lap dogs!

Yet Hughson was right. What was to be said might as well be said early as late. He followed him.

Hughson's office, behind the baggage room, contained an oak desk, some cabinets and a cuspidor, on a checkered linoleum floor. The stage man sat down and took a cigar from a box in a drawer. Frowning, he struck a match and puffed the cigar to life. While he did so, McCool stood by the door watching him.

Hughson blew smoke at the ceiling. "Now then," he said. "How did you get Artie's gun?"

"Aren't you going to ask me to sit down?" McCool grinned cynically.

Hughson waved his hand. "Get comfortable. I'm sorry."

"The hell you are. You're a damned poor actor. But I don't know how to fence either — or whatever they call it — so I'll just hack away with a blunt cleaver and see if I can get through to you. I got Judd's gun by being a little faster and a lot smarter than he is. I'm banking that I'm smarter than you are, too. And I'll bet I can sink my teeth deeper. I won't be easy to shake off."

Hughson rolled the cigar in his teeth.

"So maybe you'd better pay me what that ranch was worth," McCool suggested. "Then I'll leave you alone."

"What *was* it worth? Out of curiosity, I mean."

"Twenty-five hundred dollars."

The heavy lids of Hughson's eyes descended, then raised, and he regarded McCool through a somber mask of contempt. "What makes you think you've got that much nuisance value to me?"

"I'm selling land, not nuisance value. I'll knock off five hundred dollars," McCool said.

"For what?"

Rian grinned, his expression brash. It made Hughson think of a barefisted slugger coming off the ropes with a bloody face but a reckless glint in his eyes.

"For cash. Put two thousand dollars in my pocket and you'll never see me again."

"And if I don't?"

"Then," McCool told him, "you'll be so sick of seeing me a month from now that you'll pay three thousand."

Hughson tilted his face up and blew smoke at the ceiling. "No deal."

"So you're broke already."

"What makes you think so?"

"I told you I was smart, didn't I? I know as much about your business as you know yourself — maybe more. And I'm going to break you like a stick, and probably get your wife in the bargain."

He turned and opened the door, but lingered before going out. Hughson watched him, pondering. Something had happened to that fellow in jail. He'd gotten religion or something; had a kind of prideful confidence he'd never shown before. The change in him both alarmed and angered George Hughson. His glance dropped to the drawer, still open, from which he had taken the cigar. A bronze-framed Colt lay behind the cigar box. A rush of blood to his head dizzied him for a moment.

Why not kill him? he thought breathlessly. *All I would have to tell Marshal Fowley is: "The fool came charging in here yelling he was going to kill me!"*

His hand closed on the revolver, his eyes on the back of McCool's old blue jacket. But the shaggy red head turned abruptly and McCool was regarding him curiously. Hughson cautiously drew his hand from the drawer.

"You're a damned fool," he said. "You never broke anything but a horse in your life, and you won't break me. If you're still around town in the morning, you'll be asking for a fight in a ring where we wear brass knuckles and the bell's broken."

Rian smacked his fist against his palm. "Ah!" he said. "The kind of fight I like best."

"But probably not the kind of odds," retorted Hughson.

As soon as the door had closed behind McCool, Hughson left his desk and opened a door which gave onto the stage yard in the rear. Before the stage barn, a deep-chested man with the coarse build of a laborer, wearing brown suit pants and a clean shirt, was supervising the care of the coach and team.

He shouted at the Mexican hostlers who were handling the team. "If I catch you again turning a team in to roll without you cool it out first, I'll break your necks! That's the last time I aim to tell you."

"Biff," Hughson called quickly.

Biff Shackley, his superintendent, turned with a scowl. He was a crudely made man with an enormous chest and thick arms. His features were red and intemperate, but his gray hair was neatly cut and brushed. Without a word, he walked to the little porch behind Hughson's office.

"What's the matter?" he asked.

"There's a man just leaving the station," Hughson said. "Young fellow, about six feet, wearing a denim jacket. See him?"

Shackley's eyes quested through the group of passengers clotted around the street gate. "Yeah. Kind of red hair?" he muttered. "Say, is that — ?" The big man's features sagged.

Hughson nodded. "Keep an eye on him, Biff. I want to see where he goes. Don't let him see you."

Shackley passed a hand over his hair, dazed. "But I thought Artie —"

"So did I," Hughson said drily. "That's Artie's gun in his holster. Don't ask me," he said sharply. "Follow him, then come back and *tell* me."

CHAPTER SIX

McCool had walked a hundred feet down the warm, dusty street, the sun slanting in deeply from the west, when he realized a man was blocking his path. He halted and threw a quick look at him. Immediately he saw the marshal's shield on his coat.

The man was tall, with a dry, hard-fleshed look, and he wore full sandy mustaches. He was dressed in a gray suit, dark tie with a loose knot, a cityish gray felt hat resting on the side of his head.

"What's your name?" he asked sharply.

McCool smiled. "Judd," he said. "Artie Judd."

The marshal looked him over carefully. "It's Judd's gun, all right," he said.

"The fact of the matter is," Rian told him. "I met Judd in Vallecito and he asked me to bring his gun on for him. He said he'd be along later. What's *your* name?" he asked pleasantly.

"Marshal Fowley. I don't have a lot of use for Judd, but I don't need any smart-talking citizens like you either. I'm asking once more what your name is. Then I'll take you in for questioning."

"Rian McCool."

"How did you get the gun, McCool?"

"Artie pulled it on me," Rian said frankly. "One thing led to another and — well, he decided to rest up before he came back. He'll be along tomorrow, more than likely. Say, is there a good, cheap hotel in this town?" he asked.

"There's a good one, and there's a cheap one. Judging by the cut of your clothes, I think you might like the cheap one better. It's the Frontera Hotel. What's your business in town?"

"I'm not sure yet. I'll look into the prospects and invest where it looks like I'd get the best return."

Marshal Fowley's wide jaws bulged a little as the muscles worked. He said, "I'll probably see you later," and passed on.

Rian walked another fifty feet, glanced back, and saw him enter the stage station.

At the Frontera Hotel, he took a dollar-fifty room. It was a sort of kennel under an outside stairway, with a door to the hotel backhouse and an inside door on a dingy

54

hallway. It was furnished with a sour-smelling cot, a granite-ware washpan, and a baking powder can full of soft soap.

He lay down for a moment, resting his arm across his eyes.

His thoughts swung to Morton. Would he ever see him again? Ever see his fifty bucks? Somehow it did not seem to matter whether Morton was an artful con man or not. What he had spoken was the truth. And that, by God, was that you were as good as you made people think you were. He had noticed a sort of flinching in the eyes of George Hughson just now. It did not mean that he would back off, but it signified that he saw a change in him.

What Morton had sold him for fifty dollars was the knowledge that the thing to do with your hat was not to tip it to everybody, but to cock it over your eyes and barge right in.

He slept for a few minutes. Waking, he found himself thinking of the marshal. No question but what Fowley would come to him eventually and take the gun away from him. He would have to surrender it or go to war with the law. Scratching his shaggy head, he sat on the edge of the cot and held the revolver in his hands. His mouth slowly broke into a grin. He flipped out the loading gate, punched the heavy cartridges onto the cot, then examined the gun hammer. He shoved the gun under the pillow and left the room.

He returned in ten minutes with a fifty-cent whetstone. He took off a sixteenth of an inch. When he was finished, the hammer looked about the same, but the firing pin was too short to reach the cap. The gun would not fire. Unless Judd, who knew his weapon as a man knew his wife's lips, noticed the change and had a new firing pin installed.

Still, it was worth trying.

Marshal Fowley was in his office when Rian walked in a few minutes later. He was going through some old warrants. Seeing Rian, he started and quickly shoved the whole batch into a drawer. *He's looking for something on me,* thought Rian.

He laid the Colt on Fowley's desk, smiling wryly.

"Why fight it?" he said. "It's Judd's gun. I don't think it's very lucky anyhow. Give it to him with my regards."

Fowley smiled and picked the gun up. He hefted it, then dropped it in a drawer. "Mc-Cool, you've got a good head. A much better one than I was just hearing from an old friend of yours."

"Hughson? What'd he tell you?"

"I don't discuss such business. But I'll say this: a man that's done his time and behaves himself, draws the same amount of water in my town as a man that's never been in trouble."

"I'll shake on that, Marshal," said Rian. They shook hands and he left.

According to the hotel clerk, the office of the Empire Stage Lines — Hughson's competitor — was on an intersecting street a block south of the center of town. Rian was strolling in that direction when he saw a young woman come from a store building and start down the walk.

She moved with short strides, and there was a vitality about the brisk sway of her skirts that brought him fully awake. He recognized her by her reddish-gold hair: Justina Reese.

Rian stepped up his stride, and just before he caught her she glanced around to see who was following. Then she looked straight ahead, continued on to the corner, and turned right.

Rian followed. She glanced at him again as he caught up. When he did not pass her, she slowed down. Rian slowed, too. She gave him a quick stare of vexation and he smiled. She was remarkably attractive, her features delicately cast but without any Dresden-china look about them. She took his measure frankly, then stopped.

When Rian stopped also, she spoke calmly. "I can raise my voice, mister, and ten men will be beating you in half a minute," she said.

Rian removed his hat. "Yes, ma'am, but then you wouldn't get to meet the man that's going to knock George Hughson into a cocked hat. And that'd be a shame, wouldn't it?"

Justina frowned, started to speak, then bit her lip and hesitated. "Who are you?" she asked.

Rian glanced around, then handed her Morton's business card.

"My name's McCool. But let's think of me as a friend of Sylvester Morton's instead of plain old Rian McCool."

The girl read the card and the message on its reverse side. Then she gave him a smile which caused his flesh to crawl. It flashed intimacy, eagerness and admiration. "Any friend of Mr. Morton's," she said enthusiastically, "is certainly a friend of Father's and mine. We'll be having dinner in just a few minutes. Won't you join us?"

"You'd better believe I will," Rian said with a grin.

CHAPTER SEVEN

There was a small stage depot on a corner, a gate to a stage yard behind it, and half the number of corrals a going stage line needed for its main terminus. Under a shelter was a single coach, an old Concord wagon. Not a hostler was in sight.

All the brass and nickel brightwork Rian discerned was dull; the harness hanging on wall pegs cried out for saddle soap. As they walked to a small, flat-roofed adobe building at the rear of the yard, he picked up two or three stones and a chunk of black iron lopped off a horseshoe when the shoer fitted a horse.

Justina gazed at him uneasily. "What is it? Are you collecting ammunition for a slingshot, Mr. McCool?"

"No, ma'am. But I'm a horseman, and I hate to think of a horse getting any of this trash lodged in a frog of its hoof."

"Oh," the girl said.

The building at the rear was the Reeses' small home. A wonderful fragrance of home-cooked food filled it. After a year of jail cooking Rian almost broke down. He met the amber-eyed, tough-looking little man he had seen with Justina at the stage station: Dan Reese, her father.

Shaking hands with Reese was somehow puzzling. He had the grim face and leathery look of a retired town-tamer. But his grip was pulpy, and his eyes shied from direct contact. When you confronted him, you felt his diffidence and knew you were shaking hands with a dreamer. Just the sort of man George Hughson ate raw, without seasoning.

Old Dan Reese poured elderberry wine for McCool, who drank it thinking it would have been just right on pancakes, while he yearned for the bite of whiskey. They ate, Justina chatering brightly and Rian trying to decide how a man put pressure on people like these. But only pressure would buy him the percentage of their company, which he needed.

"Tell us about Mr. Morton," Justina murmured as they got settled in the parlor after dinner. "He seems *such* a nice man."

Rian nodded. "They don't come better than Sylvester."

"And what is your business, Mr. Mc-Cool?" asked the girl.

"I'm a stage man," Rian said, nodding and trying to believe it.

"Oh?" The girl and her father exchanged glances, puzzled. She gave a little laugh. "I hope you aren't going into competition with us?"

"No, no! The truth of the matter is, I'm thinking of buying with an existing stage line."

"But — but you said something about tangling with Mr. Hughson."

"Yes. There isn't room for three lines. Morton thinks there isn't actually room for two. I told him what was on my mind, and he said, 'Talk to George Hughson and Dan Reese. One of them might be willing to sell you an interest.' But I know Hughson and I don't like him. So I thought I'd talk to you."

"Well, well," the girl said after a moment.

Dan Reese cleared his throat. "How much money do you have to invest?" he asked in his furry old-man's voice.

"Not much. But I know staging, I'm ambitious, and I don't mind hard work."

Justina smiled with the expression of a woman who feared to hurt someone's feelings. "Perhaps," she said, "what you're looking for is a job rather than a partner, Mr.

McCool."

Rian's snub features crinkled with good humor. "No," he said, "I've held jobs, as well as running my own outfit, and you can take it from me there's no future in jobs. So I thought I'd put it to you just that way: I'll pull this stage line out of the red and practically guarantee you'll get your mail contract renewed. All it'll cost you is one-third interest. And I'll throw in a note for $1,000, payable six months after we get that renewal."

"You must be joking!" Dan Reese said. "Why, I've got thousands in this line!"

Leaning forward, Rian rested his elbows on his knees and linked his fingers. "I know. But how much is the line *worth?* Considering that you're losing money, and about to lose your mail contract?"

Justina gasped. "How do you know that?"

"Just surmising from things I've heard. It doesn't seem to me like a line that's in debt up to its hocks is worth much more than I'm offering."

The girl sat up straight, her clear, calm features weighing it. "No," she said. "It isn't. If we lose that contract, it isn't worth anything. We owe so much — and so many people owe us — that we wouldn't survive a month."

Rian's eyebrows raised. "There's money

owed you?"

"Heavens, yes! Potter's Feed owes over six hundred dollars for *higar* cane we've hauled in our freight wagons."

"I didn't see any freight wagons," McCool said, frowning.

The Reeses glanced at each other.

"There was a slide on the Johnson grade," Justina murmured. "The wagons were — well, we hope to have them back in shape soon."

"Who's your superintendent?"

"A man named Brogan. But he's stationed in Frontera, at the other end of the line."

Rian shook his head. "A super should live on the premises. I don't know," he sighed. "Maybe this outfit is past saving."

"Oh, no! It's really not so bad as that. And a man like yourself who understands business practices and all — who knows, perhaps we could have it running like a top in no time." She smiled dazzlingly.

My God! Rian thought. *Now* she's *selling the idea to* me!

Prowling to the door, he gazed out on the stage yard. He kicked the screen door open to see better. It was growing dark now. He squinted. A man on the sidewalk was standing beside the station. Perhaps he did not know he was visible; a night light in the office silhouetted his bearish profile.

Biff Schackley! Not a question in the world! One of the men who had put him in jail for a year and stripped the hide off him.

Rian tingled as he turned back. "I'll tell you what. Out of fairness to both parties, I think I ought to take the books to my hotel room and look them over. See whether I think I can help. Find out who owes you how much, all that kind of thing. I'll bring them back in the morning. If we're all in agreement, we'll have some papers drawn up."

Justina bit her lip. Her father said, "Now see here —" but the girl rose and came toward Rian. She peered into his eyes. Then she gave a soft laugh.

"It's insane!" she said. "I wouldn't be surprised if you've never so much as dusted off a stagecoach in your life."

Rian grinned. "I've dusted off a few men though, Miss Justina. And that's your real problem, isn't it?"

She did not answer. "Father and I will talk it over. You may take the books with you. Unless we come to our senses overnight, we'll probably cut you in for your outrageous third interest."

He put out his hand. She gave him hers, slender and nervous-feeling, then quickly drew it away. Rian turned and shook hands with Dan Reese. The old man began telling him about some of their troubles with wagons and stages rolling off grades. He sounded plaintive and confused.

"How are you going to fight people like that?" he asked. "The law's no help. And I'm too old to deal with the scoundrels myself."

Rian patted his shoulder. "I'm not too old, Dan," he said. "I'm just the right age. That reminds me — you wouldn't have an old hogleg you could spare for a few days, would you? I came here without so much as a blowgun."

"Sure would!"

Dan Reese left the room. Rian heard him opening and closing drawers. After a few minutes he returned. "Swore I left it in my dresser," he said. "I'll find it tomorrow and loan it to you."

"That's all right."

Rian and the girl walked from the house to the stage office. Justina went in and came out carrying a heavy ledger. Rian took the book from her hands. The moment was dark and intimate. She smiled and looked down.

Then, around the corner of the building, he heard a man clear his throat. He listened, but the girl seemed not to have heard the sound.

"I'm afraid there's more bad news than good in the book," she said. "But do read it and tell us what you think. Good night now."

He watched her return to the house. She walked a little more briskly than before, he thought. He pictured the scene in the parlor as they discussed him: con man or savior? The more he thought about it, the more he believed he would earn his money around this yard. Starting now.

He opened the latch of the gate, moved through, and turned to close it. Ten feet away, in the alcoved rectangle of the depot's door, he made out the shape of a man standing in the shadows.

Normally, a man would turn left from the gate and head toward the main street. Probably that was what Biff Shackley had counted on. Whistling, Rian turned right and moved along close to the wall of the station, approaching Shackley. The superintendent pressed back, trying to keep out of sight.

You're a hell of a tracker, thought Rian. He could actually smell the man — whiskey, sweat, and some kind of sweet toilet water.

As he came abreast of Shackley, he groped

in his pocket for a match. Then, feigning surprise at the big man's presence, he said, "Say, friend — hold this book a minute, will you?"

He thrust the big volume against Shackley's belly. Shackley automatically put his hands under it, as though to carry a baby. Rian turned calmly, cocked his fist, and drove clean and hard to his chin.

Shackley groaned as his head collided with the door. Rian hit him again. Quickly he caught the book as the superintendent dropped it. Shackley fell to his knees, making coughing sounds, blundering forward in an attempt to catch Rian around the knees. Rian drove his knee into Shackley's face. The man sprawled sideways across the walk.

Rian set the book down and hauled Shackley to his feet, staggering. He was surprised at his bulk. He was a big man, no mistake. But he was hurt, and Rian jammed him against the wall, held him with one hand, and cocked his right.

"What's the matter, Biff? Horses knock all your brains out?" he growled.

Shackley's eyes were half closed; his nose was streaming blood. He raised a hand limply and pawed at Rian's shoulder.

"Compliments of the Vallecito jail," Rian

said. "What *was* going on in the office that night?"

Shackley made a tongueless muttering.

"There was kerosene burning, wasn't there?" Rian said. "A pan of kerosene. I've thought about it for a year, and that's all I know that would burn blue and yellow. How come? Were you burning the place down for the insurance?"

Suddenly Shackley gathered himself and shoved him away. He came at him with a slow, loose swing. Rian went under the blow and smashed back at the super's face. His knuckles bit through Shackley's lips. Shackley stumbled aside, clutched at the wall, and went down again.

Rian took his gun and tossed it into a horse trough. Then he picked up the ledger, rolled Shackley's head with his foot, and said:

"Night, old buddy. Come see me at the Frontera. That's where I'm staying, if that's what the boss man sent you to find out."

In his room Rian washed up and found he had stripped some hide off his knuckles. Shackley would be out of his mind with rage. He was a muscular bull of a man, and even considered himself rather sly. And he'd been suckered into a trap like that!

Smiling to himself, Rian sat down to look

at the books of the Empire Stage Company. Before he started, he looked at his watch. Eight-thirty. Two hours till his date with Sylvester Morton at the Pastime Bar.

CHAPTER EIGHT

At nine o'clock, George Hughson heard the door of Biff Shackley's room creak open. Quickly, Hughson rolled to his feet and started out the side door to hurry to the superintendent's room at the end of the long stage building. He had been waiting an hour, wondering what had happened, and chewing on his visit with Rian McCool.

"I know as much about your business as you do!" the fool had bragged. It was a lie, of course. But what had put that particular lie into his mouth?

Hughson remembered seeing McCool talking with Sylvester Morton, the postal inspector. Any connection there? His mind handled all these factors restlessly and without satisfaction. Something was going on, and he must know what it was damned soon. He was relieved that Shackley had finally come back.

Hughson's muscular body slipped through

the door into the yard. He turned left and strode along the wall to the rear of the building. As he passed the super's window, he saw a lamp flare up behind the grimy panes. The door was still open. He hit the doorjamb with his boot, in lieu of knocking, and moved inside.

The room, dimly lighted by a wall lamp, smelled of liniment, whiskey, and sweat — a hard-living bachelor's bedroom, festooned with cobwebs in all the corners. On the scarred dresser were arrayed bottles of every kind — liquor, hair tonic, patent medicines. Shackley was bent over a washbowl on the commode.

"What kept you?" Hughson asked.

Shackley grunted something unintelligible. He scooped water up in his hands, buried his face in it, and snorted so that the spray flew. Hughson's eyes suddenly narrowed. He walked up behind Shackley and turned him angrily.

"Have you been boozing it up?" he demanded.

Then he caught his breath. Shackley's mouth was swollen as though wild bees had stung it. One eye was puffed. Tears of rage brimmed in his whiskey-fighter's eyes.

"So help me — !" he choked.

"What happened?" Hughson reached for

a bottle on the dresser. He drew the cork from a pint of Mountain Brook and put it in Shackley's hands.

Shackley drank deeply. Then he sat on the edge of his cot and told the story. His words were garbled by his puffed lips. He stopped twice and took some more whiskey.

"What kind of book?" Hughson muttered.

"A ledger," Shackley said.

"A *ledger?* Why?"

Shackley shook his head. "I heard the girl say something about 'bad news' in the book, but he could look it over and tell them what he thought —"

With a machinelike click, facts began snapping into place in the stage man's mind. He was shocked, first; then filled with a kind of joyful rage.

"That stupid jailbird!" he said. "He's planning to buy in with Dan Reese. How do you like that, Biff? He's going into competition with me!"

Shackley did not seem to know or care what he was saying. From pegs beside the door, he lifted down an old revolving carbine. He sat on the bed and used an oiled rag to dust it. He breathed loudly through his nose. Hughson reached down and took the rifle from his hands.

When Shackley rose, a frown of anger in

his eyes, Hughson smiled: "Not so fast, Biff. We'll serve him with an apple in his mouth, but not that way. We don't need to get ourselves hung, do we?"

Shackley reached for the gun again, and Hughson put it behind him, chuckling.

"I like your spirit, Biff, even if you don't show much brains sometimes. Now listen. He's got a date with Morton at the Pastime tonight. I'll try to work things so that he leaves by the back door. I want you to pick up Spence and a couple of men you can count on, and be in the alley to meet him. Take him out of town and give him a working over he won't forget."

It was getting through to Shackley now. Dabbing at a cut on his face with a towel, he growled, "He won't come back. By God, he won't!"

Hughson smiled grimly. "Don't get carried away."

The shaggy head shook. "Say, I remember him saying something else. I was laying there and I felt him take my gun out of the holster. He said something about kerosene —"

Hughson cocked one eye. "Kerosene?"

"— something about it burning blue and yellow. And he said — lemme think — he said, 'What was going on in that stage station, Biff?"

George Hughson turned and replaced the gun on the wall pegs. Without looking at Shackley again, he said, "Now I *know* he's not coming back. Take care of him."

As he went out, he heard Shackley say, "I know just the thing. Cactus . . ."

At ten o'clock, Hughson drifted into the Pastime Bar. He found Morton in a card game. The little postal inspector sat rigidly on the edge of his chair, bucking the house in a game of blackjack. His black derby rested on the back of his head and a thin film of perspiration glistened on his skin.

Hughson saw that there were very few chips in front of Morton. He watched the inspector's fingers drum on the green cloth; he peered keenly into the tormented face and recognized at once the weakness he had always suspected in the man.

He had the gambling fever.

Morton had sixteen points showing now, and the dealer was waiting for him to decide whether to stand pat or try another card.

"Hit me," Morton said, and then bit his lip in swift remorse.

A ten landed atop his cards.

He was out.

He pushed his last few chips onto the

table and Hughson watched him draw twenty and sit there cracking his knuckles, while the dealer turned up fifteen and dealt himself a six.

Twenty-one.

Morton's chips were swept away.

Morton got up. He was shuffling toward the bar when Hughson tapped his arm.

"Hello," he said cheerfully.

Morton gazed at him, his eyes vacant. "We had a date for a drink, remember?" Hughson said.

The inspector recovered. "Oh, sure. Sorry. Got a lot of things on my mind. Yes, I'll have a brandy."

After three brandies, Morton confided, "A half-hour ago I was two hundred dollars ahead. If I'd had another fifty, I'd've beat the house. You've got to have a bank roll. You can't do it on peanuts."

Hughson drew some coins from his pocket. He placed four double eagles and two gold eagles on the bar. "If you've got a blank check on you," he said, "you can still go back and make that tiger howl."

Morton stared at the money, then groped in his pocket until he found a wrinkled checkbook. He wrote a check for a hundred dollars, gripped the stage man's hand briefly, and rushed away with the money.

Hughson had a second brandy and looked at the clock. Ten-fifteen. With the fever on him heavy, Morton would probably lose the hundred in a few minutes. Especially when primed with brandy. But still it was cutting it close. McCool was due in fifteen minutes.

Before long the little man in the black suit came drifting back. He accepted without a word the fourth drink Hughson offered, staring at the back-bar as though he had just crawled from the wreckage of a stage which had gone over a bank.

Laying the check on the bar, Hughson said thoughtfully, "I suppose I might as well get the saloon to cash this for me now —"

Morton started. Then he gripped his wrist. "No! That is — it's up to you, of course, but — well, I'd appreciate it if you could give me a couple of days to cover it."

Hughson looked into his face sternly. "About how long?"

"Two weeks be all right?"

Hughson relaxed, patting the man's arm and chuckling. "A month, if you say so, Sylvester. You can make it up to me some-time."

Morton clasped his hand with drunken affection. "You're all right, George. You're okay. You bet I will."

Then his expression changed. He was staring toward the front. Hughson glanced around and saw Rian McCool standing near the entrance, that same cocksure half-smile on his face as he searched the saloon for Morton. Suddenly McCool was staring at Morton. He started through the crowd toward them.

Leaning toward Morton, Hughson murmured, "Excuse me, but you look a little ill, Mr. Morton. The outhouses are through that door, on the alley."

Morton gulped and nodded. "Thanks! I'll see you next time."

He hurried out the back door into the alley.

In the mirror, Hughson watched McCool come on. The big redhead stopped and stared at his back. The stage man stood tensely. Then McCool hurried up, opened the door, and followed Morton into the alley.

CHAPTER NINE

Rian stepped into the middle of the alley and peered through the darkness. He saw a row of outhouses across the rutted, weed-flanked alley. Wood smoke was in the air; the smell of the stage stable, a short distance up the line, came to him. There were dark glints from heaps of empty bottles. A pyramid of kegs stood against the back of the saloon building.

But there was no sign of Sylvester Morton. *The little grease ant,* Rian thought with a grin. *Maybe the whole thing was just Morton's way of setting me up for a fifty-dollar touch.*

He laughed softly and shook his head. *If it was, he's sure turned a tiger loose in the streets with his crackerbarrel philosophizing! Started a war, maybe.*

Gravel made a crisp sound near him, and his head turned. A man was standing beside the beer kegs ranked against the wall.

"Morton — ?" he called uncertainly.

Then there was hissing indraw of breath behind him and he flung an arm up for protection and dodged away. The man beside the wall stepped into his path, raising a short length of iron bar. Rian threw a fist at his face and felt a satisfying crunch of meat and bone. But the bar came down on his shoulder and he groaned and staggered into the alley.

Another man tackled him behind the knees. As he fell, someone else — he could see a bandanna mask on the man's face — stepped in close and hammered at Rian's head with his fists. Two blows hit solidly. A cold blackness engulfed him. He lay still, hoping for a moment to clear his head. A rancid perfume of perspiration and toilet water reached his nostrils. Shackley!

The man with the bar loomed over him; Rian's guts clutched in terror and he tried to roll away. A booted foot stopped him with a kick in the ribs. A man muttered, "Hold on — you'll kill him!"

But almost immediately a blow landed on Rian's head, and a bright splash of pain exploded inside his skull.

The next thing he knew was that he was being hauled along the alley, his toes dragging. His head hung loosely. A thought blew through his head like an old paper bag down an alley. *Dan Reese, you old idiot! If you'd remembered where you kept that gun, maybe you'd still have a partner . . .*

A wagon with two horses on the double-tree waited behind the stage yard. They lifted him onto the bed, wrenched his arms up behind him and tied his wrists together. With a sob of desperation he drew his knees up and kicked his boots straight out. Someone swore and fell off the wagon. He squirmed into a sitting position.

A club hit his head with a solid smack.

"Is there a man named McCool — Rian McCool — staying here?" Justina asked the desk clerk at the Frontera Hotel. She was carrying the biggest handbag she owned, a tapestry bag in the bottom of which lay her father's revolver. In the last drawer in the house, after looking everywhere, Dan had found it.

"Yes. He went out about ten-fifteen, though," said the clerk.

The girl hesitated. Then she smiled. "Well, thank you."

On the sidewalk, she stood undecided whether to look any farther. He must have felt he needed the gun or he would be in some saloon, and she certainly was not go-

81

ing to prowl around town looking through saloon windows.

She walked back to her corner and turned west toward the depot. Just before she reached it, a wagon rattled out of the intersecting street. There was enough light so that she could make out the yellow and green colors of the Hughson line on its sideboards. She wrinkled her nose in distaste.

Reaching the gate, she started to turn in. Then she saw something odd.

A man was lying on the bed of the wagon! Two men were on the seat, and a couple of others were riding backwards on the tail gate. The man driving, hunched over like a bear, was too large to be anyone but Biff Shackley.

In her breast, anxiety began to flutter like a moth in a lamp chimney. Was that Mr. McCool lying in the wagon? She knew Hughson and his superintendent were completely ruthless. Could they have gotten wind of the proposed partnership? The wagon rattled on down the dark street until it was out of sight. Justina hurried across the stage yard to the house.

"Father!" she called as she ran in.

He was gone. His hat was not on the antelope prong where he always kept it. She remembered now that he had spoken of going to the hotel to play dominoes with some of his cronies. She thought of the marshal. But by the time she got back with him the wagon would be long gone.

Justina hurried to the corral and took a bridle from a peg. She walked in among the horses and spoke the name of her saddle horse. The little buckskin mare stood passively while she pushed the bit into her mouth and pulled the crown strap over her ears. After leading the horse out, Justina lifted her side saddle onto its back and made the cinches tight. She was hardly dressed for riding, but it was no time to fret about the proprieties.

She drew the pistol from her handbag and, not finding a suitable place to carry it, unfastened two buttons of her gown and thrust it into the bodice.

As she rode down the street, she thought, *What in the world am I doing? Have I lost my mind? He isn't even a partner yet — nor a friend! Just a strange, likable young man who's dropped into my life like an unexpected gift.*

She flicked the horse with the reins and it jogged faster.

The white paring of moon above the hills

shed a faint light in the wash where the wagon was parked. Rian was conscious now, a raw, pulsing pain in his skull. They had spread-eagled him to a wheel of the wagon, facing it, ankles and wrists lashed to the rim.

Shackley caught him by the hair and yanked his head around. Thrusting his face close, he said, "How do you like this kind of party, scrapper?"

McCool spat in his face.

Shackley rammed his head against the spokes and cursed him. "Dirty, ignorant horse-buster!" he shouted. He turned and yelled into the darkness. "Spence — what're you doing?"

Spence called something from the dry jungle of sage and cactus stretching away from the bank of the wash. Presently he came back and jumped down to the sand.

Rian looked at him, wanting to remember him clearly. All the men had pulled down their bandanna masks after they'd left town. He was small and lithe, with hard eyes, bony features and a gopherish mouth. He was carrying a couple of ocotillo wands — branches from the cactus, sometimes called "wolf candle." He squatted down and began cutting away from one end the wicked fish-hooklike thorns with a pair of wire cutters.

Each wand was about four feet long.

"These do it?" he asked Shackley.

Rian's eyes squeezed out. A silent scream echoed through his whole being. The Comanche treatment: a whipping with cactus wands. There was natural poison on every thorn.

Shackley pulled on heavy gloves while Spence prepared the whips. He backhanded Rian across the mouth. "You don't like this kind of *baile*, do you?" he said. "You just like to step up and mash a man in the face without warning."

"Without warning's the way you mashed me that night," Rian said.

"You were drunk. What the hell do you know about it?"

"I know something was going on in there. I know something else, too, Biff. If you lay that whip to my back, I'll kill you for it. I'll live that long, unless you kill me outright."

Shackley chuckled. "Am I shaking?" he asked the other men, holding out his gloved hands.

"You're in terrible shape," said the wolfish little man named Spence. "Here — how's this?"

Shackley took the trimmed whip in his gloved hand. He handled it carefully, respectful of the thorns. Then he took a sud-

85

den cut at Rian's back, hitting the wagon instead. Rian made a hoarse cry of terror. Shackley went into a windy convulsion of laughter.

"Oh, my God!" he said. "This is going to be better than a horse-gelding."

He set himself, working his boots into the sand. Spence raised his hand.

"Wait a minute, Biff. Hear that?"

"Yes, I hear it. We're only a mile from the county road. It's a buckboard going by."

His eyes closed tight, Rian heard Shackley's grunt of exertion, then a whistle in the air; then he felt a pain so great that his whole body leaped as the whip seared his shoulder and back. The horses snorted and danced forward a few feet. The wheel to which he was tied revolved a quarter turn, so that he was left lying parallel to the ground.

"Back 'em up, back 'em up," the super muttered. "Can't lash a man in that position."

Two of the other men backed the horses until the figure cross-tied to the wheel was back in position. Rian felt blood running down his back. Shackley swung the whip again. The terrible pain of a hundred thorn punctures brought another scream from Rian's lips. He could feel both strokes like strips burned in his flesh by a branding iron. In dumb animal agony, he sobbed aloud.

Shackley came up and twisted his head around. "Is that the kind of *baile* you favor, scrapper?" he asked. "Because I ain't tired yet."

Biting his lip, Rian clenched the wagon spokes with both hands. The pain was spreading, scalding his entire back.

"You see, we been trying to tell you something," Shackley was saying. "We want you to go to some other town that you might like better. Any old town. Just so it's clear away from here. So when we turn you loose tonight, don't you even think of coming back."

"I guess about a dozen more ought to do it," Shackley said.

Once more he set himself. Then the wash was illuminated by a flash and roar that dazzled the eyes and made the ears ring. Even with his eyes closed, Rian was blinded. He heard the men bawling questions at each other. Then there was a second crashing explosion bursting out of a core of yellow fire, and one of the group screamed. Rian twisted his head. He saw Shackley fire a wild shot into the brush lining the arroyo, then cut and run. He saw a man lying on the sand.

In the same instant, the wagon team began to run. Rian clung to the spokes, shouting, "Ho! Ho, now!" But the horses kept running. He was spinning slowly on the wheel. The wagon wheels, deeply bogged in sand, kept the animals from running fast. But Rian, from pain and the blood in his head, soon lost consciousness.

CHAPTER TEN

When he came to his senses, he was lying face down on the wagon as it went banging along over a graded road. He groaned.

A girl's voice said, "I'm sorry we have to go so fast, Mr. McCool! I think they're all afoot, but we can't take a chance of their catching us."

Huddling on his side on the wagon bed, he gritted his teeth against the pain. In a few minutes the wagon slowed; he looked up and saw buildings. He was in too much pain to wonder about anything when Justina Reese came around to help him from the wagon. With assistance, he was able to walk into the house and lie on the floor.

Before she commenced working, she brought him a bottle of black medicine resembling a strong purgative. "Drink some of this, Mr. McCool," she said. "It's Mother Winslow's Soothing Syrup — wonderful for pain."

He was willing to do anything that would blunt the edge of his pain. He drank heartily, and in a short time the most marvelous fuzziness invaded his brain, and he sighed deeply. The stuff was probably loaded with opium, he surmised. He took another gulp and settled down to making himself comfortable on the floor, curled up like a child.

"That's right," she murmured. "Go to sleep if you can."

Working carefully, she cut his shirt away and washed him to the waist, then treated the masses of small blue punctures with antiseptic. During most of the operation, he was in a restless sleep. Then he heard her father come in and exclaim in surprise.

Justina said reproachfully, "I thought you were going to play dominoes all night! Father, I — I killed a man!"

Dan Reese sat in a chair and stared at Rian. "No, he's still breathing," he said.

"I don't mean Mr. McCool!" She recounted the story. "So if there's an inquest," she concluded, "I'll just say it was self-defense."

"Don't say anything," Rian mumbled.

"What?"

"Don't tell them a thing," he said thickly. "It's their problem. Get me back to the hotel. Back door. Nobody'll see me."

"But, Mr. McCool —"

"Coffee," he muttered.

In some recess of his mind the thought was lodged that he might be bad luck for the Reeses. Better if he were in his own room.

He loaded up on coffee. Between the hot drink and Mother Winslow's gentle ministrations, he felt relaxed and capable. Nevertheless, it required both of them to help him down the alley to the hotel. Dan Reese unlocked the outside door with Rian's key. Then he put his old Colt .45 in his holster. The two Reeses staggered into the room with him and stretched him out on the bed.

"What a horrible little room!" Justina gasped. "It smells like a mouse nest. Mr. McCool, I'll put this soothing syrup right here where you can reach it. Tomorrow I'll bring some more, in case you need it."

"I'll need it," Rian muttered.

"Do you think I killed that man?" the girl whispered.

"I hope so," Rian said. "Good night. Did you leave the gun?"

Dan Reese shoved it under his pillow. "It's loaded," he warned.

Rian's laugh was a croak of delirium. "I hope to hell it's loaded!" he said.

■ ■ ■ ■

When he awoke, it seemed to be daylight. But he saw the little forked tongue of the lamp trembling inside the sooty lamp chimney on the dresser and decided it was still night.

He reached under the pillow to check on the gun. Hot little pustules erupted in pain the length of his back; he cried out and stifled the yell in the pillow. Eyes shut, he sent his hand groping along the floor for Mother Winslow. He found the bottle and took a swallow, spilling much of it on the cotton flannel sheet. Then he set the bottle down, groaning, and waited.

Relief came. He thought of Biff Shackley. *I'm going to live, Biff,* he thought. *But you aren't.*

Time telescoped.

Once, when he was awake, he recalled having eaten a meal. Who had fed him? Someone had made him sit on the edge of the bed and spooned food into his mouth. Justina? He vaguely remembered seeing reddish-gold hair in the lamplight. He had said something about it, in his foolish delirium and weakness. The girl had smiled, touched her hair, and thanked him.

At last, when he could get out of bed, he pulled on some pants and moved about the tiny floor. He could take five short strides, the long way. His chest was bandaged with torn sheets, and he could smell liniment. He felt stronger and very hungry.

Someone tapped on the door.

"Rian? Rian, dear, are you there?" a young woman called.

Dear? he thought. My goodness, what had he been saying to her? Someone must be putting something in my opium, he reflected. He opened the door.

Abby Hughson stood there in the hall.

Dark-haired and dainty, she reached her hand toward him timidly. Her eyes filled with tears as she looked at him. "Forgive me!"

A wicked content purred in Rian. "What for? You didn't do it."

"I did something worse. May I come in?"

Gesturing, he moved aside. She came into the room and closed the door. Impulsively, she came to him and pressed her cheek against his naked chest. "I'm so sorry — so ashamed!"

"Forget it," he said. He could see himself in the cracked mirror. His face was pale, his hair dark-red and ragged; her black hair against the whiteness of his chest stirred him. Once he would have given all he owned to have her in his arms. Now he thought: *Your time's coming, sister. It's coming.*

She roused to inspect his bandages. "Heavens, your bandages are *much* too tight! Who's your doctor?"

"Dr. Winslow."

"Winslow? He must be new; I don't know him. But wounds like that shouldn't have liniment on them, and they're bound too tightly to breathe. Lie down and let me fix them."

He lay on the bed, enjoying a sensuous comfort. She clucked like a mother hen.

"Pete's sake," he muttered, "I'm not going to die."

"You are," she said, "if you don't leave town. Artie Judd's back and waiting for you to show up. He's threatened to kill you. And Biff Shackley has been perfectly wild ever since the night you were hurt."

"Guess they'll have to take their chances with me."

"Aren't you going to leave?"

"I got one of George's men, didn't I? And I made a fool out of Artie. What makes them so sure they'll do any better the next time around?"

"Because they were only trying to scare

you, up to now."

"And now you're trying?"

"Of course not."

"Then why are you here? To change my bandages?"

"To say how terribly sorry I am for the way I behaved in Vallecito," she murmured. "I was so confused — so unhappy —"

"How are things working out with old George?" he asked.

Abby sat up straight on the chair she had drawn to his bedside. "I'm afraid old George has all he wanted from me. My little bit of property."

"Then divorce him," Rian said. "Maybe we'll have another go at it, huh?"

"I know you're being bitter, but my answer would be yes, if you ever asked me again. But you see, I can't divorce him, because according to state law he owns everything that used to be mine!"

"A rough law to buck," Rian admitted. He was astounded at how cold and deep she ran. But he was a full jump ahead of her, and waiting.

"Of course, when he dies — unless I predecease him — the property would be mine . . ."

"I s'pose," Rian said.

Abby finished dressing the wounds. She

tossed the old bandages into the hall. Then she washed her hands, dried them daintily, and stood before him as he sat on the edge of the bed.

"I don't want anything to happen to you, Rian," she said. "Won't you go away, at least for a while?"

He smiled sadly. "I don't know what I'll do, Abby. I'm mad enough to kill all of them. But of course I'm not big enough."

"Maybe you are — with a little help," the girl said, smiling enigmatically.

"Now what's that mean?"

She tweaked his nose. "I'll tell you sometime. Right now, you just think about keeping out of sight and getting better."

As she was about to leave, she remembered something and pulled a pint bottle of whiskey from her handbag. With a smile, she set it on the dresser. "In case you need cheering up," she said.

"Thanks."

The door closed behind her.

I'll be damned! he thought. *She was asking me to kill him!*

"Kill my husband, and you can have me!"

He sat there, bemused. After a while he took a drink and painfully lay down to think about it.

CHAPTER ELEVEN

That night, when Justina visited him, she brought him a tray of good, solid food. It was not restaurant chow; she had cooked it herself. He put the tray on the chair and sat on the cot to eat. Justina glanced around, making a womanly check of things. Her roaming glance stopped abruptly. He felt a charge go through the room.

"You've been out," she said.

"No."

"Then where did the bottle of whiskey come from?"

Rian swallowed a mouthful of mashed potatoes. "Somebody brought it to me."

"I didn't know you were receiving visitors," Justina said.

Women definitely possessed senses a man didn't, he reflected — something like the olfactory organs of foxes, perhaps. She knew another woman had been in the room.

"Somebody came by to say hello," he told her.

"Oh."

After he ate, she made him lie down while she examined his bandages. *"What* in the *world!"* she exclaimed. "You've changed these. They're too loose. And you've sprinkled some kind of talcum powder on your punctures."

"This — this party who visited me was bound to do something for me," he muttered. "I told this party I was all right, but they went right ahead."

Justina poured cold liniment on his hide so lavishly that he groaned through his teeth. "Was this party Mrs. Hughson?" she asked.

"Now that I think back, I believe it was."

"It's strange you'd let her do anything for you. Will Mr. Hughson send his superintendent to treat you next time?"

Rian sat up. Her face was flushed. "I felt just like you do," he said. "That she might pour wolf's-bane on me. But she was talking, so I let her. I got plenty out of her, too."

"Ha!" the girl scoffed. "I expect she got more out of you than you realize, too. What did you find out?"

"Things I already knew — that they're out to kill me. And things I didn't know. I'll tell you about them some other time."

"Oh, I'm not prying," Justina said. "Suit yourself — tell me any time you feel like it. It's really no business of mine, since we aren't actually partners."

Rian lay down again. "Let's get these Shackley marks covered up," he said. "The air hurts them. I meant to bring up that partnership deal. Still interested?"

"Yes."

"I've been back and forth through your books today. Do you know there's over eight hundred dollars outstanding?"

"Of course."

"Then why don't you collect it?"

"We've tried. Potter, the feed man, has stalled us for six months. The other big account, Meanley's Hardware, is nearly a year delinquent. But Father refuses to take them to court, because we owe people, too, and he's afraid it might stir them up against us."

"But you only owe a couple of hundred. Do you think Potter has the money, if he wanted to pay?"

"He owns half the real estate in this town! Of course he could pay."

"Tomorrow morning I'll collect from Potter then."

"How?"

"I'll just walk in and ask for the money,"

Rian said.

"Rian, you actually don't dare leave this room, and you know it!" Justina protested. "For the last two days I've seen Artie Judd on the street every time I've been out. And he's carrying a gun — that ugly tortoise-shell thing."

"I think it's real pretty. I liked carrying it myself. And I'm not afraid of it, so it won't be keeping me in my room."

"Well — but there's still Shackley, and that filthy little offscrapings called Spence. And Hughson."

"My problems, lady, not yours. If you think I can't handle them, maybe you'd better not tie up with me."

Justina was silent while she finished her task.

"I hope you can handle them, Rian. I don't know how any one man can handle an army like Hughson's, though."

"It's not an army. Just a rabble. Have we got a deal?"

Justina rose, rinsed her hands, and walked to the door. She turned. "Yes. I'll have the papers drawn up tomorrow."

"Fine." Rian frowned as he noticed something missing from the dresser. "Where's my whiskey?"

"In my handbag. It's probably poisoned.

Even if it isn't, it won't help for you to be staggering around town while they're hunting you."

Rian smiled as he lolled on the cot. "I'm beginning to think you care, Tina."

"I do — about my investments. Good night."

In the morning, Rian made a list.

At the top of the list was the name Potter, Ira. He had a haircut and a shave, used his remaining thirty cents for breakfast, and strolled down to Potter's Feed Barn. It was ten o'clock. The town was redolent of warm, sweet smells and the blackbirds set up a mighty twittering. Rian felt good. His back was stiff with scar tissue and he was somewhat groggy, but with every stride he felt stronger and more confident.

He kept an eye out for Artie Judd or any others of the Hughson crowd. Reaching the feed barn, a high, square pile of adobe with a sheet-metal roof, he entered through a large sliding door and peered around the gloomy interior. In long racks were open barrels of feed piled to the rafters with baled hay.

As he stood there, he heard the twittering of barn swallows darting in and out through the door to their nests of mud anchored to the ceiling rafters. There was a rich smell of molasses feed, and the sun shafted long blurred beams through the dusty air.

"Anybody home?" he bawled.

From a door in one wall, an old man's voice called, "Right in here!"

Rian wandered into the office. There were two sections: a countered area in the forepart, a curtained cubbyhole in the back. No one but an elderly bookkeeper was in view. With a pen in his hand, a statement before him, he looked up. He was neat and smallish, rather wistful-looking in his black suit with braid binding its edges and a high white collar sawing away at the underside of his jaws.

"Was there something?" he asked.

Rian leaned on the counter. "Boss man around?"

"No. He'll be back, oh, around noon."

"I see — my name's McCool. I'm with Empire Stage — their new partner."

With a small clatter, the pen dropped on the desk. The old man's mouth fell open. "Mister — *McCool?*" he asked.

"You know about me?"

The old man shook his head, changed his mind and nodded; then he said hastily, "Look, Mister McCool, we do business with Shackley's outfit, sell him most of his feed in fact, but I — I just work here."

Rian shrugged. "That's up to you. All I want is the six hundred dollars Potter owes us. By the way, what's your name?"

"Moore. I'm the bookkeeper."

A chair scraped in the back office. Rian gazed sternly at Moore. "Thought you said the boss wasn't here?"

Moore's pouched eyes wavered. "Why — well, you see —"

Rian got the picture: Potter was not in unless he elected to be. At that moment a very corpulent man with a large, naked-looking nose appeared in the door of the private office. He wore a black suit with a half-dozen lodge buttons on the lapel, and his red, glazed features were set in a half-frightened, half-angry cast.

"Moore," he said, "I've got to run down to the bank. Tell Mr. Potter I've gone to check on a new account."

Moore murmured something. Potter — for Rian had no doubt it was he — pushed through the counter gate and headed out.

When he had departed, Rian said, "That's him, eh?"

"Yes, sir."

Rian touched a frayed place on the edge of Moore's coat lapel. "How's the pay here? Better than it is for his creditors, I hope."

"It's tolerable, Mr. McCool." Moore's voice tried to be casual but rang with misery.

"Reason I asked is that we need a bookkeeper very bad. Pay will be ten dollars more than Potter pays you — for a starter."

"Don't Miss Justina do the bookwork for Dan?"

Rian chuckled. "Women are wonderful in the kitchen, Mr. Moore, but they can sure play hell with a set of books. She hasn't sent out any regular statements in months. I'm changing everything. First job is to start suit on delinquent accounts. Does Potter have any money?"

Moore came to the counter. His hands were trembling slightly and he linked his fingers to control them.

"Mr. McCool, he owns half the real estate in town," he said, using the same time-hallowed phrase Justina had used. "He doesn't pay because Mr. Hughson don't want him to. Hughson would transfer his feed account if he did. He's in pretty thick with George, I'm afraid. I — I believe George is a little in arrears to us, you see. For over a thousand dollars. And our best chance of collecting will come after the Reeses quit."

"But they aren't going to quit," Rian said. "I'll testify to that. Do you want that job?"

"Can — can I have a week to think about it? A man my age don't like to plunge in cold."

"You're not so old, Mr. Moore. That man-my-age talk will age a man fast, though. No, in a week I'll have somebody else on the job. I'm sorry. We've got to make hay while the sun shines. Get some money coming in fast."

Moore chewed his lip. At length he said in a whisper, "All right. I'll take it!"

Rian squeezed his hand. "Good. Now your first job is to advise me on how to go about getting that money out of Potter."

Passing his hand over his thin gray hair, Moore muttered, "If I was you, McCool, I'd take the books while he's out. Then, don't you see, he can't send out any statements to collect money people owe *him!* Why, he'd be in a devil of a spot. He'd more'n likely trot right over with the six hundred — plus delinquent penalties, of course."

Rian slapped him on the shoulder. "You're all right, Mr. Moore. What's your first name?"

"Bob."

"Well, Bob, suppose you get a cardboard box about so big and put the books in it. Then take them down to the Empire office and tell Justina you're working for us and for her to hide the books."

"I'd rather you took them yourself, Mr. McCool."

"No one'll see them, and besides I'm going to be busy."

"How so?"

"By now Potter will have told Hughson I'm up and about, and Hughson will be sending Judd out to find me. Liable to be a busy morning for me."

He laid Dan Reese's gun on the counter and checked the loads. "Not that I look for any real trouble, but they aren't above pulling another bluff. And I'm not above calling it."

Moore put the ledgers in a box and laid a newspaper over them. He collected all his little possessions — pipes, tobacco, and the like — from his drawer. With a nod to Rian, he went out.

Thirty seconds later, as Rian finished checking the gun, he was back, white as paper.

"You're right, Mr. McCool! Artie Judd and Biff Shackley are standing in front of the stage depot, looking this way!"

CHAPTER TWELVE

Rian gave the old man ten minutes to slip out the side door of the feed barn and make his way to the Empire office. He did not want him involved in what might happen in the street.

As he went toward the street door, he felt his heart sledging in the cage of his ribs. For an instant he was giddy; he reached out and steadied himself against a barrel while his head cleared. He had been in bed too long, was still too drawn out like a wire, for sudden excitement.

Yet it was not fear, but a sort of elation, that he experienced. As yet he could not strike directly at Hughson, but he was coming closer all the time.

He stepped into the street. The feed barn was at the north end of the business district, and on the east side of the street. The stage office was near the middle of the town, perhaps a hundred yards south, on the opposite side of the street. There was very little traffic — a cowboy jogging in from a cross street, a heavy freight truck rumbling into an alley, a dozen people on the walks.

He saw a large, slope-shouldered man in a shirt striped like a barber's apron on the east side of the street, opposite Hughson's depot. He recognized his black trousers and yellow boots; he thought he discerned even the lavender sleeve-garters of Hughson's gunman, Artie Judd. Judd was standing in the sunlight, staring toward the feed barn.

Sitting in one of the alcoved windows of the depot was Biff Shackley. The big super saw McCool and came to his feet. Like Judd, he wore a gun.

Rian walked down the sidewalk toward Judd. There were cement curbs, but the walk itself was dirt, deeply scalloped by the feet of pedestrians. When he had gone about a hundred feet, he stepped into the street and started on a diagonal toward Shackley. Judd came to the edge of the curb, as Shackley, too, came forward. They had him in a beautiful crossfire.

He wondered whether Judd had discovered that he had no effective firing pin in his weapon.

God help me if he's fixed it! he thought.

It was in his mind to walk toward Shackley, passing him without stepping into the walk — unless Shackley went for his gun. If he did, he would deal with him.

When he was just short of Shackley, with Judd in the tail of his eye, the superintendent suddenly bawled, "Last chance, McCool! Turn back and take off or you're done."

"Turn my back on the likes of you?" said Rian.

He kept walking.

Judd called, "Count of three, horse-breaker! One —"

At the count of three, Rian saw Shackley's hand move. His heart leaped painfully; he drew his ancient, borrowed Colt. From Judd's position he heard a *click,* then a curse. He saw the sun glint on Shackley's revolver; then the gun in his own hand uttered a terrible roar and almost jumped from his fingers. A dense fog of powder smoke sprang up between them. The roar of the gun was an unmanning thing. Through the heavy, rolling echoes he heard Judd's gun click twice more; then there was an angry shout from the gunman.

He heard nothing from Shackley. But as the smoke drifted aside he saw him sitting heavily on the walk, his back against the wall of the station. The gun lay a few feet from his hand.

Rian turned toward Judd. The gunman screamed, "You dirty rat!" and backed off.

Keeping the Colt trained on him, Rian walked forward, Judd collided with the wall. Once more he raised the gun and pointed it at Rian.

Rian laughed.

Artie Judd turned abruptly and ran a few yards to an alley, ducked into it and was out of sight.

Another man was on the walk now, tall, slender, grim. He carried a shotgun, and there was a shield on his coat.

"This is loaded with nuts and bolts, Mc-Cool," he said. "Don't make me turn the town's stomach. Put your gun away."

Rian sighed and lowered the Colt. "Yes, sir," he said.

"I told you before," Marshal Fowley said, "that I wouldn't stand for any nonsense from you." They were in the marshal's office, with five or six men grouped about the room, peering at Rian, among them the newspaper editor, the marshal's deputy, and the coroner.

"This nonsense wasn't my idea," Rian said. "They were waiting for me. Ask Bob Moore."

"I'll question Moore," Fowley said sternly. "Also Judd, when I find him."

Outside, there was a brisk sound of a woman's footsteps, and Justina came into the doorway. The men removed their hats and murmured grave greetings as she entered the room. Fowley rose from his desk. "Miss Justina, can you come back later? I'm conducting an investigation."

Pushing at a loose strand of hair — she looked as though she had just been putting her hair up when the firing started — she gave him a weak smile. "I heard that my partner was involved in a shooting —"

Fowley turned his head on the side. "Your partner?"

"Mr. McCool."

The marshal looked at Rian, and sighed. "You move fast, McCool."

"In this town," Rian said, "you've got to move fast to keep alive. Are you going to lock me up?"

"No. Since it *appears* that you were the victim instead of the criminal. But there'll be a coroner's inquest, of course, and you'll either be bound over or freed, depending on the jury's findings."

Rian heard Justina let out a sigh. There was high color in her face, and as he studied her he saw her clench her hands with

111

nervousness. Somehow he had the feeling that her visit to the marshal's office was not entirely tied to the shooting.

"Can he leave then?" the girl asked quickly.

Fowley nodded.

"With or without gun?" Rian asked. "It doesn't belong to me, actually. Besides, I'd feel kind of naked without it, with people sniping at me all the time."

Fowley picked the revolver up, sniffed the barrel, scowled, and finally shrugged. "Keep the damned — your pardon, Miss Justina — keep the thing in your holster," he warned. He offered it, butt first.

Hurrying along the walk beside Rian, Justina glanced back as if to make sure they were not being followed. Then she clutched his arm and looked up at him.

"Rian, we're finished!"

"We were finished before we ever teamed up," Rian said. "This outfit is plumb snake-bit. But what's new?"

"Our Frontera office was robbed last night."

He stopped and smiled at her. "What'd we lose — couple of cans of saddle soap and a beat-up horse?"

"Three thousand dollars in gold!"

Rian blinked. "What've you been doing — hiding assets from me?"

"It wasn't our money. It belonged to a mercury mining company. The money was supposed to come here on the stage tomorrow, under special guard. Mr. Brogan, our supervisor, rode down to tell us."

"Where is he?"

"He's at home, with Father."

"Let's talk to him."

Brogan was a tall old man with a skull-like head and face. His shoulders were unnaturally broad, like the framework on which a much larger man was to be constructed. Loops of brownish skin had collected under his eyes. He was sitting on the horsehair sofa with his hat in his hands, looking solemn and defeated.

Rian knew immediately that he would have to fire the man as soon as he could replace him. You could not build a fire with wet wood.

"Well, sir, it was all over so fast I can't hardly tell you how many there was of them," Brogan said. "There was this knock. I'd just looked up. 'Who's that?' I says. 'This is Shorty, from the stable,' somebody says. Well, sir, there is a Shorty at Meyers' stable, so —"

He told how three men had come in, tied him up, and carried off the cashbox.

"Why wasn't it locked in the safe?" asked Rian.

"I was just putting it away," Brogan explained. "The mine manager brought it down at six o'clock. This was about six-thirty."

"Anybody try to follow them?"

"I told the county sheriff, and he organized a little posse. But they couldn't turn nothing up."

Justina sniffed. "That fat old sheriff! I'll wager he never wasted much time looking."

"About an hour, miss," said Brogan.

"The first place to look would be along the river," Justina said. "That's the way everything stolen slides, like the county was sloped that way. They hide everything from stolen mercury flasks to bank loot in the caves, and take it across the river after they've made arrangements in Mexico. What shall we do, Mr. McCool? We'll have to make that loss good."

"Don't you have insurance?"

"No. We're too small to qualify."

Rian told Brogan, "You might as well head back, Mr. Brogan. We'll put it in the hands of a U. S. marshal if we can ever get one down here."

"If there's anything I can do —" said Brogan.

The only thing you can do is eat and sleep, like a spavined horse, thought Rian. He said, "No, thanks. We'll mule along somehow."

After the man left, he said, "Draw me a little map of that cave section. I'll ride up the river right now and poke around."

While he assembled a few things — a couple of blankets in case he got caught out at night, some food in a paper sack — she started on a map. Then, with an exclamation, she threw it in the fireplace.

"I can't tell you where to go. I'll have to show you. It would take you three days to find the spot by yourself. There are more blind alleys than you could imagine."

Rian shook his head, the blanket roll of provisions over his shoulder. "I'm not taking any helpless females along," he muttered. "Dan, you got a rifle?"

Dan Reese lifted a repeating rifle from pegs over the fireplace and dug a box of shells from a drawer. "She ain't so helpless," he said. "Tina grew up in them caves. I was ranching over there till she was thirteen. Only worry you'd have is keeping up with her."

Rian scowled. Justina hurried into her bedroom; he could hear her pulling things from the closet. Rian lowered his voice. "What if we have to spend the night out there?"

"Let me worry about that," Justina called from the bedroom. "I may be frail, but I can fight like a tiger."

"I'll saddle your horses," said Dan.

Fifteen minutes later, Justina emerged from the house dressed in a girl's Levis, a shirt of her father's under a denim jacket, and high-heeled boots. She carried a small buggy rifle in addition to a blanket roll. There was a fragrance of rose water about her as Rian held her stirrup for her.

"I hope you brought along plenty of perfume," he said. "You can't hardly find a store over that way, I hear."

Stiff-necked, he rode from the yard to the side street Justina followed, riding loose and easy in the saddle, her hair pinned up in a tight coronet, and a kerchief drawn over her head. It was about twelve-thirty. McCool figured they could make the ten-mile ride in about three hours.

CHAPTER THIRTEEN

"You thick-headed pistol jockey!" Hughson said bitterly. He sat on the deep window-sill of his office, scowling at Artie Judd, who sat at Hughson's desk. Judd looked up, his face dark with frustration and a rage turned inward. Judd was holding his pistol in his two hands.

"But look at this thing, George! How could I have — ?"

Hughson made a quick, savage gesture. "I've looked at it! And I've looked at you till I'm sick of looking at both of you. You're drawing more pay than anybody in this outfit, and yet all I've asked of you was to make a noise like a gun when I pulled the trigger. Hell!" he snorted. "As long as the competition was an old man and a girl, you looked great. But as soon as a jailbird with a fourth-grade education came along, you started firing low, high, and sideways."

Judd's baffled anger was still focused on

the gun. "If you'd wanted him killed the day he got out of jail, why didn't you say so?"

"I didn't want him killed! Not then — not until you'd fouled the machinery so that nothing but killing would stop him. And *then,* damn it, you bungled again!"

Shackley was dead. Potter was on the run and would probably be putting six hundred dollars operating cash into the Reeses' hands tomorrow. Yet things were stirring nicely down the river in Frontera, and if he acted the part of a man in trouble, it was largely to stimulate Judd to more effective action.

Judd snapped the hammer of the Colt twice, and shook his head.

"Why don't you pack your gear and head out?" Hughson suggested.

Judd frowned. "Don't you want me to check with Spence and see how things went?"

"I know how they went. The stage office in Frontera was robbed last night. What else do I need to know?"

"Whether Spence and the others got away clean. Makin' it out of town ain't getting away, necessarily."

Hughson shrugged and walked to the desk. Quickly, the gunman vacated the chair. Hughson pulled a drawer open and took a handful of cigars from a box, which he tucked into the breast pocket of his coat.

"What're you going to do?" asked Judd.

"Go down to Frontera and see what's happening."

"Nothin'll happen there," Judd told him. "They done made it to the river, at least."

Hughson snapped an impatient look at him.

"The point is, somebody may try to make a federal case out of it. They do handle mail in that office, you know. According to what Morton told me, he'll be in Frontera this week, heading back to El Paso. If he's around town, I want to talk to him. He's the one who'll decide who handles the matter: the local law, or the U. S. marshal's office in El Paso."

Hughson reached into a closet and took out a Colt hanging from a nail in a plain black holster. His brow wrinkled. Judd watched him buckle it on.

"I'll ride up with you," he said.

"Suit yourself."

Judd spoke eagerly. "Tell you what: I'll ride as far as Carrizo Creek and cut over to the river, see what news I can pick up. Okay?"

Without meeting his eager look, yet acknowledging by a softening of his tone that Judd was being given a final chance, Hughson growled:

"Suit yourself. If you see Spence, tell him to sit tight for a day or two, and then head back. But before you go anywhere, you'd better hike over to Dominguez' shop and get a new firing pin put in that gun hammer."

The gunman left. Hughson sat down and made notes of things he wanted to accomplish in Frontera. He heard a slight sound and glanced up.

Abby stood in the doorway. She wore a black gown which nipped her waist, a double strand of pearls at her throat. The black enhanced the fairness of her skin, made her look pallid and somehow vulnerable, and Hughson felt a stab of the old intense desire he had had for her early in their marriage. It came to him suddenly to enjoy her before leaving town. He dropped his pencil and stood up.

Abby entered the room. Hughson, smiling faintly, moved to close the door. She watched him as he came toward her. He held her by the elbows and looked into her face.

"Black becomes you, Abby," he said. "Why don't you wear it more often?"

"Perhaps I shall. Poor Mr. Shackley," Abby sighed.

He was immediately annoyed. But he pulled her against him quickly and kissed her. She turned her face away with that infuriating way women had of sharpening a man's passion while they ignored it.

"For Heaven's sake!" she gasped. "Is this how we're going to meet our business problems?"

"It's one way," he said, smiling.

"A better way," his wife said, "might be to sell out and move somewhere else. I'm fed up, George. I hate this town and the people, and I hate losing money!"

His hands slipped down to her waist and he held her when she tried to move away.

"Move where? By the time we got through paying bills, we'd be washed out. Rule One of this business is that you must have a mail contract to make money. A thousand dollars a mile — and it's eighteen miles to Frontera. You'll have to take this on faith, but in a month we'll have the field to ourselves, contract and all."

His hand moved to the small of her back, while his lips sought the soft perfumed skin of her neck. After a moment Abby pushed him away and stepped back.

"Men!" she said. "While you're talking

business, you're scheming how to get a girl's clothes off her."

There was a hidden meaning in her words; he knew her too well to let the remark pass. "Who else has been talking business to you lately?" he asked.

She gazed at him. "Rian McCool," she said. "He came to me with the craziest plan. He said that if you died, I'd own all the property. That's true, of course. But you aren't going to die — are you?"

Hughson said huskily, "You — you — you're making this up! You haven't even seen him."

Her lips turned up in a teasing smile. "I took him some whiskey while he was sick — something to while away the time. Maybe it was just the whiskey talking; he got drunk before I knew what was happening. Gracious, he's more man half dead than most men are with all their faculties! *Are* you going to die, George?" she asked earnestly.

Hughson reached inside his coat and drew the gun he carried on his left hip. He walked to Abby, staring into her face, and placed the muzzle of the gun against her breast.

"I feel pretty healthy, Abby," he said. "How about you?"

"Never better, George. I wrote a letter telling how well I felt, mentioning the possibility of an accident. I left it with an attorney."

He knew he was hurting her; he could see it in the pinch-lines about her eyes.

"So what you thought," he scoffed, "was that you could prod me into a showdown with McCool, eh? And then you could turn the poor slob down, if he had the luck to kill me. Or if I killed him, they'd hang me for it, eh? Abby, don't take cards in a man's game. A woman gets her bluff called every time."

He stepped back, holstered the gun, and went behind his desk. He locked it, tossed the key and caught it, and walked out.

CHAPTER FOURTEEN

The smell in the air was of damp earth and rotting vegetation. Rian and the girl had left the county road an hour earlier, ridden south to the river road, and were following its slow kinks southeast through jungles of mesquite and thickets of the heavy yellow cane, locally called *higar.*

Justina explained that it was very good feed. On her suggestion, her father had had some Mexicans cut and truss tons of it and haul it to town. Potter had bought it for six hundred dollars and never paid for it. But she still thought it was good business.

"Now that we're going to be paid for it," she said happily.

The road consisted of two wandering tracks lurching over roots and rocks, boggy here and there with mossy seeps of river water. A stone's throw to their right lay the wide, shallow Rio Grande, islanded with sand bars. The land was generally flat, but ahead Rian could see low cliffs split by the river. They had not discussed the implications of the robbery. But both of them knew that Empire Stage Lines would die in twenty-four hours if they had to make good on a three-thousand-dollar loss. Every creditor in town would be serving them with papers, trying to get his money before they folded.

Justina halted her horse, gazing at a giant mesquite as big as an Eastern oak. "Rian, I used to climb that tree and pretend I was an Army scout," she sighed. "You can see miles down the river, and across into Mexico. Sometimes I'd see smuggler trains coming or going. Once some mercury smugglers passed right under the tree!"

"Fine place for a girl to be," commented Rian.

"Oh, they're harmless enough — just poor peasants trying to make a living. If they'd seen me, they'd have tipped their hats and said, *'Que tal, señorita?'* and ridden on."

"I've got a feeling these men won't be so polite."

"So have I. That's why I'm going to climb the tree and see what I can see." She raised her arm to point south. "The main trail into Chihuahua crossed the river right there. But there are a dozen trails to the crossing on

125

this side. Some of them start in Santa Cruz canyon — the cliffs you see. There are a thousand little side canyons leading into the main one."

Rian dismounted. "Boys first," he said. "I've got a good nose for anybody that's lashed up with Hughson. They give off a certain smell."

Justina shrugged and dismounted while he pulled off boots and socks to climb the big tree. He studied it a moment. It was a perfect climbing tree, with frequent stout limbs and not too much foliage. The leaves were small, like those of a mountain ash. He climbed; it was almost like ascending stairs. High in the tree he found a fork where he wedged himself.

Eastward, toward Frontera, the land rolled away, as brown and wrinkled as an old hide. "I can see smoke about ten miles east," he said.

Justina was lying on her back to look up at him. "That's the smelter at the mercury mines. What do you see in Mexico?"

He looked for dust, the sparkle of harness fastenings, the gleam of leather. In the dun vastness sweeping out to some distant blue mountains, islanded with small, flattopped mesas, he saw nothing.

He called his findings down to her.

126

"Good," she said. "Maybe they aren't going to move the money at all. They might just hide it here till the fuss blows over."

"Hey!" Rian called softly, peering toward the reddish cliffs where the river entered Santa Cruz Canyon. "There's some smoke over in the canyon."

Justina scrambled up. "How far down?"

"Can't say. It looks like it's from the main canyon."

"I'm coming up," the girl called.

Soon she was standing beside him, scrutinizing the river canyon. "It's in Oso Negro Canyon," she said. "That comes into the main canyon about half a mile below the cliffs. It might be cowboys, but I doubt it."

"Why?"

"Too early for a supper fire, and there's no branding going on now. It's more than likely someone who sits around making coffee and eating while he waits for a message."

"I'll have a look." Rian started back down the tree.

Justina came right behind him. "They'd eat you alive, Rian. You don't know the trails. We'll go together."

Artie Judd had left the county road an hour earlier and ridden into the thickets running out to the river. It was hot in the brush, and a cloud of gnats traveled with him, getting into his ears and the corners of his eyes. "Damn insects!" he muttered, swatting at the gnats in his ears.

He came from the brush onto a silty road paralleling the river, stopped and scowled in thought. Judd had been this way only once. Spence had brought him there and showed him some caves where, if he ever needed to hide out for a while, there was always a supply of canned food, matches, and hooks and line for taking channel cat.

A thought crossed his mind, and he grinned to himself.

Why not knock over Spence, if he was alone, and take off with the money? Nobody would ever be in a position to report the crime to the authorities; nor could they ever hang it on him.

But he felt obscurely obligated to George Hughson. He had drawn a good salary for months for doing nothing but crowd a wagon off the grade, now and then, or muscle a driver around until he quit the Reese line and left town. Now he'd been called on to earn his keep. But he'd bungled it twice — because of McCool. As much as obligation, therefore, he felt a prodding urge to square with McCool before he left.

Not much of a tracker, Judd had ridden a

hundred yards before he discovered that he was following another rider. He slipped to the ground and looked at the hoofprints.

Two horses, by God! The sign was sharp-edged and fresh. Judd swung back into the saddle. Rubbing his jaw, he gazed down the river. Nothing in sight, and the earth was too damp to show dust.

He pulled the rifle from the scabbard under his knee and rode ahead.

The river had scoured away at the red walls of Santa Cruz Canyon until it achieved a winding cleft little more than a hundred feet wide. The broad and shallow reach of muddy water became a narrow stream flecked with foam as it traveled with a low rumble of power. There was a trail littered with driftwood on the American side of the stream. A wind smelling of dampness blew against their faces as Rian and the girl rode down the canyon.

Rian shot apprehensive glances about them. He did not like the sensation of being boxed in. He feared an exposed back-trail and the unknown trail ahead. The cliffs were sheer and red, with a few tufts of Spanish bayonet clinging to them.

Several times he stopped and looked for hoofprints. But he saw none until they reached the confluence of Oso Negro Canyon. Here he saw several sets of prints leading from the side canyon to the rocks at the river's edge.

"Reckon they crossed here?" he asked.

Justina shook her head, raising her voice to be heard over the eerie fluting of wind and the rumble of water.

"It's ten feet deep and going forty miles an hour," she told him. "They just came down to water their horses and go back. It might have been cowboys."

"Any caves in the canyon?" he asked.

"It's full of them."

He scrutinized the smaller canyon with its craggy cliffs and heavy thickets, then glanced back the way they had come.

"Stay here while I go ahead," he said. "If anybody comes along, fire a shot to stop them. Then ride up the side canyon and we'll take off."

She shook her head. "I'm the general here, Rian. You stay. I know every cave between here and Frontera. Give me ten minutes. If nobody comes, ride up and meet me. I'll wait for you. Then I'll ride ahead another ten minutes."

He shrugged and let her go.

Dismounting, he led his horse fifty yards up Oso Negro Canyon and tied it. He went back and pried himself into a wedge between two boulders, from which he could watch the back trail.

Less than a hundred yards west, the canyon made one of its sharp kinks and the trail disappeared behind rubble and willows. His skin crawled; the whole layout was perfect for disaster. Anyone following them would see him almost as soon as he was seen. The river sounds would bury the echoes of gunfire a hundred yards away. If anything did happen, and their escape was blocked in this direction, it might easily be blocked in Oso Negro Canyon as well.

He glanced at his watch. Five minutes. Justina had no timepiece; if her time sense was not better than most women's, she might ride a half-hour before she stopped to wait for him.

He looked over his borrowed rifle. It was an old trap-door Springfield with specks of rust on it. He wondered whether the loads were as ancient as the gun. To check on the caps, he opened the breech of the gun. His fingertip rubbed the cap of the shell in the chamber; smooth and clean. Then, just as he started to throw the bolt home, he heard a shod hoof strike a stone.

Startled, he ducked down into the cleft. Presently he raised himself a few inches and scrutinized the trail. He saw nothing, and again shoved at the rifle bolt. It would not slide. He swore, opened the breech again, and once more pushed at the bolt. Once more it jammed.

As the hoof sounds grew suddenly louder, he looked up to see Artie Judd riding around the turn. The burly gunman had his hat pushed back; he carried a rifle like a man expecting to need it at any moment.

Rian groaned, ducked down and worked with the rifle again. Failing to break the jam, he dropped it and drew his Colt. Judd was within a hundred feet. Suddenly, on some instinct, he reined in and raised his rifle. His gaze came to rest on Rian.

Rian threw off a quick shot, the canyon exploded into tumbling echoes and Judd's horse began to pitch. The gunman fired as he fought the horse. Rian backed out of the cleft and ran hunched over for his horse. A bullet slashed the air above him. He whirled, fired at the gunman. Judd reined into cover as Rian ran again.

He untied the horse, hit the saddle, and rode up the side canyon.

CHAPTER FIFTEEN

A half mile up the canyon, a horseman reined quickly into the trail before him. He raised his old revolver, but it was Justina.

"Rian! What is it?" she asked.

"Judd's behind me! If he's here, there must be others. How do we get out of this canyon?"

He stared up at the craggy cliffs, stained red and green with minerals. Broken by erosion, they were littered with boulders and tough desert shrubs.

Justina frowned. "We could ride straight on up the canyon, but I just saw the smoke. It's a few hundred yards ahead. Wait —"

She rode a few yards ahead and turned her horse into the brush on the left side of the canyon. Beyond her, Rian perceived a curl of blue-gray smoke twisting into the air. At the top of the cliffs, the wind bent it southeast.

"There's a cow trail here," Justina called.

"Come on."

The trail ran along the rubbled base of the north cliff, then began climbing gradually. He could see several faint trails scraped into the sloping canyon wall by the hoofs of cattle and deer.

They had climbed fifty feet from the canyon floor when the first shot crashed into the baked-earth slope behind them. The horses bucked. Up through the brush and rocks came the smashing report of a rifle shot. Rian cursed the inoperative rifle on his saddle as he pulled the Colt. Down on the narrow canyon floor he could see a smear of black powder, and he fired at it.

Justina spurred her horse, but the frightened animal merely set its legs and quivered. Another slug smashed through a creosote bush at Rian's side. This shot came from farther up the canyon. Looking down, he could see the wood smoke where someone was camped; the shot had come from nearby. He gazed up and saw that before they ever reached the top they would be exposed on the hillside like flies on a wall.

He jumped down and led his horse ahead. "Get down!" he told the girl. "We've got to take cover."

White as paper, she gazed at him. Rian gave her a shake. "Come on! We've got to get out of here."

Justina turned her head. "There's a cave up here," she whispered "I — I think it's on this trail."

He led his horse past hers and ran up the trail. Glancing back, he saw her following him. Another shot ripped the brush and wailed off a rock by the trail.

He came to a cave, and was staring bleakly into it as Justina hurried up beside him. "You must have been pretty young when you called this a cave," he said.

The floor, covered with rocks, ran into the hill about twenty feet to meet the back wall. This wall rose vertically for a few feet, then sloped forward to become the ceiling. Thus there was no shelter from above, but they could lead the horses back to safety and lie behind the rocks at the front.

Without a word he took the girl's reins from her and led both horses into the shelter. Down below he heard a man shout; from another point someone answered. Spence and Judd were identifying themselves to one another.

He took the little buggy rifle from Justina's saddle and placed her behind a rock. Another shot glanced off the stones below the mouth of the cave. Through the cascade of echoes, he fired three fast shots at the smoke and crouched to reload. While he punched out the smoking shells, he told Justina:

"My rifle's jammed. See if you can clear it. Damn thing's rusted solid."

She worked at the bolt, then pulled a hairpin from the crown of her braids and began futilely picking at the follower mechanism.

"Rian," she whispered, "how are we going to get out of here?"

Rian took her chin between his thumb and forefinger. He kissed her solidly, and let her pull back, astonished.

"Well, we could take a horsecar," he said, "but I thought we'd wait till night and make a run for it. And hope one of those knotheads don't have sense enough to go for help."

Touching her mouth, she asked, "Why did you do that?"

"What if I get my head blown off in the next five minutes? It'd be awful to die *without* doing it. I've been thinking about it for quite some time."

"I think you're crazy," she said.

"Probably. Be thinking of where this trail goes, too. I want a little map of it — scratch it in the dirt, if you can find any."

The shots came sporadically — two or

three, then silence. Rocked with thunderous echoes, the cliff seemed to tremble. Suddenly Justina exclaimed with pleasure.

"It works! Look — there was a twig jammed into it."

Rian took the gun, worked the trap-door breech several times, and nodded approvingly. He spilled out half the box of old corroded shells beside him and loaded the gun.

Laying the rifle barrel across a rock, he tried to see what was going on down in the canyon. Shadows obscured the lower trail. When a gun was fired, he saw the flash, and ducked. A moment later the slug struck the sloping roof of the cave and ricocheted around. Justina gasped and pressed against him.

The shot had come from up-canyon, where the wolfish little gunman named Spence was holed up. Rian remembered him that night when Shackley whipped him — a coyote of a man with cold yellow eyes. He held his breath to steady the gun, looking for a flash of movement. Again he saw the yellow stab of flame and he fired quickly and ducked. With an earsplitting concussion, the other man's shot struck the rock before him and caromed off the ceiling of the cave.

"Let's have that map," Rian muttered.

"We may have to get out of here before dark."

The girl moved back and smoothed the earth with her hand. Taking a sharp pebble from the floor, she sketched the canyon. Rian glanced at the lines in the earth. Dusk was blurring details in the cave.

"This is where we are," she said. "Another little gully comes in here — it must be a couple of hundred yards. The gully tops out in the hills. The road's over here."

Rian nodded, squirmed around and got comfortable again. In the brush tangle below, someone was moving toward the trail to the caves. He took a rough aim, and fired two shots. The horses snorted and stamped.

The shots came more frequently now; the men had worked in closer to the cave. Uneasily, Rian realized that the cave was now in a cross fire. They would be under fire till dark; sooner or later, one of the snipers would get lucky.

"We've got to take off," he said suddenly. "Bring the horses and check the cinches."

Justina led the horses forward while he reloaded. When she had mounted, he fired the whole magazine of his rifle. The canyon rocked with echoes. No shots came back; it was apparent that the gunmen were riding out the volley under cover. He mounted quickly. From the cave mouth he fired two revolver shots before riding on up the cattle trail.

Once the hoof sounds echoed through the canyon, the gunfire below broke out with a reverberating clamor. Rian spurred his horse. Stumbling over the rocks, it bucked and lunged along the narrow cattle trail.

There was a wicked smack behind him.

Justina's horse uttered a loud grunt and went down. Rian saw the girl land in the tangle of creosote brush and begin to struggle. Swearing under his breath, he rode his horse back and reached an arm down to her, kicking free of his stirrup. She toed into the stirrup and swung up behind him. He lashed the horse with the reins.

After a few moments the girl gasped, "The side canyon's just ahead."

It was hardly more than a scar on the side of the main canyon. He could see where the run-off of summer rains had raked a notch in the earth. As he turned the horse, the guns opened up below them. In a few moments the arroyo deepened. The shots were passing high over their heads now.

Twenty minutes later they topped out among some broken hills. They stopped and dismounted to rest the horse. Rian reloaded, while Justina sat on a boulder with her face buried in her hands.

"You know," he said, "if I'd known how you ran stage lines down here, I might have gone into another line of work."

CHAPTER SIXTEEN

"This is Mr. Sharp, manager of Texas Mining Industries," Wiley Brogan said uneasily. Brogan, Justina's manager in Frontera, extended a hand of introduction toward a small, rawhide-tough little man with a brown face and black flint-chips of eyes.

It was midmorning, and they were gathered in the stage office — Rian, Justina, Brogan, and Sharp. Rian and the girl had reached town about midnight and roused Brogan, who procured rooms for them.

Justina, who knew the mining man, smiled at him as Rian offered his hand. Sharp peered into Rian's face, nodded brusquely, and took a cigar from his pocket. It was his company whose three thousand dollars had been stolen, and he had asked a meeting to discuss the matter.

"What about the money?" he asked shortly.

"We're making every effort to track it

down," Justina said. "We have some leads
—"

"You've got leads, and I had some money,"
Sharp interrupted. "What I want to know
is, why the devil you people don't carry
insurance to protect you against such
losses."

Justina explained about insurance require-
ments. Sharp lighted his cigar and spun the
match at a cuspidor.

"In other words," he said, "we're out our
three thousand?"

"No, sir," Rian said. "Not at all. If we
don't recover it, we'll make restitution."

"When?"

"Just as soon as possible."

"That's not soon enough. The money was
going to El Paso to pay for a submerged
pump we need in one of our mines. We need
the pump now — not at your convenience."

"I understand." Rian found himself employing phrases and mannerisms he had
heard successful men use.

With a serious expression, he went behind
Brogan's desk and marshaled a scratch pad
and a pencil. Jotting down $600, he said
soberly, "We've just hired a new accountant
who's going to get some things straightened
out for us. Among other things, there's the
matter of a thousand dollars in delinquent

accounts. We took in six hundred dollars on an overdue account yesterday."

He waited, then glanced up at the mining man. Sharp's eyes did not move from his face.

All right so far, Rian thought.

"We've had our problems, but we're taking steps to correct them. I'm a new partner, and I've got a background of staging."

He looked Sharp in the eye as he made the lie. In one week he had acquired more background than most men gathered in a lifetime. "We intend to stay in business despite the efforts of our competitors to drive us out."

Sharp grunted. "The Reeses have had their troubles," he agreed. "That's why I've gone along with some of their nonsense. But I can't absorb a loss like this one and keep my own job."

Rian nodded. Beneath the *$600,* he wrote: *One week from today,* and handed the slip of paper to the mining man.

"Suppose we pay you six hundred now, then two hundred a month until we've eaten up the loss? Or if we recover the money, we'll make full restitution."

In the street, a stage horn sang clean and clear. Then there was a sound of hoofs. Brogan glanced at the big Seth Thomas clock on the wall, and rubbed his jaw.

"Excuse me," he said. "Don't mean to interrupt. A man I've been waiting for is supposed to be on that stage. I want to catch him before he disappears or takes off for Kingbolt and parts west. He's a postal inspector."

"Mr. Morton?" asked Justina, in surprise.

"Why, yes," Brogan said. "According to his schedule, he'll be through on the westbound — Mr. Hughson's line, unfortunately — and I hope to get some action on this robbery. Though it wasn't a post-office loss, of course, so I can't really press him —"

Rian winced. The soft-handed approach again! *If we can't find a qualified agent to replace him,* he thought, *I'll just hire the first man I meet on the street tomorrow morning.*

"We handle mail, don't we?" Rian said sharply. "Isn't this a post-office as well as a stage line? All right, it was broken into. Mr. Sharp, what do you say to those terms?"

He moved toward the door. The stage rushed by, making for the Hughson station down the street.

Sharp's baked features wrinkled in thought. He nodded.

"It's a deal. But the first time you miss a payment I'll land on you like a cougar."

Rian hurried down the street beside Brogan, who chattered on and made little sense. Other townsmen were walking toward the depot. Frontera was a low-lying community in the broad river valley, a dun-colored town of Texas earth, and buildings made from that earth in the shape of mud bricks. It had a greater vitality than most such out-of-the-way towns had, however. Because of the mines and the trade with Mexico, there was money to be made in trading with Frontera. But not while you were fighting a war of survival.

An extremely stout man with yellowish, jaded eyes waited beside the coach as the passengers stepped from it. He was wearing a star — the "fat old sheriff" Justina had mentioned. In the doorway, a large man in a tan suit with brown velvet lapels was flipping a gold coin. He saw Rian and gave a nod and a slight smile.

Rian scowled. Hughson! When the devil had he come up? Now this was awkward. They might be able to get somewhere with Morton, but with Hughson around it would be almost impossible.

And there was Morton up on the deck,

small and birdlike in his black suit, as he dusted the crown of his high derby on his sleeve. When he saw Rian, his face tried to settle on an expression of alarm or pleasure. Next he discovered George Hughson, and slowly donned his hat; now his expression was definitely one of alarm. He saw the sheriff, and pulled his shoulders in defensively.

As the postal inspector climbed down, Brogan stepped forward. "Mr. Morton, I hate to bother you but —"

The stout sheriff shouldered him aside. Brogan moved to safety, gazing at the lawman reproachfully.

"Like to talk to you, Morton," he said sternly.

Morton's features flushed. Rian could see his lips trembling. "What's the trouble, Sheriff?"

"We'll discuss it at my office."

Rian stepped up and offered his hand. "Nice to see you again, Mr. Morton," he said.

The sheriff frowned at him. "Who are you?"

"McCool. Empire Stage. I'll go along. I've got some business with Mr. Morton."

The sheriff's office, on a corner, had more

flies than a stable, but it lacked the wholesome atmosphere. A water-stained cheesecloth ceiling sagged from rusty nails; the floor was of limed earth which badly needed watering down. A few dodgers were tacked to the adobe walls, where scabs of old plaster clung like mud to a hog's back.

Sheriff Murdo sat at his desk and fired up a cigar. He dropped the match on the floor and spat in a white china cuspidor.

"Now, then," he said to Rian, still wheezing from the walk. "What's your problem?"

Rian started to tell him about the robbery, but Murdo waved a fat hand and said, "I made an investigation."

"That's just it; you shouldn't have. This is a post-office case."

"Why?" George Hughson demanded. He had come along and now stood near the sheriff as if to support him.

"Because it was a post-office that they broke into."

"They didn't touch any mail. Only a private express shipment."

"Breaking into a post-office is still a federal offense." Rian looked at Sylvester Morton. "Am I right?"

There was an awkward silence. The inspector, sitting on a bench, frowned at his dusty boots. Hughson prodded him.

"Tell him, Sylvester. I'm all for tracking culprits down, but I buck against bringing in federal officers."

Morton looked up. His eyes were sad and tried. "Breaking a window in a post-office is a federal offense. This was a felony, and I'll have to call for U. S. marshals to handle it."

"Good," Rian said. "How soon can you do it?"

"I'm on my way to El Paso now. I'll make the request in person when I get there."

Hughson asked quietly, "You'll be riding the Empire stage as far as Kingbolt?"

Morton nodded. Hughson smiled. "I'll probably ride along."

Rian said, "I hope so. Our chances of getting through will be a lot better. By the way," he said, "I wanted to thank you for the bottle you sent."

Hughson squinted. "What bottle?" Then he caught the reference and turned away. "Forget it."

"No, it was a nice gesture. I was a pretty sick boy when Abby brought it. But after a couple of drinks I felt like a tiger!"

"Well, fine," Hughson said. "Sheriff —" he began. But Rian kept on, smiling persistently.

"That wife of yours! She's got a little tiger blood, too, George. I really envy you."

Everyone was looking at him now, seemingly embarrassed.

Hughson turned angrily. "There's a private matter the sheriff and I want to discuss with Morton. Will you excuse us?"

Brogan scurried out ahead of him. Rian sighed. "I really do envy you, George," he repeated. "Must keep a man stepping to keep a girl like that satisfied, though. Did I sleep the next day? I want to tell you I did!"

Hughson clenched his fists. For an instant Rian thought he was going to accept the challenge. Then he saw Hughson's glance flick to the gun on his hip, as though remembering Shackley.

Hughson wet his lips. "Get out of here," he said.

Sheriff Murdo jerked a thumb toward the door. "Take off, McCool," he ordered. "You're talking yourself into trouble."

After Rian had departed, Hughson sat on the bench beside Morton. From his billfold, he drew a check.

"I tried to cash this the other day, Morton," he murmured. "It came back marked 'insufficient funds.' "

Morton sat up straight. "You promised to hold it for two weeks!"

"Did I say that? All I know is, you'll have

to pay up or go to jail."

"I can't! I'm waiting for my pay check."

"That's tough. Because I need the cash. If you haven't got it, I'll go to the district attorney."

"That's a fact," Sheriff Murdo agreed. "You'd probably lose your job, Morton."

Morton leaned back against the rough wall. "So you think you'll get a new inspector down here, eh? And he'll find out how bad things are with the Reeses and cancel them out. Is that the plan? Well, it won't work, my friends! That's where you're making your mistake."

Hughson glanced at the sheriff. "Matt, it seems to me they're making a hell of a racket down there in the cantina. Why don't you go put the gad to the animals?"

Murdo blinked. Then the idea registered and he stood up and sauntered out. Alone with Morton, Hughson spoke frankly.

"I don't want to make trouble for you, Sylvester. But I've shown you a lot of favors, and I think it's time you reciprocated. As a matter of fact, I didn't try to cash that check. But I will — unless you and I reach an understanding."

Morton regarded him frostily. "Make your offer."

"Call off your dogs," Hughson said. "I

don't know who cracked the safe, and I don't care. What I *do* care about is eliminating Empire Stage Lines. 'Lines!' " he said bitterly. "An old man, a girl, and a snakebit horsebreaker running a couple of broken-down stages."

"For a thousand dollars a mile," Morton smiled.

"A thousand *I* should have. I could give the Post-Office people the kind of service they're paying for. Ask yourself: Is it a kindness to let them bleed to death, instead of giving them a quick and merciful end?"

Sucking a tooth, Morton said, "Seems to me there's a faint odor of death on *you,* my friend. You didn't make much of a fuss when McCool all but announced he'd cuckolded you. When a man won't take up a challenge like that, I begin to wonder how good a man he is."

Hughson stood up. The back of his hand suddenly whipped across Morton's mouth. Morton flinched. He put his fingertips to his lips and glanced at the blood on them. Then he smiled. There was a smear of blood on his teeth.

"You're a pretty good man at that," he said. "Providing the man you're bucking is small enough. I hope you'll be happy with

151

your new inspector. He'll have a full report on what I think's been happening."

CHAPTER SEVENTEEN

At nine-thirty that night, George Hughson stood in Biff Shackley's quarters and bleakly looked over the dim, liniment-scented room. Shackley had been about as good company as a sand rattler, but he was a single-minded man who knew his job. And he was loyal, something you could not buy. Hughson missed him. He felt as though he had lost his right arm in an accident, and as he began collecting the dead superintendent's belongings in a carton, a deep anger smoldered in his face.

Most of Shackley's possessions had been pocket-knives, tobacco cans, and patent medicines. They filled his chest of drawers and his footlocker. The room would be Artie Judd's now, if he hadn't put his foot in a trap yesterday. Hughson had not seen Judd since they split up at the trail to the caves.

Hughson looked around as someone rode from the alley into the stage yard. He quickly took Shackley's old rifle from the wallpegs, blew out the lamp, and opened the door sufficiently to have a view of the yard. The Mexican hostler was asleep in the feedroom; the other workmen had gone home.

He heard a man softly curse a tired horse as he dismounted. He knew the voice.

"Artie?" he called.

Judd turned and Hughson saw the glint of a revolver. "George?" Judd called back.

"In here," Hughson said.

In Shackley's room, with the door bolted and the lamp relighted, the two men talked. Judd was defensive about the way things had gone.

"Reckon we could have dropped them, but you go to killing women and you're calling out the hornets."

"Nobody's blaming you," Hughson said.

But there was impatience in the way he opened and closed doors, searching for liquor.

"What'd he drink — liniment?" he complained.

He found a half-empty bottle of whiskey and uncorked it. Looking for glasses, he located a tumbler rimmed with alkali and dust. He drank from the neck of the bottle and handed it to Judd. Looking tense and weary, the gunman, drank, then sighed. "Man, man." he said glumly.

"He stayed there. Like you said," Judd added.

"Why didn't you move the gold to another canyon?"

"We moved it to another cave. Spence said Oso Negro Canyon's the only one with back doors in every direction. How about that fellow Morton? He gonna make us any trouble?"

Hughson took the bottle from Judd's hand, wiped the neck on his shirt and took another pull at the liquor.

"He's not going to make trouble for anybody but himself. He's in Sheriff Murdo's tank. He'll stay there till I give the word to ship him to El Paso."

"How come he's in jail?"

"Bad-check charge," Hughson said. "Now we've got a clear track between us and Empire Stage Lines."

Judd drank again, then sprawled on the cot to peer at the pole-and-mud ceiling. "Now they lay them down and die, eh?"

"Not exactly — we don't have time for a natural death. Tomorrow — next day, maybe — they're sending six hundred dollars to Frontera. We're going to close the books on them, Artie."

"How?"

"On the road somewhere. They can't afford another big loss. You want to move your stuff in here? It'll be your room now."

Still Judd pondered in unhappy silence, and finally Hughson said, "You want to move your stuff in here or not, Artie? What I mean is — I want you to take Shackley's place."

Judd looked surprised. "Me — superintendent?"

"Why not? Anything you need to learn, I'll teach you. After the next few days there won't be any competition, and we can raise prices and start treating ourselves better. Better clothes for you, for instance. You don't have to dress like a hill rancher, like old Biff did. Money in the bank. That's after we clear Empire's plow once and for all."

Judd's simple, gaudy heart was touched. He rolled over on his belly, pulled his gun, and sighted along the barrel at the window.

"Hey, listen! That's my language you're talking."

"Mine, too. Learn your job and I'll make you a junior partner one of these days. I offered old Biff a quarter share a few months ago for a couple of thousand cash, but he couldn't scratch it up. Be thinking about it," he said seriously.

He took a last drink and went out.

The next morning Rian went to the bank.

In his pocket were four checks totaling nearly a thousand dollars, including Potter's check. Bob Moore, the new accountant, had turned up some surprising possibilities in Empire's books — angles which gave them leverage, handles to turn to squeeze money out of reluctant debtors.

The most useful of these tools was the simple device of threatening to sell overdue accounts to an attorney named John Hallon. Hallon specialized in bankruptcy cases. His reputation was such that he usually ate alone in restaurants, but he was a smart and ruthless attorney. Moore told Rian he could siphon all the blood from a man's body with the skill and speed of a six-foot mosquito.

Rian went to Hallon and received his offer of sixty cents on the dollar for all his delinquent accounts.

Then he went around telling the news to the biggest of the accounts, giving them an hour to write a check. When he returned, most of the checks were ready, a hundred cents on the dollar.

He talked to Mr. Noon, the bank manager, a deep-chested hearty old man with a white beard. Noon accepted Rian's deposit, then looked up at him in surprise. They sat by his desk, smoking cigars.

"You've got a talent for collections, Mr. McCool," he said. "I happen to know — well, I won't say I knew they were sweating old Dan Reese down — but they were hoping he'd go broke before they had to pay up. Congratulations."

Rian put the bankbook in his pocket. "Is there a bank in Frontera?" he asked.

"Not yet. We may open one down there ourselves, after we're sure the mines aren't going to play out the way the ones did at Candelaria."

"Then the only way to get money to Texas Mining is to carry the cash?"

Mr. Noon nodded.

Rian frowned and suddenly smiled. "I'll want six hundred of that deposit in gold, then. We'll take it down the river tomorrow."

Noon spoke to a teller, who glanced curiously at Rian and went back to the safe to get the cash. As he was counting out the little piles of double eagles, a stout, red-faced old man in a black suit came to the wicket next to him. Rian heard him say to the teller, "I want to transfer some funds from my savings account to commercial."

It was the voice of Potter, the feed merchant, whose money now gleamed before Rian in six neat cylinders of gold.

"Six hundred dollars," Rian's teller said briskly. "And you wanted a sack for it?"

Rian nodded. Uneasily, he glanced at Potter, but the feed merchant seemed not to have heard. Into the sack he dropped the gold pieces. He went out quickly.

Outside the stage office, Dan Reese was soaping hames and looking very gloomy. "Cheer up," Rian told him. "Better times coming."

Inside the station, Bob Moore was poring over the books, clucking over the errors he'd found. Justina gave Rian a wan smile.

"Mr. Moore's making me feel terrible. The things I did were wrong, and the things I didn't do were the things I should have done."

"The thing you should have done," sighed Moore, "was to hire an accountant. I never saw such a set of books."

"They'll look great, once we use up the last of the red ink," Rian told him. He asked Justina, "Have we got a safe?"

"Just a strongbox," said Justina. "I keep it under my bed."

"I want to put something in it," Rian told her.

They went outside.

Justina's father was now burnishing the leather he had soaped. Rian heard him sigh.

"What's on your mind, old timer?" he asked.

Dan raised his head and stared blankly across the yard. "Our driver's quit," he said. "I didn't want to tell you."

"Quit!"

Dan leaned back against the wall. "Scared out. Too many accidents on our line, he said. Too much going on."

"Where is he?" Rian asked angrily. "I'll either hire him back or make him sorry he ever saw a stagecoach."

"He's done left town," said the old man. Then he looked at his hands, curled his stubby fingers in and stretched them out again.

"Reckon I'll have to go back to driving."

"Oh, Father — !" Justina chided.

"I can drive a coach as well as any of them," Dan stated. "When I married your mother, I was driving three days a week for the old Butterfield line."

"But that was thirty years ago!" The girl looked at Rian, embarrassed by the old man's boasting.

Reese continued working his fingers. "They say a good whip never loses his hands. Let's see if it's true. Anyway, I've played dominoes till I see spots when I close my eyes. Next stage we send up, I'll be driving."

Rian slapped him on the shoulder. "I'll be riding shotgun guard then, and it'll be tomorrow."

The old man's hands dropped to his lap. "Tomorrow! Man alive, I don't know. Tomorrow — !"

"We're taking that money up to Texas Mining. I was thinking: do we have anything but that spavined old Concord stage that will run? Something faster?"

Justina spoke quickly. "We own an old Troy mud wagon. It's under a tarp behind Belder's livery stable. It's light and fast."

"I'll look at it."

He found the ancient Troy coach behind the stable. Pulling the tarp off, he inspected the dusty running gear, and the reach and bolster assembly. All appeared sound. The customary tooled-leather ornamentation of the Concord coach was heavy duck on the Troy, and the wheels were smaller. But it would do, he decided. Low-slung and fast, it would be a tough wagon to keep up with.

He spoke to the stableman, who agreed to have a couple of men clean the coach up and haul it over to the Empire yard. As he was leaving the stable, a sparkling black turnout with a buckskin mare between the shafts came up the road toward him. He waited for it to pass. When he saw that it was Abby holding the lines, he pushed his hat back and watched her.

She stopped. Smiling, she patted the seat beside her. "I was just looking for someone to talk with," she said.

Rian climbed into the buggy and took the lines from her.

CHAPTER EIGHTEEN

"You're a stubborn man, aren't you?" the girl said. They were driving down a narrow road between irrigated fields near the river. Up ahead, a large cottonwood cast a black shadow over the road.

"You know how it is," Rian told her. "Somebody says you can't do it, so you're bound to try."

"You still think you can do it?" In the sunlight, Abby's skin was fine-textured and smooth, rich with warm tones. She had a way of flattering a man with her eyes when she looked at him.

"If I do it," Rian said, "I hope you've got somewhere to jump. Because there won't be much left of Frontera Stage Lines."

"Perhaps I should jump before you do it then. But where?"

Rian looked at her, gazed again at the road and pulled up in the shade of the cotton-wood. "There's problems," he admitted.

"I could divorce George, of course," she said, "but then where would I be? Besides, I think you're fond of that Reese girl."

"Just a good friend," Rian said.

He tied the lines and looked into her face. Then he leaned over and pressed his lips against hers. Abby's arms slipped around his neck. After a moment he disengaged himself and took a deep breath.

"Come to think of it," he said, "you're still married, aren't you?"

She pouted. "Is that my fault or yours?"

"I don't know. I've been thinking over what you said about George. You know — dying before his time?"

"And what did you decide?"

"That I'd hate to swing before *my* time. There's a better way. I talked to a lawyer."

"About *me?* You didn't!"

He continued to lie, elaborating on it. "No. About a woman losing her property when she marries, and all that. He said that if a woman took a man to court she might be able to prove that the only reason he married her was for her property. And she'd get it back."

She squeezed his hands. "Really?"

"For a fact."

She pondered it. "But in the meantime he'll lose it all anyway, if you wreck him."

Rian chuckled. "It's hard to know who to back, isn't it? If you back me — and I lose — you lose, too. But if you stick with George —"

Abby pushed out her lip. "I didn't mean that at all. Would I kiss you this way if I didn't love you?"

She leaned forward, pressed her mouth to his again as she twined her arms about his neck. Rian felt the way he did after a couple of quick shots of whiskey — pleasantly dazed. Then he drove his mind back to Sheriff Crump's jail, in Vallecito. He recalled watching her walk along the street, never looking at him in his cell.

Gently, he disengaged her arms.

"The way we're going," he said, "George is going to get that divorce instead of you."

"Men are so practical," she sighed.

"It's our nature. What might be practical for you would be to slap your husband with a paper and tie up the bank account and all his assets. Then take him to court. I'd win in a walk then."

"Are you sure?"

"Pretty sure. It's worth trying, isn't it?"

"Not if I wreck my husband's line just to save yours so Justina Reese can have you. Is that what you have in mind?"

Rian laughed. "There's the female mind

for you! Listen, Abby — Justina may be pretty, but she's not my kind of girl. You're my kind, now that I've broken you to harness."

Abby's lips eased into a smile. "We'd better go back," she said.

Near the village, she said, "It would be better if you got out here."

Rian climbed down.

"I'll speak to George," Abby told him. "I'll tell him what I want: all my property back. If he won't give it to me, I'll move out and start suit."

Abby told George Hughson when he came home for lunch that day. The Mexican girl who cooked for them could not speak English, so Abby told him exactly what she had in mind. Leaning against the jamb of the door, Hughson somberly smoked a cigar while he gazed down the quiet side street on which they lived.

"In other words," he said, "you're asking me for about four thousand dollars cash?"

"Yes. If I've got the cash, I can count on your treating me the way you did before we were married. As long as you know I can move out on you any time I want, you're more likely to show your appreciation of the good wife you have."

166

Hughson turned. "Were you good in Mc-Cool's bed that night?"

Abby's eyes widened. "Who — ?"

"McCool was bragging about it," Hughson snapped.

Abby shrugged. "He was lying."

Hughson walked to her. He peered into her face. Then he slapped her, slapped her again, and watched her fall back on the sofa, weeping.

"Pack your things and get out," he said. "You can have your horsebreaker and his bankrupt business. And that's all you ever will have."

He went out and banged the screen door behind him.

Later that afternoon, Potter, the feed man, entered his office through the side door. Hughson was cool to the man as he lowered his fat backsides onto a chair.

"What's on your mind?" he asked.

Potter lowered his voice. "Anybody around?"

"No."

Potter leaned forward. "I just saw your wife checking into the Mountain View Hotel! Something wrong, George?"

Hughson rocked back in the chair. "Nothing that concerns you, Ira."

"I didn't mean to meddle. Another thing," he said. He glanced into the waiting room, closed that door, and then pulled his chair close to the desk. His watery eyes earnestly sought Hughson's face.

"McCool took six hundred dollars out of the bank this morning!"

"What of it? If you hadn't paid him, he wouldn't have had six hundred to draw out."

"You know why I did it! I was in a terrible bind —"

Hughson scraped under his nails with a gold penknife, saying nothing.

"Now I've got other people on my back," Potter complained. "Everybody I ever owed a dollar to is threatening to take me to court. They figure I'm soft, I suppose —"

"Maybe you are."

Potter sat up in injured dignity. "I paid because I had no choice. If someone's traded sharp with me, they'd better look out or I'll never pay them. There were *rocks* in that river cane I bought from Dan! That's why I let him wait for his money."

Hughson's quiet smile mocked him. Potter was fearful that he would start buying his feed from someone else. To protect himself he had just appointed himself unofficial informer to Frontera Stages Lines.

"So McCool took out six hundred dollars," Hughson said, finally.

"He asked for a bag to carry the money in! Said it was going on a trip. Just thought you might want to know," Potter said. "Of course it's none of my business. In fact, I'm going to forget I ever heard him, or that I told you."

CHAPTER NINETEEN

Artie Judd sauntered into the stage yard just before dark. He wore a new lavender shirt in addition to his customary tight, black pants and some yellow dress-boots.

Now there *is taste gone wild!* Hughson thought, watching him strut across the yard. The gunman criticized something one of the yard men was doing, halted by a rack of harness bells hung against a wall, and spoke to another man.

"I want these things polished up," Hughson heard him say. "Then hang them inside, out of the weather."

"Si patrón!" the Mexican said.

Hughson saw Judd's chest swell. *Sure, boss!* That was the stuff to feed the troops — when they were as vain and stupid as Judd. But for a while Hughson would have to take the gunman at face value. As Judd sauntered into his office, Hughson exclaimed with pleasure and moved around to look him over with feigned admiration.

"Say! Do you need a note from your mother to buy a shirt like that?"

Judd grinned. "The girls at the Pastime Bar like to tore it off me this noon," he said.

"Wish I could wear colors like that," Hughson flattered him. Then he asked, "Anything doing?"

Judd drew his Colt and spun it by the trigger guard. He gave a short laugh of contempt.

"Old Reese has lost his mind, I reckon. When I went by the stage yard he was setting on a box. He had six pegs driven in the ground with a rein tied to each. He was holding the reins like he was driving a team. He'd say, 'Ho Belle! Ho, Chunk!' and then he'd yank a rein and try to pull the right peg over!"

Hughson's brow creased. "He used to be a driver before he ranched. Has Simmons quit him?" he asked quickly.

"I don't know."

"If Simmons has quit, he's probably aiming to take his place driving. Artie!" he said suddenly, "that's it! They're sending money to Frontera tomorrow. It's dollars to washers Dan Reese will be driving."

Excitement came up full and strong in him. He sat behind his desk, spun a scratch pad before him and picked up a pencil. "Come here," he said. Judd came around the desk as Hughson sketched a map.

"Know where the road skirts Cerro Colorado?"

Judd leaned on the desk by one hand. "Reckon so," he said dubiously.

"You'd better know so before you leave town tonight."

"Didn't know I was leaving."

"You're leaving as soon as it's dark." Hughson turned the map so that Judd could see it, his pencil point tracing the stage road. "Cerro Colorado's that red slide south of the road. The road climbs across the foot of it. The rocks are as big as horse troughs, and loose. They used to have slides there all the time. Do you remember the place?" he asked intently.

Judd scratched his neck. "I know it. But —"

"It wouldn't take much to start another slide, Artie. Just one shot of blasting powder."

Judd shook his head. "All I know about blasting powder you could heap on a beer check."

Scowling, Hughson weighed the odds. It was too good a chance to pass up. Yet he did not dare to be on the ground himself when it happened. Even old Marshal Fowley might get curious about a coincidence like that if anyone saw him in the area.

He explained how simple it was to set a couple of sticks of explosive in place. He figured how much fuse Judd should attach to the cap.

"I'll give you two feet of red-dot fuse. Light it as soon as the coach comes past the dead tree I've marked — right here. I've timed it all out before — just in case," he said. "Or, if you're a good rifle shot, you can leave, the cap exposed and put a shot into it from a distance."

"I can't hit the backside of a bull from fifty feet," Judd frowned.

"Then use the fuse. Their regular stage leaves here at one p.m. They've got a watering-and-rest stop a mile or two short of the slide. So they'll be going more or less full-bore at the slide."

Judd's thick features still seemed unhappy as he studied the map.

"All you have to do afterwards," Hughson said, "is turn your horse around and come back. Take the river trail and you won't be seen. And then we're in business!" he finished, clapping the gunman on the shoulder.

Judd folded the map and slipped it in the

pocket of his new lavender shirt. His small eyes gazed into the stage man's for a moment. Then he nodded.

"Where's the stuff?"

All afternoon Justina had behaved very coolly toward Rian. At first he thought she was merely preoccupied. But when, that evening, he said, "I think we ought to hide that cash under your bed now," she retorted, "I don't care what you do with it. Why don't you buy Mrs. Hughson some matched blacks for her town buggy?"

She marched out of the office, banging the door after her. Rian stared after her as she hurried in the darkness toward the living quarters. Baffled, he gazed at Bob Moore.

"What ails the female, Bob?"

"Just that, I reckon," the old man said. "Bein' a crazy female."

"She's been a female as long as I've known her," Rian said, "but she hasn't acted like this before."

Except, he recalled, *when she found Abby'd been to see me at the hotel.*

Great snakes! he thought. *Did she see me in Abby's buggy this morning?*

He strode after her. In the darkness, he heard the screen door bang closed. A moment later he opened the door. She was not in sight, but he saw a lamp come on in the kitchen. She had placed it in a wall bracket and was tying the strings of an apron behind her as he came into the doorway.

"Hey!" he called.

Justina banged open the draft on the small iron cookstove and removed the lids in order to start a fire. She paid him no attention at all.

"What did you mean about Mrs. Hughson's buggy?" he asked.

Still she did not answer. She stuffed newspapers into the firebox, took three pieces of kindling from the woodbox and arranged them atop the paper. Rian crossed the tiny room and touched her arm.

Justina whirled and slapped him.

Then she covered her face with her hands and began to weep. Rian pulled her hands down, chuckling. "You saw us, didn't you?"

The girl turned her face from him. "Go away! The whole thing was a plan to wreck us, wasn't it? You're just doing what she tells you to."

"No! It was business. She's trying to use me, see? So I decided to let her try. And at the same time, I'm using her."

"How?"

He told her.

"Now she's moving out on Hughson. If she starts suit to recover her property, it'll tie him up legally so he can't even sign a mail contract. She may be able to attach his assets while they fight the suit. Isn't that worth taking a buggy ride for?"

Justina sniffled. "I suppose . . ."

The screen door creaked open and there was an apologetic tap. "Miss Justina?" called Bob Moore.

Justina pulled her apron up and wiped her nose and eyes. "Yes?" she called.

"A lady to buy a ticket," Moore said. "Afraid I don't know how to write it up."

"Oh. Well, I'll do it. Just a minute! Do you know the lady?"

Rian, too, thought it curious that Moore would not say who the lady was, in a town of that size. It was an event of local importance when anyone crossed the street.

"Yes, ma'am. It's Mrs. Hughson," Moore called back.

They looked at one another. Rian grinned. "You see? She's walking out on him!"

Justina put her hands to her cheeks. "Do you really think — ?"

"Go sell that ticket," Rian said. "Best if I stay out of sight."

After Justina left the house, Rian sat on the worn plush sofa. *A week ago,* he reflected, *I was sitting in a jail cell with no women at all. Now I've got a choice of two. Of course it was no choice, really. Picking Abby would be like picking a side winder. The longest day of her life, she would remember that when she wrote for him to come to her, he never answered the letter.*

He went into the kitchen and completed the fire Justina had been building. Lighting it, he replaced the black iron lids and adjusted the draft and damper. He filled the hot-water reservoir and started some coffee.

Justina came back, her eyes sparkling. "It's true! She's going to Frontera tomorrow. Do you really think that's what she's going to do?"

"Let's wait and see. Where's Dan?"

"He's been in the harness room most of the afternoon, tending the reins he's going to use. Soap, conditioner — it's ridiculous, you'd think he was getting married or something."

"It'll be good for him," Rian said. "And look at the money we'll save. Later on we can hire another driver and add service to Fort Biggs, with Dan holding down the Frontera stage."

Justina smiled. "You don't have to be a dreamer to be a stage man," she said, "but it certainly helps."

CHAPTER TWENTY

Artie Judd spent the night on Cerro Colorado.

From the top of the hill, broad and flat like an old cinder cone, he could gaze down on the shallow valley the stage road traversed on its way to Frontera. Far out in the hills he could see a few lights, like cigarette sparks, where small ranchers had their homes.

The slope climbed steeply from the stage road, a great talus of porous red blocks of volcanic stone. They seemed so precariously balanced that he postponed finding a spot for the dynamite until morning. He had the feeling that if you loosened exactly the right boulder, the little valley would be brimful of rocks a minute later.

That night he made his camp just back from the top of the slide. The old crater was filled to the brim with fine sand deposited there by the windstorms that frequently howled through this country.

Judd scooped out a hollow and built a little fire with deadfall from some alligator junipers growing on the slope. He had nothing to cook, but the fire melted the loneliness around him until he was ready to sleep.

In the morning he looked over the ground carefully, back door and front.

The back door was the bosque of the river. To use it, he would have to follow the perimeter of the cinder cone and ride down the back way into the bosque. On that side of the hill the ground was much more even. It slid out to the river right where Santa Cruz Canyon opened like a door for the river to enter.

In the clear, winey light of dawn, the gunman scrutinized the valley before him.

In the bottom, the volcanic stone had decomposed sufficiently to be called earth. There were a few cottonwoods and junipers through which the stage road took a reasonably straight path. Judd picked out the dead tree Hughson had mentioned. A quarter of a mile south of the tree, the road passed under a ledge of tumbled red boulders.

That's the spot he meant, Judd decided.

He spent another ten minutes satisfying himself that there was no one on the road; that no Mexican goat-herds were in the area, no cowboys poking around hunting stray cows. Then he picked his way down the slope with the dynamite, caps, and fuse shoved into his shirt. Once, a boulder shifted under his boot and he had to jump. Cursing, he fingered the dynamite and wondered what would happen if he fell on it.

Picking his spot with care, he tucked the two sticks of explosive under a rock and affixed the cap. Then he stretched the fuse out so that one portion of it could not ignite another portion with its sparks and cause a premature explosion.

He stood up and considered the whole scene. He envisioned the boulder jarring lazily a couple of feet into the air, coming down upon the stones below it, as the whole mass began to move.

It took him a minute and a half to regain the summit. He looked at his watch again; it was nine-fifteen. He stretched out on his back in the floury-fine sand and gazed up at some buzzards revolving on the rim of an invisible wheel.

Dan Reese spent most of the morning sitting on the box of the old Troy coach, getting the feel of it. Every time Rian passed, the old man would call to him.

"It's a great feeling, boy!" he said once. "You're the king of the mountain up here. All them horses working for you! You can make any one of them sit down and slide or stretch his neck, just by bending your finger!"

"See to it you bend the right finger," Rian suggested. He hoped the old man still had his stage man's hands, if he'd ever had them.

A boy from the hotel came to the stage depot at eleven-thirty with two large suitcases of Abby Hughson's. Rian stowed them inside the luggage boot. At twelve, Abby came and settled herself in the waiting room. Rian avoided going into the station.

A few minutes later old Potter showed up. He had a half-filled gunnysack slung over his shoulder. Stiff and red-faced, he stared at Rian, who was helping Dan tar axles on the Troy. He shook up the sack.

"I want to send this to Frontera," he said.

"What is it?"

"Feed sample. Not exactly to Frontera — to a farmer near there. You can drop it by the road at Tolson's turnoff."

Reese started a hub nut back onto the threads. "Take it into the office. My clerk will give you a tag to make out. The old busybody," he muttered, as Potter trudged into the office. "He likely saw Mrs. Hugh-

181

son coming here. He just wants to make sure before he tells on her. Feed samples!"

When Potter left, he walked at his customary dignified gait to the corner, then broke into an uneven hurrying stride. Panting, he walked into the stage yard and hurried to Hughson's side door. Without knocking, he opened it and went inside.

The stage man was not there.

Potter groaned. He was just turning away when Hughson came in, big, square-shouldered, somberly dressed. Hughson drove a glance of displeasure into Potter's eyes, saw something he had not expected there, and frowned.

"What's the matter?"

"Maybe nothing, George. Only — well, did you know Mrs. Hughson's going down to Frontera on that stage today?"

It hit Hughson with blinding force. He put out a hand to steady himself as his heart squeezed down, then exploded into violent pumping.

"How do you know?" he asked.

"She's in their waiting room right now!"

Hughson realized something about himself he had not been aware of. He still loved Abby; had somehow thought he'd make her come back, but on his terms. The magnitude of the threatening disaster overwhelmed him.

After a moment he managed to recover his self-possession. He jingled some coins in his pockets. "All right. Thanks for telling me," he said.

"I thought I'd better let you know."

"Thanks. I may speak to her, may not. Pretty hard to change a woman's mind, eh? Married men like you should know that, Ira."

Potter gave a flabby grin, chuckled, and went to the door. "Well, just thought I'd — good-bye," he said.

Hughson sank into the chair.

Now what?

Run down to the station and tell Abby that she mustn't take that stage, because it was going to be obliterated from the face of the earth? Put a weapon like *that* in her hands?

God, no!

On the other hand — let her ride into the trap with the others? He put his fingertips to his temples and massaged them. He glanced at the clock. Twelve-fifteen. Forty-five minutes before the stage left.

Anything he did involving Abby was going to be noticed, and when the stage was wrecked the finger would instantly point at him. He could not forcibly drag her home, argue with her, or try to delay the stage. Anything he did would incriminate him later.

Forty-five minutes. Time to ride up and call off the show for today? A stage traveled faster than a rider, but he would have nearly an hour's head start if he left at once. He could take short cuts across the hills and through the gullies. He would have to rest his horse frequently, but so would the stage team have to rest, since it was a two-bit outfit with no way station where a fresh team was backed onto the pole.

At last it came to him that this was the only thing he could do: ride like the devil to Cerro Colorado. If he made it in time, well and good. If he was late, he would still have a small lead on the stage. He could find a good vantage point near the road and drop one of the horses with a rifle shot. That would slow the stage enough so that the blast would go off prematurely.

A rifle. He had several, but all were at home, a fifteen-minute ride. Then he remembered that Shackley's old rifle was still in his room. Such as it was, it would have to do.

He walked to the barn and found a hostler. "Saddle my grulla," he told the man.

"Yes, sir." But the stableman hesitated.

"The grulla? You don't ride him much, Mr. Hughson. He's full of beans. Likely act up a bit."

"That's why I want the grulla. He needs to be ridden more often. He's a good, strong animal, but he needs to know who's boss."

"Yes, sir."

Hughson sauntered to Shackley's room, unlocked it and went inside. Quickly, he lifted the rifle from its wall pegs. It weighed about fifteen pounds, solid bronze, and looked as though Shackley's grandfather might have carried it in the War of 1812. However, it was a Colt revolving six-shot, with a loading lever fitting under the octagonal barrel. He cocked it and peered down the barrel. He could see light through the fire hole and knew it was unloaded.

Searching quickly through Shackley's effects, he found a box of linen cartridges. He put one in each chamber, rammed it home, pinched priming caps onto the nipples, and looked for rifle balls. Finally he found a quantity of them in the hollow stock of the gun. He inserted the first ball and worked the loading lever again; immediately the ball rolled out.

My God! he thought bitterly. *An old paper-patch model!*

He tore a few postage stamp-size patches

from a newspaper. After laying a patch over the chamber, he pressed the ball home with his thumb, then rammed it in place. This time it stayed in the gun. He finished loading and went outside.

He carried the rifle to the alley, holding it parallel to his body so that it might not be noticed. He walked a few yards down the alley and leaned the gun against the back of a building.

When the horse was ready, he told the hostler, "I may not come back after lunch. I've got some papers to work on at home."

He rode down the alley, picked up the gun, and cut through a vacant lot southwest toward the river road. As soon as he was on the road, he put the horse into an easy lope, riding well forward over the withers to ease the load on the animal's back. The horse would never be worth a damn after today but, by Heaven, it would have to make it to the slide in time!

CHAPTER
TWENTY-ONE

Five minutes before stage time, Rian carried the express box from the station. Within its battered oaken shell was the dark gleam of six hundred dollars in gold, plus a few things consigned to the post office in Frontera. The box was shoved far under the driver's seat, the mail sack jammed in on top of it. The six-horse team, held by a couple of hostlers, was already in the traces.

At stage time, Dan Reese swaggered from the house, pulling on new buckskin gauntlets as yellow as wildflowers.

Standing with Rian, Justina whispered, "Pray Heaven he's up to it! So far, I think it's just a game with him. How can a man handle a six-horse team after so long?"

As the old man prepared to mount, Rian had an impulse to help him. He suppressed it. If Dan couldn't mount the box, then, by George, he wasn't ready to drive! But Dan climbed easily to the deck, took up the lines and began separating them.

"Bo-*ard!*" Rian bawled.

Abby appeared in the depot door. Across the tawny ground she smiled at him. She waited an instant, as if hoping he would come to offer his arm. Instead, he tossed his rifle to the deck, smiled good-bye to Justina, and waited by the door of the coach.

Abby came forward. He marveled at how well she carried off the delicate situation. Still, she'd always been able to fake the part of the fine lady. Hard to believe that a few days ago the fine lady was suggesting he kill her husband for her!

Small, perfumed, and meticulously turned out in a gray and blue traveling dress, she stood before him.

"Are we all ready to leave?" she asked. "I hate to board until stage time."

"All ready, ma'am," he said with mock dignity. "That's what I was yelling about." He took her elbow and helped her into the coach. "Curtains up or down?" he asked.

"Up please," she said, smiling.

Once she was settled — the only passenger — he closed the door. He rolled up the canvas curtains and secured them. He climbed to the box and put his rifle across his knees.

"All set, Dan," he said.

The first two miles were the hardest. For a while Rian had to close his eyes. Dan was overdriving, the horses cutting this way and that as his messages traveled down the lines in a series of nervous tugs. Once a leader stumbled and there was a near pile-up.

But that somehow relaxed the old man.

He began to settle down. He even glanced at Rian with a faint grin.

"Relax, young fellow," he said over the ringing clatter of hoofs and wheels. "I got the feel of it now."

"And not a minute too soon," Rian said. "We were about to get the feel of the rocks by the road."

Judd looked at his watch every few minutes. Sometimes, when he looked, only a minute would have passed. He was nerved up like a bride. He laid out some matches for the fuse, then put them away. He was afraid they might be ignited accidentally and set fire to the fuse. He lay only a few feet from it.

His vantage point was two-thirds of the way down the slope. He could see as far as the dead tree by the road — the key to the whole attack. Judd's mouth was dry. In his hip pocket was a bottle of whiskey, half emptied during the night by his campfire. He took it out, uncorked it, then shoved the cork into the neck again, returning it to his pocket. Later.

There was damned little fire left in Hughson's grulla now. High on grain and barn sour, it had soaked up a lot of spurring before the work of carrying the big man on its back settled it down. Now its tawny sides were black with sweat, its nostrils flared.

Hughson pulled up on a lift of ground and looked at his watch. Two-forty! He figured the stage would pass Cerro Colorado at three. Give or take ten minutes, Judd would have to be a clumsier man than Hughson surmised him to be to fail in his job. The slide, once started, should spread over a hundred feet.

Scrutinizing his back trail, he saw a ragged feather of dust against the desert. Hughson groaned. It had to be the coach. He spurred the horse hard, studying the red hill a few miles ahead. To be safe, he took a route paralleling the road but a few hundred yards to the right of it. Thus, if he had to, he would be in position to shoot one of the lead horses and stop the stage.

■ ■ ■ ■

Two miles from Cerro Colorado, Dan Reese stopped the stage to rest the horses. He got down and walked around to test the tugs and traces. "They're really working," he called up to Rian. "Hitting the collars all together. Next time I'll latch 'em up looser — give 'em more freedom to move."

Rian leaned overside. "Everything all right, ma'am?" he called to Abby.

The girl was patting dust from her face with a kerchief. "Would you mind putting down the curtains now?" she asked.

"My pleasure," Rian said.

By the time he had finished lowering and tying the curtains, the horses had stopped blowing. "We'd best be rolling," said Dan. "Don't want them stiffening up."

Rian stood on the deck a moment to study the ground. He looked over the long, red slide ahead for the flash of metal or for movement. But there was no sign of trouble, and if anybody tried to stop them he had a rifle filled with bullets as big as his thumb to discourage them.

"Okay," he said, sitting down. "Let's roll."

Dan Reese kicked off the brake, and with a squeal of bull-hide thorough braces, the

191

old Troy rolled on down the road.

When it passed a dead alligator-juniper beside the road, the horses tossed their head and shied. Good sign, Rian thought, the foolish animals were feeling good. Old Dan still had his stage man's hands.

Then something happened that dynamited the quiet afternoon apart like an artillery shell.

The right lead-horse suddenly threw itself against its mate. At the same time it uttered a scream that made the goose flesh rise on Rian's arms. Distinctly, he heard a loud *pop.* Then he saw the blood spurting from its right shoulder.

The horse fell, and in an instant the rest of the team had piled up in a hopeless knot of squealing animals, kicking legs, and tangled harness. Rian crouched on the deck and looked for the sniper, as he heard a rifle shot echoing back and forth down the slope at the right of the road.

"What the devil?" Dan shouted. "Rian, what did I do? What happened?"

"Pile off!" Rian shouted. "Get behind the coach. We're under fire."

Dan scrambled to the road, lugging Justina's little buggy rifle, Rian sprawling after him. Inside the buggy, he heard Abby scream. The door opened on the far side and she stepped down. She ran past the threshing, bellowing team and stopped in the center of the road with her hands over her ears.

"Get down!" Rian shouted. "Take cover."

Abby stared wildly at the team, then at Rian; he had the feeling that nothing registered with her. Dust exploded in the road between her and the team. Then they heard the violent echoes of another rifle shot. She screamed, took a few running steps, caught her foot in her skirt, and fell. Still screaming, she got to her feet and started on.

Rian ran after her. "Come back here, you little idiot!"

He would not have believed it was possible to run so fast in skirts. Holding her skirts knee-high, the girl ran down the sandy crown of the road.

Something passed Rian with a sound like tearing linen.

A bullet struck a rock on the far side of the road and caromed off. Rian threw himself to the ground. Sprawled there like an infantryman, he searched for the source of the shot.

High among the rocks he saw a smear of powder smoke. He aimed the old Springfield with care and squeezed off a shot. Dust sprang up where it struck. He fired again, dazed by the suddenness with which disaster had come. Abby was still running, and now he realized there was no logic in following her; he was the target, not she.

He waited an instant, gathered himself and sprinted back to the coach at a staggering run. Dan was trying to cut the dead animal out of the traces to get the others back on their feet.

"Leave him!" Rian shouted, seizing him by the shoulder and dragging him into the shelter of the coach.

"They're sufferin'," Dan protested, bewildered.

"Better them suffering than us dying," Rian panted. "Stay down and look for targets."

CHAPTER
TWENTY-TWO

A half minute passed.

Rian saw movement in the boulders along the rim of the red hill. He took aim, but before he could fire, a man had risen quickly, taking a few running steps and vanishing over the crest.

Then he felt a massive jolt in the earth, a tremor which was followed by a puff of wind against his face. Motion in the slide farther up the road drew his gaze. He stared.

"Dan — look!" he gasped.

A great mass of boulders was rising from the earth on a mushrooming column of dust; smaller stones soared high, twisting and turning in the air. As the larger rocks fell back, a slide started. In a dusty tangle of brush and small junipers, the boulders plunged downhill toward the road. The rumble of their movement came through the earth.

Rian came slowly to his feet, a coldness

spreading through him. He saw Abby standing beside the road, facing the slide. She began to run. As she ran, the path of the rock slide widened. A few smaller stones bounded down the slope and landed near the road. Abby swerved, leaving the road to run across the narrow valley between the hills. She stumbled and fell, regained her feet and ran a little farther before a sotol cactus tangled her skirts and stopped her.

As she tried to pull free, the base of the slide stirred with a bass grunting sound. Here and there, puffs of dust burst from it. The mass began to settle almost wearily, seeking its own level. Already littered with smaller stones, the road now began to be covered with larger ones. Then there was a louder roar, a muted thunder, as the slide spread.

"Mother of God!" Dan whispered.

Small rocks were landing near Abby. Leaving half her dress tangled in the cactus, she pulled free. A few stones were landing beyond her now. And, as they watched, the road itself was engulfed by the rockslide. A hole had been scooped out where the explosion tore the first boulders away. Now the rocks above the hole loosened and crashed into it, and after that the slide seemed to flow like a river of mud, covering the road, spilling across it onto the level ground, burying everything in its path.

At last there was an aching stillness.

The valley boiled with dust. A few more boulders broke loose and bounded down the slope. Rian could not see the place where Abby had vanished. He was not anxious to. Trembling, he turned to the old man.

"Let's get these horses straightened out before they kill themselves," he said.

Four of the horses were uninjured, but one was dead of the gunshot which had dropped it, and another had a broken foreleg. They destroyed it, then led the others to nearby trees where they tethered them. They rolled the Troy off the road, and Rian unearthed the mail sack and express box and hid them in some brush.

"It's funny," Dan said. "Them shooting that horse. If they were going to wipe us out anyway, why fire at the horse and stop the stage?"

"I reckon that's it, Dan," he said. "Somebody *was* trying to stop it. He stopped us, but he couldn't stop Abby. I'm going to look around," he said.

"I'll go along."

Rian started to tell him to stay with the horses, but decided the old man was probably equal to a little more excitement, and he needed his gun, puny as it might be.

"Let's work around back of the hill," he said. "Take us an hour to hike up the slide. And I've kind of lost my appetite for rock climbing anyway."

They walked west a quarter of a mile, then turned south toward the river road which Rian and Justina had followed the other day. Just before they reached the road, Rian put out a hand to halt Dan.

Two horsemen had reined up in the trail a couple of hundred yards ahead. Both men instantly brought rifles to their shoulders, and Rian and Dan hit the ground.

Hughson swore as he spurred his horse into a tangle of mesquite, seeing the men in the trail. Artie Judd was right behind him, and just as they entered the brush a couple of bullets ripped through the branches. The booming thunder of a Springfield rolled down the bosque, followed by the thin crack of a lighter rifle.

Judd was afire with excitement. "Let's run over them!" he said, "Roust 'em out and gun 'em down."

"Use your head," Hughson said. "We couldn't hit them at a run. They'd knock us out of the saddle. We're going down to Oso

Negro Canyon and pick up Spence and that cash."

He was talking fast but hearing the words as though someone else were speaking them. Something told him to keep going; that the only chance to avoid being overwhelmed by what he had just seen was to drive ahead.

"We'll be in a box, George," Judd argued.

"We're in a box now. I didn't count on survivors. We've got to bring Spence out, and we're liable to need that money he's sitting on. McCool will follow us in. If three of us can't whip him and old Reese, we're finished anyway."

He dismounted and crawled to a spot from which he could see the back trail. Then he raised his gun and fired one of his remaining shots at the place where he had last seen the stage men. He sprang up.

"Let's go!"

Staying in the thickets, they entered Santa Cruz Canyon, then pulled into the trail and loped down the river. In ten minutes they reached the confluence of Oso Negro Canyon and rode up this side canyon toward the cave.

When they reached it, Spence called from a ledge above the cave where he had been lying in ambush. "I thought you'd done forgot me! I've had nothing to eat but soda crackers since yesterday."

"Stick with me, Spence," Hughson retorted, "and you'll be eating bullets before nightfall. Where's the money?"

Bewildered, the fox-faced man jumped to a lower ledge and slid to the base of the slope. "Buried in the cave," he said. And seeing Hughson's face, he asked, "What's up?"

"I'll tell you while we dig it up. I want it stowed on my saddle and the horse hidden farther up."

The sun had fallen deeply behind the rimrock above the river. Rian and Dan Reese reached the confluence of Oso Negro Canyon and scrutinized the narrow, brushy passage between the cliffs.

Remembering his experience of the other day, Rian did not intend to be trapped again. He banked on Judd and Hughson's heading up Oso Negro. There was little chance of overtaking them without horses, but there were places in this country where a horse could not go. Perhaps, if crowded hard enough, they would blunder into one of those blind alleys.

Rian chose the south side of the canyon for himself. He told Dan:

"Work up about fifty feet from the floor but stay in the brush. Don't try to move too fast. If we're fired at, dig in and wait. Let them make the mistakes."

As Dan climbed the north slope, he picked his own way through brush and broken stone to a faint cattle trail on the opposite wall. When they were both in position, he made a signal to start working up the canyon. In this fashion they advanced a half mile. The light was already failing.

The first indication that they had made contact came as a shattering volley of gunfire and blasting echoes.

He hit the ground. Across the canyon he heard Dan fire back. After a moment he raised his head and tried to see movement. No one stirred, but he saw a thin curl of smoke from a thicket. Someone had been having a smoke while he waited. Across his rifle sights, Rian watched. The light struck a spark from a spur; then he made out the shape of a man's boot. Finally he discerned the gunman huddled in the brush. It was too dark to draw decent aim. Rian found a chunk of chalky stone and rubbed his sights. Into the white pattern of sights, he set his target.

He tightened his trigger finger slowly. The shot jarred his shoulder.

With a cry, a man rose from the brush and stumbled into the trail. It looked like Judd. He fell and went sprawling down the steep slope into the thickets.

Another volley of firing came from a well-screened point farther on. Dan sent a small-caliber bullet into the brush. Lying low, Rian waited a moment, then fired back. He had little hope of hitting anything. Yet he dared not try to close in until it was darker. And by then the others would be taking advantage of the darkness to escape. Bitterly, he settled down to wait.

CHAPTER
TWENTY-THREE

Hughson wished he could recover Judd's rifle. It was an old Henry that held fifteen shots. This cannon of Shackley's, while it was a six-shot, was a bear cat to load. Now the cylinder was empty, darkness was gathering, and he wanted a full magazine before they headed for the horses.

Spence went on guard while he reloaded. Down at the foot of the slope lay the sprawled shape of Judd. Hughson felt no regret there; he had been paying for his gun, not his appetites, and from now on Judd would have been a harder man to handle.

Hughson crammed the loads into the gun and counted six balls from the gunstock. Remembering that he needed patches to make the bullets stay in, he searched his pockets for scraps of paper. There was nothing. His hand closed on his buckskin money purse. In addition to some gold coins, it contained a thin fold of goldbacks. Reluctantly, he peeled off a five-dollar bill and tore it lengthwise, tore it again into four strips an inch wide. He ripped one of the strips into postage stamp-sized patches and completed the job of loading.

From time to time McCool and the old man would open on the cave with a blasting volley that shook the canyon. When they did so, Spence and Hughson would wait, then return the fire as soon as it slackened.

Hughson had to reload once again. At last it was dark; time to try to get out of the trap.

"Spence!" he called.

There was no reply from the gunman.

"Spence!"

Still no answer, and Hughson crawled from the cave to where he lay. When he touched him, Spence did not move. Hughson's hand drew back quickly. He knew, then, that he had been alone for some time. Spence was dead.

He rose to a crouch and headed up the canyon, moving clumsily, with a feeling of panic. He hoped the horse was still tethered in the clump of desert cedar where he had left it. God help him if it was gone!

But when he reached the spot, the horse was still there, soaped with sweat. He tightened the cinches, threw off the tether, and mounted. As the horse started to climb the rimrock to the crest, gunfire broke out far below him. Hughson did not quicken his gait; only a freak shot could stop him now.

Reaching the summit, he swung east toward the stage road.

Rian struck a match and gazed around the deep, low-ceilinged cave. He and Dan had found the two dead men outside it. Until the last moment, Rian had hoped one of them would be Hughson. But the man was gone; gone with three thousand dollars; gone with his guilt and perhaps even a sick conscience for the wife he had killed.

By all the evidence, Spence had been living in the cave for several days. There were empty cans, a sack of soda crackers, and dozens of wheat-straw cigarette butts. A pack of greasy cards was laid out in a half-finished game of solitaire.

But there was no money, and nothing incriminating. Then Rian noticed some scraps of paper on the floor.

"What's this — confetti?" he said. He gathered up a half dozen scraps of paper.

By matchlight, they inspected the bits of paper and found them to be a torn-up gold-back. "Save 'em," the old man said. "If there's more'n half of a bill, the bank will give you five dollars."

Rian's brow wrinkled. "I'd give ten to know why somebody tore this up." He tucked the pieces into his shirt pocket. "Funny . . ."

The old man sprawled back against the sloping wall. "Man, man, I am so tired!" he sighed. "I ain't walked that far in twenty years."

"Or been shot at so much?"

"Or been shot at. Not since the war. Did you know I was in the First Illinois, Mc-Cool? I was a corporal at first, but in only four years I rose to sergeant. If the war'd lasted, I mighta made warrant officer."

He laughed, and Rian chuckled. "I like your spirit, Dan. I may put you on steady."

"Son, I wouldn't go back to dominoes for anything! I was going into dry rot there. Terrible. Only thing is — have we got a stage line now?"

Rian sprawled on his back, resting. "Why not? We've got a franchise and enough horses to pull the Troy."

"But we haven't got any money," the old man said.

"Maybe that goldback will buy us everything we need, Dan," Rian said thoughtfully.

"What do you mean?"

"Just surmising. Wake me up in about a half-hour, will you? I've got a long walk back tonight."

"Tonight! Reckoned we'd rest tonight and go back tomorrow."

"I want to get back as soon as I can. Likely be dawn before I make it to Kingbolt. I want you to find a nice clean cave and catch yourself a snooze. Tomorrow I'll pick you up beside the road. Okay?"

"Okay. Half-hour?"

Rian nodded. In a few moments he was asleep. Almost immediately the old man was shaking his shoulder.

" 'Bout that time, son. Sure you want to start back tonight?"

Rian sighed. "Got to, Dan."

"Here's some so-so coffee. I found some cake coffee and mixed it with hot water. It'll speed you on your way."

After Rian had drunk the coffee, he told the old man to take care of himself, and hiked down the trail toward the main canyon.

About nine o'clock he reached the stage road. He checked the horses before moving on. Chunk, the best of their lead animals, gave him a friendly nudge as he unwound the rope the horse had wrapped around the tree with his nervous stompings.

He looked the horse over thoughtfully, wondering if it had ever carried a rider. Probably not. But a tractable horse could be talked into all sorts of things. And that was a brutally long walk for a man who was tired and sick with killing and seeing murder done.

He fashioned a hackamore from a rope, and the horse accepted it. Then he led it out to the road and tried throwing a leg across the horse and sliding back, doing this repeatedly until at last it let him sit astraddle. This horse, he decided, had carried a man before. It was the kind of horse the Reeses would have had to take as second choice, rather than the strong lively animal a stage man would ordinarily pick.

At a ragged jog, he started for Kingbolt . . .

The town looked dead when he rode up the main street. Before the saloons, where few horses were tethered, some men talked quietly. All the other buildings were dark, except for an occasional night lamp. A cat scurried across the street; somewhere beyond town a pack of coyotes yelped.

There was still a light in Marshal Fowley's office.

Rian tied the big horse and stretched. The broad back of the animal had nearly split him like a wedge. Lugging the rifle, he went to the door and glanced inside. He heard Fowley's voice in the hall leading to his cells.

"I'm not going to fool around with you no more, Billy. I don't mind a man getting tanked up now and then and riding his horse down the walks. But this business of challenging everybody in town to do battle, after two drinks! Either you cut it out or I'll send you over to Huntsville next time."

A drunken voice said, "Mize well make up my ticket, Marshal. I got this town in my pocket —"

Fowley came in, muttering under his breath, and saw Rian standing in his office. Fowley needed a shave, and he looked half spent. Seeing Rian, his manner sharpened quickly.

"Am I glad to see you!" he said.

"What's happened?" Dead tired, Rian leaned against the wall.

"Thought you were going to tell *me* what's happened. A goatherder came in town tonight and told me there'd been a big rockslide at Cerro Colorado. I got to thinking —"

"It missed us," Rian said.

He told him the story.

"What makes you so sure it was Hughson?" the marshal asked, finally.

"I saw him and found the bodies of two of his men. Do you need any more proof than that?"

Fowley nodded. "Certainly I do. You saw him at a distance of a hundred feet — right? It could have been anybody. Mind you, I don't doubt your story. I'm just telling you what we'd be up against if we took him to court with no more evidence than that."

Rian drew his hand from his pocket. He dropped on the desk several of the scraps of paper he had found in the cave. "How about these?" he asked. "I found them in the hideout."

Fowley moved them around with a fingertip, studying them. "What are they?"

"Let's ask Hughson."

Sweeping the scraps into his palm, Fowley said, "All right. We'll talk to him."

Because Hughson's office was closer, they looked at the depot first. The door was unlocked and a lamp was burning on the desk, but Hughson was not in the room.

"He must be around," Fowley muttered. "Wouldn't go off and leave the place unlocked."

Through the dusty panes of Biff Shackley's room, they saw the stage man stretched out on the cot with his arm covering his face. A bottle rested on the floor beside him and his rifle was tilted against the wall.

Fowley moved to the door and turned the porcelain knob. Through the window, Rian saw Hughson quickly swing his legs over the side of the cot and reach for the rifle. Rian leveled his revolver at the man, waiting as Fowley went in.

Hughson, dazed with fatigue, managed to smile. "Oh — it's you, Marshal."

"Just checking around, George," said the marshal. "Your office was unlocked."

Hughson scrubbed his face with his hands. "Sorry," he muttered.

The marshal glanced about the room. "Sleeping down here now, George?"

"Just resting. I went home at noon and didn't come back until after closing time. Marshal," he said, "my wife's left me."

"That's too bad," said Fowley. He was still looking the room over, seemingly paying no attention to Hughson. But now he opened his hand and showed the stage man the bits of torn paper. "Know anything about these, George?"

Rian came into the doorway. Hughson did not immediately see him. Apparently stunned, he gazed at the scraps.

"No. I don't. What are they?"

At the same time, he moved toward his rifle. But what he picked up was the pint bottle of liquor. He took a small, careful drink and lowered the bottle.

The marshal glanced at Rian. "Frankly, I don't know. Want to tell him what you think they are?" he asked Rian.

Hughson's eyes drilled at Rian's face. "Take the rifle," Rian told the marshal. "Pull one of the loads and see what he used for a patch. *I* think he got caught short in that cave and used a torn-up goldback."

Marshal Fowley moved nearer the cot and picked up the rifle. Hughson made no move until the marshal began examining the cylinder. Then, in two swift motions, he hurled the bottle at Rian and smashed the lamp from the wall above the bed. In an instant the room was dark.

Hughson fired. Rian dropped to his knees. The concussion of the shot hit his body like a fist, as his ears went dead. But in the flash he saw Hughson lying on the floor with a revolver in his hand. He had fired high, at the place where Rian had stood an instant before.

Rian snapped a shot back at him. In the gun flash, he saw the marshal swinging the rifle to cover Hughson; an instant later it roared. Hughson groaned. Rian fired again, then lunged toward the man and seized his gun. Hughson's slack hand released it. He moaned as Rian pulled away.

"McCool?" the marshal asked sharply.

"Right here. He's quit. Have you got a match?"

The marshal struck a match. In the blue, sulphurous glow they gazed at the man lying sprawled on the floor. After a moment the marshal sighed, "Ain't nothin' some men won't do to get theirselves killed, is there?"

Lamps were burning at the Empire station when Rian shambled into the yard. Justina heard him and came hurrying from the house, a lantern in her hand.

"Rian, is that you?"

"Yes, ma'am. I think so," he said. He stood by the bench outside the station door; it looked so irresistible that he sank onto it with a sigh as Justina hurried up.

"I heard a story that there'd been a rockslide. I couldn't stand the suspense any longer, and I was just about to hitch —"

"Do me a favor," Rian murmured. "Don't ask me anything for a while. Dan's all right. Everything's fine. If there's any whiskey around, I'd like some coffee with about two inches of spirits in it."

"Of course," she said. "I'm so glad you're all right. Nothing happened, then?"

"The whiskey," Rian murmured. "And then the coffee. *Then* the questions. In that order."

But when she returned with the whiskey, he was sound asleep in a sitting position, a weary smile on his face. She set the whiskey down, blew out the lantern, and, sitting on the bench beside him, took his hand and patiently waited for him to wake up.

ABOUT THE AUTHOR

Frank Bonham, in a career that spanned five decades, achieved excellence as a noted author of young adult fiction, detective and mystery fiction, as well as making significant contributions to Western fiction. By 1941 his fiction was already headlining Street and Smith's *Western Story Magazine* and by the end of the decade his Western novels were being serialized in *The Saturday Evening Post.* His first Western, *Lost Stage Valley* (1948), was purchased at once as the basis for a motion picture. "I have tried to avoid," Bonham once confessed, "the conventional cowboy story, but I think it was probably a mistake. That is like trying to avoid crime in writing a mystery book. I just happened to be more interested in stagecoaching, mining, railroading . . ." Yet, notwithstanding, it is precisely the interesting — and by comparison with the majority of Western novels — exotic backgrounds of Bonham's novels which give them an added dimension. He was highly knowledgeable in the technical aspects of transportation and communication in the 19th-Century American West. In introducing these backgrounds into his narratives, especially when combined with his firm grasp of idiomatic Spanish spoken by many of his Mexican characters, his stories and novels are elevated to a higher plane in which the historical sense of the period is always very much in the forefront. This historical aspect of his Western fiction early on drew accolades from reviewers so that on one occasion the *Long Beach Press Telegram* predicted that "when the time comes to find an author who can best fill the gap in Western fiction left by Ernest Haycox, it may be that Frank Bonham will serve well." In the *Encyclopedia of Frontier and Western Fiction* (1994) it is noted that "on even the shortest list of the finest . . . Westerns ever written would have to be included *Snaketrack* and *The Eye of the Hunter*, no little achievement when it is recalled that almost four decades separate the two books." *Night Raid, The Feud at Spanish Ford*, and *Last Stage West* are other Bonham titles which possess this same high standard of quality.

We hope you have enjoyed this Large Print book. Other Thorndike, Wheeler, and Chivers Press Large Print books are available at your library or directly from the publishers.

For information about current and upcoming titles, please call or write, without obligation, to:

Publisher
Thorndike Press
295 Kennedy Memorial Drive
Waterville, ME 04901
Tel. (800) 223-1244

or visit our Web site at:

http://gale.cengage.com/thorndike

OR

Chivers Large Print
published by BBC Audiobooks Ltd
St James House, The Square
Lower Bristol Road
Bath BA2 3SB
England
Tel. +44(0) 800 136919
email: bbcaudiobooks@bbc.co.uk
www.bbcaudiobooks.co.uk

All our Large Print titles are designed for easy reading, and all our books are made to last.

BUKOVINA & BESSARABIA

MOLDAVIA

DNIE... RIVER

W9-ACI-064

Jassy

Cluj

TRANSYLVANIA

RUMANIA

WALLACHIA

Bucharest

DANUBE RIVER

SOUTHERN DOBRUDJA

Black Sea

Tirnovo

Sofia

BULGARIA

MARITSA RIVER

TURKEY

Istanbul

...C E

...alonika

Aegean Sea

THE Balkans

EAGLES IN COBWEBS

EAGLES IN
COBWEBS

~~~~~~~~~~~~~~~~~~~~~~~~~~~~

Nationalism and Communism in the Balkans

PAUL LENDVAI

Garden City, New York
DOUBLEDAY & COMPANY, INC.
1969

Library of Congress Catalog Card Number 69–10952
Copyright © 1969 by Paul Lendvai
Printed in the United States of America
First Edition

To try to bind nations by precepts of international morality was like trying to catch eagles in cobwebs.

—J. L. TALMON

CONTENTS

PREFACE   ix

I. COMMONPLACES, MYTHS, AND REALITIES   1

II. THE LAND, THE PEOPLE, THE INTRUDERS   23

III. YUGOSLAVIA: *Stormy Voyage into Uncharted Seas*   51

"THE 41 CLUB"   57
THE ROAD TO POWER   65
FROM STALIN TO GENERAL MOTORS   75
CAPITALISM WITHOUT CAPITALISTS?   89
FREEDOM IN LITTLE SPOONFULS   100
THE PARTY IN SEARCH OF A ROLE   119
THE NATIONS IN A WHIRLPOOL OF
    CHANGE AND CONFLICT   140

IV. ALBANIA: *A Traditional Fuse to the Balkan Powder Keg*   173

HOW DOES A YUGOSLAV SATELLITE BECOME AN
    ALLY OF CHINA?   182

V. BULGARIA: *Humble Vassal or Faithful Ally?*   206

HEROES, TRAITORS, MARTYRS . . .   217
NATIONAL SENTIMENTS—ASSETS OR RISKS?   234

VI. RUMANIA: *A Quiet Revolution*   262

"THE RUSSIANS SKINNED US FOUR TIMES."   279
RUMANIA STEPS OUT OF LINE   294
HOW FAST AND HOW FAR?   315

AFTERWORD   350

POSTSCRIPT AFTER THE CZECH TRAGEDY   361

NOTES   368

BIBLIOGRAPHY   379

INDEX   383

PREFACE

This book aims to contribute a more sophisticated and mature approach toward an important part of what was once called "*the* Communist world." Domestic and external pressures, aspirations, and circumstances have created a wholly new situation to which universally applicable concepts of "communism" in general or studies on the basis of purely ideological perspectives have scarcely any relevance today. It would be profoundly wrong to regard ideological orientation as having become so negligible that it has no role in relations between states and peoples. But despite two decades of professed adherence to the social gospel known as Marxism-Leninism, the quest for national identity has proved more powerful than ideological bonds. Nationalism has become a primary factor in policy, both reflecting and promoting the changing nature of relations between the Communist-dominated smaller states and the Soviet Union. And what is true of Eastern Europe as a whole seems in some ways even truer of the Balkans.

Nowhere has the political landscape changed so dramatically, yet in such a contradictory way as in this region. This book will try to show how enduring national patterns, interests, and traditions shape and influence the destiny of almost fifty million peoples of many races, languages, and religions, living in an area that is smaller in size than the state of Texas, but that remains a critical factor in the East-West balance of power. It deals with past and present developments in Yugoslavia, Albania, Bulgaria, and Rumania, all of which are modern states, products of the nineteenth and twentieth centuries. They will be considered together and separately as four Balkan states, ruled by groups that profess to be Communist yet represent traditional national interests. It is freely admitted that the term "Balkans" itself or the inclusion of Rumania and exclusion of Greece is open to question.

My main intention is to examine processes of change in Balkan politics, which are complex and ambiguous, and to discuss how nationalism in a myriad of different forms affects political developments in interstate relations and within individual states. The national problem—from anti-Soviet defensive nationalism to friction between neighbors, from tension among "state nations" within one state to minority problems—is in many ways more acute than it was when the Communists seized power twenty or twenty-five years ago. The stirring of national sentiments exacerbates frustrations and animosities, sometimes to the point of explosive conflicts.

But we should be careful in condemning the reassertion of distinctive national traditions and interests as merely a disease of the past. The defense of national individuality against domination by a big power has been the prime vehicle for both survival and attaining statehood in Eastern Europe and especially in the Balkans. Here, nationalism and democracy are still intimately linked. Thus an answer to the question whether nationalism is an ally of democracy or of reaction must today start from the specifics of each individual country. This book is meant to be a modest contribution to the study of a new situation in the Balkans in which neither the questions nor the answers are so simple or so clear as they may have appeared in Stalin's time or even in the late fifties.

I hope that, whatever errors I have committed, I have avoided sweeping generalizations, dangerous oversimplification, and partisanship for any one nation or group at the expense of another. I have also sought to warn the reader of the difference between guesses, even if cautiously stated, and facts. No book dealing with current affairs can avoid obvious pitfalls and obstacles. The contemporary nature of the subject matter involves the risk that details or even some important points may have to be corrected or revised as more information becomes available. Despite the continual change in the Balkans and in the wider power sphere of the Soviet Union, I believe that the most essential parts of this book will stand the test of time.

This book is the result of seven years of study (1961–67) and of frequent trips to the countries concerned. My interest in Eastern Europe goes back even earlier. Before visiting the specifically Balkan regions, I had personal experience and knowledge in Hungary of the forces that operate within a Communist system. I have studied the theory and practice of communism since 1946 and in this sense have never regarded events in Yugoslavia or Rumania from an "outside" perspective. But I have developed a feel for the Balkan area and a special interest in Balkan politics since my first visit to Yugoslavia. In the sixties I have regularly visited for varying periods all the Balkan countries except Albania, and in some of them, primarily Yugoslavia and Rumania, I have spent considerable time. Trips to other Communist states such as Hungary, Poland, and Czechoslovakia have helped me to gauge the impact of the changes in Yugoslavia and Rumania on the "Soviet camp" and to place them in the context of interacting pressures among and within the Communist states.

The study of special problems on the spot is indispensable if the observer seeks to understand the behavior patterns and motivation of the ruling elites and social groups of each nation and each region. This is particularly true of the most tangled issues such as, for example, Macedonia, the Croat question, or Transylvania, within this extremely complicated region. A foreigner on a hasty visit is often inclined to take the propaganda for one national group or another at face value. Setting aside the notorious unreliability of population statistics for disputed regions or of figures purporting to show the exploitation of a republic or region by the "center," the "majority nation," or the Soviet Union, what matters is that the arguments are seen as real. The mere fact that many people of the regions in dispute passionately believe that they *are* being discriminated against or exploited (for example, the Croats and Slovenes by the Serbs, the Hungarians by the Rumanians, and the Rumanians by the Russians) may be politically much more significant than the objective realities of the given situation. And this climate can be properly appreciated only if one, in addition to documents, consults human sources at first hand and checks and counterchecks their statements.

At the same time, travel without the necessary background in the history, politics, and economics of the area may produce impressionistic features or poetic eye-witness accounts but can hardly provide a sound guide to a world where the emphasis is on diversity rather than uniformity, to countries and regions with widely varying historical and political experiences. A few standard works and secondary sources are invaluable for the early period of the Communist takeover and the general history of the nations in the Balkans. With regard to the recent past, particularly the past decade or so, the most important sources are the Communist press, speeches of Communist leaders, and documents issued by the leadership. To gain insight into the complex relationships involved in power distribution in Yugoslavia, for example, a student of affairs must pay close attention not only to current events, but also to the significant differences of interpretation in newspapers and magazines published in Belgrade, Zagreb, Ljubljana, and Skopje.

The Balkans have been a traditional storm center. The twin assault of a Communist takeover and Soviet domination has not "solved" the national problem. On the contrary, it has intensified national animosities. The Yugoslav, Albanian, and Rumanian defiance of Moscow has led to a dramatic decline of Soviet influence in the area. Moreover, the cumulative effects of the rise of nationalism together with the impact of the Sino-Soviet dispute have transformed what was once the most solidly welded bulwark of Soviet power into a new center of search for external independence and internal autonomy. The four Balkan countries are seemingly peripheral and small, yet only too often events in this region have had more bearing on world politics and on the larger context of Soviet-American relations than the area's economic resources and military potential would warrant. The disruptive influences radiating from the Balkans have been an important contributory cause to stresses and tensions within the inner core of the Soviet alliance and may have long-run effects in the Soviet Union itself. It is clear that recent developments in the Balkans have been for a variety of reasons a source of uncertainty and anxiety to the Soviet leadership. Without drawing exaggerated conclusions from the movement and flux, it would be fair to say that the net effect of the rise of nationalism in the Balkans has been to limit Soviet freedom of action, to encourage a greater degree of independence in other East European states, and to change the character of intrabloc relations.

These, then, are some of the compelling reasons for studying the Balkan countries, particularly the startling developments of the past decade and a half, which in one form or another have influenced the main issues of our time. I believe there is need for a study dealing with this turbulent and fascinating period, for a work midway between journalism and history, combining background knowledge with personal impressions, necessarily relying sometimes on sources that would not perhaps satisfy the standards of a diplomatic historian, but always seeking to place current events and the forces operative in the Balkans in a broader context and historical perspective.

Vienna
May 1968.   *—Paul Lendvai*

I

COMMONPLACES, MYTHS, AND REALITIES

Far from the national state being historically out of date,
it is for a great part of humanity an objective on the horizon, a goal to achieve.

—*Raymond Aron*

At two o'clock in the morning in the autumn of 1947 the telephone
rang. The Yugoslav and Rumanian leaders, who had been discussing final preparations for Marshal Tito's forthcoming visit to Rumania, interrupted their conversation. It was the Soviet Ambassador.
Ana Pauker, then Secretary of the Central Committee of the Rumanian Communist Party and possibly the single most powerful
leader in the nation, took the call and almost immediately excused
herself. With the other members of the Rumanian Politburo she
had to leave at once to call on the Soviet Ambassador. On a telephone summons at two in the morning the Politburo, the supreme
organ of the Rumanian party, had to report to the Soviet Ambassador.[1]

Four years later, after Yugoslavia's dramatic expulsion from the
Soviet bloc, an American scholar visited the area and came to a
gloomy conclusion about Rumania's chances of surviving as even a
formally independent entity: "Before long the question will come
up whether Rumania deserves even the title of satellite. . . . [The
country] comes close to being on the same political level as the
Ukrainian or Usbek SSR."[2]

For many years the Rumanian leaders gave no sign of wishing
their homeland to play any role other than that of echo of the
Soviet Union. During the train of events that culminated in the
Hungarian and Polish upheavals in October 1956, Rumania carried
on much as before. Such at any rate, was the general consensus in
both the West and the East. As late as 1962, Rumania seemed the

most subservient and reliable of the East European satellites, except perhaps for Bulgaria.

Yet, in 1968 the leaders of this same country were hailed as the "Gaullists of Eastern Europe," the men who, since March 1963, time and again, publicly and secretly, have opposed major Soviet policies—and, what is more, with impunity. Rumania's initially almost imperceptible but in sum sensational emancipation from Russian domination as well as its brilliant and imaginative exploitation of the changes in the international situation and in the Communist world have had many facets, twists, and turns, which will be recapitulated later. A Balkan power surrounded by Communist neighbors, Rumania during the sixties has demonstrated to the world that it is possible to attain genuine independence under adverse geographical conditions without provoking either military intervention or economic blockade by the Soviet Union.

It is, of course, true that Yugoslavia in 1948 and Albania in 1961 successfully defied Soviet domination. There was, however, an open split in both cases, and the two countries had to pay a high economic price for political independence. Furthermore, Russia had no direct access to the "rebel territories." Hungary tried to go its own way in 1956—too early and too fast—but the revolution was crushed by the Red Army, while the "Polish October" petered out in midstream. Only Rumania (at the time of this writing) has managed to regain its freedom of maneuver without an open rupture and despite a common frontier of 830 miles across the wide expanses of Moldavia and Bessarabia with the Soviet Union.

How could a Communist regime, which owed its existence to the Soviet Union, with a Communist party that numbered less than a thousand members in August 1944 when King Michael's coup d'état swung the country over to the Allied side, defy Russian power and set itself up as a champion of national interest? One might have expected that after such similar "surprises" as the secret indictment of Stalin in February 1956, the return of Gomulka to power in Poland, the Hungarian uprising, the "defection" of Albania, and the Sino-Soviet schism, there would be less astonishment as the dynamic spread of polycentrism propelled hitherto neglected areas to the forefront.[3] Yet in the case of Rumania there is a general feeling that something "impossible" has become real. The Kremlin and the U. S. State Department, foreign observers, and not least the people in the country itself have found themselves respectively disturbed and surprised, fascinated and intrigued by the emerging new political landscape in the southeast corner of Europe. For it is a new landscape even if the old continues to merge with its outlines.

What has happened, and what makes the matter so serious in the eyes of the Soviet leaders, is that two decades of Communist uniformity have made no change in the central theme of political life in Eastern Europe—the spirit of nationalism. The Rumanian gamble in the face of overwhelming odds cannot be understood in ideological terms or even in purely economic ones. The gamble "paid off" not simply because the Rumanian leaders chose the right time and the right issue for their first major challenge, but primarily because they recognized that an appeal to the Rumanian sense of identity as a nation would, notwithstanding their grim domestic record, mobilize genuine popular support, and that this in turn would become an enormously powerful vehicle for their aspirations.

In contrast to the unchecked, uncontrollable eruption of pressures from below in Hungary, which in 1956 placed both the immediate power sphere of the Soviet Union and the survival of the domestic regime in mortal danger, the Rumanian challenge to Soviet hegemony has been launched and, thus far, controlled from above. Dressing up an essentially nationalist practice in orthodox ideology and representing real national interests while verbally upholding "proletarian internationalism," the Communist leaders have, for all their dialectical juggling with definitions, placed themselves in the mainstream of Rumanian history.

If, as the loss of uncontested Soviet authority and its repercussions suggest, there has been a deep and important, even irreversible change in the structure of international communism, the question arises as to whether the actual conditions in the individual countries have changed as well. However indispensable the study of documents, it cannot even remotely reflect the extent to which the political climate, particularly in the Balkan countries, has been transformed. Only frequent visits and constant comparisons, talks with the decision-makers and with the people who possess the skills to guide an increasingly complex industrial society, with representatives of the scientific community and with the intelligentsia can give a clue to the direction, scope, and pace of the changes.

Ours is an age of labels. We are often bewildered when confronted with developments that do not fit the pattern of some firmly entrenched concept. Thus we tend to look at trends, which in each country have very distinctive and often contradictory and baffling features, or even at countries, merely as the expressions of a doctrine or "heresy." For years Gomulka was hailed in Poland as a "genuine national Communist," and Kadar in Hungary as a bloodthirsty proconsul of a Soviet colony. Under the impact of the short-lived euphoria about the "Polish October," many forgot that Gomulka was not only a Pole but a Communist. Conversely, the brutal crushing of the Hungarian revolution obscured the fact that Kadar was not only the agent of Moscow in a specific situation, but also a Hungarian; never an "extreme Stalinist," but rather a cautious reformer.

When, later, Poland shifted gradually to a quite different tack in such major areas as economic rethinking, cultural freedom, and toleration of political dissent, Gomulka became an epitome of retreat and reaction, even though some of the significant gains his regime produced, including private farming, have remained. On the other hand, Kadar has been converted—at least in the mirror of mass media—from a Russian satrap into a jovial pacemaker of liberalization. In fact, he has done little more than grant some peripheral concessions, which, though they have gained his regime a certain degree of grudging acquiescence and toleration, involved no political risks. In other words, the narrow fluctuation between relative permissiveness and relative oppression, so characteristic of totalitarian regimes at a certain stage, has been identified with essential changes.[4]

There is a difference between the atmosphere in "occupied" Hungary and that in "occupied" Poland, but this is almost entirely due to Hungary's more flexible response to the same basic problems, more tactical dexterity, and better public relations in projecting an attractive image to both the native population and the world. The rigidity of the Gomulka regime and the flexibility of the Kadar group are to no small degree fashioned by the different personalities of the respective leaders. Neither the different climate in the two countries nor, for instance, the Tito-Stalin conflict and the ups and downs in Soviet-Yugoslav relations can be completely understood without taking such "unideological" factors as personal or emotional impulses into account.

The definition of ideological deviations or the classification of policies and personalities according to the stamp they are supposed to bear is a perilous matter. Thus a whole school of thought would like to make us believe that Marshal Tito is not only "the man who defied Stalin," but also an arch-revisionist who almost single-handed "broke the power of the Communist Party." Yet there is more than ample evidence to show that all along he has been essentially a "leftist" or centralist. Both his greatest triumphs and his greatest failures have been insolubly connected with the national question. The roots of his conflict with Stalin can be found in the wartime strategy and tactics of the Yugoslav Communists, which were consistently several stages ahead of the line proclaimed by the Soviet center. Yugoslav external and internal policies in the immediate postwar period had the same extremist character of being more Stalinist than Stalin.

Many vital things have changed in Yugoslavia and in Tito's personal posture, but the early traits have time and again come to the fore. Ever since 1953, at almost every critical juncture in Yugoslav political developments, Tito has opted for those in the leadership who have advocated the centralistic, the more conservative, and the less democratic alternative. Tito's deeply contradictory role and the complexities of the Yugoslav situation cannot be reduced to deceptively simple ideological expressions.

By the same token, the Enver Hoxha regime in Albania is conveniently labeled ferociously "dogmatic." It is, however, more important to note that the Albanian leaders, while invoking the "universal truth of Marxism-Leninism," are following traditional national objectives, albeit in somewhat extravagant forms. The Albanian leaders have a respectable historical lineage and are in many respects the modern successors of an elite that centuries ago played a significant role in the Ottoman Empire. Even their recklessness and bravado in their disputes with Yugoslavia, and later with the Soviet Union, are not the products of pro-Chinese sympathies, let alone of purely doctrinaire considerations, but belong to a behavior pattern natural to this poorest, smallest, and most backward Balkan country, surrounded as it is by hostile, more powerful neighbors that pose a constant threat to its precarious independence and territorial integrity.

It has become a commonplace to say that the Communist world no longer has a single tightly knit world-wide organization under one center of power with the authority to interpret the "universal truth" in the form of a single orthodox doctrine. The self-evident lesson of the decay of Soviet authority and the repudiation of a unique Soviet model is the movement—in one way or another and to varying degrees in each Communist country—toward internal diversity. The countries now enjoy a greater degree of freedom in shaping their external policies along more individualistic lines, always provided that these are not at variance with major foreign policies of the Soviet Union. Even their still wider area of choice in dealing with internal matters has not always been gained through acts of defiance against Moscow—a fact that is often overlooked. It was the second de-Stalinization campaign launched by Khrushchev at the Twenty-second Soviet Party Congress in 1961 that forced the Bulgarian, Czech, East German, and Rumanian leaders to remove the remaining symbols and to repudiate the worst excesses of Stalinism.

The spectacle of a Communist world speaking with many voices, the emergence of several trends, contradictory rather than parallel but conveniently lumped together under the label of democratization or de-Stalinization, and intensified contacts between East and West provide a fertile ground for sweeping generalizations, often mixed with a strong dose of wishful thinking. One theory currently in fashion predicts the inevitable convergence of the Communist and Western systems as the end product of universal industrialization and the increasingly similar role of state intervention. Ignoring or belittling the basic human, moral, and political differences between the two systems, some regard the per capita output of steel pipes as a yardstick to measure the extent of changes allegedly leading to a rapprochement of "socialist" and "capitalist" societies. Even belated attempts to pay attention to economic common sense, which most of the economic reforms in Eastern Europe (with the exception of Yugoslavia) have been, are often hailed as harbingers of a fundamental turn toward capitalism.

The distortion is increased by the enormously exaggerated importance ascribed to ideology. To say that the minds of the young, let alone of the older generation, are no longer animated by dreams of utopia and revolution has become almost banal. The official state religion, Marxism-Leninism, has indeed become "the camouflage for a satisfied bureaucracy."[5] A doctrine that contains no outlines for the system to succeed capitalism has inevitably become meaningless and irrelevant to the basic issues facing the Communist regimes, or indeed mankind, today. Ideology instead of being "a guide to action" is now a sterile, reactionary dogma. Confronted with such social problems as alienation, anti-semitism, or juvenile delinquency, most of the ruling Communist parties respond by pretending that they do not exist or are "isolated accidents."

It was this gap between dogma and reality, between what these societies are and what the leaders pretend they are, that generated the tortuous search of playwrights and poets, novelists and scholars, for more humane, more tolerable forms of socialist society. Even at the peak of its influence, however, the real political impact of protest literature was out of all proportion to what the elated reaction in the West suggested to the public. A Bulgarian poem attacking Stalin, a Czech drama showing the cold cruelty of an impersonal bureaucracy, or a Rumanian short story revealing that even Communist officials can be corrupt status seekers are an index to disillusionment and to the willingness of the men in power to tolerate criticism. The margin of toleration is, however, always changing, and the area of cultural experimentation can be reduced overnight practically to nothing by the stroke of a pen.

At one point, political naïveté went to such lengths that the "liberalism" of a given Communist regime was measured in terms of whether or not the works of Franz Kafka were published. When Rumania's conflict with Russia began to evolve, a Western ambassador held a confidential briefing for a dozen correspondents who were covering the Rumanian Party Congress. One of the first questions put by a British journalist was whether the Rumanians brought out any books by Kafka. One might conclude ironically that neither the questioner nor indeed the distinguished diplomat appeared to know just what Kafka had written. As later events showed, it would have been more to the point to find out why the Rumanian party leader referred to Stephen the Great, the ruler of medieval Moldavia, at that particular moment.

It is equally important to take a sober view of the significance of the so-called "revisionist" thinkers, groups, or trends. Here again, the disease of labeling has resulted in an uncritical acceptance of an "ism." "Revisionism" correctly used describes only the attempt of the great forebear of twentieth-century democratic socialism, Eduard Bernstein, to correct and rethink Marx on such essential points as the evolution of the capitalist system and the influence of social reform that makes the masses beneficiaries and not helpless victims of economic growth. He was condemned and ostracized for updating the Holy Script in terms of the social and economic facts of the 1890s, yet it is obviously Bernstein who, after two World Wars, has turned out to be right. Today the term "revisionism" is misleadingly used as a badge for Marshal Tito and the avant-garde writer Milovan Djilas in Yugoslavia and the philosopher Leszek Kolakowski in Poland, for the philosophers and sociologists grouped around the Zagreb bimonthly *Praxis,* for dissident Communist students in Warsaw.

The theories of those who seek to transform or to democratize the Communist system from within on the basis of an "enlightened Marxism" have by and large become fringe views. The efforts of the Zagreb group, for instance, which, following the footsteps of Jean-Paul Sartre and Herbert Marcuse, strives to rediscover the "humanistic core" of Marxism by returning to Marx's early philosophical writings, are interesting and stimulating, although Marx himself either did not publish those manuscripts or thought he had supplanted them by 1848. But the bitter truth is that so long as the main thrust of these attacks is directed against national feeling, economic realities, the elementary drive toward affluence, and managerial as well as political bureaucracy, *Praxis* and what its contributors stand for are bound to remain on the fringes of the main currents in Yugoslav society. To put it bluntly, the political importance of even the most vocal group in the most open Communist country is negligible in terms of power and influence. The advocates of a new reformation of communism, as sketched in the fifties, have become isolated pockets between a population pressing for more cash and leisure and a bureaucratic elite, which is willing to respond to popular pressures provided its own vested interests are protected and the concessions are kept within politically safe and economically feasible limits.

The desire of East European intellectuals for as many contacts as possible with the West cannot be doubted. It is becoming fashionable, however, to overstate the significance of the manifold cultural exchanges. Leaving aside the fact that many of the grantees or delegates nominated by the Communist governments are in no way representative of the young intelligentsia, we would be throwing dust in our own eyes if we looked upon the presence of four Hungarian doctors at a medical congress in London, or of a Bulgarian poetess at a writers' meeting in Vienna, as indications of the abandonment of restrictions on travel. Certainly one Bulgarian poetess is better than none; any contacts at any level are an improvement

over the arid deserts of total isolation. But to equate cultural or any
other contacts rationed by the Communist party apparatus with
major steps toward freedom of movement would be to lose all sense
of proportion. A passport with an exit permit (and the two do not
mean the same thing under a Communist regime!) is still a
privilege, even if it is somewhat less so than before, in every Communist country except Yugoslavia. There are no non-Communist
newspapers, weeklies, or magazines on regular and wide sale in any
East European country, once again except Yugoslavia. And the civil
rights associated with constitutional government and, even more,
political freedom in modern terms can be regarded only as matters
for future agenda in all Communist states, this time including Yugoslavia.

This does not mean that the groping for a more rational economic
mechanism, cultural experimentation, more contacts with the West,
and the growing diversification of internal policies are insignificant.
On the contrary. But we need an entirely new frame of reference
if we want to appraise or even discuss the changes, the reforms,
and the dilemmas. Three things have already become clear: First,
behind a seemingly uniform ideological commitment, actual conditions in each country are changing, at times with extraordinary
speed. While tracing the changes we should neither lose sight of
their limits nor allow our awareness of the restraints to let us forget the scope and depth of the changes. Second, the new developments have less and less in common with traditional views of a
Cold War struggle between democracy and communism, or with a
clash of concepts as to whether the stock market or central planning,
private or public ownership of the means of production, is the best
basis for a system. Some of the most pressing problems facing the
East European countries are common to all industrial societies—the
choice between international regionalism or supranational centralism; which is to be given preference, economic growth or the
standard of living; inflation versus stability; the proper balance between central and local government; social responsibility and individual autonomy. Third, the ideological vacuum created by the
lack of any realistic alternative to the Communist brand of authoritarian system and by the complete erosion of a thoroughly
discredited Communist ideology is being filled by the possibly most
primitive, but undoubtedly most powerful modern ideology—nationalism. In some countries, such as Yugoslavia and Rumania, it has

emerged in a striking manner; elsewhere, as in Bulgaria, its resurgence can be observed in a myriad of small ways.

Nationalism, in both its "traditional" form and its "new" Communist version, is stronger than communism; the quest for national identity is more powerful than ideological bonds. Nationalism has many faces and is full of ambivalence.[6] It can be simultaneously conservative and revolutionary, sterile and creative, reactionary and progressive. As J. L. Talmon aptly put it: "Nationality in the West means your passport. In Central and Eastern Europe, with their mixed populations, it means ultimately your race." Nationalism cannot be limited to the aspirations of nations deprived of their territorial statehood. It is rather "the intense awareness of a common destiny springing from some unfathomable common identity, which, it is held, must express itself fully and leave its imprint on anything that members of the entity come into contact with".[7]

What seems to citizens of long-established nation states in the West to be a disturbing remnant of the past, and to Americans a ghost from the Dark Ages, is a completely different matter in Eastern Europe. Most of these nations achieved statehood only in the twentieth century. They lived for centuries under foreign rule, and the spirit of national identity was the prime vehicle for both survival and attaining independence. Their prewar rivalries and territorial squabbles should indeed be condemned. But their sad record in mutual relations has nothing to do with the fact that for two decades this area of many languages, religions, and deep-seated national traditions has been molded into a uniform Communist world slavishly following the Soviet model.

What may be described as the national affirmation of the East European peoples, embracing a multitude of different sentiments, actions, and policies, is basically a defensive nationalism. It expresses the feeling of nations whose culture, individuality, and unique past has been—and to some extent still is—threatened by extinction. One might argue that the diversity of internal policies in the various East European countries is proof that the danger has passed its crisis point. The removal of symbols and some substance of Soviet domination has, however, actually been the result of calculated moves to take the steam out of national resentment. In a sense these steps have either forestalled or responded to popular pressures. But while appearances may have changed and the Russians may now show more tact in dealing with small nations, the essence of the domination has remained.

The defense of national individuality and the aspiration to real, not purely formal national independence can therefore be regarded as primarily an anti-Soviet nationalism—as long at any rate as the balance of power and fundamental Soviet policies remain unchanged. Stalin and his successors have forgotten over a dangerously long period Lenin's warning to the delegates of the Eighth Russian Party Congress in March 1919 when drawing attention to the delicate problems involved in the multinational character of the Soviet Union, he declared, "Above all, such a nation as the Russians, who have aroused a wild hatred in other nations, must be particularly cautious."

The roots of the hatred for the Russians cannot be properly understood in terms of cold political or economic analysis. Russia's acquisition of territories from Rumania (Bessarabia and northern Bukovina), Poland (eastern Poland), Czechoslovakia (sub-Carpathian Ruthenia), and, in the case of Germany, the incorporation, with Poland, of East Prussia and the Soviet Union's vested interest in maintaining the East-West division of the country constitute the underlying reality of these nations' relations with Moscow.

. Another significant factor coloring mutual relations is the unprecedented scale of economic exploitation of the entire area. War reparations, the notorious Soviet-East European mixed companies, the transfer of wealth, all dealt a crippling blow to the national economies. It is estimated, on the basis of incomplete evidence, that the net Soviet gain through exploitation (after deducting credits) totaled 20 billion dollars during the 1945–56 period.[8] After the upheavals in Hungary and Poland, Soviet methods of exploitation have become more "tactful," more subtle and differentiated. Nevertheless, during the 1956–60 period the East European countries are calculated to have suffered an over-all loss of almost 3.5 billion dollars through price discrimination.[9] This amount greatly exceeds the grand total of all the widely publicized Soviet loans and credits granted to the area during the same period. Rumania and Czechoslovakia received very little, and while the losses incurred through overpaid Soviet exports and underpriced Soviet imports are irretrievable, most of the Soviet loans and credits have to be and are being repaid in full. It must be noted, however, that Albania (until the break in 1961) and Bulgaria throughout the entire postwar period have been on balance economic liabilities rather than assets to the Soviet Union.

Thus historical memories, as well as territorial and economic grievances provide an objective basis for the framework of relations between an imperial superpower and a host of small nations in Eastern Europe. But there is more to it than that. The East European image of the Russians has never fully recovered from the shock of the Red Army's behavior. Only those who lived through or witnessed the first months of Russian occupation can truly grasp the psychologically disastrous consequences. The Russians came as "liberators," but behaved as conquerors. Though discipline was soon established in Bulgaria and improved in Rumania, Hungary, and Poland, the Balkans have never forgotten the first bouts of looting, raping, and other dangerous antics. Even during their brief five-month stay in Belgrade and the northeast section of their ally Yugoslavia, Soviet forces were responsible for 1,219 rapes, 329 attempted rapes, 121 rapes with murder, and 1,204 robberies with violence.[10] No other country dared to produce such statistical evidence of Russian brutality and licence as Yugoslavia did during its conflict with Stalin. But one hardly needs a vivid imagination to realize what the conduct of the Red Army was in the countries it occupied wholly, without the restraint of a powerful indigenous Partisan army. For it was in Yugoslavia that a self-confident Communist leadership sparked off a seemingly minor but explosive crisis in relations with Russia when it dared to draw the attention of the Soviet command to the political impact of the atrocities.

The failure of the Soviet Union to russify the area and convert the population to its brand of "Marxism-Leninism" should not overshadow the enormous moral, spiritual, and cultural damage inflicted upon the East European nations. Their national identities and traditions, ways of life and codes of behavior have become parts of an artificial melting pot. The model of Soviet communism has been superimposed on natural diversity, and no aspect of life has remained immune to this pernicious unifying influence. Only recently have the nations of Eastern Europe begun slowly and painfully to recover from the catastrophic effects of Soviet hegemony. The extent of damages and the degree of recovery naturally vary from country to country, but in all of them deep-rooted feelings of having been robbed and degraded by an alien superpower are still very live issues. Indeed it is hardly an exaggeration to say that nationalism constitutes the heart of the challenge to Soviet domination and that external and internal emancipation from the Soviet Union is the central theme of East European political life.

How far and how fast can this process go? Since 1956–57 a curious dualism has characterized relations between the East European countries and Russia. The long-term effect of the Hungarian revolution was twofold. One, the ruling regimes learned the lesson that their very survival was in danger without Soviet protection. The populations drew the conclusion that, with the West scrupulously respecting Moscow's immediate power sphere, there was no realistic alternative to the system. Two, as Khrushchev was the first to recognize, only by tolerating some measure of internal autonomy could the bloc be saved. In the years since the 1956 upheavals, the empire with one command center has gradually turned into a special kind of alliance, consisting of states with varying shades and degrees of autonomy. The Sino-Soviet conflict, economic friction, and internal discord in the Soviet leadership have meanwhile provided both a motive for broadening the margin of autonomy and an excuse for tightening the reins.

The more Soviet authority has weakened, the more self-assured and less fearful the East European leaders have become. To some extent, the men in power have become split personalities. Faced with a twin challenge, they find themselves in a deeply contradictory position, in which the doctrine that unites them provides little help. On the one hand, the men who engineered the Communist takeover in 1944–47 returned (with a few exceptions) in the baggage trains of the Red Army and still see the Soviet Union as the ultimate protector and guarantee of survival. Yet at the same time, they all (even such old-timers as Walter Ulbricht in East Germany) are beginning to realize that they are tolerated, accepted, or supported by growing sections of the population only to the extent that they represent or pretend to represent genuine national interests. The bonds are immensely powerful—Soviet military hegemony, dependence on both the Russian market and Russian raw materials, and last but not least a common ideology that purports to justify the monopoly of power. Yet nationalism, in any form whatsoever, has a logic and dynamism of its own. Only the future can give a definitive answer to the key question: Will the forced or voluntary toleration of autonomy save what is essential to Soviet interests, or will it rather accelerate the process of disintegration in Eastern Europe?

It is an undisputed fact that nationalism provides an area of common interest between ruling groups and their peoples. But nationalism is not purely and simply the assertion of national claims against Soviet domination. It is a powerful vehicle of old aspirations, not only between unequal partners in an alliance, but also within a multinational state. The trend toward the emergence of a national consensus and the transition from the Marxist-Leninist concept of class—the single, most important excuse for brutal discrimination against millions—to the incomparably broader, traditional sense of identity as a nation cannot be totally discarded as a contagious disease from the past. It depends on the over-all situation whether the spirit of national affirmation becomes a force opening up new vistas, or a lever to pull the peoples back to an unhappy past.

Once when I asked an outstanding Croat scholar in Zagreb whether he thought the growing liberalism in Yugoslavia would ultimately lead to a multiparty system, he laughed derisively. "We have already got one! Quite apart from the fact that the hundred and twenty deputies in the Federal Assembly [parliament] act as if they were one hundred and twenty minute parties, we have six powerful parties—the Communists of the six republics that constitute Yugoslavia!" Then as an afterthought he added smilingly, "At a poll here, our Mika Tripalo [the young party secretary in the capital of Croatia] would easily and overwhelmingly beat anyone, including Djilas. After all, even the Catholic Church supports him. . . ." His statement was not an empty witticism, but an accurate reflection of the popular mood.

As some Communist leaders have become bolder in standing up for the interests of their nations, they have come to be accepted, with however strong reservations, as genuine national spokesmen. One need only look at the turbulent but on the whole encouraging developments in multinational Yugoslavia to see that nationalism is not always a natural or literal adversary of democracy. It was neither a liberal wing in the leadership supported by a benevolent Marshal Tito nor "revisionist" intellectual groups that forced a showdown with the reactionary forces and came out on top in the long internal power struggle. The decisive event in Yugoslav political life was the fact that in the sixties the Communist leaders first in tiny but highly developed Slovenia and then in Croatia began to identify themselves with the opposition of their respective nations to a central party and state bureaucracy in Belgrade, which dictatorially siphoned off the wealth of these nations for large-scale investments in the underdeveloped regions. When the economic centralism of the federal power center was coupled with deliberate attempts to foster an artificial "Yugoslav culture" over national cultural traditions, the ghost of prewar Yugoslavia—the danger of unbridled Serb domination—began to haunt the smaller nations.

The outward-looking political leadership of the small Macedonian Republic joined the Slovene-Croat opposition, and this formidable coalition, belatedly helped by some progressive-minded Serb leaders, launched a successful counteroffensive between 1964 and 1966. Headed by a Croat general, the Army played a crucial role during the last phase, when the political battle had already been won by the champions of national equality and economic decentralization. The fall in July 1966 of Alexander Rankovic, Vice President, Party Secretary, and chief of the security police (second only to Marshal Tito in power and influence) not only marked a turning point in the habitual Communist power struggle, but also crushed the policy of Great Serbian hegemony. Whatever shifts may have occurred later in the power balance, in economic friction, in the roles of Tito and the Army, the case of Rankovic as well as the main currents in contemporary Yugoslavia can be properly understood only from the national angle.

Czechoslovakia provides another, earlier example of a direct relationship between national impulses and the adoption of more democratic concepts. Here, in the early sixties, the ever louder demands of the Slovak intellectuals for public revision of the anti-Slovak witchhunts of the Stalin era and for the political and moral rehabilitation of leading Communist personalities who had been hanged or imprisoned on account of their alleged Slovak "bourgeois nationalism" set the de-Stalinization process in motion. Initially colored by nationalism, the movement gradually took on progressive overtones that led to the discrediting and fall of several powerful leaders including the Czech Premier, and gave a crucial impulse to more liberal policies in both the Slovak and the Czech regions of the country.

After an impasse of several years, it was once again political and economic dissatisfaction in Slovakia that propelled the Slovak Communist leaders in 1967 into the vanguard of the battle against the dogmatic and centralist group in Prague headed by the First Secretary of the Czechoslovak Party and State President, the Czech Antonin Novotny. His fall in January 1968, though hastened by a combination of complex factors, was primarily due to the fact that the Slovak party leader Alexander Dubcek (his successor as First Secretary) sided with the reformist opposition.

But what is progress to one is—or seems to be—retreat to the other. On the face of it, the fall in Yugoslavia of Rankovic, who for over two decades had ruled as the undisputed boss of the dreaded UDBA, the secret police, should have heralded the beginning of a more tolerant age, particularly in Belgrade, where surveillance and control were undoubtedly tightest. Yet the surge of confidence that was so tangible in the summer of 1966, in Zagreb or in Ljubljana, the capital of Slovenia, contrasted sharply with the sense of insecurity that enveloped many Serbs in Belgrade. Meeting friends and acquaintances in Belgrade, the visitor noticed a mood of deep resentment, ranging from mild irony to embittered battle cries. A well-known doctor, an old friend who had never hidden his anti-Communist sentiments, surprised me with an unusually emotional outburst, "Look at the people who are said to be involved in the affair. All, but all are Serbs. They are not just settling accounts with Rankovic. This is a blow against us—the Serbs!" The famous writer Dobrica Cosic, a long-time confidant of Marshal Tito, sent him a sharply worded letter, accusing the President of being primarily responsible for the excesses because he had known about them but had thrown the blame solely on Rankovic. Party functionaries hinted at "attempts to weaken the Serb cadres." As an electrician said to me, "Rankovic has been no angel. But he is one of us, a strong man. Who will protect the interests of Serbia now?"

The situation was, of course, brought under control by the regime, and the climate became less charged. Yet the popular response to the sudden eclipse of a ranking, albeit widely feared national figure matched a deep-rooted code of behavior. Instinctive national solidarity, even with a potential dictator, carried the day. Not only national interests but emotions, often unchecked and stemming from a centuries-long sense of identity, shape, influence, or at the very least color policies and responses in a community of several nations.

To infuse unquestionably tired and in some cases thoroughly discredited regimes with new blood from the vessel of national impulses is an experiment not without serious risks. The twin challenge of nationalism is more than evident, for example, in Rumania. The upsurge of national self-confidence is seen by the majority nation as the natural product of what began as a defense of Rumanian national interests against Soviet domination. But the large and compact Hungarian minority in Rumania looks upon the unleashed forces of Rumanian national spirit as something akin to internal "Rumanianization," something which threatens their Hungarian national identity and traditions.

This contradiction is true of the entire East European region. In a sense, it is always the same sad story, dating back to the multinational Habsburg monarchy, torn by internal stresses that ultimately destroyed the empire. Thus, almost a century ago, what Hungary wanted from Vienna it refused to Croatia, then its ally in a common kingdom. What Croatia demanded from Hungary it, in turn, refused to the Serbs living within its borders. And this double standard in dealing with the rights of one's own nation and those of alien minorities has remained a dominant feature in the family of new states that emerged from the twentieth-century disintegration of the great empires in Eastern Europe, particularly in the Balkans.

Political frontiers after World War I were not always chosen on the proclaimed basis of ethnic boundaries but also for political, strategic, and psychological reasons. After World War II the situation was even worse, at least in Bessarabia. The geographic distribution of ethnic groups and traditional loyalties in these regions is, however, so tangled that no clear-cut and wholly satisfactory demarcations are possible. As a result, there are large and small minorities living in one country but associated with another. If the latter is a neighboring country, this makes the minority problem particularly delicate and often fraught with tension.

One need only look at the Hungarians in Rumania, the Rumanians in the Soviet Union, the Albanians in Yugoslavia, the Greeks in Albania, and the Macedonians (or Slavo-Macedonians) in Greece, Bulgaria, and Yugoslavia, not to mention the hundreds of thousands of Turks in Balkan countries, to get an inkling of how immensely complex the minority problems are. The presence of minorities keeps the vexed issue of territorial disputes on an invisible agenda, even though between Communist states they are almost never mentioned explicitly. Territorial and minority issues will be discussed in detail later, but it might be mentioned at this point that Transylvania separates Hungary and Rumania; Bessarabia, Rumania and the Soviet Union; Kosovo, Yugoslavia and Albania; southern Albania (Northern Epirus to the Greeks), Albania and Greece; while Macedonia is the cause of a recurring three-cornered dispute between Yugoslavia, Bulgaria, and Greece. This impressive list of major territorial issues could of course be supplemented by such minor differences as Dobruja (between Rumania and Bulgaria), Vojvodina (between Yugoslavia and Hungary), or the Banat (between Yugoslavia and Rumania).

The prescriptions for dealing with the problem of small-power imperialism stemming from the presence of minorities within the boundaries of national states are as far apart as the estimates of how serious the problem is. Both the Rumanian and Yugoslav governments envisage a somewhat vague regional cooperation of nation states in the Balkans, based on the principles of respect for sovereignty and territorial integrity and strict non-interference in the internal affairs of another country. The arguments for and against the realism of such ideas are certainly worth investigating. There is, however, another view, which, paradoxical as it may seem, is advocated by both Soviet and American "global strategists" (albeit for different reasons and purposes and expressed in a different political vocabulary).

This "Soviet-American" conception is allied to the notion that national bodies should be replaced by a much wider framework in which borders as such lose their meaning. Khrushchev's vision of the future was spelled out with unusual candor to an East German audience in Leipzig in March 1959 when he stated flatly: "With the victory of communism on a world-wide scale, as Marxism-Leninism teaches, state borders will disappear. In all likelihood only ethnic borders will remain for a time and even these will probably exist only as a convention. . . . It seems to me that the further development of the socialist countries will in all probability proceed along the lines of consolidation in a single world socialist system."[11]

His attempts to "synchronize the clocks" and forge a supranational, tightly integrated economic unit foundered on the rocklike resistance of Rumania, since it was evident that a meaningful integration of centrally planned economies would lead ultimately to the suppression of national identities. Khrushchev's successors are still grappling with the dilemma of how to combine "proletarian internationalism," that is, unconditional subordination to major Soviet policies, with maximal autonomy within the alliance.

From a different angle, some distinguished American policymakers and advisers regard the trends toward independence in Eastern Europe, particularly if they are tinged with anti-Soviet nationalism, as out-of-date, divisive, and dangerous. Their argument is that it is "impossible to find a solution [to the border and minority problems] in an international community based on the theory of absolute national sovereignty acknowledging no higher obligation than the interest of its own nation."[12] Whether they call it a "United States of Europe" or a "grand design," the crux of the theory is that under the conditions of a global nuclear balance only a global accommodation between the two superpowers, the United States and the Soviet Union, can provide a solution to the partition of Germany and the problems of Eastern Europe. As a matter of fact, the argument runs, both world powers help to contain local conflicts. The Soviet Union performs a "restraining function" in territorial disputes in geographically neighboring areas. The East European countries should patiently wait while the "grand design" of a new relationship between the two global powers is translated step by step into practice. Then, and only then, their problems will be solved, either within a supranational federal European system or in some other form. Nationalistic aspirations of small states, like Gaullist phrases about a "European Europe," merely raise the specter of a "Balkanization" of the European continent and upset the progress toward an American-Soviet deal.[13]

Unfortunately, these undoubtedly attractive blueprints are equations with dominant unknowns. The emergence of a "new order" in Europe based on increasingly similar societies and guaranteed by two superpowers vying with each other in peaceful competition appears for the moment to be a hazy notion of a distant future. A whole set of signs tells us that conditions in the immediate power sphere of the Soviet Union are changing. To discard or belittle nationalistic tendencies is perfectly understandable from the standpoint of a world power, which has to think in global terms. But any policy that ignores the changing realities in Eastern Europe is bound to fail in the long run.

Nationalism is a prime example of a term that means different things to different people. To the Soviet leaders it is a "narrow-minded point of view which puts national interests ahead of those of the international workers' movement." To the U. S. State Department it is a "parochial" minor irritation. To the Communist leaders it is a tempting and alarming mixture. To the populations concerned it is an inborn sense of identity that has survived centuries of foreign domination. To the student of the area it appears to be the most powerful single force eroding the pillars of Soviet domination, one that may well transform extremist Communist dictatorships into more conventional authoritarian systems.

Nationalism has the power to create hotbeds of tension or to fracture multinational societies, but to complain about it doesn't help. In a myriad of different forms, it is one of the paramount facts of life in Eastern Europe, and likely to be at the center of politics there for many years to come. Nevertheless one has to resist the temptation to treat discord among Communist-ruled states as simply a clash between old-fashioned nationalisms. Communist ideology, which simultaneously unites and divides the national ruling groups, is also an extremely important element.

The national and ideological factors reinforce each other. The contradiction between Communist theory and practice makes the problem of agreeing to disagree enormously difficult and inhibits temporary compromises on essential issues. Once the unique position of the Soviet Union as the center of both political power and doctrinal authority has been irrevocably broken, any major differences of national interests can be interpreted in different ways. None of the Communist ruling groups has abandoned unconditional loyalty to the doctrine that justifies its monopoly of power. Thus the rulers must justify major policies in terms of the sacred theory.

It is this unity of power and ideology that has made compromise between Moscow and Peking ultimately impossible and the great schism inevitable.[14] The essence of a Communist regime is still the fact that the statements the leaders declare to be the doctrinal truth at any given moment must be accepted by their subjects. Any questioning of ideology would undermine the monopoly of power. This is why public disputes are always extremely dangerous for both sides. But conflicts over major issues are supposedly inconceivable, since the old discords had economic roots and these were, of course, erased with the disappearance of capitalism. As all Communist countries are by definition "brothers," they must conceal differences that would be considered perfectly natural among non-Communist countries.

This is the reason that Communist economic conferences, even relatively unimportant ones to discuss, say, what kind of marine engines should be manufactured in which country, are shrouded in secrecy. Disputes about the location of a steel plant or friction over import duties levied on ball bearings become fateful issues simply because countries that call themselves brothers cannot confess their egoism, selfishness, and profit-seeking to the detriment of another partner. Can a Communist country be imperialistic? Can territorial disputes make enemies of two Communist countries? Can a Communist state discriminate against a national minority associated with a brother country? All this is inconceivable, yet it continually happens, not only between the smaller countries and the Soviet Union, but also among the small Communist states. Once a ruling party refuses to recognize that there is only one center authorized to define in any situation and at any given moment the "universal" truth or supreme interest, ideology ceases to be a binding element and becomes a factor that makes action and compromise more and more difficult. It is also increasingly a fig leaf, for the "brothers" must hide the recurring conflicts among themselves under ideological formulas.

At the same time, the ruling groups never really explain the roots of past public disputes or the reasons for a new reconciliation to their subjects, who must profess unshakable faith in the infallibility of the leadership. This in turn pollutes the political climate both within the country and in its relations with its neighbors. The thesis that Soviet power restrains local conflicts may be correct if seen only in terms of prewar developments. But on balance Soviet domination and communism have combined to separate the East European, particularly the Balkan, nations from one another more than ever and to increase mutual ignorance and suspicion. By pushing the real issues below the surface instead of dealing with their causes, these twin pressures have erected new barriers rather than dismantling the old ones.

After World War II, the four Balkan countries—Yugoslavia, Albania, Rumania, and Bulgaria—were "model satellites," constituting what seemed to be the most solidly welded bulwark of Soviet power and influence in the world. It was Yugoslavia that directed the first deadly blow at the most sacred dogma—that communism implies unconditional support of the Soviet Union. Then came the sensational break between Albania and the Soviet Union, the weakest and the strongest Communist powers. A few years later Rumania began its battle for emancipation. Only Bulgaria, which is not even a direct neighbor of the Soviet Union, has remained a loyal vassal.

Like all Communist-ruled countries, these four Balkan states share three basic assumptions: that political power should be in the hands of a single party; that the means of production should be publicly owned and the economy centrally planned; that there is a basic contradiction between capitalism and socialism, which will inevitably lead to the decay of capitalism and the final victory of socialism. Yet despite these common tenets, Yugoslavia has remained outside the military blocs, non-aligned and independent; Albania, though nominally still a member of the Warsaw Pact and Comecon (the economic cooperation body), is not even on speaking terms with the inveterate "revisionists" in Moscow and has become firmly allied to China;* Rumania, still seemingly a full-fledged member of all international Communist bodies, has not only blocked supranational economic and military integration, but has also taken a neutral stance in the Sino-Soviet conflict and defied Soviet policies on such major international issues as the German question and the Middle East crisis.

Why have the Balkans become the new center of the search for external independence and internal autonomy? How deep is the new mood? Why did Rumania and not Bulgaria take the road to emancipation from Soviet control? Is Bulgaria perhaps not quite so stagnant as it appears to be?

The answers to these and many other questions can be found only in Balkan history and traditions. "Nationalities endure while regimes pass."[15] Not only must we see the present; we must also look back at the past to find the reasons for the different kinds of Communist regime and the startlingly diverse developments. One cannot understand Balkan affairs without at least a minimal acquaintance with the origins of the forces that are still operative.

---

* In the wake of the invasion of Czechoslovakia, the Albanian parliament on September 14, 1968, formally annulled Albania's membership in the Warsaw Pact.

II

THE LAND, THE PEOPLE,
THE INTRUDERS

The first and most elementary requirement in government
is a routine of decent administration.

—*L. B. Namier*

Driving from the west toward Belgrade, the visitor is struck by the
air of modernity when he reaches the outskirts of the Yugoslav
capital. Most of the dilapidated houses, which a few years ago still
pocked the countryside, have been pulled down and replaced by
highrise apartments with colorful façades and a host of attractive
shopping centers. Just before crossing the bridge to the old city
proper, one passes the new Museum of Modern Art on the left, an
inpressive example of the best in contemporary architecture with a
beguiling combination of beauty and sweep. This steadily expanding mixture of residential suburb and federal administration center
is now called New Belgrade.

The other side of the river Sava is the "real" Belgrade where
most of the 700,000 inhabitants live. An impressive old fort, dominating the skyline, is a reminder that Belgrade, situated at the
confluence of the Sava and the Danube, has served since ancient
times as an often-besieged bastion, protecting the gateway to Southeast Europe. Despite a confusing jumble of pseudomodern and
oriental styles, laced with some unpleasant relics of the short-lived
Stalinist architecture, the city proper still radiates a Byzantine and
Turkish atmosphere, mingled, of course, with Serbian. The more the
visitor wanders around, the stronger he feels—this is truly the
Balkans.

When he crosses the short bridge over the Sava, he is said to be
leaving one world and entering another, moving from the "West"
into the "Orient," from Central Europe into the Balkans. Zemun, the
small town on the west bank where a modern airport now stands,
was for centuries the frontier station between the Austrian and the

Ottoman empires, and the old dividing line determined aspects of political life in this area that are still valid and important. The Sava was a vital part of the famous Military Frontier against the Turks, a special marchland of forts and watchtowers, created toward the end of the sixteenth century and defended by frontiermen enjoying special privileges. The "frontier" was under direct Austrian control, which was extended or reorganized many times throughout the centuries in response to the success or failure of Turkish raids. The frontiermen, the new settlers in the depopulated border regions of Croatia and southern Hungary, were mainly Orthodox Serbs who had fled northward, attracted by the promises made by the various Austrian emperors of religious liberty and land held on a special tenure. The descendants of the migrants who crossed the Danube to settle in Hungary in the fifteenth and sixteenth centuries played a stirring role in the history of the Serbian people, while the descendants of those who fled to Croatia have become a highly complicating factor in the "Croat question" of our time.

The union of areas with different national consciousnesses, administrative traditions, and religious loyalties, all forged by a centuries-long division between different worlds, has proved to be a troubled one in the new Yugoslavia and "Great Rumania" of the twentieth century. The Rumanians of the Old Kingdom expected gratitude from their kinsmen in the "liberated provinces" of Transylvania and Bukovina, as the Serbs did from the Slovenes and Croats in Yugoslavia. Yet even the Rumanians, not to mention the Hungarians and Germans, the Croats and Slovenes, who had been molded by a "Western" pattern in areas that had belonged for a long period to the Austro-Hungarian monarchy, responded with scorn when, after 1918, the newcomers from Bucharest and Belgrade began to superimpose "Eastern" methods on their "Western" ways.[1] To this day, the Slovenes and Croats in Yugoslavia, the Transylvanians and the few remaining Bukovinians in Rumania feel superior to their respective administrative centers. When these inequalities happen to coincide with national divisions within one country, any crisis, external or internal, can transform precarious coexistence into fratricidal strife. The razor edge between resentment and violence was tragically shown during the Yugoslav civil war in the massacres of Serbs by Croats, who were later joined by the Muslims, and in the mass executions of Croats by the Partisans.

For a foreigner in Ljubljana, the Slovenian capital, or in Cluj, the principal Transylvanian city, to refer to the Balkans as something even remotely related to these towns and areas is an almost unforgivable social blunder. As a Slovenian scientist put it to me many years ago, on my first visit to his city, "Except for the *cevapcici* (tasty meatballs), you will find here nothing that would remind you of the Balkans." North of the Sava and the Danube, the expression "Balkan" is unanimously regarded as an insult.

Yet the word simply means "mountain" in Turkish. This is also the name of the majestic range that separates northern Bulgaria from the rest of the country and extends some 370 miles eastward, running parallel with the Danube almost to the Black Sea. The Balkan Mountains give the entire southeast European peninsula its name. In geographical language, the Balkan Peninsula is bounded on the northwest by the Alps, on the north by the Sava and the lower Danube, and on the east, south, and west sides by the Black, Aegean, and Adriatic seas. Neat geographical definitions should not, however, be taken too seriously. While Rumania, strictly speaking, belongs to the Danubian basin, it is primarily a Balkan country. Conversely, Yugoslavia and Bulgaria are also in a sense Danubian states. The Danube, the ancient line of invasion and great trade artery, flows through these three countries and links them to one another.

Strangely, neither Greece nor Turkey can properly be regarded today as a Balkan country. The Byzantine and Turkish empires and all that they stood for had a profound influence on the Balkan states. But modern Greece has always tended to look toward the West. Thanks to its traditions, long coastline, merchant shipping, traders, and the many Greek settlers, first in the great Mediterranean ports and later in the United States, Greece has been incomparably more cosmopolitan than any other state in southeast Europe. During the past twenty-five years, after British and American intervention and aid combined to keep the country on the Western side of the Iron Curtain, the differences between Greece and its northern neighbors have become even more pronounced. Similarly, modern Turkey is no longer a Balkan country. It has abandoned all territorial outposts in Europe, except for eastern Thrace and the European part of Istanbul (which will often be referred to below as Constantinople).

Regardless of geographical niceties, the word Balkans is instinctively and historically associated not with a mountain range or peninsula, but with disorder and poverty, with tales of warfare and violence, heroism and treachery. The Balkans have had—and with good reason—an international reputation of being a tinderbox, the powder keg of European politics, and a hotbed for revolutionary ideas. The prediction attributed to a British traveler returning to his London club toward the end of the last century after a visit to the Continent, "There will be trouble in the Balkans in the spring!" was rather vague, but turned out to be surprisingly accurate.

For five hundred years the Balkan countries, of small importance individually, were as a whole of major significance as a battle-ground of the rival Austrian and Turkish empires. From the eighteenth century on, Russian interest in gaining control over the coveted Straits—the Bosporus, Sea of Marmora, and Dardanelles—made the fight into a three-cornered battle. Later, the Balkans was the scene of fierce struggles for power between Nazi Germany and the Western democracies, and the Soviet Union. Ever since the gradual breakup of the ailing Ottoman Empire in the nineteenth century put the so-called "Eastern Question" on the agenda of European politics, the expression "Balkanization" has been understood as describing unhealthy and undesirable political fragmentation, the division of an area into small antagonistic states.

The phrase Balkan politics became identical with disapproval, censure, and condemnation. It described the haphazard and quick changes of weak and usually rotten governments. Worse still, it carried the odium of misrule and oppression, unspeakable corruption and abominable poverty, and these indeed have been the characteristic features of the Balkan countries. The legendary exploits of the Hajduks, brigands of a Robin Hood variety, or the many fantastic—and sometimes true—stories of espionage and adventure may have lent this scenically beautiful area an air of romance. But history has played cruel tricks on the peoples of the Balkans, who "formed a buffer zone between the West and Asia, allowing the Western nations to develop in comparative security their own civilization while the fury of the Asian whirlwinds spent itself on their backs."[2]

Geography has been undoubtedly the major cause of the misfortunes and diversity. It still poses some of the important problems faced by the modern Balkan states. It is the intricate and rugged mountain ranges—formidable highland bastions in Macedonia and Montenegro, barren limestone mountains blocking the Dalmatian coast from the interior, steep slopes shadowy with alpine forests in Bulgaria, and stark high mountain barriers in Albania—that have left a permanent mark on the peoples and given the land its character. The mountainous part of the country (above 1,500 feet) comprises almost half the territory of Yugoslavia and nearly one-third of the area of Bulgaria.

Yet these great mountain ranges, from the Carpathian Alps to the Balkan and Rhodope massif, from the Dinaric Mountains to the Pindus range, have never truly protected, though they have isolated, the different peoples from one another. Natural barriers, they have hardly ever corresponded with national or ethnic boundaries. From time immemorial, the peninsula was penetrated by countless migrating tribes and invading armies, following, now in one direction, now in another, the great natural highways, the river courses: from Austria and the plains of Central Europe along the sweeping valley of the Danube to the heart of Serbia, there to continue east through the Iron Gates to the delta of the Danube on the Rumanian coast of the Black Sea, or southeast across Bulgaria by way of Sofia and the Maritsa River to Adrianople and Turkey, or south down the strategic furrow formed by the Morava and Vardar rivers to Salonika and Greece. From the Adriatic, two mountain rivers, the Neretva and the Bosna, provided the principal route to the interior.

This accessibility by both land and sea and the inner fragmentation and diversity of peoples separated by formidable mountain barriers, have had a profound impact on history. The nations never were independent long enough to shape their own destinies but time and again fell easy prey to foreign domination and were deeply affected by the radiations of outside cultural centers—Byzantium and later Constantinople, Venice, Vienna, Budapest, and Moscow. The Balkan Peninsula has always been a link between Europe and Asia Minor, a vital trade route, a bridge between West and East.[3]

When the Congress of Berlin in 1878 tried to solve the territorial issues arising from the decay of the Turkish Empire, it awarded large portions of present-day Albania to the neighboring states. The Albanians, still under Turkish rule and encouraged by the Sultan, formed the League of Prizren, which began to bombard the Western statesmen with documents in defense of the Albanian nation and language. The Congress, not surprisingly, ignored the protests as coming from the most obscure corner of the Balkans, and Bismarck settled the matter with the scornful remark, "There is no such thing as Albanian nationality."

Yet modern Albanians are the oldest inhabitants of the Balkans, the descendants of the ancient Illyrians, who in the fifth century B.C. were mentioned by the Greeks as inhabiting the peninsula together with the Thracians. Shkodra in northern Albania was the capital of the Illyrian kingdom incorporated into the Roman empire in 168 B.C. Five Illyrians, including Diocletian, whose palace at Split on the Adriatic bespeaks past magnificence even sixteen centuries later, ruled as Roman emperors. Despite innumerable foreign invasions and long Turkish rule, the Albanians have remained Thraco-Illyrian by stock, and their language, though Indo-European, is quite unlike any other tongue. They have no ethnic or strong religious bonds to their Slav, Greek, and Italian neighbors.

The origin and history of the Rumanians (called for a long time Vlach or Wallach, the Gothic word for foreigner) has been an issue passionately contested well into our time. They regard themselves as being of Daco-Roman stock: descendants of the Dacians, relatives of the ancient Thracians, who were conquered by the Roman legions under Emperor Trajan in A.D. 106. About 165 years later the Emperor Aurelian withdrew the legions, and the territory was overrun by barbarian tribes. The Rumanians did not reappear in the triangular region of Transylvania, bounded on three sides by the Carpathians and another mountain range, until the thirteenth century. What happened during the ten intervening centuries has been called by the first great modern Rumanian historian, A. D. Xenopol, "the enigma of the Middle Ages." There is indeed "no parallel to the mysterious silence, which shrouds the Rumanians for the one thousand years following the withdrawal of Aurelian and his legions—a period in which there are neither chronicles nor charters nor architectural remains. One lacks the very basis for reconstructing even the barest outlines of history."[4]

Whether the bulk of the Daco-Roman population held out in the mountains where the Rumanians preserved their racial identity, or whether they all withdrew with the legions would seem to be of only academic interest today. There was and is no convincing proof as to who did or did not accompany the retreat of the Roman legions; how many of them there were; or how many emigrated beyond the Carpathians. Yet even in the twentieth century this obscure controversy has kept the tempers of Hungarian and Rumanian historians near the boiling point and provided a so-called "ideological basis" for bitter territorial discord.

The point is that Transylvania belonged for almost a millennium in one form or another to Hungary. The Hungarians who settled in the ninth century in the great Pannonain (or Danubian) plain soon moved into adjacent Transylvania, where they constituted the ruling class. The culture of the region has consequently been essentially Hungarian. But by the nineteenth century the Rumanians, mainly serfs and nationally oppressed, constituted the majority of the population, speaking what was essentially, albeit with many Slavic words, a Latin tongue. With the rise of nationalism and after the dismemberment of historic Hungary, which was accompanied by the emergence of Great Rumania, the historic argument about the first surviving owners of the soil, the debate over who—the Hungarians or the Rumanians—got to Transylvania first, became a live issue and a cause of internal strife. Even today it casts a shadow over Hungarian-Rumanian relations and has involved the only non-Slav nations in Eastern Europe—the nations that separate the Russians, Poles, Czechs, and Slovaks from the South Slavs—in an unsolved and probably insoluble national dispute.

While the Albanians appear to be descendants of the ancient Illyrians and the Rumanians consider themselves the ancestors of the romanized Dacians, the historical lineage of the South Slavs is perhaps slightly less respectable but not controversial at all. They have inhabited their present homelands for an uninterrupted period of some thirteen centuries, having appeared in the sixth century. With the exception of the Albanians, the Latin character of the coastal city-states in Dalmatia, and the scattered pockets of Vlach kinsmen of the Rumanians in northern Greece and Macedonia, the whole area gradually became Slav in character and language.

Despite the racial and linguistic kinship, the South Slavs became divided by historical, cultural, and religious differences. The Slovenes in the eastern valleys of the Alps and the Croats of western Illyria came under Latin and Roman Catholic influence. The Slovenes, who from early times formed part of the Holy Roman Empire and never lived under Ottoman rule, speak a language that differs considerably from that spoken by the Croats and Serbs. They have been and still are by far the most advanced South Slav nation. The Croats have clung strongly to Roman Catholicism since the ninth century.

They enjoyed the status of an independent country (the extent of the early kingdom under Kresimir Peter and his successors has long been disputed between chauvinistic Croatian and Serbian historians) for about two hundred years until 1102, when Croatia was united with (the Hungarians say conquered by) Hungary. This political marriage lasted for over eight hundred years.

The Dalmatian coast, its population becoming in time predominantly Croat, was the scene of no fewer than twenty-one wars between Venice and Hungary before the fifteenth century. Then it came for about 370 years under Venetian rule, during which it was constantly threatened by Turkish raids. The Renaissance and Baroque palaces and churches along the coast and on the islands, often still surrounded by walls or protected by forts adorned with magnificent doorways, graceful columns, and carved portals, are reminders of a Dalmatian civilization which was on a par with intellectual life in the West and far superior to that of the rest of the Balkans. After a short but politically significant Napoleonic occupation, the coast was allotted to Austria in 1814. Its unification with Croatia proper was prevented for political reasons until the birth of modern Yugoslavia on the ruins of the Austro-Hungarian monarchy.

Two great Slav missionaries, Cyril and Methodius, and their disciples in the ninth century not only developed a Slavic literary language and the Cyrillic alphabet, but also succeeded in converting the Serbs and the Bulgars to the Eastern Church of Greek Constantinople, subjecting both nations to the rich influence of Byzantine culture. After the open schism between Rome and Constantinople, the difference of faith cut the Balkans in two, separating the Croats and Slovenes (as well as the Hungarians and the northern Slavs) from the Serbs, Bulgarians, Rumanians, and Albanians (and also the Russians). The line separating the two branches of Christianity has remained a source of mistrust and hatred between the Croats and the Serbs. Though they speak essentially the same language, (known as Serbo-Croatian or, in Croatia, Croat-Serbian), the Serbs use the Cyrillic alphabet and the Croats the Latin. There are significant differences of vocabulary, construction, and dialect even in the regions inhabited mainly by Croats. And what may seem to the foreigner irrelevant linguistic niceties are suspiciously regarded by many Croats as a "creeping Serbianization" of the Croat literary language. One of Yugoslavia's stormiest postwar political scandals was sparked by an apparently linguistic argument in the spring of 1967.

There are two other nations in contemporary Yugoslavia with constituent republics of their own, yet their national character is still hotly disputed by some of their neighbors. The Montenegrins speak Serbian and are Orthodox in religion. Following the breakup of the medieval Serbian empire, the Montenegrins lived in an independent principality, ruled later as a theocratic state by prince-bishops. The tiny principality numbered only about 120,000 inhabitants in the mid-nineteenth century, and even today as an enlarged republic its population does not exceed half a million. The Montenegrins, however, pride themselves on having never been subjected to any foreign power. Their mountain bastions—Montenegro means "Black Mountain"—remained outside the Turkish grip, for the invaders soon discovered that in the mountains "a small army is beaten; a large one dies of starvation." The Montenegrins have had a different political past and different traditions from their kinsmen in Serbia, and many of them regard themselves as a separate nation. Officially at any rate they are recognized as such in Yugoslavia.

The Macedonians or Macedo-Slavs speak a variety of dialects, closely related to Bulgarian as well as to Serbo-Croatian. The so-called Macedonian literary language, which evolved after World War II, is now classified as a separate language in Yugoslavia. To speak about a Macedonian language, let alone nation, in Sofia the Bulgarian capital, however, is even today regarded as treacherous impudence and proof of total ignorance. In 1966 the talented poet and president of the Bulgarian Writers' Association, Georgi Dzhagarov, during a seven-hour talk enlivened with innumerable glasses of the native plum brandy, tried to convince me that the Macedonian nation, among other things, is an invention. Himself partly of Macedonian origin, Dzhagarov quoted facts and figures, spoke with passion and eloquence about the most natural fact of life—that the Macedonians are none other than . . . Bulgarians. When, a few months later, he and his friends elaborated on the same theme in talks with a delegation of Macedonian writers from Yugoslavia and insisted on publishing a communique about future cooperation in Bulgarian and Serbo-Croatian because the Bulgarian and Macedonian languages are the same, the guests left in an uproar. A violent controversy followed, one of the many periodical flare-ups between Yugoslavia and Bulgaria over the past and present fate of Macedonia.

The maze of national problems in the Balkans, like the Macedonian dispute in which no one can be right and no one wrong, are topical issues that force the observer to burrow far into the past to grasp their origins. One must go back to the medieval Bulgar empires, which still fire the imaginations of their descendants, and then to the medieval Serb rulers, whose memories, too, are kept alive by epic poems and mangnificent monasteries.

Driving from the Black Sea port and resort of Varna through the fertile plains and uplands which slope gently from the Balkan Mountains toward the Danube, the traveler would hardly think it worth while to turn off the main road after less than sixty miles. What do place names such as Pliska or Preslav mean today? Little is known in the West of the Bulgarian people themselves, as one poignantly realizes when talking to the shabbily dressed caretaker among the desolate ruins of monumental fortifications and public buildings in Pliska, the first Bulgarian capital. Here stood in the seventh and eighth centuries what the Bulgarians claim to have been the largest basilica in Europe at that time. Some 300 feet long and 90 feet wide, it was built of finely hewn stone blocks at the center of the Outer City, which spread over an area almost 8 miles square. In the much smaller Inner City one sees the ruins of palaces and chapels complete with secret passages, a water supply system, a big cistern, and other relics indicating a surprisingly high level of culture. Today there is no money to continue the excavations begun at the end of the nineteenth century. Pliska and the second Bulgarian capital at near-by Preslav, with its even more impressive and better preserved citadel walls and the marble columns of the Golden Church, are off the "beaten track," visited mainly by occasional groups of school children.

Yet there amid the wheatfields and wooded hills were the centers of the first medieval Bulgarian empire, which has left a legacy of pride and frustration to modern Bulgarians. A Mongol tribe, the Bulgars overran the area in the seventh century and later adopted the language and customs of the Slavs whom they conquered. The fortunes of the young Bulgarian kingdom were closely associated with Byzantine political and cultural influence. For eleven centuries, until the Turks took Constantinople in 1453, Byzantium was the focus of worldly prestige and cultural tradition in the Balkans.

But as early as 811 the young Bulgarian state under Khan Krum was strong enough to defeat the army of the Byzantine Emperor Nicephorus I. One medieval fresco shows Krum and his warriors proudly drinking out of the hollowed skulls of the defeated nobles. Krum used the silver-lined skull of the Emperor himself.

Under Simeon I (893–927), who assumed the title of tsar, the Bulgarian empire reached its height. A major power in the Balkans and a serious threat to Constantinople, it extended from the Black Sea in the east to the region of Belgrade in the west, from the slopes of the Carpathians in the north to Macedonia in the southwest. Large portions of Serbia, Albania, and the whole of Macedonia were parts of the empire, which, as present-day Bulgarian history books proudly and with slight exaggeration state, was bounded by the Black, Aegean, and Adriatic seas. After Simeon's death, Byzantine recovery and revolts broke up the empire, but toward the end of the tenth century, under Samuel, Bulgaria emerged again as a major power, with its center in Macedonia and its capital at Ohrid, the site of the first Bulgarian Patriarchate. The revival was short-lived, however, and soon the Byzantine empire again ruled most of Bulgaria and Macedonia. In the twelfth century, a revolt headed by Vlachs and Bulgars exploited the growing weakness of Byzantium and led to the establishment of a second Bulgarian empire, which, notably under Ivan Assen II (1218–41), held sway over an area almost as large as Simeon's, including large parts of Macedonia. Its capital, Tirnovo, high in the Balkan Mountains, remained, even after the eclipse of the empire, the picturesque fortress capital of medieval rump Bulgaria and was the site late in the 19th century of the first Bulgarian constituent assembly, which accepted the so-called Tirnovo Constitution.

Bulgaria was replaced as the dominant power in the Balkans in the fourteenth century by the Serbs, who won a great, final victory at Kustendil over the combined armies of the Bulgarians and the Byzantine empire. The great event in Serbian history was the emergence of the Nemanjid dynasty between the twelfth and fourteenth centuries, which led not only to the liberation of eastern Serbia but also to the establishment of a large medieval empire. Under Tsar Stephen Dushan (1331–55) medieval Serbia was able to occupy the whole of Macedonia, Albania, and beyond. The Serbian archbishopric, the basis of a national church, established in the early twelfth century, was raised in 1346 to the dignity of a patriarchate. In the same year Dushan was crowned at Skopje (today the capital of the Macedonian republic) as "Emperor of the Serbs and Greeks," a title soon changed to the even more impressive "Emperor and Autocrat of the Serbs and Greeks, the Bulgarians and Albanians."

The empire fell to pieces after his death. His successors led by Prince Lazar were decisively beaten by the Turks at Kosovo in June 1389. The anniversary of the battle is still celebrated each year in Serbia on June 28, the feast day of St. Vitus or Vidovdan. The battle of the fatal "field of blackbirds" inspired the most famous ballads in Serbian folk poetry and the memory of the disaster has a peculiar hold on the Serb people to this very day.

It is difficult, if not impossible, for the West with its continuous national history to understand what an enormous impact the conflicting "ancestral charters" of the Bulgarians and the Serbs have had on modern Balkan history. Unfortunately, the Nemanjids in the fourteenth century conquered for the Serbs much of the same land that Simeon and Samuel had ruled in the ninth and eleventh centuries for the Bulgarians. Nineteenth-century French statesmen did not refer to the legacy of Charlemagne, or British governments to the memories of Plantagenet England, as vital arguments in forming their policies, but resurrecting the heroic achievements of tsars and princes long dead became a political program for the Serbs and Bulgarians. For peoples whose national histories have been brutally interrupted, past glories are an inspiration in the struggle for national revival and have provided tools for the nationalists to embroil Serbs, Bulgarians, and Greeks in a hopeless conflict over Macedonia.

Because Macedonia, with a total area of less than 28,000 square miles, occupies the center of the Balkan Peninsula and controls the Vardar valley, the main route from Central Europe to Salonika and the Aegean, it was the most important area of European Turkey. Neither before nor after the 530-year Ottoman rule has it been a single administrative or political unit. Though Turkish, Bulgarian, Serb, and Greek statistics, which differ widely on the area's population, are not to be taken seriously, they do reveal the bewildering confusion of races in Macedonia. Of the estimated two million population in 1910 about half were Slavs—claimed by both the Bulgars and the Serbs. Thus at the turn of the century, Bulgarian ethnographers found 1.2 million Bulgarians and 700 (!) Serbs in the coveted area. The Serbs, on the other hand, produced two million Serbs and 57,000 Bulgarians living on the same territory. All agreed that there

postwar Yugoslavia changed the picture dramatically, but it was the creation of a Macedonian Republic within the Yugoslav Federation that set off the train of events leading to the blueprint of a Balkan Federation and culminating in Yugoslavia's expulsion from the Soviet bloc.

The central event of Balkan history was the Turkish invasion, which destroyed the medieval states in Serbia, Bosnia, Bulgaria, and Rumania. The final Turkish conquest of Bulgaria began in 1371, and after the battle of Kosovo in 1389 the neighboring Serbian and Bulgarian principalities succumbed one after another. The seizure of Tirnovo in 1393 sealed the fate of Bulgaria as an independent state until 1878. Constantinople's fall in 1453 was followed rapidly by the complete domination of Serbia. By the sixteenth century the entire Balkan Peninsula was under Ottoman rule, and the battle of Mohacs in 1526 marked the defeat of Hungary and the disappearance of the last independent state in the Danubian basin.

Centuries of alien domination have left a profound imprint on Balkan social patterns, economy, cultural evolution, and codes of behavior. Under Turkish domination the entire area entered a period of decline—although not solely for the reasons usually associated with the patterns imposed by the Turks—from which it began to emerge only in the twentieth century. One of the most significant effects of the Turkish conquest was the destruction of the native landed aristocracy. In both Bulgaria and Serbia their extinction had a lasting influence on the rural structure, leading ultimately to the development of egalitarian peasant societies with deeply rooted social traditions and strong democratic tendencies. A sense of social justice and group loyalty coupled with fierce individualism has remained a characteristic feature of the Serbian and Bulgarian peasant.

For several reasons, developments in Rumania and Bosnia took a different tack. The two Rumanian principalities—Wallachia and Moldavia—were deeply involved in the various three-sided conflicts between the Turks, the Habsburg monarchy, and the Poles, who were later replaced by the Russians. The decline of a free peasantry and the growth of serfdom were the products of a system that subjected the peasants to a double exploitation: by the Greek magnates, who acted as vassals of the sultan, and by the native boyars, who were completely subservient to them.

As the Phanar, or Lighthouse, section of Istanbul, including the seat of the Oecumenical Patriarch, was inhabited by Greeks, the Greek rulers and middlemen were called Phanariots by the Balkan people. It was Phanariot rule, during which, between 1711 and 1821, twelve families provided seventy-seven rulers for the two principalities (in half the cases they were the same persons, merely swapping positions), that created an almost legendary flair for corruption in Rumania. The Phanariot princes who doubled a new Turkish levy or raised it fourfold, pocketing the difference or sharing it with the boyars; who banned the import of a product and then organized the smuggling of the same article; who even deposed the Orthodox metropolitan only to appropriate his large revenues during an enforced and prolonged vacancy, were the ancestors of those modern Rumanians who, after independence, raised graft to a consummate artistry. Between the two world wars literally everything in Rumania from contracts for public buildings to liquor permits was for sale. It is said that the police once jailed a foreign correspondent because he tried to change his money legally at the bank instead of resorting to the black market![7] The traces of corruption are still evident, even in such petty forms as overcharging, which is carried out in Rumania more regularly and more brazenly than in any other Communist-ruled country in the whole of Eastern Europe.

The majority of the Balkan Christians remained faithful to their religions, but 70 per cent of the Albanians and a sizable portion of the Bosnians converted to Islam. After the fall of Constantinople, tiny Albania held out for fifteen years, largely because of the heroic resistance organized by George Kastrioti, called Skanderbeg by Western historians. Though raised a Muslim at the sultan's court, he returned to his native country at the head of an army, liberated it from alien occupation, and as an independent Prince in the mountain capital of Kruja repulsed repeated Turkish invasions during his lifetime. After his death in 1468, about 70 per cent of the Albanians became Muslim. Unlike their Slav neighbors, Muslim Albanians were treated as equals in the ruling class of the multinational Ottoman Empire and rose to high positions. Eleven of the forty-nine grand viziers between 1453 and 1623 were Albanians and one, Mehmet Ali, ruled Egypt in the early nineteenth century and founded a ruling dynasty that was deposed only in 1952 by the officers' coup.

Bosnia, inhabited by both Catholic Croats and Orthodox Serbs, has always been a highly sensitive spot in the complex of interracial relations in Yugoslavia. The presence of the largest compact group of Muslim Slavs in the Balkans, accounting even today for well over one-third of the 3.6 million inhabitants of the republic of Bosnia-Herzegovina, has confused the picture all along and exerted an important influence on the development of the region. The heretic creed of Bogomils spread in the twelfth century, not only in Bulgaria but also in Bosnia where, defying both Rome and Constantinople, it inflamed religious differences to the boiling point until the Turks conquered the land in the fifteenth century. The members of this heretic "Bosnian Church" found Turkish rule more to their liking. Most of them adopted the Muslim faith and, although remaining Slavs in language and race, became "more Turkish than the Turks in outlook" and intolerable oppressors of their fellow Slavs whom they despised.

Thus Bosnia presented the world with a unique case of a new nobility, Slav by race, speaking Serbo-Croat, yet Muslim by religion and, alone among the Slavs, partners and not subjects of the Turks. For centuries some 7,000 Muslim beys or agas lorded it over the Roman Catholic or Orthodox serfs, and even after Austria-Hungary occupied the land in 1878, the free peasant families were exclusively Muslim. Whereas serfdom was abolished in Serbia in 1817 and in Croatia in 1848, in Bosnia as late as 1914 one-third of the arable land was worked by some 100,000 serf families.[8]

This curious religious triangle, accentuated by sharp social differences and brought to a pitch by the rise of the Serbian state and the rivalry of the Great Powers, served as the igniting spark of a rapid succession of crises that rocked nineteenth-century Europe and culminated in World War I. The assassination of the Austrian Archduke Francis Ferdinand in June 1914, which unleashed the "Great War," remade the map of Europe, and brought two million American soldiers to the Continent, was the act of a Bosnian Serb in an obscure Bosnian town. During World War II Bosnia was the scene of some of the worst massacres and provided the essential launching pad for the triumphant sweep of Tito's Communist Partisans, who alone among the warring nationalist factions advocated the concept of a united Yugoslavia with equality for all. Though Bosnia's role in international affairs has luckily become nil, it still provides a floodmark for measuring the given levels of nationalistic passions. As before, the Roman Catholic Croats look toward Zagreb, the Orthodox Serbs toward Belgrade for protection, while the Muslims, many of them, cherish memories of past glories when they were among the chosen Muslim rulers and oppressed the Christian peasants. They feel like a deposed elite, dominated or overwhelmed by those they formerly ruled.

In spite of the setbacks in Bosnia and Albania, the Catholic and Orthodox churches in the Balkans provided a continuity of national traditions through the centuries of Turkish and Austrian bondage and successfully resisted the attempts of the Phanariots to impose the Greek language on the Serbian and Bulgarian churches. In Rumania, where Bulgaro-Slav rites were in force until the middle of the seventeenth century and where even in the nineteenth century liturgical books were printed in Slav characters, Greek influence was extremely strong. The first Rumanian books were printed in the seventeenth century. Yet, Rumanian literature, paradoxically, owes its survival to the fact that the clergy spoke even less Greek than Slav.[9] The churches everywhere also survived as popular institutions with a legitimate historical lineage. The history books, grammars, and dictionaries produced by Catholic priests and Orthodox monks like Father Paisi in Bulgaria, Dositej Obradovic in Serbia, or Valentin Vodnik in Slovenia served as clarion calls for a national awakening. The Orthodox priests in Transylvania, who in the seventeenth century recognized papal supremacy but were allowed to retain their liturgic order, to marry, and to keep their beards, organized the Rumanian Uniate Church, which was the spiritual leader of the resistance against Hungarian domination and a pioneer of Rumanian nationalism. When Rumanian seminarists in Rome realized that they were speaking a Latin language, when they saw that the conquered Dacians of the ancient past commemorated in the bas-reliefs on the famous column of Trajan were wearing fur hats similar to those still worn by Rumanian peasants, they acquired a sense of national identity, which subsequently spread in the Rumanian lands of Wallachia and Moldavia.

While the Orthodox Church has been primarily a national institution and the preserver of national tradition, the Roman Catholic clergy has been a prime factor—although not always a positive one—in shaping the destiny of modern Croatia and Slovenia. It was the Croatian Bishop Strossmayer (1815–1905), perhaps the foremost creative figure of the nineteenth century in the Balkans, who founded the Yugoslav (South Slav) Academy of Science and Art, a national university, with schools and seminars, which made Zagreb one of the great centers of Slav culture and a bulwark against the repeated attempts to impose Hungarian cultural supremacy. Strossmayer was also a strong advocate of the "Illyrian" ideal of the union of Croats, Serbs, and Slovenes, which was one of the basic factors leading to the birth of the Yugoslav state in 1918.

After the Nazi conquest in 1941, when a separate "Kingdom of Croatia" was set up under an absentee Italian princeling and ruled by the Fascist terrorist group Ustashe (the word means rebels), the Zagreb Archbishop Stepinac, some of the bishops, and many of the Catholic clergy were dazzled by the prospect of converting hundreds of thousands of Orthodox Serbs. Stepinac welcomed "the splendid opportunity of furthering the Croat and the Holy Catholic cause in Bosnia," which had been given to puppet Croatia although the Serbs outnumbered the Croats two to one. Despite their growing misgivings about Ustasha methods of "conversion" through wholesale massacres and the threat of annihilation, the archbishop and the higher clergy failed to disassociate themselves with sufficient vigor from the terrorist regime. After the war, this was used by the Communists to launch a full-scale assault on the Church.

Scores of admittedly extremely compromised priests were summarily shot and many imprisoned, including the archbishop himself who was sentenced to sixteen years. Though he was released in 1951 and exiled to his native village, the regime refused to recognize him as archbishop, and when Pope Pius XII appointed him cardinal the following year, Tito broke off formal relations with the Holy See. After the death of the controversial cardinal in 1960, the liberalization of the political climate improved the position of the Catholic Church. After long, drawn-out negotiations the Vatican and the Belgrade government signed an important agreement in the summer of 1966, providing among other things for the re-establishment of diplomatic relations.

The Catholic Church has triumphantly weathered the campaigns of vilification and abuse and the crippling blow of nationalization without compensation. Since 1963 it has been allowed to publish periodicals. The Croat ecclesiastical biweekly *Glas Koncila*, although it can be sold only in churches or chapels, has trebled its regular circulation to 150,000 and its pre-Christmas issues usually pass the 200,000 mark. The Catholic gazette in Slovenia sells over 100,000 copies. In a country where parties were traditionally organized along national and religous lines, and where over one-third of the population (about 7,000,000) are Roman Catholics, the Catholic Church has remained, if not in a political then certainly in a spiritual sense, a power in its own right.

No rewriting of history can erase the socially progressive, if politically conservative role played by the Catholic People's Party in Slovenia in the interwar period. Deeply influenced by a Catholic political philosophy, it successfully pushed popular educational programs and the organization of voluntary sales and credit cooperatives for the peasants. Its leader, Father Anton Korosec, secured virtual autonomy for his people within an authoritarian Great Serbian state by forging what might be called a Ljubljana-Belgrade axis. He was undoubtedly the ablest Slovene politician of this century.

Yet despite the significant Croat and Slovene exceptions, the general religious and cultural pattern in the Balkans has been predominantly fashioned by strong Orthodox traditions. About 35,000,000 of the 49,000,000 present inhabitants in the four Balkan countries (Yugoslavia, Albania, Rumania, and Bulgaria) are estimated to be Orthodox, while Roman Catholic and Uniate, Muslim and Protestant minorities account for the rest. The Jews, whose number before World War II was well over 900,000 (of whom 800,000 lived in Rumania alone), were decimated during the holocaust, and most of the survivors have emigrated to Israel; by the mid-sixties there were perhaps 110,000 or 120,000 left in the entire Balkan Peninsula.

As the majority Orthodox population hated both the Turkish sultan and the Roman pope, the appearance of Russia as the champion of the oppressed Orthodox subjects of the sultan posed a major challenge to Austrian interests and constituted perhaps the single most important external factor influencing the national awakening of the Balkan peoples. In addition to its purely religious aspects, the sense of Slavic kinship has been a powerful emotional factor in modern Bulgaria, and, in a more romantic than practical sense, in tiny, geographically distant Montenegro.

The six Russian invasions of the Balkans in the eighteenth and nineteenth centuries liberated Bulgaria and hastened the formal independence of Serbia and Rumania. They also fatally weakened the attraction of the pan-Slavists, who had advocated the union of all Slav peoples under the undisputed leadership of the Great Russians. The defense of Orthodox interests served—as did, later, the cause of the international revolution for "the fatherland of the proletariat"—

as a vehicle for expansion. The behavior of the armies and the intrigues of the agents of "Mother Russia" alienated even the grateful Bulgarians, who at one point in the 1880s had to accept two Russian generals ruling them as prime minister and minister of war.[10] The Rumanians, as a Latin nation, could not even soothe their wounds with the balm of racial kinship.

As a rule, the farther off a great power was, the more sympathetic toward it the Balkan peoples were. This has been true of Russia, Austria, and Germany. And it was undoubtedly France that provided Balkan intellectuals with the greatest inspiration for national sentiments and modern political ideas. This has always been true particularly in Rumania, which to a great degree owed its unification and independence to Napoleon III. In 1848 the French consul in Bucharest reported to his superiors in Paris, "Whether she accepts or repudiates it, France has here on the banks of the Danube an inevitable clientele which attaches itself to her as the head of Latin nations."[11]

The proverbial saying that the Rumanians feel themselves "a Latin island in a sea of Slavs" has become a shopworn platitude, repeatedly used as a lead in stories by newspapermen visiting Rumania for the first time. But, like every cliché, it contains an element of truth. Regardless of temporary alliances with Austria and later even with Nazi Germany, France has remained the pole of attraction for most modern Rumanians. France was the great, albeit ineffectual patron of the Little Entente of Rumania, Yugoslavia, and Czechoslovakia after World War I formed to thwart the irredentist aspirations of a dismembered Hungary and to block the expansionist aims of Bulgaria, the great loser in all Balkan conflicts. Thus France was a natural choice for the Communist government when it began to reestablish contacts with the West as an important part of its endeavors to emancipate Rumania from Soviet domination.

In Yugoslavia, which had unsolved territorial disputes with each of its neighbors, the memory of the brief French occupation of Dalmatia and the adjacent Croat and Slovene territories, which in 1809 were merged into one unit called the "Illyrian Provinces," played a considerable role in the emergence of the Yugoslav state. Quite apart from some lasting administrative and material improvements, the French occupation was the first experiment in uniting Croats, Serbs, and Slovenes in a common community.

Although one still meets wizened peasants in the far-flung corners of Rumania who cherish memories of the long-dead Austrian empire, which with the passage of time has come to seem almost a Golden Age of calm and prosperity, the influence of rump Austria and rump Hungary, in terms of power or spiritual impact, has been marginal in the Balkans since 1918. Britain's role in the area has been consistently negative. Traditional British interests, including the protection of communication lines to the Middle East and India, resulted in Britain's unflinching support of the Ottoman Empire to combat the advance of Russia—a policy that ran counter to the national interests of the Balkan peoples in the entire period leading up to World War I.

When Prime Minister Chamberlain in 1938 publicly wondered whether Britain should go to war because of the problems of Czechoslovakia, "people of whom we know nothing," he was truly speaking for the people of Britain. Yet the situation was, if possible, even more distressing in regard to the still farther away peoples of the Balkans, a medley of races represented by spokesmen with unpronounceable names. This ignorance about both the Balkans and Soviet aims there has been responsible for the suicidal initiatives undertaken by various British governments during the past fifty years. The realities of geography and military power may have made Soviet domination over Eastern Europe unavoidable in the long run. But the easy rape of these countries was in no small degree due to deliberate Western decisions, primarily to Churchill's personal diplomacy and his infamous deal with Stalin, settling the fate of the area in a few seconds in exchange for Western, mainly British, influence in Greece.

Until the advent of the Cold War, American influence in the Balkan countries was negligible. A few schools and missionaries, including the unfortunate Miss Stone whose kidnaping and subsequent release for an exorbitant ransom in Macedonia made headlines in the press of 1901, were the means whereby some inhabitants of the Balkans learned of Western ideas and a civilized way of life. But when, after 1875, American wheat exports virtually eliminated the previous sales of the predominantly agricultural Balkan countries in Western markets, the United States dealt a crippling blow to Balkan economy. At the same time, however, hundreds of thousands of Croats and, to a lesser extent, Slovenes and Bulgarians began to emigrate to the distant land of promise. Whether they later returned and retired with their savings or became Americans, the early emigrants and their children have provided an emotional link between two widely disparate worlds.

But it was Germany that in the 1930s stepped into the power vacuum left by the Austrian empire. Nazi Germany became the best customer for the food surplus and raw materials of the Balkan states. With seemingly favorable trade pacts and large-scale investments, skillful propaganda and subtle subversion sweetened with bribes, the Third Reich exploited national rivalries and gained first an economic, then a political hold on the Balkans.

There have always been many shades and differentiations among the Balkan countries in regard to the Germans. Quite apart from the German princely dynasties (the Hohenzollern-Sigmaringen in Rumania, the Coburgs in Bulgaria), German cultural influence and administrative efficiency always attracted large segments of the Bulgarian and Rumanian ruling classes. Bulgaria in 1941 made the same choice it made in 1915. It sided with Germany to regain the "lost territories" in Yugoslav Macedonia and on the Aegean. Virulent anti-semitism and hotly disputed territorial issues with Russia and Hungary provided the Nazis with an easy access to Rumania. As for Yugoslavia, regardless of their subsequent alienation, it is a historical fact, which no Communist juggling with Partisan offensives can erase, that most of the Croats and quite a few Slovenes in the spring of 1941 greeted the German troops as liberators from the Great Serbian yoke. Actually, even the Nazi conquerors were soon entangled in the maze of rival national claims and were subsequently split into pro-Croat and pro-Serb, pro-Bulgarian and pro-Hungarian factions. An astute former Nazi diplomat and Hitler's principal trouble-shooter in the Balkans, H. Neubacher, regards the attack on Yugoslavia and even more the dismemberment of the state as the most fatal mistake committed by Nazi Germany. The carving-up of Yugoslavia, the satisfaction of the Bulgarian, Hungarian, and Italian nationalist claims, including the cession of Dalmatia to Italy, "squandered the capital of good-will in Croatia and Slovenia" and left everybody dissatisfied, while the Ustasha massacres of the Serbs in enlarged Croatia and the ruthless killing of hostages as a retaliatory measure by the Germans provided for a steady stream of recruits to the Partisans of Marshal Tito.[12]

The Balkan states are the products of the accidents of Great Power diplomacy. None has ever known a period free from outside pressure sufficiently long to devote its main energy to catching up

with the modern world or to developing strong democratic traditions. All were born on the ruins of multinational empires; all are
permeated with the spirit of violent nationalism in various forms;
and all have been subjected to long or short bouts of intervention in
their domestic affairs.

The two Balkan Wars, and later the two World Wars, destroyed
much of the progress in economic and social development. The
Turkish rule left an almost insuperable backwardness in the villages.
By 1913 the length of railroad tracks per 1,000 inhabitants or per
unit of surface was roughly three times smaller in the Balkans than
in the West.[13] Despite great efforts, even as late as 1920, illiteracy
stood at 54 per cent of the population in Bulgaria and 50 per cent
in Yugoslavia, where though Slovenia had a mere 8.8 per cent,
Serbia had 65 per cent and regions of Macedonia and Bosnia 80 per
cent. A Rumanian census taken in 1930, reported nearly 40 per cent
illiterate.

Until recently all the countries were almost wholly dependent
on agriculture, and virtually everything hinged on the year's harvest.
Industrialization and the development of capitalism was fastest in
the regions belonging to the Austro-Hungarian monarchy and the
Old Kingdom of Rumania, but considerably slower in Serbia and Bulgaria. In the first two decades of the twentieth century vast areas of
Southern Bulgaria, Bosnia-Herzegovina, Montenegro, Macedonia,
and Albania were just emerging from the Middle Ages. The small
states, which immediately started to build up bureaucracies and
armies, were soon faced with the problem of enormous foreign debts.
Foreign investments were also decisive in industry and banking.
About 83 per cent of the total capital invested in the Rumanian industry, worth 127 million dollars in 1915, was of foreign origin.[14]

The emergence of immensely enlarged states after World War I
confronted the rulers in Yugoslavia and Rumania with the tremendous problem of attempting to fuse vast regions at different stages
of historical development into viable modern nations. No coordinated transportation linked the few developed centers and industrialized regions to the distant backward provinces. Strong
protectionist policies and nationalistic ideas of economic self-sufficiency depressed the levels even in the more developed areas, which
had been geared to the large market of the monarchy and relied
for credits on Vienna and Budapest banks.

The Great Depression hit the weak, lopsided economic structures of the new nations with a vengeance. Though industrial production rose in the interwar period, on the threshold of World War II, 80 per cent of the working population in Rumania and Bulgaria and 76 per cent in Yugoslavia were still engaged in agriculture, while industry only accounted for 8 to 10 per cent of the labor force. An accurate index of the retarded development was the fact that barely 2 per cent of Balkan exports consisted of manufactures.[15] National income per capita ranged from 100 to 130 dollars annually. A Rumanian economist estimated just before the war that, on a given unit of land in the Balkans, four times as many people produced three times less wheat than in Denmark. As a result of backward farming methods and a rapidly growing population, large-scale, if disguised, rural unemployment became the key social problem.

Thus nothing would be less fair than to paint an idyllic picture of prewar conditions simply because the Communist regimes have failed to solve some of the basic problems and even created new ones. The same can be said of the political systems and the ruling classes. Faced with a terrifying legacy of backwardness, prewar economic policies were consistently wrong and external politics both short-sighted and nationalistic, building up insurmountable barriers to mutually advantageous cooperation.

The new states were created under the promising banner of national self-determination, democracy, and agrarian reform. These dreams, however, were cruelly disappointed under the twin impact of misrule by inefficient and irresponsible ruling classes and such external factors as the economic crisis and the rise of Italian Fascism and German Nazism. Though the Balkan countries were predominantly peasant countries and most of the ruling elite the sons of peasants, they were never in any sense true peasant democracies before the Communist takeover.

Bernard Shaw's comedy *Arms and the Man* takes place in Bulgaria at the time of the brief war with Serbia in 1885. When a Swiss officer asks for the hand of her daughter, the mother loftily declares: "I doubt, sir, whether you quite realize either my daughter's position or that of Major Sergius Saranoff, whose place you propose to take. The Petkoffs and Saranoffs are known as the richest and most important families in the country. Our position is almost historical: we can go back for nearly twenty years."[16]

This, indeed, was the position in the Balkan countries, which were subjected to the arbitrary rule of upstarts. But as Lewis Namier once put it, "All Government is based on some form of oligarchy, and the moral and intellectual level of the men who compose it and the view they take of Government and their responsibility toward the governed matter far more than their social origins."[17] This diagnosis also holds for most of the Communists who have been running the affairs of the Balkan countries since World War II.

A deep antagonism between the village and the city, which was inhabited mainly by bureaucrats, intellectuals, and the military, all of whom feel immensely superior to the class from which they came, has dominated Balkan politics. Molded by the age-old traditions of struggle against alien occupation and of hiding the harvest from invading armies, the semieducated or illiterate Balkan peasants have remained distrustful of government in general. The suspicion against the city as such frustrated the scattered and disorganized prewar attempts to teach them modern farming methods. Similarly, the small holders' obstinate clinging to their scraps of land has bedeviled Communist attempts at total collectivization.

Bitter social hatred and deep national divisions were accentuated by a false educational system, which preached nationalism as a state religion and produced a steadily growing surplus of graduates in the professions rather than badly needed industrial experts, farm engineers, and technicians. Concentrated in the few urban centers, faced with meager prospects of jobs in the civil service, industry, or the army, seething with discontent, the intelligentsia tended to split into extreme nationalist, later Fascist, or extreme left groupings.

Elections were usually farcical, or, if not, the electoral law was conveniently changed to give the party in power a comfortable majority of seats regardless of the popular vote. The Balkan bourgeoisie consisted of the higher and middle echelons of the government bureaucracy, army officers, and a sort of urban upper middle class of well-to-do merchants, industrialists, business and professional people. These accounted for an estimated 5 to 10 per cent of the population in Yugoslavia and Bulgaria.[18] Rumania was ruled by what was undoubtedly the most corrupt and most cynical ruling class in the Balkans, retaining the main features of a social system originally shaped by Greek Phanariot rule.

The peasant parties, once the bright hope of the future, succumbed to corruption in Serbia and Rumania, exhausted their energies in a purely political and increasingly nationalistic struggle for national interests in Croatia, and were crushed by terror in Bulgaria. The lack of a strong working class and, in Yugoslavia, the division along national lines excluded the possibility of the Social Democrats playing a major political role. And the Communist parties, after spectacular early electoral successes, assassinations, and bomb outrages, were banned from public life in Yugoslavia and Bulgaria. Even so, these two parties had some roots and influence, particularly among the intellectuals. The Communists in Rumania, on the other hand, thanks to the suicidal slogans advocating secession of separate nationalities issued by the Comintern in Moscow, never had a chance up to the end of World War II.*

In the late twenties and early thirties, the Balkan countries came one after the other under the dictatorial rule of hereditary monarchs. In Albania, which though nominally independent since 1912 received its final frontiers only in 1926, a young Muslim chieftain from the mountains, Zogu, seized power as President of the Republic and in 1928 had himself crowned as King Zog I. King Alexander of Yugoslavia suspended the constitution and imposed a royal dictatorship in 1929 (he was assassinated in 1934 and succeeded by Prince Paul as Regent), as did King Boris in Bulgaria in 1935, and later King Carol in Rumania. Despite the excesses of the Iron Guards in Rumania and the Macedonian terrorists in Bulgaria, these were conventional autocracies and not Fascist regimes; the monarchs represented the interests of a small military and administrative caste and relied, if necessary, on the police as the chief implement of terror. The arbitrary role of both the various semiparliamentary regimes and the royal dictatorships was made more bearable by the curious Balkan mixture of inefficiency and corruption that even in our time helps individuals cope with the Communist administrations in their daily life.

In view of the historical, political, and economic liabilities, it is perhaps small wonder that everywhere in the Balkans the experiment in democracy ended in dismal failure. The breathing spell to create a healthier, more resilient body politic was desperately short, and by the late thirties the Balkan states, one after another, gradually became client states of an expanding Nazi Germany. By the summer of 1941 the Axis powers had brutally and quickly dissolved the independent states of Yugoslavia and Albania and reduced the others to the position of vassals, mere cogs in their war machine.

* The history of the Communist parties and some vital features of the interwar period will be dealt with in later chapters.

Barely three years later, as so often in the past, the wartime strategy and diplomacy of the Great Powers determined the fate of these states above the heads of the people concerned. Actually, the Communist Partisans had won their political battle for power by the end of 1943 in Yugoslavia and by mid-1944 in Albania. But Soviet communism, like the Turkish empire and the Austrian monarchy before it, has failed to change significantly, let alone to erase, the enduring national patterns, historic facts, ethnic and cultural diversity of the Balkans. It is the irresistible reassertion of distinctive national traditions and interests that marks the differences and similarities in the development and outlook of each of the four Communist-ruled Balkan countries.

III

YUGOSLAVIA
Stormy Voyage into Uncharted Seas

Today nationalism is at least question number two. If we
don't win the battle for The Reform, then it might become
question number one.

—*Vladimir Bakaric*
(March 1966)

"Aren't you really afraid? Where will all this end? What will remain
of socialism?" asked the Polish guest and nervously lit another cigarette. His attractive hostess Miss Savka Dapcevic-Kucar smiled.
"It is not so tragic after all," she said, and proceeded to explain the
great economic and political reforms that have thrown Yugoslavia
into what seems to so many Communists of other nations an unbelievable chaos. In the silence that followed, a good deal of her
guest's doubt and suspicion, or rather plain ignorance, must have
remained. "Everything we do appears to most of the comrades from
the socialist countries as a sheer puzzle," the red-haired professor
of economics, now the first woman Premier in Europe, told me
when we met in early 1967 after her encounter with the Pole.

His amazement was the natural product of the self-imposed isolation of many foreign Communists from the turbulent developments of the last fifteen years or so in Yugoslavia. The able Yugoslav
trade union leader, Dusan Bilandzic, had an even more humorous
meeting with some distinguished French Communists. Visiting union
headquarters in Belgrade just before the latest batch of drastic decentralization measures were launched in July 1965, the guests,
obviously still under the impact of the Stalinist propaganda about
Yugoslavia's "sell out" to the "imperialists," were pleasantly surprised to hear that the federal state still controlled about a half of
the nation's investment resources. When their host told them, however, that he himself was not at all happy but, on the contrary, very
upset about this degree of centralization and deeply worried about

the slow dismantling of the concentration of power, the French became visibly disconcerted. "They must have left more confused than when they arrived," Bilandzic said, smiling.

These two episodes are characteristic of the bewilderment of the orthodox Leninist Communists (or those who pretend to be such) when they are confronted with numerous sets of strange Yugoslav institutions, which are constantly and sometimes tumultuously in flux. All this is utterly remote from anything in the Holy Script of Lenin, let alone in Marx. In fact, there are great built-in contradictions in the Yugoslav experiments, which fascinate and appall observers of every school. If one adds to the internal ferment the well-known fact that Yugoslav foreign policy, too, constantly moves forward, backward, and upside down, it is no wonder that this maverick of the Communist world has bewildered the men in the Kremlin as much as the policy-makers in the West.

Yugoslavia seems to be all things to all men. The Chinese regard it as a "thoroughly rotten capitalist outpost of American imperialism" and a living example of the future of a degenerated Soviet Union ruled by a "treacherous revisionist clique." The Russians and their allies welcome Belgrade's consistently pro-Soviet stance on major international issues, but are secretly worried about the possible snowballing effects of Yugoslavia's political and economic reforms, as Brezhnev's lightning visit in the autumn of 1966 to get an on-the-spot impression of the repercussions of Rankovic's fall and of the projected revamping of the party vividly illustrates. Finally, quite a few influential American congressmen cannot forgive Yugoslavia for not "going capitalist"; worse still, they consider that it has returned, fully repentant, to the Soviet camp. Therefore the enforcement of a ban on the sale of surplus farm products, or even on dollar credits to Yugoslavia amounts in their eyes to a hard blow at "world Communism."

There are plenty of arguments to support such assumptions. What self-respecting Communist country would admit the unpalatable truth of widespread unemployment—which is by definition impossible under a socialist system—or allow 300,000 of its experts and workers to seek employment abroad and even organize their temporary migration? With public ownership of the means of production, banks, commerce, etc., workers should not strike against themselves; but this allegedly socialist country reports some two hundred work stoppages per annum and debates them hotly

THE SIX CONSTITUENT REPUBLICS
OF YUGOSLAVIA AND THE TWO
AUTONOMOUS PROVINCES
(Vojvodina and Kosovo-Metohija)
BELONGING TO SERBIA

in public. Can a Communist government ever find itself outvoted in parliament and even resign if it fails to get a vote of confidence? In a Communist state, can peasants not only own their land but privately import and operate tractors; can individuals run trucking businesses, restaurants, and motels? Can a Communist country ever contemplate allowing foreign investments of risk capital and setting up partnership projects? Can a ruling Communist party admit that it has turned into a brake on social development instead of remaining the infallible vanguard and motor of advance toward full communism? Whatever the answers, all this has already happened or is happening in Yugoslavia.

Before hurrying to agree with the Chinese assessment, one should, however, glance at the debit—to the Communists, of course, credit —side of the accounts. Yugoslavia is still, and is likely to remain for quite some time, a single-party system. The ministers and the bankers, the administrators and the deputies in parliament, the leadership of the unions and the other organizations are predominantly Communist. For all the open controversies on many public issues, there is no open contest between different political forces with free debate on major issues. The clashes among group interests are not allowed to go beyond the limits set by the Communist leaders. Thus criticism and debate cannot be tolerated once it becomes "anti-socialist," that is, advocates, for instance, the setting-up of an opposition group that also subscribes in broad terms to socialism but with significant differences in approach or methods. The key question as to just what is "constructive" or "destructive" criticism is still decided by a consensus among the leaders. The fate of Milovan Djilas, Mihajlo Mihajlov, and a host of lesser-known cases involving the censoring or suppression of various periodicals, is highly instructive. There may be several candidates on the ballot, but nominations are tightly controlled by open or disguised commissions of the ruling party. Major foreign policy decisions are not discussed publicly, let alone questioned, once a decision has been made. In short, Yugoslavia appears to be after all a fully fledged Communist dictatorship.

Whose reasoning, then, is correct? The arguments of the ferociously revolutionary Chinese leaders or those of the deeply disappointed American congressmen? The paradox is that both are, in some respects, right; yet at the same time both assumptions can be challenged. The controversial issue of the future direction of the system is indeed at the heart of the great debate that has been going on around and within Yugoslavia. Aside from conventional labels and ideological phraseology, the seeming chaos is in fact the very real evolving attempt of the largest Balkan country to relate outward and to adapt its own brand of communism to the modern world.

Despite their outward diversity, all Communist regimes are still based on "four fundamental deceptions achieved by four arbitrary acts of redefinition."[1] A tightly knit general staff, the supreme leaders, is equated with the party machine (Central Committee, Politburo, Presidium, Secretariat, etc.). This, in turn, runs the party, which purports to rule on behalf of the proletariat, which is equated with the people at large. This system of one party and one leadership based on one doctrinal truth that can be interpreted at any given moment and in every conceivable situation only by the general staff of dedicated high priests, fits almost perfectly what may be called an essentially Stalinist economic model: total centralized planning with enterprises and factories geared to clear targets, obligatorily prescribed by one administrative center and its branches.

In Yugoslavia, however, for reasons that will be spelled out below, there has always been a crucial, albeit often hidden, contradiction between the single-party political dictatorship and the economic and administrative system created by this dictatorship. The more economic and administrative decentralization a regime allows, the more necessary it will become to assure political centralization in order to halt the erosion of the party's power to control the economy. The tightening of the reins to counter the trends toward disorganization and anarchy, however, nips in the bud any meaningful attempt at economic and social pluralism. Every major innovation involves major political risks, ultimately posing a threat to the very principles upon which a bureaucratic Communist dictatorship is built. The truth of this has time and again become apparent, even in the timid experiments of two steps forward, one step back launched by Khrushchev, his successors, and their East European friends.

The point, however, is that in Yugoslavia the devices of workers' councils and communes, the prime movers of self-management and decentralization, are not mere window dressing but in name and to a growing extent in fact the basis of the system. But, to paraphrase

Lenin's words, they are reproducing "hourly, daily, and on a mass scale" forces that sap the very foundations of the political dictatorship. Herein lies the crucial difference between Yugoslavia and the other Communist-ruled countries. In the other countries the "chaos" lurking behind any serious attempt to transfuse the economy and politics with new blood is recognized, and for the time being and with great difficulty the lid is held down. In Yugoslavia, the "chaos" is life itself, and more and more of its elements, which have, of course, always been there, are emerging.

The moment of reckoning has come more than once during the past fifteen years when the experiment in grass-roots democracy and local government began to succeed too well and to get away from its creators. The crux of the crisis is that, once having set in motion the liberalization process, the party can no longer hold it down to the slow speed originally prescribed. The dynamics of society are running well ahead of the party's capacity to diffuse the power of economic decision-making and to dispense freedom in general without sooner or later committing institutional suicide.

Caught in a very cold wind of economic obsolescence and a crisis of political nerve, Yugoslavia is faced with three major and intertwined sets of problems (not to mention a host of lesser matters of concern): those it has in common with single-party dictatorships of the Soviet model where the monopoly of power is based on international utopian Communist goals combined with the need for periodic ideological mobilization; those that many industrial societies face, such as local versus centralized government, social justice versus economic efficiency, or inflation versus stability; and finally the dilemmas that are peculiarly its own, created by the forces of history, factors of geography, and accidents of nature.

This country, the size of the state of Wyoming, with a population of 20 million, is composed of six republics, five nations, and a dozen-odd nationalities with three religions and two alphabets. Its regions are widely disparate—some already over the threshold of development, others still with one foot, at best in the last century, at worst in the Middle Ages. When such a country seeks to become a "developed socialist state" beyond its present average national income of $500 per person annually, the few constants in the development must necessarily be embedded in a shifting pattern of contradictory tactical moves quite unrelated to ideological labels and propaganda slogans but increasingly shaped and jostled by psychological tensions stemming from deep-seated national and tribal differences.

"The 41 Club"

"I was not an old fighter. Nor was I barefoot. What will happen with us?" This is the recurring line sung by a young man with a guitar every evening in Jazavac (The Hamster), a restaurant with a floor show, furnished in a deliberately old style on the main shopping street of Zagreb, the capital of Croatia. He finishes the song with grim defiance: "I was born in 1941!"

The year 1941 marks a watershed in Yugoslav history. It was the beginning of a drama that "even a librettist for Verdi would have considered complex."[2] By 1941 the Kingdom of Yugoslavia, barely two decades old, was falling apart in the desolation of shattered loyalties after having failed to solve the national question compared to which other burning domestic issues paled to insignificance. Yugoslavism, the idea of the union of South Slavs, who never before 1918 had been united into one state, had become thoroughly discredited and little more than a fig leaf for unbridled Serbian political hegemony. Aside from the treatment of the smaller nations and nationalities such as the Macedonians, Montenegrins, Albanians, etc. as second-class citizens, the central problem was whether the Croats should be suppressed or conciliated. The only serious attempt at a working solution was undertaken too late and too timidly in August 1939 under the impact of the critical international situation. The compromise, the famous Sporazum (The Agreement—its significance is still a highly controversial issue dividing Yugoslav historians) concluded between the Croat peasant leader Ivan Macek and the then Yugoslav Prime Minister Dragisa Cvetkovic was a limited solution which left the nationalist Croats dissatisfied and the ruling Serbs, or the majority of them, embittered.

Precariously poised on the edge of the abyss of self-destruction, the Yugoslav government, under growing economic and political pressure, succumbed to threats and on March 25, 1941, Cvetkovic and his foreign minister on instructions from Prince Paul, the prince regent, and the Cabinet, signed the Tripartite Pact of Germany, Italy, and Japan in the baroque Belvedere Palace in Vienna. The pact of the Axis powers forged in the preceding year had by then actually been joined by three neighbors of Yugoslavia—Hungary, Rumania, and Bulgaria. Whatever motives (military unprepared-ness, keeping Yugoslavia out of the war, or maintaining the royal dictatorship) may have inspired Prince Paul and his advisers,[3] they had reckoned without the people of Serbia.

Within forty-eight hours patriotic officers, headed by Air Force General Simovic overthrew the government and the regency and brought young King Peter to the throne.

The coup was overwhelmingly supported by public opinion in Serbia where there had been a violent reaction to what the generals and students, opposition politicians and the Orthodox Church had regarded as an act of dishonor. Thousands of demonstrators appeared spontaneously on the streets of the capital shouting im-provised slogans: Bolje rat nego pakt—Bolje grob nego rob! (Better war than the pact—Better death than slavery!). The lightning coup evoked a reverberating echo around the world. It was greeted with a particular ovation in Britain, then facing practically alone a tre-mendously powerful Nazi Germany that had already overrun West-ern Europe. Yugoslavia had found its soul, Churchill proclaimed.

It was, however, only Serbia and not Yugoslavia that had found its soul,[4] Serbia, the nation that staged the first successful Balkan insurrection against the Turks in 1804 and whose coat of arms proudly states, "Only solidarity saves the Serb." Although he had not originally planned to attack Yugoslavia and was already fully occupied with the "grand design" of invading Russia, ten days after the Belgrade coup an enraged Hitler struck. In the early morning hours of April 6, a Sunday, wave after wave of German bombers blasted the unprotected capital. Large sections of Belgrade were destroyed and an estimated twenty thousand persons killed. The militarily unprepared country with poor communications and vir-tually indefensible principal cities was attacked from all sides. The massive thrusts of the German army smashed the main defenses while the Italians, Bulgarians, and Hungarians dealt parallel blows, completing the swift military defeat. Yugoslavia, eleven days after the invasion had begun, was forced to capitulate.

The discordant elements of Yugoslavia were torn asunder. Few of the non-Serbian inhabitants could feel devotion for a Serbian dictatorship, and many were only too willing to destroy it. Military collapse was inevitable. But insult was added to injury by the behavior of the Croat units, which in many cases abandoned their

coast to Italy as the price of a semblance of independence soon chilled the first flush of genuine enthusiasm. Even the compensation offered in the form of the whole of Bosnia-Herzegovina with its Serb and Muslim majorities failed to soothe ruffled tempers. With the surrender of Dalmatia, Pavelic lost his claim, if he ever had one, to being a national leader. When the Ustashe began to slaughter the Serbs, who had initially amounted to one-third of the population of the new state, they not only forced them to take to the hills to save their lives but gradually alienated large segments of the Croat population. Hitler's chief representative in the Balkans estimates that the Ustasha terrorists massacred some three-quarters of a million defenseless people, mainly Serbs but also almost twenty-five thousand Jews and other "alien elements."[6] Thus in retrospect the Ustasha regime constituted a valuable tactical support for the Axis powers, yet carried within it the seeds of strategic disaster.

The rest of Yugoslavia was also quickly partitioned among the victors. Slovenia was portioned out between Germany and Italy, Montenegro went to Italy, the heart of Vojvodina to Hungary, Macedonia to Bulgaria, while the region of Kosovo—a decision welcomed by the largely Albanian population—was allotted to the nominally independent Albania under Italian military control. Serbia itself, more distrusted and hated than ever by Hitler with his "anti-Serb complex"[7] was reduced to a rump protectorate, smaller than even the old state before the Balkan Wars. Within a span of two weeks, on paper at least, Yugoslavia ceased to exist.

But before the summer was out a national insurrection, kindled partly by news of the German attack on Soviet Russia, almost swept the Germans out of Serbia and the Italians out of Montenegro. What started as a national rising, a war of liberation against the invaders soon became insolubly linked with and superseded by a social revolution against the old order. This social war was in turn connected with the evolving civil war between the Croats and Serbs that arose from Ustasha excesses and was further complicated by periodic clashes between other national and religious groups. Thus at least three simultaneous wars were in progress.

Due to the peculiarities of geography and the shifting patterns of a fluid situation, there was also another special kind of war: the mountains against the plains, the countryside against the enemy-held towns. The ultimate triumph of the Partisans was essentially the victory of the mountaineers: people from the barren limestone regions of the Dinaric Alps, stretching for 350 miles and accounting for one-fourth of Yugoslavia's territory. The mountain peasants came down and took over the cities, and it is they who today constitute the bulk of the exclusive "41 club," the hard core of old fighters who have become the real rulers of the new Yugoslavia. It is they who are resented or derided today by the new generations and the urban classes as the main block to real progress.

How was it possible for a small band of Communists, an insignificant cog in a world-wide revolutionary organization that lacked popular support in the country, to put itself at the head of a national resistance movement, to survive great ordeals, to outflank and destroy its non-Communist rivals, who had been in the field first? How was it possible for these men finally to seize power in the name of socialism and the proletariat in a backward Balkan country with a working class that amounted to less than 2 per cent of the population and remained largely passive throughout the national liberation struggle and the civil war?

Aside from a variety of significant external factors, the key to the domestic victory of Marshal Tito and his Partisans lay in their approach to the national question. In the bloodshed of enemy occupation and tribal rivalry, the Communists were the only force that raised the banner of a united Yugoslavia. Their rallying slogan— "Brotherhood and Unity!"—urged Serbs, Croats, and Muslims to submerge their ancestral quarrels in a common struggle against the occupying powers and their domestic allies, whether Serb Chetniks or Croat Ustashe.

This should not, however, lead us to believe that the masses immediately rallied to the banner of the Yugoslav idea, as the official accounts suggest. The truth was more complicated, composed of many different elements. But the parts themselves were relatively simple or at any rate comprehensible.

Serbia, the heart and soul of the initial resistance to the occupation, had become quiet by November of 1941. As a matter of fact, until mid-1944, the Germans "enjoyed greater security in Serbia than anywhere else in the country."[8]

This sudden and drastic change was not due entirely to the fact that the Germans had rushed reinforcements into the Morava Valley and crushed the uprising. The German counterattack was greatly facilitated by the deep cleavage that developed between the Communist Partisans and the followers of Draza Mihajlovic, a general staff colonel, who had in May 1941 issued a stirring appeal for continued resistance. His followers, wearing long hair, flowing beards, and armed to the teeth, were generally called Chetniks (or armed bands) and had a long tradition of fighting for Serbian independence during the Turkish occupation. Actually, the official head organization of the Chetniks, which was thoroughly discredited during the interwar period and linked with the Germans and their Serbian puppet administration under General Nedic, was distinctly different from Mihajlovic's guerrilla forces, which nevertheless came to be referred to both in Yugoslavia and abroad as Chetniks.

While the Communists insisted on all-out action regardless of the enemy's reprisals against the civil population, this Serb royalist who "distrusted the Croats and detested the Communists" wanted to preserve his forces to strike only when the wheels of fortune turned in the world war, and then to rebuild the old rightful order, the monarchy. Though his arguments were in many respects pertinent to the situation, his passive tactics proved in the end fatal for his position. As one of the few acute observers among the British liaison officers in Yugoslavia aptly put it, "a resistance leader cannot retain leadership unless he actively resists."[9]

Two meetings between such disparate leaders as Mihajlovic, the high staff officer who looked solely to the West, and Josip Broz Tito, the dedicated professional revolutionary, failed to produce any tangible results. By the first of November Tito's Partisans and Mihajlovic's Chetniks were fighting each other instead of launching common actions against the Germans. The fateful battle at Kraljevo split the resistance movement from top to bottom. From then on the Partisans became the enemy number one for the Chetniks, and vice versa. Were it not for the countless victims, one could say that the open feud later led to operetta-like situations. The Chetniks, led by Mihajlovic, who was subsequently promoted to general and minister of war in the royal government-in-exile and to whose headquarters British liaison officers had been assigned, were fighting alone, or often together with German and Italian units, against Tito's Partisans, to whose headquarters British observers were also attached.

Under the pressure of the two-front battle against the Germans and the Chetniks, the Partisans were soon forced to evacuate their first stronghold in Serbia. The indiscriminate, brutal German reprisals against the civil population, above all the terrible massacre of five thousand inhabitants of the town of Kragujevac, including hundreds of schoolchildren, turned the popular mood in the area against the Partisans whose actions had provoked the merciless retribution. Afterward Mihajlovic's Chetniks concluded a "gentleman's agreement" with the puppet administration and its motley supporters, as well as with the Germans retaining control over the Serbian countryside. This tacit cooperation was successful, not least because the population itself, apart from a few scattered guerrilla bands, clearly opted for passivity and even collaboration rather than for all-out resistance.

With Croatia in the firm grip of the Ustashe, at any rate until 1943, and Serbia controlled by the Chetniks, the Partisans were forced to retreat into the wild mountainous regions of East Bosnia and Montenegro. It is often overlooked that the bulk of the operations, the greatest battles, took place in the barren zone of the Dinaric Alps, among the bleak hills of Montenegro and most of the time in the wildest forests of Bosnia. This had a twofold effect.

The war in the mountains was fought by mountaineers and peasants. While the Communists may justly claim to have engineered the second victorious "proletarian revolution" in history, it was a "proletarian revolution" carried out, except for the leading cadres, mainly by backward peasants. Thus it happened that mountain warriors from Montenegro, "men of the woods" from the sterile Karst zone, and peasants from the regions of Kordun, Lika, etc., in Croatia constituted the bulk of the "new class" that took control of the administration and the economy after the war. For all their merits as guerrilla fighters, the effects of their rule as chief decision-makers will long plague the country.

By going to the mountains, the Communists operated chiefly in areas either traditionally prone to the Yugoslav idea or through special circumstances slanted in that direction. Up to the end of 1942 the Partisan units consisted mainly of the Serb population of Bosnia and Croatia, which had taken to the forests. As Bosnia-Herzegovina had been assigned to the Pavelic regime, most of the decisive operations took place ironically in the very heart of the puppet Kingdom of Croatia. By 1943, however, the all-Yugoslav character of the Partisans' officer corps was reflected in the ethnic composition of the forces. The Croats of Dalmatia, the one-time cradle of the "Illyrian movement," formed no less than five divisions.

They were impelled to join the Partisans by the twin pressure of Italian occupation and the atrocities committed by the local Chetniks, who, collaborating with the occupying forces, repaid in kind the massacres of their kinsmen in Bosnia. There were also a fair number of Slovenes, Bosnian Muslims, and Croats from Croatia proper. According to one rough estimate, by the end of 1943, Croats, Slovenes, Muslims, and other non-Serb nationalities accounted for two-fifths of the Partisan forces.[10]

In short, the Partisans were the carriers of a Communist nationalism of Yugoslav character against both Great Serbian nationalism and Croat separatist nationalism, represented respectively and in excessive forms by the Chetniks and the Ustashe. It is important to remember, however, that neither the Chetniks nor the Ustashe operated in a vacuum and they reflected, however repulsively, old national aspirations. The bulk of the Serbs in Serbia and the Croats of Croatia proper were, until the very last stage in 1944 when Communist supremacy became inescapable, more or less spectators on the fringe of the great battle. Thus Yugoslav nationalism, reborn with the assistance of the midwife of Communist ideology,[11] triumphed because of special circumstances in specific territories from which the Communists later conquered the core of the country—Serbia and Croatia.

The road to power

The policing instrument that restrained the deep national cleavages and forged tribal loyalties into a Yugoslav loyalty was the Yugoslav Communist Party. Neither the grave problems besetting Yugoslav society today nor the wartime triumph and the successful revolt against Soviet domination can be truly understood without a glance at that party's turbulent history and character and at the man who, more than anyone else, created it.

From its birth in June 1919 the party's victories and failures vividly demonstrated the great paradox of the world Communist movement. The Communists failed where they should have succeeded, in the developed regions where the working class is most "conscious"; and they succeeded where they should have failed, in the most backward and mainly rural areas.[12] The new party, incorporating the bulk of the Social Democratic parties that had

operated in Serbia and the other regions now united into the Kingdom of Yugoslavia, called itself the Communist Party of Yugoslavia
after its second Vukovar congress in 1920. It joined the Moscow
Comintern and immediately lost a predominantly Serbian group
that refused to accept the famous twenty-one conditions set by the
founders.

At the first and, up to now, also the last free elections in the
history of Yugoslavia, the Communists polled 12.4 per cent of the
popular vote (the Social Democrats less than 3 per cent) and with
fifty-eight seats became the third largest party in the Constituent
Assembly. They achieved their greatest successes (36 per cent in
Montenegro and 33 per cent in Macedonia) in the least industrialized provinces with the highest percentage of illiterates. Though
these spectacular successes were facilitated by special local factors,
the trend was instructive since the party polled only 10 per cent
of the vote in Slovenia and 7 per cent in Croatia.[13]

After young Communists had made an unsuccessful bomb attack
on the Regent and murdered a leading politician, their deputies
were expelled from parliament and the party was driven underground. Within a couple of years membership, which in 1920 had
stood at sixty thousand, melted to a mere tenth of that number. Until
the fateful year of 1941 the Communists never managed to have
more than about six thousand members. For many years the party
was condemned to insignificance and almost completely destroyed
between the Comintern hammer and the national anvil.

As the national question became almost immediately the most
burning issue of the day, the Communists were confronted all along
with a crucial dilemma: Should they maintain their original position in favor of national unity based on the rights of all nations and
nationalities as formulated, somewhat vaguely, in the Vukovar
program of 1920? Or should they support the demands of the disgruntled nationalities for self-determination even up to their secession from the state? This issue split the leadership from the very
beginning. The perennial dispute, heightened, of course, by outbursts of South Slav temperament, provided a fertile soil for factional
struggles. "Two Yugoslavs—three factions" was the derisive description coined by Comintern functionaries for the state of affairs in the
minute Yugoslav party.

The struggle between right and left was decided by the Comintern leaders. Secretaries General came and went; the Politburo was

revamped time and again according to the line gaining the upper hand at a given moment in Moscow. The founder of the party, Sima Markovic, a Serbian mathematics professor was Secretary General no less than three times. Although he defended a federalist yet Yugoslav solution, he was in the end expelled from the party. The Seventh Comintern Congress in 1935 vindicated his arguments, but Markovic was nevertheless purged in 1936. His fate confirmed the old Communist rule of thumb: once a heretic, always a heretic —even if the heresy later becomes the order of the day. Fox said of Burke that he was "a wise man, but he is wise too soon." In much later times the crucial importance of timing, particularly in view of the religious character of the Communist dogma, has been borne out again and again by developments. One has only to recall the fate of Imre Nagy in Hungary or of Milovan Djilas in Yugoslavia.

The factional struggles in the Yugoslav party reflected the dissensions within the Comintern itself. Under the instructions of the Moscow center, the Yugoslav party in 1932 demanded the establishment of separate Croat, Slovenian, and Macedonian republics; in short it opted for the breakup of Yugoslavia. For more than ten years the Communists, who were then, in the words of Leon Blum, the "nationalists of a foreign power," agitated as the mortal enemies of their own country. The Fifth Comintern Congress in 1924 proclaimed the secession of nationalities the binding line for all Communist parties. It was obviously in the interest of the Soviet state to fan the fires of nationalist tensions in the Balkans and to destroy the new multinational states of Yugoslavia and Rumania, which were the key props of the French cordon sanitaire directed primarily against both the Soviet state and Communist expansion.

This decision was at the same time an essentially pro-Bulgarian stand. Macedonia was supposed to become the heart of a Communist-dominated Balkan federation. The Balkan Communist Federation, a regional branch of the Comintern, which operated from 1920 until the abortive September rising in 1923 in Sofia, was the tool to implement this blueprint. The scheme was inspired by leading Bulgarian Communists like Georgi Dimitrov and Vasil Kolarov, who had been running the Comintern agency. And it was, of course, not doctrinal but national considerations that put the Balkan Communists at loggerheads over the controversial project. It is no exaggeration to say that the history of the Yugoslav and other Balkan Communist parties contained the elements, the excitement, and the drama of a Balkan folk epic.[14]

The Communists were compelled to hobnob with the extreme nationalist Ustashe and Frankovci in Croatia, and with the terroristic VMRO (Internal Macedonian Revolutionary Organization) operating in Macedonia. The traditional Balkan flair for conspiracy and tangled commitments had its heyday in the twenties and thirties, beautifully illustrated by the amazing career of the Macedonian revolutionary, Dimitri Vlahov. Once a deputy from Macedonia in the Turkish parliament, during World War I he was the Bulgarian governor in Pristina, the capital of the occupied Kosovo region. In the early twenties he was Bulgarian consul general in Vienna. In 1924 he formed a leftist wing of the VMRO, the socalled United VMRO, and later emigrated to Moscow, only to emerge as a member of Marshal Tito's government in 1945. His son, Gustav Vlahov, educated in Vienna and Moscow, is to this day fervently devoted to the Macedonian cause. Following his father's footsteps, he also became a member of the Yugoslav government as minister of information and currently occupies the key post of president of one of the parliament's chambers.

During the turbulent twenties a young mechanic, Josip Broz, better known under his conspiratorial name of Tito, started to climb the rungs of the hierarchical ladder in the party. In many respects, he was an ideal type of the new all-round Communist leader, particularly qualified for high party service in a multinational state. Alone among his many rivals in the party, Tito represented no single national or tribal group. He had been born in 1892 in the little village of Kumrovec, the seventh of the fifteen children of a Croatian father and a Slovenian mother, both of peasant stock. Although his formal education consisted of only four years in the elementary school of his native village, which he left at the age of twelve to work as a locksmith in Zagreb, inclination, circumstances, and the upheaval of the war combined to convert the good-looking village boy into a man of the world who today speaks three—or, if one counts his early knowledge of Czech, four—foreign languages. Throughout his life, he has shown a penchant for easy living, good food, attractive women, and foreign travel.

Even before he was called up for military service in a Croat regiment of the Austro-Hungarian army, he had acquired a cosmopolitan outlook while working as a skilled mechanic in Germany,

Czechoslovakia, and Austria. Tito speaks excellent German with a strong Viennese accent, picked up while he was employed as a test driver for the Daimler motor company. Working near the Austrian capital, he spent many evenings taking dancing lessons or going to cafés and theatres. In the Austrian army, he was fencing champion and rose to the rank of sergeant major. Almost fifty-five years later, when he returned on a triumphal formal state visit to Vienna, his visible delight was occasionally tempered with a touch of melancholy. Memories of his youth cannot have failed to return as he was rapidly driven from one reception to another, dressed in the resplendent uniform of a marshal.

On Easter 1915, Tito, severely wounded, was captured on the eastern front by the Russians and spent five formative and stormy years in a disintegrating Russia that soon plunged into the turmoil of revolution and civil war. In 1920 he returned to Yugoslavia with a Russian wife and an abiding faith in communism. In the same year, while he was again working as a mechanic, he joined the party. His organizing ability soon caught the eyes of his Communist superiors, and after a host of minor assignments, he was appointed secretary of the Zagreb branch of the metalworkers' union in 1927. He now became a full-time party functionary and a professional revolutionary. His rise was meteoric. Taking a prudent centrist, middle-of-the-road position in the raging battles between right and left, Tito was given the key position of secretary of the Zagreb organization of the Communist party barely one year later. Though the party could boast of only about 250 members in the Croatian capital and less than 3,000 in the entire country, he now ranked as a middle-class professional on the payroll of the Moscow Comintern.

During the worst periods of factional struggle in the Yugoslav and the Soviet party, from 1928 to 1934, Tito had what one might with hindsight call the good fortune to be serving a five-year prison term. In jail he met a brilliant Jewish intellectual from Belgrade, Mosha Pijade, later one of his closest collaborators, who helped to fill some of the gaps in his training as a "Marxist-Leninist." More important still, he did not become involved in the factional struggles. As a young functionary of peasant-worker origin with a good activist record, exemplary behavior at his trial, and no factional stigma attached to his career, Tito upon his release was regarded as a bright hope of the party by the then Secretary-General, Milan Gorkic, a man of Ruthenian origin brought up in Bosnia, whose real name was Cizinsky, and also by the Balkan buro of the Comintern.

Almost immediately, Tito traveled (as usual, on a forged passport) to Vienna where he was coopted as a member of the Politburo, the supreme authority. By 1935 he was in Moscow as a member of the Balkan Secretariat of the Comintern, in charge of Yugoslav affairs. This was the period when the Comintern, with great fanfare, adopted the "popular front" program, or what Communists like to call the "strategic general line," which was to last for virtually the entire period until 1947. This strategic change meant corresponding alterations in tactics, including the national question. Communists were converted from one day to the next from sworn enemies of the Kingdom of Yugoslavia into staunch defenders of a multinational state and uncompromising critics of separatism, still combined, of course, with condemnation of the existing political regime.

At the Comintern congress in 1935, a Yugoslav group proposed Tito as a member of the Executive Committee of the Comintern in opposition to the officially sponsored candidacy of Secretary-General Gorkic, the Yugoslav party leader. The issue was solved by the Comintern leadership, but there were clear straws in the wind. Next year Tito was appointed organizational Secretary, in practice the number two man in the hierarchy. These were the days of the Spanish Civil War and the era of the Great Purge, which not only decimated the Soviet Communists but also practically wiped out the lodgers at the seedy Hotel Lux in Moscow, the residence of the foreign Communists.

It came as no surprise when, in July 1937, Gorkic was called back from Paris, unmasked as an "enemy" and summarily shot. Together with the elite of the other East European exiled Communists, the Yugoslav party was caught in the whirlwind of the Stalinist terror. Over a hundred Yugoslav Communists perished, including twenty former members of the Central Committee. It is reckoned that "Stalin succeeded in killing more Central Committee members than either the Yugoslav police in the interwar period or the Axis during the war."[15]

And yet, at the very height of the great purge, after Gorkic had been shot and the Yugoslav Politburo dissolved, Tito was appointed—at first provisionally—Secretary General of the Yugoslav Communist Party. The fascinating questions of just how Tito man-

aged to survive and, more, to be entrusted with the task of "rebuild-
ing" the party, whether he played any role in the Gorkic affair, and
what he was doing on his frequent trips to Moscow in 1938–39, have
always been and are bound to remain a closely guarded mystery.
In any case one can well believe his statement that his days in a
small room on the fourth floor of the Hotel Lux, in permanent fear
of arrest, were "the most difficult days" in his life.

With all his colleagues shot or under lock and key, Tito was
forced to start from scratch to create a new leadership and to
broaden the popular base of a weak party. His political acumen and
flair for the essential was evident in his reaffirmation of the all-
Yugoslav character of the party. The setting up of the Communist
parties of Croatia and Slovenia in 1937 not only broadened the
attractiveness of the party, but also foreshadowed the postwar
federal structure with each republic having its own party, which
together constitute the Yugoslav Communist Party. Yet this politically sensible form of organization contributed more than anything
else to the later developments that transformed the party from an
integrating force into a factor of division. These, however, sprang
from what may be called the "iron law" of a multinational Communist dictatorship and cannot in any way detract from Tito's merits
as a far-sighted organizer aspiring to national leadership.

The fact that the entire new high command of the party was,
with a few exceptions, mainly young, hand-picked by Tito, and
unconditionally devoted to him was extremely important in the long
run. His principal lieutenants, who in the spring of 1938 already
formed a temporary leadership, were two Serbs (Alexander Rankovic and I. Milutinovic), two Slovenes (Edward Kardelj and
Franz Leskosek), one Serb from Croatia (Rade Koncar, who was
killed in the war), and a Montenegrin (Milovan Djilas)—together
with Tito, three intellectuals and four ex-workers and union officials,
only three of whom had been to Moscow, while the others had not
even been abroad. Non-Serbs accounted for almost two-thirds of the
29 members of the Central Committee elected in October 1940, all
of whom were professional revolutionaries, mostly ex-workers and
ex-students and mainly in their late twenties and early thirties.[16]

Though the party had only 12,000 members before the uprising
in 1941, its influence was considerably greater. Perhaps no other
Communist party has ever been based to such an extent on
students. One should not forget that the prewar regime, a royal dic-

tatorship, was nothing like a modern totalitarian system. Its dictatorial rule was mitigated by inefficiency and corruption. A certain amount of criticism was allowed in the press, and the intellectuals as well as the scions of the ruling classes enjoyed some freedom. This was particularly evident at the Belgrade, and to a lesser extent Zagreb, universities, the strongholds of the young Communists. At the elections to the student bodies in the early twenties and again in 1940, the Communists were the strongest group. They included the sons of rich merchants and high civil servants, the sons of low-rank officers, and peasants like the Montenegrins Djilas and S. Vukmanovic-Tempo. "Few Communist parties can boast of having organized street riots in which a participant arrived in a chauffeur-driven Cadillac. Nor did many Belgrade students of bourgeois origin possess a self-contained apartment as did the secretary of SKOJ (the Young Communist League), Lola Ribar." When the children of the bourgeois landed in prison they were soon released on the pleas of their influential fathers. Once several highly respected citizens of Belgrade called on the Yugoslav Prime Minister to release Koca Popovic, a millionaire's poet son so that "he would not have to spend Christmas in jail"; Popovic later became Partisan general, Foreign Minister, and Vice President of Yugoslavia.

In the autumn of 1940 the organization of young Communists could already boast about 18,000 members. These students, particularly the 200 veterans of the Spanish Civil War who had returned to their country, proved of great value as vital cadres for the Partisan army, providing many outstanding commanders and the bulk of the proletarian brigades—two elite divisions.

Despite claims put forward later, the Yugoslav party, like all other Communist groups, dutifully followed the Comintern line from the time of the Hitler-Stalin pact until the German invasion of Russia. Even after the coup in March 1941, in which the party took no part, and the German conquest of Yugoslavia, the Communist attitude was at best obscure (the official version describes those two and a half months as "the phase of final preparations"). Even such an unquestionably well-disposed biographer of Tito as the British brigadier, Fitzroy Maclean, reluctantly came to the conclusion that "for the first two months and more after the German invasion there is no convincing evidence of any organized Communist resistance movement."[17]

The German attack on Russia overnight changed the "second

imperialist war" to the "great fatherland war." The Yugoslav Communists may well have felt chagrin, bitterness, and restlessness under the months of enforced passivity, but it is a historical fact that they appeared as an organized resistance force in the field only after the German-Soviet war had broken out. Under the code name Grandfather, the Comintern instructed Tito to launch an all-out campaign of resistance in the enemy's rear, urging him, however, to "remember that at this stage what you are concerned with is liberation from Fascist oppression and not socialist revolution." Regardless of the instructions, which were dutifully repeated in an order of the day to the first Partisan units, Tito said then to his biographer, Vladimir Dedijer, that the time "had come for the party to seize power and to seize it in such a way that the bourgeoisie would never regain it."

Many events during the Yugoslav epic of 1941–44 remain obscure. There were never clear-cut fronts during the few great battles and the myriad of small engagements against Germans and Italians, Ustashe and Chetniks, and at times even against the combined forces of the four main enemies. The occupiers and their allies never governed the country as a whole. At the same time, liberated territories were lost and recaptured several times. The Yugoslav leaders claimed 80,000 Partisans at the end of 1941, some 150,000 in mid-1942, and almost 350,000 by the end of 1943. When in March 1945 the People's Liberation Army was changed into a regular Yugoslav army it numbered 800,000 men. One might add that twenty-five years later the Veteran's League, despite the fact that a number of its members must have died, had no less than 1.4 million "Partisans" registered in its files![18] The question as to just who had actually fought and who jumped on the bandwagon after the fighting was over, or at best once gave some food to the fighters, or who is authorized to be a holder of the 1941 Partisan Medal, is still a controversial issue. Today it is a question of tangible rewards, greater or smaller privileges from pensions to housing, and thus a matter of considerable political importance.

The decisive fact, however, was that the Communists had been running the show all along and controlling the Partisan units. Of the 12,000 prewar cardholders, only some 3,000 survived the ordeals of the fighting. Yet in June 1945 the party already had 141,000 members. This was an almost completely new hard core of activists who had been admitted to the party during the years of the social revolution and liberation war. Though Communist statistics about social composition are notoriously unreliable, because they either deliberately operate with "origin" instead of "occupation" or include in the category of "workers" both landless peasants and salaried employees, even in 1948 the peasants accounted for almost half of a membership three times larger than in 1945. There is no doubt that peasants made up the bulk of the fighters and the party activists.

But, in accord with the prewar character of the party, the real decision-makers, the general staff, during and immediately after the war was dominated by the middle class, either students or intellectuals of bourgeois origin, or "self-tutored professionals" of peasant or worker stock, who "used the party to climb into the ranks of the middle class." Thus in 1948 almost 52 per cent of the members of the all-Yugoslav and republican Central Committees belonged in the middle class category.[19]

If one considers how the tangled national factors, splits and rivalries among the occupiers and their allies, and the influences of Allied diplomacy and wartime strategy acted and reacted upon one another in a whirlpool of change during the war years, it is not so surprising that a dedicated minority of Communists, guided by Lenin's conspiratorial elite theory, accustomed to clandestine work, and with a clear-cut program was able to become the spearhead of the national resistance movement and to seize power in the name of a practically non-existent or passive proletariat. The Yugoslav road to power fully confirms what Bertram D. Wolfe wrote about Leninism: "All that was needed was a power vacuum; a supply of arms (the Second World War took care of that); a supply of malcontents (and where are there no malcontents?); an apparat to seize power; some fragments of Lenin's doctrine; and Stalin's example."[20]

The small group of 12,000 Yugoslav Communists grew to 141,000 in 1945 and reached about 470,000 in 1948, the year of the open conflict with Stalin. But the old-timers by then amounted to less than a fraction of 1 per cent. The party was formed and led, more than any other Communist party in the world, by a single man—Josip Broz Tito. Its young high command was devoted first to him and only through him to Stalin, the Comintern, and the Russian "mother party." The Great Purge of the thirties became a boomerang, which later turned against its creators. No other high-ranking and respected Comintern agents were left either within the Partisan ranks or in the country at large to contest the leader of this indigenous revolution or to halt the development of a cult of Tito. The fact that almost none of his followers had known any other leader was the basis of the amazing solidarity and cohesion of Tito's leading team. This in turn was a key factor, which Stalin to his own peril chose to ignore.

From Stalin to General Motors

If a traveler chooses to spend the end of April and the beginning of May in the Balkans and happens to cross from Bulgaria into Yugoslavia, he is invariably struck by an amazing contrast. In Sofia, or in the smaller towns and villages near the Yugoslav border, he sees red banners everywhere, slogans hailing the Soviet Union and Bulgaria marching shoulder to shoulder proudly toward communism. On the 1st of May he is confronted with columns of people bearing the traditional flags and pictures.

There is quite a difference in the Yugoslav towns, particularly in the capital. To be sure, May Day is a public holiday, yet there is hardly any red or decoration of any color. At the most one sees here and there a solitary weather-beaten picture of the Holy Trinity of Communism displayed on the façades of party or union headquarters. When one reaches Belgrade, the picture changes even more dramatically. Instead of the apostles of revolution, with or without beards, the main boulevards are lined with huge billboards displaying such symbols of capitalism as General Motors and Ford, sprinkled with advertisements for Mercedes and Citroen and other leading motor companies. For the past few years, May Day has coincided with the Belgrade motor show and the "masses" march to the fairground to admire and in some cases even to buy cars, rather than to imitate their fellow Communists in neighboring countries.

It is difficult to believe that only fifteen years ago this same country was ruled by the most orthodox, the most intolerant Stalinist regime in Eastern Europe. Today those days seem distant, if not totally irrelevant. Yet the past is still alive in an outwardly different present. The early phase of Yugoslav communism is worth summarizing at some length because it both shows how far the process of liberalization has gone and helps to give an insight into the underlying strength of the opposition to concrete reform and the roots of the great struggle still going on in the country.

The significance of the Yugoslav revolt against Russian domination of world communism was truly historic. It shattered the thirty-year-old dogma, which not even Trotsky dared to challenge, that communism implies unconditional support of the Soviet Union; that the interests of the two are inseparable. When on April 12, 1948, the members of the Central Committee convened for the possibly most crucial meeting in Yugoslav party history, Tito explained the crux of the dispute in plain language: "This is not a matter here of any theoretical discussion. . . . Comrades, the point here, first and foremost, is the relations between one state and another." In short, the issue was not ideology but independence. The central position was then spelled out unambiguously in the Yugoslav answer to Soviet accusations: "No matter how much each of us loves the land of socialism, the USSR, he can, in no case, love his own country less."[21] As pointed out earlier, the very fact that Yugoslavia demonstrated to other Communist-ruled countries that one can be a good Communist and for all the vicissitudes remain a Communist without taking orders from Moscow contributed more than anything else after the death of Stalin to the disruption of the former bloc unity.

Much of the confusion still obscuring a sober view of current and past developments in Yugoslavia is due to a wrong assessment of the character of the Tito-Stalin conflict, and of the political, ideological, and, last but not least, emotional factors that have left an imprint on later developments. The great duel between David and Goliath was not the revolt of a Yugoslav nationalist against alien hegemony. Nor was Tito an early fighter against Stalinist bureaucracy. The battle was fought between two totalitarian parties in terms of Communist power politics of the twentieth century, not the nationalism of the nineteenth century.[22] In other words, it was a conflict between two different concepts by Communist leaders subscribing to the same strategic aims but divided by differences as to timing and tactics.

Soviet hegemony and infallible authority were actually shattered among the wooded hills of South Serbia and the wild forests of Bosnia in the winter of 1941–42 when Tito and his Partisans defied Moscow's clear instructions to cooperate with Mihajlovic's Chetniks, and thus launched a policy that ultimately enabled them to seize power without Soviet assistance and in a fashion that conflicted with Stalin's strategy. That the Partisans became involved in fierce fighting with their non-Communist rivals was not an act of conscious defiance of Moscow, let alone a nationalist revolt against the Comintern. On the contrary, the Yugoslav Partisans were fanatically devoted to Stalin and Russia. They formed their elite division, a special proletarian brigade consisting solely of Communists, on Stalin's birthday in December 1941, they wrote slogans such as "Long Live Stalin!" on the walls in captured towns and showed their enthusiasm for "Mother Russia," the "Fatherland of the Proletariat" in every possible way.

What, then, happened? The fact is the chain of command between the Comintern and its agents broke down in the first decisive months after the German invasion of Russia. Nothing had been further from the ideas of Josip Broz, the trusted Comintern official, and his close associates than to work against Soviet policies. In a crisis situation, however, lacking any instructions from his superiors, Tito was left on his own and followed his instincts and political preferences, that is, those of a dynamic leftist, an extremist, or, in Communist parlance, a "left-sectarian" functionary. It is the great merit of the late Franz Borkenau to have been the first Western analyst to show the real roots and postwar international implications of Tito's leftist tendencies.

Never fond of a waiting game, Tito, first unwittingly, later consciously, pitted his party against the cautious and temporizing Soviet general line, which wanted to avoid offending the democratic "prejudices" of the British and American allies whose support was so vital to a Soviet Russia engaged in a life and death struggle against the Nazi invader. When Tito attacked Mihajlovic, when his Partisans not only liberated some towns in Serbia during the 1941 rising, but proceeded to destroy the old administrative structure and erect an undisguised Communist dictatorship he was, without being aware of it, already in the process of breaking completely with the line of cautious respectability and cooperation with "all patriotic forces" advocated by Moscow.

Ironically, it is a thin twenty-four-page Yugoslav leaflet written by the late theoretician Mosha Pijade at the height of the conflict with Stalin that shows with utmost clarity that the Yugoslav Communist leaders, and first of all Tito himself, had been extremists all along. They wanted a short-cut to a full-fledged Communist regime, to destroy the old system and to annihilate domestic rivals or enemies regardless of broader Soviet interests. In March 1942, as soon as radio contact had been reestablished with the Comintern, Grandfather (the code name for Moscow) doubted that the Yugoslav Communists were really doing everything to organize a genuine national united front. The broadcast warned that the defeat of the invaders was the main task. "Take into account that the Soviet Union has treaty relations with the Yugoslav king and government, and that taking an open stand against them would create new difficulties in the joint war efforts and the relations between the Soviet Union on the one hand and Britain and America on the other. Do not consider your fight only from your own national point of view, but also from the international standpoint of the British-American-Soviet coalition. . . . Show more elasticity and ability to maneuver."[23] Clearly, Stalin had not wanted to have complications in the crucial joint war efforts because of some guerrilla bands in the backwoods of the Balkans.

Though Tito assured Grandfather that he had drawn the wrong conclusions from his reports and that the situation was in fact quite different, the basic conflict between local Yugoslav considerations and over-all Soviet objectives was a recurring cause of friction throughout the war. No wonder Stalin was "stamping with rage" when the Partisans upset his carefully calculated maneuvers, which, of course, in the long run also aimed at the establishment of Communist and Soviet domination over the Balkans. When Stalin was still contemplating sending a military mission and supplies to Mihajlovic, whom the British were preparing at that very moment to drop in favor of the Partisans, Tito decided to convoke a session of the Anti-Fascist Council for the National Liberation of Yugoslavia (AVNOJ). The session took place on November 29, 1943, in the little Bosnian town of Jajce. The Council was transformed into a provisional legislature, and its executive into a provisional government headed by Tito, who received the title of Marshal. Moscow, however, was informed only forty-eight hours before the fact. The cable also omitted to mention the trifling matter that the meeting would declare the royal government-in-exile illegal and forbid King Peter to return to Yugoslavia. On the eve of the crucial Teheran Conference of the three great powers, this was regarded by an "unusually angry" Stalin as a "stab in the back for the Soviet Union."[24]

The strategy and tactics of the Partisans were undoubtedly correct from their point of view. The Balkans being a minor theater of operations, Tito could not really influence the decisive battles of World War II. What he could do was to decide who would rule Yugoslavia after the war—the Communists, the Monarchists, or some kind of popular front dominated behind the scenes by the Communist party. Both politically and militarily he followed a sensible policy in choosing his domestic enemies as the main target for his actions. By the end of 1943 the Communists had succeeded in compromising and practically destroying any organized force or center of authority that could have blocked their takeover. The special position of Yugoslavia became evident in October 1944 when the Red Army "requested" permission to enter the country for a limited period for operations against the German forces in Hungary. Though Belgrade was jointly taken, the Partisans were at no point under Soviet command, and the Russians were expressly forbidden under the Tito-Stalin deal of September 1944, which was made on the occasion of their first meeting in Moscow, to exercise any administrative power on Yugoslav territory. By March 1945 the Russian troops were evacuated. Yugoslavia thus became the sole East European country (with the exception of Albania) that was never fully or for any considerable length of time occupied by Soviet troops.

Improbable as it sounds today, the Yugoslav party stood on the left of the international Communist movement throughout the whole postwar period as late as 1949. True, the conflict with Stalin assumed historical significance regardless of its original motives. But one must always remember the sparks that ignited the accumulated differences to the point of explosion. Emotional motives, like the chagrin and disillusionment over the lack of Soviet aid, or the discovery that at the very moment of joint Soviet-Yugoslav operations around Belgrade Stalin and Churchill were neatly arranging to go halves in their interests in Yugoslavia, undoubtedly influenced the attitude of the Yugoslav leaders toward Stalin. Similarly, the postwar examples of Russian duplicity in regard to the rearming of the Yugoslav army or to exploitation in the form of the notorious joint companies hastened the break.

The point of the matter was that the Yugoslavs were, in every major domain, far ahead of the policies of the Soviet Union and its satellites. Consider some of the evidence. While the weak Communist parties in Hungary and Rumania, Bulgaria and Poland were bidding desperately for the support of non-Communist groups, in the very first phase even for that of the Conservatives, and while Moscow was operating with the term "people's democracy," Yugoslavia became, in the summer of 1945, the first and then the only open Communist totalitarian dictatorship. Tito and his lieutenants did not have the patience to respect even the façade and to play the comedy of Communist and non-Communist "cooperation." After the Yalta declaration, as a price for formal recognition by the Allies, some representatives of the former government-in-exile were included in the new government. Within a few months, however, the non-Communist politicians were forced to resign, the press was muzzled, a single-list totalitarian election staged, the monarchy abolished, and every remnant of an opposition destroyed.

Once again it was not a question of principle but of timing and tactics that split Tito and Stalin and divided Yugoslavia from the rest of the Soviet power sphere. The leftist Yugoslavs put their own interests ahead of those of international communism. Worse still, they regarded other Communist parties, as having "deviated" from true Leninism. As late as July 1949, Edward Kardelj, one of Tito's leading and closest collaborators, proudly and derisively told the Yugoslav parliament: "Yugoslavia stood far ahead of the others. And we, who contended that we had won our socialist revolution, that our people's democracy was of the Soviet type, were told that we were narrow-minded sectarians and entirely incapable of inventing something new."[25]

What did "narrow-minded sectarianism" mean? It meant that the Yugoslav hotheads compromised if not completely unmasked the Soviet and Eastern European line of early coalitions, of stressing the distinctive national patterns of development, of even in some cases (Hungary) staging free elections. For the population at large it brought wide-scale terror, swifter in pace and worse in its scope than in any other East European country. The Yugoslavs were the first to nationalize practically the entire economy except for a handful of tailors and watchmakers. They were the first to launch a campaign of vilification and trials against the clergy, the first to collectivize agriculture and take the land away from the peasants. By June 1948 Yugoslavia had advanced further on the road to full collectivization than any other satellite. As to the scope of the terror, the man in charge of the "mopping-up" operations, Alexander Rankovic, was later to declare at a session of the Central Committee in February 1951 that 47 per cent of the arrests made by the dreaded UDBA (the secret police) in 1949 had been unjustified. One may well imagine the corresponding percentages for the arrests undertaken during the earlier period. The liquidation of the old economic and administrative bureaucracy was, of course, the essential condition for the mountaineers taking over the "commanding heights."

Yugoslavia was second only to Poland in losses of population in proportional terms. No less than 1.7 million people, about 11 per cent of the population, were killed, fled, or were deported. The losses hit mainly the younger age-groups with better education and skills. A large part of industry and agriculture was devastated, and one-sixth of the housing almost totally destroyed. But Yugoslavia drew up the most ambitious industrialization plan in Eastern Europe. In addition to building new factories in the most underdeveloped regions, the Five Year Plan proposed an almost fivefold increase in gross industrial output. Steel output was to be trebled and power production increased four times.

The dizzy and totally unrealistic plans provoked the first clash in the top leadership. The chief planner, president of the Economic Council and Minister of Industry Andrija Hebrang opposed the projected targets. One of the ablest Yugoslav Communists, previously Secretary of the Croat party, Hebrang also complained that Tito had treated him with "personal animosity." In the best Stalinist style criticism was taken as tantamount to treason, and Hebrang was demoted. Another leading functionary, Sreten Zujovic, a Serb, was also severely reprimanded. By the time the Russians wanted to build them up as an alternative leadership to Tito in 1948, the two disciplined leaders had lost every lever of influence. As always in Communist power struggles, compromising documents were conveniently found, revealing that Hebrang had shown cowardice and collaborated with the Ustashe while in prison. Arrested in the spring of 1948, he is alleged to have committed suicide in prison, while Zujovic was released two years later after having exercised self-criticism in the press.

As the ambitious targets were based on the assumption of Soviet aid and trade with the bloc that accounted for half of Yugoslavia's foreign trade in 1948, the blockade imposed on the country after its expulsion from the bloc proved disastrous. But the plan could not have been fulfilled under any circumstances. Nevertheless there was a logic in the ruthless Sovietization, the rapid collectivization, the wildly unrealistic industrialization targets, in keeping well ahead of the other Communist-dominated countries—"the logic of extremism."[26]

It was this basic general line, a leftist strategy, that shaped Yugoslav external policies during this period and inflamed the tensions with Moscow to an unbearable pitch. This was the real background to the Yugoslav intransigence in both Trieste and Austrian Carinthia, which raised the risk of hostilities between the British and Yugoslav armies and of involving the Russians in a useless and early conflict with the West. Yugoslavia's territorial ambitions in Italy and Austria provoked the first serious clash with Stalin, after Tito in May 1945 had issued the unmistakable warning that "we don't want to be used as a bribe in international bargaining."

There was also the missionary zeal of the Yugoslavs in the international Communist movement. Though the postwar period still has many obscurities, the available evidence seems to confirm the conjecture, first put forward by the late Professor Borkenau, that Tito's adventurist initiatives were only part of the aggressive global strategy advocated by a strong group in the Soviet leadership headed at that time by A. Zhdanov. It was his lengthy speech at the founding meeting of the Cominform, the new institution of Communist cooperation set up in September 1947, that gave the signal for the change in the strategic line from a defensive posture to aggressive dynamism. The two Yugoslav representatives at that meeting, Kardelj and Djilas, were only too willing, at Zhdanov's request, to criticize the Italian and French parties sharply for their timidity. The Yugoslavs fed the fires of the Greek civil war. They shot down American transport planes flying over Yugoslavia in broad daylight and kept the tensions over the Trieste issue near boiling point.

As the Berlin blockade and the Korean war so clearly demonstrated later, there was no difference of principle between the extremism of the leftist faction and that of Stalin. But Stalin always wanted to rely on the levers of Soviet power and not on the local parties and revolutionary ideology as the main tools of aggression. Also, he wanted the spoils for the Soviet Union and not for a local Communist chieftain in the Balkans, who had a flattering image of himself as a leader of the Communist world second only to Stalin.

Aside from the sudden death of Zhdanov in August 1948, the Yugoslav brand of expansionism in the Balkans gradually turned a dispute about revolutionary tactics into a barely disguised challenge to Soviet hegemony over the area. There were two major elements in the conflict. The first concerned Albania. Whatever differences there may have been between the Yugoslav treatment of its tiny neighbor and the Soviet attitude toward Yugoslavia. Albania was in fact a satellite of Belgrade, and the Yugoslavs were preparing a unification of the two countries. Albania was to be incorporated into the Yugoslav Federation as a separate republic merged with the mainly Albanian-inhabited Kosovo region.

There was a sizable group in the Albanian party—created, organized, and controlled by the Yugoslav Communists from the very beginning—that secretly but deeply opposed the Yugoslav designs and was seeking Soviet support.* There was not a single meeting of the Russian and Yugoslav leaders between 1944 and 1948 at which Albania was not discussed.[27] Then, in early 1948, without informing Moscow, the Yugoslavs, allegedly acceding to a request from Tirana, decided to send two divisions to Albania and actually moved a wing of airborne fighters there to "defend the southern borders against a possible attack by Greek monarcho-fascists." Before the divisions could be moved, Moscow threatened an open breach unless the two governments immediately canceled their agreement.

The second major dispute revolved around the Yugoslav-sponsored project of Bulgarian-Yugoslav federation, later to be expanded into a more ambitious Balkan union. During the war years there had been a fierce dispute between the Yugoslav and Bulgarian Communists as to who should run the party and the resistance movement in Macedonia, then completely occupied by Bulgarian troops. The friction got worse as the defeat of Germany approached.[28] In December 1944, Tito sent Kardelj to Sofia with a proposal to solve the thorny issue of Macedonia within the framework of a Yugoslav-Bulgarian federation. At that time Stalin approved the project. Quite apart from Western, mainly British, protests, the main stumbling block was the question of on whose terms

* See also the chapter on Albania.

the federation should take place. The Bulgarians, who never had been truly enthusiastic about the merger, wanted a union in which Bulgaria would be equal with Yugoslavia. The Yugoslav draft, however, proposed that Bulgaria should become simply a seventh republic within the Yugoslav federation. Subsequently the whole issue was shelved until the summer of 1947.

When at that time Tito and the ailing Bulgarian leader Georgi Dimitrov not only revived the old project but also began to drop hints about a future project embracing Rumania, Hungary, Poland, and Czechoslovakia, as well as Greece should the guerrillas seize power, Moscow became increasingly suspicious—and not without reason. Tito was touring the neighboring countries with a maximum of publicity, concluding treaties everywhere before the Soviet Union did, and in the case of Rumania, "for lack of time" even failing to inform the Soviet leaders about his forthcoming trip. When finally in January 1948 Dimitrov gave an obviously prearranged interview alluding to a future federation or confederation of the Balkan-Danubian countries, he was publicly rebuked five days later by *Pravda*. Though he hastily issued an abject apology, both the Bulgarian and Yugoslav leaders were immediately summoned to the Russian capital.

Here they were severely criticized by Stalin for their hectic activity in regard to the federation, and the Yugoslavs further reprimanded for their single-handed venture in Albania. "You do not let anyone know what you are doing and we have to find out everything on the streets," Stalin complained. He described the statement in the Yugoslav-Bulgarian treaty declaration about "supporting all actions against the hotbeds of aggression" as a call for a preventive war. The uprising in Greece, Stalin added, had no prospects of success and must be stopped as soon as possible. But while rejecting the idea of a federation or customs union between Rumania and Bulgaria, let alone the scheme of a broader union, Stalin was enthusiastic about a Yugoslav-Bulgarian federation. It should be created "right away, if possible tomorrow," he said, and then both should unite with Albania. His demand for an immediate Yugoslav-Bulgarian federation was, however, rejected by the Yugoslav Central Committee on March 1, 1948, because, as Tito bluntly stated, this would be to allow a Trojan horse to enter the Yugoslav party.[29]

These, then, were in very broad terms the main issues that led to the final split. Stalin dealt with the crux of the matter at the last fateful meeting in the Kremlin: the issue, he said, is "not your mistakes, but your policy." By 1948 the postwar phase of diversity based on limited local autonomy had been replaced in Eastern Europe by the Stalinist pattern of mutual relations, in which the specific aspirations of the ruling regimes must bow before the supreme and absolute authority of the Kremlin. What earlier may have seemed to Moscow a desirable tactical ploy against Western pressure was tending to become a grouping of Balkan states with a will of its own, undermining essential Soviet power interests. Tito was no Luther of communism. He wanted to be a partner and not a servant. But his inflated sense of mission and self-importance, his missionary zeal, stemming from the conscious pride of a national leader who had made a revolution on his own, proved incompatible with the essence of Stalinism, a rigid institutional and ideological hierarchy. With his internal and external dynamism, Tito was in fact challenging Moscow's monopoly of running the international Communist movement.

Stalin was faced for the first time in Communist history with the dilemma of dealing with a rival or deviationist who was a genuine national leader with a party, an apparat, and an intelligence service of his own. At first he played his hand cautiously, trying to influence Tito from the outside and at the same time penetrate the key Yugoslavian cadres from within. With tensions mounting, the battle shifted more and more to subversion. Soviet intelligence multiplied its efforts to infiltrate, subvert, and dominate the rival UDBA, the army command, and the Yugoslav party leadership. It was only after these attempts had manifestly failed, that Stalin ordered the Cominform to issue a writ of excommunication.

The conflict was fought between two totalitarian Communist parties. But as both were ruling parties, it necessarily and immediately acquired the character of a national conflict, of a showdown between the then only Communist great power and a small Balkan country. It is the basic rule of thumb in communism that a heretic must by definition be a renegade and a traitor. If he is a leftist like Tito, he must be condemned as in fact a "rightist"; if he pretends to defend the interests of a small nation, he should be shown up in his true colors as an enemy of communism. Thus within a year, the Yugoslav leaders, still desperately hoping that interstate relations would not be affected, were already not only "sliding into the camp of the enemies of the Soviet Union," but had become old agents of imperialism. After a spate of show trials in Albania, Hungary, and Bulgaria, the Cominform by November 1949 had approved a resolution with the characteristic title: "The Yugoslav Communist Party in the power of murderers and spies."

The Yugoslav leaders were, however, also past masters at this game and played their cards surprisingly well. While the UDBA was swiftly rounding up some twelve thousand Cominform-followers, the ill-fated "Informbirovci," the party did its best to show that it was not guilty of "rightist" softness or of any nationalist or anti-Soviet feelings. Three weeks after the open break, Tito gave an eight-hour address to the Fifth Yugoslav Party Congress, devoting only the last twenty minutes to refuting the charges leveled by the Cominform. He finished his speech amid a rhythmical shouting of "Stalin! Tito! Stalin! Tito!" As late as 1949 pictures of Stalin were still carried in Belgrade in the May Day parade.

The Yugoslav leaders deliberately left the initiative to Stalin. As Tito later said to his biographer, he had to give Stalin time to behave in such a way that "people in Yugoslavia would say 'Down with Stalin' of their own accord without my having to suggest it to them." Needless to say, the charge of nationalism helped the regime to regain at least some of the popularity among the non-Communist majority it lost after the early waves of terror. External threat or promise of expansion, political and economic dynamism are the essential conditions for the existence of a totalitarian regime. Thus the leadership decided to launch a stepped-up collectivization campaign after the break to show the satellites that the Yugoslavs were "better collectivizers," hence better Communists than they and also to give the party activists large practical tasks. The years 1949–50 saw the greatest pressure in agriculture and the most wildly irrational measures in the economy in general. Within roughly a year, the number of collective farms showed a fivefold increase to 7,000 and the arable land in the socialized sector, which already accounted for one-fourth of the total, jumped seven times to 2.2 million hectares. The hard line succeeded in keeping up the morale of the party cadres and in convincing even the few doubters that the Yugoslavs were unjustly accused of being "soft" on the pace of marching toward communism.

The price, however, was the disruption of the farming output and dislocation in industry, which for years plagued even the first modest attempt at economic reform. Yet the very failures of the politically motivated collectivization, heightened by disastrous droughts in 1950 and 1952, helped psychologically to prepare the ground for a change of policy. The danger of demoralization recurred toward the end of the two-year transition period from 1948 to 1950, but absolute faithfulness to Stalinism made the acceptance of Western aid virtually impossible. After the economic catastrophes and in particular after the outbreak of the Korean War, it became more and more evident to the Yugoslav leaders that without massive economic and military aid from the West they might well be faced sooner or later with a military attack and economic disaster.

There was no alternative but gradually to tell the bitter truth about a degenerated Soviet system based on bureaucracy and chauvinism. The attacks from 1950 onward were directed first at Stalin's personal dictatorship and later shifted to a general condemnation of the Soviet system. This, in turn, led to the necessity of making the Yugoslav system different from the discredited Soviet model, of abandoning rigid schemes and methods, and of changing the ideology so as to adapt the orthodoxy to fit the concrete measures. What followed was an essentially syndicalist idea—to be sure, dressed in appropriate quotes from Marx and Lenin—about social ownership, the management of the factories through elected workers' councils. The Five Year Plan was abandoned and the collectivization drive stopped. The hated compulsory deliveries were abolished in 1951, and early in 1953 peasants were allowed to leave the collective farms. By the following year most of the land was back in private hands, although a 10-hectare (c. 25 acres) upper limit was set for the individual holdings, which is still in force. Workers' self-government and economic decentralization became the great new dogma, which lies at the root of the many contradictions characterizing the entire period from 1950–52 to the present time.

Then came the definite rapprochement with the West in the form of grants, loans, and food sales as well as military aid. In the 1949–55 period, economic help from the United States reached almost 600 million dollars while military aid totaled 588 million dollars.[30] The long period of Stalinism in theory and in economic practice came to an end.

Thus Tito and his team, extreme Communists, dynamic leftists, were forced first into the position of nationalists, then, once out in the cold, into the position of liberalizers and reformists who until 1955–56 depended exclusively on the West. The road, however, from the pictures of Stalin to the posters of General Motors has never been straight, but always fraught with contradictions. When some Yugoslav leaders try to reverse the gears or throw their weight around in international politics, often against the interests of their former benefactors, it is not enough to remark, "After all, one shouldn't forget that Tito is a Communist." The question is what kind of a Communist?

The man who until the end of the fifties and the beginning of the sixties—but no longer!—dominated Yugoslav politics has remained, like so many of his closest collaborators, a Communist molded by the Comintern school and the old orthodoxy. One of his many revealing statements was made at the thirtieth anniversary of his appointment as Secretary-General of the party. Referring to the current party reform, Tito claimed that the key to the "enormous success" of such a small prewar Communist party was simple: "with conscious discipline, purging the ranks of wavering factionalist petty bourgeois elements, the party developed into a monolithic revolutionary unit."[31]

In short, if there were absolute discipline, absolute obedience, and absolute unanimity in carrying out the decisions, everything in the country would be in order. This concept of a "strong hand" policy is consciously or subconsciously shared by many Yugoslav decision-makers. On the other hand, the rigidity of the new dogma of self-government and decentralization restricts the freedom of maneuver of the genuinely progressive forces. But, as we shall see, there are also enlightened centralists and dogmatic decentralists and vice versa. It must not be forgotten that the upper echelons of the ruling elite came to power in their late twenties or early thirties. Their origin, recruitment, view of the world, schooling, cohesion, and circulation were shaped in the formative Stalinist period of 1941 to 1950. The main cross-currents of the recent past and the present are therefore not a mere conflict of generations, but a conflict of concepts and of personalities. While the crucial battles are waged more and more in terms of national colors, the pace of the changes is also influenced by the remnants of a long forgotten phase: the dizzy and heroic days of fighting, missionary zeal, leftist extremism within the country and in the Balkans as a whole.

Capitalism without capitalists?

In broad daylight on a Friday in August 1967 the director of a transport enterprise in the Serbian city of Nis, Blagoje Popovic, was literally thrown over a wall onto the street by a group of embittered workers. The twelve culprits later conceded that they might have been somewhat "wrought up" at having received lower wages than they had expected. The same day four directors decided to leave their jobs in the industrial town of Smederevo, near the capital, giving as the chief reason their inability to cooperate with the workers' councils that had appointed them. Three days later, in Zagreb, the capital of Croatia, 250 workers of a battery plant went on strike demanding that their plant separate from the larger concern with which they had merged barely a year before, after the production staff unanimously voted to do so. During the same month workers in three other factories struck because they were dissatisfied with their take-home pay, which had been calculated according to the profit-loss yardstick, theoretically the standard basis for income distribution.

The attack on the director, which subsequently kept the courts in Nis busy for many months, the resignations, and the strikes are only a few examples within the span of a single month of the tensions in Yugoslav factories. But how to explain the case of the Union Bank of Belgrade, one of the largest banks in the country, which holds one-fifth of the aggregate savings deposits? On a certain day the bank had no liquid funds and its current account was frozen by the Public Auditing Service. On the following day, however, the accounts showed a substantial surplus. Somewhat later, the governor of the Central Bank explained that there had been no question of the Union Bank being insolvent. It was merely a "momentary situation" owing to the fact that his proposal that a system of special reserves be held in the securities of the Central Bank had been rejected by the bankers for fear of a "disguised centralization of funds." Another amusing and highly revealing story was reported in the same period. From this small Balkan country no fewer than two hundred firms submitted competitive bids to build a factory for Libya. Only one-third of these enterprises would suffice to carry out such construction in Yugoslavia itself.

A few weeks later, many Yugoslav households and industries felt tangibly what J. K. Galbraith has called the "natural inclination" of the modern corporation toward "a brutal and anti-social egotism," even under the conditions of socialist self-management. From one day to the next, the Electric Power Community, representing power companies in the different republics, cut off power for four hours, blaming shortage on the weather. An angry government hastened to make it clear, however, that the companies had given no advance warning and that for a considerable time the thermoelectric (coal using) plants had been working below optimal capacities. The power companies had deliberately kept the output of thermoelectric plants at low levels and overused hydroelectric power. Why? Simply because of prices and costs. Since water-generated electricity costs one-third to one-fifth as much to produce as thermal power, and since the rates charged to the customers are nevertheless the same, this meant a large—and unauthorized—profit for the electric companies. Furthermore the electric power system is not truly unified. As *Borba*, the leading Belgrade daily, pointedly remarked: "Certain power communities behave in this field as if they owned it. Poor connections among the various regions, mutual bargaining and relations, which have nothing to do with real business relations, explain the curious fact that in some republics power supply has often been cut while at the same time there has been plenty of power in other republics."[32]

The strikes by embittered workers who in theory are supposed to run their factories themselves, the exodus of numerous directors, the "momentary insolvency" of a leading bank, the behavior of the power companies and the lack of any coordination in that key sector are only some of the many facets of what seems to many casual observers—and to even more Yugoslavs—to be chaos. The Yugoslav brand of socialism is a unique system with institutions and structures that are as different from those of the Communist East as they are from those of the United States or Western Europe. Even the word "system" is not an accurate description of what is in fact a vast undertaking that has been going on for more than fifteen years, taxing economic resources, political nerves, and the fabric of society.

The so-called Yugoslav road to socialism is in fact a unique series of experiments in economic and social development undertaken by a Communist regime that, since the early fifties, has not looked to the Soviet model and has remained independent of Soviet dictation.

Its central features are: the experiment in industrial democracy called workers' self-management; an attempt at grass-roots democracy without overthrowing the Communist monopoly of power, which might be described as local self-government in the framework of communes (urban or rural districts); and finally, a search by trial and error for a viable alternative to either private or state capitalism (the latter is the Yugoslav term for the Soviet-type system), referred to as socialist market economy.

The distinctive and exciting feature of the Yugoslav political scene is the continual flux and evolution of an unfinished system and a doctrine built piece by piece. Experiments of all kinds, from industrial reorganization to the revamping of the delicate mechanism regulating relations between nations and republics, are freely tried out and discarded. The official doctrine is still, on the face of it, the Holy Script, Marxism-Leninism. But by drawing on bits and pieces from scattered statements of Marxist thinkers and at the same time borrowing freely from the economic theories of the bourgeois West, the Yugoslavs have devised many sets of constantly changing institutions, adapting them with uninhibited daring to practical needs. However much Yugoslav reality has differed and still differs from theory, in one crucial sense at least the Yugoslav Communists have remained faithful to the statement spelled out in the last sentence of their lengthy 1958 party program: "Nothing that has been created should be so sacred to us that it cannot be transcended and superseded by something still freer, more progressive and more human."

As a result of the many experiments within the great experiment, Yugoslavia has become a most puzzling, bewildering, and confusing country—in appearance at any rate—to fellow Communists, Western businessmen, orthodox economists, and political scientists of every school. Events do not take place in terms of either orthodox Communist doctrine or Western "conventional wisdom." It takes time to realize, or rather feel, that there is a crucial difference between what seems to be there, what is reflected in diplomatic dispatches or occasional news reports, and what is really going on. It is the continuing reality rather than isolated policy statements that provides the key to the Yugoslav enigma.

Nowhere is it so easy to fall prey to one of the two main extremes as in Yugoslavia, and this author has been no exception to the rule during his many visits to the country. The first, which may be called simplicistic optimism, tends to accept statements at face value and regard progressive slogans as facts pointing to a new form of democratic socialism. The other dismisses the elaborate system of workers' management and local self-government as meaningless window dressing for a Communist dictatorship, which for all its verbal acrobatics would never dream of giving up its monopoly of power.

The confusion is if anything intensified if the visitor listens to Yugoslavs when they attempt to expound their ideas and explain their system. Self-management, self-government, direct democracy, socialist market economy are the "in" words, while such terms as étatism or statism (standing for uncontrolled interference of the state), authority (meaning command based on concentration of power), and centralism (deciding in Belgrade or in the capitals of the republics over the heads of those concerned about vital economic and political matters) are the "dirty" words. At the same time, each of these words means something different to different persons or interest groups. A bank director in Zagreb may thunder against the concentration of funds in Belgrade and give the impression of being an ardent decentralist. But actually he may well be a "mini-centralist," a republican centralist, who wants to administer the funds from above, or to grant credits geared to political considerations and not to economic common sense—the difference being that he does it himself and within the framework of his own republic or region.

One hears Yugoslav Communists say things that would warm the heart of any "free enterprise" advocate. State intervention? Must be cut to an absolute minimum. Price controls? Very undesirable—imposed temporarily for some vital goods, but to be removed as soon as possible. Taxes? Accepted with great reluctance and should not stifle efforts to maximize profits. Yet, one also catches, in addition to Adam Smith, echoes of every conceivable socialist idea—not just Marx, let alone Lenin, but the early socialists and syndicalists, Owen, even more Proudhon, plus a strong dose of anarchism or anarchosyndicalism.

"There were in their times some interesting anarchists. We all read about them or some of their works. But to my best knowledge, Yugoslavia is the first country in the world where anarchists have been and are still in power!" This is how a Western ambassador, himself an erstwhile socialist, introduced one of his dispatches to his government. A distinguished American political scientist dryly remarked ". . . it can be said that were Yugoslavia not a one-party state, its constitutional and administrative structure would lead to a most appalling chaos."[33] Another observer came much closer to the crux of the problem when he described it as one of equilibrium coupled with momentum, "for the state is in the position of a cyclist who cannot move forward until he has learnt to keep his balance, and yet can only find his balance by moving."[34]

The recent and current history of Yugoslav communism may be compared to a stormy voyage into uncharted seas with many of the key personnel still doubtful about the wisdom of having embarked. The captain and his senior staff initiated the voyage, originally intended as a cruise along the coast. But they did not take into account the strength of the wind, the shape of the ship, the abrupt changes in mood among sailors and passengers, and countless other factors. On top of everything, their original compass was either defective all along or proved useless once they encountered unexpected storms. For quite some time they have been cruising the high seas far away from the coast. The other shore is not yet in sight, and meanwhile the captain has lost much of his former self-confidence and even more his undisputed authority. Neither he nor the younger officers, who would like to take the helm, can agree among themselves just which course would be the fastest and safest. Yet however long the journey, a return to the coast is impossible.

This voyage started on June 26, 1950, the day after the outbreak of the Korean War, when Marshal Tito first proclaimed the slogans, "Factories to the workers—management of production by the producers!" On the same day a law was passed handing over the management of all factories and business enterprises to the workers and establishing the institution of workers' councils. This was a momentous departure—in the making of which the "direct producers" had, of course, no voice—from the Soviet model.

To be sure, the beginning of the great experiment in industrial democracy, economic decentralization, and eventual democratization of political and social life stemmed from political and moral aspirations rather than economic expectations. After they had begun to expose the basic defects of the Russian pattern and to condemn Stalinism as a dictatorship of bureaucracy over the proletariat, the Yugoslav Communists had to devise some way out of the ideological blind alley. A Communist regime cannot stand still; it needs a doctrine. The Yugoslavs had to find an innovation that would avoid even the slightest suspicion of a return to capitalism, set them as far apart as possible from the Soviet model, and present an acceptable alternative, however hazy in form, to the hundreds of thousands of party faithful.

Tito's chief ideologists at that time, Milovan Djilas, Edward Kardelj, and the late Boris Kidric, found the tool. The Stalinist system, so ran the Yugoslav argument, corrupted and polluted the ideas of the great Marxist thinkers, and the remedy lay in the return to the original "unspoiled" concept. Stalin identified the state bureaucracy with the state and the "withering away" of the state with its consolidation under the pretext of a continual sharpening of the class struggle. But the state must not only "wither away" as an instrument of suppression; its apparatus, its functions, and its interference in such fields as economy, education, culture, etc. must also vanish. Self-management, and not the state and an all-powerful state bureaucracy, must be the main instrument in the building of socialism.

The trouble was, of course, that neither Marx nor Lenin had said much about this. Apart from some snatches of Marx's *Civil War in France* and Lenin's *State and Revolution*, there was nothing in their voluminous writings about workers' self-management. Even their few relevant statements were either revised later by Marx or not put into practice by Lenin. Communists are, however, always able to get around such seemingly painful conflicts between theory and practice by a reference to Engels who said that Marxism was "no dogma but a guide to action" or to Lenin's dictum that Marxism cannot be regarded as something "completed and sacrosanct." This is what Communists call "creative Marxism" or "creative application of the theory," which means in plain words that practically anything can be done in the guise of "creativity," provided it is promoted from above by the men in power.

Thus it happened that the Yugoslav leaders who had opted for the maintenance of their power, and consequently for national interests as against unconditional ideological solidarity with Moscow, within two years already posed a major ideological challenge to Stalinism both as a dogma and as an socioeconomic system. The system of workers' councils and of delegates to producers' chambers had, of course, nothing to do with Marx or Lenin. It was an updated version of pure syndicalist and anarchist ideas. The erstwhile leftists, extremists, or "sectarians" embarked on an experiment to revamp the economic and state structure, and the further they progressed the more they violated the very principles upon which their system had been built.

To be sure, the rhetoric has all along been more impressive than the reforms. The bold summons to wage war on state bureaucracy and to erect a genuine system of self-management was followed by actual measures that were super-cautious and highly conditional.

The experiment in industrial democracy and economic decentralization, accompanied by a marked but limited increase in freedom for the average person, was launched and controlled by the party leadership. But its creators underestimated the inherent dynamism of economic competition, which is pregnant with political risks. As Dusan Bilandzic, one of the country's top labor experts, once remarked, "The entire period from 1950 to 1965 marks in fact only the birth of the self-management system." Nevertheless the competitive forces unleashed by the establishment of workers' councils mercilessly demolished the façade of the "Great Lie" and exposed three sets of contradictory problems insolubly linked with one another: how to combine the advantages of a decentralized system regulated by the market mechanism with the general lines of a plan that established over-all priority targets; how to fit the Communist party into a decentralized market economy and decide what role it was to play in an increasingly diversified society once actual decision-making was no longer in the hands of the party hierarchy; and how to strike a viable and acceptable balance between economic efficiency and social considerations, between the "have" and the "have not" nations and areas. The first problem cannot be solved without the second, yet both are interwoven with and increasingly dominated by the national tensions that as early as 1961–62 came into the open as the central problem of Yugoslav life. Despite these dilemmas and the countless additional problems characteristic of any technologically primitive society subjected to rapid modernization, the over-all record has been impressive, both compared to the past and, even more, compared to the performance of the Communist-ruled countries adhering to the Soviet model.

To see how much of the Yugoslav system is appearance and how much reality, one has to turn first of all to the changes in the economy, one of the main pillars of bureaucracy. By paraphrasing a term coined by Galbraith, this system, where the producers are at the same time collective entrepreneurs, could be called "capitalism without capitalists" or "socialism without the control of society."

When the Yugoslav leaders decided to find an ideological alternative and felt compelled to bridge, partially at least, the gulf between the rulers and the ruled, they offered the people working in
the economy the illusion of power. The irresistible logic of the economic and social forces, however, transformed the illusion of power
into a power of illusion that gradually became a prime mover of developments, animating them from below. This is not a matter of
mere semantics, but constitutes the underlying core of the shifts,
changes, and struggles of the past fifteen years. Workers' councils without a meaningful autonomy would be a mockery of self-
management. To fill the form with some content, the party was
soon forced to put powers into the hands of enterprises.

The innumerable changes in enterprise autonomy were connected
with the problem of striking a balance between too much and too
little decentralization and with the political conflict between those
who said that liberalization had gone too far and those who maintained it had not gone far enough. The essence of the changes proclaimed in 1950 and carried out in a piecemeal fashion was the
transition from administrative orders to economic regulators, from
command to initiative. For anyone accustomed to the highly
sophisticated economic tools in the developed West it is difficult to
gauge the enormous theoretical and practical significance of this
departure from the Stalinist model.

In the Stalinist economic system, millions of economic decisions
were taken on the basis of faulty data derived from an irrational
pricing system and coordinated by a centralized high command
through a myriad of orders. The main features were: political interference at all levels, suppression of initiative, and the fact that the
orders issued from the center "were not binding on those above, but
had to be implemented without question by those below."[35] Production had an absolute priority over consumption, heavy industry
over light, industry over agriculture. The role of the individual enterprise was of a cog in an elaborate administrative structure in which
government machinery was completely merged with the party organization and economic management. Literally everything an enterprise did, from the prices of materials and costs of production to
wages and sales, was set by the higher authorities with profits paid
into and deficits automatically covered by the state budget.

Given the single-party Communist system as such, based on the
public ownership of the means of production, the device of workers'

councils represented Yugoslavia's first major step toward more freedom, not only in economic but also in political and social life. The introduction of workers' management and the gradual widening of their powers changed business organizations from receivers of commands from above into increasingly independent risk-takers.

The technique of organizing this new form of management and of running current operations has remained the same and is fraught with built-in contradictions between "participatory democracy" and efficient management. In every enterprise (in factories as well as in commerce, transport, schools, hospitals, civil service, etc.) a workers' council, which, depending on the size of the labor force, can have fifteen to seventy members, is elected by secret ballot. It has a mandate for two years with half of the membership renewed every year. Decisions are made by majority vote. The council elects a management board of at least five, including the director, who is responsible for day-to-day management. The council usually meets once every month or six weeks, while the board meets at least twice a month. There is no financial compensation for being a member of either body, and no one can be elected twice in succession or more than twice in all to the council or the board. The job of director is advertised in the press, and applicants are interviewed by a committee made up in equal proportions from the local authorities and the workers' council. The director has to be reappointed every four years, but the council can dismiss him any time. Previously, dismissals were subject to approval by the communal authorities. But since the commune (the district administrative unit) often had disputes with the enterprises—being directly interested in their operations through communal taxes and levies—many directors tended to side for obvious personal reasons with the "outsiders" rather than with the workers' councils. As a result of many such bones of contention, responsibility for the dismissal of the director and other competences have been transferred to the councils. The director can, however, go to court to claim restitution or appropriate compensation.

Thus workers are supposed to play the role of shareholders; although they lack the education to make or even understand a complex technical choice, they are quite capable of comparing their earnings with others in the same branch. One may, of course, immediately point to the danger of putting the cart before the horse, that is, concentrating on distribution rather than on the creation of profit. This does indeed represent a brake on progress. Yet, once again, within the given system, profit incentives are infinitely superior to the Soviet method of compulsion to meet planned targets (more often than not geared to faulty signals) and bonuses for overfulfillment of the plan.

As the wages paid to the employees are tied to the productivity and profitability of the enterprise, the workers, as stockholders, push the management to seek higher earnings. The management in turn has to "sell" its ideas to the workers' council and convince it that they are good. The incentive of seeking higher pay via higher profits is bound to improve efficiency and compel staff and management to maximize cost-saving innovations[36]—at least, in theory.

Despite many defects and considerable political "back-seat driving" by powerful vested interests, the Yugoslav model has changed the rigid Stalinist system beyond recognition and produced a considerable sum total of economic decentralization. Through a series of laws in 1952, 1954, 1958, and 1961, enterprises were given important powers to operate on the market according to their own decisions and at their own risk. The real changeover actually started in 1954, when state financing was abolished and investment funds were separated from the state budget. Starting with the meager concession of being able to elect or dismiss the workers' councils, by the end of the fifties the enterprises planned their production independently, marketed their products, bought raw materials, decided on employment, made their own arrangements with foreign firms, and enjoyed increasing freedom in investing their capital and distributing their profits. Though projected bold reforms in 1961 were temporarily frustrated by bureaucracy, the enterprises could henceforth divide their net earnings independently once they had paid their federal and local taxes.

Parallel reforms from 1953 to 1964 gradually introduced a working market mechanism with government control maintained through price and investment, fiscal and monetary policies. State administration was drastically reduced; the six republics and the communes (there are at present 517 such local administrative districts) were given increased powers in political and economic decisions. Ministries were abolished and only a few administrative state secretariats remain. Enterprises are no longer in any way subordinate to the central institutions; they form their own branch associations and set up business chambers to represent their interests.

The constitutional reform of 1953 established a bicameral basis in local self-government and also at republican and federal levels, and the new Constitution of 1963 made the entire system even more complicated, with a corporate structure resembling in some ways Mussolini's Italy. The communes described as "the basic social-political community based on self-government by the citizens" constitute "the political foundation of the uniform social-political system." Each commune has an assembly elected by universal suffrage and a so-called Council of Producers elected on a vocational basis in enterprises, thus excluding self-employed peasants and artisans. The actual parliaments—the Federal Chamber and the Republican Chambers—are also elected directly, while the members of the four vocational chambers (education and culture, economic matters, social welfare and public health, and political administration) are elected by indirect suffrage from the local Councils of Producers.

The point is that local government, at least in the economic sense, has had a growing impact on business operations, investment decisions, and economic developments. The communes have received steadily increasing financial revenues from their local enterprises, from local taxes and a variety of levies including the license fees paid by private artisans. Managing schools and welfare institutions, controlling a large segment of prices, and investing from their own independent funds in housing and public services, the communes have gradually surpassed many enterprises and the weak branch offices of an imperfect, albeit chronically overhauled banking system as the financial nerve centers of their respective areas.

The wide executive powers and large financial resources given to the communes in the course of administrative and economic decentralization may well have been intended as political window dressing, but economically they were in many cases almost suicidal, thanks to reckless investment commitments. For many years both the local authorities and the republican bureaucracies were stimulated by their share in the personal earnings of the employed to put pressure on the enterprises to employ excess labor. The new regulations introduced in 1961 eliminated the pressure but encouraged the communes to "double" their share in the earnings of the enterprises by creating or financing unnecessary new firms.

Despite the great strides made in the field of enterprise autonomy, their freedom remained limited because government bureaucracy at all levels kept control of over 70 per cent of investment capital.

The workers could dispose of their net profit only after the social community (the Federation, republics, and communes) in one form or another had already appropriated on the average half, but in many cases well over half, of the enterprises' net profit. At the same time, until 1965 investment resources remained centralized and decision-making on size, location, and financing of investment projects was decided ultimately by political factors rather than economic considerations.

Investment financing was decentralized on paper, with part of the funds for fixed investments shifted from the state bureaucracy to the communal and republican authorities. The credits provided from the centralized funds, that is, from the money earned by but taken away from the efficient producers, were used partly to channel subsidies to inefficient enterprises, partly to build large new projects, while modernization and reconstruction of existing capacities were neglected.

Sailing under the unofficial slogan of "A little to everyone," the disease of "investomania" infected the communes and republics. As the Croat leader, Vladimir Bakaric, put it in 1961, "Everyone wants to develop his own region, and that is the reason each region believes that some factory, no matter what kind, must be built there."[37] Factory chimneys became status symbols in the mountain bastions of Montenegro and the wooded hills of Bosnia. The building and fate of countless "political factories" and the future of the centralized funds and overambitious commitments have become the central issues of economic policy since 1961, polluting the general atmosphere and eventually sparking off the great and continuing clash between centralists and decentralists.

Freedom in little spoonfuls

"You should judge us not in terms of our achievements but by our motives," Dr. Najdan Pasic, then director of the Social Science Institute in Belgrade, said to me once when we were discussing the countless contradictions between lofty declarations and hard facts in Yugoslav economic and social life.

Despite war devastation, the enormous damages caused by the Soviet blockade, and the military threat posed by Stalin's Russia, which necessitated defense expenditures to the tune of some 1.2

billion dollars between 1948–53, the country has achieved some of the highest growth rates recorded by any nation at a similar stage of economic development. To be sure, Western aid, predominantly American, loans, grants, and surplus sales totaling 1.8 billion dollars in addition to some 700 million dollars worth of military supplies, helped to save the country from famine, if not from economic disaster through a critical period.[38] But the country is burdened with underdeveloped regions, which account for 40 per cent of the territory, and its growth rate, averaging 7.6 per cent yearly in the 1952–65 period, could well have been more balanced and less costly both economically and socially had it not been for this handicap. Nevertheless the record is impressive by any standards.

The growth of the Gross National Product during the ten-year period 1952–62 was the second highest in the world; the increase of industrial production at an annual rate of 12 per cent, and that of farm output at 3.7 per cent, the third highest. Industrial output in 1967 was eight times higher than prewar levels; agricultural performance was up 54 per cent. National per capita income, a mere $140 (at present prices) before the war, stood at $149 when the decentralization experiments were launched. By 1966 it had jumped to $550, and the planners reckoned that by the end of the sixties Yugoslavia would reach the 1965 development stage of Austria or Italy.[39]*

Figures, however, cannot remotely illustrate the economic, sociologic, and psychologic impact of the consumer civilization that has gradually begun to dominate the life and expectations of the average person, so long smothered by the slogans and commands of a Stalinist administrative system. Though accumulation (investments through forced savings) had priority over consumption until 1963, the decentralized system gave a powerful push to consumption, which doubled between 1953–63. Choice, variety, and quality of goods improved vastly, due partly to the appearance of imports in the shopwindows. In addition to market economy, income sharing, and production incentives, consumer credits also stimulated demand and spurred the employees to earn more money. Mass consumption, mass communications, leisure pursuits, and last but not least the test of comparison, first as a result of the influx of foreign tourists,

---

* The target is, however, unlikely to be reached in view of the subsequent performance in 1966–67 when GNP grew only by 4 per cent in two years, instead of the projected 7–10 per cent *annually.*

then from the increasing number of Yugoslav workers abroad, have combined to change the consumers themselves.

The advent of the consumer civilization has been accompanied by a cultural revolution, which created a new technocratic, scientific, and educational elite. There are now 170,000 students taught by 15,000 professors as against 17,000 and 1,200 professors before the war. By the end of 1966 the number of university graduates reached about 400,000. A parallel demographic revolution reduced the proportion of the agricultural population from the prewar 76 per cent to less than half of the total population, with over 1,000,000 people shifted to towns.

For anyone who has made a number of visits to the country the evidence of progress is striking. The main cities of Croatia and Slovenia with their well-stocked shops, traffic, parking problems, and unrestrained sale of Western newspapers are almost on a par with the average Austrian or Italian city. Coming from Bucharest or Sofia or even Budapest, the traveler finds himself in an utterly different world. Nothing could illustrate the gap between Yugoslavia and the neighboring Communist countries better than the sight of the many East European tourists storming the shops and supermarkets, which offer a choice and variety of goods still regarded as scarce or luxury products in their own countries. Every summer in the beautiful ancient cities on the Adriatic coast one sees many Hungarians and Czechs, and occasionally Bulgarians, standing amazed before the shopwindows, virtually ignoring the priceless treasures of Venetian and Dalmatian architecture.

Considering the incredibly low starting levels and the fearful odds against which the country had to fight, the growth of car ownership and the spread of consumer durables is particularly astonishing. There were only 8,500 cars registered in 1952. By 1961 the figure stood at 75,000 and then jumped fourfold to 274,000 in mid-1967. This means that one in 72 Yugoslavs owns a car, compared to one in 246 seven years ago. The leading Yugoslav car factory is currently producing 50,000 cars under a license from the Italian Fiat company and intends to increase its yearly output to 100,000 units by 1969. The number of such consumer durables as refrigerators, washing machines, other household appliances, and television sets doubled on the average between 1964 and 1967.

Compared to even small neighboring non-Communist Austria, let alone to the more developed West European countries, the figures are, of course, still modest. Every eighth Austrian has a car, which means that in terms of relative population there are almost thirty times as many cars as in Yugoslavia. Bearing in mind, however, that the bulk of the cars are registered in the more industrialized north-western parts—Slovenia and Croatia—which account only for one-third of the total population, the gap is much narrower. In fact, the density of traffic and parking problems in Ljubljana, the Slovenian capital, are as bad as in any Austrian or Italian city of the same size. Over-all comparisons are misleading in the case of a country where the national income per head in the north is still three times as high as in the south.

While still lagging behind the West, Yugoslavia is a consumer paradise compared to the other Communist-ruled Balkan countries, which started more or less at the same development level immediately after the war. Yugoslavs grudgingly admit that the general standard of living has increased compared to prewar levels, but people do not think in terms of comparisons over a span of twenty-five years. Even aside from the fact that over one-third of the employed is under thirty (i.e. either was not alive or was a small child before the war), the Yugoslavs, like people everywhere, judge the improvement in their living conditions mainly from one year to the next, or at best over a period of two to five years. Objectively speaking, no realistic comparisons with prewar levels for the population as a whole are possible—partly because of the many changing components (real wages, consumption, and the transformation in consumer habits, housing, social security, etc.), partly due to the lack of sophisticated statistical tools to measure millions of variables in real terms.

If one talks to the people and compares earnings and prices it soon becomes evident that even the relative affluence—by Balkan standards—is enjoyed by a minority. Official statistics stated that in 1967, for example, average monthly earnings in the social sector (excluding private farmers, artisans, and professional people such as lawyers, etc.) were 73,000 dinars (1 dollar = 1,250 dinars).* But 10 per cent of the employed earned less than 40,000 and 19 per cent more than 100,000. At the same time a man's suit costs 38,000 to 50,000 dinars, a raincoat 23,000 to 35,000, a shirt

---

* Prices and wages are meaningless if converted into dollars; here and elsewhere they serve as guidelines to the purchasing power of wages and salaries in a given country.

from 2,800 to 6,000, a pair of shoes from 5,000 to 8,000. As for women's clothing, a coat costs 35,000 to 45,000, a dress 20,000 to 33,000, light summer dresses 13,000 to 18,000, pullovers and cardigans from 4,000 to 12,000, and shoes from 5,000 to 7,000. The prices refer to goods of poorish or medium quality, but in fairness one must also add that their quality has continually improved and more and more fashionable goods, mainly shoes, leather goods, and casual clothes, are attractively designed.

If one adds that an average employee has to pay roughly four months' wages for a television set or refrigerator and no less than the equivalent of thirty to forty months' earnings to buy such small continental cars as the Volkswagen or the Renault, it is clear that cars and consumer durables are beyond the reach of most people. The power to spend freely is enjoyed by a very thin layer indeed. Yet even such telling comparisons between earnings and prices are no reliable yardstick to gauge progress in this country.

Until the great economic and social changes known as The Reform* that began in mid-1965, a considerable part of the standard of living was an economic illusion created by state subsidies, that is, by money taken away from the efficient producers. One of the country's leading economists, Janez Stanovnik, told the author that 40 per cent of the standard of living had not been earned but subsidized by the state. Thus, for instance, a worker's family of four spent a mere 5 per cent of its income on rent. Health services, transport, and social security in general were financed by funds from the national income, but the debts piled up by the various institutions ultimately became an intolerable burden. Once a real effort is made to put the economy on a self-supporting basis, rents, fares, and social security contributions by individual persons have to go up steeply. This in fact has been happening since The Reform was launched, knocking out some of the key props of an artificially created "standard." This, of course, has caused widespread discontent, particularly among the worst hit categories of lower paid workers.

The admittedly low earnings of the vast army of unskilled workers, however, by no means tell the whole story of their daily lives. Soon after The Reform was officially launched, I visited Pliva, a phar-

* The Reform with capital letters stands for the latest and most radical revamping of economic and social life, as distinct from the previous experiments and changes. Officially it began in July 1965.

maceutical factory in Zagreb. The management was, of course, very much in favor of The Reform, which by reducing the fiscal burden on enterprises sought to increase the share of the income allocated to them from 51 to 71 per cent. There was much talk about the foreign exchange system, investments, and exports. Yet it was a short encounter with an unskilled female blue-collar worker that gave me a real insight into the social realities behind the statistics. She was working more or less as a cleaning woman in the factory, having come to Zagreb about eighteen months earlier. When she told me that she was earning between 45,000 to 50,000 dinars and staying in a rented room with her husband, also employed by Pliva, I vividly imagined how difficult they must find life in the Croatian capital. Then she added that they had just bought land and were building a house in the suburbs. "How can you afford to build a house?" I asked, not hiding my amazement. "We got a bank credit of 60,000 dinars and another loan," she replied. "But how will you pay back the credit plus interest?" Her answer was again straightforward. "We have not sold our farm, but leased it to relatives and neighbors." One did not need to calculate long to figure out that this unskilled worker lived considerably better than the engineers of Pliva with a take-home pay of 100,000 to 110,000 dinars.

No less than 1.65 million of the employed belong to the mixed income category. They are in fact worker-peasants or peasant-workers, taxing the communal services and paying contributions from only a part of their actual earnings. It is estimated that 40 per cent of the workers still live in rural communities; in Zagreb the Croat union leader Milutin Baltic told me that about three-quarters of the unskilled workers are commuters from nearby villages. The rapid urbanization was due not only to the attractions of urban communities, but perhaps even more to the prohibitive taxes levied on the five million private farmers working on almost 90 per cent of the arable land with their holdings restricted to 10 hectares. On top of this, agricultural prices were until the mid-sixties kept at artificially low levels, and only a fraction of the funds was channeled to the agrarian section, mainly to the favored socialist segment, the state farms operating in the most fertile regions of the country.

The rural exodus went ahead at a much faster pace than the demand for workers in the socialist sector, swelling the "pool" of unskilled labor. This in turn led to steadily increasing unemployment, decreasing productivity, and a rising spiral in the cost of urban housing and communal services. One cannot in fairness put all the blame for the difficult problem of unemployment on the new Yugoslavia. Rural overpopulation has long plagued all the Balkan countries. According to conservative estimates, 43 per cent of the peasants, or five million people in the countryside, before the war were "superfluous." Overpopulation in this context means the surplus over the number of rural producers who, under European conditions, can meet average standards.[40]

The obsession, even under the decentralized system, with over-all industrial growth instead of selective growth did not, however, help to solve chronic ills. Indeed in the long run it aggravated some of them. Agriculture was neglected and exploited, despite the fact that a rapidly rising demand for food for the growing urban and industrial population, not to mention the millions of foreign tourists, could not be satisfied and made ever increasing imports of food necessary, thus contributing to a rising balance of payments deficit. To make things even worse, Yugoslavia has one of the highest rates of population growth in Europe, owing to the "demographic explosion" in the most backward areas among the Macedonians, Bosnians, and the one million Albanian minority.

The rising rates of unemployment and later emigration were a bitter pill for a Communist government to swallow, the more so since Communist theory holds that large-scale unemployment is "inherently impossible" under the conditions of a socialist system based on public ownership of the means of production. Yugoslavia has, however, faced up to the unpalatable truth. It became the first Communist country to publish exact figures about the number of workless, employment trends, and emigration. Even before The Reform really started to hit the inefficient plants, there were by the end of 1967 about 260,000 unemployed officially registered with the labor exchanges, not including 60,000 university or college graduates looking in vain for jobs. If one adds to this figure those working abroad, the "real" rate of unemployment would be almost 15 per cent, or, if one counts only the migrant workers who left during the last two years, just over 10 per cent.[41]

In plain words, this means that there are nearly 600,000 people either jobless or working abroad compared to an over-all labor force of three million in the socialist economy, excluding administrative and social services. The government has wisely made a virtue out of necessity and undertaken a variety of measures to organize and control emigration and to attract back as much as possible of the migrants' earnings with the bait of special interest rates and favorable terms for purchasing cars and consumer durables. Migrants' remittances almost doubled to 100 million dollars in 1966 and are making an increasingly precious contribution to the shaky payments balance. While other Communist governments let out only a trickle of tourists and for the time being at least would not even dream of allowing hundreds of thousands of their proud socialist citizens to be "exploited" by foreign capitalists, the Yugoslavs are becoming more and more business-minded, weighing the advantages and disadvantages of migrants. The press and the officials freely admit that, given the existing domestic situation, they can see only blessings, such as fat remittances, acquisition of new skills, and a reduction in the amount of unconcealed unemployment. In fact, any slackening of demand in the West for foreign workers would be a severe loss. It is amusing, but also typical, that Yugoslav newspapers followed the 1966–67 recession in Germany with anxiety instead, as one might have expected, of being light-hearted about this confirmation of the "inevitable doom of capitalism."

Aside from the ominous sign of highly skilled people accounting for a steadily larger proportion of the emigrants, the medicine required for a real cure of the economy and its long-term integration into the international division of labor would be a drastic cutting down of featherbedding in industrial enterprises, and thus even more unemployment. Over the years I have heard many unofficial estimates from economic experts. Some estimated that 500,000 workers, office employees, and low-ranking bureaucrats in the state and local governments would have to be dismissed or shifted to other branches; others, that 20 to 30 per cent of the existing enterprises will ultimately have to be closed down if The Reform is to be a success. Until there is a major structural change, Yugoslavia cannot hope to be internationally competitive, yet nobody is willing to face the immense political risk of launching a frontal and politically premature attack on the ailing and in fact incurable segment of the economy.

"Our basic and continuous problem is that a poor small Balkan country wants to get rich quickly, and how should one reduce the pain to a minimum? Or in other words: Should the government be a government of the rich or one of the poor?" This is how Leo Mates, former Undersecretary of State and Ambassador to the

United Nations, one of the far-sighted thinkers, sees the nature of the dilemma. The conflict between what is spiritually desired and what is economically needed, between social considerations and economic viability, between mitigating the effects or dealing with the causes, is at the root of the economic problem. But the only way to change the causes is political.

What makes a Communist system, even at its mildest as in Yugoslavia, difficult to bear for the average citizen is that it is so conditioned and animated by the device of campaign and concerted mobilization that in a sense it simply cannot stand still. Thus since The Reform got underway it has become fashionable for everyone to insist that he is in favor of this "surgical operation." This is the repeat performance of the shadow boxing that characterized the previous battles between centralists and decentralists. On countless trips to Yugoslavia, I have never met a single manager, economist, or political bureaucrat who would speak out against self-government as such or against The Reform. As the central organ of the party pointed out barely three months after The Reform started with a batch of economic measures, including the promulgation of some forty laws, "There is, of course, no frontal attack against The Reform, but attempts to dilute and distort its aims through compromises and concessions. Nobody denies the necessity of certain sacrifices provided it is not 'my collective, my commune, my region.' Similarly, everyone recognizes that one should not yield to localistic and separatistic demands endangering over-all aims, provided they affect someone else."[42]

The Reform's original intention was a genuinely creative attempt to put the country on an internationally competitive level. As such, it is not a campaign but a painful and long-drawn-out adjustment to economic realities. As Leo Mates told me with an ironic smile, "Many politicians cannot or do not want to grasp the fact that The Reform is not a storm which will later subside, but an entry into the open sea where there will no longer be calm." One of the architects of the great experiment, forty-eight-year-old Kiro Gligorov, said in a private conversation two years after the official launching that The Reform might last for well over a decade and that its most difficult phase was still ahead. This able Macedonian rose in the ranks of the federal state apparatus from being one of the numerous assistant secretaries of the government to Finance Minister and then to Deputy Premier within a period of five years. His successful career was in no small degree due to remaining faithful to the golden rule he formulated as early as 1961 in a talk: "We have no dogmatic prejudices, none whatsoever. . . ."

Who could imagine that a high-ranking Communist leader would go on television and discuss, before millions of viewers, without a touch of false optimism, the crisis in employment. That is what Kiro Gligorov did in April 1967, the day after our conversation. The whole thing would have been as incredible two years earlier as the now-routine weekly television programs or open-ended discussions about party reorganization, prices, and the salaries of top officials. Unemployment and the threat of a rise in the number of workless was perhaps the main topic in the country in 1967. "We should rid ourselves of the illusion of full employment," Gligorov stated flatly and added that "a complete solution is a question of decades."

What then is a partial solution? The only avenues of escape seem to be inducements to the peasants to return to or stay on the land, the creation of new jobs in the service, or tertiary activities. Both remedies are, of course, risky in a Communist country where the state and local bureaucracy in administration and in economy has been imbued with a crusading spirit against private property and the pernicious capitalist methods of "exploitation of man by man," and is also genuinely alarmed about the threat to "socialist relationships." The campaign against the rapidly expanding private sector has not, to be sure, sprung from purely ideological motivations, but rather from a very real fear of a dynamic competition that might show up many small enterprises as being inefficient. This in turn would place the position of local functionaries and "socialist businessmen" in grave jeopardy.

Though the farmers are still second-class citizens in the political sense of the word, who are not represented in legislative bodies—which means that almost half of the population is outside the self-government system altogether, there is no doubt that they and the producers of basic raw materials were the "winners" of the initial phase of the economic spring-cleaning. Under the impact of more realistic prices and the breaking of many financial shackles, the peasant holdings became more interested in production, and aided by good weather the entire agricultural sector surged ahead. A record maize harvest in 1965 and peak wheat production the following year, as well as steeply rising exports of basic and processed farm products, helped the balance of payments and gave a push to consumer demand. Over-all farm output in 1967 was up 11 per cent over the figures for 1965, and the private farmers are estimated to have earned 180 million dollars more than during the preceding period.

One of the more depressing features of trips to Communist-ruled countries are visits to the collective farms patterned after the Russian kolkhoz. While it may be true that every revolution must break up the peasantry, because only by the destruction of the peasant economy can the society gain sufficient surplus from agriculture to invest in industry, the Communist regimes "succeeded" so well in taking the scraps of land from the smallholders by naked force and threat that they have plunged their countries into a chronic agricultural crisis. On paper, the fiercely individualistic peasants have become wage earners and obedient members of the collective farms, who are usually allowed to move to the towns or change their residence only with an official permit. In reality, they are prisoners of war, still hoping for a change and riveting all their attention and care on tiny private plots, usually up to half a hectare, they have been permitted to keep. Thus whenever Communist governments are forced to do something about the plight of agriculture they are compelled to make concessions to the proprietary instincts of the peasants; they increase their tiny private plots, allot more fodder to their private livestock (usually one cow, a couple of pigs, and some poultry), and increase purchasing prices.

Since Yugoslavia abandoned forcible collectivization in 1953, the socialist sector has been increased only by the purchase of land or by economic cooperation. But even as late as 1963–64 agriculture accounted for only about 9 per cent of the total investments; during the period of Stalinism until the early fifties, the figure stood at a mere 4 per cent.[43] The policy of increasing the socialist sector through more subtle pressures on the pirvate farmers has undergone many changes; there has never, however, been a return to the open coercion of the past.

In the long run, small peasant holdings with an average of 4.4 hectares (almost 30 per cent of the farms have fewer than two hectares) are uneconomic and must cooperate with one another in some form to exploit their unused capacities, to utilize improved techniques of production, to market their surplus, and to get sufficient credits. By "socialism in the village" the Yugoslav leaders, sobered by past experiences, mean respect for and maintenance of private land ownership, combined with a close cooperation with the socialist enterprises. This cannot be done through exhortations, let alone covert threats, but only with the bait of attractive financial incentives and tangible advantages for the peasants who, not without reason, are suspicious and distrustful of government initiatives as such. The example of the state farms, where the productivity is at least twice as high as on the collective farms, sounds highly attractive in the official Yugoslav publications, but less so to the obstinate and often semi-educated peasants tenaciously clinging to land they have owned for at least a generation.

On a Sunday in April 1966, about nine months after the drastic change in agricultural price policies as part of The Reform, I drove to the village of Martince in Serbia, about fifteen miles off the main road between Belgrade and Zagreb. The untarred, potholed road shook the car mercilessly, and the little village surrounded by flat, rich land lay in guileless isolation. It looked like most of the villages in the Pannonian Plains, which comprise the fertile regions of Hungary and Rumania—a couple of grocery stores, a few shops, a movie house, and the ubiquitous "House of Culture" serving the threefold purpose of a snack bar, conference hall, and club.

Though only some 3 per cent of the land in Yugoslavia is farmed collectively (6 per cent by state farms and other agricultural enterprises), I had decided to see what a Yugoslav "collective farm" looked like. The talks began in a small circle with the chairman of the cooperative and three members of the managing board. It being a Sunday morning, however, we were joined by more and more peasants. By the end there were some two dozen people in the small room and I was able to gauge the temper of the place.

Martince has about 4,500 inhabitants, and until 1953 the whole village was one large collective farm. Now there are 238 full members who work the land acquired by nationalization or through compulsory sales over the 10-hectare limit. But there are also 600 private farmers associated with the cooperative. Half of them leased over 50 per cent of their holdings, the rest less than that, to the cooperative. The entire area farmed by the cooperative embraces 5,470 hectares, of which 3,270 belong to private farmers who are members of the cooperative. It is run under workers' management similar to that in industry; it produces maize, wheat, and sugar beet, and raises livestock.

Aside from the fact that anyone can quit the cooperative at any time, the important point is that it is organized and run along strictly business lines. In some cases it farms the land of private farmers on a share-crop and cash basis for the duration of one or two crop years, according to a contract. Cooperation has many different forms, but it is always based on the principle that profit is shared in proportion to the contribution made by each partner, and profits are calculated for each individual business deal. The cooperative provides tractors, seeds, fertilizers, weed killers, etc., and employs twelve agricultural engineers to advise members on technical matters and provide other services.

The Martince cooperative also buys and sells the crops and livestock from the farmers and acts as chief distributor of investment funds and loans to private farmers. One of the most profitable forms of cooperation is supplying pedigree stock to private farmers for breeding. One of the most successful breeders, a thirty-four-year-old private farmer, joined our round table discussion toward noon. He had delivered 140 pigs to the cooperative. Well-dressed and self-confident, he had just sold his Volkswagen and bought a new model.

As a result of price adjustments, the cooperative had increased its net earnings by 15 per cent. After a heated debate, my hosts calculated that the average cash earnings amounted to 100,000 dinars monthly. Although the figure was as much as a skilled worker or a young engineer in industry earned at that time, I suspect it was an exceedingly cautious estimate. The cooperative can export its products freely and import whatever it desires, provided foreign exchange is available. For example, the Martince farmers sold 200 wagonloads of maize to Bulgaria and other countries. They wisely insisted on payment in dollars, and the management was able to import some badly needed heavy machinery from Western Germany.

In contrast to Bulgarian and Rumanian villages where one sees only bicycles, scooters, and motorcycles, Martince—that is, its inhabitants and not the cooperative as such—could boast at the time of my visit, according to a quick improvised count among my conversation partners, of possessing seventeen small and medium tractors, fifteen cars, and five trucks. In short, the cooperatives that are based on voluntary association in the form of contracts with peasants resemble the cooperative ventures one would expect to find in the Scandinavian countries and have hardly anything in common

with the collective farms of the Soviet Union or elsewhere in Eastern Europe.

The two and a half years since the major change in agricultural
policies have given a tremendous push to the purchase and import
of tractors and other machinery by the private peasants. Whether
or not they are working with the cooperatives, the farmers, particularly in the fertile regions of Serbia and Croatia, are spending
more freely than at any time since the war. The imports of trucks
and tractors in 1967 trebled in comparison with the previous year.

Yugoslavia in the sixties is passing through a fundamental social
upheaval in which many cherished myths and old assumptions are
at last being questioned. Within this ferment, the liveliest and often
most vicious controversies revolve around the private sector, in both
agriculture and the services. Granted that without furthering
private initiative there is no hope of absorbing even a part of the
labor surplus, at what point will the coddling of the private entrepreneurs pose a danger to the socialist system? Can one encourage
small-scale commodity production which, as Lenin once said, breeds
capitalism "every hour, every day"? What is to be done if it obviously also breeds prosperity, provides jobs, and stimulates demand for products of the socially owned industry?

Repression is unquestionably the safest and surest way to quell
political fears. But it also ruins a potentially significant segment and
adds to the grave problems besetting the rest of the economy. Decentralization inevitably brings in its wake a variety of attitudes
toward private farmers and entrepreneurs. As soon as private producers are doing well, especially if they indulge in "conspicuous
consumption," some communal authorities immediately clamp down
and levy hefty local taxes, thereby stifling initiative at the very beginning. Other communes, particularly in the more developed and
outward-looking areas, try to protect the hens that lay golden eggs—
for the local authorities as well as for themselves.

The most frustrating agricultural restriction is, of course, the 10-
hectare limit for peasant holdings. This is prescribed even in the
new Constitution of 1963. But none other than a commission
of the party's Central Committee, or, more correctly, the majority
opinion, came to the conclusion in the autumn of 1967 that "there
should be no fear even of increasing the maximum limit for private
arable land to 15 or 20 hectares."[44] The makers of agricultural
machinery realized that the rising demand for their products and

for building materials offered an unexpected chance. The peasants grasped the simple fact that German or Italian machinery was cheaper than the homemade product. The mutual and simultaneous realization of this truth not unnaturally tangled the issue in a mesh of disputes about the advisability of restricting imports, increasing tariffs, or introducing import quotas. The basic fact is, however, that a new and steadily enlarging market for all kinds of agricultural machinery has appeared. A Croat official underlined the situation by comparing Yugoslavia, where there is one tractor for every 400 hectares, with Germany (one for 7 hectares), France (one for 18), and Italy (one for 28). With the six republics of Yugoslavia gaining ever-increasing competences, it is quite possible that, even if there were a stalemate at the federal level, Croatia or Slovenia might take the plunge and single-handedly increase the size of the holdings.

Tempers are still more inflamed and problems more varied when private artisans or caterers appear on the scene. If an enterprising individual decides to build a small motel with a snack bar on the Adriatic coast or opens a shop in a Serbian city, he virtually places a time bomb in the midst of the local political "establishment." There it is, the country-wide political agony in a minute mirror— What to do with this "personalized" private sector? Soon weighty political discussions tinged with envy start in the countless committees of political organizations. The communal committee puts the case on its agenda and consults the local party organization. Then follow the sessions of the veterans, the socialist women, the socialist youth, the "Socialist Alliance of Working People," and all other bodies with the exception of the Boy Scouts, all dealing with the same "socio-economic issue": Should one allow the entrepreneur to earn more money than the "working people," or should one nip this "socio-economic" danger in the bud under some convenient pretext? All this is not a malicious satire, but very real, albeit with the important proviso that the impressive list of political bodies actually embraces only a very small circle, often consisting of the same people; they may step forward at one meeting as old fighters, at the next as tested Communists, and at the third as "puzzled" socialist citizens.

There have been what the Yugoslavs call "two crusades" against private artisans and caterers; the first in the immediate postwar period, the second in 1962 when Marshal Tito and the centralists made what was apparently their last concerted effort to tighten the reins on everything. The campaign went ahead at such a dizzy pace that soon not only electricians and pastry shops, but also barbers and watchmakers became "scarcities," and the public vented its anger in a flood of letters-to-editors. Tito himself was compelled to issue warnings against the local hotheads in January 1963, and soon afterward parliament alleviated the excessive fiscal burdens put on the private sector and passed more liberal regulations about the maximum number of employees. Caterers were allowed to have a staff of three and artisans five.

The confidence of the people in the promises of the government and particularly in the economic common sense of the local authorities had, however, been thoroughly shaken. By 1964 only some 102,000 private workshops were registered, less than in 1959. But economic liberalization and the staggering increase in the number of foreign tourists spending their holidays in Yugoslavia have gradually created the conditions for a new upswing.

Although old-timers still eye the private entrepreneur with unconcealed disgust, the dynamism of private initiative has surpassed the most optimistic expectations and caught even the powerful opposition off its guard. With 20 million foreigners passing through and millions staying in the country, with the foreign currency intake multiplying within a few years to over 200 million dollars in 1967, the provision of lodgings, motels, restaurants, snack bars, and other services has become the single most crucial bottleneck and limiting factor on the boom. Yugoslavia is participating in the European tourist traffic only to the extent of 1.2 per cent. With a scenically magnificent 1,238-mile long Adriatic coast and breathtakingly beautiful mountainous regions, there are virtually no limits to the expansion of tourism—provided the Yugoslavs improve the tertiary sector and communications and do not price themselves out of this intensely competitive business.

In the fifties the coastal area was as beautiful and certainly more romantic than today, but almost completely devoid of roads, let alone facilities. One by one the beaches began to be connected by a highway, built partly by World Bank loans. By 1963 a large stretch was completed, and the spaces of a seemingly limitless coast have now been filled in. Yet the greatest difference has been the emergence of countless small and attractive motels, cafeterias, and restaurants, owned and run by private entrepreneurs. Many municipalities help people building four- to six-room houses with the explicit purpose of catering to tourists. The price of an overnight stay in such a private house is usually about $1.25, of which the communal authorities pocket 30 to 40 cents. The builders are mostly employees in the "socialist sector," mainly from the "peasant-worker" category.

There are also far more ambitious ventures, and many entrepreneurs violate the legal restrictions by employing ten or even twenty persons with the tacit approval of the communes. The expansion has been so unexpectedly rapid that there are no over-all statistics. In Serbia alone, more than 12,000 handicraft shops were set up in 1965–66. There are many new restaurants in the suburbs of Belgrade, Zagreb, Ljubljana, and other big cities as well as in the countryside. In Croatia, by the autumn of 1967, about 80 per cent of the road haulage was done by privately owned trucks whose number had doubled to 17,000 in eighteen months. The association of Croatian authorities issued decrees entitling artisans, caterers, and teamsters to health, retirement, and accident insurance. The association of private artisans in Belgrade estimated that at least 100,000 new workshops would be opened once health insurance regulations became more liberal there.

This private sector could eventually offer several hundreds of thousands of people employment. Since the beginning of 1966 the most authoritative Communist papers have stressed that "there is nothing inherently wrong or immoral if someone—by our standards —earns a lot of money, provided it is a reward for his own efficiency." Whether enterprises are going concerns can be tested only in the market—this is, at least in theory, one of the key principles of The Reform. When, for instance, a socialist enterprise in the town of Sombor leased to private entrepreneurs four cafeterias that had been operating at a loss, and the same places with the same staff became flourishing businesses within a few months, the advantages of private initiative could not be denied. As a popular Belgrade daily remarked, "The working day has certainly become longer, but the monthly take-home pay, previously often a mere 25,000 dinars, has also increased to 250,000 dinars!"

No wonder the newspapers do their best to convince those local politicians who, in the words of *Borba*, believe they are performing great services for socialism when they hinder the opening of workshops or levy prohibitively high taxes on the owners. "Does the

ghost of capitalism haunt the private shops?" The Zagreb paper
Vjesnik u Srijedu posed the rhetorical question only to reply with a
firm "No," since it is self-evident that private catering establish-
ments flourish where socialist ones fail, and one cannot judge "the
level of socialist relationships" by the presence or absence of private
enterprise in retailing, handicraft, or catering. Economists point out
that "under the conditions of a socialist economy, private property
need not necessarily lead to a capitalist relationship, but can be
completely integrated into the socialist system."[45] It is quite
evident that despite the mortal danger of the "exploitation of man
by man" the socialist citizens of this socialist country gladly take
that risk and suffer from "exploitation" if they can double or treble
their earnings.

These issues are not secondary matters on the fringes of great
political debates but the hard core of transition, doubt, and dissent
in a society where nothing seems as simple as it used to be. Economic realities and technological compulsion, not political will or
ideological precepts, trigger the chain reaction that challenges the
values of the system itself.*

Socially, politically, economically, Yugoslavia is in a state of flux.
It is no longer a separate and self-sufficient entity, isolated from the
whirlpool of change in the West. I never understood this so clearly
as in a chance encounter with an old Serbian farmer. Coming from
Rumania, I gave him a lift from near the border to the next village.
When I told him how lucky the Yugoslav peasants were compared
to their opposite numbers in Rumania and Bulgaria, he nodded approvingly: "I know it. We got back our land after the trouble with
Stalin. Yes, you are right, we live better than those over there. But
I also know through my son and other relatives who worked there
how the Austrian and Swiss peasants live. But how can I scrape
together three and a half million dinars for a small tractor? The ten
hectares are just not enough. . . ."

His remarks reflected in microcosm the crucial dilemma of the
Yugoslav regime. The old man, like my next hitchhiker, a young
student who had just returned from a trip to Vienna and was planning to travel to Italy during the holidays, was so far removed
from conditions in other Communist-ruled countries that he was

---

* During the student riots in June 1968 in Belgrade, the pent-up bitterness
of the young erupted primarily in such slogans as "Down with the Red Bourgeoisie! We demand social equality!"

not even aware of the tremendous differences. Friends in Belgrade teased me after I held forth about their "privileged life" compared to the conditions I had just witnessed in the neighboring countries. They would organize lectures to be held in small circles, they said, so that "our morale will be improved."

Alexis de Tocqueville long ago noted that a little progress is a dangerous thing: ". . . experience teaches us that, generally speaking, the most perilous moment for a bad government is one when it seeks to mend its ways."[46] The social upheavals in Yugoslavia, so often ignored by casual observers who subdivide this dynamic process into static, isolated elements, strikingly confirm the truth of Tocqueville's celebrated dictum. A good statistical case can be made that in the past decade Yugoslavs have made significant gains. But this has helped only to whet their appetite for more, rather than to satisfy it.

Alone among the East Europeans, Yugoslavs can get out of their country; passports, valid for two years and an unlimited number of journeys, are issued almost as readily as in a Western country. For twenty countries visas have been abolished. Almost 3 million people, 15 per cent of the total population, traveled abroad in 1967, mainly to Italy, Austria, and Germany. In other words, Yugoslavs look to the West and not the East as a yardstick to measure the scope and pace of domestic progress. Given a glimpse of the "promised land," what earlier could be borne in apathy—relative poverty, lack of opportunity, backward environment, the ignorance of the decision-makers—becomes intolerable.

The daring program to save the system by radical reform, to create some kind of unity and stability out of dissension and restiveness, is implemented amid controversies so acute that victors and losers alike are embittered. On occasion, these terms even become interchangeable. But there have been changes in the decision-makers as well as among the population at large. The passage of time has had a profound impact on the political climate, once exclusively dominated by leftist radical extremism.

The crusading zeal of the Communist activists has ebbed. They no longer set the tone of the country. The opening of the borders has been accompanied by a heightened sophistication about the world and Yugoslavia's place in it. A spreading skepticism and disenchantment is setting its stamp on the youth who are fed to the teeth with slogans and blocked from the jobs for which they had been trained. Once awakened and given a breath of hope, educated Yugoslavs are not willing to suffer patiently the barriers of ignorance erected against a civilized existence.

As Bakaric once put it, "Centralization versus decentralization is often posed in the fashion of should I alone or five of us have the power to decide. But the basis does not change. Giving freedom in little spoonfuls cannot be a genuine solution."[47] The savage conflicts of the new Yugoslavia are not about a single party or multiparty system, capitalism or socialism. The battle waged at all levels is between the solidarity of "equal stomachs" and progress by higher productivity linked to higher incomes, between ignorance and efficiency, between rule by consent and rule by command, between technocratic dynamism and bureaucratic immobilism.

What happens when group pressures collide, when the interests of different plants or regions clash? Who should decide if there are conflicts and tensions between group interests? The reformers say: the market mechanism, controlled and influenced by an increasingly pluralistic society. The conservatives say, or rather whisper: the party controlled by a self-appointed, tested top leadership. This contradiction lies at the heart of the power situation in Yugoslavia.

The party in search of a role

"The party wants to lead—but it does not know where to," remarked the high-ranking Yugoslav official, and then almost as an afterthought added, "in fact, the real problem is what to do with the party as such." In a sense the relationship between the Communist party and the decentralized system resembles a marriage in which neither partner can live with or without the other. Instead of remaining an infallible supreme mediator of group interests and a center of unity keeping economic and administrative decentralization within bounds, the party with over 1 million members, 35,000 cells, and countless committees finds itself in a blind alley, in public search of a role, in the midst of a desperate attempt to save itself through radical reform.

In theory, the party is the vanguard, the motor, the inspirer of progressive social developments. In fact, it has used the elaborate devices of self-management and decentralization merely as a front to mask the unimpaired monopolistic concentration of superior power in the hands of the top party chiefs. In theory, since 1952, the party has carried out its political and ideological activities chiefly by persuasion and is not a direct leader. In fact, its entire machine, the apparat, has had a vested interest in maintaining the party as the one and only center of political power on as large a scale as possible.

The trouble with the decentralization experiments was that they succeeded too well. The dynamic forces unleashed by the leadership in the early fifties began to erode the center's power to control the economy, the regional and national conflicts, and ultimately the party itself. It is the measure of this failure that the institutional clashes, which the party wanted to confine if not eliminate, became, through the very efforts of those in power, ever more aggravated until they reached the point at which not only the reform but the federal state of six republics was at stake.

The halfway and quarterway solutions so typical of the entire period from 1952 onward cannot be explained by the confusing pattern of reconciliation and discord with Moscow or by Marshal Tito's ambitions in the international arena. It is the deep contradiction between product and creator, the democratic core of a theory of industrial democracy and market socialism however imperfect, and the totalitarian character of a single party dictatorship, no matter what image it projects, that provide the breeding ground for the problems and also for the lack of trust. Regardless of the self-management legislation, there has been a sharpening split between the real decision-makers accountable to no one and the risk-takers who have had to bear responsibility for implementing decisions.

Witnesses to a yawning gap between lofty principles and disappointing practice, the people refuse to believe what the party tells them it is doing and plans to do. The mass media and a vast organization fed the population an endless diet of lengthy explanations about the party's functions. Yet in the autumn of 1967 when an opinion poll was organized among 340 Slovenian high school students, the results were astonishing. Asked if they knew all the tasks and the role of the party, 81 per cent answered, "Not well enough," and 9 per cent flatly declared "they were not aware of its role at all." A somewhat different poll was carried out by the Social Science Institute in Belgrade. The pollsters asked a sample cross section of adults what they knew about the party reform, which by then had been in the foreground of public discussions and elaborated in numerous articles and speeches for over a year. Sixty-six per cent admitted they had no idea whatsoever what the party reorganization meant.

The confusion is if anything worse in the ranks of the party itself. The leaders have been split for a fairly long time over the basic political and economic issues. Marshal Tito and the majority of his closest collaborators in the Belgrade center, mainly Serbs and Montenegrins, never intended to allow the various experiments to weaken the chain of top-to-bottom political command or alter the basic organizational structure of the totalitarian state. The tensions, difficulties, and dissonances appeared to these men, accustomed to unlimited and uncontrolled power, as temporary in nature; to be resolved by the old technique of applying new names to the same realities, devising some new institutions, and issuing proclamations promising palliative measures. The leadership as a whole, not to mention the tens of thousands of activists, have all along conspicuously lacked the psychological readiness to take the medicine required for a cure.

One of the ablest and perhaps most down to earth of the Yugoslav philosophers, Mihajlo Markovic, has exposed the dilemma facing the leaders succinctly and soberly. "An underdeveloped predominantly rural society cannot avoid that phase of development in which an elite, in the best of cases a genuinely revolutionary elite, will try to create, through maximum mobilization of the masses and use of coercion conditions necessary for self-government, i.e. industry, working class, an intelligentsia, school system, and mass culture. The question however arises, that once those conditions are attained, will this elite find moral strength to decide voluntarily to go on to the essential part of a socialist revolution: the establishment of self-government and consequently its own elimination as a power elite? Or will a few decades of intense power concentration change its social structure to the point where it will want to be the personification of society, to preserve its political and material privileges forever and be not only the brain but also the iron fist of the historical process?"[48]

For fifteen years the answer to this basic question was a qualified "Yes." In fact, however, at every crucial juncture, whenever the issue was at razor's edge, the answer was a firm "No." In no society, and least of all in one ruled by a militant ideologically inspired party, do bureaucrats wish to deprive themselves of their functions, power, and jobs. The paradox of the Yugoslav experiments lay in

the often-forgotten fact that they have had to be implemented by the
state bureaucracy and the party machine. In plain words, the opponents of the reform are the ones to decide how far the experiments
can go—experiments which, if successful, would cut the very
branches on which they are perched.

The turbulent developments in Yugoslav economic and political
life fully confirm the truth of the assessment made by a keen observer of Communist economics: "In general, effective decentralization in a centrally administered economy can take place only
when carried out on a very broad front all at once, which requires
intervention from higher quarters and calls for big political battles.
Centralization, however, can and often does proceed in little steps,
virtually unnoticed but important in aggregate impact."[49] By putting
on the brakes discreetly or giving the gas too soon, high government
bureaucracy at all levels frustrated the attempts at creating a workable market mechanism and strove to discredit industrial democracy.

It is difficult enough to secure balanced growth and rational and
optimum allocation and use of resources in a democratic country.
Under the conditions of technologically primitive Yugoslavia and in
the framework of a unique system in flux, political interference has
caused abrupt alterations between "stop" and "go" policies, between
too high investments or too rapid growth of distributed incomes.
The domestic consequence of extremely high investment rates,
reaching 30 to 35 per cent of the GNP in most years, due partly to
inefficient employment of capital, has been a chronic inflationary
pressure. To curb excessive demand, price controls had to be introduced, which in turn slowed down the transition to rational
prices. This, however, is the essential condition before "market
socialism" can become a reality.

Thus measures giving the economy more elbowroom have been
followed by backsliding into economic and political recentraliza-
tion at the top level. High bureaucracy blamed enterprise autonomy
and reckless spending, and identified technical progress with centralism. The workers became puzzled and increasingly embittered
outsiders, reacting emotionally to the intricate complex of technical
problems with which only experts can competently deal. Many
workers' councils began to avail themselves of the possibility of
taking funds from their enterprise money bags indiscriminately, regardless of how much they had put in.

Between 1961 and 1966, during the great battle over the future direction of the entire system, Yugoslavia at times seemed to have the worst of both worlds—of decentralization at the bottom and centralization at the top, freedom to spend at enterprise level because a "socialist factory cannot go bankrupt" and someone will save it, and freedom to allocate investments by the political decision-makers without due regard for economic efficiency because the center was outside the mechanism of social control. No matter how formidable the economic problems (which in any case could not be solved within the borders of a small market), the real roots of the economic and social evils lay in the political distribution of income by a handful of decision-makers at the apex and in political interference at all levels.

Bureaucratic centralism and not "anarchic self-management" was primarily responsible for the sharpening economic and political tensions between the nations within the federal state. As Edward Kardelj, then President of the Federal Parliament, pointed out in November 1965, the common cause of mounting tensions was to be found in the administrative system: "So long as there is a big 'federal cake' created by administrative methods, it can be distributed only on the basis of subjective administrative-political decisions. So long as there are federal cakes, there will also be republican and communal cakes. . . . Our main weakness is that we are always complaining about national, republican, and local pressures, but then either negate them or deal with them on the basis of equalization [of incomes]. The economy must be freed of political intervention, it must be de-politicized."[50]

What does the ugly word "de-politicization" mean in plain English? It means that everybody, from managers to communal officials, from bankers to ministers, should make and not only implement decisions without the direct interference of the political bodies. "Party discipline must not replace the responsibility toward the voters. The government must not hide behind the Executive Committee of the party or the managers behind the local party organisation."[51] In other words, responsibility should be placed actually and not only verbally where it belongs—on the shoulders of the republican governments and parliaments, of enterprises and communes. The formal institutions of workers' self-management and administrative self-government should be infused with real meaning, because economic reform cannot be successfully carried through without political reform.

All this has been particularly sharply stressed by many authoritative party spokesmen since the plenary session of the Central Committee in October 1966 decided to prepare a radical reorganization of the party. As the newly elected Secretary of the Executive Committee, Mijalko Todorovic, put it: "From top to bottom the party organs should divest themselves of executive functions. If the League of Communists wants to take the lead in reforming society, it must reform itself during this phase. . . . Without reorganization, the League would turn into one of the main impediments to social development." The Macedonian party leader and one of the foremost reformers, Krste Crvenkovski, enunciated the bitter truth: "Nothing essential has happened since the Sixth Congress in 1952 when we proclaimed that the party should no longer be a factor of authority but rather a political, ideological guiding force. Our problem is the realization of this concept. . . . Reorganization should break the long monopoly held by small groups of men at the highest level." He even went so far as to plead for a full-scale reassessment of the classic organizational formula of democratic centralism, on the ground that democracy had been merely a shield for rigid centralism. In numerous public statements he stressed the need to replace the "pretence of a monolithic unity which actually never existed" by a pluralistic party in which interest groups would be free to maneuver so that ultimately legalized factions or a "loyal opposition" might emerge.[52]

Yet it took nearly fifteen years to reach the point at which the crucial issues could be posed publicly. Three or four years earlier, people went to prison, journalists lost their jobs, and periodicals were suppressed if they dared to refer to the party as the backbone of the bureaucratic system, a dead weight on progress, and the inviolable shelter for bureaucracy and conservativism.

There were two turning points—in 1952–53 and 1961–62—when Marshal Tito still had enough authority to give the regime a broader and more democratic basis, to translate lofty principles into facts without tearing asunder the very fabric of the system. The first occasion arose after the Sixth Party Congress, in connection with the Djilas affair; the second chance was offered when the reformers launched a major initiative to put the country on a self-supporting basis and gradually to eliminate the economic roots of the national tensions. On both occasions, Tito remained true to his early leftist extremism, although now in the guise of an elder statesman. He opted for bureaucratic immobilism as against forward-looking dynamism, for centralism instead of decentralization, for the vested interests of the party machine as opposed to the democratization of social control. His choice was to no small degree shaped by his Comintern schooling, by his personal aspirations to play the role of a triumphant and vindicated pacemaker in a changing Communist world movement, by his willingness to jeopardize the interests of a small Balkan country for the sake of a dubious and precarious partnership with Moscow and his ambitions as a ranking leader of the Third World.

One of the misconceptions among casual observers is to regard Tito as a man who has been moving the party in the direction the "liberals" want to go, but who has set a pace slow enough to win the grudging consent of the old guard. This assessment has not been borne out by actual developments. It was only in the period of deadlock between 1964–66, when Tito at last perceived the dimensions of the danger threatening his single most important noncontroversial achievement, the reforged unity of the Yugoslav state, that he became a balance wheel in the basic split at the top. When the cumulative evidence of Rankovic's success in building up a power center of his own, relying on the secret police and the Serbian party apparat began to pose an overt danger to the party line committed to The Reform and a covert challenge to Tito's supreme position, the then seventy-four-year-old leader sided for the first time in party history with the forward-looking forces whom he had only a few years earlier helped to push onto the defensive. The people of Yugoslavia have had to pay an exceedingly high price for Tito's tendency to force the real issues underground and to maintain a highly centralized power structure.

The stormy period from the preparations for the Sixth Congress in November 1952 till the bloodless purge of Djilas serves even today as a reminder and a warning of how a meaningful political reform can be destroyed from within. It is this memory, as well as the subsequent course of the next decade, that explains and no doubt justifies the widespread popular cynicism with regard to the current reorganization of the party.

In 1952–54, while it was revamping the economic and administrative system, the leadership issued a bold summons for a major structural alteration in the role, power, organization, and methods of the ruling party. To make the "Yugoslav road to socialism" different from what the Central Committee had in June 1952 described as the "bureaucratic caste system" of the Soviet Union, the party officials had to transform themselves from bureaucrats into educators, from local commanders into "missionaries." The party had to cease ruling and governing directly, to rely not on orders but on persuasion and setting the proper example. To symbolize the significance of the reforms, the party changed its name to the League of Communists of Yugoslavia, and the Politburo, the supreme organ, was henceforth to be called the Executive Committee. The People's Front, which then had some seven million members and acted as an inefficient "transmission belt" for the party, was renamed the "Socialist Alliance of the Working People of Yugoslavia." The new body was intended to provide a "broad enough platform" to enlist the masses in the task of government and to deal—under the "general ideological leadership" of the Communists—with "concrete political and other social questions."

The new League of Communists proclaimed in the congress resolution: "The League of Communists cannot be and is not the direct operational leader and director of economic, government, and social life. It is rather, by its political and ideological activities, primarily by discussion, to work in all organizations, agencies, and institutions for the adoption of its line and standpoint, through the activities of individual members." The League did not claim a monopoly in determining the political line of "the struggle for the construction of socialist relationships." It also "considers it untenable dogma . . . that absolute monopoly of political power by the Communist party is a universal and 'eternal' principle."[53]

Though the leaders made abundantly clear that there was no question of giving up one-party rule, let alone returning to a multiparty system, the activists among the then 780,000 members, who accounted for almost 8.5 per cent of the adult population, were not surprisingly plunged into a bewildered passivity and ultimately a steadily worsening disarray. It was an unprecedented situation: a party that had built up power through the ruthless suppression of opposition within and without was now supposed to guide, argue with, and prevail over, but not command and bully, the vast majority of the population. Though the congress did not mention the "withering away of the party," Tito himself put this delicate issue on the agenda in the higher party councils. In his authorized biography he is quoted as saying, "The party cannot go on in the same

old way. If the state does not wither away, then the party becomes
. . . an instrument of the state, a force outside society. If the state
really withers away, the party necessarily withers away with it."[54]

By June 1953, under the combined impact of mounting opposition
among the hard core of the party and the international relaxation
following Stalin's death, the Central Committee decided to tighten
up party discipline and curtail "petty-bourgeois-anarchist ideas of
freedom and democracy." The concept of the withering away of
the party, the leadership announced, had been misunderstood. As
Tito said later, "There can be no withering away or winding up of
the League of Communists until the last class enemy has been im-
mobilized, until the broadest body of our citizens are socialist in
outlook."[55] In other words, the new names remained, but nothing
essential had changed in the Communist dictatorship. The radical
statements had in practice no effect at all, and by the end of 1953
about 70,000 "wavering and petty bourgeois" members, who had
taken the go-ahead signal seriously, were expelled from the party.

It was then that a fiery Montenegrin sensed the impasse and,
recognizing the fundamental contradiction in workers' self-management run by the factory cells of a monolithic party, proposed qualitative innovations and not merely verbal juggling with the role
of the party. He was Milovan Djilas, then forty-two, a war
hero and a member of the leading foursome at the apex of the
party, a Partisan general and President of the Federal Assembly, an
ideologist and poet. This rebellious spirit and long-time favorite of
Tito, an erstwhile Stalinist and extreme Communist who in February 1942 was instrumental in proclaiming Montenegro an "integral
part of the Soviet Union" but later became the chief ideologist in
the battle against Stalinism, challenged the ruling faction in a series
of sensational articles.

Whether Tito, as he later said, really read Djilas' articles published in the party organ only "superficially," or whether he wanted
to test the reaction to the impassioned calls for more democracy, is
today irrelevant. The fact remains that Djilas was the first to reveal
the basic conflict between the one-party dictatorship and its brain-
child, the decentralized system and its theory. "There is no alternative but more democracy, more free discussion, more free elections
to social, state, and economic organs, more adherence to the law,"
Djilas wrote. "New ideas are always the ideas of a minority."

Though at that time Djilas had not yet come out in favor of a socialist opposition party, he called for freedom in the party itself, the elimination of unconditional discipline, free conflict of opinions, and the dismantling of the vast apparat of professional functionaries. While his last attack on the mode of living of what he was later to call "the new class" precipitated his fall, a showdown with the overwhelming majority of leadership was in any case inevitable. The "fighters against Stalinism," already blinded by the dizzy prospect of a reconciliation with the heirs of Stalin, wasted no time in isolating and destroying their comrade-in-arms in the best Stalinist fashion. The articles by Djilas, a man with immense authority and prestige, evoked a wide response among many Communists and non-Communists with "deplorable consequences," which Tito observed "increased as fast as a snowball on a sloping roof."

In January 1954 Djilas was expelled from the Central Committee and stripped of all his functions. Living under close police surveillance and socially ostracized, he began an evolution that soon led him to become an advocate of democratic socialism and a multiparty system. His was a unique case in the history of communism. His challenge was a moral and personal act rather than a political defiance in terms of seeking power. As a politician he may have failed. As a thinker, he was far ahead of his time in recognizing the crucial problems of the Yugoslav system. Everything the reformers today say and advocate was spelled out years ago by Milovan Djilas.

More than thirteen years after his fall, Djilas, now a mature and almost serene man, still sees the granting of political freedom, the emergence of currents within the ruling party as the basic issue. While still convinced of the need for at least two socialist parties, Djilas in the spring of 1967, regarded this as a matter for the distant future. "Democracy is a process . . . first of all there must be freedom for the ruling class," he maintains, and he sees no prospects of "revolutionary changes." After nine years and twenty-five days in jail, interrupted by an ill-fated fifteen-month parole in 1961–62, Djilas is unbroken, sovereign and self-contained in his manner, and no longer views the world as black and white. Though now universally recognized as an outstanding writer, he is still deeply involved in politics.

After a four-hour conversation, I left him with the feeling that the last chapter of the Djilas affair is yet to be written. He may land in prison again, or he may live in relative liberty. It is unlikely that in the foreseeable future he will once again beome a leading political figure. But whether in or out of jail, his ideas, his writings, his books, and his presence are bound to have a certain influence on the evolving scene. His personal history—he has spent almost one-third of his adult life in jail, partly under the prewar regime as an illegal Communist, but mainly under the rule of the party he helped to bring to power—conveys a poignant sense of the legends of Yugoslavia, which turn heroes into traitors and traitors into heroes.

Developments have strikingly confirmed Djilas' warnings about the "new enemy," bureaucracy. Despite the adoption of a new party program at the congress in April 1958, which was verbally as progressive as ever and condemned by the Soviet bloc as "thoroughly revisionist," the bureaucracy rapidly became more and more powerful. The number of employees in state and local administration almost doubled between 1952 and 1961, from 119,000 to 193,000. After a slight drop for two years, it reached 188,000 in 1964; following the introduction of The Reform, it fell at last to 168,000 by the end of 1966. The number of "professional functionaries," those fully employed by the party and other political organizations, not counting the federal bodies, increased between 1961 and 1964 by 61 per cent to 4,716.

Instead of leading the fight against bureaucracy and exercising a real check on its power and privileges, the party itself became a shield for and an instrument of bureaucracy. After the Djilas affair and during the period of reconciliation with Moscow between 1953 and 1955, about 273,000 members were expelled, and, even allowing for the admission of new members, the number of card-holding Communists dropped from 779,000 to 642,000. Though membership gradually increased to 1,040,000 in 1967, the party has become predominantly an organization of officials, administrators, clerks, and officers. More than half of the expelled members in 1964–66 were workers, and an increasing number of them are currently quitting of their own accord. About 7,000 people left the party in 1966, mostly blue-collar workers.

The figures about the social composition of the party speak for themselves. Between 1947 and 1966, the proportion of "officials" almost trebled, from 14.9 to 39.2 per cent of a much larger total. Though the percentage of blue-collar workers rose slightly from 30 to 33.9 per cent, that of peasants fell from 46.9 to a mere 7.4 per cent. If these changes are cause for anxiety, then the gradual disappearance of the young from the ranks is justifiably described as "alarming."

Many of the top leaders and the great majority of the rank and file of the Yugoslav Communists were extremely young when they came to power. Young people under twenty-five years of age accounted for almost 40 per cent of the membership in 1951, and the average age stood at twenty-nine. By 1967 the proportion of the young, who accounted for a steadily increasing share of the population at large, dropped to 11 per cent in the party. There are some 3.2 million young people (between fourteen and twenty-five) of whom about 750,000 work in the socialist sector, 1.5 million live in the countryside, and the rest are in schools and universities. But the party has only 120,000 young members. "Unable to understand the great difference between the proclaimed and the real life . . . between the moral and political profile of a Communist today and the one they meet in books, the young men withdraw into their privacy and are often forever lost to society."[56]

As a Croat priest once told me, "Both of us, the Church and the party, have failed to win the young people of today. But on reflection I think that the party, for all its organizational and financial supremacy, has failed even more resoundingly than we have." The young do not want to be bothered by the hollow rhetoric of an old-fashioned power elite that continuously talks about reforms but clings to power. They seek to build new human relationships and long for a civilized existence and personal freedom. "Stop boring us with the past" is a slogan typical of the young generation.

"I regard Bob Dylan as a revolutionary, more revolutionary than our fathers who are very happy and proud of their bourgeois comforts, of their Mercedes cars with or without chauffeurs as you like. . . ." So opens an article written for the Zagreb *Vjesnik* by D. Tralic, an eighteen-year-old high school student. "At present we have more illiterate people than immediately after the war. Education is completely neglected. Our cultural life is ruined. And what can be said of our medical care or social insurance? I am accusing the generation of our fathers. True, they carried the revolution on their shoulders . . . but they have failed to continue it successfully. Where are the revolutionaries today? Our parents have become the most ordinary breadwinners, while the League of Communists seems to many people I know a repulsive meeting place of careerists." This young student finished his article with a reference to a new revolution to be carried out by the new generation, to a communism to be built "by honest people."[57]

The party has become the stronghold of middle-aged bureaucrats. From the bottom to the top, however, the dynamics of economic and administrative decentralization, the sharpening clashes between enterprises and communes, between the republics and the Belgrade center, and among the "rich" and the "poor" regions and nations, have caused a deepening rift within the power elite. This split has had much greater scope, effects, and ramifications than the competition for influence between interest groups within other ruling Communist parties. The differences in dimensions and intensity are due partly to the unique features of the administrative self-government which provide new forms of political institutions and procedures for group conflicts, partly to the multinational character of Yugoslavia.

Decentralization and self-management, competition on the market, and industrial democracy in the enterprises originally impelled an even tighter political control over all activities. Bureaucrats in the factories, local government, and state administration changed hats, names, and positions, but kept their mental habits and unconditional loyalty to the top-to-bottom chain of command in the ruling party. On the basis of membership statistics, one can reckon that the ruling class consisted predominantly of those 141,000 people who belonged to the party in 1945. When after 1954 members began to be listed according to occupation and not social origin, the figure for workers and peasants decreased by 138,000 while the number of white-collar employees and army officers increased correspondingly. Within this group, the "holders of the Partisan Memorial Medal 1941," the old fighters who immediately joined the uprising, constituted the "establishment," the hard core of the new elite.

From industry to commerce, local to federal administration, the Partisans, the "mountaineers" without training, experience, and education, were placed in the key positions, while the ranking party leaders, often but not always with high school or university degrees, became the decision-makers at the top level. The passage of time, mass education, the change of generations, and the emergence of an educated technical proletariat and intelligentsia have, however, increased the number and influence of those who possess the professional skills to guide and manage an increasingly complex industrial society. Decentralization has created a permanent situation for building up group pressures and institutional clashes. But the outward trappings of authority and executive functions have not been identical with the concentration of real as opposed to formal power. Regardless of the strides in self-management, the crucial questions have been: Who formulates the options, who chooses the alternatives, who has the power to hinder certain decisions and where does this power lie?

It lay in the hands of the party apparat, which gave up formal responsibility to run current affairs. Under the conditions of a single-party system, workers' councils were in the beginning simply one more transmission belt for the ruling party. With the trade unions having no real competences at all, the enterprises were taken over by the party organizations. These in turn owed allegiance to a party built on the principle of democratic centralism—the absolute binding force of all directives of a higher organization to a subordinate cell. As Lenin once put it, "in order that the Center . . . may really direct the orchestra, it is essential to know exactly who is playing which fiddle and where, who is learning to master which instrument or has mastered it and where, who is playing out of tune, where and why . . . and who should be transferred to correct the dissonances, how and where. . . ."[58]

In Yugoslavia, however, more and more players—party secretaries, managers who, as Tito said, "are sometimes more managers than Communists," communal functionaries, etc.—began to play out of tune despite the neat hierarchical structure of the party. It has become increasingly difficult to direct the orchestra in a society in which "bureaucratic centralism has given way to bureaucratic polycentrism."[59] Self-interested executives and ambitious local bureaucrats formed temporary alliances that ran counter to the proclaimed guidelines and instructions of the center. As the funds began to be dispersed, business and local, republican and federal officials also appeared as still unequal partners but already sharing a fluid and shifting power. The emergence of many centers of power run mostly by small "informal groups" of political bureaucrats, technocratic executives, and local officials made a mockery of "direct democracy," but at the same time diluted the power of the center from within.

The party organizations in the enterprises became increasingly schizophrenic. If they followed the decisions made by the superior organs outside the factory, they lost all real influence over the workers. If they sided with the "irresponsible demands" of the labor force or with the "narrow group interests," they were scolded by their superior party organs for violation of party discipline and for giving in to a backward environment. Communists, of course, should lift themselves above such earthly matters as individual egoism and group interests. They should struggle against both bureaucracy and irresponsibility, "against everything that in the life of self-managing collectives and on a broader social plane stands for the outlived relations of the old society—against petty-bourgeois lack of perspective and selfishness, against social irresponsibility, and against the expropriation and restriction of self-management rights in the name of false liberalistic and technocratic formulas."[60]

When, with the launching of The Reform, economic problems began to be tackled in earnest, the inherent contradictions in the positions of the party organizations in the economy became almost intolerable. As the Belgrade paper *Politika* put it, there was serious opposition on the part of "good Communists" against their election as secretaries of a basic organization. "They understand their tasks as members of the various elected organs, but the function of a secretary seems to them rather foggy. In the past, there was no decision in the enterprise without him. Now the situation is different; a political fight is needed. It is more difficult and complex than when authority could replace the lack of justified arguments. Many Communists have split personalities. On the one hand, as members of the self-management organs they are responsible for the decisions taken; on the other, membership in the League of Communists does not give them the right to put themselves above the elected bodies and force the adoption of another attitude."[61]

Still clinging to the myth of the "working class" as the most progressive force and the vanguard of social developments, the leaders are shocked and appalled when confronted with irresponsible behavior and naked anti-social egotism. They are beginning to discover the bitter truth which is so evident in pluralistic democratic societies. The leading Slovenian ideologist, now Premier of the Slovenian Republic, Stane Kavcic, as well as many others, have come to the conclusion that "when they are salesmen, the workers demand full freedom and are upset about state intervention. When, however, they appear as buyers of raw materials or half-finished products on the market, they call for aid from the state, think that the market is too free, and use ideological arguments to prove that everything that is happening is not socialist and not even logical." What do the Communists do in such a situation? In the words of Kavcic, some of them are for "strong-arm methods" and demand that the party take everything into its hands. Others act simply as "transmission" for the management fight for investment funds and higher wages. "Communist political activity must not be exhausted in the defense of equality in poverty, of some absolute moral, of absolute justice."[62]

Economic decentralization and a single-party system have combined to produce three main situations in the enterprises. In many cases, everything is decided by the famous "informal groups," that is, usually by the manager, party secretary, chief of the personnel department, and chairman of the workers' council, often joined by spokesmen of the Veterans' Federation. As the former leader of the trade unions, S. Vukmanovic-Tempo, said, the workers consider them almost "class enemies, because political, technological, and managerial power is concentrated in the hands of a small number of the political activists which exerts the greatest influence upon the collective."[63] In the large corporations and banks the outlines of what Galbraith calls "technostructure" have emerged—experts, planners, and administrators whose decisions due "to the technical complexity and associated scale of operations" are actually "removed from the reach of social control."[64] Finally we find "real self-management," where unskilled or semiskilled workers "democratically" almost equalize their wages with the salaries of the highly trained personnel.

When the economic situation is critical and prices are going up, the main concern of the 150,000 workers' council members is naturally enough the pay check rather than the long-term interests of the enterprise or the state of funds. Lacking any real collective bargaining mechanism or a fully developed union system, the workers, including most of the party members, go on strike, as it were "against themselves," reject the principle of pay according to work performed, and, through what is described as a "spontaneous revolt," force the "informal groups" or "technostructure" to sanction higher wages. From the first publicly admitted strike in January 1958 in the Trbovlje mine in Slovenia until the end of 1966, there were 1,365 strikes in Yugoslavia. The moment the policing instrument of the party and the secret police are withdrawn, centrifugal forces whirl around, carrying through a policy of "equal stomachs."

"What we need today are socialist bankers and not honored old fighters who can only telephone; able administrators and not popular tribunes without any profession," one of the country's foremost economists, Branko Horvat, told me several years ago. Yet the stifling iron hand of the "informal groups, vertically and horizontally linked and passing the most important decisions"[65] led in many firms to what *Borba* described as the "rule of mediocrities in the cloak of self-government." When one talks about the "managerial class" as a whole pitted against "state and party bureaucracy," one must remember that many of the managers even today rose to top positions by virtue of their political reliability and the right connections. Even in Slovenia, by far the most developed region of the country, 40 per cent of the directors have completed only elementary schooling, but, as I was told by one of the leading officials, with the help of the Veterans' Federation and often the party they manage to keep the factory gates shut to young trained experts.

The over-all statistics clearly show that this Balkan "managerial class," like the working class, has no real traditions and consists mainly of peasants with a high proportion of illiterates. About 40 per cent of the managers (in Macedonia 55 per cent!), 25 per cent of the commercial and technical directors, have only elementary schooling; one-third of the factories in 1964 did not have a single highly qualified person on their staffs and even at the re-election of directors in 1966, only 29 per cent of the newly elected were trained for their jobs, while 18.5 per cent had had no more than four years in an elementary school, and many of them not even that. In mid-1967 it was estimated that out of each 100 jobs requiring professional skills, only 54 were filled by men with appropriate training. Out of 264,000 skilled and highly skilled young people who left vocational schools and universities during the 1965–67 period, 150,000 could not get jobs; it is said that "it is easier to get a degree than to get a job."[66] No wonder that the proportion of technically trained workers seeking employment abroad rose from 16 per cent in 1965 to 37 per cent in 1967.

The built-in incentives for making more money, which are often tied to faulty signals in the form of irrational prices, have created a unique situation in Yugoslavia. Perhaps no other society is so income-orientated as this supposedly socialist one. But the structural defects in the investment, banking, and price systems channel the scramble for money in the wrong direction—into distribution instead of profit-making. Month by month, often biweekly, the papers publish "the leaders and laggards" in the incomes league. A report in the October 5, 1967, *Borba* vividly illustrates what the lack of an income policy tied to over-all productivity might mean in a primitive environment. It said that in July 1967 average incomes were 82,000 dinars monthly. But earnings varied from 56,000 in the timber industry to 138,000 in the oil industry. Workers in the textile, leather, non-ferrous metal, and wood-processing industries and coal mines had an average take-home pay of less than 70,000 dinars, but white-collar and blue-collar workers in air transport or in banks could boast of 155,000 dinars.

On the one hand, pay for the same quality of work in different regions, industries, and enterprises makes for striking differences due to natural advantages or a monopoly position enjoyed by some enterprises or whole sectors. On the other hand, freedom to set wages leads to situations in which a cleaning woman, if she happens to be employed in a bank, earns more than a university professor. The wide publicity given to the bizarre excesses keeps the distribution of incomes at the center of public attention.

While this problem can be reduced to manageable proportions once wages are linked to the real efficiency of the enterprises, the main danger lies in what is called Uravnilovka. This expression stands for the thoughtless equalization of incomes within enterprises regardless of professional skill and position. The general manager of an electrical engineering plant in Belgrade told me that he was earning not quite two and a half times as much as the worst-paid unskilled laborer among the 1,400 employed. In the largest chemical factory in Slovenia, near Ljubljana, at the time of my visit in 1965, an unskilled worker had a net monthly income of 50,000 dinars, an engineer 112,000, the technical director 160,000, and the general manager 170,000. I found a range of one to three in the Credit Bank of Zagreb and of one to four in a modern synthetic fiber plant at Skopje between the wages of the least skilled worker and the salary of the general manager.

In a country that badly needs trained personnel, the market and also official policy should tend to break the extremely narrow hierarchy of incomes and to reward technical and administrative staffs more appropriately. But with workers' management, "one worker, one vote" favors equalization, since unskilled or semiskilled workers are, of course, the most strongly represented on the council. With trained intelligence much more scarce than either capital or labor in Yugoslavia, Uravnilovka has become a burning problem. A Yugoslav journalist sees the only solution in a change of the voting system, making representation in the council or the member's vote of greater or smaller value in proportion to his group's effective contribution to production. As the journalist aptly remarked, "Without making a distinction between skilled and unskilled work, the principle of payment according to work performed is a mere fiction."[67]

Interests within individual enterprises also press for a direct and institutionalized part in policy formation. But as Professor Mihajlo Markovic warned, the talk about direct democracy "can be not only a progressive slogan but also a dangerous myth . . . a suitable ideological instrument for bureaucracy because overt étatism (state intervention) has been defeated. Influence of individuals on the state is very modest, the process of de-professionalization (the elimination of politics as a profession with privileges) has just started, the League of Communists is still an organ of social power and not merely an ideological force and has been playing a decisive part in picking candidates for elections. . . . Because of the given degree of literacy and education, even the existing and possible forms of popular participation and political action are not utilized. The key question is the democratization of relations in supreme political bodies."[68]

How indeed can one speak about social control from below, let alone expect prudent behavior from the worker "shareholders," when many of them cannot even read or write. According to the 1961 census, about one-fifth of the population over ten years of age was illiterate. The percentages varied, of course, between the developed and backward areas. Thus Slovenia had only 1.2 per cent illiteracy, but Macedonia and Montenegro from 21 to 24 per cent. Bosnia-Herzegovina had 32.5, while in the Kosovo region it was well over 50 per cent. It was estimated that 5 per cent of the labor force were illiterates. In fact, the total number of illiterates and semi-illiterates, 500,000, is about 15 per cent of the labor force. Six years later in 1967, several official statements stressed the fact that the real level of illiteracy is considerably higher because the number of adults who learn to read and write is ten times lower

than that of the children who fail to attend schools.[69] The deep
cultural and economic cleavage between the developed north and
underdeveloped south has a profound impact on the performance of
the factories, enterprises, and banks, and also on the pace and meaning of political reforms.

It was only natural in this situation that the federal bureaucracy
in 1960–61 came forward with a concept "which was not publicly
announced, that enlightened bureaucratic technocracy is more
effective than self-government."[70] Faced with pressures from below getting out of hand, multiple clashes of interests at all levels,
and the erosion of central control, a powerful wing in the party
and state machine made a concerted effort to subvert the democratic process on the vital questions of economic and political
decision-making.

It was, however, bureaucratic centralism coupled with totalitarian party dictatorship that was primarily responsible for increasing and sharing out the "federal cake," the central moneybag; for
keeping the economy geared to faulty price signals for an unduly
long period of time; for relying on "informal groups" and pushing
decentralization to absurd lengths in order to step in and impose
"order" through a tightening of the reins. Instead of solving socio-
economic problems, central bureaucracy created new ones by
promoting its special interests with no regard for economic considerations; by committing immense investment "mistakes," employing
capital in "political factories" and in prestige projects mainly in the
less-developed regions.

By the end of 1965 Yugoslavia with a small domestic market
could boast of 14 factories manufacturing valves, 12 turning out car
bodies, 5 manufacturing gearboxes, 20 producing agricultural machines, and 14, electric cookers. There were 366 foundries, countless
textile plants, and no less than 250 chemical factories. There were a
dozen-odd steel plants with a total production of only 1.7 million
tons; by 1970 their production should go up to 3.7 million tons
at a projected investment cost of almost 600 million dollars, but
the output will still be split up among the dozen producers at a
time when elsewhere one plant's optimal capacity equals their combined output. Seven new railroad lines were projected. In the field
of refineries and petrochemical plants, the investment race continued at an unabated pace even in 1967, more than two years after
The Reform had been launched. Domestic consumption of petro-

leum products will reach some 5.5 million tons in 1969, but the refineries built or expanded in various regions will have a total capacity by 1970 of 13 million tons.[71]

The battle over who cuts the cake and how has gradually become the central feature of the domestic political scene. What was first called "localism" or "particularism" was gradually transformed into national friction, because the competing investment projects coincided with the borders between the six constituent republics. The more decentralization progressed, the greater the demands became for retaining a larger share of the money earned within the republic, instead of transferring it to the central funds. The "have nots," on the other hand, clung to the concentration of funds, hoping to secure by political pressure the largest possible share—of the other people's money.

Instead of restraining the centrifugal forces at all levels, the ruling party itself became the carrier of the various savage conflicts and multiple contradictions. By the end of the fifties and the beginning of the sixties the degree of autonomy in the republics caused a major split in the top leadership, among the then fourteen members of the Executive Committee. In 1964, when only 8 per cent of the population were over fifty, the average age of these fourteen leaders was over fifty-seven, and that of the 135 members of the Central Committee, fifty-two.

It would be misleading, however, to speak about a rift between "liberals" and "conservatives." From top to bottom the conflict was primarily between centralists and decentralists, between those in favor of a "strong-hand" policy directed from the center and those demanding more powers and freedom for the republics, communes, and enterprises, coupled with a sweeping de-politicization of the economy. In a certain sense, this was also a contest between economic strength and political influence. With Tito's support, the centralists won the first battle when they succeeded in blocking the projected economic reforms in 1961–62. Within two years, however, the reformers initiated an offensive, which culminated in 1966 in a decisive showdown with the real master of the Belgrade center, Alexander Rankovic. In the course of years Rankovic had accumulated an immense power over the central party machine, the secret police, and the state bureaucracy. Former differences between Communists and non-Communists were completely overshadowed by much more important lines of division, recalling the internal stresses of prewar Yugoslavia. The main actors in the great drama became the nations who invoked a more powerful and ancient allegiance than the party card. The reassertion of national identity has in the final analysis contributed more than anything else to the crisis of the party and to the accelerated process of political liberalization and economic modernization.

The nations in a whirlpool of change and conflict

The time—the spring of 1966 with mounting political tensions in the air. The place—the capitals of three republics. The actors—leading Croat, Serbian, and Macedonian politicians, all Communists, all Marxists, yet espousing totally different ideas. Aside from the language and political jargon, each in his own way sounds like any U. S. Senator or Congressman speaking on behalf of the special interests of his state or district. The talks with the visitor, as well as the heated debates in parliament and other political bodies, revolve around money. From the late fifties to the late sixties, the topic has remained the same. But with the passage of time and the sharpening clashes of interest, the degree of candor has become steadily greater.

Zagreb: the bright hope of the Croat Communist party, Mika Tripalo, born in 1926 and now Executive Secretary of the Communist party of the whole Republic. The very model of the young executive-politician, quick on the draw, highly competent, sometimes too clever. Stressing that The Reform is not progressing at a very satisfactory rate, Tripalo does not mince words: "The key question is giving back the immense centralized funds to the economy. What we need is modernization of the existing capacities and not the building of vast new projects. But then a prominent politician at the recent congress of the Socialist Alliance of Serbia stands up and proudly proclaims: 'We want to build this, we shall do that, we must launch this . . .' In short, he rattles off some ten or twenty huge investment projects. Our answer is: 'Go ahead, if you have the money.' But then it develops that they haven't got enough funds. . . . The same applies to the underdeveloped regions. We have a central fund, budgetary subsidies, a favored rate of interest for credits, etc. But we have to put an end to parasitism. Those who are able to earn cannot be punished all the time. . . . As to nationalism, the only solution is that our multinational Yugoslavia must be based on the full equality of each nation and not on some being more equal than others, on socialist self-government and not on bureaucratic centralism."

Belgrade: "You are asking questions that we regard as delicate; they are even more so if discussed with a foreigner, particularly if he is a newspaperman." The dark-haired hulking man then proceeds to present the "Serbian angle" for the next two hours. He is the "prominent politician" whose statements drew the ire of Mika Tripalo. President of the largest mass organization, the Socialist Alliance of Working People, Mihajlo Svabic is fifty-four, former Vice-Premier of Serbia, member of the Executive Committee of the Serbian Communist party, and widely regarded as one of the most influential men in the capital. A Partisan turned elegantly dressed professional functionary, Svabic is credited with having saved the life of Alexander Rankovic (at that time still the "strong man" of Yugoslavia). Sitting in one of the countless conference rooms of the highest skyscraper in New Belgrade, which serves as the headquarters for the federal and Serbian political organizations, Svabic holds forth calmly but firmly on Serbia's position. "Basically, all this boils down to the question of priorities. You can't wear white tails and go barefoot, or to put it another way, a top hat and peasant moccasins [opanak] do not go together. First we have to develop the infrastructure, build railroads and waterways to connect East with West Serbia, and with Montenegro and Herzegovina. We have here enormous hydroelectric potential, great lead, copper, and other reserves. Despite the fact that Serbia accounts for almost 42 per cent of the population and one-third of the area of Yugoslavia, in certain periods until 1956 we received only 29 per cent of the central investment funds. Now through a 'coincidence of circumstances' the largest projects in the current Five Year Plan—the Iron Gates power and navigation scheme on the Danube, the Danube–Tisza canal, the Belgrade–Bar railroad, the big thermal power plants in Kosovo, etc.—happen to be concentrated in our republic and accordingly we have a share of 52 per cent in the total federal investments until 1970."

Skopje: Three years after the earthquake which killed 1,700 people and destroyed the city in 1963, the Macedonian capital is a booming urban center with attractively designed settlements of prefabricated houses and satellite suburbs which house a population of 275,000 (almost 100,000 more than at the time of the disaster). Reconstructed with the help of massive foreign aid and a 500-million-dollar government fund, Skopje seems so prosperous that a Belgrade satirical weekly caustically remarked: "Going around on foot I provoked astonishment among the inhabitants of Skopje, for most of them are driving cars. . . . Stretching over a length of fifteen miles, Skopje resembles an American city; because of the long distances people use the American way of travel, that is, cars instead of public transport. Everything would be all right if only everything else also reminded the visitor of the United States. One has the impression that since the great earthquake the people here have become a bit spoiled. There is even a new slogan: Whatever you can do, let other people do it."

Needless to say, these ironical remarks, which contained an element of truth and reflected a widespread opinion in the country, caused an uproar in both Skopje and Belgrade. The paper was accused not only of distorting the facts but also of Great Serbian chauvinism. Faced by a visitor arriving in the midst of the bitter controversy, information officials attempted to perform a virtually impossible task: to demonstrate the scope of reconstruction, and at the same time refute the allegations that the Macedonians are living too well—on other people's money.

The Premier of the Macedonian Republic with a population of 1.5 million, Nikola Mincev, talks in a somewhat different fashion from our last conversation in August 1962, when he was the planning chief of Yugoslavia. Now he speaks exclusively about the problems of his republic and seeks to prove his case with an impressive list of statistics: "Every factory can be called a political factory but in our republic there are none; only one cigarette factory had losses last year. . . . Despite federal aid, our relative position in Yugoslavia has not improved but on the contrary become worse. If you take the over-all Yugoslav average national income as 100, then Macedonia stood at 68 after the war, but dropped to 62 per cent last year. We are not afraid of The Reform, but we are not convinced that the community as a whole is truly aware of its obligations toward the underdeveloped areas. At the same time we are against the administrative command economy; the more economic the instruments of aid, the better and more pleasant for us."

The Macedonian party chief, Krste Crvenkovski, born in 1922, belongs to the younger and also the most progressive group of leaders. A swarthy broad-faced man, a former youth leader and long-time Minister of Education in Belgrade, he speaks as frankly as Mika Tripalo about the national question and the Serb menace to the smaller nations. "The main danger lies in Great Serbian hegemony. The recent attack on Skopje is unimportant, but it does reflect a certain mentality. We are also allergic to the economic hegemony of Slovenia. One should not always talk only about aid, but also about the fact that we had to pay 40 per cent higher prices for machines delivered by Yugoslav contractors for our steelworks here than the prices in the world market. The spirit of nationalism, a defensive one, mind you, may well become stronger in Macedonia because we are a young nation, feeling, not without reason, sometimes insecure. But we are convinced that the greater the rights and equality of the nations in our country, the stronger the Federation."

Figures, figures, figures dominate the conversation wherever one travels. The three talks quoted above contain in a nutshell problems discussed continuously in the country. The regular visitor to Yugoslavia hears again and again complaints, demands, and suggestions, not always in the measured tone of these three "samples," but invariably seen from different angles. The Croats complain about the "squandered billions" spent on uneconomic investments in the south; the Slovenes quietly refer to their disproportionately large contribution to the central funds; the Bosniaks blame the fact that raw material prices are kept artificially low; the Serbs figure out how much they are losing because of the low prices for farm products and lack of adequate transportation. Invariably one recalls Bakaric's angry outcry: "Who *does* receive something in Yugoslavia, if we are all plundered?"

In a sense, no one is right and no one is wrong. With the best will in the world, it is extremely difficult, if not indeed impossible, to equalize the goods of a society in which the bases on which these goods are portioned out are themselves maldistributed. On top of this, as the able scholar and Yugoslav Ambassador to the UN, Anton Vratusa, aptly remarked, "Due to the distorted price structure and artificial amortization rates, there are no over-all, exact and reliable figures. Thus each side usually operates with different figures."

Nevertheless there are certain incontestable truths about the dimensions of the efforts to take the income and funds from the "have" regions and transfer them to the "have not." The program to equalize development levels between the north and the south prevailed for over fifteen years. Under the wartime slogan "Brotherhood and Unity," exploitation of the resources in the developed northern areas was subordinated to the "over-all goals" determined by the top political leadership. Nowhere perhaps was the attempt more ruthless and brutal than in Slovenia.

The 1.6 million Slovenes belonged until 1918 to the Austrian monarchy and were more closely connected with the Central European tradition than any other Slav nation. Both after the first world war and during the second, they firmly opted for a South Slav state, prompted by their fear of losing their national identity under the twin onslaught of German and Italian territorial ambitions. The geographical distance from Belgrade, the difference in language, and a shrewd political leadership combined to preserve a relatively large degree of internal autonomy in the interwar period. Thrifty and industrious, emotionally stable, and better educated than their fellow Slavs, the Slovenes can be justly called the "Swiss of Eastern Europe."

Their resources, once on a par with those of neighboring Austria and Italy, were put on the "economic chopping board" as soon as World War II ended. The situation was worst in the immediate postwar period, when entire printing plants were dismantled and sent as a "gift" to Albania. But the exploitation continued during the decentralization of the economy. Thus in 1952 Serbia was allowed to retain half of its national income after the deduction of central taxes and levies, while Slovenia kept only one-third. In 1957, Serbia was given back 36.6 per cent of the turnover tax collected in its territory, while Slovenia received a mere 1.2 per cent. In 1958, Slovenia with 8.6 per cent of the total population had to contribute no less than 37.2 per cent to the federal budget, which meant that almost half of its national income was siphoned off by Belgrade.[72]

The money went to the less developed regions—Montenegro, Macedonia, the province of Kosovo (part of Serbia), and Bosnia-Herzegovina. Between 1952 and 1964, capital assets increased by 230 per cent in Yugoslavia but the growth in the underdeveloped regions was 325 per cent. Kosovo, Macedonia, and Montenegro with 15 per cent of the total population received no less than 28 per cent of the investment outlays between 1957–61.[73] But Croatia, too, has large underdeveloped regions, and the Serbs claim that roughly one-third of their communes—excluding the Kosovo province—are well below the countrywide average.

In theory, the attempt to strike an acceptable balance between economic efficiency and the satisfaction of social needs sounds sensible enough. The developed regions must not stagnate nor be held back to "wait" for the backward areas to catch up. On the other hand, the development of the "have not" republics should be speeded up to narrow the gap. In practice, it is somewhat different.

Consider the tiny mountain bastion, the Republic of Montenegro, which has half a million inhabitants and is approximately the size of the state of Connecticut. Montenegro profited tremendously from the fact that Montenegrins occupied key positions in the top political bodies of Yugoslavia. Between 1958 and 1963, 70 per cent of Montenegrin investments were financed from central funds.

A Slovenian engineer who spent six years in Titograd, the Montenegrin capital, related to me matter-of-factly the way the mountain warriors handled their industrialization. "We spent billions of dinars building a steel plant at Niksic, which operates at a yearly deficit of 3 million dollars. Then followed the textile boom, and about half a dozen spinning mills and clothing factories were erected around the capital. But there were no roads and no railroads. Then they launched the overambitious project of building up the little port of Bar to a big harbor, with no regard for actual needs. Now, after eleven years of construction, the railroad connection from Niksic to Bar has been completed. But who will calculate the daily losses and the earnings we could have gained if we had spent these huge sums on sound investment projects."

The Five Year Plan, launched in 1957, disregarded Croat suggestions about improving port and rail facilities and gave the go-ahead signal for enlarging the comparatively unused port of Bar. This in turn served as a trump card in the intermittent battle for constructing the Belgrade–Bar railroad, an old ambition of land-locked Serbia seeking an outlet on the Adriatic. In 1966, the Montenegrins succeeded in having their long-standing bid to build an aluminum plant at Titograd accepted. It was to have been built in the late fifties, but during the renewed dispute with Tito in 1956–58, the Russians twice suspended 285 million dollars' worth of credits that had been granted in part for the purpose. "What is a Yugoslav joke?" a high-ranking official once asked me. "To build an aluminum plant with Russian credits and Montenegrin labor . . ." Faced with three bids, from the Croatian port of Sibenik, the Bosnian city of Mostar, and Montenegro, for the location of an aluminum plant, the Yugoslav Investment Bank, without properly investigating the economic soundness of the different proposals, immediately opted for Montenegro. This created an uproar in Zagreb. To calm ruffled tempers, in 1968 the Federal Assembly went to the other extreme, giving the go-ahead signal for the construction of no fewer than three aluminum projects, each of relatively small capacity. Meanwhile, although the Montenegrin coast is ideal for tourism, the local officials were completely ignoring its possibilities. As Milka Kufrin the then Minister of Tourism told me in 1964, over a period of seventeen years Montenegro had provided funds to accommodate only 1,200 tourists.

The lavish scale of uneconomic investments aroused growing resentment in the north. The Slovenes and Croats became increasingly interested in what the money taken from them yielded in tangible fruits. Early in 1964, the Zagreb *Vjesnik* reported, "There has been no lack of good will, but why are the results not satisfactory? The national product during the past fourteen years rose twice as fast in the areas north of the Danube-Sava line as in the south. In 1962, investments per head of the population in Montenegro were more than twice as high as those in Slovenia. Yet the output per man in Slovenia was much larger."

To make matters worse, the "have not" regions are far from satisfied with the aid they have received. Spokesmen of the less developed republics, seething with discontent, are unimpressed when told how much they have progressed compared to the past. What they are interested in is the average national income per head in the various republics, and they know that between 1947 and 1967 the proportions have remained basically the same. Slovenia and Croatia have somewhat accelerated their advances, and the development level of the south measured in these terms is still one-third below the Yugoslav average, while that of Slovenia is almost twice as high. The ratio between Slovenia and the south is about three to one.

What is fact to one is illusion to the other. From the point of view of narrowing the differences there has been no improvement at all. Thus considerable advances in the standard of living are accompanied by increasing resentment and bitterness that the progress has not been greater, that the gap between "rich" and "poor" still exists. This is the crucial point in a country consisting of such widely disparate regions, which more or less coincide with the divisions between different nations. The Slovenes and Croats do not think in terms of abstract postulates or complicated economic calculations. They feel, justifiably, that they have been exploited and robbed of the rewards of their work. The man in the street in Zagreb sees that the National Theater is closed for months and the construction of a concert hall is stopped, that books are getting more expensive and publishing firms have to prune the number of books they want to print by one-third. The Slovene hears that the only large investment project in his republic, the gas complex at Velenje, has to be canceled, although 25 million dollars' worth of imported equipment has already arrived and must be paid for. In the central square of his capital he is daily confronted with two huge structures of steel beams and girders resembling bizarre abstract sculptures, two half-finished, high-rise buildings whose construction was stopped in 1964.

All this is due to "lack of funds." From the blue-collar worker to the university professor, the visitor gets the same answer: "Belgrade takes everything it possibly can from us." The Macedonians and the Serbs nevertheless feel strongly that "the Slovenes make money at the cost of the less developed people." Or, as the editor of the leading Belgrade economic weekly *Ekonomska Politika,* puts it, "The Slovenes want to sell in Yugoslavia and live in Switzerland." The point of the matter is that the Slovenes could live almost as well as the Swiss, but they do not. Their cash incomes are 20 or 30 per cent above the rest of the population, not three times higher as they should be in terms of actual economic performance. Also, their consumer habits and traditional living standards cannot be compared to what the illiterate or semiliterate men of the south are accustomed to.

This state of affairs could not last indefinitely, and the real power of the more developed regions increased as the economy grew more sophisticated. What matters in any economy is the output (product per worker) and input (asset per worker) ratio. The figures are self-evident. Slovenia and Croatia with just over 30 per cent of the population and 40.4 per cent of capital assets, accounted for 46.3 per cent of the country's industrial output in 1965. On the other hand, the south—Macedonia, Montenegro, and Bosnia-Herzegovina (excluding the province of Kosovo)—with 28.8 per cent of the population and 26.7 per cent of assets had a share of only 20.2 per cent in industrial production. The contrast is, of course, even more striking in the case of Slovenia, which by 1966, with a population amounting to a mere 8.4 per cent of the total figure, produced one-fifth of the aggregate industrial production and contributed 17 per cent to the combined foreign trade total.[74] Even these figures do not give a complete picture, for one should also take into account such factors as, for example, quality, design, and packaging, or the fact that Slovenia ships two-thirds of its exports to the West, thus securing badly needed foreign exchange.

It was only natural that the Slovene Communist leaders were the first to challenge Belgrade's administrative distribution of national income. Later joined by the Croats, they were the spearheads of the accelerated decentralization measures in 1959–60 which culminated in the comprehensive economic reform formally approved by party and state organs in early 1961.

As this concept was essentially a model for a developed socialist system, the opposition came from those "who used to get more from the central moneybag than they put into it; and from those who gained more from their political influence than from their industrial skill."[75] The visitor in the spring and summer of 1961 was struck by the boldness of some official statements, the scope of the projected swing to the market mechanism, the opening toward the world market, and the optimistic expectations of many officials and public opinion. Edward Kardelj compared the changes "to the greatest revolutionary events of our social development." Yet by October 1961 the optimism had begun to evaporate, and by March 1962 the entire ambitious operation was brought to a grinding halt. What remained of the reform program was a limited foreign exchange reform.

What had happened? The Slovene-Croat initiative was stopped under the pretext of economic difficulties skillfully exploited by mainly Serbian centralists. By March 1962 what had begun as a tactical maneuver against the reform became a full-blown strategic offensive concerning not just the economy but the entire political course and future existence of the smaller nations of Yugoslavia.

Postwar Yugoslavia was deliberately created as the opposite of the interwar state dominated by the Serbian ruling elite; reconstituted along federal lines, real autonomy was granted to the six republics, and the national units were given the constitutional right "to self-determination, including the right to secession." In accord with these principles, the six republics have not only parliaments of their own, but also separate constitutions, courts, and legislative powers. There is no single state language, indeed the Constitution proclaims Serbo-Croatian (Croat-Serbian), Slovenian, and Macedonian as the official languages of the Federal Republic.

Regardless of the economic bickering, it seemed in the fifties that the Communist leaders had solved the basic national problems as best they could under the tangled conditions of a multinational community with a tragic history of fratricidal strife. But with bureaucratic centralism and the politically motivated distribution of income above the heads of those concerned, the vexed issues of the past have reappeared, in somewhat different forms.

The striking thing about the renewed national tensions, first in the economic field and then in the political domain, was the emergence of the republican party leaderships as centers of national dissent. The Yugoslav Communist Party has a federal structure similar to the state itself. Until the mid-sixties, all crucial decisions were made by the federal party center in Belgrade. Yet the republican leaders all along had a machine and influence of their own. In other words, within the country-wide hierarchy there were regional or republican hierarchies. A man like the Croat leader, Dr. Vladimir Bakaric, or his Slovene colleagues had an independent power base, which could not be infiltrated by outsiders—in this case by the Serbian centralists in charge of the federal party bodies. The dynamics of economic decentralization steadily increased the importance of the republican parties, which in turn broadened their popular support to the extent that they were standing up for the interests of their nations.

The abrupt stopping of the 1960–61 decentralization policies led to a barely veiled split between the republican leaders and the federal party center; it also caused a rift within the center itself. The federal yet hierarchical structure of the Yugoslav state and party apparatus has helped to protect the smaller nations, but it also acts as a brake on circulation even within a relatively small elite and tends to stimulate the promotion of sectional interests. As a leading Yugoslav scientist once publicly told Marshal Tito, "In our country it is known that in every ministry every assistant secretary of state from a given republic fights for the interests of the republic from which he comes; for later on he will return to his republic and thus he naturally must carry out what he is told to."[76] This is, of course, also true of ministers, who are delegated by their respective regions. With the exception of the Montenegrins, who naturally prefer the amenities of the capital to their backward native environment, there is no "mixing" of the national elites. It is inconceivable that a Slovene would occupy a leading position in Macedonia, or vice versa.

But Belgrade is not only the federal capital; it is also the capital of Serbia, by far the largest republic. Despite the presence of a few thousand high officials and scientists from other nations, Belgrade has been and is still regarded by the Croats, Slovenes, and Macedonians as an essentially alien center, in which a predominantly Serbian central party and state bureaucracy holds the reins. The increasing influence of the republican parties and the presence of a handful of "token" Slovenes or Croats at the top, have not changed the power relationships in the federal center. The bureaucracy that had to implement the decisions consisted mainly of Serbs who, consciously or subconsciously, identified "federal interests" with those of Serbia. Even eighteen months after the showdown with Rankovic, a Belgrade paper admitted that "the federal apparatus (with the exception of leading officials and the Foreign Ministry, which is attractive for other reasons) consists mostly of people from Belgrade." After an allusion to the need for a more effective representation of social talent from the various nations in the central administration, the paper stressed the bad consequences in two basic directions: "First, the professional level and capability of the federal administration are certainly not what they should be; and second, this need emphasizes a feeling that the Federation is 'no man's land' or alien, or even, among extremist and chauvinistic circles, that it is 'Belgrade's government.' "[77]

The Serbian tradition of "a strong and sinister hand in government and large-scale corruption in public affairs" was established by the first ruler of the semi-independent principality, Milos Obrenovic (1817–39 and 1859–60). This had a fatal impact on the first "Kingdom of Serbs, Croats, and Slovenes" born in 1918. Even before the new state emerged, the Serbian Premier Pasic strove for political supremacy and regarded the new state as merely a "Greater Serbia." But the Serbs in the interwar period failed miserably to run a state which within six years had swollen to five times the size of Serbia before the Balkan Wars with a four times larger population. Between 1918 and 1941, the Serbs held the premiership in every single cabinet, the ministries of the Army, Foreign Affairs and, except for eighteen months, the Interior. Of 165 active generals in 1938, 161 were Serbs. All the important diplomatic posts and key positions in the economy were occupied by men from Serbia.[78] With tensions between the Croats striving for autonomy and the Serbs clinging to their idea of unity, "one king, one state, one people," inflamed to a pitch, King Alexander in 1929 not only proclaimed a royal dictatorship, but also changed the name of the state to the "Kingdom of Yugoslavia." He wanted the distinct but related people to think of themselves as Yugoslavs and not as Serbs, Croats, or Slovenes. In practice, however, nothing changed in the policy of Serbian hegemony.

The Yugoslav or common South Slav nationalism triumphed temporarily, under specific circumstances—and even then only in some parts of the country—during the ordeals of the liberation war against the invaders and the civil war. The conflict with Stalin contributed once again to the merging of national feelings in loyalty to the federal state, now exposed to mortal danger. But once international tensions subsided and the competitive forces of economic decentralization started to operate in earnest, loyalty to nation proved stronger than loyalty to state or class, even among the Communists. As Bakaric said, "Nationalism began to grow some time after 1952 and developed more vigorously after 1962 or 1963." On another occasion he added "this is no longer a remnant of reactionary forces, but is our 'own nationalism,' because of the decay of the old administrative system and of the demoralization of certain people affected by this decay."[79]

The chance to eradicate the main economic roots of nationalism in time was deliberately missed in 1961–62. Regardless of the federal structure of the state and party, the decisive questions— distribution of investments, the course of economic policy, and relations to the West and East—were determined in the federal center by the Executive Committee and Secretariat of the party. The die was cast at a three-day enlarged session of the supreme party organ in March 1962, to which not even stenographers were admitted. Acting, however, on the instructions of Rankovic, the UDBA, the secret police, recorded the conference on two tape recorders, and Rankovic received a typed transcript the following morning.[80]

Four years later at the plenary meeting of the Central Committee in July 1966, Tito said that the session "discussed relations in the leading circles and various anomalies. . . . We made a mistake not going to the very end because of certain tendencies to compromise and fear for unity, which was already damaged. The subject [the Rankovic case] is nothing new, it has its origins a few years back, almost a decade. We made the mistake of leaving security services for twenty years with Rankovic as its principal leader. . . ." Others, including Milos Minic, a Serb, said, "The crisis was ripe for a settlement; matters ought to have been settled then and there in March 1962."

But Tito at that crucial session, and in fact even earlier, did not support his claim that his position was a moderate, middle ground between two opposing extremes. Far from restraining, let alone opposing, the centralists grouped around Rankovic, Tito in November 1961, presented a new foreign policy program to an astounded public. Its essence was to use the new de-Stalinization campaign launched by Khrushchev a month earlier and the deterioration of relations with the United States (because of the anti-Western, pro-Soviet stand Tito took at the Belgrade conference of the neutralist countries) for a major attempt to seek reconciliation with Moscow. His speech was followed by intensified visits at all levels between Belgrade and Moscow, culminating in Tito's "holiday trip" in December 1962, the first time in six years he had been to Russia.

While the ardent desire of an aging Communist leader to retrieve his sense of mission and self-importance certainly played a part in the sudden reorientation of foreign policy, this seems to have been a secondary factor. The primary one was the tension-ridden situation in the party and the country at large. Leaving economic policy and administration to his chief lieutenants, Tito was interested first and foremost in maintaining the party's absolute power, keeping the centrifugal forces in the economy in check, and preserving the re-forged national unity. Recognizing the dangers posed by the unleashed forces of decentralization, Tito opted for bureaucratic centralism. The changes in the Communist world, above all the evolving Sino-Soviet conflict, came as a timely basis for the old pretext of using the international situation as an argument to justify unconditional unity and thus to strengthen the center.

Whatever Tito may really have thought, his record in 1961–63 was one of a dedicated centralist. A few weeks after his pro-Soviet statements, he spoke out for tightening the reins in the party, and following the famous session of the Executive Committee, he made a celebrated speech in Split in May 1962, which was the signal for the old-timers in the apparat to launch a massive witch hunt against everything suspected of "petty-bourgeois liberalism." Applying the classic self-saving method of a totalitarian Communist dictatorship, the general atmosphere was kept "revolutionized" from above; young shock "squads" intimidated people on the street or in restaurants who greeted each other with "Gospodin" (Mister) instead of "Drug" (Comrade); private incomes, but not, of course, those of the high officials, were scrutinized and people held for questioning by the police.

The reformists were defeated, but in contrast to the past, they refused to defend publicly policies they privately opposed. At the plenary session of the Central Committee in July 1962, four months after the crucial debate in the Executive Committee, "economic integration" was the word, and Tito thundered against a "wrongly conceived decentralization, for our country must form a unit as far as economy is concerned." The scene was dominated by Rankovic, who in a lengthy speech sketched out the program of tightening "the leading role of the party." Neither at this nor at the following plenary meeting in May 1963 did any of the reformers and decentralists from the north speak. The new Constitution was hailed as a major step forward on the path of democratization, but the power balance shifted once again in favor of the centralists. In mid-1963 Rankovic was elected Vice President of the Republic and the Serbian leader, Petar Stambolic, rose to the position of Premier.

The centralists, however, overplayed their hand. Tito made a number of speeches that served no purpose other than to float new, or rather, dangerous old ideas into the public consciousness and thereby lift the bickering over economics to the level of a national crisis. Standing above the separate nationalities, Tito has never felt himself or been regarded as a Croat. Borrowing a phrase from King Alexander a generation ago, he may well have said that he was the only Yugoslav in the country. From the end of 1962 on, he lent his authority to the hitherto covert attempt to revive the idea of "Yugoslavism," of a "uniform Yugoslav culture," a "uniform Yugoslav socialist consciousness" which "should be the common property of all nationalities."

All this was in essence a complete break with the postulates of

national individuality and cultural distinctiveness upheld ever since
the Communists had come to power. Given the numerical majority
of Serbs, the power balance in the center, and the political context
of centralism, economic and cultural integration was a fundamental
challenge to the constitutional rights of the smaller nations. Thus
the Croats, Slovenes, and Macedonians, not to speak of the Albanian
and Hungarian minorities, had good reason to be wary of the campaign for Yugoslavism. In fact it was nothing but a resurgence of
the prewar "integral Yugoslavism" of King Alexander that was a
façade for Serbian domination, although exerted this time by Serb
Communists and not by royal officers or bourgeois politicians. The
new ruling elite of Serbia calculated in the same terms as its
prewar predecessor: "Greater political power plus smaller economic
wealth equals greater economic wealth plus smaller political
power."[81]

These fateful initiatives opened the lid of Pandora's box, destroyed the outward consensus within the ruling elite, and released
the age-old historical and emotional tensions between the nations,
which now merged with the determination to defend tangible economic interests. The differences between "have" and "have not"
nations were superseded by the need for common defense against
the danger of Serb hegemony, which overrode all other considerations. Aside from some young people, mainly of Serbian origin, and
the Bosnian Muslims, the visitor rarely encounters a self-proclaimed
Yugoslav. The average citizen identifies himself and is regarded as
a Serb or Croat, Macedonian or Albanian. At the time of the 1961
census 6 per cent of the population, or 317,000 people (mainly
Muslims), declared themselves Yugoslavs. The campaign for a Yugoslav consciousness, mainly stimulated by Serbian writers and intellectuals, ran counter to the real sentiments of the population and
served dangerous political ends. Crvenkovski, the Macedonian
leader, drew the logical conclusion: "Yugoslavism is a socially conservative, politically reactionary ideology. Its starting point is the
merger of the existing nations into some new Yugoslav nation."[82]

The dramatic revival of national tensions was closely connected
with the question of Tito's successor. Many observers tended to regard it as a clear-cut battle between two crown princes, Alexander
Rankovic, a Serb tailor, and Edward Kardelj, a Slovene school-
teacher, who were almost the same age—born respectively in
1909 and 1910. During the war Rankovic built up the security serv-

ice, the UDBA, and for two decades was primarily responsible for security, the judiciary, and personnel policy. Kardelj was alternatively Foreign Minister, Vice-Premier, and President of the Federal Assembly. Rankovic was the top man in daily charge of the party and a secretary of the Central Committee, while Kardelj, also a secretary, became the leading theoretician of the decentralization experiments after the fall of Djilas. But it would be a misleading simplification to say that Rankovic was "dogmatic" and Kardelj a "liberal."

The real situation never matched this deceptively neat equation. Kardelj was always an advocate of the decentralization, but his approach often reflected the same high degree of intolerance and sectarian rigidity that characterized his "extremist phase" in the immediate postwar period. He pushed the principle of decentralization, of "payment according to work," to ridiculous and self-defeating extremes. Yugoslavia became the only country in the world for quite a time to have twenty-six separate railroad enterprises, which were later reduced to six republican companies; where teachers were paid according to lessons per pupil; doctors for every phase of treatment of patients, starting with taking the pulse; judges on the basis of the number of "settled cases"; and administrators according to their paperwork. As *Borba* caustically remarked, "If only the police were to calculate its 'output,' socialism would be complete." Rankovic, on the other hand, was interested in controlling the decisive levers of the power structure, in gaining a hold over the top planners and administrators, and in forging an alliance with those technocrats who held that modern technology requires centralized decision-making. In some respects his concepts were more pragmatic and realistic than those of Kardelj.

But regardless of the personal traits of the two contenders, the real division was between centralism and federalism, between unity forged by a "firm hand" policy and the harmony of distinct but related nations. Rankovic was a Serb and stood for the Serbian apparat, while Kardelj, no matter how long he operated from Belgrade, was regarded as a Slovene, the representative of a small and "peripheral" nation. The Slovenes themselves, however, Communists and non-Communists alike, have never regarded him as being truly one of them because he has not identified himself with the interests of his native national unit.

The so-called "national key," distribution of top positions according to the proportional strength of the various nations, was formally held in high esteem. In reality, it was a farce. The Executive Committee until 1964 consisted of four Serbs, three Croats, three Slovenes, three Montenegrins, and one Macedonian. But the UDBA, the single most important "unifying instrument" and "sword of the party," like the central apparat, was run by Rankovic and his associates, all Serbs. At the Eighth Party Congress in December 1964, the reformers achieved a political victory but the organization remained firmly in the hands of the Serbian centralists. The Executive Committee was enlarged to nineteen members: six Serbs, four Croats, four Montenegrins, three Slovenes, and two Macedonians. This meant that the Montenegrin party with 34,000 members had the same representation as the Croat with 218,000 members. The Croats formally included Tito, who was not an exponent in any sense of the Croat interests, and his close friend General Ivan Gosnjak, also a Croat but loyal to no one but Tito.

After their defeat, the champions of economic decentralization and national equality combined a holding operation with a build-up and channeling of pressures from below. While Rankovic never succeeded in subverting the Croat and Slovene party and police apparatus, it was evident to the reformers that the battle could be won only in the center. Rankovic's real adversary was not Kardelj but Vladimir Bakaric, whom we have already quoted several times. The son of a judge and a graduate in law, Bakaric was born in 1912 and joined the Communists as a high school student. It is the irony of fate that his father was once in charge of an investigation into the underground activities of Tito in the late twenties. First postwar Premier of Croatia, head of the party there since 1945, and member of the all-Yugoslav Executive Committee since 1952, this plump man of medium height with heart trouble may well be the ablest leader Croatia has produced since the times of Bishop Strossmayer (1815–1905). An outstanding expert in agricultural policies, Bakaric is credited with having halted the disastrous collectivization campaigns in 1953. Since he stood above local interests, Bakaric was for a long period regarded by the "pure Croat nationalists" as a servant of Belgrade and even today is sporadically accused of "giving in." Yet he was unquestionably the mastermind behind the strategy that, after four years of tangled maneuvering, led to the ouster of Rankovic.

This quiet and modest man, who from time to time retires to the

Adriatic island of Hvar to ponder basic economic or theoretical problems, is not a natural rebel, by either temperament or political conviction. A particular set of circumstances made him a "rebel" in spite of himself against the stifling iron hand of Serb-dominated central bureaucracy. Since the Croats account for just over 23 per cent of the population, Bakaric could never aspire to the mantle of a Yugoslav leader. Like all Yugoslav leaders with the notable exception of Tito, he is classified according to ethnic nationality. But he has an unfailing instinct for the essential; he has relied on intellectual "task forces" in dealing with a multitude of problems, and has picked out and promoted young, able, and well-educated executive-politicians like Mika Tripalo and Savka Dapcevic-Kucar. Perhaps most important he has recognized the enormous potential of the press and television in an increasingly pluralistic society.

In a series of interviews, Bakaric issued repeated warnings against the rising tide of nationalism and shifted the real thrust of popular and national dissent toward the revamping of the federal structure. When the reformers switched to a political offensive in 1964, Bakaric warned "if an operation is necessary one does not operate with a blunt scalpel but with a sharp one. . . . Foreign policy is a matter for all the peoples of Yugoslavia." He injected the catch phrase, "the Federation must be federalized," into the disputes. On the surface, the country was divided into two camps, centered respectively at Belgrade and Zagreb. The actual division was, however, more complicated.

The republics are not always identical with compact national groups. The Serbs in Croatia, who make up almost 15 per cent of the population, are, out of self-interest, behind the Croat reformers in their quest for a fairer distribution of the national income. But because they vividly remember the nightmares of the 1941–44 war, they tend to look to Belgrade as a symbolic protector of their distinctiveness as Serbs outnumbered by Croats. Their situation is ambivalent and complicated by the fact that many of them were Partisans and occupied prominent positions in the administration and—which the Croats particularly resent—in cultural fields, such as the university, mass media, publishing houses, etc.

A special case is Bosnia-Herzegovina, where Serbs outnumber Croats two to one, with a large Muslim group poised precariously in the middle. In Bosnia the unbridled rule of Serb UDBA officials inflamed national tensions, heightened by the covert discrimination against Croats in the party and state administration, to an alarming degree. Thus though the Croats constituted almost 25 per cent of the population, their share in the personnel of UDBA amounted to a mere 5 per cent, and at the security service headquarters in Sarajevo there was only one Croat official.

In a crudely simplified form one may therefore conclude that Rankovic and the Serb advocates of centralism were in power in Serbia proper and had a strong hold on the power structure in Montenegro and Bosnia. "The camp of Zagreb" on the other hand could count on firm allies in Slovenia, and sympathizers among the Macedonians, forward-looking Serbs who resented Rankovic's strong-arm methods, and the non-Slav nationalities, numbering some 2 million people, most of them living in the two autonomous provinces—Kosovo and Vojvodina—attached to Serbia.

What the nationalities and smaller nations could be expected to endure under the domination of the UDBA, which according to the party documents was "not only a state within a state but a force above society," was vividly illustrated by the intensity of the oppression of Albanians in the Kosovo province. Though the Albanians here are almost 70 per cent of the population, and the Serbs only 23 per cent, the national and political equality upheld by the Constitution was a farce.

The Secretary of the provincial party committee, Veli Deva, a native Albanian, provided some highly illuminating details: "At all levels, the use of our language was reduced to a minimum. There were many conferences where all the participants, even the stenographers, were Albanians, but they spoke Serbo-Croatian. The names of the streets, schools, firms, and even towns were written in Serbo-Croatian. These may seem trifling matters, but are in fact grave political problems. In the entire federal administration, there was not a single Albanian representative." In 1955–56, under the pretext that "the Albanians are preparing a coup d'état," a large-scale campaign was launched to collect weapons, and a number of Albanians were killed. No over-all figures have been published, but information divulged about the murders in the commune of Djakovica may serve as a pointer. Here, throughout the years, fourteen presidents of the communal assembly and secretaries of the party organization were persecuted, imprisoned, and tortured; nineteen people were killed, and others committed suicide. There were 120,-000 files kept in evidence about "unreliable" Albanians.[83]

Not only was the Serbian Communists' treatment of the Albanians on a par with the revolting record of prewar Yugoslavia, but Albania had no representation in top party and state bodies. There are almost as many Albanians (1.1 million) as Macedonians and twice as many as Montenegrins. Yet until the recent reorganization of the top party organs, there was no Albanian in the top leadership. It was only in October 1966 that, for the first time since the war, ethnic Albanians and Hungarians were elected to the enlarged Presidium of the party. Though things have only just begun to change in the Kosovo region, the Serbs are already upset about "a threat to the position and life of the Serbs and Montenegrins in Kosovo," and disgruntled conservative elements are mounting pressure on the new Serbian party leaders "to defend their brethren." For all the publicity given to the fact that Serbian Communists were "revolted and ashamed of the abuses in Kosovo," there is still a double standard in dealing with UDBA murderers and those guilty of political dissent.

The young university lecturer, Mihajlo Mihajlov, whose importance was wildly exaggerated in Western press reports, stood on trial for the second time in April 1967 for "spreading falsehoods and carrying out hostile propaganda against the state." Already serving a prison term, he was sentenced to four and a half years in jail. Nine days later, two UDBA officials were tried for having tortured two Albanians to death in the town of Prizren in 1954. They were sentenced respectively to a five- and a four-year prison term.[84]

The coalition of Croat, Slovene, and Macedonian Communists forced the Eighth Party Congress in December 1964 to come out unequivocally against the idea of a "single Yugoslav nation" and to adopt an outwardly unanimous decision in favor of a drastic revamping of the economy. This was followed, in July 1965, by the launching of The Reform. Professor Rudolf Bicanic, one of the country's foremost economists, called this "a process of the four Ds: Decentralization, De-étatization, De-politicization and Democratization."[85]

The formal unity proclaimed at the congress and plenary meetings of party and state bodies soon began to wear very thin indeed. Tito gradually recognized that to reduce The Reform—as in 1961—to a mere superficial stabilization and to block the steadily mounting pressures from below for meaningful and not merely verbal national equality would be to risk political disaster and a grave

national crisis. Deadlock between reformers and centralists polluted
the atmosphere. At the plenary meeting of the Central Committee
in February-March 1966, it was abundantly clear that, as King
Alexander said a generation earlier, "the machine no longer works."

The details of the final showdown with Rankovic and his independent apparatus of power read like a detective thriller. The
radical novelty of the power struggle in the center was that it was
—at any rate in the last crucial phase—a straightforward battle between the security service and the army intelligence, or, in a broader
context, between the two key levers of power. The UDBA's decision-
makers constituted a tightly knit unit pledging unconditional
obedience only to their chiefs and ultimately to Rankovic, who "was
identified with the party leadership" as being responsible for the
entire sector. Though the security service in Croatia and Slovenia
was also accused of "deformations," it was the UDBA center, run
solely by Serbs, that was the key element in the "conspiratorial
struggle for power." Rankovic and his two closest collaborators,
Svetislav Stefanovic, the long-time operative director of the security
service, and his successor, Vojin Lukic, later "elected" organizational secretary of the Serbian Central Committee, sought points of
control in the central and Serbian party apparat, in the federal and
Serbian ministries of interior, and last but not least in the Foreign
Ministry. Rankovic was built up by security agents and informers,
acting on clear instructions from above, as the successor to Tito. A
cult was created around his person, and the regular "situation
reports" on "popular sentiments" prepared by the top UDBA officials for the party leaders were naturally tailored to fit their purposes.

Opponents or waverers were ruthlessly and rapidly removed and
degraded. Predrag Ajtic, a native Albanian and an old party member, who in 1963 refused to cooperate with the Rankovic group
when serving as ambassador in Bulgaria, was recalled, expelled
from the party, and became a social outcast. He was not fully
rehabilitated until three years later, after the fall of Rankovic. From
1964 on, Party Secretary Simic in the Foreign Ministry and Deputy
Foreign Minister Bosko Vidakovic brought the diplomatic service,
above all its personnel, coding, and communication departments,
completely under UDBA control. Ambassadors were appointed
over the head of the Minister, Koca Popovic, though he was a close
friend of Tito and a prominent figure in his own right. Even diplo-

matic cables were first checked and if necessary destroyed before they reached Popovic. In the winter of 1964, three leaders of the UDBA, headed by the then Minister of Interior, paid a visit to Moscow and at a party, when they were slightly drunk, flatly remarked that "Tito is getting old, and it is time Rankovic took over the helm." The Yugoslav Ambassador, Cvijetin Mijatovic, himself a Central Committee member, sent an angry cable to Koca Popovic relating the episode. But the message never reached him.

The cumulative effect of these developments, coupled with mounting economic, political, and national tensions, convinced Tito that "we were heading for difficult times, that around Rankovic a personality cult and factional group was beginning to emerge." He was worried "about the party's prestige, internal and external repercussions," and thought that the situation "could be dramatic." Rankovic also established close contacts with the Soviet intelligence and was often visited by the Soviet Ambassador. As a Central Committee member put it at the crucial plenary meeting in July 1966, "He was shaping a line in foreign policy different from that of the party and government."[86]

The Belgrade security service had installed listening devices in Kardelj's offices by 1958, and in 1961 his private telephone was connected with the Rankovic home. From that year on, every room in the new government building was also "bugged." In November 1965 when Tito came out clearly in favor of the reform course, microphones were placed in his premises and his official and private telephone line was linked with Rankovic's office.

The high bureaucracy lives in Dedinje, a luxury suburb of Belgrade. From his home at 25 Uzicka Street Rankovic could listen in on all the telephone calls in the houses with lower numbers, including Tito's in number 15. With a switch in his bedroom, he could relax and simultaneously eavesdrop on his colleagues in the top leadership.

But the security service failed to infiltrate the army intelligence and the top command headed by General Ivan Gosnjak, a Croat and a long-standing party leader. While Rankovic had Tito's premises "bugged" and the telephones of other leaders tapped, his own line as well as those of Stefanovic and Lukic were monitored by army intelligence. The man who may well have given the final push to the assault on the UDBA strongholds was Milan Miskovic, newly appointed in 1965 as Minister of Interior. Being outside the

UDBA clique, Miskovic soon noticed that he was ignored by his subordinates, who went directly to Stefanovic, the chairman of a new federal commission in charge of all departments dealing with security, police, and militia. Later he discovered that wiretapping devices had been installed in his office and that he—the Minister of Interior!—was under constant surveillance.

Vaguely perceiving the gathering clouds, the UDBA conspirators gave instructions to tap army intelligence headquarters from May 30 to June 8, 1966. Party Secretary Lukic, sent as a member of a party delegation to Mongolia around the same time, was already suspicious and asked the Belgrade UDBA officials to see whether his telephone was being tapped. By then, however, the line-up of forces was complete, and the decisive blow was skillfully executed. In addition to the presidential guard battalions, a significant force in itself, elite army units were moved to the capital and the island of Brioni, Tito's other main residence. At the beginning of June, microphones were discovered in the Marshal's office and home, even in the bedroom. According to one version, a pipe system with the ominous implications of a possible "gassing device" was detected. Tito immediately set up a technical task force to investigate the affair. Listening devices were found not only at Kardelj's premises, but also in the homes of the Serbian party leader Jovan Veselinov and Premier Petar Stambolic. (During a debate about the Rankovic affair in the small circle of Tito's closest collaborators, Kardelj is reported to have remarked, "I had noted years ago that my telephone was being tapped." "Why didn't you tell me?" snapped Tito. "I thought *you* might have ordered it . . ." Kardelj said quietly.) One week later, on June 16, Rankovic was confronted with the evidence at a session of the Executive Committee. He voted for the setting up of a party-state investigating commission and resigned as secretary and member of the Committee.

The plenary meeting of the 155-member Central Committee on July 1–2, 1966, confirmed the fall of a potential dictator, the wreckage of a brilliant career, which had led a tailor's apprentice to the position of second in command. After forty years of party membership, Rankovic was forced into unwanted retirement at the early age of fifty-seven and three months later was expelled from the party. Both he and Stefanovic, after destroying much of the evidence against them, attempted to present the "bugging" of Tito's premises as the main issue, strongly hinting that the listening devices had been planted by "someone else." Rankovic made a desperate and futile attempt before the plenary meeting to iron out the affair in a personal talk with Tito. Contrary to their hopes, Tito still had enough prestige to keep everybody in line, and none of their former close associates spoke up in their defense.

Whether the microphones were placed there by the army intelligence—Stefanovic, according to private information, named Tito's aide-de-camp as being directly responsible—is today irrelevant. The Brioni meeting of the Central Committee represented a stunning defeat for the policy of Great Serbian hegemony and bureaucratic centralism. In many respects, it may mark a watershed in postwar Yugoslav history, hastening the transition from the rule of individuals to the rule of institutions, from a monolithic dictatorship manipulated by a handful of people to a more pluralistic system.

In the long run, perhaps the most important consequence will prove to be the demonstration that the Serbian relative majority cannot, by numerical superiority, impose its will on the smaller nations. At the same time, the press campaign that showed up the UDBA officials as utterly corrupt profit-seekers, getting kickbacks from directors they helped to appoint, importing tax-free cars and selling them at a large mark-up, gambling in exclusive casinos reserved for the security officers, building private houses and seaside cottages at community expense, and using prisoners as unpaid laborers, blew to smithereens the myth of "the sword of the party."

Barely three months after the Rankovic affair, Tito demanded a stop to the destructive campaign against privileges and called for the strengthening of the security service, which had been demoralized by the purge. "It was essential," he said later, "to make people as fond of the UDBA as they were during and after the war. . . ." But regardless of its reorganization, which involved cutting personnel in half, the UDBA can never again become an inviolable symbol and center of power. More important still, it has been drastically decentralized, with most of its powers transferred to the republics, which have also taken over border and customs control. A parliamentary watchdog commission checks its over-all operations, and similar bodies have been formed at regional levels.

The fact that even the speeches made by the defeated faction at the plenary meeting, as well as all the lurid details of the UDBA tyranny and "dolce vita," were published by the mass media was a product of and factor in the process of democratization. The Rankovic affair was not a purge like the staged trials still characteristic of "conventional" Communist power struggles. Rankovic and his seventeen high-ranking collaborators were pardoned in December 1966 by presidential decree, after criminal proceedings had been instituted against them. The federal parliament approved the decree, although nine deputies abstained from voting. There are many explanations for the amnesty, some conflicting and each probably containing an element of truth. One version is that the victors wanted to appease Serbian public opinion, which immediately reacted to the fall of the top Serbian leader with instinctive national solidarity. Another is that Rankovic demanded a public trial; but he knew too much, and thus had some trump cards. The official arguments for the amnesty referred to "the strength of self-government, humanism, past services rendered by Rankovic and some of the other accused." While the compromise solution deprived Rankovic of the chance to defend himself, many Serbs interpreted it as a sign of the weakness of the "anti-Serb victors."

Be that as it may, the Brioni plenum gave a tremendous push to democratization and the trend toward national equality. At the elections in April 1967, voters were given a much wider range of choice on republican and federal levels than in 1965. Representatives are elected for a four-year term, but every second year half of them come up for re-election. While the number of candidates at the communal level in 1965 was already twice the number of seats, there were only 64 candidates for 60 seats in the top political chamber of the federal parliament. In 1967, however, voters elected 60 deputies out of 81 candidates for the federal parliament, and 325 out of 425 candidates for the republican parliaments. Though the number of candidates proposed at nomination meetings was drastically reduced by the Communist-controlled electoral commissions, there was still an incomparably greater freedom of choice than before. In quite a few districts it came down to real contests between 2 or even 3 to 5 candidates on the ballot. Three prominent party functionaries, including Minister of Foreign Trade Nikola Dzuverovic, were beaten.

The resignation of the Slovene government on December 7, 1966, after its defeat in the social-health chamber of the republican parliament dramatically revealed the extent of pluralism in political life. The chamber voted 44 to 11 in favor of rejecting the government's bill to increase the contribution paid by individual workers to the cost of the health services. In 1964 and 1965, even the federal government had been outvoted on various measures, but this was the first time that a Communist government took the unprecedented step of tendering its resignation. The "government crisis" in Slovenia lasted three weeks, providing astounding evidence of the progress toward making parliamentary institutions more genuinely democratic and influential centers of decision-making.

As a first step toward the reorganization of the party, the top bodies were broadened. Using once again the old technique of giving new names to institutions, a Presidium, consisting of thirty-five members, replaced the old Executive Committee as the policy-making body. The new Executive Committee, now composed of eleven members, was given purely executive functions, and the members barred from operative positions in the state apparatus and other political bodies.*

But as Krste Crvenkovski repeatedly warned, "The abolishment of personal union between party and government leadership is only the first step. . . . Democracy should cease to be the privilege of a self-styled elite." This also depends on the handling of the so-called "system of rotation" under which leading officials can have only one, or, under special circumstances, two terms in office, which had been a game of musical chairs with the same small group of people switching from a top position in the government to a similar high post in the party, the unions, or mass organizations. Professor Rajko Tomovic, writing in the official party organ, fittingly compared the rotation "to a closed circle which opens only if and when someone new is introduced into the circle, but not to break the circle itself."[87]

* Further important changes were announced after the plenary meeting of the all-Yugoslav Central Committee in July 1968. The Central Committee as such will be abolished. The next party congress, in 1969, will elect instead an enlarged forty-nine member Presidium and sixty-seven members of the so-called standing group of a completely new body—the Conference of the League of Communists. While the congress is held every four years, the supreme policy-making organ between two congresses, controlling the activities of the Presidium and the Executive Committee Secretariat, will be the annual Conference. The mandate of the 250–300 delegates will last only one year except for the standing group elected by the congress. The Conference can also change the composition of the Presidium—up to 40 per cent of its membership. The new structure and other provisions should make the selection and renewal of key personnel more genuinely democratic.

The first really comprehensive reshuffle took place in May 1967. Except for Tito and three other officials whose terms had not yet expired, a completely new team took over the leading posts in parliament and the federal government. For the first time, the top party leaders were freed of any administrative responsibilities in the state administration at federal and republican levels. The actual government, called the Federal Executive Council, is headed by a president and two vice presidents and consists of fourteen members. The ministers, secretaries of state, and presidents of various commissions are regarded as officials. In all, thirty-eight people constitute the top administrative team.

Only two of the thirty-five-member party Presidium are in the government—Mika Spiljak, fifty-one, the Premier, and one of his deputies, Rudi Kolak, forty-eight. It is true that eleven of the thirty-eight top officials also belong to the party's Central Committee, but the generation of prewar Communist leaders have been largely replaced by younger men who joined the party during the war and held only low or medium ranks as Partisans, since administrators, planners, and scientists outnumber party professionals three to one. Their average age is forty-seven, and one of the ministers, Bora Jelic, former Deputy Governor of the Central Bank, actually joined the party only after the war.

Will the "glorious heroes and pompous fools," as a well-known Yugoslav describes the majority of the Old Guard, really step down? Will selection now be guided by ability rather than by "the clique"? There are several important factors that are still a deadweight on upward mobility. First of all there is the more or less proportional representation of the nations at the federal level. The designated Premier, the architect of The Reform, was the able Slovene, Boris Krajger. He was killed in an automobile accident just before the election, and the careful balance between the republican representatives was upset. The Croat Spiljak, generally regarded as a man of mediocre abilities, was put forward as candidate for the premiership. The new Secretary of the party's Executive Committee, Mijalko Todorovic, was a Serb. Another ranking party leader, Veljko Vlahovic, a Montenegrin, was to be President of the Federal Parliament, which meant, after the post of Vice President was abolished, that he would have ranked as formal deputy to the President, that is, to Marshal Tito.

The line-up would have been: a Croat President (because Tito is formally counted as a Croat), a Croat Premier, a Serb party Secretary, and a Montenegrin as President of Parliament. On top of this, moreover, one of the deputy premiers, Kiro Gligorov, is a Macedonian and the other, Rudi Kolak, represents the republic of Bosnia, although he is also of Croatian stock. The proposals were published at the end of January 1967. Talking to Bakaric about a month later, I asked, "Won't the Serbs be dissatisfied with their representation having only Todorovic in a top position?" Bakaric in reply stressed that "Todorovic's position is an extremely important one. . . ."

In March, however, a major scandal erupted when eighteen Croat scientific institutions, headed by 130 prominent scholars including 80 Communists, issued a declaration asking for a constitutional change to make Serbian and Croatian separate languages instead of Serbo-Croatian/Croat-Serbian. They claimed that the Croatian dialect was discriminated against in everyday use and the Serb version imposed as the common language. The initiative, staged or spontaneous, was not only disastrously timed and practically superfluous in view of the evolving changes in the federal structure, but played directly into the hands of the Serb nationalists. An hysterical mass campaign was launched. The people who had signed the declaration were expelled from the party, while forty-five Serb writers, almost half of them Communists, including one member of the Serbian Central Committee, reacted in a similarly couched counterproposal, demanding instruction in Serbian dialect and in Cyrillic letters for the 650,000 Serbs living in Croatia. The dispute also involved the ethnic nationality of the Montenegrins, whose party leadership came out in a strongly worded statement against "Great Serbian hegemonists who deny the Montenegrins' national individuality."

Inflamed national passions, especially the already wounded pride of the Serbs who had "lost" Rankovic, brought a "reappraisal" of the original suggestions for the top position. Taking into account the principle of "numerical representation of individual nations and republics in supreme state and political bodies," the Socialist Alliance, the mass organization that formally proposes the candidates, dropped the Montenegrin Vlahovic and nominated a leading Serb functionary, Milentije Popovic, for President of the Federal Parliament. Thus within three months, the leadership had to yield to the pent-up national feelings of the Serbs.

All this was not a "palace intrigue" or a trifling personal matter, but an index to the enormous role the national question plays in

every single field, including the selection of leaders: ethnic nationality and not ability remains the often overriding consideration. As a
result, the smaller nations, the Slovenes and Macedonians, were
"the losers" in a Serb-Croat deal that neatly divided the four top
positions. The affair once again confirmed that the existence of
Yugoslavia depends on the balance between Serbs and Croats. It is
their relationship that ultimately determines the given temperature
of national tensions.

The second factor within the given Communist system that has
a covert but nonetheless important influence on decison-making
and social mobility is the role of the Old Guard. Tito's collaborators are, as far as their record goes, old-timers, but actually they are
all in their mid-fifties. Former members of the previous almighty
Executive Committee, such as ex-Premier Stambolic, the Serb leaders Veselinov, Kardelj, or the Montenegrin Vukmanovic-Tempo, are
today members of what the Yugoslavs hopefully but not quite real-
istically call the "Upper House." This special sort of "Senate"
called the Council of Federation consists of sixty-seven members and
according to the Constitution has only advisory functions. The Old
Guard also dominates the party Presidium.

Events during and after the Arab-Israeli war in 1967 showed, however, that persons with prestige can exert a great influence on important decisions whether or not they have executive functions. The
role of the Old Guard is insolubly tied to Tito's. His position has a
two-fold impact on developments: as the only figure standing above
the separate nationalities, his prestige helps to smooth the transition
from a federal form with centralist content to something more akin
to a confederation whose base is to be a unanimous and not majority
rule. Yet because he is a historic figure above overt criticism, he has
been, in a sense, the single greatest stumbling block to a meaningful
democratization of decision-making, both within and outside the
party. Tito, who regards the army as the only remaining effective
instrument of unifying the country, and the handling of major foreign policy issues as his personal domain, has refused to reduce his
activity to that of a benign "father figure." His single-handed initiatives in the Middle East crisis, his participation at two Soviet bloc
summit meetings in June and July 1967, without first consulting
the proper party and government bodies, harmed Yugoslavia's standing in the world and compromised her alleged "non-aligned" position. Worse still, Tito still clings to the obsolete Leninist structure

and character of the party, resisting real and not merely technical changes.

The creation of a six-member executive body of the Council of Federation consisting of his oldest friends—Kardelj, Koca Popovic, General Gosnjak, Vlahovic, Vukmanovic-Tempo, and his Cabinet chief, Vladimir Popovic—in July 1967 raised the ominous specter of a "super-cabinet," a power center subordinate only to Tito. He has complained several times that "people say that no one listens to me any longer."[88] Thus it is somewhat naïve to believe that either Tito, as long as he is alive, or the relatively youthful "Old Guard" will ever be mere spectators watching the "legitimate" party and government bodies dealing with important policy issues.

Yet it is also a fact that Tito no longer possesses total authority and his influence within a looser form of federalism is bound to wane much faster than it did before the fall of Rankovic. A new structure of checks and balances influenced by clear-cut national and regional interests is emerging. The question of Tito's "successor" is no longer on the agenda; the problem of succession, however important, is only a part of finding an acceptable solution to the "peaceful coexistence" of the nations of Yugoslavia.

The Reform is still in its first phase. The long-term options between a developed and an underdeveloped economic model, between over-all or selective growth, between the market mechanism and centralized investments, between economic efficiency and the policy of equal stomachs, have yet to be made. But the Federation is changing its character so rapidly that even these crucial questions are likely to be posed in a different fashion. The Chamber of Nationalities in the Federal Parliament has already secured increased powers to block any bills passed in the Federal—that is, the policy-making—Chamber. The composition of political and other bodies will be based more and more on the principle of republican delegations, instead of on the "superiority of nations which have a numerical majority."[89]

The six republican parties, although all are Communist, in some ways resemble the prewar line-up of forces organized along national lines. The UDBA has already been decentralized, and the decision that 25 per cent of all recruits do their military service in the territory from which they come may be the first step toward the creation of standing republican armies. The Croats point out that, under the Austro-Hungarian monarchy, Croatia had regiments of its own with Croat officers who commanded in the Croat language. The Slovenes, who began their campaign for real equality of languages in the autumn of 1966, are fervently supported by the Macedonians.

There are, of course, two points of view on the trend toward confederation. "Some people ask: Can Yugoslavia afford to have six film industries? But others say: Can anyone hinder a nation expressing itself through this medium?" as Crvenkovski once put it, adding acidly, "there are no wise centers, or provinces that are always wrong."[90] The same dispute affects television, publishing, education, and so on. The Serbs, accustomed to being the "leading nation," ask, "What price federalism?" to which the others respond, "What price centralism?"

The danger is that the power of control over the national currents can easily slip from the hands of the Communist leaders of the respective ethnic groups. This happened, for example, in the case of the Croat declaration in favor of linguistic equality. Bakaric and his associates intended to use the "pure" Croat nationalists as political tools and discard them once the battle with Rankovic for the "federalizing of the Federation" was won. But the temporary allies got out of control with frightening ease. Serbian hegemony in the guise of Communist centralism poured oil on the smoldering fires of aggressive Croat separatism, defensive Slovene nationalism, Macedonian national feelings—not to speak of the disgruntled Albanians suffering from Serbian oppression. The transition from majority decisions at the apex to unanimous rule—the technique of confederation—is fraught with dangers, and the advent of television magnifies and dramatizes the issues.

National feelings act and react upon one another. The Macedonian Orthodox church proclaims itself autocephalous, that is, fully independent, in 1967 although the Serbian mother church refuses to recognize it as such; the Albanians for the first time try in earnest to assert their rights in terms of the Constitution. And to add insult to injury, a Croat sits in Belgrade as Premier. Serbian public opinion is deeply offended and aroused in "the defense of Serbia." The centuries-old feelings of national superiority toward the former provinces of the Austro-Hungarian monarchy, not to speak of such "dubious" ethnic groups as the Macedonians or the Albanians, those latecomers to "Old Serbia," are more powerful than the tenuous bonds of Communist party discipline. The situation is particularly dangerous in Serbia where, before and during the war, the party was much weaker than in other parts of the country. And now there are no Serbian leaders in power remotely comparable in prestige and stature to the deposed Rankovic. Thus, in contrast to the early sixties, Serbia may well become a storm center particularly in view of an unnatural—yet in national terms logical—alliance of Serbian nationalists of the old school and the Rankovic vintage. What the regime describes as a "political underground" is precisely this phenomenon, which poses a potentially serious threat to the post-Rankovic moderate Communist leadership in Serbia.[*]

The test of a truly federal structure of nations with equal rights, like the most difficult period of The Reform, is still ahead. As the moderates on all sides realize, the national conflict is "unwinnable" in a much deeper sense than is commonly understood by the man in the street. Yugoslavia's problems can be solved by consent only if there is national equality and a necessary minimum of consensus among the nations and their protagonists. The single Yugoslav state, tension-ridden as it may be, exists and is bound to survive, barring an unlikely upheaval on European scale, because a secession or break-up would expose the component national units to an even more dangerous future. No one, aside from the most extreme Croat separatists, is ready willfully to destroy the federation, however they may feel about it.

Yugoslavia is a single-party dictatorship, but compared to countries at a similar stage of economic development such as Spain or Portugal, Greece or Turkey, its political record is by no means as disappointing as conventional ideological labels would suggest. By trial and error, search and experiment, it has covered an amazing

[*] Sharpening tensions were evident in the recall of former Yugoslav Premier Stambolic, not exactly a liberal, from the "Upper House" to the presidency of the Serbian party in January 1968. The behind-the-scenes conflict over the national problem came to a head at the May plenary meeting of the Serbian Central Committee when two leading members—the historian Jovan Marjanovic and the well-known writer Dobrica Cosic—publicly complained about an "anti-Serbian trend" in political life, particularly in the autonomous provinces of Kosmet and Voivodina. Though the Central Committee formally condemned their "slanderous" statements, both men have remained members of the Committee. This leniency provided ample evidence that most of the Serbian party leaders are not able (or perhaps even willing) to fight the nationalistic tide in their republic. Soon afterward a spate of terrorist bombings in Belgrade perpetrated by Croat nationalists further inflamed popular feelings and made meaningful action against rampant chauvinism more difficult, if not impossible.

distance, racing ahead of all other Communist-ruled countries toward a more tolerant, more humane, and more liberal system. Given the multinational context and historical background, the emergence of an all-Yugoslav opposition to communism as such can be safely discounted; a multiparty system would inevitably have to be organized along national and not political lines. Even allowing for the potentially crucial role of the army in a power struggle, it seems more likely that the League of Communists, like parliament, will be the arena of an open give-and-take between competing groups, all calling themselves Communist, but representing different groups and national interests. The greatest immediate problem is how to fit the party into the specific Yugoslav framework. But what happens within the party is determined by the national environment. In this sense, the spirit of national affirmation, for all its tensions and risks, has opened up new vistas by shattering the myth of formal unity and unconditional discipline that never really existed. Thus the future depends not only on the outcome of a "showdown" between Communists and non-Communists, between young and old generations, between technocratic-minded executives and politically minded bureaucrats. All these crosscurrents are but elements in the great unsolved task of transforming the "necessity" of Yugoslavia into a "harmony" of its distinct yet associated peoples, into a unity in diversity.

IV

ALBANIA
A Traditional Fuse to the Balkan Powder Keg

The only religion for an Albanian is Albanianism.

—Enver Hoxha

"For those who stand in the way of unity, a spit in the face, a sock in the jaw, and, if necessary, a bullet in the head." This ominous warning was not given at a secret meeting of the Mafia in Sicily or at a Casa Nostra convention in a New York restaurant, but at the Fourth Congress of the Albanian Communist Party in February 1961. The number two man in the leadership of the smallest ruling Communist party in the world, Premier Mehmet Shehu, threatened any would-be waverers at home and simultaneously cautioned the Soviet guests and delegations of the other "fraternal parties" that his tiny country would not yield to mounting Soviet pressure.

Nine months later came the open break between the Soviet world power and the smallest, poorest, most backward and isolated country in the Balkans. In spite of the aid and protection of distant China, few believed at the time that the ruling group of the most primitive of all European Communist states would be able to ride out the storm and survive for long. But six years have gone by, and while Khrushchev, the excommunicator whom the Albanian party leader, Enver Hoxha, described as "the greatest counterrevolutionary charlatan and clown the world has ever known," has disappeared from the stage, the Albanian regime continues to thrive.

Far from getting more conciliatory with the passage of time, Albanian words and deeds are as ferociously defiant as ever. Three Soviet overtures for re-establishing trade contacts, including the offer of badly needed spare parts, were scornfully flouted by the Albanians. When not invited to the Warsaw Pact or Comecon meetings, they protest violently, for Albania is nominally still a member of both organizations. When they do receive an invitation, they answer haughtily that first the other Communist states should

YUGOSLAVIA

Priština

Prizren

ADRIATIC SEA

Scutari

ALBANIA

Durrës

Tirana

Vlora

GREECE

CORFU

ALBANIA

‒ ‒ ‒ Frontier in 1941-43
showing the regions
ceded (from Yugoslavia)
to Albania by the
Axis powers

——— Postwar frontier

mend their ways and offer public apologies to Albania.* Enver
Hoxha and his associates rejected "with contempt the dirty invitation
of the Soviet revisionists" to participate at the festivities celebrating
the fiftieth anniversary of the Russian Revolution and simultaneously
appealed to "the Soviet brothers" to launch a "new revolution to
destroy the treacherous revisionists."[1]

This Communist outpost on the Adriatic, the size of Maryland
with an estimated population in 1967 of about 2 million, has the
psychology of a besieged fortress. All opponents, real or imaginary,
not only its immediate neighbors the "Tito clique and the Greek
monarcho-fascists" but also "the U.S. imperialists and the Khrushchevite revisionists have plotted and are plotting against the
People's Republic of Albania." This feeling of permanent external
insecurity is reflected in the exhortations to the workers and soldiers
to work harder "in a revolutionary way with a revolutionary discipline and military rhythm . . . building socialism with a pick in one
hand, a rifle in the other."

If the Balkans have been the traditional powder keg of European
politics, then this most obscure corner has more often than commonly realized been the fuse that exploded the tinderbox. The process, like so much else in modern Balkan history, began with the disintegration of the Ottoman Empire. The Albanians as the oldest
inhabitants of the Balkan Peninsula feel that their history has been
one of perpetual insult. Aside from the short glorious chapter when
Skanderbeg repulsed the waves of Turkish invasion in the fifteenth
century, the descendants of the ancient Illyrians have from early
days been an apple of discord among their more powerful neighbors. While the Greeks' imagination is still fired by the memory of
Byzantium, the Bulgarians evoke the great medieval empires of
Simeon and Samuel, and the Serbs dream of the Golden Age of Tsar
Dushan, the history of Albania has been one of constant foreign
domination or partition.[2] After having played a significant role as
Muslim equals in the ruling elite of the Ottoman Empire, the
Albanians had by the end of the nineteenth century fallen behind
the emerging neighboring nation-states and developed a defensive
nationalism and a sense of grievance which was to outlast their later
gain of nominal independence.

Albania provides an excellent case study of small-power imperialism, of attempts at territorial aggrandizement by Serbia, Greece,

* See footnote on p. 22.

and Montenegro, small states that themselves fought in self-defense against great-power intervention. The fight for the control over the area inhabited by the Albanian tribes, which throughout history lacked religious and social unity, has always been stimulated by open territorial disputes. The most important of these concerns the Kosovo region and northwestern Macedonia. When in the sixteenth and seventeenth centuries the Orthodox Serbs left the area around Pec, Prizren, and northern Macedonia, the Albanian Muslims gradually occupied the vacant lands.

To the Serbs, this region was Old Serbia, which had been Slav since the seventh century and included the sites of their first patriarchate at Pec and of the fateful battle of 1389. Thus in the wake of the Turkish defeat in 1877–78, the Serbs and their brethren, the Montenegrins, immediately claimed substantial areas, while the Greeks coveted large portions of southern Albania, which they called Northern Epirus. Aware of the weakness of the decaying Ottoman Empire, the Albanians resorted to arms, formed the League of Prizren, and demanded autonomy under Turkish sovereignty. The Congress of Berlin in 1878 greatly reduced the territorial awards to their rapacious neighbors. In fact, the Albanians were doing so well in the fighting that it took a naval demonstration by the six Great Powers to force the cession of Ulcinj, the small Adriatic port, to Montenegro, thus giving that landlocked mountain bastion a coveted outlet on the sea.

Though the Turks had stimulated the rise of Albanian nationalism as an instrument to stave off the loss of their last European possessions, they soon became alarmed at the drive for cultural autonomy. The Sultan dissolved the League of Prizren and suppressed the society formed for the defense and development of the Albanian language, while the Patriarch of Constantinople threatened to excommunicate anyone found reading or writing Albanian.[3] The Albanians suffered the embitterment of loyalty betrayed and went on the defensive not only against the Turks, who by denying their national identity and cultural autonomy alienated the most reliable remaining subjects of the Sultan in the Balkans, but also against the infidel who wanted to impose his will upon them, whom they considered inferior.

Unable to catch up with the neighboring nation-states and resenting the injustice to its national cause, Albania with two revolts in 1909 and 1911 in Kosovo and the adjoining regions precipitated the war between the Balkan states and Turkey. But in all the changes of fortune in the two Balkan Wars over the control of European Turkey and the division of the spoils, the Albanians were the losers. Serbia and Montenegro in the north and Greece in the south took by force well over one-third of the territory inhabited mainly by Albanians and, not satisfied with these territorial gains, aimed to dismember rump Albania.

Three factors helped Albania survive the following decade of anarchy and emerge as an independent state in 1920. The same factors have enabled the country to outlive the constant menace to its independence in our time. These were the perennial discord among its more powerful land and sea neighbors, Yugoslavia, Greece, and Italy, over how to dismember it; the intervention of one or more of the great powers to maintain a precarious balance in the Balkans; and last but not least the staunch determination and sheer will power of the small menaced nation to resist foreign invasions.

Though a Constituent Assembly held in November 1912 in the port of Vlora (Vallona) proclaimed the independence of rump Albania, large portions of the country were still occupied by her neighbors. Later Austrian and Italian intervention forced the invaders to evacuate the occupied territories, after which the great powers agreed that Albania should be a sovereign principality with a prince. Naval demonstrations and an Austrian ultimatum to Serbia kept the neighbors in check. Nevertheless, a northern chieftain, Esad Pasha, bribed by Serbia, rose in revolt against the international commission that in theory ruled the country. The first formal ruler, chosen by the great powers, the German Prince Wilhelm zu Wied landed in Durres (Durazzo) in March 1914. But the new state did not even have any agreed-upon frontiers when World War I broke out. Prince Wied was forced to leave the country barely six months after his arrival.

During the war Albania was occupied first by its neighbors and Italy, subsequently in the north by Austria, the southeast by France, the south by Italy. The rival claims of the would-be conquerors—Italy, Greece, and Yugoslavia—dominated the endless disputes about Albania's future at the Versailles peace conference. The situation was slanted in favor of Italy, which, in the secret Treaty of London in 1915, had secured the promise of a mandate over central Albania, including the annexation of the two strategically situated Adriatic ports of Vlora and Sasseno. The Serbs at

first relied on their vassal, Esad Pasha, who presented himself at the
peace conference as the only legal representative of Albania, but the
Greeks, claiming the need to protect the Orthodox Albanians,
who amounted to one-fifth of the population, concluded a deal
with the Italians that would have meant dividing the country between Greece and Italy. After this agreement was announced, the
Serbs also presented their claims.

Albania's fate seemed to have been sealed, as the great powers
were more than willing to get rid of the nuisance of the dispute and
satisfy all the claimants. The Albanian delegation at the conference made a twofold bid: for the territorial integrity of rump
Albania, and the right to self-determination for the areas ceded
previously to Serbia, Montenegro, and Greece. The shifts in the international situation, the bickering among the neighbor states, and
the rising resistance of the Albanians in the country itself
strengthened President Woodrow Wilson's determination to resist
the dismemberment of the country. At the beginning of 1920, an
Albanian national congress held in the town of Lushnja spoke out
firmly against any kind of mandate over the country and demanded
ethnic borders for Albania.

A series of events then combined to help the Albanians. France
wanted to evacuate its zone of occupation; Greece was fully occupied with the gathering storms in Asia Minor; Esad Pasha was
assassinated in Paris by an Albanian nationalist; sporadic revolts
by brigands financed and equipped by the Yugoslav government
were crushed in northern Albania; Italy was forced to evacuate
the coastal strip under the growing pressure of the national movement and canceled the partition agreement with Greece, concluded
barely a year earlier. The Albanian parliament elected in 1920
formed a government dominated by a young Muslim chieftain from
the north, Bey Ahmed Zogu, a former officer in the Austrian army,
who became Minister of Interior and later commander of the army.
Albania was recognized as a sovereign independent state and
admitted to the League of Nations in December 1920. The conference of the Great Power ambassadors proclaimed that "the existence of a free and independent Albania is the basic condition for the
maintenance of peace in the Balkan peninsula."[4] But it took a further six years until the Greeks and Yugoslavs, after many skirmishes,
which even involved the bombardment and seizure of the island
of Korfu by Mussolini's navy as retaliation for the assassination of an

Italian general heading the international frontier-drawing commission, were forced to recognize the final and exact boundary lines. Thus one can say that the birth of modern Albania lasted almost fifteen years.

To understand the violent nationalism, deep-rooted loneliness, and ruthless code of behavior of present-day Albanians, one must remember their long history of humiliating injustices. Hemmed in since time immemorial by more powerful neighbors and deserted so often by outside powers that had proffered help, the Albanians, regardless of religion and politics, grew suspicious of everyone. The history of interwar Albania as well as that of the Communist regime has also been overshadowed by the interference of foreign powers, by the Albanian search for a powerful foreign protector, and by the perennial concern of its neighbors on land and sea over the potential menace of Albania's becoming the puppet of a big power. Ethnic factors have always injected an element of tension into Albania's relations with Yugoslavia, which contains over 40 per cent of the small Albanian nation. While the Kosovo region and the fate of its Albanian inhabitants feed the spirit of extreme nationalism and territorial irredentism, the ever-present menace of a Greek move to annex southern Albania (Northern Epirus) puts the tiny country on the defensive. As a result, the 460-mile land frontiers cutting through black jagged mountains and lakes are regions of almost permanent insecurity. Italy, only forty-two miles away across the Straits of Otranto, has on the whole, in spite of Mussolini's suicidal adventure in 1939, preferred an independent but weak Albania, permitting Italian domination of the Adriatic and keeping foreign intruders out of this sensitive region.

Aside from strategic considerations and the insatiable territorial appetite of small-power imperialism, there was no compelling advantage in securing control over what was the most underdeveloped of all Balkan regions. The mountainous area, with only a fraction of land under crops, has always been an economic liability to the given protector or conqueror. As late as 1938, well over four-fifths of the population were illiterate; one out of every two babies died in their first year; the extraction of raw materials (oil, chromium ore) had only just begun; there was no industry, only some handicrafts; the entire labor force totaled barely 15,000; and there were altogether some 80 engineers, economists, and agronomists among the 380 foreign-trained university graduates.

In addition to the extremely backward environment, the Shkum-bini River, just sixteen miles south of Tirana, the capital since 1920, constituted a historic dividing line between peoples with two different dialects and great variations in social structure and behavior patterns. In the north lived the Gegs, mainly Muslims with a small Catholic minority, in a primitive tribal society based on clan loyalty and ruled by the chieftains of the different clans. The institution of the blood feud, going back to the fifteenth century, dominated the code of behavior and provided a savage counterforce against one of the traditionally highest natural population growths in the world. The chief of a clan was an absolute ruler, allowing no appeal against his judgments. A variety of offenses to women served as an igniting spark for the blood feuds. Women were engaged in their infancy. If later the girl did not wish to marry the man whom her parents had chosen for her, she had to swear perpetual virginity. If she nevertheless married another man, a blood feud broke out at once. According to one estimate, in some parts of northern Albania about 20 per cent of the annual male death rate in the 1920s was caused by blood feuds.[5] A German soldier mentioned in his wartime diary that he had witnessed in 1942–43 "women markets" with sales arranged on the spot.

In contrast to the Geg highlanders (who also form the great majority of the Albanians living in the Kosovo region of Yugoslavia), the plainsmen of the south speak the Tosk dialect and have always been more susceptible to foreign, mainly Greek and Italian, influences. The Tosks constituted the bulk of the landless and subsistence level peasants, many of them belonging to the Orthodox minority and living mostly in villages, not in isolated homesteads as in the north. They were economically and socially ruled by a small group of great landowners, almost without exception Muslim beys.

Since the time of Skanderbeg, the national hero, the more primitive Gegs and their chieftains had dominated movements for independence and statehood. The first government of independent Albania was, however, headed by a Tosk, the Orthodox Bishop Fan Noli. A progressive educated in the United States, his government recognized the Soviet government and proclaimed a radical land reform. His left-wing regime was short-lived being overthrown in 1924 by Ahmed Zogu, a Geg chieftain who had received arms and financial support from the Yugoslav government. For almost

fifteen years, Zogu, first as premier, after 1928 as King Zog, ruled
Albania. Living in constant fear of assassination, Zog rarely appeared
in public. That his suspicions were well-founded was vividly demonstrated during a short visit to Vienna in 1931 when he and his body-
guards fought a gun duel with assassins on the steps of the Vienna
State Opera house.[6]

Zog's main energies were devoted to keeping on as friendly terms
as possible with his neighbors, but in the given international context
his political problems were insoluble. Zog first looked to Belgrade,
then, from the mid-twenties, to Italy as his main source of financial
and military aid. Under the Treaty of Tirana concluded with Mussolini's regime, Albania became in effect if not in name a client state
of Italy. With the exported raw materials covering only 40 per cent
of the annual import bill, Italian loans poured in. The Albanian currency was printed in Italy and even its National Bank was set up
there. Recognizing the danger of full colonization, Zog made a desperate attempt to switch more of the country's trade to Yugoslavia
and Greece. But Fascist Italy tightened the economic screws and
staged a naval demonstration along the Albanian coast. The diaries
of Count Ciano, Mussolini's son-in-law and Foreign Minister, give an
illuminating account of just how much the conquest of Albania
kept dominating Mussolini's dreams. The invasion project was alternately on and off as the Fascist dictator witnessed Hitler's stunning successes in Central Europe. When King Zog stubbornly refused
to accept full colonization in exchange for bribes, Mussolini invaded
the country in April 1939, using the attack also as a launching pad
for a further thrust toward Greece in 1940 under the pretext of
"protecting the maltreated Albanian minority."

The experiment in independence was brief and disastrous. Despite some advance toward a functioning government and economic
improvement, Albania remained the most primitive backwater in
Europe, serving, as before, as a thoroughfare for invading armies—a
minor theater in a world conflict with no one paying much attention
to the interests of the local inhabitants. Zog fled with his young
Hungarian wife, Countess Geraldine Apponyi, and his infant heir;
he died only a few years ago, in exile. As to his record, one may
quote the foremost expert on Albania, Professor Stavro Skendi, who
summed up Zog's reign in the following words: "Whatever his flaws,
he made a nation and a government where there had been a people
and anarchy."[7]

How does a Yugoslav satellite become an ally of China?

Communism achieved one of its most "unhistorical" victories in tiny backward Albania. The Albanian Communist Party was born during the convulsions of World War II and the principal midwives were the Yugoslav Partisans and British army and intelligence officers. From its birth to the present, however, the history of Albanian communism provides a classic example of ideology serving as a mask for ancient historical factors, geographical conditions, and local pressures.

The first Albanian Communists were the followers of the deposed Bishop Fan Noli who made their way via Vienna and Paris to Moscow. Here they formed a National Revolutionary Committee, which later became subordinated to the Balkan Federation of Communist parties and thus also to the Comintern. The most important figure was Ali Kelmendi, a Geg from the north, who was trained in Moscow and subsequently sent back to Albania to organize the first Communist cells. Forced to flee in 1936, Kelmendi fought in the Spanish Civil War and was, until his death in 1939, the acknowledged leader of the small group of Albanian Communists living in France. Another early Communist leader was Bishop Fan Noli's former private secretary, the poet Sejfulla Maleshova, who was purged from the Central Committee in 1948. The leader of the Communist students abroad, Lazar Fundo, was at odds with Kelmendi and narrowly escaped death in Moscow during the Great Purge. He broke eventually with the Communists, acted as a political adviser to the nationalist guerrillas during the war, and was killed by his former comrades in 1944.

But the bulk of the people who ruled Albania after the war were Tosk intellectuals. Sons of well-to-do landowners and government officials, they were sent to the West or to the French and American schools in Tirana for their higher education. Many of them went abroad with the aid of state scholarships and returned home revolutionaries and violent opponents of the backward Geg chieftains who ruled what was still a tribal society. Most of them found no career opportunities in the state administration and became still more resentful of the obsolete social structure.

One of these frustrated intellectuals was the startlingly good-looking son of a Tosk Muslim landowner from the town of Gjiro-kaster, near the Greek border in southern Albania. His name was Enver Hoxha, and in 1930, after he had completed his studies at the French lycée in Korca, he was sent on a state scholarship to France. After a year at the University of Montpellier, he went to Paris where he joined the small group of Albanian exiles that included Kelmendi and Fundo. By 1933 he was in Brussels, studying law at the university and working as private secretary to the Albanian honorary consul. Three years later he returned to Albania and taught French, first at the high school in Tirana, then at the lycée in Korca.

In actual fact, the Communist movement before the war consisted of four isolated discussion groups, the most important of which was set up by Hoxha and other intellectuals and the tinsmith Koci Xoxe in the Tosk town of Korca. At a time when the entire movement contained only a few hundred people, it had some seventy members. The small groups, torn by bitter internal friction, were subsequently welded into a single party by two Yugoslav Communists whom Tito sent to Albania to organize both a Communist party and a Partisan movement. Miladin Popovic and Dusan Mugosa actually founded the Albanian Communist party on November 8, 1941, after the Axis powers had invaded both Yugoslavia and Albania, and from then until the Tito-Stalin conflict, the Albanian party was a mere extension or branch of the Yugoslav party. Throughout the war the Albanian Communists got their instructions from the Yugoslav party, and Tito's emissaries played a major role at every party meeting and decisively influenced every tactical and political move.

As the Germans, in the course of dismembering Yugoslavia, reincorporated the Kosovo area and western Macedonia into the new "autonomous" Albania, the old national conflict hampered the Communists in their bid for popular support. The Yugoslav Communists, both at their Fourth Congress held in 1928 in Dresden and at their 1940 party conference in Zagreb had endorsed the return of what was officially called Kosovo-Metohija (Kosmet) to Albania.[8] But during the war Tito radically revised the previous policy statements. If the national problem within Yugoslavia was to be solved by a federal state structure, nothing could be more natural—and, of course, more advantageous for a highly ambitious Communist leader—than to resolve the tangled issue of a large and compact Albanian minority in Yugoslavia by the unification of the entire Albanian nation as a member state of the Yugoslav Federation.

Thus the fate of Kosmet was not mentioned in the first ringing declaration issued by the young Albanian Communist Party and its Yugoslav founding fathers. It called on the people to revolt against the Axis occupation. Small guerrilla bands started to operate from 1942 onward, but the Communist silence on Kosmet made it hard to cooperate with other Albanian resistance movements. Meanwhile the Albanian Communists patterned their guerrilla forces completely on the Yugoslav model: red star on the caps, Communist greeting, the institution of political commissars, etc. After receiving Tito's "fatherly advice," they stopped calling the partisan units "armed forces of the party" and began to prepare for the creation of a National Liberation Movement. In the beginning, the Zogists, followers of the King, and especially the movement headed by the staunchly pro-Western Geg chieftain Abbas Kupi, were much stronger than the Communists.

The history of the Communist road to power in Albania is at the same time a chronicle of the monumental short-sightedness, political naïveté, and outright stupidity of the British command in charge of Balkan operations. In addition to the Communists and Kupi's tribal warriors, there was a third initially powerful organization of Tosk beys, called Balli Kombatar, whose program was directed against both the Communists and the Royalists. The National Liberation Movement (NLM) was formally launched at a Communist party conference in March 1943 at which about seventy delegates claimed to represent six to seven thousand NLM members. The conference confirmed the provisional Central Committee of the party and elected Hoxha Secretary General and supreme commander of the NLM army.

After the Communist representatives had agreed to decide the future status of Kosmet by a postwar plebiscite, the nationalist mountaineers and Hoxha's Partisans set up a joint National Liberation Council (NLC), thereby providing the Communist party with a convenient national façade. The Yugoslavs, upset by this "nationalist deviation," immediately dispatched Vukmanovic-Tempo to Albania to bring their "pupils" into line. After his intervention, the Communists, particularly Hoxha, exercised self-criticism and repudiated the so-called Mukje agreement. Meanwhile Italy collapsed, and the Italian units in Albania capitulated, delivering the bulk of their military equipment to Hoxha's forces. There were sporadic clashes between the Balli Kombatar and the Partisans when German airborne units landed in Tirana to protect the flank of the retreating German armies, should the Allies decide to launch an attack through the narrow Strait of Otranto.

At this point Hitler's top Balkan troubleshooter, H. Neubacher, performed a series of impressive political feats. By his willingness to recognize Albania's "neutrality," the creation of a Council of Regents, and other concessions to the tribal chieftains and dignitaries, he prevented the creation of a Communist-dominated united front and secured the benevolent neutrality of the Balli Kombatar nationalists, who recognized that the Communists—and not the Germans, who were bound to leave in the near future—constituted their number one enemy. The Communists immediately attacked the Balli Kombatar, drove them into the occupied zone, and manipulated them into a more or less open collaboration with the Germans.[9] On the reports of British liaison officers stationed with both the Partisans and Kupi's warriors in the mountains, the Allied Command denounced the Balli Kombatar as collaborators even before they had been driven into that position. Thus within a year the initially weakest resistance movement became one of the two main forces in the country.

The incredibly inept British moves that led to this were described in a fascinating book by the senior British officer attached to Kupi, Julian Amery.[10] Though the Geg chieftain had refused all German overtures to join the puppet government and remained steadfast even when attacked by Hoxha, the Allied Command in the Balkans continued to direct the bulk of the military supplies to the Communists and was more than willing to suspect Kupi of being a covert collaborator of the occupying forces. Despite the urging of the British mission with the Zogists, the British command kept sending the Communists weapons right up to the last phase of the civil war, which, as in Yugoslavia, was inextricably linked with the larger war, with the battle against domestic political foes often gaining precedence over the military campaign against the occupiers.

Following Tito's example, the NLC proclaimed itself the national government in May 1944, forbade King Zog re-entry into the country, and consolidated its hold on the liberated territories, which contained some 400,000 people. The British, who were celebrating the Communists' victories, sent scores of nationalists and non-collaborators who had fled to Italy back to their death before firing squads in order "not to embarrass our relations with Hoxha." Amery relates that British headquarters in mid-1944 "still seemed to believe that Enver Hoxha was their friend, and in a cable to him summed up their policy toward the Partisans as follows: 'Gradual build up of NLC and its army will now take place. Our relations will be strengthened for postwar purposes.'" Amery adds, "Our own experiences allowed us no such illusions, and we could only smile when the Director of All Balkan Operations telegraphed us his congratulations which said: 'We are now reaping the benefits of eighteen months' hard work.'" As the German defeat grew near, the Partisans surged forward with the British command, refusing to evacuate their staunchest ally, Kupi and his officers.

The Communist Partisans, who claim to have had a strength of 70,000 by the end of the war, took Tirana, the capital, in November 1944 and seized power in the name of a non-existent proletariat in the most primitive of all European countries. Less than two years later, their British friends indeed "reaped the benefits" of their unfailing support when two British warships were sunk in Albanian minefields in the Corfu channels with the loss of forty lives. As Amery said: "Never before had there been so many British observers in the Balkans, and yet never can responsible Englishmen have cherished so many misconceptions and illusions about the problems of that bloodstained region."[11] In view of the recent revelations about "Kim" Philby, the Soviet agent in the heart of the British Secret Service, who also betrayed to the Russians in the late forties the Western-aided attempt by Albanian anti-Communists to foment an uprising,[12] one is tempted to think that perhaps more than just "misconceptions and illusions" influenced the suicidal British policies in the wartime Balkans.

Be that as it may, Albania emerged after the war as a Communist client state of Yugoslavia. The projected unification of Albania proper with the now autonomous province of Kosmet into a constituent republic of the Yugoslav Federation may well have been devised to mollify Albanian nationalism, but in effect it intensified the deep-rooted spirit of defiance against foreign domination. Albanian leaders had the same intense feeling of pride and self-confidence from having seized power on their own as their Yugoslav masters. To enjoy the appearance of power without its substance was therefore something they profoundly resented from the very beginning.

The first factional struggles over Kosmet and, in a broader context, over the entire relationship with Yugoslavia had led to a purge of the leaders of two of the small Communist discussion groups from Korca and Tirana as early as 1942. It was one of the few leaders of proletarian origin, Koci Xoxe, who gradually emerged as latter-day successor of Esad Pasha, the Albanian vassal of the prewar Kingdom of Yugoslavia a generation earlier. Immediately after the controversial Mukje agreement about the projected plebiscite, Xoxe vigorously condemned the Communists who had signed it. During the following five years Enver Hoxha, who was always distrusted by the Yugoslavs, survived Belgrade's tightening grip and the growing power of Xoxe by yielding when he had to and subtly resisting when he could the fast pace dictated by Tito.

The postwar political line was characterized by the same ruthless crushing of all opposition and the same extremist political and economic moves that were typical of the Yugoslav "father" party. It was not doctrinal differences, but purely national considerations that turned a substantial part of the Albanian leadership against Yugoslav communism. Yugoslavia, like Fascist Italy previously, provided credits covering half of the state income; over 1,500 Albanian students were being educated at universities and high schools in Yugoslavia; Serbo-Croatian was made a compulsory subject in the Albanian schools; and no less than twenty-seven bilateral treaties provided for common price and currency systems, a customs union, and the setting up of joint Yugoslav-Albanian companies. Even the Albanian party as such remained a junior branch of the Yugoslav party, which represented it at Cominform meetings.[13]

As we have seen, the Albanian question was the final igniting spark that brought the powder keg of Soviet-Yugoslav relations to the point of explosion. It was a curious situation. The Albanian leaders were fired by the same desire as the Yugoslavs to escape from the stifling iron hand of a more powerful "fraternal" Communist state. Conversely, the Yugoslavs, regardless of their original intentions and the fact that they offered Albania more favorable conditions than those the Soviets had held out to them, were guilty of the same sins of which they accused Stalin. As Djilas aptly remarked many years later, "The problem lay not in the degree of justice but in the very nature of these relations. . . . And what if the Albanians wanted their state to be separate from us just as we wanted ours to be separate from the Soviet Union? If unification was carried out despite Albanian wishes and by taking advantage of their isolation and misery, would not this lead to irreconcilable conflicts and difficulties?"[14]

By 1947 the factional struggle within the Albanian leadership had become closely linked with the rising tensions between Moscow and Belgrade. While later Yugoslav and Albanian accounts are naturally slanted and filled with mutual recriminations, the main facts remain clear enough. Koci Xoxe, the Yugoslav supporter among the top Albanian leaders, pressed from 1947 on for an accelerated merger of Albania with Yugoslavia. His main adversary was Nako Spiru, the Politburo member in charge of economic affairs and the husband of another high-ranking Communist leader, Liri Belishova. At the height of the factional disputes, Enver Hoxha remained prudently in the background, having already established close contacts with the Russians, who were all along excellently informed about everything, despite their accusations that the Yugoslavs "forgot" to consult them about the details of their policies.

The maneuvers and countermaneuvers were profoundly Balkan in character, taking place in extremely close quarters in the tiny capital of a minute country. Albania was only then making its first strides in road building, industrial development, and land reclamation, after having carried out a radical land reform and, thanks to UNRRA* aid, narrowly escaped a mass famine. The Communist party had only 29,000 members and 16,000 candidates. But if the country was the most backward of all Communist states, its ruling group of some two dozen Communists was the most international and best educated of any of the East European Communists. More than four-fifths of the twenty-three leading cadres were of middle-class origin. Then as now, the character of this small group was a "combination of old Ottoman elite feeling with Western education and Marxist-Leninist ideology."[15]

Its real feelings about the overbearing Yugoslav comrades had, however, to be hidden because the levers of power were firmly in the hands of Koci Xoxe, who was simultaneously Deputy Premier, Minister of Interior, and Secretary of the Central Committee; the army command was controlled by Yugoslav advisers. The economist

* United Nations Relief and Rehabilitation Administration.

Nako Spiru was the first to speak out openly against the joint economic projects and thus implicitly against the merger of the two
unequal neighbors. Sharply scolded by Xoxe and faced with the
likelihood of being purged as a "chauvinist," Spiru killed himself.
His suicide was more than a dramatic protest against the loss of Albanian independence; it brought the Tito-Stalin conflict to its breaking point.

The Yugoslavs and Xoxe stepped up preparations for the final
act of "unification." Milovan Djilas was sent, partly on Stalin's personal request, to Moscow to discuss the rapidly worsening Albanian-
Yugoslav situation and the entire Soviet-Yugoslav relationship. The
closing stages of the three-cornered battle took place on three different but interconnected planes. In Tirana, Xoxe launched what
he believed would be the final showdown with his adversaries. At a
plenary meeting, he had Liri Belishova, Sejfulla Maleshova, and
other veteran Communists expelled from the party and Mehmet
Shehu removed as chief of the general staff. During this same
period, the Yugoslavs, "complying with an Albanian request,"
moved a squadron of fighter aircraft and made plans to send two
army divisions to Albania. While the moves were in progress, Djilas
was negotiating with Stalin in Moscow. It was difficult to refute
Stalin's logic.

Why, he asked, were the Yugoslavs forming joint companies with
Albania when they refused to form them in their own country with
the Soviet Union? Why were they sending instructors to the Albanian army when they had Soviet instructors in their own? How
could Yugoslavia provide experts for development of Albania when
they were themselves seeking experts from abroad? How was it that
Yugoslavia, itself poor and underdeveloped, suddenly intended to
develop Albania?

As Djilas began to explain the advantages of unification, Stalin
quickly replied, "We have no special interests in Albania; we agree
to Yugoslavia's swallowing Albania." At this he gathered together
the fingers of his right hand and brought them to his mouth as if
to swallow them. When Djilas protested that it was "not a matter of
swallowing but of unification," Molotov interrupted him cheerfully, "But that is swallowing." Almost fifteen years later Djilas
recalled that after the discussions with Stalin and Molotov two
thoughts had occured to him for the first time: "The first was the
suspicion that something was not right about Yugoslav policy toward

Albania, and the second that the Soviet Union united with the
Baltic countries by swallowing them."[16]

The news of the Yugoslav-Albanian military pact provoked an
angry rejoinder from Stalin, who threatened Belgrade with an open
breach unless the agreement was immediately canceled. The Albanian question and the dispute over the controversial Balkan Federation project provided the main subjects for Stalin's last tense
encounter with Kardelj, Djilas, and Bakaric before the final split in
June 1948. Only twenty-four hours after the publication of the
Cominform resolution expelling Yugoslavia from the "great Communist family" the Albanian Central Committee followed suit, de-
nouncing the protectors of yesterday as "traitors and Trotskyites."
Xoxe was the first to bite the hand that had been feeding him. He
at once launched a sharp attack on Tito, but his desperate maneuvers
failed. Within two months he had been demoted and in November
of the same year he was arrested. In June 1949 he was secretly tried
and executed, the first of the long series of bloody purges in the
late forties.

Thus 1948, the year of Tito's rebellion against Stalin, was also the
year in which the second indigenously based Communist regime
in the world, Communist Albania, escaped from the clutches of the
Yugoslav Federation. There is no doubt that Stalin's break with
Tito saved Enver Hoxha and many other leading Communists from
being purged, even perhaps from the firing squads of Koci Xoxe. If
the price for independence from Belgrade was to become a dependency of Moscow,[17] this was clearly the lesser evil. The further
off Albania's protector, the more room she had for maneuver. Stalin
provided a protective shield, not only against Yugoslavia, but Greece,
whose determination to take Southern Albania was strengthened
when, during the Greek civil war, Albania served as a sanctuary for
Communist guerrillas. Besides, Moscow was clearly better able to
pour more money into non-viable Albania at less political risk than
was Belgrade.

The Tito-Stalin conflict marked the progress of Albania from a
"subsatellite" to a Soviet satellite. At the same time the break with
Yugoslavia, the unilateral abrogation of the bilateral treaties, the
the expulsion of the entire army of Yugoslav "advisers," and the
purge of Xoxe removed the main barriers to Hoxha's rise to undisputed eminence at the apex of the party hierarchy. Most
Albanian functionaries shared a profound sense of liberation from

Yugoslav tutelage, and the resulting upsurge of national feeling was more than welcomed by the Soviet leaders who were soon to use Albanian and Bulgarian territorial irredentism as potent weapons in their hate campaign against the isolated Tito regime.

Aside from a small group around Xoxe, most Albanian leaders had never been prepared to trade their independence for the economic advantages of belonging to the Yugoslav Federation. For a variety of personal and political reasons some of the losers in the subsequent intraparty struggles, such as Tuk Jakova, second in command of the party apparat until 1951, and General Bedru Spahiu, the former attorney general who prosecuted Xoxe and deputy chief of the general staff, later looked to Belgrade for help in deposing Enver Hoxha. There is also no doubt that after their reconciliation with Khrushchev the Yugoslavs encouraged the anti-Hoxha factions. It was no accident that General Panjut Plaku, a member of the Central Committee who had been purged at the same time as Jakova, fled in 1957 to Yugoslavia.[18]

During Stalin's lifetime the Albanian leaders revelled in their violent nationalsim, now openly directed against Yugoslavia; expelled some six thousand "people's enemies" and "disloyal elements" (altogether 8 per cent of the party's membership); and, with the Russians covering almost 40 per cent of the state revenues, made undoubted progress in industrialization, trebling their output between 1951 and 1955.[19] Through a combination of skill and terror, Hoxha consolidated his position and by 1955 was the sole survivor of the original top leadership.

This period was marked by the spectacular rise of General Mehmet Shehu in the party hierarchy. Once number two among the projected victims of the Titoist Xoxe, Shehu, also a Tosk, replaced Jakova as Minister of Interior in 1951 and after a short spell as Deputy Premier became the successor to Enver Hoxha in 1954 when the latter, copying the Soviet fashion of "collective leadership," relinquished the premiership while remaining First Secretary of the party. Shehu, now in his late fifties, was educated at the American vocational school in Tirana and, like Hoxha, spent his formative years as a young Communist in the West. After training as a professional soldier at the Naples military college, from which he was expelled after a few months for Communist activity, and at the Tirana officers' school, he fought as deputy battalion commander in the Spanish Civil War and joined the Spanish Communist Party. After a three-year internment in France, he became a member of the Italian Communist Party and made his way back to Albania, where he rose to eminence almost immediately as the ablest Partisan commander.[20]

These two men—Hoxha, the undisputed supreme leader, and Shehu, the second in command, had much in common: Western education, bourgeois habits, the old elite feeling, and ruthless extremism in dealing with external and internal foes. Both were suddenly confronted with mortal danger when Khrushchev made his spectacular attempt to reconcile Tito and visited Belgrade in May 1955 without informing the Albanians and disregarding their later protests. Hoxha had everything to lose by a real improvement in Soviet-Yugoslav relations; not just his policy, but his life was at stake. Following the Soviet example, he announced a change of line toward Yugoslavia. In a *Pravda* article in July 1955, he, like Khrushchev, blamed "the imperialist agents, Beria and Abakumov" for "the unpleasant occurrences of the break . . . for the misunderstandings among brothers." At the Third Party Congress in May 1956, Hoxha again reiterated that "all accusations were unjust and we were mistaken in this question"; promised to establish friendly relations with Yugoslavia, and pledged full support for the Twentieth Soviet Party Congress line, including the condemnation of the cult of Stalin.

Behind the scenes, however, Hoxha stubbornly resisted Yugoslav demands and subsequent Soviet pressure for the public rehabilitation of Koci Xoxe. By purging Jakova and Spahiu, the two senior leaders who could have been built up as an alternative leadership, he outmaneuvered the Russians and Yugoslavs, survived a stormy party conference in Tirana in April 1956, and managed to pack the party congress in May with his followers who endorsed the purge. The Yugoslavs, courted by Moscow and dizzy with success, pressed hard for the rehabilitation of "the friends of Yugoslavia" and demanded from Moscow the removal of Hoxha, the Hungarian Rakosi, and the Bulgarian Chervenkov as the "minimum" price for rapprochement.

Enver Hoxha realized that a rehabilitation of his most prominent victim would be the curtain raiser to his own fall, and, in contrast to Rakosi and Chervenkov, managed to ride out the storm. This was only partly due to his undoubted tactical brilliance and single-minded ruthlessness. The isolation of Albania, its backwardness and marginal importance as well as the growing tensions in Hungary and Poland were the main factors that enabled him to gain time.

This breathing spell ultimately proved crucial; the upheavals in Poland and Hungary put a speedy end to the Soviet-Yugoslav honeymoon. Hoxha lost no time in aggravating the rift between Belgrade and Moscow. The first and most vicious attack on Yugoslavia after the Hungarian revolution was Hoxha's article in the November 8, 1956, issue of *Pravda*.

If in 1948 Hoxha was rescued by the Stalin-Tito conflict, so in 1956 the Hungarian uprising saved him from disgrace and almost certain death. Immediately after the crushing of the Hungarian revolution, Hoxha and Shehu liquidated the covert opposition in the top leadership. A laconic communique announced that Liri Gega, a member of the ruling Politburo, her husband, Dali Nreu, also a Central Committee member, and the Yugoslav-born Major Bulatovic had been shot as "foreign spies." Khrushchev later revealed that the Soviet leadership had at that time asked the Albanians to spare the life of Gega, who was expecting a child, a request that probably served only to confirm the well-founded suspicion that she had been involved in a Soviet-sponsored attempt to overthrow Hoxha. The Albanian leaders may well have been, as the Russians complained, "worse than tsarist satraps," but they had learned the cardinal rule of the Communist power struggles: swift liquidation of the potential allies of the external foe that seeks to subvert and dominate the leadership of a weaker party.

The Albanian leaders have never forgotten their experiences on the brink of the abyss in 1955–56. Even during the period of the renewed Yugoslav-Soviet discord between 1957 and 1960, when they reaped the benefits of Soviet and East European aid, they remained on their guard and watched Khrushchev's foreign policy line particularly in regard to Yugoslavia, with suspicion. When Khrushchev began once again to switch to a policy of "peaceful coexistence" and improved relations with the West, Hoxha and Shehu immediately recognized that this would inevitably lead to renewed friendship between Belgrade and Moscow. Remembering the troubles in 1955–56, Khrushchev visited Tirana in May 1959 in what was essentially a countermove against any dangerous repercussions of a renewed rapprochement with Yugoslavia.

The trip was a complete failure. Khrushchev advised the Albanians to improve their relations with Yugoslavia and to convert their country into a "flowering garden" rather than force industrialization. The man who was so obviously planning to sacrifice Albania's interests in order to heal the breach with Tito exceeded Hoxha's and Shehu's worst fears. They felt strongly what Shehu later told Mikoyan with brutal frankness: "Stalin made two mistakes. First, he died too early and second, he failed to liquidate the entire present Soviet leadership."

The danger that has always been the greatest for Albania—"a firm alliance between one or more of its rapacious neighbors and the major power under whose influence they already were"[21]—loomed once again on the horizon. Fully aware that they were skating on thin ice both politically and economically, the Albanian leaders began to pin their hopes on allies farther afield. China was beginning to emerge as a rival center of world communism after Khrushchev's equally unsuccessful trip to Peking.

The Sino-Soviet conflict erupted at a closed session during the Rumanian Party Congress in Bucharest in June 1960. Neither Hoxha nor Shehu showed up in Bucharest, but the number three man in the hierarchy, Hysni Kapo, spoke out for the Chinese side. His greetings to the public session of the congress differed from those of the pro-Soviet delegates in emphasis rather than in essence, although his position on the "character of imperialism and Yugoslav revisionism" was a significant straw in the wind. At the secret session, however, he fully backed the extremist arguments of the Chinese.

It was at the Bucharest meeting that the Albanians first gave notice to the Russians that they had made their policy decision. Faced with the choice between Soviet aid, which amounted to an estimated 600 million dollars during the postwar period, and their survival in power relying on a distant protector, the Albanian leaders predictably opted for the latter course. Khrushchev responded with a concerted attack to force Hoxha back into line. In the midst of a severe drought and serious food shortages in the summer of 1960, Moscow suddenly reduced its aid. At the same time Khrushchev tried to carry out a "palace revolution" in Tirana, and failed. In September, Liri Belishova, one of the secretaries of the Central Committee, and another veteran Communist were expelled from the Albanian leadership "for grave faults."

Pent-up Albanian anger finally exploded at the Moscow world conference of the eighty-one Communist parties in November 1960. Four meetings between Khrushchev, Hoxha, and Shehu only exacerbated the mutual animosity. According to the Albanian version, the Soviet leader was so furious that he snapped at them that "he could reach a better understanding with Macmillan (then British

Prime Minister) than with the Albanians." Never before in the history of world communism had a top-ranking Soviet leader been attacked as violently as Khrushchev was by Hoxha. From ideological issues to his policy toward Yugoslavia, from the impermissible subversive activity against the Albanian leadership to threats of excluding Albania from the Warsaw Pact and the socialist camp, Hoxha leveled all possible accusations at the Soviet leader.

The Albanian indictment culminated in the dramatic story of the summer famine when only fifteen days' supply of wheat was in stock. After a delay of forty-five days, the Russians promised 10,000 tons instead of the 50,000 needed and made no deliveries until September and October. "These are unbearable pressures. The Soviet rats were able to eat, while the Albanian people were dying of hunger; we were asked to produce gold," Hoxha proclaimed bitterly.[22]

The Albanian rebellion was on. In many ways it resembled the Stalin-Tito dispute, and it had the same catastrophic results on Soviet prestige. The sheer recklessness of the Albanians and the petty spite of Khrushchev provided it with a series of comic opera episodes. Consider the case of the projected Palace of Culture that the Russians in 1959 had promised to build in Tirana as a "gift from the Soviet people." In the autumn of 1960 the Soviet chief engineer left for Moscow, taking all the plans with him. When, a few months later, a Soviet ship arrived with materials on board, the Soviet government canceled the unloading.

What turned out to be the last attempt to prevent an open split occurred at the Albanian Party Congress in February 1961. The Albanians remained adamant. While the Soviet delegates complained that they were being humiliated, the Chinese were treated as honored guests. Finally Hoxha announced that a "criminal plot," organized by "some Albanian traitors and external foes such as the Yugoslavs, the Greeks, and the American Sixth Fleet," had been discovered and foiled the previous autumn. Almost the entire press of the Soviet bloc ignored this dramatic revelation and censored it from the printed versions of Hoxha's speech. It was widely regarded even at that time as a Soviet plot to overthrow Hoxha. Soviet trained Rear Admiral Sejko and some other "culprits" were later given a "show trial" in a Tirana movie house.

The Albanian Communists began to play a significant role in the widening Sino-Soviet rift as the spearhead of the Chinese offensive against Soviet supremacy in the international Communist movement. In the course of 1961 Soviet and East European experts were withdrawn from Albania and gradually replaced by Chinese specialists. From March on, Hoxha and Shehu boycotted Soviet summit meetings. Soviet submarines left their base at Vlora, and Soviet, Czech, and East German credits promised for the 1961–65 Five Year Plan were canceled. A few days after the formal Soviet note about the cancellation of aid had been received, China stepped in and officially announced credits of 125 million dollars, roughly the same amount the Soviet bloc had promised.

There was still no open excommunication of recalcitrant Albania from Moscow, solely because Khrushchev had realized that an open conflict with Albania would be tantamount to an open challenge of China. At the Twenty-second Soviet Party Congress in October 1961, Khrushchev brought the dispute with Albania into the open as an integral part of his second de-Stalinization campaign. Two days later, the Chinese Premier Chou En-lai defended the Albanians, stating in no uncertain terms that "public one-sided censure of any fraternal party" does not help unity; then he left before the congress was formally ended.

The Albanians issued a ferocious rebuttal the next evening along with the full text of the Soviet attack and the Chinese rejoinder. They called Khrushchev "a base, unfounded anti-Marxist," a "plotter and common putschist," "a real Judas" who revealed differences among Communists to their enemies; and charged that by brutally violating the 1960 Moscow Declaration he had begun an open attack against the unity of the socialist camp. Within a month even diplomatic relations were broken off.

Three essential preconditions enabled Albania's ruling group to survive this rift. Perhaps the most important factor was the unity of the top leadership that challenged Khrushchev. A series of bloody purges had eliminated the anti-Hoxha, pro-Soviet elements. Of the thirty-one members of the Central Committee elected at the first congress in 1948 only nine survived, fourteen were liquidated and eight forcefully "retired" from political life. Those who had come out on top were bound together by the traditional ties of clan nepotism and their common complicity in the ruthless purges. Among the sixty-one Central Committee members were five married couples—including the wives of Hoxha, Shehu and Kapo—and no less than twenty persons related to one another as sons-in-law or cousins. Some families are said to have up to seven representatives of their clan in the committee.[23]

This predominantly middle-class Tosk leadership has created a peculiar world of its own. Relying on a self-imposed isolation from the rest of the world, particularly their neighbors, and combining a highly effective appeal to the deepest nationalistic instincts of the population with the ever present threat of terror, Hoxha and his clique run the country as absolute rulers. The remnants of popular opposition were mopped up immediately after the war, and there has been no visible evidence of disunity in the Communist party since the purge of the Belishova group in 1960. At the last two party congresses, in 1961 and 1966, the composition of the top leadership did not change at all.

Yet even the impressive unity of the Politburo would hardly have sufficed had it not been for the geographical factor that made direct Soviet military intervention impossible. Its situation in a remote corner of the Balkan Peninsula is a perennial source of Albania's defensive posture. In addition, the emergence of an increasingly polycentric international Communist movement, coupled with the demonstrative Chinese support for Albania, restrained the Kremlin and gave the Albanian leaders time and opportunity to prepare key cadres for the inevitable break with Moscow.

The turbulent history of Albania's relations first with Yugoslavia and then with the Soviet Union is a classic case study of the often intimate, but always permanent link between Communist ideological arguments on the one hand, and economic, political, and military realities on the other. It is true that the Albanian leaders are the fiercely radical successors of a deposed Ottoman elite, whose imagination is fired by memories of past glories and who have all along nurtured a natural, inbred sympathy for Chinese extremism and been opposed to the Soviet ideological position. They are "left extremist" deviationists, particularly in the eyes of a status-quo power like the Soviet Union, which, for all its upsurges of revolutionary rhetoric, has long outlived its early phase of genuine revolutionary fervor.

But all the violent, self-righteous Albanian attacks on the "Titoist and Khrushchevite modern revisionists" mean nothing unless they are translated into the relatively simple terms of power interests and national conflict. In the context of the Sino-Soviet rift, the Albanian party in the 1961–63 period played a role quite disproportionate to its small membership. It became, temporarily, a significant force in the great conflict between the two rival centers of world communism. When the Russians and Chinese were still avoiding direct polemics, they leveled their ideological guns at Albania (meaning China) and Yugoslavia (meaning the Soviet Union) respectively. At the same time, the Albanians identified the main issues openly and every party by name. In the early stages of the dispute with Moscow, they in fact presented the Chinese line more sharply than the Chinese themselves were prepared to do. When, for example, the Albanian party organ in October 1962 spoke about "fixing once and for all the demarcation line with revisionism," the voice was the voice of Hoxha, but the script was Mao's. During that phase the Albanians appeared to be always one step ahead of the official Chinese position, but in effect they represented the actual Chinese line. From January 1962 on, the Peking press regularly reprinted all Albanian policy statements.

When the Moscow-Peking conflict became open, this intricate division of labor became superfluous. The Albanian Communists ceased to play a seemingly independent role in the rift, and it was only after the fall of Khrushchev in October 1964, when his successors made a desperate attempt at a reconciliation with Mao, that the Albanians for six months or so again acted as Peking's mouthpiece, making it increasingly evident that the new Soviet leaders had failed to heal the breach.

Like Tito fifteen years earlier, the Albanians accused the Russians of having deviated from "true Marxism-Leninism." But they were in an incomparably better position than the Yugoslavs to maintain the morale, self-confidence, and militancy of the party rank and file. Aside from the extreme ethnic nationalism kept alive by the issue of Kosmet, the Albanian leaders could claim to have been "side by side, in quiet as well as stormy days, with the invincible economic, political, military, and moral might of the 700 million Chinese people, united as one single body around the glorious Communist Party of China, led by Comrade Mao Tse-tung."[24]

At their first party congress after the break with Moscow, in November 1966, the Albanian rebels could bask in the flattering presence of thirty-one "Marxist-Leninist"—that is, pro-Chinese—splinter parties and groups. Most of these could hardly claim to be more than insignificant sects. There were, however, four important ruling parties represented: those of China, Rumania, North Vietnam, and North Korea. In addition, the Albanians have what they call "normal relations" with Cuba. Thus, far from feeling outcast, the Albanian Communists glory in being "equal and independent, united with the Communist party of China and the People's Republic of China in an iron bloc" against "the Soviet-American domination of the world."[25]

But the country has paid a high economic price for the political triumph of "going-it-alone." Leaving aside gifts, Soviet loans between 1956–60 financed 8 per cent of all investments and an even higher percentage of industrial investments. Albania's Five Year Plan was geared to deliveries of Soviet and East European machinery and equipment. The small domestic industry, agricultural machinery, and transport equipment, was based on imports from the Soviet Union, and the lack of proper spare parts has become an increasingly acute problem. In fact, the bottlenecks reached such a critical stage that in October 1967 the main engineering plants were switched to the production of spare parts. Hoxha himself declared at the congress in 1966 that the 1961–65 period was the most difficult the party had faced since the war of liberation. Though industrial output rose by 39 per cent, it fell short of the originally projected growth of 52 per cent. Investments accounted for almost 29 per cent of the national income, and even the modest projected rise in the standard of living was not achieved because of the Soviet blockade.

Though farm output is claimed to have risen 2.3 times over pre-war levels, the country is faced with grave supply difficulties. A rising birth rate, a steady decrease in the death rate, and the virtual elimination of blood feuds have combined to give a powerful push to net population growth, which at 32 per 1000 is one of the highest in the world. Total population between 1923 and 1960, the year of the last census, doubled to over 1.6 million, and was scheduled to reach 2 million by mid-1968. This naturally aggravates the problem of a chronic grain deficit. China replaced only part of the large-scale aid that the Soviets withdrew, supplying annually some 130–140 thousand tons of wheat during the 1961–65 period.

The emphasis is now on self-reliance, particularly in agriculture. The current plan proclaimed that by 1970 the country should be self-sufficient in grain production and that imports should be reduced to a minimum. For the first time since the war, the projected rate of growth in agriculture (41 to 46 per cent for the five-year period) is almost on a par with that of industry. For all the "brotherly and internationalist aid" of the Chinese friends, the Chinese goose has not proved a very golden one. Except for the first loan of 125 million dollars granted in 1961, no details or figures have been published about the extent of the Chinese contribution to the financing of the current Five Year Plan. And everything the Albanian leaders have been saying since mid-1966 about "reliance mainly on one's own efforts and resources" seems to reflect less than full satisfaction with Peking's response to their shopping list. According to a Yugoslav account, Chinese credits amount to only one-fifth of the Soviet aid received during the previous Five Year Plan.

The very backwardness of the country, however, helped to absorb the blow when Soviet-bloc aid was cut off. Industrial output may well be thirty-five times higher than before the war, as Hoxha claims, but the point is, of course, that the starting level was practically nil. Over 70 per cent of the population is still occupied in subsistence agriculture. The country finances its import through the shipments of raw materials. Crude oil production rose from 108,000 tons in 1938 to 800,000 in the sixties; that of chromium ore, from 7,000 to 330,000 tons. The output of nickel and copper has also risen steeply. But the living standard, even in terms of the Balkans, is still pitifully low. An average unskilled laborer in Yugoslavia earns about 80 per cent more monthly in terms of purchasing power than his Albanian colleague.

Albania is still a mixture of the fifteenth and twentieth centuries. Oxen and horse-drawn carts dominate the landscape, and there must be more than 1,000 inhabitants to every car. Its roads are the quietest "highways" in Europe. Compared to the size and population of the country, it probably has the relatively largest security police, called Sigurimi, in the world. Since 1965 the regime has made some hesitant moves to attract Western tourists, 2,000 of whom are estimated to have visited the country in 1966. Not a single Albanian is permitted to travel abroad privately. Not even low-ranking bureaucrats, let alone the top leaders, have ever agreed to see a Western newspaperman, who can in any case visit the country only as a tourist and is whisked off immediately to the coast.

Faced with grave economic difficulties and no promise of any appreciable rise in the standard of living until 1970, the Communist regime has resorted to the old technique of "revolutionizing life from above" and embarked on a cautious version of the Chinese "cultural revolution." An open letter from the Central Committee to the people in March 1966 proclaimed a large-scale campaign against proliferating bureaucracy, arrogance, favoritism, and nepotism. In the course of a drastic reorganization, about 15,000 persons were transferred from administrative to productive work, high salaries were trimmed down, and the number of government offices was radically reduced. Copying the Chinese pattern, party leaders took the politically risky step of abolishing all ranks in the army and reintroducing the institution of party commissars in all army units. As most of the officers were trained in the Soviet Union, the army still constitutes a potentially dangerous element.

From the beginning of 1967, the Albanians could no longer ignore the domestic upheavals in China and therefore began to issue calls for "revolutionary actions" by the youth and for a stepped-up campaign against "old and harmful traditions and habits." The most significant results were the accelerated social emancipation of women, who were promoted to occupy more leading positions, and a full-scale assault on religion, directed primarily against the Muslim clergy and institutions. In September 1967 it was claimed that during the preceding six months 2,169 churches, mosques, monasteries, and other religious institutions had been closed in order to turn them into cultural youth centers. "The Albanian youth has created the first atheist state in the world," the literary monthly *Nendori* (November) proclaimed solemnly.[26]

In contrast to China, however, the Albanian leaders have not given a free rein to a "cultural revolution from below," and there has been no evidence of the campaign running against the power base of the regime. The party has also avoided "the tragedy of revisionist degeneration" by remaining an elite rather than becoming a mass organization. There are still only 66,000 party members, accounting for just over 3 per cent of the total population. This is the lowest ratio of Communists per inhabitants in Eastern Europe.

Regardless of ideological fashions, relations with more powerful neighbors have remained the constants in the shifting pattern of Albanian politics. Since the break with Moscow, they have undergone some interesting changes. Impelled by the old fear of encirclement, the Albanian leaders put out feelers to Italy, politically and geographically their least dangerous neighbor, and after a series of annual quota agreements that have steadily increased the volume of trade exchanges, Italy has become Albania's second largest trading partner.

Relations with the two land neighbors are, however, infinitely more complex. Keeping Yugoslavia and Greece divided has always been an important counterforce against the danger of partition. Thus close collaboration between Athens and Belgrade, as at the time of the now-defunct Balkan Pact between 1953 and 1956, heightened the feeling of insecurity. Subsequently this danger subsided and was supplanted by the number one menace: an alliance between Yugoslavia and the Soviet Union. After Albania survived the dreaded reconciliation—admittedly more limited than originally feared—between Belgrade and Moscow, the Greek military coup in April 1967 confronted the country with a new situation.

In contrast to Yugoslavia, the Greeks have never officially resigned themselves to the fact that what they call Northern Epirus belongs to Albania. The issue, which had slumbered for quite a time, reappeared in 1967. Regardless of whether the military regime in Athens wanted to whet territorial appetite or merely divert attention from the domestic scene through irredentist hints, its vague allusions to Northern Epirus immediately injected an element of tension into Albania's exposed situation. As before, the Greeks regard persons of Greek Orthodox religion as Greek nationals, although the old Turkish statistics used the term "Rumi" for every Orthodox subject without distinction as to language and nationality. The actual number of ethnic Greeks still in Albania is something of a mystery. The Greeks refer to the bulk of the 300,000 or so inhabitants of the two prefectures Korca and Gjirokaster as "their brethren." Most outside observers, however, agree that the real number totals only some 30,000 to 50,000. At any rate, the disputed area embraces one-sixth of Albanian territory.

Yugoslavia, with a natural interest in preserving a Balkan status quo, not only issued immediate veiled warnings, thus lending meaningful support to violent Albanian reactions to renewed Greek pretensions, but also used the opportunity to initiate a concerted campaign for a "normalization" of Albanian-Yugoslav relations. While there were 615 frontier incidents between 1948 and 1960, the border situation had later become more or less "normal," in the sense that the shooting stopped on both sides. Since 1965 the two countries have signed several interstate agreements and conducted negotiations about a final demarcation of the exact boundaries, water regulations, road and transit traffic. Though mutual trade in 1967 still totaled only 6.5 million dollars, the figure nevertheless marked, for the first time, an increase of 25 per cent over past levels. The Albanian mass media did not, however, tone down its rude and offensive language when speaking about the "revisionist Tito clique." Anything that would lend a political character to the slight improvement in relations was avoided.

In October 1967, the leaders of the Albanian minority in Yugoslavia held out an olive branch to Albania proper, bidding for good and normal relations between the two countries. A series of conciliatory articles in the Belgrade press followed, culminating in a statement issued by the foreign affairs committee of the federal parliament, announcing new proposals for establishing good-neighbor relations with Albania. The Yugoslavs, however, reaped nothing more than a heap of scornful abuse from Tirana. Instead of moderating their anti-Yugoslav campaign as suggested by Belgrade, the Albanian leaders made it clear that, whereas trade could be extended similarly as "with other capitalist countries," they would "fight without compromise on the ideological and political front against Tito's band of traitors, in the defense of Marxism-Leninism." Worse still, the Albanians made some fairly overt allusions to the fact that the Kosmet region and other adjacent areas, which in 1912 remained outside the state borders, were purely Albanian territories and accused the Yugoslavs of a policy of denationalization and genocide against the Albanian minority.[27]

Albanian-Yugoslav relations are likely to oscillate as before between bad and less bad rather than between bad and good. The widespread echo the Yugoslav friendship call evoked in the Western press, and their anxiousness to convince their Chinese protectors that Albania would continue "a principled policy" against the main ideological adversary, added to the venom with which Albanian leaders rejected the Yugoslav overtures. Yet the Albanians are now in a more advantageous position. The fall of Rankovic and the resounding failure of the supranational Yugoslav nationalism he and Tito had hoped to foster, in the Kosmet region as well as elsewhere, led to a revival of intense national feelings among the large Albanian minority in Kosmet. Revelations about the outrages committed against Albanians by the Serb UDBA officials confirmed that at least a substantial part of the Albanian accusations about the treatment of their brethren was true.

It is not just the size of the Albanian minority in Yugoslavia but the fact—a rather rare phenomenon in the modern world—that it accounts for 40 per cent of the numerical strength of the entire Albanian nation, that lends a crucial importance to the Kosmet region. The Albanian Communists in Yugoslavia are now pressing for full recognition of their national identity, attempting to solve the tricky question of the character of Kosmet by presenting it as "a bridge for unity among Albanians, Serbs, Montenegrins, and other Balkan peoples, . . . a bridge between Yugoslavia and their mother country."

With the Albanian minority taking its constitutional rights in earnest and pushing for real, not merely declarative, equality, the situation is highly dangerous. The Communist leaders in the Kosmet autonomous region have to steer an extremely difficult middle-course between fighting not only Great Serbian hegemonist tendencies but also primitive ethnic nationalism, which would logically lead to covert separatism.

The Albanians are called "sons of the eagles," which is the meaning of the Albanian name for the country, Shquiperia. Official Yugoslav usage makes a distinction between Albanians living in Yugoslavia, who are called "Shquiptai," and those living in Albania proper who are referred to as "Albanci." During the revival of the minority's national identity, a member of the party committee for Kosmet touched upon this sensitive issue, describing such artificial distinctions about the same ethnic group as "baseless, only creating unnecessary problems."[28]

The Albanians living in Yugoslavia may well emerge as a factor on their own, with control slipping from the hands of the Belgrade authorities, and may complicate an already tension-ridden relationship between the two countries. The mounting pressure for more and closer cultural and personal contacts between Kosmet and Albania has already provoked a suspicious echo among the Serbs. The Albanian leaders, too, are confronted with a new situation. They already supply books and periodicals to Kosmet, but resist border traffic and tourism. The reference to the "Titoists using tourist visits as a cover for sending agents and spies to Albania" is a worn-out and hollow argument, but it reflects deep-rooted suspicions. In any case, for the first time since 1948, relations are in flux and a new factor—the Albanian minority asserting its rights—has appeared on the stage.

As far as Albania's over-all position is concerned, the country has for the first time in its history an almost ideal protector, powerful but at safe distance, that, even if it wished to, could not restrain Tirana in a possible search for political and economic alternatives. Should the twists and turns in Balkan rivalries or other national interests require it, the Albanians are free to make a choice. For China, Albania has proved a political asset. As the Chinese people have little idea of the real strength of Mao's sole outpost in Europe, the staunch Albanian ally, "this great beacon of socialism in Europe," while costing little in money, renders great service in Mao's public relations gambit, both at home and in the Afro-Asian countries.

It remains to be seen how long the small ruling elite can resist the wind of political and cultural change blowing both in their vicinity and throughout the Soviet bloc. Their experiences with the more powerful Communist "brothers" have reinforced the extreme nationalism of the ruling group and the population at large. As Enver Hoxha said at the outset of the latest anti-religious campaign, "The only religion for an Albanian is Albanianism." The continuity of the defiant spirit of nationalism, which seeks inspiration from the past and takes a fierce pride in the country's achievements under communism, however modest, is the single most important trait in Albanian politics. Repeatedly Albania has played a significant role out of all proportion to its size, population, and resources. The survival of so poor a country during the whirlwinds of traditional power conflicts and the Sino-Soviet split is in itself no mean feat. Past and present appear to guarantee that this tiny nation will remain a maverick in a changing world, continuing to surprise its friends and foes.

V

BULGARIA

Humble Vassal or Faithful Ally?

I am bound to the Soviet Union in life and death; the same
is true of our party and our people.

—Todor Zhivkov to the author

The big portly man with a mop of white hair over his forehead
and a pock-marked, broad face was offered, as usual, a place of
honor at the table of the party presidium. He was visibly enjoying himself, putting his arm over the shoulders of the Minister of
War and bantering with other dignitaries. At every formal reception
I attended, whether in honor of the Emperor of Ethiopia, a Polish
party delegation, the French or Austrian Foreign Minister, this
same man was always treated with a mixture of friendly reverence
and affectionate attention. He was Nikolai Organov, the Soviet
Ambassador to Bulgaria between 1962–67, or, as a Western ambassador told me with a mischievous smile, "the Governor."

Bulgaria is the only Communist-ruled country in the world where
the Soviet Ambassador still sits on the platform at all important public occasions and accompanies the Premier on his tours of the provinces. It is the only country where on festive occasions the streets
and public buildings are hung with giant portraits of the members of
the Soviet Politburo side by side with those of their Bulgarian opposite numbers. It is the only country where the ruling party, for
many years the most profuse in its protestations of loyalty to the
"wise leadership of Comrade Khrushchev," hurriedly approved his
dismissal without expressing any emotion whatsoever and assured
his successors of the Bulgarian party's unfailing devotion.

Two weeks before Khrushchev's sudden fall, I toured the country and saw the photograph of the Soviet leader in most government offices. Returning six months later, I broached the delicate
matter in conversations with several high functionaries: "Nowhere
was Khrushchev so often and so warmly hailed as in Bulgaria, yet

you have been the only ones in Eastern Europe, aside from the Rumanians, who have ignored the whole affair, not even mentioning his name in your Central Committee resolution and keeping silent about the whole issue."

"We informed the people at party meetings and also at conferences organized by the Fatherland Front [the Communist-run mass organization] about the affair and we spoke also about Khrushchev. But we did not want to interfere publicly in the internal affairs of the Soviet Communist Party; we did not wish to add to their difficulties. After all we do have a special relationship with our Soviet comrades." This was the answer given by Petar Vutov, then Minister of Culture. His colleague, Foreign Minister Ivan Bashev, was equally swift with his reply when asked about the Soviet Ambassador accompanying Premier and party leader Todor Zhivkov on his country trips. "No one finds it in the least odd. If he wanted, our ambassador in Moscow could also escort the Soviet leaders on their journeys to the provinces. In view of the difference in size, however, it would perhaps look ridiculous. What's more, the representatives of the other socialist countries could also claim the same privilege."

Even the first visual impressions of Sofia show that there is a very special relationship between this small Balkan country, roughly as big as the state of Tennessee, and its giant friend. Walking along the broad main street, paved with orange-colored tiles and lined with double rows of chestnut trees, the visitor encounters three monumental palaces built in the mid-fifties in the depressing Soviet "wedding cake" style. These house a huge department store, government offices, party headquarters, and the largest hotel. The policeman who directs the sparse traffic is in a uniform also modeled on the Soviet pattern. The official cars, with curtains always drawn, are without exception heavy, black Soviet-made limousines. Just around the corner a permanent large neon "advertisement" hails "eternal Soviet-Bulgarian friendship."

Farther along the main street, opposite the former royal palace, now the National Gallery, is a white marble structure with two soldiers in dress uniform guarding the entrance. This is the Bulgarian equivalent of Moscow's Lenin mausoleum, where the embalmed body of Georgi Dimitrov lies in state: Dimitrov, the hero of the Reichstag fire trial, previous Secretary General of the Comintern, and the country's first postwar Communist Premier and party

ON THE EVE OF THE RUSSO-
TURKISH WAR, 1877

BULGARIAN FRONTIER PROPOSED
BY TREATY OF SAN STEFANO, 1878

TREATY OF BERLIN, 1878

BOUNDARIES AFTER WORLD
WAR II (showing Macedonia as
one of the Republics of Yugoslavia)

FRONTIER CHANGES INVOLVING MACEDONIA

leader. When he died in somewhat mysterious circumstances in July 1949 in Moscow, Stalin lent the Bulgarians the official embalmer who had preserved the corpse of Lenin.[1]

A few hundred yards farther the visitor realizes that the "special relationship" between Sofia and Moscow did not start with Dimitrov and Stalin. On the same side as the mausoleum, Tsar Alexander II sits on his great stone horse atop a mighty pedestal inscribed "The Liberator." In his hands he holds the declaration of war on Turkey that helped free Bulgaria in 1877–78 from five hundred years of Ottoman rule. Across the street is an impressive Russian-style Orthodox cathedral with green domes and golden crosses, set on high ground in a large open space. The Alexander Nevski cathedral was built at the end of the last century as a gesture of gratitude to and in honor of the Russian soldiers who had fallen in the war that liberated Bulgaria.

Thus when party leader Todor Zhivkov proclaims that "Bulgarian-Soviet friendship is sacred and indestructible . . . that Bulgarian-Soviet unity is a symbol of our freedom, independence and Communist future," he also evokes historic memories of loyalty and gratitude to "Mother Russia"; the Bulgars were always her favorites in the Balkans, her vanguard of expansion and defense against Constantinople. Is then the ubiquitous cult of friendship with Moscow a genuine reflection of traditional pro-Russian feelings? How much of this effusion is voluntary and how much enforced? Is Bulgaria an enthusiastically faithful ally or an eagerly obedient vassal?

Any attempt to define the essential characteristics of the political situation must begin with the traumatically humiliating defeats Bulgaria has suffered since its re-emergence as an independent nation. Between 1912 and 1944, Bulgaria was involved in two Balkan conflicts and two world wars to regain the territories promised by the stillborn Treaty of San Stefano in 1878 and lost at the Congress of Berlin the same year.

The yearning to regain the frontiers of what would have been the biggest state in the Balkans, to liberate the "lost territories" of Macedonia, Thrace, and southern Dobruja was a dominant factor in Bulgarian politics until the end of World War II. Heightened by the memory of medieval greatness, the unfinished liberation of the country became "a national myth which held the imagination of Bulgarian leaders in so powerful a grasp that they appeared at times to forget completely their major tasks of social and economic progress."[2]

In the wars of 1912–18 Bulgaria paid an exorbitant price in terms of casualties and economic losses for a very slight territorial gain. Not including the many thousands of civilians who died in the typhus and influenza epidemics, the country registered 160,000 dead and 400,000 wounded out of a population of 5 million, in which the number of males between twenty and fifty was only 763,000 in 1915.[3*] In the entire interwar period, Bulgaria smoldered with resentment against its more fortunate neighbors, which had emerged as victorious and enlarged states. It became the revisionist state par excellence in the Balkans with irredentist longings directed against Yugoslavia, Greece, and Rumania. It was the sense of national frustration so strongly felt by the taciturn and stubborn Bulgarian people that converted the country into a tool of the Central Powers in the first world conflict and paved the way to an alliance with Nazi Germany in the second.

In both wars, Bulgaria chose the wrong side and at their close had to evacuate the territories it had occupied in Yugoslavia and Greece. It was allowed to retain only the region of southern Dobruja, lost in 1913 to Rumania but regained in 1940 with the assistance of Germany. The ruthless behavior of the Bulgarian occupation troops in Thrace and Macedonia has never been forgotten in Greece and Yugoslavia and has left a legacy of suspicion and resentment against the Bulgarians, once called "the Prussians of the Balkans."

The national spirit and territorial irredentism are the key to the seeming enigma that the Bulgarians are the only East Europeans who have traditional sympathies with both Russia and Germany (neither of which has a common border with Bulgaria). Modern Bulgarian history is a chronicle of unfulfilled hopes and cheated expectations that have bred a deep-rooted psychology of defeat. As an elderly non-Communist Bulgarian historian put it to me: "There is nothing to fall back on in our modern history. We cannot heave ourselves up out of our historic tragedies. Therefore we tend to look at Russia as a protector. The result is, of course, that we have become in fact, if not in name, the sixteenth union republic of the Soviet Union."

* The population in 1967 was just over 8.2 million.

There are, however, weighty political and economic factors that determine the degree and the nature of this psychological dependency. The distinctive feature of the Bulgarian national movement in the last century and of the rise of the socialist parties in this was the powerful influence exerted on the Bulgarians by the Russian revolutionaries, reinforced by the sense of Slavic kinship. Most of the national leaders, like Khristo Botev and Liuben Karavelov and the outstanding personalities in the first decades of independent Bulgaria such as Premier Stefan Stambolov, the moderate socialist leader Yanko Sakazov, and the founder of the Communist party, Dimitar Blagoev, were among the five hundred Bulgarian students who had been educated at Russian high schools and universities.

It is important to remember that, in the past, gratitude for Russian aid and friendship with the liberator was not equated with servile subordination to Russian strategic interests. As Karavelov, the revolutionary leader, once wrote: "If Russia comes to liberate, she will be met with great sympathy; but if she comes to rule, she will find many enemies."[4] This prophetic warning was borne out by subsequent developments. Although all officers above the rank of lieutenant in the young Bulgarian army, organized even before the birth of the state itself, were Russians, the occupying authorities and the tsarist diplomats were soon faced with mounting difficulties. When the first ruler of independent Bulgaria, Prince Alexander of Battenberg, albeit a nephew of the Tsar, sided with the liberals in whittling down Russian influence, a group of officers directed by Russia forced his abdication in 1886. This was the first but not the last army coup in restless Bulgaria.

It was against Russian opposition that Prince Ferdinand of Coburg was then elected to the throne and that a young liberal, Stefan Stambolov, governed the country for seven years (1887–94). Despite his authoritarian methods and his violation of the Tirnovo Constitution of 1879, one of the most liberal of its time, Stambolov gave the country a spell of badly needed stability, several successful moves toward general modernization and an independent foreign policy. In retrospect, he is regarded by many Bulgarians as perhaps the most outstanding statesman in their country's history. True, growing resistance to his strong-arm regime and discord with Ferdinand led him to tender his resignation, but both his dismissal and his assassination a year later, to a large degree were attributable to extreme nationalists who were aroused by the Turkish authorities closing the Bulgarian schools in Macedonia. The Prime Minister responsible for the short-lived Serbo-Bulgarian rapprochement in the early twentieth century was also assassinated. A generation later the same fate befell the great peasant leader Alexander Stamboliski, Prime Minister between 1919 and 1923, who for all his controversial domestic policies, worked for peace in the Balkans based on a modus vivendi with Yugoslavia and was, in consequence, violently opposed by the Macedonian terrorist organization.

If we could gauge a nation's penchant for violence by the number of assassinations in its political record, interwar Bulgaria would lead the international league. First to be conquered by the Turks and last to be liberated, Bulgaria inherited a political tradition of brutality, violence, and corruption. It is generally agreed that none of the East European countries between the two world wars had "a record of such systematic and uninterrupted brutality as Bulgaria."[5]

When not at war, Bulgaria was torn by bitter divisions and almost unbearable stresses. A soldier rebellion, an abortive Communist insurrection, four army coups, and innumerable minor political upheavals marked the road that ultimately resulted in King Boris proclaiming a royal dictatorship in 1935. At the height of its power, VMRO,* which started as a genuine revolutionary Macedonian organization but later degenerated into a gangster band, was a state within the state. Split into rival factions, the Macedonian gangs assassinated no fewer than 864 persons between 1924 and 1934.

Yet, in contrast to most other East European countries, prewar Bulgaria was a strongly egalitarian peasant society, if never a real peasant state. There was no deep social cleavage between rulers and ruled, no relics of an oppressive feudalism. Only 1 per cent of the farmers had individual holdings of more than thirty hectares and these accounted for less than 6 per cent of the land. As a result of the absence of striking contrasts in wealth, class distinctions have always been very slight. Ethnically and culturally Bulgaria was also more homogeneous than its neighbors. About 90 per cent of the population consisted of ethnic Bulgarians, speaking one language and belonging to the Orthodox Church. The Turks (now numbering about 750,000) have never posed a serious minority problem to the government in power.

* See section on Yugoslavia.

But in this small country suffering from overpopulation and under-employment there was not enough room for all the would-be politicians, not enough "respectable" jobs for the university and high school graduates trained chiefly to be "administrators." Politics was one of Bulgaria's leading industries—in the early 1930s there were seventeen government officials per 1,000 inhabitants.[6] The presence of over 250,000 refugees from the lost territories, coupled with the dangerous antics of the pseudo-revolutionary Macedonian gangs fighting for "the unification of all Bulgarians" and the widespread irredentist aspirations shared by most Bulgarians, combined to aggravate a tense situation.

Frustrated nationalism, domestic tensions, political discord, and economic difficulties after a lost war could well have provided ample opportunities for a conspiratorial elite of dedicated revolutionaries. But the single most important feature of Bulgarian communism is that it emerged as a party in the Russian tradition, an offspring of the Russian revolutionary movement, in contrast to the other Communist parties in the Balkans, which were molded primarily by German and French socialism.[7] The Bulgarian socialist party, founded in 1891 when there were fewer than 5,000 workers in the country, split in 1903 (the year of the schism in the Russian movement) into a radical and a moderate group. The first was called "narrow," being accused by its adversaries of being too narrow-minded, and the second, accordingly, "broad."

The leader of the "narrows," Dimitar Blagoev (1855–1924), was a teacher and the founder of the first known Marxist circle in Russia (when he was studying there). Even before the Russian Revolution, the "narrow" party was renowned as doctrinaire, fanatic, and obstinate in its fight for dogmatic orthodoxy. On a visit to Bulgaria in 1910, Trotsky noted that the Bulgarian socialists copied even the rhetoric and phraseology of their Russian tutors,[8] and to this very day, they have remained faithful to this tradition. Blagoev, who was proud of having gone to the theater only once in his life was an apostle of intolerant orthodoxy, waging a relentless fight against the moderates and flouting the idea of any cooperation with the peasant organizations, let alone with other political forces. He had already spelled out his program in no uncertain terms in 1902: "The socialist party would rigorously fight for the complete abolition of private property from the biggest machine to the tailor's needle, from

the large tracts to the last inch of land."⁹ Before World War I, the
"narrow" socialists had a membership of only 3,400.

It was not doctrinal purity and political intransigence but the
humiliating defeats between 1912 and 1918 and their manifold
repercussions that helped Blagoev's party to win unexpected
electoral successes. In 1913, the "narrows" and the "broads" polled
one-fifth of the total ballot and were represented by thirty-seven
deputies in parliament. In contrast to the reformists, the "narrow"
party was consistently against both the Balkan wars and Bulgaria's
participation in World War I, a position that enhanced the party's prestige after the defeat. By 1919 its membership had risen
to 21,000. But for all his revolutionary rhetoric, Blagoev was not in
the same class with Lenin and his party stood idly by when the
so-called Radomir rebellion led to a real revolutionary situation in
the autumn of 1918. After a soldiers' mutiny, an improvised army
15,000 strong proclaimed a republic, chose the Agrarian Union
leader, Stamboliski, as its head, and marched on the capital. The
rebellion was crushed in three days' fierce fighting on the outskirts
of Sofia. The Communists regarded it as "a fight within the bourgeoisie."

The ultra-leftist line with its contempt for the peasants' movement
led the Communists into a second, even more fateful blunder. At its
congress in May 1919, the "narrow" party changed its name to the
Communist party and joined the Comintern. Not handicapped by
traditional anti-Russian nationalist feeling as its sister parties in
Hungary, Rumania, and Poland were, it emerged soon after its formation as the country's second largest party. The Communists
polled a large share of the popular vote and sent forty-seven deputies, one-fifth of the total, to parliament. Until it was outlawed in
1923, the party was surpassed only by the Agrarian Union in polling
strength. Operating from the late 1920s on under the label of "Labor
Party," the Communists succeeded in the first relatively free elections in 1931 in sending thirty-one deputies to parliament and in
capturing an absolute majority of the seats in the Sofia Municipal
Council a year later. Though the mandates of the crypto-Commu-
nists were subsequently invalidated by the courts, there is no doubt
that the Communist party, which never numbered more than
30,000 to 35,000 members, enjoyed a certain popularity in those
turbulent days. It is, however, equally true that, in contrast to the

exaggerated claims of its spokesmen, it represented no serious threat
to the state.

One of the crucial junctures in interwar Bulgarian history was the
plot that overthrew the government of Alexander Stamboliski. Like
Stambolov a generation earlier, Stamboliski is considered one of
Bulgaria's most outstanding and controversial statesmen. As an
advocate of a radical peasant and anti-urban ideology, Stamboliski held that the welfare of the peasant majority should take
priority over all other issues. His Agrarian Union, which governed
from 1919 until 1923, passed a series of measures to the benefit of
the villages and established a compulsory labor service and the
institution of public works to circumvent the ban on military service decreed by the peace treaty. At the same time he held the extreme nationalists in check and signed an important agreement with
Yugoslavia. His ultimate aim was the establishment of a corporate
peasant state associated with the neighboring agrarian states in a
"Green International."

His strong-arm methods, club-wielding "Orange Guards," and
anti-city demagogy provoked and antagonized all other party
groups. With the active or tacit support of the political parties, the
crown, and the urban population, the League of Reserve Officers
engineered a coup in June 1923, which in forty-five minutes un-
seated the Stamboliski government. The chief technical organizer
of the plot was Colonel Damyan Velchev, the commander of the
Sofia Military Academy. Stamboliski was caught and murdered after
horrible torture.

Stamboliski's Agrarians were a radical, definitely anti-bourgeois
force with 40 per cent of the popular vote. Yet the Communists,
as so often in their history, sized up the balance of forces incorrectly
and regarded him as their main enemy. The second largest party
not only stood aside in the showdown between the Agrarians and
the nationalists, but in its first statement expressed hardly veiled relief and even called off resistance in those cities where the local
party organizations had come to the aid of the Agrarians. At the
time, the Comintern called the event "the greatest defeat ever suffered by a Communist party."[10]

The decision to stand by idly was taken unanimously by the
party's Central Committee. Its Secretary General and effective
leader, in view of Blagoev's advanced age and failing health, was
his closest collaborator and disciple, Vasil Kolarov. Luckily for his

personal career, Kolarov, a graduate of Geneva University, happened to be in Moscow at the time of the coup. He returned in August, rebuked his comrades for their inactivity, and presented them with the Comintern's order to foment an armed uprising. The neutrality policy previously endorsed with almost complete unanimity was immediately reversed on Moscow's orders, and what was from the beginning a hopeless insurrection was launched in September 1923. The uprising, with its center in the Vratsa district near the Yugoslav and Rumanian borders, was quickly suppressed.

Nevertheless it provided the Bulgarian Communists with a historical myth and prestige, enabling them to play a role in international communism quite out of proportion to their size or importance. Priding themselves on being the only party aside from the Russians that entered the Comintern as a unit, the Bulgarian Communists ensured the lasting favor of their Russian masters by their historic merits, orthodox record, and unfailing obedience.

After the party was forced to go underground, it perpetrated an act of terrorism without precedent in Communist history. In April 1925 a bomb exploded in the cathedral of Sofia, killing 128 persons and wounding 323 others who were attending a funeral service for a general assassinated by the Communists two days earlier. The plot, organized by two Communist lieutenant colonels in the army and their associates, sparked off a renewed reign of terror against the Communists and Agrarians. For over twenty years, the Communists emphatically denied any responsibility. It was only at the first postwar party congress in December 1948 that Dimitrov acknowledged that this "act of desperation" had been perpetrated by "ultra-left members and the military department of the party."

This, then, was the domestic political record of the Bulgarian Communists, regarded in Moscow as the "best Bolsheviks" in international communism. The obedience of the Bulgarian Communists "was to become unique even in the Comintern and is the real reason why, despite their frequent blunders, the Bulgarians were always Moscow's favorite Balkan disciples and its regular gendarmes and purgers within the Comintern."[11] The Balkan Communist Federation and Communist policies in that region in the interwar period were dominated by the Bulgarians, who skillfully combined the fight for the Comintern's line of dismembering the Rumanian and Yugoslav succession states with pursuing traditional Bulgarian national objectives. On and off, the Bulgarians quarreled with their

Balkan comrades over a period of twenty years and usually succeeded in dominating them. The interests of revisionist Bulgaria
neatly coincided with Soviet policies and enabled the Bulgarian
Communists to merge their absolute loyalty to the Comintern with
their nationalistic impulses.

During the interwar period close personal and ideological links
between Bulgarian and Soviet communism were forged. The ranking Bulgarian leader, Vasil Kolarov, occupied top positions in the
Comintern hierarchy; he belonged to the Comintern Executive Committee and for some time headed the Balkan Secretariat. Bulgaria's
internationally best-known Communist politician, Georgi Dimitrov, was made subordinate to Kolarov and devoted his main attention to the unions, emerging in the limelight only after his defiant
self-defense at the Reichstag fire trial. After his extradition to
Russia, he became Secretary General of the Comintern and proclaimed the famous "popular front" line in 1935. It is estimated that
during the 1930s six hundred Bulgarians occupied important positions in the Soviet state administration. Undeviating obedience,
related language, historical and sentimental links, common irredentism, and personal ties thus combined to produce a relationship without parallel in Moscow's links with other "national detachments."[12]

This factor had a profound impact on Bulgarian communism after
the seizure of power and reinforced the historical and psychological
dependence on the Soviet Union. Despite the many personal changes
in the top leadership, the Bulgarian Communists' loyalty to Moscow
has remained a constant. The degree of the dependence has, however, split the ruling hierarchy more than once. At the same time
the record of brutality and the spirit of schism so characteristic of
the underground movement have remained the principal traits of
the Bulgarian Communists since their takeover.

Heroes, traitors, martyrs . . .

On December 27, 1947, the Bulgarian party organ *Rabotnichesko
Delo* carried a front-page letter of the Central Committee and the
government congratulating Traicho Kostov, Central Committee
Secretary and Deputy Premier, on his fiftieth birthday and praising
him as "an outstanding leader of the party." Two years later, almost to the day, Kostov was hanged as a police informer, Titoist

spy, and foreign agent who had conspired with the American Minister in Sofia. At his trial, Kostov repudiated in open court the confession he was alleged to have signed in prison—the only time that such an event occurred during a Communist show trial. As so often in Bulgarian history, the papers produced the text of a "new" confession *after* the defendant had been executed.

After a partial and discreet rehabilitation during the first de-Stalinization campaign in April 1956, Kostov was fully and demonstratively cleared in November 1962 at the Eighth Party Congress. And on December 27, 1967, *Rabotnichesko Delo* once again carried a front-page editorial on the seventieth anniversary of Kostov's birth, hailing him as a "brilliant fighter for communism, a remarkable leader" and a martyr to the "abuses committed against socialist legality during the personality cult period."

In a party rent since its birth by violent factional struggles, there are many more recent variations on the hero-traitor-martyr cycle. For example, the case of Dobri Terpeshev: one of the oldest members of the party, he was the supreme commander of the Partisan units during the war and negotiated with Tito in the autumn of 1944 about the evacuation of Macedonia. After the Kostov affair he went into a rapid eclipse, but his final purge as a "right-winger" did not take place until 1957 when he lost all his positions. As late as 1961, he was attacked as a "former party member." Yet when he died in January 1967, he received a state funeral and was praised as an "outstanding veteran and former member of the Politburo."

The case of former Premier Anton Yugov is illuminating in a different way. As Minister of Interior he was responsible for the worst period of repression in Bulgarian history. Yet after the Kostov purge he was attacked by Dimitrov's successor, Vulko Chervenkov, for "his lack of vigilance." Six years later Chervenkov himself had to resign as a token of de-Stalinization in the midst of attacks on his "brutality," and was replaced by Yugov. After another six years or so it was again Yugov's turn to be purged. His colleagues in the Politburo suddenly discovered that he had been too much involved after all in "the violation of socialist legality."

If one accepts Bernard Shaw's witticism that assassination is the extreme form of censorship, one must conclude that the Bulgarian leaders have made some progress in abandoning wholesale execution as a means of silencing the losers in power struggles. Kostov was hanged, and no amount of posthumous praise can resurrect him, but Yugov lives in a comfortable, spacious house, has a chauffeur-driven Mercedes and a gardener at his disposal, receives a large pension, and makes an occasional appearance in restaurants or at the theater.

Kostov, Terpeshev, and Yugov were victims of the occupational hazards every Communist leader faces. What distinguishes the factional struggles in the Bulgarian party is the scope, intensity, and persistence of the power conflicts and the perennial search for scapegoats. Neither past purges nor the current situation in the Bulgarian Communist Party should be viewed merely in the context of ordinary struggles for power. The shifting allegiances and multiple crosscurrents have been colored by the relationship with Moscow and Belgrade, by differences over the crucial issue of how to industrialize the country—and to what extent and in what direction—as well as by chronic discord over the definition of the point beyond which even a limited internal liberalization must not be allowed to go. The question as to who or which group comes out on top in a given factional struggle has always been decisively influenced by Soviet preferences. At the same time, local pressures, rooted in the different political and personal backgrounds of persons and groups in the upper echelons, have influenced Moscow's choice.

The origins of intraparty struggles can be found partly in the circumstances in which the Communists seized power. In contrast to Yugoslavia and Albania, communism was "imported" into Bulgaria. The Soviet Union maintained diplomatic relations with Bulgaria until the very end. Not until victory was certain did it suddenly declare war and "assure itself the rights and privileges of conquest."[13] On September 9, 1944, after the Russians had invaded the country, the Bulgarian government was overthrown by the Fatherland Front, an underground movement composed of the Zveno group, the radical Agrarians, the Social Democrats, and the Communists.

The Zveno group, named after a prewar periodical of the same name (zveno means "link"), was associated with the Military League headed by Colonel Damyan Velchev and played an important role in Bulgarian politics. Velchev, perhaps the most accomplished military conspirator in modern East European history, engineered the plot against Stamboliski, organized another military coup ten years later, and was instrumental in the smooth seizure of power in 1944. The leader of Zveno, Kimon Giorgiev, became the head of the Fatherland Front government while Velchev occupied the key position of Minister of War. The left-wing Agrarians, headed first by Dr. G. M. Dimitrov (no relation to the Communist leader) who was sentenced to death in absentia in 1941 and returned after the coup, also received several posts, as did the socialists.

With Bulgaria occupying the long-coveted territories in Macedonia and Thrace and reaping certain economic advantages from trade with Germany and a wartime boom, yet not participating in the war against the Soviet Union, the small Communist guerrilla bands had never been able to exert great influence. There had been few German troops in the country, and the activity of the Partisans consisted mainly of raiding villages and harassing and fighting the local gendarmeries and scattered army units. At its peak, the Partisan movement, for all the carefully fostered myths, never numbered more than 10,000 to 15,000 men. The party itself claimed some 25,000 members in September 1944, but non-Communist sources put the figure at about 8,000.[14]

Yet this hard core of dedicated Communists, reinforced, it is true, by scores of Soviet-trained functionaries and officers, played a key role in imposing countrywide control and destroying the old administration. While the Soviet Army "paralyzed by its very presence the forces of reaction in the country," as Chervenkov said later, the Communists in charge of the Ministry of Interior launched what was, even by Balkan standards, a ferocious campaign to ferret out and liquidate the political cadres of the non-Communist bourgeois parties. Within six months of the Russians' entry, "people's courts" held 131 trials and condemned over 10,000 persons, 2,138 of whom were executed. Many of these people were persecuted merely because they were mistrusted by the Communists and the Russians and suspected of being pro-Western. The only potentially dangerous counterforce, the army, was not only purged of its most "unreliable" elements, but was sent out of the country to fight the Germans in Austria and Hungary. By the time the units returned, the Communists had seized effective control of central and local government. Within a year the Fatherland Front became a mere screen for unbridled Communist rule; Dr. G. M. Dimitrov was forced into exile and subsequently once more condemned to death in absentia. Rigged elections in disregard of Western protests and opposition boycott lent a pretense of legality to what was already a single-party dictatorship.

While the proclamation of a republic met with genuine popular consent, the terrorism against political rivals and opponents alienated even those who had had sympathies for a left-wing government. Only Communist eagerness to conclude a peace treaty and gain Western recognition saved the life of Nikola Petkov, the daring Agrarian leader who succeeded Dr. G. M. Dimitrov, and the lives of other opposition leaders. The campaign of terror and intimidation made the victory of the Fatherland Front in the October 1946 elections a foregone conclusion. Nevertheless 1.3 million people defied the pressure, enabling the opposition to win 22 per cent of the popular vote.

Having renounced his Soviet citizenship two days earlier, Georgi Dimitrov took over the premiership. After the signing of the Peace Treaty and the securing of British and American recognition, came the symbolic turning point in postwar history: the trial and execution of Nikola Petkov, the peasant leader who had been defying Communist policies for six months on the floor of parliament. As an acute observer on the spot remarked: "The Anglo-American intervention in Bulgaria (and also in Rumania) in the years between the armistice and peace treaties had about as much effect as a badly worn brake on a heavy bus hurtling downhill."[15]

The effective leader of the Communist party during the closing stage of the war and in the immediate postwar period was Traicho Kostov; Dimitrov and Kolarov, both old and ailing, returned only in the autumn of 1945 when Communist control had already been firmly established. Kostov, crippled since 1925 when he jumped out of a window to escape torture by the Sofia police, was a "home" Communist. Though he spent several years in Russia, he ran the party during the crucial wartime period.

As ruthless as his successors, he committed the unpardonable sin of trying to protect his country's political and economic interests. In contrast to Dimitrov who had worked for close cooperation with Yugoslavia and a Balkan Federation, Kostov was against what he regarded as an unfair deal. As Djilas later recalled: "Kostov was considered [by the Yugoslavs] an opponent of Yugoslavia and by the same token a Soviet man. Yet he was also for Bulgarian independence and disliked the Yugoslavs because he thought that they were Stalin's chief henchmen and even trying to dominate Bulgaria."[16]

It was, however, his stand, not against the federation project, which by then Stalin opposed, but against exploitation of Bulgaria that sealed his fate. Stalin regarded Bulgaria as a political satellite and economic colony. In 1946–47 Soviet representatives bought up much of the Bulgarian tobacco crop and its famous attar of roses at ridiculously low prices. When the Bulgarians tried to market the rest of their tobacco and rose essence, they were shocked to discover that they were competing against their own products, offered by the Russians on Western markets at less than prevailing world prices. As acting Premier, Kostov tried to put an end to these practices by applying the law on state secrets to Soviet economic officials, who together with intelligence agents and military experts had already infiltrated the entire state apparatus. This was the only matter he brought up at the crucial Soviet-Yugoslav-Bulgarian talks in February 1948. His complaints about the injustice of some agreements were brushed off by an irritated Stalin fully engaged in the showdown with the intransigent Yugoslavs, but the episode was not forgotten.

Though Kostov was tried on the false charge that he was in the service of Tito and "the imperialists," his real guilt consisted of "national deviation in relation to the Soviet Union." After his public rebuke by *Pravda* for supporting a federation project, sixty-six-year-old Dimitrov had been "written off," and his brother-in-law, Vulko Chervenkov, who had spent two decades in Moscow, had become Stalin's chief Bulgarian agent. The liquidation of Kostov was entrusted to this able and ruthless apparatchik. Kostov, the anti-Soviet nationalist, who did not realize "that secrets and commercialism do not exist in our relations with the Soviet Union," as the party paper solemnly proclaimed, was forced to resign in March, was expelled and arrested in June, after Chervenkov had returned with the "script" of his trial, and hanged in December 1949. His closest collaborators, Finance Minister Stefanov, who had stabilized the currency; Professor Petko Kunin, the top planner; and many other officials were sentenced to long prison terms.

After the deaths of Dimitrov and Kolarov, Chervenkov became the undisputed dictator. Party membership in 1948 was over 500,000, twenty times higher than at the time of the seizure of power, since tens of thousands of opportunists had jumped on the bandwagon. Within two years, more than 90,000 members were purged, including many able and reliable Communists suspected of harboring secret sympathies for Kostov, of being "waverers" or guilty of some unspecified "deviation."

Bulgaria under Chervenkov became a model satellite and the spearhead of the campaign of vituperation against Yugoslavia. Regardless of differences over other matters, the overwhelming majority of Bulgarian Communist leaders, whether of the "native" or Muscovite variety, felt that the Stalin-Tito conflict had saved Pirin Macedonia (the 2,700 square miles of Macedonia that Bulgaria managed to secure in 1913) from being merged with Tito's Macedonian Republic. The Sofia press began to refer to Yugoslav Macedonia as Western Bulgaria. Meanwhile all contacts with the West were cut. The United States broke off diplomatic relations after the Kostov affair. Relations with Greece deteriorated to the point where not even rail or postal communications were maintained. After the brutal expulsion of some 150,000 of the Turkish minority, serious tensions arose with Turkey. Internal policies were even more Stalinist than in Rumania. Collectivization of agriculture surged far ahead of other Communist countries. As early as 1950, 44 per cent of the arable land belonged to the collective and state farms, while in neighboring Rumania the figure stood at only 12 per cent. By 1957 the Bulgarians were the first in the entire Soviet bloc to proclaim the "full collectivization" of private farming.

In no other Communist country was the Stalinist model of industrialization copied to such an extent as in Bulgaria. In terms of percentages, the performance was impressive. But even aside from the fact that Bulgarian statistics were and are notoriously unreliable (reports and figures released for varying periods often conflict widely with one another), the wisdom of the manner and degree of the entire industrialization policy is very much open to doubt.

How to improve agricultural methods, absorb surplus labor, and industrialize in a way suited to the needs and resources of the country had been a central question facing Bulgaria ever since it became independent. The Communist answer to these questions was a forced "all-round" industrialization—and this in a small country devoid of hard coal, iron, and oil, with a very low per capita income and little industrial experience, and with no reserve of specialists and skilled workers. The by-products of building a "heavy industrial base" without any regard for resources, of increasing the proportion of investments three to four times prewar levels, of neglecting agriculture and placing enormous burdens on the consumer may plague Bulgaria almost indefinitely.

Bulgaria could offer the Soviet Union cheap labor, non-ferrous metals, and processed agricultural and chemical products, often of shoddy quality. Exports to the Soviet market had priority over domestic supply, and plans were drawn up according to the given needs of the Soviet planner. While in 1937 what is now the Soviet bloc accounted for only 12 per cent of the country's foreign trade, the proportion rose to 92 per cent by 1951, with the Russians alone having a stake of almost 60 per cent. The price paid for a questionable pattern of industrialization was exorbitant: a high rate of waste, the destruction of traditional handicrafts, a depressed standard of living, and growing tensions and imbalances between high-cost heavy industry and neglected light industry and between industry and agriculture. This was coupled with serious social dislocations as housing lagged far behind the massive population transfer from farming to industry.

While these problems were typical of all Communist countries during the heyday of Stalinism, political developments in Bulgaria were in some respects unique and at times enigmatic. When in 1954, the Soviet "new course" obliged the rulers of the satellites to break the previous practice of combining party leadership and the premiership, Chervenkov surprisingly decided to remain Premier. He chose his successor as First Secretary of the party carefully, picking a junior functionary, the then forty-three-year-old Todor Zhivkov, instead of making room for a potential rival. Of peasant stock, with a minimum of formal education, Zhivkov was elected a full member of the Central Committee only at the end of 1948 and his subsequent rise in the hierarchy was due solely to his being a favorite of the party leader. He became one of the party secretaries and then member of the ruling Politburo in 1950–51, during the wholesale purge of the party.

From 1955 onward the Soviet-Yugoslav rapprochement began to cast a menacing shadow over Chervenkov's career. The "little Stalin" of Bulgaria, like his colleagues in Albania and Hungary, saw his survival at stake in the wake of Khrushchev's spectacular journey to Belgrade in May 1955. Furthermore the Bulgarian leadership as a whole was second only to Albania in its traditional enmity toward Yugoslavia. Thus it was not surprising that Khrushchev stopped in Sofia on his way back from Belgrade, to keep the situation under control. "The road toward development of friendly relations between the Soviet Union and the people's democracies on the one hand and Yugoslavia on the other, has been opened," he proclaimed at a public meeting. At the same time he also made a secret speech to a select party audience, where he is alleged to have pointed out the limits rather than the scope of the reconciliation, stressing particularly the maintenance of Soviet ideological and political primacy.

The first Soviet-Yugoslav reconciliation did not erode Soviet influence in Bulgaria, but it did raise the thorny question of who should be the chief Soviet agent once Chervenkov had been sacrificed to the cause of Yugoslav friendship. This was the period when the Soviet leadership itself was split over the scope and pace of de-Stalinization, with the warring factions favoring different leaders in the various satellites. Nowhere was the matter so difficult to solve as in Bulgaria where there was no other leader "in reserve" with a stature remotely comparable to Chervenkov's.

After the Twentieth Party Congress the Soviet leaders chose a compromise solution. At the plenary meeting of the Bulgarian Central Committee in April 1956, Chervenkov was removed from his position as Premier, castigated for his cult of personality and for "having considered that his word was law," and was replaced by Anton Yugov, Minister of Interior from 1944 to 1948. Chervenkov remained, however, a member of the Politburo and was appointed Deputy Premier. The Yugoslavs immediately complained that the plenum "did not go far enough" in condemning Chervenkov, rehabilitating Kostov, and settling accounts with the secret police.

The "April plenum" has become one of the sacred fictions in party history, the turning point in the fight against the "personality cult" and the return to "socialist legality." All that it actually produced as far as the population was concerned was merely atmospheric improvements, and even the limited advances in the field of cultural dissent were quickly reversed when a writers' rebellion the following year exceeded the limits of party tolerance.

The real significance of Chervenkov's demotion and of the entire April plenum was that it struck at the prestige of Bulgaria's strong man without changing his policies—he was demoted but not disgraced. This led to a dramatic revival of factional struggles, plunging the party into a chronic crisis of authority. The other East European rulers of the Stalin era were either replaced by their re-habilitated victims (in Hungary and Poland) or were able to ride out the storm (Ulbricht in East Germany, Hoxha in Albania, Gheorghiu-Dej in Rumania, and Antonin Novotny in Czechoslo-vakia). Every country had its undisputed victors and losers, which meant either the re-establishment or reinforcement of a single chain of command, the most important precondition for the existence of a totalitarian party dictatorship.

In Bulgaria, Chervenkov was no longer fully in command, but he remained in the wings as a Politburo member until the end of 1961 (in the Central Committee until November 1962), decisively in-fluencing factional struggles and major policy decisions. His still immense authority in the party handicapped the nominal party leader, Todor Zhivkov, in asserting himself in the party apparatus and building up an independent power base. The man in the street, and indeed most of the functionaries, regarded him as merely an errand-boy for Chervenkov.

The anti-Yugoslav campaign in 1957–58 gave the old-timers in the Bulgarian leadership a new lease on life. Once again Khru-shchev picked Sofia as the place to proclaim the changed line toward Yugoslavia, this time not "opening the road to normaliza-tion" but blocking it. At the Seventh Party Congress in June 1958, he announced that the 1948 Cominform resolution expelling Yugo-slavia had been "basically correct," charged Tito with abetting the Hungarian revolution, and accused the Yugoslavs of being a Trojan horse in the Communist movement. Bulgarian speakers happily echoed his vituperative attacks. As Tito in a sharp rejoinder ironi-cally remarked: "There was so much mention of Yugoslavia at the Bulgarian Party Congress that it resembled a Yugoslav faction's congress."

Soon after the congress, the country was thrown into a complete turmoil. Bulgaria embarked on her version of the Chinese "great leap forward." The ambitious Five Year Plan was scrapped and replaced by targets that all foreign observers and many Bulgarians regarded as not only enormously exaggerated, but outright ridicu-lous. The so-called "Zhivkov theses," published in January 1959, envisaged the fulfillment of the plan in four or possibly three years; agricultural production was to be doubled in 1959 and trebled by 1960. The collective farms were merged into 867 vast farms, each with an area of over 4,000 hectares. Despite 68,000 conferences and meetings at which the "masses" enthusiastically endorsed the "stupefying" undertaking, covert opposition was strong from the very beginning and continued to grow as the disastrous consequences of the "great leap" became more and more evident. Premier Yugov prudently remained in the background, but a prominent "doubter," Boris Taskov, a Politburo member, was demoted for "his lack of faith" in April 1959.

It is generally agreed that Chervenkov had a hand in this extraordinary experiment. He had visited China before the campaign started and the Bulgarian press had reported progress there in glowing terms. But in view of the tight Soviet control over Bulgaria, it is difficult to believe that the Bulgarian "leap" was the reflection of a conscious pro-Chinese trend.[17]

Sympathies for an underdeveloped China trying to overcome its backwardness and agonizing awareness of how far Bulgaria was lagging behind the developed "brotherly" countries may both have played a part, but the Bulgarian experiment was primarily the fruit of the domestic political deadlock that had eroded the self-confidence and dynamism of the party cadres. The "leap" was essentially a desperate attempt to retrieve the party's sense of mission and self-importance, to "revolutionize" the situation from above, and to replace growing discord with unity of purpose.

The experiment was probably backed initially by the Russians, but the pace got disastrously out of control in the hands of a party so deeply imbued with a tradition of "narrow" extremism and doctrinaire romanticism. The idea was identified with the name of Zhivkov and with his mentor, Chervenkov, who himself presented the blueprint to parliament in the spring of 1959. But instead of leaping forward, the authors of the venture soon found themselves in the ditch. Economically, the program was a dismal failure, leaving a legacy of wasted funds, senseless investment projects, and organizational chaos. The political repercussions were even more ominous. Zhivkov's standing fell, if possible, even lower than it had been before, and only the unfailing support of Khrushchev, who regarded him as a personal favorite, kept him at the helm of the party.

Throughout the whole decade between 1956 and 1965, there were three main factors behind the ups and downs in internal developments: the lack of a universally acknowledged leader, the economic impasse, and the external influences of a troubled relationship with Yugoslavia. Old and young Stalinists, dogmatists, and conservatives did not belong to any single faction either opposing a "reformist" Zhivkov or throwing its weight behind Premier Yugov as a symbol of the "old order."

Numerous ranking functionaries, "natives" and Muscovites, tended to regard Zhivkov as an "upstart" who had conspicuously failed to project an image of himself as a party leader, let alone as a national figure. This sizable and influential middle group of senior Communists with different backgrounds and views made it difficult for the Soviet leadership to opt unequivocally and swiftly for a solution. Even the Twenty-second Soviet Party Congress failed to tip the balance in favor of Zhivkov. As a token of de-Stalinization, in November 1961 Chervenkov was stripped of his seat in the Politburo and his post as Deputy Premier. He remained, however, a member of the Central Committee.

The factional conflicts and economic tensions culminated in 1962. Realizing the scope of the two-pronged crisis of authority and the economy, Moscow sent no less than eight fact-finding missions to the country, one headed by Khrushchev himself and two others led by his closest associates in the Soviet leadership. Once again using the occasion to announce yet another change in the line toward Yugoslavia, Khrushchev held out an olive branch to Tito and wished "the Yugoslav comrades successes in building socialism." The real purpose of his visit, however, was to dampen the factional struggle, to bolster Zhivkov's position, and to forestall any possible repercussions of the second major Soviet-Yugoslav reconciliation.

In the autumn of 1962 the Bulgarian party was preparing for its impending Eighth Congress, and the usual conferences at local levels were sprinkled with customary references to party unity. But the widening rift between Moscow and Peking and the aftermath of the Cuban crisis convinced Khrushchev that the deadlock in Bulgaria must be broken, and broken in a manner that would help the Soviet party in its campaign against its rivals in Peking. Even so the decision was made at the last possible moment.

On the eve of the opening day of the congress, the front of the former royal palace was as usual decorated with huge pictures of Lenin and Dimitrov. To the left of them were displayed portraits of the ten members of the Bulgarian Politburo, and on the right those of the Soviet Presidium. Next morning came the dramatic blow: Zhivkov denounced Premier Yugov, his deputy Georgi Tsankov, who had been Minister of Interior for over a decade, and others, as a dogmatic faction conspiring together with Chervenkov against the party line and in the defense of the "personality cult."

With the main culprits absent from the congress hall, Zhivkov's opening salvo was followed by a series of concerted attacks. The accusers were the young rising leaders who had rallied around Zhivkov during the past few years: Mitko Grigorov, the chief ideological spokesman; Stanko Todorov, the top economic planner; Boris Velchev, the secretary in charge of organization; and other functionaries who subsequently filled the positions vacated by the disgraced "conspirators." Grigorov, then forty-one years old, leveled the most impassioned accusations at his fallen colleagues: "During the Chervenkov era, an atmosphere of fear, mistrust, and suspicion prevailed in the party." But Chervenkov had already been criticized in 1956 and again in 1961. Why had it taken so many years for his sins and the sins of Yugov and Tsankov, who had been in the top leadership long after the worst period of their alleged violation of "socialist legality," to be discovered?

"We wanted to avoid a shock in the party," declared the president of the control commission in charge of disciplinary actions. The truth of the matter was that the final showdown had taken place three days before the congress, at a meeting of the Central Committee. The plenary session was interrupted, and Zhivkov flew to Moscow to ask for help in the face of powerful opposition. Inspired "leaks" tried to spread the impression that Yugov had also spoken out against the Soviet policy of peaceful coexistence, criticizing Khrushchev's behavior during the Cuban crisis. This, like many of the charges against the deposed leaders, was demonstrably false. Yugov was simply lumped with his old adversary, Chervenkov, and projected as a dyed-in-the-wool Stalinist, because the losers in the power struggle had to be disgraced under the banner of de-Stalinization.

In the course of the most sweeping purge since the Kostov affair, three Politburo members and twenty-seven Central Committee members, almost one-third of the total membership, were either purged or replaced by newcomers. Zhivkov took over the premiership of a government in which thirteen key posts were now occupied by new men. The two Premiers between 1950 and 1962 and all Ministers of Interior and their deputies throughout the entire postwar period now rank in the official history as "dogmatic plotters guilty of serious infringements of legality."

For the first time since his emergence from obscurity in 1954, Zhivkov seemed to have firm command of the party. With his most dangerous rival and his erstwhile protector expelled, he was in a position at last to exercise a pervasive influence over the party line and the apparatus, to throw overboard the ideological baggage of Stalinism, and to steer the long overdue reform course in domestic and external policies. Yet during the next two years the line swung wildly backward and forward, from more freedom to renewed tightening of the screws.

There were in fact multiple lines. The campaign against the men previously in charge of the security service and their "criminal excesses" brought a welcome relief to the average citizen. Some of the detention camps were closed, about four thousand prisoners, including an estimated five hundred political inmates, were pardoned, and a greater freedom of speech was tolerated. But in the middle of 1963 the regime recognized the timeliness of Tocqueville's warning about the acute dangers posed to a weak government when it seeks to mend its ways and relax the iron grip of repression. Making cracks at the expense of a nervous regime again became a risky venture, with the papers reporting a series of prison sentences and deportations of "hostile elements." A popular joke began to make the rounds in Sofia: What is the difference between a pessimist and an optimist? The pessimist says: "The situation was bad, is bad, and it will become even worse." The optimist says: "The situation was bad, is bad, it cannot possibly become worse."

The attitude toward intellectuals, above all writers, also varied. While de-Stalinization was in fashion a spate of poems, short stories, and plays were published reflecting the horrors of the Stalinist period. Then in the spring of 1963 Zhivkov spelled out the permissible limits of criticism in a major speech. But, in contrast to the past, the rebellious writers, rather than producing "party-minded" literature, either resorted to the tactic of silence or retreated to apolitical themes.

Contradictory tendencies were also apparent in foreign policy. The most important and durable change occurred in relations with Greece. After over twenty years of intermittent tensions, in July 1964 the two countries signed a package deal incorporating twelve interstate agreements on the restoration of direct road, rail, and air traffic, postal communications, trade exchanges, water regulation, etc. The re-establishment of normal relations with Greece marked the beginning of a more active Bulgarian policy in the Balkans and put an end to the long period of isolation.

But relations with the United States underwent bewildering alterations. For almost ten years after Kostov's trial there were no diplomatic relations at all between the two countries. The Bulgarians had implicated the then American Minister Donald Heath in the "plot," harassed the legation staff, and imprisoned its native employees, and Washington had broken off relations. The legation was reopened in 1960 after the Bulgarians had rehabilitated Kostov and withdrawn the false charges against Heath.

In 1963 a series of lively cultural contacts and exchanges of high level visits between the two countries began. On the Fourth of July, the American Minister, Mrs. Eugene Anderson, appeared on Bulgarian radio and television, the first Western mission chief to be accorded such a favor since the war. Then, almost overnight, the atmosphere dramatically changed. Assen Georgiev, a leading Bulgarian diplomat to the United Nations, was publicly tried as an American spy and executed in December. It was not so much the trial itself, but the excessive publicity devoted to it, coupled with savage attacks on the United States in the heavy-handed style of the Stalinist hate campaigns, that raised the ominous possibility of a full return to strong-arm police methods. An organized mob, controlled and directed by the secret police, stormed the American legation and shattered most of its windows. Two similar outbursts of officially instigated mob violence against the legation followed in 1964–65.

Fluctuations between improvement and retreat were also evident in other important areas, from the complex relationship with Yugoslavia to the first cautious steps toward economic reform and more reliance on material incentives. In conversations with writers, students, and economic experts, the visitor could hardly fail to notice that the defiant pride in achievements was almost always tinged with frustration that the progress was not faster, and at times with barely veiled anger at a leadership so subservient to Moscow, so vacillating in its policies, and so weak in surmounting the opposition to its stated reform program.

What happened to the much-publicized break with the past? To begin with, Zhivkov's sweeping victory over his rivals was more apparent than real. His troubles grew, not out of his failures, but out of the very character of his triumph. He had not won the power struggle on his own, but solely by virtue of Khrushchev's support and direct Soviet intervention. As a result, his personal and political dependence on the Soviet leader became greater than ever before. This in turn weakened rather than strengthened his authority in the party.

The mood of general dissatisfaction with food supply difficulties, the housing shortage, and the lack of appreciable improvement was coupled with an unprecedented opposition to Zhivkov's reformist initiatives within the power structure itself. Faced with rising popular pressures and the still powerful resistance of the party machine, mainly at the medium and lower levels, Zhivkov and his associates had three options: to return to the safe and cheap course of repression; to embark on a resolute program of liberalization; or to mark time by compromises. The old-timers were no longer powerful enough to enforce a full-scale retreat, nor did the Zhivkov group yet have the strength or the necessary Soviet backing to push for a meaningful change. Thus the leadership was forced, and also partly inclined, to choose the third option: to plod along on a middle-of-the-road course between the extremes of Stalinism and reform. This was politically the least disastrous and hence the most acceptable line to the vested interests of a power elite that in both its composition and its divided loyalties bore the stamp of two decades of bitter factional struggles.

Even this state of affairs was infinitely superior to the not-so-distant Stalinist past. But the population at large and, even more, the close to four hundred thousand university graduates and people with specialized training were measuring progress in terms of the regime's frequent promises and their own expectations, not in comparison with the worst period of postwar history. As in most other Communist countries, streamlined simplifications about clear-cut battlefronts between "dogmatists" and "reformists" often only obscure the real problems if indiscriminately applied to a myriad of major and petty conflicts in administration, economy, and everyday life.

Many Bulgarians from ministers to local officials and managers, did not oppose change in the past or do not resist it today because they are "dogmatic." It is rather the other way around: they take up positions that can be described as dogmatic or conservative for fear of losing jobs gained solely by virtue of their Partisan record and the right connections. The battle between the forces of progress and retreat is often really a contest between stupidity and ability, between pompous inefficiency and creative dynamism. As a Sofia literary weekly suggested in November 1962: "A state committee for the struggle against stupidity should be formed to investigate all state employees."

The seesaw in internal politics, a heightened sophistication about world affairs, the first impact of the early tourist boom, which brought in its wake tangible proofs of the Western standard of living, resulted in a spreading skepticism and disenchantment among the youth. As a young student put it to me in the autumn of 1964, "We Bulgarians are the thriftiest and the most hard-working people in the Balkans. We have uranium, non-ferrous metals, a beautiful coast, and many natural assets. But look at the Yugoslavs, how much better they have fared. Why do we have to live so miserably?" His girl friend, also a student, was even more outspoken: "My mother is of Russian origin and I like the Russians as people very much. But why do we have to imitate them in every single thing? Why can't a movie critic say that this or that Russian film is bad? We have always been a proud nation, yet today we count only as a copy of Russia. The worst thing is that in the end we are beginning to lose faith in ourselves as Bulgarians."

What was perhaps most surprising to a visitor were the frequent almost nostalgic references to Chervenkov, the disgraced "little Stalin." In the words of the girl student, "My parents do not feel any improvement in our life since he has gone. I was too young to remember, but it could not have been so much worse than it is today. Chervenkov was at least someone with a standing in Moscow, a strong personality who was respected, even if feared." An old doctor, surprisingly, echoed her opinion in much the same words: "I always hear not only on our radio, but even in foreign broadcasts to Bulgaria that the Russians are our liberators and best friends. But no one ever asks us *which* Russians liberated us from the Turks." With almost nothing but contempt for the Communists, the old man nevertheless sounded a note of grudging admiration when speaking about Chervenkov. "At least he was a strong man, a real leader." But he considered Zhivkov a nonentity.

No other East European leader, not even the Hungarian Janos Kadar, who was put in power by the Red Army, has been so personally dependent on Khrushchev and so identified with him as Zhivkov. Thus, nowhere did the fall of the Soviet leader cause such a shock, or pose such a direct danger to the number one man of the local regime, as in Sofia. There was complete and stunned silence for five days after the laconic Soviet communique had been issued. Aside from publishing a *Pravda* editorial the next day, and reprinting the shortest possible versions of Kadar's and Gomulka's speeches with all references to Khrushchev omitted, the Bulgarian mass media kept absolutely silent. Finally on October 21 a resolution of the Central Committee was published proclaiming "great respect" and "confidence" and full support to the Soviet party leadership and its decisions. The idol of yesterday was not rated worthy of mention.

The resolution did, however, stress the continuation of the line of the April plenum (1956) against the personality cult which had been carried out by the party and state leadership "headed by Comrade Todor Zhivkov"—a clear hint that Zhivkov for the time being had survived the immediate aftermath of his protector's fall. But with the fall of Khrushchev, the "special relationship" between Zhivkov and Moscow ceased to exist. Furthermore, other senior leaders like the veteran Politburo member Colonel-General Ivan Mihailov, for twenty years a high-ranking Soviet officer, had their separate lines of communications to the Kremlin and the Soviet intelligence services, and as in 1949, 1956, and 1962, the final word was still spoken in Moscow and not in Sofia.

Within six months, the deceptive calm in Sofia was blown to smithereens by what went down in history as the first genuine military conspiracy ever to occur in a Communist state. After a hiatus of twenty years, the army once again re-emerged as an independent factor on the political stage in Bulgaria.

National sentiments—assets or risks?

"Thank God, we are still alive!" With a broad smile on his face, the balding white-haired man swallowed his glass of native plum brandy and posed the rhetorical question: "Do you think that our army is a Latin American army? How could an army coup possibly take place or succeed in our socialist country?" We were talking in July 1965 about what my jovial and friendly host, Premier Zhivkov, described as "an insignificant episode": the recent conspiracy organized by high-ranking officers and wartime Partisan commanders. The nine main conspirators had been tried in camera less than four weeks before our meeting.

Sitting in his spacious office underneath a life-sized color portrait of Georgi Dimitrov, Zhivkov struck me as a somewhat colorless middle-aged man who nevertheless made an over-all impression that was considerably better than his reputation. He revealed remarkably little personal presence, but, to a degree unusual in a man of his position, during the one-and-a-half-hour interview, projected —effortlessly and I believe genuinely—an image of himself as a modest and self-effacing, even shy, and to some extent amiable politician. His statements during the free-wheeling conversation, with no questions submitted in advance, did not shine with anything resembling superior ability, let alone intellectual brilliance, but he was neither a fool nor a complete nonentity. He spoke and argued like a kind of small-sized Khrushchev, without Khrushchev's temperamental outbursts, but with a similar down-to-earth common sense, peasant slyness, and the shrewd manner of an undoubtedly competent and highly experienced Communist functionary.

What, I asked, did the conspirators want? Zhivkov presented them as "people with a disturbed consciousness and a primitive way of thinking," "men who did not know what they wanted . . . hatching out confused combinations." As proof, he mentioned that in one version of their plans he himself was to remain as top leader, "although I am known for being bound to the Soviet Union in life and death; the same is true of our party and our people." In his opinion, it was the sensation-seeking hostile Western press that had exaggerated the "totally insignificant episode" out of all proportion, probably because of the suicide of one of the conspirators and the attempted flight of another. As to their political program, Zhivkov flatly labeled them "pro-Chinese." He heaped abuse on the "main centers of calumny" in Belgrade and Vienna, but studiously ignored my reference to the interesting fact that the news had been broken to the world by the correspondent of an American news agency in Sofia, a Bulgarian citizen.

When one extracts and clarifies some of the issues embedded in the amorphous mass of inspired leaks, wild rumors, clumsy denials, and hard facts, the "insignificant episode" turns out to have been strikingly different in character and scope from what Zhivkov and official propaganda tried to imply. Though much of the background and the exact sequence of events is still obscure, the available evidence and reliable on-the-spot information are more than sufficient to allow a reconstruction of what actually happened. The conspirators were not just a handful "of miserable adventurers, careerist elements, and unprincipled power-seeking persons," as Zhivkov described them in his first public reference to the conspiracy. They were in fact senior, influential, and respected generals and former Partisan leaders, all lifelong Communists.

The nine who were subsequently tried included five high-ranking officers, at least three of whom had the rank of general. The leaders of the plot were Ivan Todorov-Gorunia, a member of the Central Committee and the government; General Anev, the commander of the Sofia military garrison; and Tsolo Krastev, a departmental chief in the Foreign Ministry. All three were famous for their wartime exploits as commanders and political commissars of a Partisan detachment operating in the Vratsa region, a traditional Communist stronghold and the erstwhile center of the abortive Communist insurrection in 1923. The conspirators allegedly timed their coup for April 14, 1965, when a meeting of the Politburo was scheduled. Select and reliable army units were to occupy the radio building, airport, and government and party headquarters in order to force the leadership to resign. It was said to be Soviet military intelligence, rather than the Bulgarian security service, that got wind of the discussions and struck on April 7, forestalling the coup. While the information is of necessity speculative, it is a fact that Todorov-Gorunia committed suicide and at least one general tried to escape when the plot was uncovered.

It is easier to see what they rebelled against than what kind of domestic policies they stood for. Todorov-Gorunia, General Anev, and their friends were certainly not "pro-Chinese." Impelled by the examples of Yugoslavia and Rumania, which had to varying degrees successfully emancipated themselves from Soviet tutelage, and revolted by the humiliating degree of Bulgarian subservience to Moscow, the chief conspirators wanted to establish a more independent Communist regime. Not only were most of them outstanding soldiers, but at one time or another they had occupied more senior positions than Zhivkov and many of his associates. While some of them had had close wartime contacts with the Yugoslavs, it would be wrong to label them "pro-Yugoslav." Regardless of possible inspiration from abroad or even foreign contacts, these lifelong Communists were essentially pro-Bulgarian conspirators steeped in the historic tradition of viewing the army as a sacred national institution.

There is no way of knowing how many officers and former Partisans were implicated; before the sound and fury of the conspiracy had died away, rumors mentioned 200 to 500 arrests. Both the way the case was handled and the subsequent reshuffles in the army and security command clearly indicate, however, that a much larger group than the ten publicly named conspirators was involved.

The first news about a "pro-Chinese" abortive plot reached the West in a highly unusual—and for a Communist country unparalleled—way. The story was sent on April 14 by N.E., the Bulgarian stringer in Sofia, to his agency's Vienna office. It is, of course, not customary for native employees of Western agencies to send out such highly explosive news from a Communist country unless it is officially inspired, in other words unless it is authorized to prepare public opinion before the publication of the official version.

The confusion that characterized the subsequent official statements was a clear indication that something had gone wrong. The reporter himself clearly acted on orders. The fact that I saw him later in Sofia still working as a stringer for the same Western news agency confirmed the impression that it was not he who bungled the story. Yet the fact remains that the inspired leak was followed by a mysterious silence in the Bulgarian capital. This started a spate of wild rumors, with a number of other generals and ministers mentioned both in the Western press and among the Bulgarian public as possible accomplices. It was only eight days later that the Bulgarian press agency, while confirming the suicide of Todorov-Gorunia and the arrests of General Anev and Tsolo Krastev, issued an ostensible denial in its foreign service. Party members were then called to closed meetings, but the Bulgarian press maintained a complete news blackout. At the end of April, Zhivkov held a speech at a factory opening referring to the plot for the first time. The reference was, however, expunged from the published account.

The Bulgarian public was told officially only some four weeks after the event, on May 9, when the papers published Zhivkov's speech at the Sofia Military Academy ridiculing "the fantastic tales concocted by the enemies of socialism about our army supposedly being not loyal to the party . . . endeavoring to set the army against the party and its Central Committee, against the people and the government," and describing the "handful of miserable adventurers" as having no support whatever in the army and among the people. The many tributes to the army, the "guardian of the socialist system," were coupled with profuse pledges of loyalty to the Soviet Union and promises to improve the living and working conditions of the officers.

The speech amounted to an indirect confirmation of dissatisfac- tion in the army, now dominated by native officers, either former Partisans or younger commanders trained after the war. The most striking proof of an atmosphere still pregnant with risks was the dispatch of the high-ranking Soviet leader, Mikhail Suslov, by the Kremlin at the end of May to Sofia for an on-the-spot investigation. Suslov, who had a guiding hand in the 1949 and 1962 purges, did his best to bolster Zhivkov's position in a series of speeches support- ing both his person and his policies. He also called the conspirators "political adventurers, who have lost every sense of reality." As a visible and somewhat tactless demonstration of Soviet backing, the Soviet Ambassador Organov emerged as Zhivkov's permanent traveling companion, escorting him to countless meetings and often making speeches himself.

But Soviet and Bulgarian leaders in all official pronouncements, including the court verdict, shrank from referring to the central fact of the case, the political orientation of the conspirators. In con- trast to the Georgiev trial in 1963, the proceedings went on behind closed doors, partly to belittle the importance of the "episode" and also allegedly because some of the chief defendants refused to make a public admission of guilt in a way that would have served a politically useful purpose. In any event, they were depicted only as "miserable and power-seeking adventurers," not as "foreign agents" or "relics of the bourgeois past." If one remembers that the con- spirators were tried in a country where even telling jokes is severely punished, and where two peasants who had wounded a frontier guard while trying to escape had been shot in 1963, then the sen- tences must be regarded as extremely mild. The two chief con- spirators were sentenced to fifteen years each and General Anev to twelve, the rest receiving terms ranging from three to ten years.

This strongly suggests that the conspirators' grievances struck a responsive chord in the army, the traditional barometer of general unrest, and that there were divided counsels in the top Soviet and

Bulgarian leadership as to ramifications of the plot. Soon after the trial, a new Committee for State Security was set up, detached from the Ministry of Interior and directly subordinated to the "Buro of the Council of Ministers," that is, to the inner Cabinet headed by Zhivkov.

Subsequently a number of leading generals, including the first Deputy Minister of War, another vice-minister, the political chief of the army, the deputy chief of staff, and the chief of the Central Committee's military section, were either sent "into exile" as ambassadors, or transferred from the army to less important functions. Four senior army commanders were dropped from the Central Committee at the last party congress in November 1966. Early in 1967 the number two man in the army, Colonel Ivan Vrachev, was demoted to the post of deputy chairman of the committee for tourism. And, it may have been more than coincidence that the only full-scale reshuffle in a regional party organization since the congress took place in the autumn of 1967 in the district and city of Vratsa. Almost all the secretaries of the local committee were replaced or demoted, and a Politburo candidate member was installed as leader of the regional organization. As mentioned earlier, the three chief conspirators all came from this particular area.*

The abortive conspiracy opened a qualitatively different and in some respects radically new phase in Bulgarian politics. The immediate response was, predictably, a drastic purge coupled with financial concessions to the disgruntled officers and the usual prop-

* Since this chapter was written a report delivered on April 4, 1968, at the plenary meeting of the District Party Committee by the new First Secretary and Politburo candidate member Ivan Abadzhiev dramatically revealed that the district of Vratsa was the power base for the plotters and has remained a stronghold of opposition to the Zhivkov leadership. "During the last two or three years a number of close friends of the plotters remained in various responsible positions despite their obviously formal declarations. They used the heightened international tensions and particularly the events in the Middle East in June 1967 as an excuse to increase their activities." He reported that thirty-three people were expelled from the party, thirty-nine others were penalized, fifteen persons in responsible positions were removed, and "several people deported from the district." In the presence of Zhivkov, the leader of the regional organization warned that the purge would continue because "there are traces [of the conspiracy] which still have not been eliminated." Thus three years after the conspiracy, the allegedly "insignificant episode" is still a matter of concern to the party leadership. (For details see *Otechestven Zov*, April 18, 1968.)

aganda drive. Nevertheless, the important point to grasp about the coup is that it genuinely frightened both the Soviet and Bulgarian leaders. As a result, the long-term repercussions were very different from what one would have imagined during those tense days in the spring of 1965.

Sensing which way the wind was blowing and realizing the extent to which their regime had been discredited in the eyes of the general public, the Communists, for the first time since their seizure of power, made a conscious attempt to bow to the spirit of intense patriotism and the specter of public opinion. Cautiously at first and then with growing momentum, the party leaders and the controlled mass media began to shift the emphasis to foster national pride and the "rediscovery" of a distinct historic past.

Revisiting the country four times since the officers' conspiracy, I have felt time and again the cumulative effects of the rebirth of Bulgarian nationalism. Perhaps the most demonstrative "curtain-raiser" to the new official policy was the centennial celebration of the birth of the great Bulgarian poet, Pencho Slaveikov, in April 1966. Slaveikov, a man of towering stature, profoundly influenced by Western, predominantly German, philosophy and literature, had previously been either a bone of contention between more dogmatic and less dogmatic critics of the Stalinist period, or had been crudely falsified as a product of purely Russian influence. This time he was celebrated as a Bulgarian of world renown.

Staying in Sofia at the time of the celebrations, one was almost overwhelmed by the number of memorial articles, decorations, and portraits of the poet. The newly elected president of the Writers' Union, Georgi Dzhagarov, himself a gifted poet and playwright and barely two years earlier a target of vicious attacks, freely admitted to me that Slaveikov had not always been regarded so highly. Imbued with virulent national feelings like most Bulgarian intellectuals, Dzhagarov reveled in evoking his nation's great, but in the West utterly unknown, past. "Slaveikov was our greatest national literary figure, but also the first bridge-builder connecting us with the mainstream of Western culture," he said and then added with a touch of resignation, "Now UNESCO, the World Council of Peace, and other international bodies are joining us in the celebrations. But who really knows his works? Who indeed has any knowledge of our past and present literature in the West? We have lost twenty years in making ourselves known to the world."

Reverence for the glories of the past and the resurrection of the national heritage in literature, theater, history, and science were the hallmarks of other celebrations of national holidays, such as the ninetieth anniversary of the April 1876 uprising against the Turks. The patriotic wave is the new factor in the leadership's bid to broaden its base and project itself as more than just an echo of the Soviet Union. Over and beyond this purpose there are, however, two other widely conflicting aspects to this stimulation from above of "healthy national sentiments."

What is called "socialist patriotism" is intended not only to help consolidate the party's hold on the population, but also to act as the single most important counterforce against Western "bourgeois" influences. For the barriers once isolating Bulgaria from the rest of the world have been lifted. The number of foreigners visiting this scenically beautiful country with its broad sandy Black Sea beaches jumped from 324,000 in 1962 to almost 1.8 million in 1967. When the first hotels were erected along the coast in 1954, the country earned less than 130,000 dollars. By 1963 the intake was 21 million and rose to 53 million by 1966. There were an estimated 1 million vacationers in 1967, and, what is most important, well over half of them had come from the West.

The influx of badly needed hard currency has not blurred the party's awareness of the evident political risks involved in easier contacts with foreigners—picking up "decadent" habits and influences, not to speak of the "many Western spies disguised as innocuous tourists." A curious ideological duel takes place, for example, in the small shopping street in the center of Sofia where the American legation is located. Coming from the principal square, one sees a small group of people before a large shop window where the Bulgarian news agency displays its latest photographs. Horror scenes from the Vietnam war are sprinkled with portraits of visiting foreign statesmen and Bulgarian leaders shaking hands or making speeches. Just ten yards farther is the American reading room, where a window exhibit shows strictly non-political pictures of assembly belts and cars, medical experiments, and technical innovations. The group of people standing here is much larger than that before the news agency, although no ordinary citizen dares as yet to enter the reading room itself. Were he to do so, he would certainly be interrogated by the police on leaving the building.

In a country where there are still no foreign non-Communist

newspapers, no jazz records from the West on sale, and where
foreign trips are regarded as a privilege, it is only natural that the
Bulgarians, particularly the young people, are eager to meet and
talk to foreigners. Indifferent to politics and scornful of the regime,
they mix freely with tourists in cafés and restaurants, particularly
in the port cities and holiday resorts. Nothing could indicate the
ebb of fear and timidity more poignantly than the scene I witnessed
in 1967 before the beginning of the tourist season in Varna. A young
student approached an elderly British couple sitting in a hotel
restaurant, politely introduced himself, and asked permission to sit
down at their table. A lively conversation started, and it soon turned
out that what he wanted was any books or periodicals his new
acquaintances might have finished reading. A similar scene
would have been inconceivable two or three years earlier. In contrast to the wave of black-market operators, speculators, and street-
walkers who appeared in the first wake of the tourist boom, these
young people present a very different picture.

Though Bulgaria is the only Communist country which continues
to jam Voice of America broadcasts, the influence of Western mass
culture and mass civilization reaches the population not only via
the tourists but also through foreign radio broadcasts and in a
myriad of other ways. Aside from shoddiness, the style of clothing,
hairdos, and general behavior of the young people in the coffee
shops and dance halls on the main boulevards are almost indistin-
guishable from those of the youth in the West.

On and off, the regime has launched campaigns against the "revolting servility toward everything foreign," and in the early sixties
young people wearing tight trousers, beards, or long hair ran the
risk of being arrested, beaten up, or having their heads shaved by
an overzealous militia acting with the tacit approval of the authorities. In the more relaxed atmosphere of 1965–67, police
brutality and raids by volunteer thugs, what the Communists euphe-
mistically used to call "administrative measures," have become
rarer. Yet even in September 1967, the new and, by Bulgarian
standards, lively popular weekly *Pogled* reported that a despairing
mother had come to the paper for help after her son had been arrested by the militia for wearing a pair of blue jeans. Discussing the
fanciful clothing, exaggerated hair styles, and general aping of
foreign fashions, the paper dared to raise the cardinal issue:
"Aren't those who seek the reasons only in bourgeois influences

wrong? Do we not risk becoming ridiculous if we cut the hair and shave off the beards, yet ignore the minds which they ornament? Are we eradicating the bourgeois influences or rather our own?"

This indeed is the dilemma. The young undoubtedly idealize the West excessively, the main avenue of escape from what is, for all the improvement, still a drab everyday life with bleak professional prospects. While the rebellion of a disenchanted youth is a worldwide phenomenon, its intensity in Bulgaria, as in most other Communist countries, has been heightened by the regime's inability to satisfy even relatively modest consumer demands and by a previous overdose of unimaginative indoctrination that presented the Communist takeover as the real beginning of the nation's history.

Thus the leadership regards the revival of national pride as not only a general political asset but also the principal tool in fighting alienation among the youth and a "nihilistic" attitude toward Communist reality. It is considerably easier to issue ringing patriotic phrases than to improve quality and service, management and efficiency, supply and distribution. As Zhivkov put it in his address to the last party congress in November 1966: "We should mercilessly burn with a hot iron all manifestations of admiration for what is foreign, of disrespect for our national dignity, of a nihilistic attitude toward our country and the past achievements of our motherland and people." Patriotic education of the youth and the fostering of a legitimate pride in their historic past rather than stale Communist ideology have become the prime weapons in the battle to regain the young, who in the words of a high school student hold that: "You did nothing but lose our confidence. We can no longer stand the vexation of listening to worn-out phrases."[18]

But there is a potentially dangerous aspect to all the talk about national pride, dignity, and past glories. If nationalism is an asset in the fight against "admiration of foreign influences," it also entails the risk of turning the people against servility to the most pervasive foreign influence of all, the Russian domination over the country. The solution seems to be deceptively simple. Zhivkov and his colleagues have declared with the utmost clarity that "our patriotism is inseparable from our affection and respect for the Soviet Union and its great Communist party"; that "the patriotism of the Bulgarian youth is inseparable from friendship and unity with the Soviet Union and its glorious youth"; that "we consider our army to be a part of the Soviet armed forces."[19]

In other words, nationalist sentiments should be ferociously defiant as regards the pernicious influences of the West, but docile, benevolent, and affectionate in the context of relations with the Soviet Union. Yet if there is one central fact about Bulgarian history, it is surely that, once the national feelings of these proud and persistent people are aroused, they are hard to calm, let alone channel in politically desirable directions. The officers' plot showed that subservience to the Russians carried to excessive lengths could prove self-defeating and ultimately suicidal, even for a regime not handicapped by anti-Russian traditions. If the leadership were to try to submerge the patriotic "new look" in a renewed artificial tide of pro-Soviet propaganda, it would discredit itself completely. If, however, the revival of the sense of national identity gains real momentum and by its very nature eludes total "stage management" from above, it may well subject an unequal relationship to growing strains and delicate tests.

In any event, nationalism has once again become a dominant unknown in the shifting pattern of Bulgarian politics. The virulence of deeply entrenched national feelings shimmers through many conversations. In the spring of 1967 I visited the museum in Tirnovo, the attractive medieval capital of the second Bulgarian empire, in the company of the editor of the local party paper. Leaving the building, we watched a platoon of young cadets from the officers' school as they marched along the main street in their traditional red caps and blue uniforms. My companion turned to me proudly, "We are the strongest nation in the Balkans. I mean this in a historical sense. No other nation was for five hundred years under the Turkish yoke and yet managed to preserve unimpaired its national identity, language, and traditions." Then, as an afterthought, he added, "And today we have one of the highest growth rates in the world!"

Nowhere in Bulgaria did I detect overt anti-Soviet feelings. But as an able Yugoslav diplomat in Sofia observed, "For the time being, these two trends—virulent nationalism and declarations of absolute devotion to the Soviet Union—are being pushed forward hand in hand. Sooner or later, however, two such conflicting tendencies must clash." Or as a young Bulgarian columnist remarked in the course of a long conversation, "Since 1965 the general atmosphere has substantially changed. Even with regard to the Soviet Union, the phase of uncritical idolatry is over. At least in small circles, if not yet in print, we now speak about certain things—in regard to culture, for example, or the shoddy quality of some Soviet products—in a tone that would have been unthinkable a couple of years ago, that would have brought charges of nationalistic deviation. But I must also say that quite a few Soviet newspapermen and writers themselves have ridiculed our habit of worshiping everything Russian."

All this is part of an unobtrusive but important process in a nation that is beginning to regain at least some of its self-confidence. Between 1965 and 1967 there have been important and promising changes behind a seemingly rigid façade. This is particularly evident in Bulgarian foreign policy. To be sure, the improvements in relations with the other Balkan states and more intensive contacts with the West have in no way deviated from Soviet policies, and were initiated with Soviet approval. Yet they have contributed to the relaxation of tensions and enhanced Bulgaria's prestige. While some of the moves, such as the reconciliation with Greece, date back to the first half of 1964, there is ample evidence that it was the combination of Khrushchev's fall and the abortive coup that spurred Zhivkov and his associates into a more energetic foreign policy and a faster realization of the domestic reforms so often promised in the past.

The Bulgarian leaders deeply resent the implications in remarks made by foreign visitors that they are a mere dependency of Russia. The able and well-educated Foreign Minister, Ivan Bashev, once told me with visible irritation, "Of course, we have as before excellent relations with the Soviet Union and co-ordinate our policies on great international issues. But part of the Western press treats our relationship as if I had to ask Moscow for permission to travel to Turkey or even received my passport there. . . ." A spate of visits by Western statesmen to Sofia and Bashev's frequent trips to the West as well as the normalization of relations with neighboring countries have certainly helped to accentuate the role and presence of Bulgaria in the international arena.

The most important shifts of emphasis in foreign policy have affected Bulgaria's direct neighbors. The further development of relations with Greece was halted by Greece's domestic upheavals and the military coup in 1967, but even the present "frozen" stage compares most favorably with the past, when the two countries were not even on speaking terms. With Turkey there has been a noticeable change, effected through an exchange of visits between the Foreign Ministers, followed in the spring of 1968 by Zhivkov's state visit to Turkey. A series of bilateral agreements were signed regulating border markings, consular matters, trade, and the re-establishment of railroad connections. A new direct railway line is to be built, avoiding Greek territory, and the repatriation of the Turkish minority, albeit for the time being only some 30,000 of the 750,000, has been resumed.

Relations with Rumania and Yugoslavia are more complex. Neither Minister Bashev nor other officials make any great effort to hide the differences, political and national, that exist with regard to both these neighbors. At the same time, they insist that these should not in any way hinder bilateral political, economic, and cultural co-operation: in plain language, collaboration with each of the two countries must not go beyond the point at which major Soviet policies—rightly or wrongly identified with those of Bulgaria—would be disturbed or embarrassed. Thus Zhivkov met the Rumanian leader, Nicolae Ceausescu, officially or informally, nine times between 1965 and 1967. In spite of this, the two parties and governments remained as far apart as before on such controversial issues as the Sino-Soviet conflict, the Communist world conference, relations with Western Germany, and intrabloc relations. Nevertheless, in the long run Rumania's demonstratively independent and successful foreign policy may become an important factor in Bulgaria's trend toward greater freedom of action in a rapidly changing Communist world.

Relations with Yugoslavia have oscillated between improvement and deterioration. Beginning with Tito's state visit in September 1965, his first since 1947, there have been a series of high-level meetings, including visits by the Macedonian party leader Crvenkovki and republican Premier Mincev. Yet the pace of progress has been slow, still hindered by recurring tensions over the Macedonian question and suspicions about the repercussions of Yugoslav political and economic reforms. Despite repeated and emphatic agreements to keep the lid tightly shut on the historic differences over Macedonia, there have been frequent polemics in the press and between Bulgarian and Yugoslav historians.

Much of the reason for this lies in two new factors. The first is the growing assertiveness of the Macedonian leaders within Yugoslavia, which makes it more difficult for the federal government in Belgrade to ignore their grievances for the sake of better relations with Bulgaria. The Macedonians never fail to attack the Sofia press if it refers to the great figures of the Macedonian ecclesiastic or national movement as Bulgarians. As anniversaries provoke many such occasions the attacks are virtually unlimited. The other factor is the status of the 200,000 inhabitants of Pirin Macedonia in Bulgaria. At the time of the 1947 Tito-Dimitrov agreement, they were regarded as Macedonians by both sides. Yugoslav Macedonia sent about a hundred teachers as well as books and newspapers to the Pirin region, and there was a lively exchange of students. But even then most Bulgarian leaders, and indeed all their countrymen, considered Macedonian only a dialect of Bulgarian and the Macedonian nation an artificial creation.

After the break with Tito, the population of Pirin Macedonia was treated like other Bulgarians, and the first steps toward cultural autonomy were quickly reversed. Since then the Bulgarian leadership has steadfastly rejected demands to grant a minority status to the people in the area. The Macedonians in Skopje regard this as an intolerable suppression of a minority. "Where have the Macedonians disappeared to?" the Belgrade *Borba* asked ironically in 1967 when the latest Bulgarian census of 1965 claimed that there were fewer than 9,000 Macedonians living in the whole of Bulgaria. The paper pointed out that nine years earlier the census had mentioned the existence of 180,000 Macedonians in Bulgaria.[20]

The truth of the matter is that neither Communist party can risk a loss of prestige in its own country by abandoning traditional national claims. Thus the best one can hope for is, as Foreign Minister Bashev told me, that "the question will gradually die away since it is also a problem of generations." Unfortunately, the resurgence of national feelings, among both the Macedonians and the Bulgarians, keeps the problem uppermost on the agenda. The new wave of nationalism in Bulgaria is therefore the second reason for the virulence of the polemics. Aside from the important fact that schoolchildren in the two countries learn totally different versions of the history of Macedonia, the shift of emphasis to the "glorious past" in Bulgarian history and general propaganda is bound to embroil the two neighbors in ever sharper disputes. Following Zhivkov's appeal that historians compile a comprehensive history of the Bulgarian nation and the Communist party, the Institute of History at the Bulgarian Academy of Sciences has begun to prepare a nine-volume history of their country.

An article published by the authors in the Institute bimonthly makes it clear that the project is loaded with political dynamite. The emphasis is put on fighting "reactionary Western bourgeois historians, who falsify Bulgarian history" and spread "anti-scientific theories about the historical roots of an allegedly separate Macedonian nation in our times" and about "the national-liberation movement waged by the Bulgarian population in Macedonia and Thrace."[21] Needless to say, it is primarily the Macedonian scholars in Skopje and their colleagues in Belgrade who are the "falsifiers." In short, this is a "declaration of war" and the beginning of a counteroffensive by Bulgarian historians. It is worth mentioning that the first known Bulgarian criticism of Soviet historians was sparked off by their references to "Macedonians in Bulgaria" and a "separate Macedonian nation."[22]

It is only through talking to Bulgarian scholars and intellectuals, however, that one gains a real insight into the passions that envelop the historical dispute. One can travel unshadowed most of the time in Bulgaria, yet when I visited the Pirin region in 1966, the officials I saw the next day in Sofia were fully informed as to what I had been doing there. Talking to a group of high school students, I had made a spot check by asking them whether they were Macedonians or Bulgarians; out of the ten boys, only two described themselves as Macedonians. Somewhat wrought up, the writer, Dzhagarov, shot at me, "Did you also ask the people in Skopje whether they were Bulgarians or Macedonians?" When a year later, after *Borba's* query about the "missing Macedonians," I raised the issue again, a high Bulgarian official retorted angrily, "First of all it is not *Borba's* business what nationality the people in Bulgaria declare they are. And what about the eight hundred thousand Bulgarians in Macedonia?"

The situation is made even worse by the Bulgarians' widespread ignorance of political and economic developments in Yugoslavia. There are hardly any Yugoslav books and no newspapers, in the original or in translation, on sale. Many people are convinced that there is chaos and crisis in Yugoslavia and have only the haziest notions about life in general there. Yet the influx of Yugoslav tourists, well over 200,000 a year, usually driving their Fiats and dressed as Western tourists rather than as fellow Slavs, provides tangible proofs that the "crisis" has apparently raised rather than lowered their standard of living. The Bulgarians who are allowed to travel to Yugoslavia, about 70,000 to 100,000 yearly, also see for themselves that the gap between what the average person can afford in each country has become steadily larger.

When speaking about Bulgarians traveling to the West, one must measure progress in terms of the Bulgaria of two or five years earlier. Using this admittedly modest but realistic yardstick, the freedom of movement has become considerably greater. Between 1964 and 1965 the number of Bulgarians going abroad rose from 123,000 to 200,000, and that of travelers to the West almost doubled to 21,000. For a population of 8,000,000 these figures are, of course, exceedingly small, though still greater than the comparative statistics for Rumania.

Quietly and almost imperceptibly, Bulgaria has also embarked on a policy of broader trade and political relaxation with the West. The share of the non-Communist world in the total trade turnover rose from 13 per cent in 1956 to 17.4 per cent in 1962 and 23.3 per cent in 1965. According to preliminary figures, the proportion reached almost 28 per cent in 1966, with Western suppliers accounting for 30 per cent of imports. Germany, which accounted for half of the Bulgarian trade in the late 1930s, emerged again as the country's most important Western trading partner by far. West German imports are second only to those of the Soviet Union and amounted to 10 per cent of the 1966 total. Imports from Italy, Austria, France, and Britain also increased considerably. (Annual trade statistics are usually published two years later.) At the same time, the Bulgarian government, keenly interested in utilizing Western technology and science, signed a surprising number of co-production agreements, including the setting up of joint sales companies in Britain, Australia, and France. Western capital and know-how will also play a role in expanding and improving the quality of the tourist industry.

Aside from Soviet economic domination, import quotas and tariff barriers in the West, coupled with the small range of marketable Bulgarian products, set limits to the expansion. The payments deficit in hard currency trade is estimated to have reached about 300 million dollars in the 1962–66 period. Though the government regards such figures as "top secret," the fact that the deficit incurred against West Germany alone rose from 13 million dollars in 1965 to 60 million dollars in 1966 indicates the magnitude of the payments problem.

Political relations with the West have also been characterized by a remarkable intensification of visits at all levels and the signing of numerous cultural and technical cooperation agreements. In accord with Soviet policy, the most striking improvement took place in relations with France. It was quite deliberate that in October 1966 Zhivkov's first official visit as Premier was to France.

Violent attacks on the American Legation have stopped, and there has been a superficial improvement in personal contacts since 1965, but both political and economic relations between Bulgaria and the United States are still at a low ebb and by no stretch of the imagination can they be described as even remotely normal. Mutual trade yearly totals a mere 3 million dollars, compared, for example, to German-Bulgarian exchanges worth 150 million dollars. The only important product Bulgaria can hope to sell in an appreciable volume on the American market is tobacco, her main cash crop. But since it does not qualify for most-favored-nation treatment, it cannot fight tariff discrimination and compete with the 100 million dollars worth of tobacco the United States imports from Turkey, Greece, and Yugoslavia. "As long as we are discriminated against and cannot sell our tobacco, we are not prepared to negotiate about cultural exchanges or political topics," Bashev told me. The State Department, in turn, expects a modicum of civilized behavior and at least a token of political good will, such as ceasing to jam Voice of America broadcasts. At the moment neither of the two sides can or will break through the vicious circle.

The situation has, if anything, become worse during the last years. While in 1965 Bashev regarded the granting of most-favored-nation treatment as the main precondition for a normalization, he told me in 1967 that the war in Vietnam is another major stumbling block. As to the jamming of the Voice of America, Washington should first stop the Bulgarian-language broadcasts of Radio Free Europe.

The issue is, of course, of marginal importance to Bulgaria, let alone the United States. It is the relationship with West Germany that serves as the real test of the courage and determination of the Bulgarians to promote their national interests even if they are at odds with those of other Communist countries and with the European policy of the Soviet government. The hour of decision struck early in 1967 when the West German government offered to reestablish diplomatic relations with both Bulgaria and Rumania in spite of their recognition of and relations with East Germany. Unlike Czechoslovakia or Poland, neither Balkan country had disputed issues with West Germany. Yet even after Rumania had gone ahead and Bonn renewed its offer to Sofia, the Bulgarians still hedged, referred to their treaty obligations, and—with a visible lack of enthusiasm—signed a friendship treaty with East Germany instead of responding to the West German initiative.

Thus while the Bulgarian leaders would like their country to play a more individual and enterprising role, they lack the will, courage, and, in all probability, the ability to veer away from the main Soviet line, let alone to defy policy decisions made by the Kremlin. This is frustrating to some of the outward-looking and more imaginative members of the leadership. But after the Yugoslav, Albanian, and Rumanian breakaways, Bulgaria, bordering on two shaky Western allies—Greece and Turkey—has become more important than ever to Moscow as a strategic and political mainstay of Soviet influence in the Balkans.

As Bashev once put it to me, "You may be right in saying that we are the Soviet Union's best friends. But don't forget that this friendship costs them a lot of money. They are helping us in many ways and to a tremendous degree." Bulgaria is indeed the only East European country that has profited throughout the entire postwar period from the Soviet alliance. The Kostov affair notwithstanding, during Stalin's lifetime Bulgaria was never exploited to the same degree as the other satellites, and it has received more Russian aid since than any other Communist country. Even allowing for the fact that the Bulgarians also suffered from a discriminatory pricing policy (paying until 1966, for example, twice as much for Soviet crude oil as Western buyers), and had to make do with obsolete Soviet equipment, they have on balance fared rather well economically. The Russians have injected enormous sums, reaching almost two billion dollars, into Bulgaria, financing one-quarter of its total industrial investment. Virtually the entire ferrous and non-ferrous metallurgical industry, 70 per cent of its electrical engineering, and half its chemical plants were built up with Soviet assistance. No one knows the real amount of the total debt, the repayment of which Moscow has several times postponed.

No East European country is integrated so closely with the Soviet economy as Bulgaria. Over half its foreign trade is with the Soviet Union, which provides 70 to 90 per cent of its essential imports and purchases 60 per cent of its engineering exports. Bulgaria has become the world's third largest producer of electric telphers and trucks, the bulk of which, along with other electrical products, textiles, tinned fruit, and vegetables are shipped to the Soviet Union. Three projected power plants are to operate with Soviet coal, and the Burgas petrochemical plant, which went into operation in 1965 with an initial capacity of two million tons to be increased later to six million tons, is based completely on imported Soviet crude oil. From the building of a nuclear power plant to the permission granted to a Bulgarian enterprise to utilize a Soviet forest region as a source of timber, Russian assistance is of crucial importance in the country's drive for industrialization.

History has shown that the industrialization and modernization of such a small country can be solved satisfactorily only if it belongs to a wider economic area. "Bulgaria has been prosperous only when it has been part of the larger European community, whether in the freer system that existed before the First World War or in the artificial unity temporarily provided by German policy in the 1930s."[23] In theory, the Soviet bloc, more precisely the Comecon organization, could provide a suitable framework for a broad division of labor and a more efficient allocation of resources.

Unfortunately, Bulgaria is not integrated with the more developed Communist countries such as East Germany or Czechoslovakia, but primarily with the Soviet Union, which is not exactly a pacemaker in managerial efficiency and modern technology. Worse still, the massive investment decisions are still based on the disastrous priorities of the past, duplicating at high cost industrial facilities in steelmaking and heavy engineering that are already available in the Communist area.

A case in point is the Kremikovtsi iron and steel works, which officials proudly call "the pride of our industry," but malicious Bulgarians describe as "the graveyard of our economy." After visiting the project, which was started in 1960 and has some installations already working, and talking to the local engineers, the visitor is apt to agree with the pessimistic judgment. It was decided to build the plant, with a capacity of 1.85 million tons of steel per annum in the first phase, about ten miles from Sofia because of nearby iron ore reserves amounting to 250 million tons. On closer analysis, however, the iron content of the ore turned out to be about 30 per cent, thus necessitating substantial imports of better quality ore from abroad. About 40 per cent of the coke will also have to be imported. This in turn makes the location a disastrous burden. The imported ore and coke must be transported by rail from the Black Sea ports of Varna and Burgas 200 miles away. Construction costs alone are put at about 400 million dollars.

Even some Bulgarian officials, like Professor Davidov, the deputy chairman of the new special commission for economic reform, admit that "were the decision made today, we would not build Kremikovtsi." And it is hard to understand why the Russians, who are supplying 80 per cent of the equipment, gave the go-ahead signal in the first place. Considering the bitter discord with the Rumanians over the erection of a similar steel plant in Galati, it is even more surprising. But Russian willingness to turn a blind eye to the incompetence and follies of the Bulgarians is less astounding than it may seem at first glance.

There is a reverse side to the "special relationship"; the Russians, too, have, on occasion, a psychological complex about their traditional favorites in the Balkans. This is evident in the scope and character of their credits and gifts. After the controversy with Rumania and in the broader context of the Moscow-Peking rift, the latest batch of credits, worth 580 million dollars, was granted in 1964 clearly to emphasize the fact that loyalty to Moscow is appropriately rewarded and to refute the charge, made openly by China and covertly by Rumania, that the Soviet Union makes colonies of smaller countries by hindering their "all-round industrialization."

Statistically, Communist Bulgaria can boast of impressive strides in industrialization. Industry's share in the national income rose from a prewar 15 per cent to 50 per cent of a much larger total in 1966. Though agriculture is still important, the number of industrial workers has jumped seven times to 1.5 million. Even during the 1961–65 period, in which the rate of growth in other East European countries fell significantly, Bulgaria proudly reported that industrial production had risen annually by almost 12 per cent. But the question remains—risen for what?

Before the war, heavy industry, except for mining, was practically non-existent, because, in view of the limited resources and lack of capital, it was considered unprofitable. Mechanical imitation of the Soviet model, with no regard for costs and resources, neglected traditional industries such as food and tobacco, which used exclusively domestic raw materials, and created a relatively large high-cost machine and engineering base, dependent mainly upon imported materials. As a result, heavy industry in 1965 accounted for 38 per cent of the aggregate industrial output and is scheduled to rise to 48 per cent by 1970. Though the country paid an onerous price in terms of enormous investments and repressed living standards, even the tacitly revised production indices reveal the glaring disproportions between the input of labor and capital on the one hand and actual results on the other. For example, during the last Five Year Plan (1961–65) gross fixed investments doubled, but national income rose only by 38 per cent as against the originally projected 60 per cent.

Visits to Bulgarian factories and a review of the unreliable official statistics seem to indicate that the return on capital investment in Bulgaria has been smaller than in any other Communist-ruled country except perhaps Albania. Though after the early 1960s the regime began to pay more attention to a better utilization of labor and more efficient economic management, the factional struggles at the top and the general political uncertainty hampered even the first hesitant attempts to give the peasants and workers more incentives. It was a measure of the failure of agricultural collectivization that Bulgaria, a traditional exporter of farm products, which before World War II, despite increasing exports, satisfied domestic needs, in 1964 was forced to purchase 450,000 tons of Canadian wheat for the 1964–66 period. At the same time there is no doubt that two good harvests in 1966 and 1967 played a crucial role in helping the government to keep economic difficulties within manageable proportions.

Nevertheless, inflexible planning methods, a cumbersome bureaucracy, inefficient investments and low productivity combined to create a situation that could no longer be ignored. Since 1963 a flood of articles by leading economists, including Professor Kunin, the erstwhile economic overlord (imprisoned with Kostov, subsequently rehabilitated, and since 1962 again a member of the Central Committee) have urged the government to revamp the obsolete planning system and decentralize the economy. Bulgaria, along with the Soviet Union and other Communist countries, began to experiment with a decentralized new economic system in 1964, when fifty-two enterprises were given more independence in production and wage policies. By the end of 1967, the system claimed to embrace 70 per cent of the economy. In general, it is based on more powers for enterprise managers in production and sales; incentives within the new vertically integrated trusts; the use of the profit motive instead of quantitative planning indices; bank credits instead of budgetary subsidies; and a wage structure more closely tied to production results.

It is also important to remember what is *not* going to be changed. As Zhivkov told me in July 1965, the Bulgarian leadership remains firm on certain basic principles: the preservation of central planning, that is, all important proportions of the economy established by the political decision-makers; administrative price-fixing of producer goods and essential consumer goods; and maintenance of the state monopoly on foreign trade. Other Bulgarian officials also made it clear that investment and wage guidelines will continue to be decided at the center. There are, however, great differences in approach among the economic experts. Professor Davidov, one of the leading architects of the new planning system, is in favor of introducing a three-tier price structure with fixed, variable, and "free" prices. He estimates that about 25 per cent of the prices, mainly of consumer goods, will be regulated by supply and demand. In the first phase (1968–69) about 40 per cent of the investment funds should be decentralized, that is, transferred to the trusts and enterprises.

As so often happens in Bulgaria, the official rhetoric has so far been much more impressive than the actual measures. A Yugoslav reporter aptly remarked that the new system was "not just a necessity, but rather an emergency."[24] Despite many decrees and exhortations, poor quality and low productivity, high costs and inefficient management have remained the chief defects plaguing an overextended economy. Nothing could better illustrate the dimensions of the problem than the admission made by Zhivkov at an economic conference held behind closed doors that the over-all productivity of labor in Bulgaria is only about half the Soviet figure![25]

After many debates, behind-the-scenes struggles, and wavering, the reform theses were finally approved by the party Central Committee in the spring of 1966. Eighteen months later a "decree on the profitability of economy" revealed that the advances in implementation had been very modest indeed. How could material incentives play a meaningful role when only 3 to 6 per cent of the average wages are really linked to better performance and a mere one-tenth of investments are financed through bank credits, which have to be repaid in contrast to budgetary subsidies? Many elements of the much publicized new system are still obscure and controversial. But even in the best of circumstances, Bulgaria will only

enter the early phase of the very stage Yugoslavia is already abandoning. In other words, it is lagging over ten years behind its more
enterprising and daring neighbor.

One major reason for moving so gingerly is a justified fear of
inflation; the pressure of over-all demand on the available resources
is undoubtedly very strong. Yet this is the consequence of the
scale of ambitious national goals, which in turn reflect the past
disastrous pattern of priorities, rather than a real response to
the material aspirations of the population. The current plan (1966–
70) is still based on the priority of heavy over light industries, the
predominance of production over consumption. The projected annual industrial growth rate of 12.5 per cent shows a continuing
obsession with over-all maximization of growth and grandiose investment projects. If one adds to all this the vast sums spent on
defense and aid commitments to the Afro-Asian countries, it is
evident that a thoroughgoing decentralization of economic decision-
making and the creation of a workable market mechanism, geared
to more realistic price signals, are still for the distant future.

The best one can expect from the present blueprint is that some
of the most glaring irrationalities and inefficiencies of economic
management and the planning system will be done away with. As
a Bulgarian economist put it, with a fair dose of optimism, "There
will, of course, be shifts of emphasis, even perhaps retreat. But the
clock cannot be put back." Many ideas, including some form of
workers' management and the election of managers, which were
regarded as dangerous "heresies" only a few years ago, are now
publicly discussed. Opponents of the reforms are fighting a rearguard battle, and none of them ventures to defend the discredited
Stalinist model openly.

The pace and scope of even a limited economic spring-cleaning
depends on the outcome of the struggle for gradual replacement
of the thousands of incompetent managers and officials by able and
economically trained experts. There is an "overproduction" of
young graduates, yet a survey on the professional qualifications of
the administrative and managerial "elite" produced a fairly distressing balance sheet: about one-quarter of those in charge of central
government institutions and organizations, half of their deputies,
and over one-third of the departmental chiefs had only elementary
schooling. Less than 24 per cent of the top officials had higher education. The situation is even worse at enterprise levels; about half

of all managers attended only elementary schools.[26] Thus, as mentioned earlier, opposition to a revamping of the economy and ideological rigidity are more often than not due to fear of losing position or status rather than to more complex considerations. What the leadership castigates as the "apathy and conservativism" of responsible functionaries and managers is an instinctive self-defense and often deliberate sabotage on the part of an entrenched bureaucracy.

Economic reform has been the single most important political issue to emerge in the mid-sixties. The very fact that there was and is a real conflict of opinions in the party and that even the radical reformers, thanks to Zhivkov's direct intervention, can publicly defend their proposals is widely regarded as a point of some political importance. The Ninth Party Congress, in November 1966, gave a strong stimulus to the technocrats' widening influence on policy-making. Through a substantial increase in the Central Committee membership, from 101 to 137, the Zhivkov group managed to pack it with fifty-four new and presumably more progressive members.

But there is no Bulgarian party congress without some element of drama. It was the sudden fall of Mitko Grigorov, the number two man in the party secretariat and widely regarded as Zhivkov's "crown prince," that electrified the atmosphere at the 1966 congress and surprised public opinion. Without advance warning, Grigorov was not re-elected to the ruling Politburo and was subsequently "banished" to Prague as Bulgarian representative on the editorial board of the international Communist monthly *Problems of Peace and Socialism.* Barely four years earlier the chief accuser of the "dogmatic anti-party Chervenkov-Yugov group," this able and ruthless ideologist had emerged as an ambitious rival of the party leader who pushed for separation of the premiership and the party leadership. Grigorov's fall was greeted with an audible sigh of relief by the intellectuals, who had already suffered too long from his strongarm methods and ideological orthodoxy.

Another promising development was the promotion of Professor Ivan Popov, the head of the Commission on Technology, to Politburo membership without his previously having been a member of the much larger Central Committee. Of the eleven members elected in 1966, only two were survivors of the 1954 Politburo. The personnel changes have underlined the fact that Zhivkov's position is stronger than it has been at any time during his twelve-year tenure. Yet the fact that two veteran functionaries, the ideological "pope" of the Stalin era, seventy-eight-year-old Todor Pavlov, and Mrs. Tsola Dragoicheva, seventy, were elected to the top policy-making body was a demonstrative concession to the old guard, whose influence is still considerable.

When asked about the significance of these tributes to the old generation, the editor of a Sofia paper stated frankly, "They have only honorary positions. In all key functions you find progressive people. And this is the important thing." Such candor, and in the presence of two other prominent intellectuals at that, would have been impossible a couple of years earlier. To get a sense of proportion, however, one should also quote a keen Yugoslav observer who caustically remarked, "Progressive leaders? It depends to whom one compares them. Sure, compared to such inveterate dogmatists as Pavlov, some of the new people may be regarded as perhaps progressive."

Though sixty-one is the average age of the Politburo members since the inclusion of Pavlov and Dragoicheva, the seven candidate members (without voting rights) have an average age of only fifty. They and the members of the enlarged secretariat are relatively young, trained administrators and technocrats committed to the moderately reformist line. It would be unwise, however, to ignore the fact that many influential functionaries at the upper and intermediate levels pay only verbal tribute to the reform course.

Petty tyrants in quite a few provinces are still unable to grasp, often out of sheer ignorance, the crucial importance of the small privately owned plots of the collective farm members. Since the early 1960s the Bulgarian leaders, like their colleagues in other Communist countries, have taken a variety of measures to protect and help private plots as the best and fastest way to increase rural production. Though these private plots (usually up to half a hectare) account for less than 10 per cent of the arable land, they produce 20 per cent of the vegetables, 26 per cent of the milk and meat, and 50 per cent of the eggs—an astounding proof of the property-owning instincts of the peasants and the imperative need of recognizing private interests. Though often still pitifully poor, the peasants on the whole live better now than at any time since 1948, and during the past few years their standard of living has risen faster than that of the urban population. Both the rural population and the economy would profit from more liberal and flexible price and purchasing policies aimed at specialization in crops that are good potential earners of foreign exchange.

One of the most criminal follies was the destruction of the traditional handicrafts and trades, which even before the war gave over 90,000 people employment and contributed almost as much to the national product as industry. It was two decades before the combination of tourism and popular dissatisfaction with available services compelled the government to rediscover that such "relics of capitalism" as private carpenters, electricians, and plumbers can be more useful than dangerous. A decree in the summer of 1965 allowed the establishment of private workshops in eight sectors, provided they did not employ more than one person and one apprentice each. The number of private craftsmen and artisans subsequently rose within a year or so from 10,000 to 26,000. But in a country where broken installations, faulty fixtures, and shoddy goods account for so many everyday problems, the first timid concessions to private enterprise mark only the beginning of progress toward a more civilized way of life.

As one moves away from politics, it becomes harder to discern just how much, if at all, the standard of living has risen. Sofia, the capital, seems a spacious city of trees and gardens. Modern suburbs and attractive new buildings are beginning to make the visitor forget the small center of monumental Soviet-style palaces. But the city population since the war has trebled to 800,000, and it is a woefully overcrowded capital, plagued by a host of major and minor defects in essential municipal services. Despite an impressive construction rate, housing is one of the main problems. The rural-urban migration swelled town population by two million, but construction fell short of demand. Thus in the years 1957–62, 157,000 apartments were needed, but only 92,000 were completed. Rents at 3 to 5 per cent of the average income are extremely low, and higher rents are generally regarded as the only solution to supplement the limited funds the government can spare from other priorities for housing construction. Yet rents are an extremely important part of a modest standard of living.

Basic food is relatively cheap and since 1965 has been plentiful. Queues for bread, fresh fruit, and vegetables are still to be seen, however, and an average urban inhabitant is estimated to spend four hours a week lining up for services and goods.[27] This is mainly due to a chronically inefficient distribution and transport network. Though wages and salaries of some categories of employed were raised in 1966–67, the most noticeable improvement was in the over-all supply, greater variety, and considerably better quality of the goods offered to the customers. If the traffic policeman at the main crossing a few years ago resembled a conductor waving to a non-existent orchestra, traffic today no longer consists solely of official limousines. Private cars have increased from virtually nil to a few thousand, exact figures still being regarded as "state secrets." In the smaller cities this changes the general picture considerably. More important still, it holds out some hope to the people that even Bulgaria is catching up with the twentieth century. The news that the government had signed agreements with Renault and Fiat to manufacture under license 10,000 French and 30,000 Italian cars was greeted by many Bulgarians as the dawn of a new age.

It is the new "upper class" of successful writers, journalists, actors, singers, and scientists, coupled with a few doctors and engineers, who have profited the most conspicuously from the relative easing of restrictions. Nevertheless, Bulgaria has remained the most egalitarian society in Communist East Europe. By any standard, the general living conditions still leave much to be desired. The bitter outburst of a building engineer in the port of Varna reflects the opinion of many professional people: "No nation is working so hard and so strenuously as ours, yet none lives so miserably."

In 1967 this highly qualified expert was earning about 120 leva (1 dollar = 2 leva). At the same time a pair of shoes costs 15 to 20 leva, a shirt 16 to 18 leva, a pullover 30 to 36 leva, a suit 80 to 100 leva, a television set between 310 to 450 leva. He has to work over four years to be able to buy a Bulgar-Renault, or forty months to purchase a small Czech or Russian car. The lack of financial rewards for expert knowledge and the brutal leveling influence of communism are the main factors behind the technical intelligentsia's indifference, often tinged with bitterness. Average wages in industry range from 70 to 90 leva, and the managers earn only twice as much as the blue-collar workers.

"The Bulgarian will hunt the hare in an oxcart—and catch him," says an old proverb. He has none of the easygoing tolerance and cynicism of the Rumanians, nor much of the unpredictable volatile temperament of the Serbs. Thrifty and hard-working, the average Bulgarian is imbued with a spirit of dogged persistence and a sense

of social discipline. Despite the demographic revolution and destruction of the old rural society, the traditions of a stubborn natural
conservativism still linger on and sometimes impede the necessary
changes. No matter how high the price in terms of liberties, the
country has made perceptible, in some respects even striking, progress. How much it might have improved under a different system
must remain in the realm of conjecture. It is not industrialization as
such, but rather its manner, pace, and scale that have resulted in so
much unnecessary waste and unjustified sacrifices. It would be unfair, however, to overlook the fact that much of the blame for past
follies belongs to the Soviet masters and protectors.

The fostering of the powerful emotional appeal of national
identity could prove to be crucial in long-term developments. The
crusading zeal of communism has ebbed, and the vacuum is beginning to be filled by an upsurge of intense national feelings. For the
first time in postwar Bulgarian history, traditional nationalism,
clumsily camouflaged as "socialist patriotism," has become a genuine
force in political life. It acts as a brake on meaningful cooperation
with neighboring countries, above all with Yugoslavia. But it may
also help more than anything else to put Soviet-Bulgarian relations
on a more equal and more dignified footing.

To return to our original question: How much is reality and how
much appearance in the cult of Soviet-Bulgarian "brotherhood"? Is
Bulgaria faithful ally or subservient satellite? As must be obvious
by now, there is no clear answer. The degree of genuine friendship
toward the Russians is in inverse ratio to the degree and character
of the Soviet influence. The more national dignity and elbow room
the Bulgarian regime has, the less danger there is of an eruption of
pent-up anti-Russian resentment. Should the Bulgarian leadership
continue to indulge in an overdose of humiliating subservience to
the Soviet Union to the detriment of self-interest, what remains
of the traditional good will toward Russia will inevitably be squandered and anti-Soviet sentiments aroused. Even so, Bulgaria would
remain a client state, but an increasingly restive one, susceptible to
the contagious disease of national self-assertiveness so rampant in
Rumania and Yugoslavia.

Experience has shown that Bulgaria is not just a flotsam, as so
often thought, driven by the torrent of Balkan history and the cross-
currents of world communism. It has been and is a factor on its
own, always exerting a steady influence, at times even a profound
one, on Balkan politics.

VI

RUMANIA
A Quiet Revolution

No decision about us without us.

—*A Rumanian proverb*

"I am no Communist. I regard the conditions in my country, particularly in respect to personal freedom, as far from satisfactory. For us, however, the most important point is that our ship—Rumania—is at long last heading in the right direction, and there is a Rumanian and not an alien captain at the helm. As regards the state of the ship and life on deck, it's a different matter. We Rumanians will take care of that ourselves. But do not forget the all-important fact that this is now a Rumanian ship!" The speaker was a well-known Rumanian violinist, who had not been to the West for over twenty years. The conversation, in one of the few superb restaurants that have survived war and communism in Bucharest, revolved around the "new course," which has stirred emotional fervor and a new dawn of national consciousness in a country about as large as the state of Oregon.

Nowhere in Eastern Europe are the sense of nationhood and the spirit of national identity, the glories of an ancient past and a cultural heritage so deliberately and conspicuously patronized, promoted, and displayed by a Communist ruling group as in Rumania. The fostering of national individuality and distinct traditions, which for almost two decades were threatened with extinction under the twin onslaught of communism and Russification, began with the rediscovery of the heroic achievements of remote ancestors. For example, *The Dacians*, a monumental epic film set in the reign of King Decebalus of Dacia in A.D. 106, was the number one hit of the 1967 season in Rumanian movie houses.

Memories of the Dacians' resistance against the Roman invaders and their Daco-Roman heritage have fired the imagination of present-day Rumanians as unfailingly as they did that of their forerunners several centuries ago. The film portrays in a highly emotional and romantic manner the life and times of Decebalus, who after stubborn resistance was defeated by the Emperor Trajan. He was allowed to retain his crown, but a Roman garrison and a civilian adviser were stationed in his kingdom to assure Roman control. Four years later Decebalus made a desperate attempt to shake off the yoke. Alerted by special messengers, Trajan returned with his troops, besieged, and finally took the capital. Decebalus escaped in disguise, continued to fight the Romans, and was eventually captured. He committed suicide to save himself the humiliation of being taken prisoner to Rome.

The Dacians is by no means merely a tribute to the heroic deeds of distant history. It, like the praise showered on the great figures of the more recent past, is a conscious appeal to national sentiments, an attempt to rally the population around an indigenous leadership which is standing up to neighboring Russia. Current films, plays, poems, novels, articles, and studies that evoke the national past abound in unequivocal references to the similarity of past and present dangers. People whose national history was so often interrupted instinctively grasp the meaning of ostensibly irrelevant statements and allusions. Thus when in the film the Roman envoy is admiring Decebalus' jewels and gold treasures, the king thanks him for his kind words but, raising his voice, declares, "We Dacians are hospitable and willing to share everything with our guests. We would rather die, however, than lose our independence and freedom." At these words, at every single performance, the audience spontaneously broke into thunderous applause.

Without a Rumanian "captain at the helm" such a defiantly patriotic film could not have been made. Yet it was the deep-rooted traditions of a flamboyant nationalism and an equally profound aversion to Russia—both the products of a series of humiliating injustices—that enabled the initially weakest Communist ruling party in Eastern Europe to exploit the changes in the Communist world, to challenge Soviet domination, and to set itself up as a champion of national interests.

The course of the entire Soviet-Rumanian dispute confirms the extraordinary survival of traits in Rumanian history that are unparalleled in any other country. As the late Professor R. W. Seton-Watson put it, "To some, Rumanian history may seem obscure and often inglorious, but there is a certain dynamic force in its vicissi-

tudes, and Europe cannot show any more striking example of the corroding effects of foreign rule, of the failure of a policy of systematic assimilation, and of the gradual triumph of national sentiment over unfavorable circumstances."[1]

The emergence of an independent Communist Rumania has been a very different process from the rebellions in Yugoslavia and Albania against Soviet tutelage, and not merely because, unlike these two countries, Rumania has a long common border with the Soviet Union. When reports of Rumania's discord with the Soviet Union over economic problems first appeared in the Western press in March 1963, most observers, including the present author, were astonished, and quite a few remained skeptical as to just how serious the political implications of a seemingly straightforward economic controversy were. Within a few months, however, Rumania had progressed from apparent docility to open defiance.

Through a series of seemingly small but politically extremely important gestures, the Rumanian Communist leadership began to feed the strong anti-Russian feelings of a population that since 1945 had been ordered to look to Russia as liberator, guide, and model. Almost overnight, the lavish demonstrations of cultural solidarity with Russia were replaced by a deliberate policy of "Rumanianization," a new emphasis on national traditions with anti-Soviet overtones. Streets, movie houses, theaters, and cultural centers were renamed. The A. Popov movie theater became the Dacia; the Maxim Gorky, the Union. A Russian language institute in the capital was closed and a large Russian book store demolished; the Rumanian edition of the Soviet propaganda monthly *New Times* was discontinued; schools dropped compulsory Russian-language studies; Rumanian orthography was "re-Latinized," eradicating the previous "Slavification" of the alphabet and of culture in general.

This sudden and dramatic change delighted the nation, dismayed Moscow, and stunned observers. Yet the element of surprise had roots in Rumanian history. In the opening decades of the nineteenth century, for example, the two Rumanian principalities ruled by the Phanariot princes as vassals of the Turkish Porte "turned a Greek face to the world."[2] The Greek revolution of 1821 headed by Alexander Ypsilanti started in the principalities of Moldavia and Wallachia. But "suddenly in the twinkling of an eye Greek is gone and has been replaced at every point by Rumanian. The leaders of the Greek revolt addressed a hostile people." Tudor Vladimirescu, a

Rumanian officer in the Russian army, declaring that "the hour has come to shake off the Phanariot yoke," launched an uprising and occupied Bucharest. When the two rebel leaders, the Greek Ypsilanti and the Rumanian Vladimirescu, met in the capital, the Rumanian declared, "We have no idea of betraying the Greeks, but their cause is not ours. Greece belongs to the Greeks, but Rumania to the Rumanians."[3]

More than a century later a surprised world witnessed a very similar metamorphosis. Rumania turned a Russian face to the world and "in the twinkling of an eye" Russian was gone and replaced by Rumanian. But in both cases the lightning transformations were the result of a "gradual triumph of national sentiments."

In Rumania the forms of emancipation and the methods used by the people in power show startling parallels throughout the long, drawn-out struggle for national unity and independence. The challenge to Soviet domination has been as profoundly Rumanian in character as the centuries-old fight for survival and unification "between the Turkish hammer and the Polish anvil" and later in the three-sided conflicts of the rival Ottoman, Habsburg, and Russian empires.

Faced with the perennial danger of vassalage and complete enslavement, the Rumanians since time immemorial have learned to temporize and to appease more powerful adversaries. To appear to yield in order to survive, to gain a breathing spell by diplomatic acrobatics aimed at keeping the would-be conquerors divided, have always been the hallmarks of Rumanian tradition. The rulers, be they Moldavian and Wallachian princes, kings, liberal politicians, authoritarian hereditary dictators, or Communist party leaders have had in common a penchant for mixing firmness toward the basic issues with subtlety in tactics and a dash of shrewd opportunism. They have none of the Polish or Hungarian weakness for a romantic but hopeless fight to the bitter end. The Rumanians have often seemed to be the losers and laggards of Eastern Europe. But when the dust settles, they more often than not turn out to be the real winners. Their traditional mastery of tactics and legendary flair for supple diplomacy and excellent timing have remained important constants in Rumanian history.

Ever since the reappearance of the Rumanians as state-builders after the "thousand years of mysterious silence," Rumania's principal aims have been the unification of Moldavia and Wallachia, the two principalities under Turkish rule, and the establishment of Great Rumania, including the disputed province of Transylvania.

Nothing could better illustrate the overriding importance of the struggle for national unity than a visit to the Museul Unirii (Museum of Unification) in Jassy, a picturesque city built on seven hills. Jassy, the capital of Moldavia, less than sixteen miles from the Soviet border, is not only the cradle of Rumanian culture and science with the country's oldest university, but also the scene of the first historic triumph on the tortuous road to unity and independence. It was here that the movement for unity started, which in 1859 brought to the throne of Moldavia Jan Alexander Cusa, who united the two principalities two years later.

The attractive house where Prince Cusa reigned until 1862 was converted into a museum on the hundredth anniversary of his election as ruler of Moldavia, but its present collection of old maps, etchings, and pictures has been on display only since 1964. Looking at the ancient documents and talking to the guide in the museum and intellectuals in the city, the visitor gains an insight into the vicissitudes of Moldavian history and better understands why the relationship with Russia has dominated the changing fortunes of modern Rumania to such an extent. A visit to Jassy and Suceava, the principal city of rump Bukovina, which has been ravished so often by Russian invasions, exposes the roots of the almost pathological hate for Russia.

Touring the regions along the Soviet-Rumanian border in the tense summer of 1966, the youthful party leader Nicolae Ceausescu time and again evoked the memory of the great figures of the Moldavian past: Prince Stephen the Great, who in the fifteenth century repeatedly beat the Turks, ruled over vast territories, parts of which now belong to Russia, and was praised by Pope Sixtus VI as "Athlete of Christi"; his illegitimate son and successor, Petru Rares, who performed dangerous tightrope-walking feats between the Turks and the Hungarian princes of Transylvania, between the Habsburgs and the Polish kings, alternately fighting or supporting them. Though in the words of the greatest historian of Rumania, "his perfidy was almost unique even in the annals of the sixteenth century," Rares nevertheless fought for Moldavian independence and initiated the building of the magnificent monasteries of Voronet, Humor, and Moldovita whose unique exterior frescoes are not only artistic marvels but also sophisticated appeals for resistance against Turkish encroachment.

When Ceausescu conjured up the "glorious past" of Moldavia or invoked the memory of the great Princes, he constantly projected the present as the continuation of the heroic past and presented the Communist leaders as the legitimate inheritors of that past and fighters for traditional national aspirations. If these aspirations have been only partly realized, the territorial expansionism of rapacious Russia is to blame. This is why every reference to Moldavian history, past and recent, is loaded with political dynamite. When the party leaders visited the towns and cultural monuments of Moldavia and issued one emotional appeal after another, people for the first time since the war worked themselves up to a frenzied national enthusiasm. Crowds responded with thunderous applause when Ceausescu paid tribute to the "historical fight for the creation of the Rumanian nation and its national unity," appealed for "a consolidation of the freedom and sovereignty of the fatherland," and issued a meaningful warning: "We have had to overcome many difficulties in our history. But our nation knew how to unite its forces and to brave all the storms."

These storms have come predominantly from the direction of Russia. Since Peter the Great's drive to control the mouth of the Danube and particularly since the late eighteenth century, the rulers of Russia have regarded the Rumanian principalities and later the united Rumanian state as a natural sphere of Russian influence. Catherine the Great and the Habsburg emperors, Tsar Alexander and Napoleon, Tsar Alexander II and Bismarck, Stalin and Hitler at one time or other haggled and bargained over the dismemberment of the Rumanian lands and the fate of the easternmost province of Bessarabia.

The repeated Russian invasions and occupations of Rumania, the treatment of the country as a Russian dependency, the wholesale plundering and exaction of compulsory labor, the annexation of Bessarabia, and the fomenting of internal strife by means of bribes and agents, both before and after the birth of independent Rumania, have combined to instill the profound Rumanian suspicion and resentment of Russia, which the experiences of the years under communism were to deepen still further. The area lying between the rivers Pruth and Dniester and the Black Sea, occupied in the early fourteenth century by the Moldavian ruler Bessarab and called

Bessarabia, has been a permanent bone of contention between Rumania and Russia. Conquered by the Turks in the late fifteenth century, at the Treaty of Bucharest in 1812 Turkey ceded its seventeen thousand square miles to Russia. Bessarabia was always strategically important; it provided Russia with direct access to the Danube delta and a powerful lever of control over Danube navigation.

Tsar Alexander regarded Bessarabia as a base for further annexations. The Crimean War, however, halted the thrust of the Russian empire to the south and cleared the way to the unification of the two Rumanian principalities. The Treaty of Paris in 1856 restored the southern strip of Bessarabia, three districts bordering on the Danube, to Rumania. During the fight for the unification of the two principalities and full independence from the Turks, the Bessarabian question was necessarily, but only temporarily, in abeyance.

Though the domestic reforms carried out by Prince Cusa—the emancipation of the peasantry and the establishment of institutions of higher education—helped to consolidate the autonomous principalities, Cusa alienated his supporters by a series of scandals in his private life. He was deposed by a coup d'état, and in 1866 the Rumanian crown was offered to Prince Carol of Hohenzollern, a Prussian officer and cousin of Napoleon III. Under his rule, the movement from autonomy to independence gained momentum from the combined support of France and Prussia. The Russo-Turkish War of 1877–78 led to the unilateral declaration of independence, which was subsequently recognized by the European great powers.

Nevertheless the Rumanians felt cheated of the fruits of victory. Although they had rushed to the aid of the Russians in the Battle of Plevna, the Russians "rewarded" them by taking back the three districts in Southern Bessarabia ceded to Rumania in 1856 and launching a policy of brutal Russification of the entire area. The award of Northern Dobruja, one of the most neglected regions in the Balkans, to Rumania failed to soothe the general revulsion against what most Rumanians regarded as a stab in the back by a treacherous ally.

Thus the birth of modern Rumania was already overshadowed by intense mistrust and resentment toward Russia. It was this fear of the powerful neighbor that impelled King Carol and his advisers to shift the previous pro-French and, to a lesser extent, pro-Russian orientation and enter into a secret alliance with Germany and Austria. As early as 1883 a secret treaty was signed with Austro-Hungary and Germany providing for protection against a possible attack by Russia. The alliance was one of the best-guarded secrets in modern European history; until the outbreak of World War I only a handful of people knew of its existence.

The Old Kingdom or so-called "Regat" entered a period of rapid economic expansion, stimulated by the influx of foreign capital. Despite the pretense of constitutional government and the formal establishment of parliamentary institutions, power remained in the hands of the landed aristocracy. The Jewish minority, 5 per cent of the population, was barred from citizenship, and the merciless squeeze of the peasantry led to recurring social upheavals. Despite the great peasant revolt of 1907, quelled with the help of over 100,-000 troops, the Old Kingdom remained an authoritarian state, denying the most elementary political rights to the vast majority of its population.

Foreign policy aimed at the establishment of "Greater Rumania" through the acquisition of the coveted territories of Southern Dobruja from Bulgaria, Transylvania from Hungary, Bukovina (ceded in 1775 by the Turks to the Habsburg empire) from Austria, and, of course, Bessarabia from Russia. The Balkan Wars spurred the national movement. Rumania first embarked on the road of territorial aggrandizement in 1913 at the expense of defeated Bulgaria. The territorial gains in Dobruja, like future successes, were primarily due to a fortunate combination of external factors. As the Bulgarians had already been defeated by the Serbs and Greeks, the Rumanian army's only losses were from cholera.[4]

The pro-French nationalistic wing of the aristocracy pressed vigorously for a shift of allegiance after the outbreak of World War I, since it was the Austrian ally that thwarted the "reabsorption" of Transylvania. After the death of King Carol, Rumania entered the war in August 1916 on the side of the Allies who had promised it practically all the coveted territories except Bessarabia, which belonged to Russia. Once again the Rumanians emerged as winners because of unbelievable luck combined with tactical dexterity. Despite vigorous resistance by the Rumanian troops at Marasesti in Moldavia, the country had been defeated and forced to sign a separate peace treaty with the Central Powers in May 1918, but just before the armistice six months later Rumania declared war a second time and attended the peace conference as one of the Allies.

At the same time, the October Revolution in Russia gave Rumania an unexpected opportunity to reoccupy Bessarabia where a Military Committee had already proclaimed the region's autonomy in October 1917. Faced with complete chaos and the danger of Bolshevization, Rumania moved divisions into the area where a newly formed National Council, a more or less representative body, in April 1918 voted overwhelmingly for the union of Bessarabia with Rumania.

Rumania was a unique example of a country defeated in war that appeared as a victor and was aggrandized at the expense of one of its allies. Most foreign historians agree that its triple shift of allegiances within the span of four years was tolerated by the Allies only because of their fear of Russian communism and its possible spread westward. The unification of Transylvania with Rumania was solemnly proclaimed at a mass meeting in Alba Iulia on December 1, 1918, and carried out without opposition since Hungary, torn by revolutionary upheavals, was attacked from three sides after the dissolution of the Dual Monarchy. After the fall of the short-lived Communist regime in Budapest in 1919, Rumanian troops occupied the Hungarian capital and distinguished themselves by ruthless wholesale requisitioning as their method of paying off old scores against the former ruling nation in Transylvania. By the Treaty of Trianon, Rumania not only managed to gain Transylvania proper, where Rumanians accounted for just over half of the population, but also incorporated several important cities with an overwhelming Hungarian majority along the western fringe of the territory.

Thus Rumania emerged from World War I with more than double its prewar territory and population. While the Old Kingdom had an almost completely Rumanian population, Greater Rumania was a conglomeration of widely disparate provinces with non-Rumanians accounting for one-fourth of the total population. The tensions that dominated the entire interwar period arose mainly from vexed minority problems and fear of possible encroachments on territorial integrity from the open or covert revisionist claims of Russia, Hungary, and Bulgaria. Like the Serbs in the new Kingdom of Yugoslavia, the rulers of the Old Kingdom continued the previous centralized policy in a multinational new structure and were reluctant to share political power with anyone except the Transylvanian Rumanians.

Despite the territorial changes and spectacular economic prog-

ress during the 1920s, the social system inherited from the Turkish-
Phanariot past remained virtually intact. The atmosphere of easy-
going corruption pervaded the poorly paid civil service and life in
general. A small, privileged ruling group, cosmopolitan, sophisticated, and cynical, was firmly entrenched in power. For all the differences between then and now, some key features of domestic and
foreign policy, launched respectively by the Bratianu family whose
Liberal party governed the country until 1926 and by Nicolae
Titulescu, Foreign Minister in 1928–29 and again in 1932–36, bear a
striking resemblance to some important aspects of present-day Rumanian policy.

If one ignores the Communist vocabulary with which the present
Rumanian leaders garnish their statements about political sovereignty, economic independence, and all-round industrialization, it
soon becomes evident that the new course is primarily the continuation of the so-called integral economic nationalism advocated by
the Bratianus after World War I. It was not the late Communist
leader, Gheorghiu-Dej, or his successor Nicolae Ceausescu, but Ionel
Bratianu, the Liberal Prime Minister in the early 1920s, who first
launched a three-pronged offensive under the banner of "national
independence," "nostrification" (Rumanianization) and "by our own
means."[5]

Bratianu's policies of economic self-sufficiency and strong protec-
tionism were coupled with sweeping nationalization measures
involving not only the holdings of former enemy states but also
companies owned by citizens belonging to the ethnic minorities,
Hungarians and Jews in particular. In one form or another, about
one-third of the country's industry (two-thirds in Transylvania) was
affected by the laws promoting "Rumanianization" and strengthening
the Bucharest-centered leadership of Rumanian entrepreneurs.[6] The
discriminatory practices against minorities, including their exclusion from public office, bred mutual resentment and intensified
the mutual antipathy between them and the Rumanian majority.

On the international scene, Rumania during the interwar period
was regarded as a bulwark of the West against Soviet Russia and the
key prop of the French-inspired 1921 Little Entente of Rumania,
Czechoslovakia, and Yugoslavia. At the initiative of Foreign Minister Titulescu, undoubtedly one of the most outstanding statesmen
in Rumanian history, the Little Entente was supplemented by a

Balkan Pact between Rumania, Yugoslavia, Turkey, and Greece in 1934.

The Soviet Union never recognized the loss of Bessarabia and as early as 1919 issued an ultimatum demanding the withdrawal of the Rumanian troops within forty-eight hours. The ultimatum expired without any further move. Bilateral negotiations held in Vienna in 1924 failed to lead even to a resumption of diplomatic relations, which were not re-established until 1934. The far-sighted Titulescu, who was also President of the League of Nations for two consecutive years, quickly recognized the danger of Hitler's rise to power and the need to find some form of modus vivendi with Soviet Russia. Before his dismissal in 1936, he and Litvinov, then Soviet Foreign Minister, had initialed a pact in which Moscow, de facto if not de jure, recognized Rumanian authority over Bessarabia.

Communist Rumania's foreign policy today is a continuation of Titulescu's diplomatic acrobatics performed in a complex and dangerous international situation. There is a legitimate historical lineage in a foreign policy that is always devised to ensure Rumania against any potential encroachments. The differences in the character of a given political system may have changed the framework but not the essence of the national interests to which proven skills in the arts of compromise and muddling through have always been subordinated. A comparison of the statements made by Titulescu and those of the present Communist leaders makes the continuity self-evident.

"We shall never renounce for the sake of any of the Great Powers, or of all the Great Powers together, the principle of equality of states, that is, the sovereign right to decide our own fate and to refuse decisions concerning us in which we have been involved without our consent." This is how Titulescu formulated the credo of Rumanian foreign policy on June 11, 1936. Thirty-one years later, Nicolae Ceausescu, Secretary General of the Communist Party, opened a major foreign policy debate in the Bucharest parliament with the following defiant declaration: "The small and medium-sized states refuse to play the role of pawn in the service of the interests of big imperialist powers any longer. They rise against any form of domination and promote an independent policy. By vigorously defending their legitimate rights and interests, the small and medium-sized countries can play an outstanding part in international life, can considerably influence the course of events."

The Great Depression and its grave political repercussions, which inflamed domestic tensions, put an end to Titulescu's efforts to seek a limited reconciliation with Russia and paved the way for the establishment of the royal dictatorship and Rumania's entry into World War II on the side of Nazi Germany. German economic and political penetration weakened the pro-French sentiment and gave a powerful fillip to the extreme right-wing, anti-Semitic groups like the Iron Guard and the League of National Christian Defense. The monarchy, previously regarded as a stabilizing force, became an increasingly important factor in the gradual erosion of the parliamentary system, primarily thanks to the dangerous antics of King Carol II whose celebrated affair with Magda Lupescu helped to fill the gossip columns of European newspapers. As Carol had renounced the right to the throne one year before the death of King Ferdinand, his son Michael was proclaimed King and a Council of Regents was installed in 1927. Three years later Carol was allowed to return, but, despite his promises, he continued his association with Lupescu. This provoked the resignation of Prime Minister Iliu Maniu, the leader of the National Peasant Party, caused a constitutional crisis, and hastened the rise of extremism.

The Iron Guard, partly financed by the Nazis, directed the discontent of the impoverished peasantry and of many urban white- and blue-collar workers into the traditional channels of anti-Semitism, which, since the Jews were identified with Soviet Russia and communism as such, became an ominously powerful force in the late thirties. As in neighboring Bulgaria, assassination and murder were the extremists' political weapon. The 1937 election was the last parliamentary election still free enough to defeat the government in power. But the defeat of the moderate National Liberal Party through an electoral pact between the National Peasant Party and the Iron Guard was a dire portent of extremist strength. The Iron Guard was not just a lunatic fringe but a dynamic movement supported by about one-fifth of the voters.

An extreme right-wing, rabidly anti-Semitic government took over, only to be replaced by a royal dictatorship in February 1938. Domestic tensions were accentuated by the deterioration of the international situation and the increasingly vocal territorial claims of the neighboring states, particularly Hungary and Bulgaria, which enjoyed the Axis powers' support. After Munich and the Hitler-Stalin pact, Rumania, and indeed the whole of southeast Europe, was left at the mercy of the two totalitarian powers. Room for maneuver shrank to nil.

The dream of "Great Rumania" lasted barely two decades. The secret protocols to the Soviet-German pact of August 1939 sealed the fate of Rumania; the Nazi leaders gave the Russians a free hand to annex what they liked. The vague formulation of the German statement in the protocol, disclaiming any interest "in those areas," whetted the Russians' territorial appetite, and the night of June 26 the Soviet Government presented a twenty-four-hour ultimatum to Rumania, demanding the cession of Bessarabia and also of Northern Bukovina, which had never before belonged to Russia. To add insult to injury, the map attached to the ultimatum included the town of Herta and twelve adjoining villages that were parts of the Old Kingdom and of the earliest nucleus of the Moldavian state. Despite the desperate pleas of the Rumanian government, Hitler, Mussolini, and the members of the Balkan Pact refused help.[7]

On June 28, 1940, Soviet troops began to occupy the 19,500 square miles of annexed territories. The bulk of the "reabsorbed" provinces were added to the small Moldavian Autonomous Soviet Republic, the rest went to the Soviet Ukraine. In August, the enlarged Soviet-Moldavia became a constituent republic of the Soviet Union. Its population today is just over 3 million with Rumanians, whom Soviet statistics classify as "Moldavians," making up over 65 per cent of the total. In all, there are 2.3 million "Moldavians" in the Soviet Union according to the 1959 census. The rankling sense of grievance over the denial of even elementary minority rights to their kinsmen has remained an important psychological factor in Rumanian hostility toward Russia.

The Russians, however, dealt only the first blow in the dismemberment of Greater Rumania. The annexation of Bessarabia and Northern Bukovina was followed by the Vienna Award, by which the Axis Powers allotted Northern Transylvania, an area of some 16,000 square miles, to Hungary. Germany also made a move to satisfy the territorial demands of its other client state, Bulgaria, by forcing Rumania to cede Southern Dobruja, which had been conquered in the Second Balkan War. Rumania's claim to this relatively small area, often called the "ethnographic museum" because of its medley of diverse ethnic groups, was never historically strong. Thanks to the compulsory exchange of populations, Southern Dobruja, in contrast to the other disputed areas, has ceased to be an open issue.

Within two months Rumania lost more than one-third of its territory and five million of its population, including two million subjects of non-Rumanian origin. One gets the impression that Rumanians, regardless of political creed, have never recovered from the shock of 1940. The enduring bitterness was very evident in Ceausescu's celebrated speech in May 1966 when he castigated the Comintern whose directives in 1940 criticized the Rumanian Communists for "their stand in the defense of the national independence of the fatherland." Recalling the "theft of Northern Transylvania" (but ignoring the annexation of Bessarabia), the party leader made a revealing statement: "At this grim moment in the fate of their country, the Rumanian people found themselves alone, without any outside support, abandoned by all the powers of Europe."

Hitler exploited the age-old rivalries between the Hungarians and Rumanians whose mutual antipathy was rivaled only by their common hate and fear of Soviet Russia. King Carol was forced to abdicate in favor of his son Michael, and the former Minister of War, General Ion Antonescu, became—after a short but terrible spell of fanatical Iron Guard dictatorship—the effective ruler of the country. Rump Rumania under Antonescu became a client state of Germany no less devoted than Hungary, joining the Tripartite Pact only one day after its hated neighbor. The Vienna Award left both sides discontented. The Hungarians had wanted the whole of Transylvania. The Rumanians were outraged that they had to cede anything at all. But by a supreme irony of history, after the German invasion of Russia, these two mortal enemies fought shoulder to shoulder on the same front under the same master against the common enemy.

Fired by the opportunity of reoccupying Bessarabia, the Rumanians were clearly more eager to fight on the side of Nazi Germany than the Hungarians, and their contributions of troops and material were considerably greater. After recapturing Bessarabia and Bukovina in less than four weeks, General Antonescu, ignoring the pleas of the young king and many political leaders, refused to halt his troops at the Dniester. Some fifteen Rumanian divisions fought the retreating Russians, seizing about ten thousand square miles of Russian territory, including the port of Odessa. The establishment of Transnistria, the area between the rivers Dniester and Bug, as a semi-independent territory under Rumanian administration and some terrible atrocities committed by the Rumanian occupiers was a further, often forgotten, emotional factor accounting for the violence of the mutual resentment between Rumanians and Russians.

Pinning his hopes on a German victory, Antonescu had become heavily committed in the war against Russia partly in order to outbid the Hungarians in their support of Germany, in the expectation that the Nazis would reward Rumania by annulling the Vienna Award. With a German defeat in sight and the Soviet army approaching Rumanian territory, the contacts between the Western powers and Rumania's democratic opposition, primarily the old peasant leader, Iuliu Maniu, which had never been broken off completely, were intensified, and a number of Rumanian envoys were sent to Cairo to prepare an armistice. Meanwhile, following a cooperation agreement between the Social Democrats and the minuscule Communist party, a broad coalition including these two groups and the two traditional prewar parties, the National Peasants and the National Liberals, was formed. Nevertheless the dramatic overthrow of the Antonescu dictatorship and Rumania's last-minute swing to the Allies was primarily the work of King Michael and a group of senior officers. It was the young monarch who, on August 23, 1944, when General Antonescu came to the palace for an audience, seized the chance and had him arrested there and then. He then broadcast an appeal to the nation and the world, declaring that Rumania had broken with Germany and joined the Allies. The Communist-inspired National Democratic Front played only a minor part in this patriotic undertaking which, as *Pravda* stressed at the time, led to a "collapse of the entire German defense system in the Balkans." The coup enabled the Red Army to reach the Bulgarian, Yugoslav, and Hungarian borders within a week.

Interpretations of the August coup varied significantly in later years. Its character and importance became a crucial issue in the power struggles within the Communist party between the "home" Communists and the Muscovites. It also served as a curtain raiser to the Soviet-Rumanian dispute when, in December 1962, a Rumanian party periodical publicly rebuked the Soviet historian Ushakov for ignoring the August 23 uprising in his book, *The Foreign Policy of Hitlerite Germany*, and giving all the credit for Rumania's liberation to the Red Army. The book was a Stalinist version of what happened in Rumania. The new version, almost equally incorrect but politically extremely important, is that the

armed uprising was carried out by the "Communist-led domocratic
and anti-Hitlerite forces"; even King Michael and the army command are credited with cooperating with the "Communist-inspired
and -led patriotic action."[8]

The coup certainly hastened the victory of the Allies and
saved Rumania from even more damage than it had already suffered
during the fighting and air raids. The last-minute break with Germany, paralleling to some extent Rumania's shift of allegiance in
World War I, was also a key factor in regaining the Transylvanian
territories. Just as Hungary in 1940 gained because it lay nearest to
Germany on Hitler's march east, so in 1944 Rumania profited because it lay nearest to Russia on the Red Army's march west.[9] From
the very beginning, the Soviet government held out the bait of returning all or the "major part" of Transylvania to the vacillating
Rumanians. The promise was confirmed in the armistice terms, and
the peace treaty of February 1947 restored the Hungarian-Rumanian
borders as they stood before the Vienna Award.

But the Rumanians had to accept the final loss of Bessarabia and
Northern Bukovina, which were duly reabsorbed by Soviet Russia.
After numerous frontier changes and population shifts between
1940 and 1944, Rumania emerged from the war with a "net" loss of
almost one-fifth of her interwar territory and 15 per cent of her population. Wartime civilian and military losses totaled over 550,000,
and official figures put the total war damages, including reparations
to the Soviet Union, at a figure exceeding three and a half times the
country's national income in 1938.[10]

Worse still, the August coup was not able to protect future independence since, as so often in the past, Rumania was once again a
pawn on the chessboard of spheres of influence. Military and political realities made Soviet domination and a Communist takeover
inevitable. This was implicitly recognized in May 1944 when Anthony Eden, then British Foreign Secretary, suggested to the Russians that they should "temporarily regard Rumanian affairs as their
concern while leaving Greece to us," or, as Churchill put it in a cable
to Roosevelt, the Russians should "take the lead in Rumania." In
October 1944 Churchill agreed with Stalin "in no more time than
it takes to set [the figures] down" to settle the fate of the Balkan
countries in terms of neat percentages. "How would it do for you to
have 90 per cent predominance in Rumania?" Churchill asked Stalin,
and it was in "such an offhand manner" that the two men "disposed

of these issues so fateful to millions of people."[11] The 90 per cent preponderance authorized the Russians to treat Rumania as a protectorate to be occupied and ruled. And the general record of Soviet domination exceeded the population's worst expectations.

"The Russians skinned us four times"

The young guide switched on the lights behind the glass-covered map of Rumania. One after the other, red, blue, and green arrows shone brightly. The red marked the positions of the Red Army; the blue, the actions of Rumanian army units; the green, the concentration of German forces trapped in a hopeless situation after the August 23 coup. The explanations were expounded in faultless Russian by the girl who was showing a group of young Soviet tourists around the new museum in Bucharest devoted to the history of the Rumanian workers' movement and the Communist party. She was telling her listeners, whose attention was visibly wandering in the scorching heat of mid-summer 1966, how the armed uprising led by the Communist party shattered the German defense system and took tens of thousands of German soldiers prisoner long before the Red Army appeared in the Rumanian capital. In other words, Rumania was liberated primarily by the Rumanians themselves, who then fought with "the glorious Soviet Army" against Nazi Germany, adding over 170,000 dead or wounded to their losses before the end of the war.

A few minutes later the Russian tourists were led into the next room where the banners of the Rumanian divisions that switched to the Allied side, photo montages about the fighting, and pictures of the army commanders regarded as "arch-reactionary militarists" only a few years ago are displayed to the public. Here, as in each of the fourteen tastefully arranged halls, Russian visitors find only the sparsest references to the "fatherland of the proletariat" which so profoundly and for so long molded the political, cultural, and economic pattern of postwar Rumania. There are only two placards about the Russian Revolution, but an entire hall depicting the exploits of the Rumanian army in World War I; one group photo with Stalin (and, for the sake of balance, also one of Mao Tse-tung), but a long line of paintings and photos of the great national figures from Stephen the Great to Titulescu.

This red-brick building, used as a mint before the war, is situated on a broad avenue between the city center and a copy of the Arc de Triomphe. Three thousand people a day are said to visit the permanent exhibition, which is perhaps the most ambitious attempt ever undertaken by a ruling Communist party to "master the past" —naturally in a Communist fashion—and project itself as torchbearer of the finest national and progressive traditions.

Particularly remarkable to a visitor is the fact that the Communist regime with the weakest indigenous roots, born as a creation of Soviet postwar occupation, should have the audacity to downgrade Russian and Soviet influence and champion resurgent nationalism. While the sense of identity as a nation always exposed to external dangers has been the principal factor in Rumanian history, it cannot explain why and how the Communist ruling group, so long feared and disliked by the population, managed to capture the sentiment of the country and win genuine popular support in its dispute with its erstwhile protector and master.

The point of the matter is that for four decades after it was founded on May 8, 1921, the Rumanian Communist Party was considered not only un-Rumanian but anti-Rumanian.[12] It was discredited as un-Rumanian because its founders and principal leaders were either Jews or Ukrainians, Bulgarians or Hungarians, in a country in which anti-Semitism and xenophobia had extremely deep and strong roots. Otto Katz (or Cass), a Russian Jew who moved to Rumania at the age of twenty and became, under the name of Constantine Dobrogeanu-Gherea, the leading thinker of the left-wing Socialists with his son Alexander, established a splinter group of Social Democrats as a Communist party. The other principal figure was the Bulgarian-born Christian Rakovsky, who before World War I dominated both the Bulgarian and Rumanian Social Democratic parties and after the October Revolution entered Soviet service and occupied key positions, including the premiership of the Soviet Ukraine. Both Alexander Dobrogeanu-Gherea and Rakovsky died during Stalin's Great Purge in the mid-thirties.

Especially after the party was outlawed in 1924, its real leaders were the members of the Foreign Buros who lived in Moscow and were subordinate to the Comintern. As Ceausescu bluntly stated in his speech marking the party's forty-fifth anniversary, the Comintern in the interwar period imposed its own policies and leaders on the Rumanian Communist Party in complete disregard of "the economic, social, political, and national conditions in Rumania." He also spelled out the disastrous consequences of the Comintern's practice "of appointing leadership cadres, including secretaries general, from among people abroad who did not know the Rumanian people's life." The Secretary General from 1924 until 1928 was a Hungarian, and the two subsequent leaders "elected" at the fourth and fifth Congresses were not even members of the Rumanian party but belonged respectively to the Ukrainian branch of the Soviet party and the Polish party.

The new party museum exhibits commemorating the dates of the prewar party congresses list the former leaders, including those who were purged, and indicate in brackets when a Secretary General was a member of a foreign Communist party. The predominance of Jews and foreigners among the principal leaders was, of course, not due to anti-Rumanian prejudices in the Comintern, but merely reflected the fact that communism had a limited appeal in Rumania, and that only to the minority groups whose pro-Russian sympathies were the product of the brutal racist and minority policies of the interwar Rumanian regimes.

The Communist party was also considered anti-Rumanian, however, because of its allegiance to Russia and its support of such policies as the incorporation of Bessarabia into the Soviet Union. After the Third Party Congress in 1924 the party upheld for over fifteen years the right of self-determination including secession. As late as December 1939, Boris Stefanov, a Bulgarian, who was imposed on the Rumanian Communists as Secretary General in 1931, published an article in the official paper of the Comintern urging Rumania to return to "an out-and-out policy of self-determination," especially in regard to Bessarabia.[13] In his sweeping indictment of the Comintern's interference in the Rumanian party affairs, Ceausescu stated the bitter historical truth that the orders from Moscow instructed the party "to fight for the breaking away from Rumania of certain territories inhabited by an overwhelming majority of Rumanians . . . and in fact promoted the dismemberment of the national state and the breakup of the Rumanian people."

This made it inevitable that communism, despite the great social discontent in the country, remained an insignificant clandestine movement on the fringe of political life. In the elections of 1929 and 1931, the Communists under the name of the Workers' and Peasants' Bloc, managed to gain only 2 per cent of the total votes.

The single, most important action undertaken by the Communists was the railroad strike of 1933 in the workshops of Grivita, a working class suburb of Bucharest. It was then that a young railwayman, Gheorghe Gheorghiu, acting as secretary of the national action committee of the railroad workers, won his first laurels in the Communist movement. Though he was arrested just before the strike started, Gheorghiu who called himself Gheorghiu-Dej (after the small Transylvanian town of Dej) went down in party history as the hero of the occasion. Actually, the storming of the workshops and the strike itself were led by Constantin Doncea, Chivu Stoica, and other Communist comrades. The strike was crushed, and the imprisonment of scores of leading Communist activists virtually destroyed the party.

While the Rumanian colony in Moscow was rent by factional struggles between "leftists" and "rightists," the practically leaderless party in Rumania rapidly disintegrated. In 1944 it had only about one thousand members. When the Soviet army was approaching Rumania, Gheorghiu-Dej was still serving his twelve-year prison term with his future closest associates, Stoica, Gheorghe Apostol, and Nicolae Ceausescu, the youth leader, also behind bars. Thus an important group of future leaders of the party had slight, if any, contact with Moscow and could be regarded as home-grown Communists in the full sense of the word.

The real leaders of the party were, however, the "Muscovites" who returned to the country in September 1944 in the baggage train of the Red Army. The hard core of Soviet-trained Communists was led by Ana Pauker, the daughter of a Jewish rabbi whose upper middle class husband, Marcel Pauker, had been one of the founders of the movement and a high Comintern functionary who was killed during the Great Purge. "Red Ana" returned to Rumania in 1934 and was arrested. Five years later she was extradited to Moscow under an exchange agreement between the Rumanian and Soviet governments. There she became the head of the Foreign Buro. Her principal collaborators were Vasile Luca, a Hungarian from Transylvania, and Teohari Georgescu who ran the secret police between 1944 and 1952. The Moscow group also included Emil Bodnaras, a former Rumanian army officer (partly of Ukrainian origin), and the Bulgarian-born Petre Borila. With a Russian victory in sight, Bodnaras was sent to Rumania to establish contact with the Gheorghiu-Dej group in the internment camp at Targu Jiu. At about this time the home Communists fired what turned out to be the opening shot in the long battle against the Soviet-trained leaders. Acting on their own, Dej and his friends ousted the then leader of the party, Stefan Foris, claiming he was a traitor.* The leading group outside and in the internment camp then acknowledged Gheorghiu-Dej as the new leader. Meanwhile a three-member provisional secretariat including Bodnaras was set up to direct clandestine activities and establish close contacts first with the Social Democrats and then with other democratic parties.

Whatever role the Communists played in the preparation of the August coup, it is a historical fact that they carried out their activities without Moscow's knowledge or approval. It was a young lawyer of middle class family, a lifelong Communist, Lucretiu Patrascanu, who had been received by King Michael in secret audience in August, who acted as chief contact-man with other political groups, and who joined the first coalition government after the successful coup as Communist representative. Another Communist lawyer, Ion Gheorghe Maurer, also distinguished himself in those tense days by personal boldness. Dressed as an army officer, Maurer appeared in mid-August at the Targu Jiu camp and brought Gheorghiu-Dej out. This act of daring helped to forge a close personal friendship between the two men that subsequently proved of some significance during Rumania's emancipation from Soviet tutelage.

The preeminence of the native Communists lasted only until the arrival of the Pauker group from Moscow and the establishment of Soviet administration. Within six months the coalition had cracked up under relentless Soviet pressure, three governments had been overthrown; two weeks after the Yalta Conference Stalin gave the signal for the final showdown with the King and the pro-Western parties. Stalin's Rumanian stooges organized demonstrations and concerted press attacks against General Radescu's Cabinet, while the Communist ministers and their associates sabotaged the administration. The decisive act was staged by Stalin's personal emissary, the ill-famed prosecutor in the Moscow Trials in the thirties, Deputy Foreign Minister Andrei Vyshinsky.

At the end of February 1945 Vyshinsky arrived in Bucharest, saw

* As revealed on April 26, 1968, by a party panel into the purges, Foris was summarily killed in 1946, as it is claimed now, on the instructions of Gheorghiu-Dej and Ana Pauker.

the King and demanded that he dismiss the Radescu government as "it was unable to maintain order." With about one million Soviet troops in the country, Vyshinsky made it brutally clear that Moscow was determined to cash Churchill's check for "90 per cent Russian preponderance" without further delay. He gave King Michael a two-hour-and-five-minute ultimatum to appoint Petru Groza, the leader of the Plowmen's Front, the Communist puppet party, Premier, brusquely rejecting the King's alternative suggestions. When the monarch declined to accept the list of ministers, Vyshinsky warned him that this was an unfriendly act to the Soviet Union and unless he accepted the entire cabinet by noon the next day "Rumania might cease to exist as a sovereign state."[14] To add emphasis, Vyshinsky pounded the table and slammed the door so hard on leaving the room that the plaster of the wall cracked.

The pro-Soviet National Democratic Front government headed by Groza took over on March 6, 1945. To sweeten the bitter pill of the Soviet ultimatum and enable the Groza government to make a "good start," Moscow announced that Transylvania would be returned to the administration of the Rumanian government.

Immediately after the formation of the Groza Cabinet a sweeping purge of the police, army, and local administration was started. Through the same mixture of threats, terror, and splitting tactics applied in the other satellites, organized political opposition and the parliamentary system were destroyed step by step. The consolidation of power and the transformation of covert Communist rule into an overt single-party dictatorship was hastened after the conclusion of the peace treaty in February 1947.

The main features of this process—the arrests and trials of the leading opposition figures, the subversion of the Social Democratic party and its enforced merger with the Communists, rigged elections, and the widescale liquidation of active opponents—were depressingly similar throughout the entire Soviet orbit. As the monarchy gradually became the only symbol of national opposition to communism, the formal Communist takeover culminated in the forced abdication of King Michael and the establishment of the People's Republic on December 30, 1947. Despite the hopeless rearguard battles of the anti-Communist parties and pathetic Western protests, Rumania's fate had already been sealed on March 6, 1945, when Moscow's agents seized the "commanding heights" of power. By the time the monarchy fell, the country had entered the dark phase of its history, which was at least as Russian as it was Communist.[15]

Of course, every country in the Soviet sphere of influence was subjected to the twin assault of communism and Russification. What distinguished Rumania from the other satellites was the scope, degree, and duration of Soviet economic exploitation. The various confidential circulars the Rumanian leadership addressed to the party meetings during the conflict with Moscow amply document that no other East European country was plundered so ruthlessly and so long by the Russians. "The Russians skinned us four times," the Rumanian leaders complained already in 1947 to a Hungarian statesman visiting Bucharest.[16]

After four skinnings not much was left for the Rumanians. What a French observer wrote about the Russian troops' wholesale requisitioning in the early nineteenth century, "everyone took what he found where he found it," could have been said with equal justification in the immediate postwar period. Hit by droughts, famine, war losses and a runaway inflation, Rumania had almost at once to start paying reparations to the Soviet Union. These were fixed at 300 million dollars calculated at 1938 prices, which meant about 50 per cent more in current prices. Plants and equipment were dismantled, merchant marine and rolling stock appropriated, stores of industrial and semi-manufactured goods removed and shipped off to Russia. Some estimates put the total loot in the first few months at 2 billion dollars.[17]

The open plunder was, however, only the prelude to a complete takeover of the Rumanian economy through the notorious device of joint stock companies. The companies, which were set up in several satellite states, were split in equal shares between Moscow and the respective governments with German assets the Russians had seized providing the Soviet capital. Nowhere except in East Germany was the industrial subordination and economic exploitation so blatant and so total as in Rumania. The sixteen joint companies, called Sovroms, controlled such economic sectors as crude oil, shipping, timber, chemicals, and uranium. After the death of Stalin, the mixed companies everywhere were dissolved and the Soviet assets returned to the countries in question—needless to say on highly unfavorable financial terms, thus further augmenting Soviet gains. Once again Rumania was singled out for particularly insidious currency manipulations. The sudden devaluation of the

Rumanian lei in February 1954 doubled the ruble price for the sale of Soviet rights in the Sovroms seven months later.[18] Two key companies—uranium and oil—were actually returned to Rumania only after the Hungarian revolution in 1956.

In addition to the heavy requisitioning, reparation payments, and exploitation through the Sovroms, Rumania also suffered from price discrimination in trade with the Soviet Union and was forced to contribute to the maintenance of Soviet occupation troops. Even after Moscow had begun to reverse its policies toward most of the other satellites, Rumania's status did not change. Though Moscow canceled Rumanian debts together with those of the other satellites after Stalin's death, Rumania like Czechoslovakia continued to represent a net asset to the Soviet Union. Despite the fact that its economic potential had suffered one of the most severe losses in the entire area, Rumania benefited the least from the aftermath of the Polish and Hungarian upheavals and from the changed emphasis in Soviet economic policies.

Rumania was the leader among satellite contributors to Soviet economic strength, but it received next to nothing when Moscow began to bolster up the crumbling satellite economies. Between 1956 and 1960, for example, the East European countries as a whole received Soviet commodity loans and investment credits of more than 2 billion dollars. Rumania's share of the total was a mere 95 million dollars. During the same period Soviet loans and credits accounted for 10 per cent of the gross state investments in Bulgaria, almost 6 per cent in Hungary, and a fraction of 1 per cent in Rumania. Other statistical comparisons reveal that between 1945 and 1962 Soviet aid to Rumania totaled 10 dollars per capita of the population, as against 78 dollars for East Germany, 73 dollars for Bulgaria, and 38 dollars each for Hungary and Poland.[19] At the same time Rumania was one of the prime suppliers of oil products, timber, uranium, and foodstuffs to the Soviet economy.

Economically, the gap between Rumania and the more developed Communist countries widened steadily, and despite its rich resources of raw materials Rumania lagged behind the other East European countries in industrialization. By the late fifties with per head industrial output in Rumania three and a half times smaller than in East Germany and less than half of the Soviet figure, it became painfully evident that, barring concerted action on a broad front, Rumania would remain a permanent food and raw material base for the more developed Communist countries.

Politically, the Soviet economic grip swelled the anti-Russian nationalism of the angry but powerless population. More important still, the frustrations of being discriminated against in comparison to the other satellites went very deep among the leading home Communists and younger functionaries who had come to the fore in the fifties.

Gheorghe Gheorghiu-Dej, a "home" Communist, was elected Secretary General of the party at the national conference in October 1945. He was, however, largely a figurehead. Ana Pauker and a handful of other Muscovites controlled the party apparatus, the secret police, the Foreign Ministry, and the key economic sectors. During and after the seizure of power, Gheorghiu-Dej and his associates had to devote their main attention to physical survival in the midst of the purges against native Communist leaders that engulfed Eastern Europe in the wake of the Tito-Stalin break. They gained a crucial breathing-spell in February 1948 when one of the architects of the August coup, Lucretiu Patrascanu, was made the chief victim in the campaign against "bourgeois ideology" and "nationalist-chauvinistic" deviations. Nevertheless, Gheorghiu-Dej and his friends were also exposed to mortal dangers and had to live down what the Pauker clique regarded as their "political mistake" —the party's involvement in the August coup. According to the later official account, which is probably substantially correct, the Muscovites maintained that it would have been better "to leave the overthrow of the military fascist dictatorship to the Soviet Army because thus the working class would have been able to seize power immediately, avoiding the phase of collaboration with the bourgeois parties."[20]

In addition to being led by "foreign elements," who "usurped" the dominant positions, and acting as a tool of Soviet domination, the Rumanian Communists also discredited themselves by their recruiting drives among the former members of the fascist Iron Guard and by the admission of thousands of floating careerists and opportunists. Party ranks swelled from 1,000 old-timers to over 200,000 members by the end of 1945 and no less than 714,000 by the end of 1947. After the merger with the Social Democrats, membership passed the 1,000,000 mark. As with many other excesses committed during the heyday of Stalinism, the leadership later

shifted all responsibility for the welcomed entry of so many Iron
Guardists into the party onto the shoulders of the "Pauker group."
After 1948, over 300,000 "alien, careerist elements, including Iron
Guardists and hostile persons" were weeded out of the ranks.[21]

The May 1952 purge of the Muscovite leaders—Ana Pauker,
Vasile Luca, and Teohari Georgescu who were secretaries of the
Central Committee and in charge of, respectively, foreign policy,
planning, and the secret police—marked the first crucial turning point in postwar Rumanian communism. It was then that
Gheorghiu-Dej and his closest collaborators assumed real control
of the party and state apparatus. The removal of the Pauker trio
was also a landmark in the Rumanianization of the top leadership.

The information now available indicates that the elimination of
the Pauker group was one of the strategic moments of crisis and
decision in postwar Rumanian history, but a word of caution should
be added about the use of broad generalizations. The significance
of the 1952 events is still being debated, and the observer is faced
with a choice between two theories. One regards the purge of the
three top Soviet-trained leaders as a chapter in the internal power
struggle without any political, let alone nationalist overtones. The
other tends to accept the official version (presented ten years after
the purge) and sees the purge as the origin of the Rumanian defiance of the Soviet Union.

A Western observer has very few hard facts to go on in accepting
either theory. The main danger, however, is to expect to find tidy
and simple answers to complex situations. Both tendencies were
present in some degree, but the main trend at any one time depends upon the particular context in which it is viewed. In other
words, the assessment of the change at the apex of the party has
been different at different times. In the context of 1952, the eclipse
of Pauker and her associates did not mean a change in policy, let
alone in the power relationship between the Soviet center and the
Rumanian party. Nothing would be more naïve and misleading
than to imagine that the outcome of a power struggle in 1952, almost a year before Stalin died, could have been decided without
the knowledge or against the will of the Kremlin.

The policy decision as to just which leaders should be thrown to
the wolves as scapegoats for the policy failures, the deterioration of
the economic situation, and the discontent following the currency
reform, which had aggravated the plight of the urban population,

was made in Moscow. What made the change in the leadership possible was the shift of allegiance by another group of Muscovites, the so-called Bessarabian wing, whose most important leader was General Emil Bodnaras, Moscow's trusted agent in charge of the army and security. It is also highly probable that the fall of Ana Pauker and the ascendancy of a native Rumanian but unquestionably orthodox Communist like Gheorghiu-Dej was facilitated by Stalin's obsession with anti-Semitism in his last years. It was certainly more than just coincidence that the Secretary General of the Czechoslovak Communist Party, the Jewish Rudolf Slansky, was purged during the same period as the Jewish Pauker.*

Whatever the causes of the personnel changes, it soon became clear that they did not mean any substantial modification of policies or methods. Within five days of the purge, Gheorghiu-Dej quickly consolidated his supremacy by taking over the premiership, combining the position with his post as Secretary General. He faced two main problems. First, he had to maintain the unity and cohesion of the "new" leadership in a difficult situation. The second and more pressing problem was to convince Moscow that the strengthening of the "native wing" would not jeopardize the tight Soviet grip on the country. That he managed to solve both problems and establish himself as a trusted and accepted figure even during the instability after Stalin's death was something of an achievement. His natural gift for compromise and timing helped him ride out the storms and consolidate his hold on the party. The essential consideration governing Gheorghiu-Dej's political behavior during the turbulent fifties was prudence.

Through a combination of peripheral concessions and ruthlessness, Gheorghiu-Dej managed to keep the post-Stalin ferment within politically safe bounds. Rumania remained a quiet satellite with the safety valves never opened as wide as in other Communist countries. To dispel any doubts about the continuity of basic policies and to intimidate those who might want to push relaxation too far, Lucretiu Patrascanu, already disgraced in 1948, was executed after a secret trial in April 1954. The liquidation of the one man who had been generally regarded as a genuine nationalist

* Pauker and Georgescu were never tried, and Pauker died in 1960. Only Luca was sentenced, at a secret trial, to death in 1954, commuted later to life imprisonment. He died in prison.

dramatically underlined the Rumanian leadership's freedom from any overt taint of "nationalist deviation."*

Aside from the Patrascanu affair, relative calm reigned in the country. With Soviet troops stationed in the land until the summer of 1958 and the army and the security apparatus firmly controlled by trusted Soviet agents, Moscow's influence in the post-Stalin period seemed as pervasive as ever. The peak of the terror campaigns against the recalcitrant peasants who opposed collectivization and the mass deportations of unreliable elements, including tens of thousands of Serbs from the border areas, was followed by what might be described as "sleepy Stalinism."

Faced with the new Soviet line of "collective leadership" and separation of government and party functions after Stalin's death, Gheorghiu-Dej gave an impressive display of shrewd political management. In April 1954 he decided to remain Premier but relinquished the post of First Secretary of the party (the Secretary Generalship was simultaneously abolished) to one of his closest associates, the Trade Union leader Gheorghe Apostol. In contrast to Chervenkov in Bulgaria, however, he realized soon enough the dangers of losing his grip on the party apparatus and eighteen months later engineered a new realignment at the top.

In October 1955, on the eve of the party congress, which had been postponed several times, Gheorghiu-Dej resumed his former position at the helm of the party and gave the premiership to another of his trusted lieutenants, Chivu Stoica, a former railwayman. This game of musical chairs, performed with such apparent smoothness, was not only without precedent in an Eastern Europe torn by tensions and stresses, but also showed the uncontested supremacy of Gheorghiu-Dej. Both the shifts at the top and the election of the new Politburo combined to strengthen the native wing without giving any reason for raised eyebrows in Moscow. It was at this congress that Ceausescu, who had been a member of the Secretariat since 1954, was promoted at the early age of thirty-seven to full membership in the Politburo.

Though the Rumanian leadership steered a prudent middle course between too much repression and too much relaxation during the post-Stalin period of political instability and power struggles in

---

* A Central Committee resolution of April 26, 1968, formally rehabilitated Patrascanu and condemned Gheorghiu-Dej and the then Minister of Interior, Alexander Draghici, for the trial and execution.

the Kremlin, it also had to weather the dangerous storm of de-Stalinization. After the Twentieth Soviet Party Congress, a plenary meeting of the Central Committee in March 1956 heaped blame for "violations of Socialist legality and internal party democracy" on the purged leaders. With tensions mounting in neighboring Hungary, the ferment among intellectuals and students began to grow in Rumania. During and after the Hungarian revolution, the situation rapidly approached the danger point, particularly among the Hungarian minority in Transylvania.

Nevertheless, the Communist regime survived the tense but short-lived period of sporadic demonstrations and general restiveness. What would have happened if the Hungarian revolution had not been crushed or had lasted longer is a moot point. As it was, the caution in keeping de-Stalinization within narrow limits paid handsome dividends. As there had been no show trials and the Pauker group provided a convenient scapegoat for past excesses, there was no crisis of authority at the top. Gheorghiu-Dej declared five years later, "We did not have to repair serious injustices or rehabilitate anyone post mortem."[22] Other factors working in favor of the regime were the lack of a body, either church or full-blown revisionist group within the party, for the opposition to rally to, and the absence of non-Communist neighbors.

The appearance of a solidly united leadership coping with a potentially critical situation was, however, deceptive. From early 1956 until mid-1957 Gheorghiu-Dej faced an extremely serious challenge to his position. Two powerful Politburo members, Miron Constantinescu, organizational secretary and Minister of Culture during the intellectual ferment in 1956, and Iosif Chisinevschi, the chief of the propaganda section, are alleged to have launched a concerted attack against him and his policies. Whether these two men of different backgrounds—the first a "home" Communist, the other a Soviet-trained Bessarabian Jew—really formed a joint minority faction, or whether a "leftist" immigrant and a native reformer were lumped together to enable Gheorghiu-Dej to kill two birds with one stone—is still not clear. The case for the second version is fairly strong, but not conclusive.

In any case, the manner and timing of the removal of the two rival claimants for power revealed Gheorghiu-Dej's consummate skill as a tactician. The two men were toppled in July 1957, at the same time the Molotov "anti-party" group was purged in Moscow.

Chisinevschi and Constantinescu were accused of both left and right deviation, of past abuses and "anarchistic-petit bourgeois" tendencies—a familiar Communist ploy to ward off later criticism from either direction.

This purge was the second important landmark in the postwar history of the party. With his last dangerous rivals out of the way Gheorghiu-Dej became the absolute dictator of Rumania. When the Soviet troops left the country in 1958 as part of Khrushchev's "peace strategy," Gheorghiu-Dej was the acknowledged head of a genuinely united leadership. In March 1961, in the course of a comprehensive government reorganization, he combined the party leadership with the presidency of the republic in the new office of Chairman of the State Council.

The consolidation of his personal power was accompanied by the rise of two men who were to play a significant role in the confrontation with the Soviet Union. The first was Nicolae Ceausescu, a symbol of the young generation of native Communists, who after the 1957 purge emerged as second in command of the party apparatus in charge of personnel and organization. The other was Ion Gheorghe Maurer. Born in 1902 the scion of a professional family, of part French and part German extraction, Maurer had been a defense counsel for the Communists in the 1930s and had liberated Gheorghiu-Dej from the concentration camp in 1944. After acting as chief assistant to Gheorghiu-Dej in the first postwar years and being elected to the Central Committee, he dropped out of public life for almost a decade. In 1955, he was even demoted to a candidate member of the leading party body. His meteoric rise later, often over the heads of those who could claim greater seniority, coincided with the consolidation of Gheorghiu-Dej's position. As soon as Gheorghiu-Dej and his friends decided to strike out on their own on the home front and in international politics, this highly competent, ruggedly handsome, personable man rapidly became Rumania's chief "traveling salesman" and principal troubleshooter. Appointed Foreign Minister in 1957, he succeeded Petru Groza as head of state one year later and also rose quickly in the party ranks. In June 1958, at a Central Committee plenum, he was again made a full member, and barely two years later, at the party congress in 1960, he entered the ruling Politburo. In March of the following year, he replaced Chivu Stoica as Premier. The available evidence suggests that Maurer has been all along, both before and after Gheorghiu-Dej's death, one of the chief architects of Rumania's increasingly independent foreign policy.

In trying to understand the forces that shape Rumanian policies, the intimate and intangible something that might be called the "character structure" of the principal actors has to be taken into account. Thus when the analyst seeks to date the beginning of the Rumanian "heresy," he cannot separate the shifts in political emphasis from the psychological and emotional elements, even the passions, involved in changing secret resentment of Soviet hegemony into a dominant political trend. In the light of the revelations made at the Central Committee meeting held in November-December 1961, in the wake of the Twenty-Second Soviet Party Congress, it is not surprising that the Rumanian leaders launched their daring move toward national emancipation sooner than anyone might have expected.

Gheorghiu-Dej coped easily with Khrushchev's second de-Stalinization campaign. After towns, streets, and institutions named after Stalin, or after any other living person (that is Gheorghiu-Dej himself), had been renamed, there was virtually nothing more to be done. Gheorghiu-Dej asserted that he had been a helpless prisoner of the Pauker group and, by purging them, had restored "collective leadership." In fact, if not in so many words, he claimed that he had been the first to de-Stalinize—and that during the height of Stalinism.

The real political significance of the Central Committee plenum lay, however, in its portrayal of the entire history of the party as a battle between the "alien elements" or "immigrant groups" on the one hand, and the "native" Communists on the other. Speaker after speaker elaborated on the long struggle between the various Muscovite leaders and those "comrades who risked arrest and execution, who suffered the burden of prisons and concentration camps (in Rumania) . . . who fought with international brigades against Franco in Spain or in France against the German occupation." It was the exiles in Moscow who after their return had propagated the cult of Stalin, enjoyed the sympathy of Molotov's anti-party group in belittling and disapproving the exploits of the home Communists, including the August uprising, and "opposed and hindered the promotion of those activists who were connected with the working class and the people."[23]

In retrospect, it appears that this Central Committee meeting with its strongly nationalistic and implicitly anti-Soviet overtones was a covert manifesto of independence addressed to the initiate among the by now almost 900,000 party members.[24] The plenum, whose significance was overlooked at the time, was the first major step toward the party's full identification with the Rumanian people. Freed from the stigma of being "un-Rumanian," the party leadership started a coordinated effort to release the latent spirit of national identity.

Regardless of the prevailing circumstances in 1952 when the Pauker group was purged, the important fact is that the victors, the veterans of the Communist underground inside the country, saw the move even then as a strategic defeat of the "foreign elements." In other words, Gheorghiu-Dej and his friends had *felt* all along— even though they had acted differently—frustrated and embittered by their political servility to and economic exploitation by Moscow. The interpretation of the long-forgotten Pauker affair thus became a political factor of prime importance in the startlingly different context of 1961. What had looked like a "normal" power struggle for so many years was now used as a device to restore a sense of purpose and newly found self-confidence in the party and to offer hope to a sullen and demoralized nation. Within fourteen months the question at issue was no longer the nationalistic rewriting of party history, but the whole problem of relations with the Soviet Union and the nature of the relationship.

Rumania steps out of line

Rumania's drive for national independence was not initiated by a dramatic act of defiance. Rather, it grew out of a series of calculated moves that initially combined a short-term defense with a long-term offensive strategy. The emancipation from Russia was a "quiet revolution," profoundly Rumanian in its character and style, a mixture of restraint in manner and toughness in intent, so brilliantly controlled, so matchlessly executed that the Rumanian search for autonomy was startlingly different, not only from the successful Yugoslav and Albanian rebellions but also from the abortive Hungarian uprising.

By the end of 1961, Gheorghiu-Dej and his associates, exuberantly reclaiming a national identity as Rumanian Communists who had saved the party and, by implication, the country from Moscow-trained "foreign elements," were probably irrevocably committed to a course of independence. What appears to have been decisive in influencing the major policy decisions were three important considerations:

(1.) The Rumanian leadership early showed a profound grasp of the nature of the Sino-Soviet conflict and the whole new range of possibilities for maneuver it held out to the East European nations.

(2.) The policy-makers and the party functionaries in Bucharest were firmly united and prompted by genuine national pride.

(3.) The main issue that sparked off the open confrontation with Moscow was the Rumanian leaders' unflinching determination to pursue an all-round industrialization, and their handling of this pivotal issue represented something like a national consensus.

It is very difficult, if not impossible, to date the beginning of the coordinated efforts to gain independence of action. To pick out particular events, such as the withdrawal of Soviet troops in 1958, and generalize from them would be as unwise as to regard subsequent Rumanian moves purely as dazzling improvisations. Many important aspects are still shrouded in secrecy and, at best, obscure. But if the past is re-examined with the benefit of present knowledge, based partly on "off-the-record" conversations with informed Rumanian Communists, it seems probable that the 1956 crises in Hungary and Poland were the precipitating factors in laying the domestic foundations for the anticipated shift by the Gheorghiu-Dej group.

The purge of the last potential rivals in the summer of 1957 consolidated the supreme position of the home Communists. The departure of the Soviet troops the following year provided another important psychological and political precondition for furbishing the party's image and enabling the leadership to hitch its long-term strategy to the dynamics of nationalism. Though the Rumanian leaders concealed their goal for a time behind a screen of cloudy phrases and courtly attitudes toward the Soviet Union, in the late 1950s they moved with sure instinct and remarkable dexterity, testing new possibilities abroad and breaking out of political isolation at home.

The accelerated creation of an industrial base involving full industrial exploitation of domestic raw materials, coupled with the lessening of economic dependence on the Soviet Union and the

more developed East European countries, became the core of a
broad national line, which dominated the preparations for drawing
up an ambitious six-year plan covering the period 1960 to 1965. An
increasing reliance on Western technology and trade was already
evident during the 1958–60 period when a purposeful reorientation
of over-all foreign trade reduced the Soviet share of the total from
51.5 per cent in 1958 to 47.3 per cent in 1959 and 40.1 per cent in
1960.

It is worth underlining the point that the blueprint for an industrialized Rumania was not only rooted in legitimate national
aspirations, but also corresponded to Lenin's frequent references to
heavy industry as the precondition for the construction of socialism.
On both national and ideological grounds the Rumanian position
was unassailable. Another fundamental consideration was singularly
favorable material conditions. Until 1960 the growth of investments
in Rumania lagged behind all other Communist countries in
Eastern Europe, mainly because of the staggering inheritance of
ruthless Soviet exploitation.[25]

Yet the country's natural wealth was greater than that of any
other East European country. Abundant natural resources—oil,
natural gas, timber, bauxite, coal, manganese, copper, lead, zinc,
uranium, and hydro-energy potential plus the fertile plains that
make the country self-supporting in cereals and the 150-mile coastline on the Black Sea—have played a crucial role in Rumania's
willingness and ability to resist plans that would have placed the
country at the mercy of its "rich" neighbors. Also, measured by
Balkan standards, it had a relatively large industrial base, accounting for 30 per cent of the national income before World War II.
Untapped potential wealth and an abundance of labor (peasants
accounted for almost 70 per cent of the population in 1956) were
further inducements to a many-sided industrialization. Moreover,
by the beginning of the sixties the government could rely on
sizable technical and managerial cadres, trained since the war,
who were eager to get to work and whose active loyalty was
indispensable.

The ambitious Rumanian program gradually became part of a
broader conflict of interests between the "have" and "have not"
members of Comecon, the organization for cooperation founded in
1949 as the Communist answer to the Marshall Plan. Encompassing
the eight Communist-ruled countries of Eastern Europe, Comecon

(or, as officially called, Council for Mutual Economic Assistance—CMEA) took the first steps toward meaningful cooperation and specialization shortly after Stalin's death, only to have them brought to an abrupt halt by the upheavals of 1956. At a summit meeting of the East European leaders in 1958, an ambitious program to promote industrial specialization and coordination of the long-term plans of the member countries was drawn up. But it soon became apparent that a real and not merely verbal "socialist international division of labor" would require multilateral arrangements that in one way or another would involve the right of the individual Comecon member states to determine priorities of allocation and the chief directions of economic development. The more developed countries, like Czechoslovakia and East Germany, worked more and more vigorously to convince the less developed members of the need for specialization by whole industries and not just of the production of certain types of products. From the very beginning, the attempt to cut waste and duplication implied that Rumania and Bulgaria should devote their main resources to agriculture and raw materials, restricting their industries to those few that fit bloc-wide needs. In the dispute between the advanced and the underdeveloped countries that ensued, the Kremlin at first remained in the background, partly because economically the dispute about the scope of industrialization was of only marginal importance to the Soviet Union. But when the Soviet attitude toward supranational planning shifted, the "normal" wrangling between the have and have not members of Comecon was transformed into a highly charged Soviet-Rumanian political confrontation.

At the Twenty-first Soviet Party Congress in February 1959 Khrushchev had spoken about a "more or less simultaneous" transition to communism by all socialist countries, indicating that the less developed countries would be allowed to catch up with the more industrialized members of Comecon; and the statutes of the integration body, adopted in 1960, stressed the principle of voluntary cooperation and the unanimity ruling. This legal escape hatch later proved crucial when Rumania successfully opposed decisions being made by majority vote. Though the optimistic Rumanian six-year plan and a simultaneously published fifteen-year program of economic expansion encountered some Soviet opposition, particularly the construction of the big Galati steel plant (initially planned to produce 4 million tons of steel by 1970),[26] Khrushchev paid warm tributes to both documents and praised Gheorghiu-Dej at the Rumanian Party Congress in June 1960.

Already entrapped in heated polemics with the Chinese delegation at the same congress, the Soviet leader was clearly bent on stressing the solidarity of the bloc rather than adding to his troubles by criticizing his hosts. Whatever reservations the Russians may have had about the Rumanian requests for substantial supplies of equipment and raw material, they went on record as supporters of the Rumanian program and duly signed a number of important agreements, including the delivery of installations worth 500 million dollars for the controversial Galati plant. By the end of 1961, however, the Rumanians had good reason to suspect that the Soviet leadership was reassessing its previous ambiguous attitude and moving closer to the viewpoints held by the supporters of over-all economic integration. As early as the Central Committee plenum in December 1961, the then chairman of the State Planning Committee, Gheorghe Gaston Marin, had sounded a note of warning, criticizing "certain erroneous theories" which would deny each socialist country the right to build its own heavy industry, and which "present in a distorted manner the principles of specialization and cooperation within the socialist international division of labor."

In early 1962, Gheorghiu-Dej's main concern was to head off any full-scale conflict, to reassure the Russians about the prudence of the Rumanian industrialization course and at the same time dissuade them from pushing the integration controversy to the point of final decisions. One of the most consummate political tacticians of postwar communism, he had not forgotten Lenin's remark that "those politicians of the revolutionary class who are unable to maneuver, to compromise in order to avoid an obviously disadvantageous battle, are good for nothing."

In retrospect, it is clear that some of the Rumanian moves on the home front at this time were designed to brace the party for the forthcoming showdown, which by then was regarded inevitable. To extend the party's appeal across class lines, the token de-Stalinization was coupled with changes in the rules of admission to the party, making it possible for members of the prewar "bourgeois" parties to join. While the technical intelligentsia was purposefully recruited, functionaries holding key positions were rigorously screened and, in a number of cases, quietly replaced by younger men whose loyalty to the leadership was beyond doubt. Some Rumanian sources claim that even the sudden completion of agricultural collectivization in the spring of 1962, more than three years ahead of the original schedule, must be seen in the context of the domestic consolidation of the regime—in both the ideological and technical sense—on the eve of open friction with Moscow.[27]

The Sino-Soviet conflict had a dual impact on Soviet-Rumanian relations. On the one hand, it weakened Moscow's willingness and ability to cope swiftly and ruthlessly with lesser malcontents. On the other, it strengthened Khrushchev in his determination to consolidate Soviet control—military, political, and economic—over Eastern Europe. In addition to the Warsaw Pact, Comecon was to be the principal economic and political instrument of Soviet hegemony.

Khrushchev, who always tended to regard restraint as evidence of weakness, in mid-1962 moved to prepare a qualitative change in the character and scope of Comecon. At a summit meeting of the East European party leaders in June 1962 it was agreed to establish an Executive Committee, consisting of the Deputy Premiers of the Comecon member countries, to coordinate planning. The conference also published a document about the principles of the division of labor, the unanimity ruling, and the independence and sovereignty of the individual member states. But what Khrushchev and his Czech and East German allies regarded as a minimum, a first step on the road to an integrated bloc-wide economy, the Rumanians saw as the absolute maximum of external interference in national economic planning.

In the months following the summit meeting, the differences gradually came to a head. Immediately after the meeting, Khrushchev paid his last official visit to Rumania. Publicly he advocated the advantages of closer coordination and specialization (at much greater length than his hosts did). Privately, like Walter Ulbricht on a similar mission to Rumania three months later, he combined economic arguments with threats. A long article by Khrushchev in September 1962 calling publicly for the integration of the economies of the Comecon countries along supranational lines may well have been the spark that ignited the long accumulating tinder. Henceforth, a supranational planning agency would select investment projects, allocate resources, and prescribe the economic policies of the individual members by majority rule.

The Soviet scheme would have put an abrupt end to Rumania's industrialization program, already surging ahead at an impressive pace, and relegated the country to the role of supplying food and raw materials to the economically more advanced Comecon members. Whatever the advantages in raising bloc-wide efficiency, integration on Soviet terms would have frozen the widely disparate levels of development instead of helping the less developed countries to catch up.

The political implications were even more ominous. Progress toward supranational economic decision-making was bound to lead to a covert political unification, ultimately to the disappearance of national state boundaries. Lacking either a market mechanism or a reliable yardstick for measuring the real cost of a given investment (because of the manifold discrepancies between costs and prices), a truly bloc-wide division of labor was impossible without infringing on national control over economic policy. This indeed was the main point so cunningly enmeshed in arguments and pleas about the advantages of pooling economic resources. The Rumanian leadership, perceived the underlying trends in the situation at an early date, took a defensive stance combined with a long-term advance, moving with deftness and flexibility to exploit what was becoming a deep and irrevocable split between Moscow and Peking.

The hour of decision struck in early March 1963 when the Rumanian Central Committee published a resolution after a three-day-long enlarged plenum of the supreme leading body. It ostentatiously pledged full support to the stand taken by the Rumanian representative, Vice Premier Alexandru Birladeanu, at the previous meeting of the newly founded Comecon Executive Committee. Reliable reports agree that at that stormy session in February in Moscow, Birladeanu flatly and definitely rejected the blueprint of supranational integration and in particular the proposed device of majority decisions. The resolution pointedly declared that the main means of developing the division of labor successfully was the "coordination of national economic plans" based "on respect for national independence and sovereignty, of full equality of rights, comradely mutual aid, and reciprocal advantage."[28]

Immediately after the publication of the communique the party held a series of closed meetings throughout the country to explain that the future of Rumanian industrialization and, by implication, national independence was at stake; that the party was pitting itself against "erroneous conceptions" which would "profoundly harm the elementary interests of our nation" and run counter to the unanimously adopted principles about the complete equality of the Comecon member states. According to Rumanian sources, the atmosphere at the meetings was often initially one of stunned surprise, soon changing to powerful emotional support tinged with nationalistic and anti-Soviet outbursts.[29]

By bringing the long simmering differences into the open and presenting the nation with the truth, Gheorghiu-Dej and his associates reached a point of no return. This was the beginning of the daring venture to replace Soviet protection by popular backing. Up to then "Moscow had protected its vassals from popular anger; now the people (and the West) should protect the regime from the fury of the Kremlin."[30] The Rumanian party had known its greatest isolation when as a detachment of an international movement centered in Russia it had defied traditional nationalism. Conversely, its only chance of winning a measure of popular acceptance and becoming politically effective was when it followed a patriotic line as in the summer of 1944.

Thus, beneath the deceptive surface of a docile satellite, the leadership by early 1963 had embarked on a line of economic and political independence, which, despite a grim domestic record, from then on steadily broadened the popular basis of what the public came to regard as a national and flamboyantly pro-Rumanian, even if Communist, regime. The rebuke to a Soviet historian at the end of 1962 who, as mentioned earlier, ignored the August 23 coup and the role the Rumanian Communists claim to have played was an opening shot, a warning understood only by a handful of the initiate in Bucharest and Moscow.[31] Now, however, the leadership presented the nation with a new conception not only of itself and its potentialities but also of the dangers posed by foreign meddling. No matter how great the risks involved, the Communists gave a sullen and demoralized population a sense of national purpose that transcended all divisions, personal grudges, and bitter memories.

At the same time the Rumanian leaders began staking out an independent line, a policy of non-alignment in the Sino-Soviet dispute. Through a series of seemingly small but deviously calculated gestures, they avoided total identification with Moscow in the worsening quarrel with Peking and gave notice to the world that the Rumanian-Soviet friction was political as well as economic. In contrast to the rest of the bloc press, the Rumanian papers published no attacks on Peking and Tirana. On the contrary, at the very time the Soviet Union and its allies were radically curbing their trade with China, Rumania increased theirs. The Rumanian Ambassador, who had been withdrawn from Albania along with the other Communist chiefs of mission at the end of 1961, quietly returned to his post in Tirana in March 1963, and almost at once a new trade agreement involving considerably higher exchanges was signed by the two countries. While the controversy at subsequent meetings of the Comecon Executive Committee gathered steam, the Rumanians held their ground. Despite a visit by a high-level Soviet delegation, Gheorghiu-Dej, with consummate timing and remarkable political flair, moved swiftly to exploit the conflict and win considerable freedom of action.

Though there is no public evidence, it is probable that in 1962 the Chinese gave the Rumanian leaders direct encouragement in their bold resistance to Khrushchev's plan of supranational economic integration. By mid-1963, the integration controversy figured prominently in the polemical broadsides issued from Peking. The famous twenty-five points in the Chinese letter of June 14 to the Soviet party about the issues that should be discussed in the forthcoming bilateral talks contained several barely veiled references to integration which implicitly supported the Rumanian position: "Such economic cooperation must be based on the principles of complete equality, mutual benefit, and comradely mutual assistance. It would be great-power chauvinism to deny these principles and, in the name of the 'international division of labor' and 'specialization,' to impose one's will on others, to infringe or harm the interests of their people."[32]

The Rumanians lost no time in underlining their neutral position on the eve of the abortive Sino-Soviet talks. Every East European regime except Rumania (and of course Albania and Yugoslavia) followed Moscow, which officially stated that the letter containing "slanders and distortions" would not be published. *Scinteia,* the central Rumanian party organ, on June 22 published a long account of the twenty-five points. Despite the fact that the paper also reprinted the Soviet policy statements, this was an act of open defiance and dramatically weakened the Soviet position at a crucial juncture in the conflict with Peking. A few days later, the Rumanians added insult to injury: alone of the East European Communist leaders,

Gheorghiu-Dej failed to appear at the meeting in East Berlin at the end of June on the occasion of Ulbricht's seventieth birthday.

At no point did the Rumanian party leave any doubt that the leaders in Bucharest were in broad agreement with Moscow on the main political and ideological issues—peaceful coexistence, the non-inevitability of war, the nuclear test ban treaty, or even the rapprochement with "revisionist" Yugoslavia. What divided Bucharest and Moscow was the equally basic issue of the right of each party in power to act independently in pursuing its own rather than Soviet interests. The distinction between proletarian internationalism, which meant loyalty to the Soviet Union, and national independence, which meant independence from Soviet domination, was the basis of Rumania's opposition to the way the Soviets handled the conflict with China and the dispute within Comecon.

The peculiarly Rumanian tactic of audaciously pressing forward, yet always stopping short of unforgivable provocation caught Khrushchev on the horns of a predictable dilemma. Fully preoccupied with China and faced with Rumanian opposition, he reluctantly shelved his ambitious plan for a supranational planning body at the Moscow meeting of the party leaders in July 1963. Although controversies over East European integration have been going on ever since, the outcome of the showdown was an important victory for the Rumanians with far-reaching consequences. The Soviet plan for a closely integrated bloc-wide economic structure as a prelude to political unification was in ruins. Comecon remained an organization of national economies cooperating with each other along both bilateral and multilateral lines. The Rumanians have shown no intention so far of leaving it. Why should they, if they can enjoy membership on their own terms? Rumania participates in several joint ventures such as the Comecon bank, the rolling stock pool, and the unified power grid, but has not joined multilateral groupings in metallurgy and ball-bearing production. Its general attitude toward all proposals has always been decided in terms of purely national interests and considerations. Or as Premier Maurer was reported to have said once in private conversation, "Why should we ship our corn to Poland so that the Poles can fatten their pigs in order to buy machinery in the West, when we can sell our corn to the West and buy machinery that we need?"

The July summit meeting in Moscow marked the end of the primarily economic phase of Soviet-Rumanian differences. To the bitter disappointment of Khrushchev, the Rumanians were not restrained but encouraged by their victory to press forward more boldly in their quest for national identity and freedom of action. There followed the process of de-Russification and the revival of national traditions gradually encompassing various fields of culture and science. The twin issues of economic dynamism and national spirit were the main instruments of the new course which enlivened the country and kindled the hopes of the population.

Without the Sino-Soviet conflict, Rumania would hardly have been able to challenge Moscow with impunity and to embark so demonstratively on a "Rumania first" policy. The critical question for the future was the power struggle between Moscow and Peking. A real reconciliation, giving Khrushchev a much freer hand to deal with the Rumanian "deviationists," was no longer in the cards in late 1963. But what posed a mortal danger to Rumania's precarious freedom of maneuver was the Soviet campaign for the public excommunication of China from the Communist movement, coupled with mounting pressure to close the ranks among the "faithful." After having sabotaged supranational integration, the Rumanians now emerged as "honest brokers," attempting to prevent the final split. Premier Maurer published a remarkable article in the November 1963 issue of *Problems of Peace and Socialism*, the international Communist monthly, calling for an end to public polemics and indirectly lecturing both sides. In March 1964 he headed a Rumanian delegation that made a last-minute attempt at mediation, meeting with Mao in Peking and with Khrushchev on the way home. Under Rumanian pressure Moscow agreed to postpone for six weeks the publication of a policy statement made by Central Committee Secretary Mikhail Suslov, which was a full-scale vitriolic attack on the Chinese leadership and called for a Communist world conference with the obvious purpose of expelling China from the movement.

Though the Rumanian initiatives failed, they provided a stunning proof of Rumania's rapid progress from a seemingly docile satellite to an independent force in world communism. While the Sino-Soviet conflict gained impetus, Rumanian-Soviet relations entered the phase of venomous tensions. As in the case of Stalin's break with Tito and the Albanian-Soviet split, the differences in interests and policies were complicated and heightened by personal factors. Gheorghiu-Dej was a latter-day successor of Petru Rares and the other medieval Rumanian princes who, by a virtuoso performance in intrigue, deceit, and maneuvering, divided their powerful adversaries and survived in the face of overwhelming odds. Rumanian delegations fanned out around the world on shopping and political missions. Maintenance of good or "correct" relations with such opposites as Albania and Yugoslavia, the United States and China, bolstered Rumania's bargaining power and world standing. The changes in the international situation as a result of the Cuba affair, the test ban treaty, and a more imaginative and differentiated Western policy, combined with the erosion of Soviet authority in the world Communist movement, defined the boundaries of effective Soviet response to the Rumanian challenge. And the Rumanian leadership took great care to avoid publicly offending Moscow and giving any pretext for a frontal attack.

The fact remained that Rumania was not a minor irritant, but an important new element of instability and the carrier of a dangerously contagious disease—pragmatic nationalism. There were, of course, serious factors that limited the Rumanian challenge: adverse geographical conditions, economic dependence on the Soviet Union, which still accounted for over 42 per cent of the country's trade in 1964, and the military preponderance of the Soviet power center, to which Rumania was still ostensibly tied by the "unshakable bonds" of a common ideology. Yet at no point during the dispute was Moscow able to alter the main direction of Rumania's new course.

Khrushchev's impetuous attempts, lacking imagination and consistency and pervaded by hostility and a feeling of betrayal, did not deter but inflamed the seething resentment the Rumanian leaders had harbored so long. They recognized that Khrushchev could not afford a second Albania, especially on Russia's doorstep. To the Kremlin both an open rupture and a continued toleration of Rumanian defiance involved great risks.

Several accounts given me by Rumanian sources agree that the mutual animosity between Gheorghiu-Dej and Khrushchev exacerbated the clash of interests that lay at the heart of the dispute. According to one version, Khrushchev during his official visit in the summer of 1962 accused the Rumanians of being "unreasonable, egotistic, and self-exalted." By mid-1963 the personal relationship between Gheorghiu-Dej and Khrushchev was near the freezing point.

In the autumn of 1963, Khrushchev, according to reliable reports, made one of his fateful misjudgments. After his secret visit to Bucharest, which failed to bridge the widening gap, the Soviet leaders organized a concerted attempt by their agents in the security service, the general staff of the army, and the party apparatus to unseat Gheorghiu-Dej. Though they also solicited support from some highly placed functionaries, it was too late to infiltrate and subvert the top leadership. Many rumors circulating in Bucharest and reported in the Western press alleged that it was General Emil Bodnaras, for many years Moscow's trusted chief Rumanian agent, whom the Russians tried to use to overthrow the Gheorghiu-Dej regime. Certain cryptic allusions in speeches made by Gheorghiu-Dej and Bodnaras at the latter's sixtieth birthday in February 1964 appear to lend credence to the rumors. Bodnaras, however, threw his prestige and weight behind his country's new course and participated in important missions to Peking, Moscow, and Belgrade.[33]

The Russians may also have tried to persuade the other ranking Soviet-trained Politburo member, Petre Borila, previously in charge of the armed forces. He rarely appeared in public after 1962 and was dropped from the Politburo at the last party congress in July 1965. But he remained a member of the Executive Committee and made a covertly anti-Soviet speech at the national party conference at the end of 1967. Whether his loss of stature was due to a serious illness, as Rumanian officials maintain, or rather to his having been at some point susceptible to Soviet enticements is bound to remain in the realm of speculation.

The fact of a major but unsuccessful Soviet-sponsored conspiracy is beyond dispute, and this made it abundantly clear to everyone concerned that the question at issue was the destruction or survival of the Rumanian leadership. The mood of revulsion engendered by Soviet meddling spread rapidly from the party functionaries to the inarticulate masses.

Traveling in the country during the tense weeks of April 1964, in conversations with officials, intellectuals, and friends, I was struck by the emotion, even passion, with which they discussed their country's present course. A mixture of exuberant nationalism and excitement over economic expansion combined with an air of living dangerously was the overriding impression. At the construction site of the Galati steel plant, the chief engineer did not show the slightest trace of uncertainty about the promised Russian deliveries of machinery and iron ore, but added significantly, "We have every chance of becoming a developed industrial country, and no one can stop us utilizing our resources." The Foreign Trade Minister, asked about Czech and East German complaints over the Rumanians switching their purchases of machinery to Western suppliers, dryly remarked, "We equip our factories with nothing but the best and most modern machinery wherever it may come from. This has nothing to do with politics, or with our friendship with the socialist countries. In this field there is only one principle—business is business."

Even then Rumania was perhaps the most thoroughly de-Russianized state in Eastern Europe—except, of course, for Yugoslavia. Aside from the automatic loyalties in the conflict with Moscow, however, the popular mood had not yet turned into one of hope and confidence. The repression was so serious; the corruption so corroding; the grip of the Securitate, the dreaded secret police, so tight that the national line had only begun to thaw the top layer of ice.

The conflict with Moscow had a dual impact on the home front. The need for popular support meant that the Rumanian leaders had to meet some of the aspirations of the people for more freedom and affluence. But the very fact that the Communist rulers were engaged in a life-and-death contest with the people who had originally put them in power was a compelling reason to continue tight control and a cautious approach to internal reforms.

With the Soviet offensive against Communist China in full swing, there was suspense in the air. The Rumanians were left no choice but to take a stand. After the failure of the Rumanian mediation attempt, the Soviet press on April 3, 1964, after a delay of six weeks, published Suslov's violently aggressive speech and the call of the Central Committee for a world Communist meeting. A spate of anti-Chinese editorials and speeches in all East European capitals followed. Khrushchev, then touring Hungary, made a series of major speeches attacking the Chinese, and his Hungarian hosts faithfully echoed his accusations.

For three weeks the Rumanian press ignored the open eruption of the Sino-Soviet conflict. This silence was the beginning of a new gambit. Rumania was to become the first Communist country to use "news management" as an integral part of over-all policy. A unique mixture of omissions and leaks has since become a familiar and useful instrument for the policy-makers. The deliberate silence in April 1964 indicated that Rumania was not going to join either side in the great Communist schism. The Bucharest papers, although as monotonous as ever, presented their readers with news pages unparalleled in either the East or the West. On April 10, for example, *Scinteia,* the party organ, reported in thirty-two lines President Johnson's press conference, and in eighteen lines the "elections" in Malavi (formerly Nyasaland). A major speech by Khrushchev about "goulash communism" in Hungary got only fifteen lines. When asked about this curious way of news reporting, the editor told me matter-of-factly, "We do not like long speeches. We prefer news. Furthermore we have other means to inform our public." Four years later the Rumanians still remained faithful to their rule—any references to the Sino-Soviet conflict were expunged from statements and speeches of Soviet and Chinese spokesmen.

To underscore Rumania's neutrality, Gheorghiu-Dej not only failed to turn up at festivities celebrating Khrushchev's seventieth birthday (attended by all East European party chiefs) but deliberately scheduled the plenum of the party's Central Committee for that time. This unprecedentedly long meeting, which lasted from April 15 to 22, was preceded by Khrushchev's last desperate attempt to maintain at least a façade of unity in the campaign against Peking. According to an account given this writer by a well-known Communist journalist almost a year after the event, the last personal confrontation between Gheorghiu-Dej and Khrushchev had all the trappings of what may be called a Communist melodrama.

One morning in late March the telephone rang on the desk of the Rumanian President's personal secretary. It was a call from the then Soviet Ambassador Shegalin, who wanted to speak to Gheorghiu-Dej himself. The ambassador informed the Rumanian leader that Khrushchev had just landed at a military airport near the capital. He would like to ask Comrade Gheorghiu-Dej to call on him in the Soviet Embassy at a convenient time. Gheorghiu-Dej's answer was curt and icy, "Rumania is a sovereign state and expects that even the leaders of friendly states should land on her territory only after mutual agreement. In any case the head of state is not accustomed to conducting talks in the buildings of foreign embassies. Comrade Khrushchev may come, if he wishes, at 4 P.M. to my residence."

There is, of course, no way of verifying the accuracy of this version. All accounts I heard agreed, however, on the main point: Khrushchev made a second, secret mission to Bucharest, and after a dramatic encounter, the two men parted irreconcilable foes. Whatever the truth in the many lurid details that circulated later among the public at large, the Soviet leader was certainly received in a way that would have been inconceivable two years earlier.

The decisive step in Rumania's drive for independence and the most daring gesture of defiance was the famous statement issued by the enlarged plenum of the Central Committee on April 26, 1964. It has been aptly called a "Declaration of Independence," since it staked out and proclaimed Rumania's right to national autonomy and full equality in the Communist world. Behind the stale platitudes of Communist language, the declaration publicly and fiercely rejected not only economic integration and suprastate planning, but also every form of Soviet supremacy. It provided something like a coherent ideological basis for a "go-it-alone" economic policy. Such schemes as a joint plan, a single planning body for all Comecon member states, and internationally owned joint enterprises "would turn sovereignty into a notion devoid of any content," it declared, stressing that "the planned management of the national economy is one of the fundamental, essential, and inalienable attributes of the sovereignty of the socialist state," and that, in order to exercise these attributes, the state must hold in its own hand "all the levers" with which economic and social life is managed.

The resolution went far beyond the framework of the integration dispute, which had already been settled in favor of the Rumanians. It spelled out the Rumanian party's independent course in the Sino-Soviet conflict and, while supporting by and large the Soviet stand on the substance of the controversial issues, condemned both sides with equal force for engaging in public polemics. Countering the Soviet proposal to organize a new world Communist meeting as a "collective rebuff" to China, the Rumanians insisted that a conference must include "all" Communist and workers' parties.

Politically the most important and novel aspect was the forthright rejection of any form of satellization and the proclamation of the complete independence of all Communist parties. "No one can decide what is and what is not correct for other countries and parties. There is not and cannot be a 'parent' party and a 'son' party, a 'superior' and a 'subordinate' party. No party has or can have a privileged position, or impose its line and opinion on other parties."

The turgid prose of the declaration, and indeed of all subsequent policy statements, is punctuated with the vocabulary of nationalism —"sovereignty," "equal rights," "national interest." In view of the "concrete conditions of great diversity," the strict observance of equal rights, of non-interference in internal affairs, and of each party's exclusive right to solve its own political problems and work out its own political line is the "only" basis for unity.

The defiantly nationalistic tone of the entire document indicates how fierce the Rumanian opposition to Soviet-sponsored projects of economic and political unification must have been when they were discussed behind closed doors. Once again meetings were held all over the country to rally public support for the leaders, who had burned their bridges by bringing their vigorous arguments against foreign domination into the open. Compared to the campaign a year earlier, the tone was even more outspoken and bitter. The private party brief to the membership went considerably further than the April Declaration. Soviet policies, past exploitation of the country, Khrushchev's attempt to subvert and unseat the leadership were criticized in the strongest terms. The speakers presented the 1.4 million party members with the picture of a small but potentially rich country humiliated and threatened by a powerful and rapacious neighbor. No compromise was possible—it was Rumania or Russia. The same terrible historical truths aroused the same powerful emotional response. The verve and ingenuity the leadership displayed putting its pro-Rumanian policy in action won general support and new respect, even grudging admiration for the party.

The "Declaration of Independence" was both a product of the new polycentric era in international communism and a factor that hastened the fragmentation of Soviet hegemony in Eastern Europe. Because of the timing, the Rumanian leaders, unlike Tito, did not have to pay the penalty of expulsion from the camp. But they were nevertheless skating on very thin ice indeed, and the momentum generated by their pragmatic nationalism brought Soviet-Rumanian relations near the breaking point more than once.

The mounting tensions in the aftermath of the declarations were evident in the sharp polemics between the Rumanian-language broadcasts of Radio Moscow and Radio Bucharest, in the suspended publication of the Rumanian edition of the international Communist Journal, *Problems of Peace and Socialism,* and culminated in the so-called Valev controversy in June–July 1964. E. B. Valev, a Soviet economist, published an article in a Moscow University academic journal about "interstate economic complexes." He specifically mentioned the establishment of such an economically integrated region on the lower Danube that would comprise about 42 per cent of

Rumania's and one-third of Bulgaria's territory combined with a small part of Soviet Ukraine. It is difficult to believe that such an ambitious scheme of economic unification, implying the disappearance of state boundaries, could have been put forward independently by a professor in a country where even statements of less import have to be cleared by superior authorities. Whatever its background, Valev's scheme represented prevalent Soviet thinking along these lines and showed what the future might have held in store for Rumania—and indeed for all other East European countries—had Khrushchev's grand design been implemented.

The Bucharest economic weekly *Viata Economica* of June 13 published a violent rejoinder to the proposal, which it stated was nothing less than "a plan for the violation of the territorial integrity of Rumania, for the dismemberment of its national and state unity." Though *Izvestia* in Moscow barely three weeks later repudiated the proposals, the episode gave a severe jolt to bilateral relations. It was a warning that has never been forgotten, and Rumanian officials still allude to the "Valev scheme" as a proof of the dangers to which their country was exposed.

Meanwhile anti-Russian ferment reached such dimensions that Khrushchev conveyed several warnings (allegedly also through Tito, who in June met both the Soviet leader and Gheorghiu-Dej) that there was a limit to what the Russians were willing to tolerate. The dispatch of two high-level Rumanian delegations to Moscow, led respectively by Premier Maurer and Chivu Stoica, temporarily eased the strains, but the Rumanians continued on their independent road. When Moscow in July formally proposed that a preliminary conference of twenty-six parties (the members of the preparatory commission for the 1960 Moscow Communist meeting) meet in December 1964 to prepare for a new world conference, the Rumanians refused the invitation. After Khrushchev's fall, his successors eventually convened the meeting on March 1, 1965, in Moscow, but the Rumanian party along with the Chinese, Albanian, and four other invited parties, did not participate.

Though the Russians, however irritated, were unlikely to push the Rumanians to the point of an open break, Gheorghiu-Dej and his associates took no chances. They administered their policy with equal deftness and flexibility toward the West as toward the East. The two most significant steps taken to strengthen relations with the West were the mission of Deputy Premier Gaston Marin to Washington in May–June 1964, followed by the visit of Premier Maurer to France a month later. These, like similar missions to Austria, Italy, Japan, and other non-Communist countries, were as much political as economic in character. The restoration of traditional ties and the emergence of Rumania on the international stage (on three occasions in 1963–64 its representative deviated from the Soviet bloc vote in the United Nations) also involved a subtle bid for moral and psychological support by a small country swimming in uncharted waters.

Nowhere perhaps was the Rumanian combination of will, nerve, and cunning more impressive than in maintaining "cordial relations" with both China (and Albania) and the very country the Maoists regard as the epitome of "revisionist treachery and capitalist degeneration," Yugoslavia. It is often forgotten that Yugoslavia was a telling example of the benefits to be reaped from an independent position. Furthermore, in contrast to Russia, Hungary, and Bulgaria, which were embroiled in territorial disputes of varying intensity with Rumania, Yugoslavia was a traditional friend, a former ally in the Little Entente and the Balkan Pact in the interwar period. When Yugoslavia was attacked on all sides in 1941, even General Antonescu, though a staunch Nazi ally, refused to cooperate in the carving up and in the attack. After World War II, however, Rumania like the other satellites obediently followed Stalin's order and switched from friendship to implacable hostility. The seat of the Cominform was transferred to Bucharest, which became one of the centers of the campaign vilifying Tito, and Gheorghiu-Dej, as a native Communist, was chosen to deliver the sharpest Cominform denunciations in November 1949.

Yet Tito in June 1956 preferred to pass through Rumania rather than Hungary on his way to Moscow, and on the return journey stopped in Bucharest. He clearly regarded Gheorghiu-Dej as the erstwhile prisoner of the Muscovite Pauker-Luca group, by then purged. Some Rumanian sources say that the subsequent visit of a Rumanian delegation headed by Gheorghiu-Dej to Belgrade in October 1956, though overshadowed by the Hungarian revolution, had a profound impact on future Rumanian policy. It was then that the two leaders began to discuss the realization of an old dream: the building of a power and navigation project at the Iron Gates on the Danube. After the Moscow-Belgrade quarrel over the Hungarian uprising, and even after the Soviet campaign against the 1958 Yugoslav party program, the Rumanians issued relatively few, late, and carefully worded rebuttals. Relations on state level remained more cordial than between Belgrade and the rest of the bloc.

It was certainly not sheer coincidence that at the very time when Rumania was beginning to stake out its independent line, the two neighboring countries were in close touch and in June 1963 signed an agreement on the building of the Iron Gates project. At an investment cost of 400 million dollars, the gigantic plant should go into operation with a yearly capacity of 10,000 million kWh in 1971. Gheorghiu-Dej paid a formal state visit to Belgrade in November to sign the final agreement. Within ten months he and Marshal Tito had met twice again to discuss bilateral relations and the sharpening discord between Bucharest and Moscow. This laid the foundation for a new relationship between the two largest Balkan states, which in turn has contributed greatly to the easing of tensions in the Balkans, the emergence of a new diverse pattern, and the curbing of Soviet influence over the entire area.

At the same time, the Rumanian leaders have managed to remain on good terms with China and Albania. While the rapprochement between Moscow and Belgrade was repeatedly and vocally condemned as a "sell-out to the arch-revisionist Tito clique," no Chinese or Albanian paper has ever directly castigated the Rumanians for their friendliness toward Yugoslavia. For Khrushchev's foes, the disruptive potential so impressively displayed by Rumanian opposition to Soviet hegemony was more important than ideological purity. By the same token, the Rumanians, while disagreeing with most of the extreme Chinese positions, unabashedly exploited the fostering of ties with China as a lever to counter Soviet pressures. Thus both sides gained definite advantages from a strictly pragmatic assessment of their mutual interests. On the twentieth anniversary of the August 23 coup, the Rumanian regime performed the considerable feat of imposing a tacit truce on the entire international Communist movement by playing host to delegations from all Communist countries, including the Soviet Union and China, Yugoslavia and Albania. The festivities were intended to provide the first but not last demonstration of the unique position occupied by Rumania in the Communist world.

The sudden fall of Khrushchev in October 1964 caused no repercussions in the country; the Rumanians were privately pleased at a turn of affairs which they regarded as a dramatic confirmation of their rejection of Khrushchev's steamroller tactics. Perhaps alone in the whole world press, the Rumanian mass media reported only the official Soviet communique without any commentary whatsoever. Khrushchev's fall and his successors' cautious moves toward a normalization of Sino-Soviet relations almost automatically lifted some of the pressures on Rumania and implicitly strengthened her bargaining position. By the end of the year the changes began to affect the internal atmosphere. Virtually all political prisoners (about 11,000) were released, jamming of foreign radio broadcasts ceased, and control over intellectual life in general was appreciably relaxed.

In the meantime the bid for independence from and discord with Moscow was spreading to other areas. At the end of October 1964, Rumania unilaterally reduced army conscripts' term of service from twenty-four to sixteen months, the shortest term of service in any Warsaw Pact country. Snippets of information from Rumanian sources confirm Western press reports that at the Warsaw Pact summit meeting held in Warsaw in January 1965, Gheorghiu-Dej not only defended his country's right to change the term of military service, but also made the first tentative moves to change the previous practice of decision-making, which the Rumanians maintained had infringed on their country's sovereignty.

The success of the new course and the national revival encouraged the Rumanians to resurrect their historic claims to Bessarabia. Once again this was done in a peculiarly cunning way. In August, Mao Tse-tung told a Japanese delegation that the "places occupied by the Soviet Union are too numerous," and referred in this context to "parts of Rumania." Prudently, the Rumanians, continuing their purposeful silence on the Sino-Soviet dispute, ignored Mao's hints and the violent Soviet diatribe published a few days later in *Pravda*.[34] In late autumn 1964, however, a Bucharest publishing house brought out Karl Marx's *Notes on Rumanians*. These previously unpublished notes and letters, found in the Amsterdam Archives, sharply condemned the annexation of Bessarabia by the Russians. The twenty thousand copies were sold out in a couple of days. Somewhat later, the Institute of Party History managed to find and publish a letter written by Engels in January 1888 in which he cautioned the Rumanian Social Democrats "to beware of Tsarism. . . . You have suffered much as a result of Kiselev's rule, the crushing of the 1848 revolution and the twice repeated annexation of Bessarabia, not to mention the innumerable Russian invasions of your country, situated as it is on the route to the Bosphorus."[35]

Within two years of the first public sign of discord with Moscow, the Rumanian Communists gained independence on a broad front, initiated a national revival, vetoed supranational economic integration, denied the right of any party or state to be the center of communism, claimed exclusive right for themselves to carry out their political line, remained uncommitted in the Sino-Soviet conflict, re-established the old contacts with the West, and touched on the most sensitive nerves in their relations with the Soviet Union—the age-old territorial issue of Bessarabia and the scope of their commitment to the Warsaw Pact.

Then suddenly, on March 19, 1965, Gheorghiu-Dej died. Despite his grim domestic record, he had come to be regarded during his last years as a national figure. Everyone, including the dignitaries hurriedly dispatched by all Communist countries to his state funeral, felt that his death marked the end of an era and left a large question mark hanging over the country's future. Would the unity of the leadership survive the crucial test of a succession crisis? Who would chart the political course at home and in foreign relations, and how? But sooner than anyone could have expected the doubts at home were gone, and in Moscow the last glimmer of hope about a more pliable Rumania vanished.

How fast and how far?

There was an atmosphere of pride, self-confidence and suspense in the modern, air-conditioned Congress Hall in Bucharest. The Ninth Party Congress[36] of the Rumanian Communists, the first to be held since the party had launched its independent course, opened on July 19, 1965, four months after the death of Gheorghiu-Dej. For more than one reason it marked the beginning of a new era in postwar Rumanian history.

Delegates from fifty-seven "fraternal" parties, including such opposites as the Soviet party leader Brezhnev and his Chinese counterpart, Teng Hsiao-p'ing, the Yugoslav Kardelj and a member of the Albanian Politburo attended and, complying with their hosts' request, avoided open polemics. Instead they vied with one another in paying tribute to the Rumanian party.

From the very beginning of the proceedings the most surprising aspect was the sudden and ruthless eradication of the cult of the dead leader. Gheorghiu-Dej had been buried amid unprecedented nationwide mourning; the new leaders had eulogized his memory and promised to carry on in his spirit. But to Western observers, permitted for the first time to be present at a party congress, it was as if he had been in his grave for four decades instead of four months. There were no pictures, no slogans, no decorations recalling the deceased dictator. After a minute of silence at the opening session, no Rumanian speaker mentioned his name. As so often in Rumanian politics, omission marked a significant departure.

In this case it gave notice to the population and the world that his successors were beginning a new era introducing a new style. The criticism of some of Gheorghiu-Dej's policies also allowed his successors to blame everything that went wrong on the legacy of failures associated with his name. Rumanians had, however, learned from Khrushchev's disastrous handling of de-Stalinization; they terminated their own version of the "cult of personality" in a more prudent fashion. As a high functionary put it to me, "It was a mistake to present Gheorghiu-Dej as a superhuman, faultless hero figure. It would be equally false to make him now into a kind of second Stalin, a demonized scapegoat. What we are doing is gradually to place his role in a new and more realistic frame."

Since then his policies have been repeatedly criticized and a number of functionaries including Miron Constantinescu (purged in 1957) and the organizer of the Grivita strike, Constantin Doncea (purged in 1958) quietly rehabilitated. The party museum repeatedly refers to him as one of the many outstanding figures in the history of the workers' movement, and there is a small memorial room with his personal belongings (situated, however, in such a way that the average visitor would hardly notice the door behind the thick curtains). On the anniversary of his death, there were articles, written in a restrained tone, but other references to Gheorghiu-Dej have been sparse, and tributes even more so.

Suppression of the Gheorghiu-Dej cult was essential if his political heirs were to convince the party and the public that they were leaders in their own right. This was particularly true of Nicolae Ceausescu, who in March 1965, at the age of forty-seven, succeeded Gheorghiu-Dej as party leader. Although he had been in the Secretariat of the Central Committee since 1954, Ceausescu was relatively unknown. He was not only the youngest member of the Politburo; he was also overshadowed by the two other members of the triumvirate that after Gheorghiu-Dej's death seemed to have taken over the reins of power: the veteran leader Chivu Stoica, who had been Premier from 1955 to 1961 and who became head of state; and Premier Maurer, who was internationally recognized as the man who, more than anyone else, had won world recognition for Rumania's independent course.

There was also a fourth leader waiting in the wings—Gheorghe Apostol, who had been a serious contender for the first secretaryship. Five years older than Ceausescu, he could claim greater seniority in the Politburo, and had in fact been First Secretary for eighteen months in 1954–55.

Ceausescu was therefore faced with the delicate but urgent task of establishing his personal authority. With driving energy and youthful dynamism, he lost no time in projecting himself as a symbol of movement and change. In the four months before the party congress, he made many public appearances and delivered a series of major speeches to the military, scientists, writers, and party activists. Although he made frequent references to the need for "collective leadership" and was always accompanied by other Politburo members, he began immediately to establish himself as the "strong man" of the ruling team.

The congress dissipated any lingering doubts about his position. He alone appeared at the rostrum and received a standing ovation from the nearly four thousand delegates and guests, while the other Politburo members remained for a few minutes in the background. Even at his first appearance in the international limelight, the small, good-looking, dark-haired man displayed poise and self-assurance. Though he, too, is a self-made man, his personality is strikingly different from that of the late Gheorghiu-Dej. According to all accounts, he lacks his predecessor's charm and sense of humor. Gheorghiu-Dej's private life and the behavior of his two daughters were for many years favorite topics of Bucharest gossip. By contrast Ceausescu and his engineer wife are models of sobriety and puritanism. The draconian laws of 1966–67 against divorce and abortion, the campaigns against smoking and the happy-go-lucky behavior of the youth clearly bore the personal imprint of Ceausescu and his influential wife.

But whatever faults sophisticated and cynical Rumanians may

find in his style and accent, Ceausescu has proved to be a passionate torchbearer of militant nationalism, a national figure, and, last but not least, a shrewd manipulator of political forces within the party. His five-hour policy statement at the congress reiterated time and again what was to become the theoretical basis for the "Rumania first" line: "The nation and the state will for a long time to come continue to be the basis for the development of socialist society." Henceforth the socialist nation and its place in the family of "equal, independent, and sovereign socialist nations," of the "sacred, inalienable right of people, now tasting freedom and national independence, to decide their own future and the fate of the fatherland" has become the theme of countless speeches he and his associates have made.

Industrialization was described as the basis of future prosperity and "the decisive factor in guaranteeing independence and national sovereignty." To show that the party was the inheritor and executor of patriotic traditions, Ceausescu burrowed back into the past century to quote the "bourgeois" historian Xenopol and the forefather of Rumanian socialism, C. Dobrogeanu-Gherea, who had warned that "reliance on agriculture alone . . . would make us an eternal slave of the outside world, getting only crumbs from the table of the civilized peoples," and "industrialization is a question of to be or not to be for our country."

The second major theme in Ceausescu's speech and in the congress proceedings was the broadening of the party's popular base. The party was depicted as a broad national movement encompassing one adult in every ten and over one-third of the intelligentsia. Paradoxically, the weakness of the prewar Communist movement helped lend credence to the new patriotic appeal and quelled underground fears among the old-timers. Their number was well under 1 per cent of the 1.45 million members, 64 per cent of whom were under forty in 1965. (By the end of 1967, membership rose to over 1.7 million, or every eighth adult citizen.)[37]

The attempt to merge Communist policies with traditional national aspirations and to present the party as the legitimate heir to the national traditions was coupled with emphatic calls for the strengthening of its leading role. The stress on "socialist legality," more tolerance toward the creative arts and science, and the provisions of the new Constitution all indicated that the slow process of internal relaxation would be continued. At the same time

Ceausescu made it very clear that ultimate power would remain with the party and no encroachment upon decision-making would be allowed.

A series of organizational changes underlined the Rumanian Communists' individualism compared to other ruling parties. The party (called the Workers' Party since 1948) changed its name back to the Rumanian Communist Party, and shortly after the congress the new Constitution declared Rumania a "Socialist Republic," instead of a People's Republic—a distinction claimed up to then only by Czechoslovakia and Yugoslavia. The new party statutes erased references to the Soviet Communist Party and abolished the candidate-status for future members. The title of the party leader was changed from First Secretary, which had come into fashion after Stalin's death, to Secretary General. And the entire organizational structure of the highest party echelons was radically revamped.

The changes were partly intended to symbolize a new era and show the will to maintain the momentum generated by the national line. But the new chain of command and other measures were also master strokes of political management devised to make Ceausescu's personal authority unchallengeable. To allay fears among his colleagues, he time and again reiterated that "collective leadership" was the "highest principle of party organization" and suggested a clause in the party statutes forbidding leaders to hold dual positions in party and government. This stipulation was used to force one of the most powerful men in the country, Alexandru Draghici, to give up the post of Minister of Interior (which he had held for thirteen years) and thereby his control over the secret police. His successor was Ceausescu's former personal secretary. While Draghici remained in the supreme party organs and even became a secretary of the Central Committee, membership in the Secretariat, was simultaneously doubled to ten, depriving Draghici of the chance to build an independent power base.

The most important device to strengthen Ceausescu's position was the creation of a completely new organ, the Executive Committee. The old Politburo was abolished and to some extent replaced by a Standing Presidium composed of seven former Politburo members. Two old-timers, Petre Borila and A. Moghioros, an ethnic Hungarian, were dropped from this supreme organ but elected to the Executive Committee. This was, however, a much wider body with fifteen full members and ten alternates. It was meant to serve as a "connecting link" between the Presidium and the Central Committee whose membership was increased from 79 to 121, with most of the newcomers regarded as supporters of the Secretary General.

Subsequent developments showed clearly that the new institutional framework helped to curb the influence of the Old Guard and at the same time to promote the rapid ascendancy of the Secretary General and the younger men who were closely associated with him. Soon after the congress, Ceausescu began a series of much-publicized tours to the various provinces and made numerous major speeches announcing more or less important measures aimed at streamlining the economy, particularly agriculture. The main effect was of a young leader of a young party endeavoring to introduce innovations in style and substance. The concerted campaign to project him as a national leader was accompanied by a number of changes within the second tier of party and government leaders; former regional party secretaries, who had been devoted to Ceausescu from the time he was in charge of personnel and organizational affairs, were promoted to important positions in the Army, the Planning Commission, the Cabinet and the central party agencies.

It would have been surprising if there were no antagonisms between the rival claimants for power or at least considerable differences of emphasis among the various leaders. But the factors that united the leadership were far more powerful than those that divided it. Without a general consensus it could hardly have survived mounting Soviet pressure.

There were, however, factional fights in connection with Soviet attempts at subversion. This was indirectly confirmed by Ceausescu in an important article in May 1967,[38] when he warned about the danger of factionalism, called for stricter discipline, especially among party leaders, referred to outside interference, and emphatically stressed that no member was allowed "to maintain contacts with other parties without the knowledge of the leadership." While there is no conclusive evidence as to which leaders in which particular period and on which issues opposed Ceausescu, it became fairly evident who his closest supporters were.

There were two important landmarks in the process that led to the emergence of a new inner nucleus within the "collective leadership," both of which coincided with periods of intense tension in Soviet-Rumanian relations. Ceausescu scored his first major success in consolidating his power at the Central Committee plenum of June 27–28, 1966. His two close collaborators, the then forty-three-year-old Paul Niculescu-Mizil and forty-one-year-old Ilie Verdetz were made members of the Standing Presidium, raising the number from seven to nine. At the same time, two other "Ceausescu-men," including the new planning chief, Maxim Berghianu, entered the Executive Committee. The fact that Verdetz was promoted to the highest echelon—the select Presidium—without having been a full member of the Executive Committee was the most telling proof of Ceausescu's overwhelmingly strong position.

Rumanian sources rapidly identified the three representatives of the "second generation"—Ceausescu, Niculescu-Mizil, and Verdetz —as the real "troika" of decision-makers, rather than the formal triumvirate of Ceausescu, Premier Maurer, and President Stoica. The troika displayed great ingenuity in manipulating forces from both below and above. In the course of 1966, 85 out of the 150 district party secretaries were replaced and a number of important officials removed from the ministries of Interior and Defense. The Executive Committee and the Secretariat were increasingly brought into play to counterbalance the numerical weight of the senior leaders inherited from the Gheorghiu-Dej era. Even with this leverage, the ascendancy of the Secretary General could not have been as swift as it was without support from other members of the Presidium. It has been suggested by reliable sources that Premier Maurer, General Bodnaras, and, at least until the end of 1966, First Deputy Premier Birladeanu sided with the Secretary General. It would be somewhat misleading to treat the rest of the Presidium as a group, but it appears likely that most of them, particularly Stoica and Draghici, at one point or another resented the swift upward climb of the younger men.

Throughout 1966–67 Ceausescu visibly gathered strength and confidence. Every week or so, at conferences and on trips to the remotest corners of the land, he appealed to national pride and identity in a tone unparalleled anywhere else in Eastern Europe. This was, however, no longer just a bid for personal authority, or a rallying cry for national unity in the face of Soviet threats, but rather the beginning of a personality cult. Wherever the "party and state leaders" went, at every major conference, whether of building workers, collective farmers, railwaymen, or students, it was invariably Ceausescu who made the main speech. The advent of television provided previously unavailable opportunities for "image-building." His colleagues in the leadership began to praise Ceausescu's various statements and recommendations more and more frequently. Letters and telegrams from various party and youth conferences began to be addressed not just to the Central Committee but to Comrade Ceausescu personally. In factories, high schools, and youth hostels, posters and permanent decorations displayed not only quotes from Lenin but an increasing number of extracts from the speeches of the Secretary General.

The second and by far the most important reshuffle came in December 1967. At the national party conference, the supreme collective party organ next to the congress, Ceausescu presented a complex scheme for territorial and administrative reorganization and a reform of the planning system.

Embedded in his lengthy speech were proposals for revolutionary changes in party and state organization that would result in an unprecedented concentration of power. The essence of the proposals was the fusion of party and government functions from top to bottom. Yet there was an extraordinary paradox in the new "model": on the one hand, it proclaimed decentralization, "collective leadership," and a greater participation of the masses in economy and administration; on the other hand, it broke one of the basic principles of rule in Communist countries—the formal separation of party and state. To overcome "duplication" and "overlapping," "one and the same comrade should be entrusted with a specific field of activity in both the Central Committee and the government." This meant that, in contrast to all other ruling Communist parties, the Rumanian party leaders from the level of the Standing Presidium to the newly constituted 39 counties and larger cities (replacing the previous division into 16 regions and 150 districts) would take on direct operational responsibilities. The top party organs would henceforth handle matters of defense, state security, foreign policy, personnel selection, and culture, while the government bodies would deal with concrete details of economic policy, leaving overall guidance to the Central Committee.

The main and immediate reasons behind this move became immediately evident. Chivu Stoica suggested on the second day of the conference that, in accordance with the principle of dual responsibility, Secretary General Ceausescu should also take over the post of President of the State Council. This was "enthusiastically" endorsed by later speakers, and a few days later parliament duly elected Ceausescu head of state.

Thus in less than three years and on the eve of his fiftieth birthday, Ceausescu was exercising as much power as Gheorghiu-Dej had. Using the exact reverse of the arguments presented three years earlier, the conference unanimously eliminated the clause in the party statutes forbidding leaders from holding dual party and government executive functions.

The reshuffle in the wake of the administrative reorganization showed beyond a shadow of doubt who the losers were. Chivu Stoica, a former Premier and since March 1965 as head of state outwardly the number two man of the regime, was forced to return to the Secretariat of the Central Committee as one of the eight secretaries. Ilie Verdetz remained the only First Deputy Premier as heir presumptive to Maurer while the other three senior Presidium members suffered obvious setbacks. Gheorghe Apostol, once a First Secretary of the party and a rival of Ceausescu's in 1965, was demoted to his erstwhile position as Chairman of the Trade Union Federation. The chief Rumanian protagonist in the Comecon disputes, A. Birladeanu, remained in the government but only as one of the six Deputy Premiers, while Emil Bodnaras was spared the humiliation of serving under Verdetz and was transferred to the State Council as one of the three deputies to Ceausescu as head of state. Finally, Alexandru Draghici after having lost control over the secret police was transferred back from the Secretariat to the government as a Deputy Premier.

Ceausescu's unchallenged ascendancy was, however, only a prelude to a dramatic public showdown in April 1968. A plenum of the Central Committee shattered the sacred myth of an unblemished postwar record of Rumanian communism, the line that "we do not have to rehabilitate anyone post mortem." The politically most important move was the full rehabilitation of Stefan Foris, the erstwhile Secretary General (executed without trial in 1946), and of Lucretiu Patrascanu the Communist leader during and after the August 23, 1944 coup who, after six years of imprisonment, was executed in 1954. Scores of other Communist functionaries were also rehabilitated—many of them posthumously—including Miron Constantinescu, purged in 1957 from the Politburo.

The power struggles in connection with the rehabilitations started two and a half years earlier when a special investigating commission was set up. The Central Committee primarily blamed Gheorghiu-Dej and Draghici for the "unfounded, gross fabrications" and the murder of Patrascanu. Draghici as the main scapegoat, who on top of everything "behaved cynically and irresponsibly" when the commission's findings were discussed, was ousted from the leadership and the government. After the long silence following his cult, Gheorghiu-Dej is now regarded as a leader who had "undeniable merits" but also committed "grave excesses and serious errors."

Though only Draghici was expelled from the leading bodies, there is no doubt that the three old-timers in the Politburo in 1954—Stoica, Apostol, and Bodnaras—are also bound to lose their prominent positions sooner or later. The resolution of the plenary meeting stated that they also bore "great responsibility" for approving the decision to execute Patrascanu. The implication is that their careers are now virtually closed.*

At the same time Ceausescu, who claims that in 1956 at a stormy Politburo session he warned against the abuse of the secret police and the lack of party control, is trying hard to project himself as a pacemaker of "democratization" in addition to being a torchbearer of nationalism. The rehabilitations lend some credibility to his emphatic assurances that "no citizen can be arrested without well-founded and proven cause" and "no one should be afraid of being arrested before returning home from his job."

As Ceausescu and his associates pushed Rumania along the road of independence faster than even the most hopeful Rumanian nationalists had bargained for, the discord with Moscow gradually permeated almost every major international issue. The new leaders multiplied and broadened their rebellious moves, and with each successive victory, their voices took on a harsher note of criticism in deviating from or, more frequently, clashing with Soviet foreign policy.

The breathing spell after Gheorghiu-Dej's death was in fact only a deceptive calm; it gave Ceausescu time to "put his house in order."

---

* The rehabilitation process was brought to its logical conclusion in September 1968 when the Supreme Court annulled the sentences against Vasile Luca, the former Deputy Premier and Secretary of the Central Committee in 1952, and three other high party functionaries as "groundless and unjustified." Thus Luca, Pauker, and Georgescu, like Gheorghiu-Dej are likely to rank in the often promised but not yet published party history as leaders who committed "serious errors" but were not "traitors."

In the spring of 1966, the Rumanians not only rejected public Soviet demands for strengthening political and military cooperation, but also launched a sustained campaign to transform the Warsaw Pact from an instrument of Soviet hegemony into a "partnership of equals." The Rumanian offensive evolved on three different, inter-connected planes. There were first of all Ceausescu's defiantly nationalistic speeches in which he again and again evoked a sense of identity with a mythical past and proclaimed: "The Rumanian people have taken their fate in their own hands and we have got everything we need." This wave of exuberant nationalism reached its crescendo in his famous speech of May 7, on the forty-fifth anniversary of the founding of the Rumanian Communist Party, which combined a sweeping indictment of the Comintern's interference in Rumanian party affairs with a passionate commitment to "national re-awakening" and the right of each party to run its own affairs at home and in foreign policy. Three days later a worried Brezhnev made an unannounced visit to Bucharest. (Subsequent developments made it clear that his mission failed.)

The next two months saw a series of meetings held by the Foreign and Defense ministers of the Warsaw Pact states to prepare a forth-coming summit meeting of the Political Consultative Committee, the supreme organ of the alliance. These conferences, which were unprecedentedly long and intense, provided the second main plane on which the Rumanian campaign against Soviet preponderance developed. The Soviet leaders had hoped that American "aggression" against North Vietnam and the alleged expansionist plans of the "revenge-seeking aggressive German militarists" would help to forge a greater degree of cohesion and tighten Soviet control in Eastern Europe. Brezhnev and most of his allies in the East European capitals pressed for "increased vigilance" and a "perfecting" of the Warsaw Pact organization. Accordingly, the preparatory conferences for the summit meeting were devoted to two main topics: the strengthening of the multilateral and supranational character of the Warsaw Pact and the drawing-up of a sharply worded policy statement attacking the German Federal Republic as the main source of political tensions in Europe.

The third aspect of the Rumanian opposition to these plans was a faultlessly orchestrated policy of deliberate leaks, followed by half-hearted denials coupled with meaningful hints, which bewildered and infuriated their allies. In his speech of May 7,

Ceausescu described the existence of military blocs, of the stationing of troops on foreign soil as "an anachronism incompatible with
the independence and national sovereignty of the peoples and
normal relations among states." The statement was by no means a
novel departure in Rumanian foreign policy. What alerted the
attention of observers was the fact that the Secretary General connected the abolition of military blocs so emphatically with national
independence, that he failed to refer to Rumania's role in the Warsaw
Pact, and that his generally militant speech was followed by Brezhnev's trip to Bucharest.

Nine days later, on May 16, "mysterious" leaks from Moscow revealed that Rumania had submitted proposals to its allies for a
sweeping reorganization of the Warsaw Pact. These were said to
include demands for the evacuation of Soviet troops from foreign
territories, the termination of contributions by other member states
to the cost of troop stationing, a periodic rotation of the supreme
command, and more influence on decision-making with regard to
nuclear responsibilities. Thirty-six hours later a Foreign Minister
spokesman in Bucharest denied that a note had been sent. The reports, particularly about the withdrawal of Soviet troops, were said
to be "unfounded."

The denials were, however, ambiguous: "As long as NATO
exists, there will have to be a Warsaw Pact, but Rumanian policy is
to work for the relaxation of tensions and the abolition of all military
blocs." This restatement of the well-known Rumanian position was
coupled with a deliberate stress on the character of the pact as an
alliance of independent states where binding decisions could be
made only unanimously. To complete the masterly exercise in semi-
denials and semiconfirmations, the Bucharest correspondent of the
Yugoslav news agency *Tanjug* was told that there was no formal
denial because in that case all foreign correspondents would have
been informed. As regards the statements made to a handful of
Western reporters, "these were merely conversations to deepen their
understanding of Rumania's attitude to military blocs."[39]

While the delicate negotiations to prepare the Warsaw Pact summit meeting were in full swing in Moscow, the Rumanian leaders
played host to both Marshal Tito and Chinese Premier Chou En-lai.
Tito paid his first formal visit to Rumania since the end of 1947 just
before Ceausescu's speech of May 7. Chou En-lai made a "friendship
visit" at the head of a party and state delegation in June, although

the Chinese leadership had indignantly refused to dispatch delegations to the party congresses held earlier in the Soviet Union, Czechoslovakia, and Outer Mongolia.

The visit enhanced the international prestige of Rumania, which alone of the member states of the Warsaw Pact had managed to maintain "cordial relations" with China. But Chou En-lai's eight-day stay subjected the "marriage of convenience" to a severe test. The Rumanians staunchly rejected the Chinese Premier's attempts to use Bucharest as a rostrum for launching attacks against the Soviet Union. They censored their guests' speeches as ruthlessly and as scrupulously as they did the statements made by the Soviet leaders, insisting that Chou abstain from open or covert polemics and threatening to call off the final festive "friendship meeting" if he did not accede to their ultimative demands. In the end, after the audience had waited in suspense for almost two hours (an event without precedent in Communist Rumania), the furious Chinese leader gave way and made an impromptu noncommittal speech. The fact that no joint communique was published but only a press notice stating that "during the exchange of opinions each side expressed its respective viewpoints," indicated that the visit had ended in discord.

The Chinese disillusionment with the Rumanian policy of "sitting on two chairs" was reflected in several meaningful hints dropped by Chou En-lai and his Albanian friends when Chou proceeded from Rumania to Tirana. No longer under constraint, he poured abuse on the "Soviet revisionists" and obliquely reminded the Rumanians that "the struggle against modern revisionism, as against imperialism, is a matter of principle, which allows no double attitudes." Albanian Premier Shehu spoke disparagingly about "acrobatic politicians who mask their revisionism under the guise of neutrality."

Chinese-Rumanian relations have never recovered from the shock of the near debacle in Bucharest. Relations have remained correct, but distinctly cooler than before. Reciprocal self-interest has restrained the ruling group in Peking from openly criticizing the Rumanians, and Premier Maurer, accompanied by several high-ranking leaders, has paid at least three visits to Peking since June 1966, indicating the keen Rumanian interest in keeping the channels of communication open. But in contrast to his previous missions in 1964, none of these visits was publicly announced.

The Rumanians have succeeded in maintaining their tenuous contacts with China and Albania throughout the period of their spectacular foreign policy initiatives in Europe and the Middle East— initiatives that by no stretch of the imagination can be reconciled with China's official posture. Perhaps even more important, the Rumanian leaders have strengthened their position with Moscow by standing up to Chinese pressures. The discord during Chou En-lai's visit provided irrefutable evidence that their policy of strict non-alignment in the Moscow-Peking conflict was meant to be taken seriously by both sides.

As one of the deputy Foreign Ministers in Bucharest put it to me on the eve of the Warsaw Pact summit meeting: "We are neither neutralists nor nationalists, but Rumanian Communists. People in Moscow and in the West, and elsewhere, have overlooked this simple fact—perhaps for an unduly long period. We have to represent our national Rumanian interests and—if necessary—protect them."

It was in this spirit that at the Bucharest session of the Political Consultative Committee of the Warsaw Pact in July 1966 the Rumanians set out to frustrate Soviet attempts designed to strengthen military cooperation and to restore a greater degree of discipline and unity in the foreign policy of the members.

From the outset, the committee, the supreme organ of the Warsaw Pact and as such the single most important institutional device for maintaining Soviet military control over Eastern Europe, had failed to be an effective instrument of joint policy-making. From May 1955 when it was founded until mid-1966, it had held only seven regular sessions, although the statutes provided for "conferences held according to necessity but at least twice a year." The key positions—supreme commander, chief of the general staff, and Secretary General—were always held by Soviet marshals and functionaries. Yet the Soviet Union was never able to use the Pact as a potent weapon in either preventing or responding effectively to Albania's rebellion and Rumanian acts of defiance.

The eighth session in Bucharest, held eighteen months after the previous meeting, resulted in a precarious modus vivendi that was little more than an agreement to disagree. After acrimonious debates at the numerous preparatory conferences, the Russians reluctantly decided to bury temporarily their ambitious design of improving military and political coordination through new organizational arrangements. The seven member states published a joint resolution condemning American "aggression" against North

Vietnam and expressing willingness to send volunteers if and when they were requested by Hanoi. A nineteen-page declaration about the European situation, formulated in the habitually turgid prose of Communist policy statements, was clearly the result of a compromise. Altogether the document in some ways resembled the ill-fated Moscow Declaration of 1960, issued by the eighty-one Communist parties. Each signatory could make use of different paragraphs to justify diametrically opposed policies, but the lack of any reference to closer military integration within the framework of the Warsaw Pact represented a major concession to the Rumanians. A high Rumanian official privately remarked, "We are an independent and sovereign member of the Pact, in the same way that France remains in the North Atlantic Treaty Organization. But our army has, of course, its own national command, and no supranational headquarters can interfere in the affairs of or give orders to the Rumanian armed forces."

Behind the scenes the delicate issue of the competences and structure of the Supreme United Command of the Warsaw Pact has remained on the agenda. The text of the Warsaw Treaty (Article 5) states only that a united command will be created for "those parts of the armed forces (of each member country) which as agreed between the signatories are placed at the disposal of the united command acting on the basis of principles established in common." With the exception of the East German army, it does not specify whether all or part of the armed forces of the signatories are integrated, nor does it contain any stipulations about the possibility of withdrawal or revision of the treaty. The Defense Ministers of the member states are automatically deputies of the Supreme Commander. But there is no stipulation about a permanent Soviet commander, nor are there any references to the possibility of a rotation.

The Treaty's ambiguity and brevity has naturally provided an escape hatch. When the death of Marshal Malinovsky, the Soviet Defense Minister, in March 1967 necessitated a reshuffle in the Soviet High Command, and thus also in the Supreme Command of the Warsaw Pact forces, the Rumanians appear to have raised objections to the appointment of a third Soviet general in succession as head of the united command. The hitherto Supreme Commander, Marshal Grechko, was appointed Soviet Defense Minister on April 13, and the same day the promotion of General Jakubovsky to the rank of Marshal and first Deputy Defense Minister was officially announced. There was, however, a three-month delay before Marshal Jakubovsky was confirmed as new Supreme Commander of the Pact forces. In June the news of his appointment was released, to be revoked only a few hours later by the official Hungarian news agency. Soon after this unusual occurrence, Ceausescu, at a party meeting in Brasov, for the first time referred to the necessity that each member country "have its own command able to answer any call."[40]

Though in August 1967 Rumanian army units, for the first time in four years, participated in joint military maneuvers with Soviet and Bulgarian troops in Bulgaria, the Rumanian leadership continued to balk at any measures that in its opinion were an infringement of national sovereignty. Significantly, on the eve of the spectacular foreign policy debate in the Bucharest parliament that summer, a *Pravda* editorial stressed the "tremendous" political significance of the Warsaw Pact and Comecon. At a time when imperialism was seeking to weaken the bonds between the socialist countries, the article said, these states saw their participation in the Warsaw Pact not as some "formal presence" but as "a live, creative and working cooperation in military and political matters." The truth is, however, that Rumania's adherence to the Pact has become increasingly a "formal presence." As Ceausescu put it, "a country deprived of part of its national prerogatives ceases to be free and sovereign," while Presidium member Chivu Stoica referred to "the full exercising of sovereign rights of each socialist country over the levers of leadership covering its entire territory" and to "the inadmissibility of renunciation of any constitutional attribute of a socialist state."[41] It is evident that such terms as "all the levers" and "constitutional attributes" were intended to cover not only economic-decision-making (as in the April 1964 declaration) but also military command and foreign policy.

Rumanian sources have "leaked" information about dissatisfaction with the high cost of partly outmoded equipment provided by the Soviet suppliers, and Defense Minister Ionita has revealed that the country has begun to develop its own armaments industry in order to save foreign currency for the purchase of weapons systems that Rumania cannot manufacture. In early 1968, the Rumanians bought six British jet airliners for their civil aviation fleet, lending some credence to the rumor that in time they may also buy arms in Western Europe.

The year 1967 saw a series of momentous changes in Rumanian foreign policy. Responding to the more imaginative and forward-looking "Eastern policy" of the new West German coalition government, Rumania on January 31, 1967, split with its Warsaw Pact allies on the single, most important issue of European politics and re-established diplomatic relations with the German Federal Republic. To justify this significant departure, the Rumanian leaders referred to the Bucharest declaration of the Warsaw Pact in July 1966, which called for the development of multilateral and bilateral relations between European countries regardless of differences in social systems. They also claimed that the move marked the end of the Federal Republic's so-called Hallstein doctrine, which threatened reprisals, including the breaking of diplomatic relations, with any country that recognized the East German "Democratic Republic."

The resumption of formal relations between Bonn and Bucharest was a daring violation of bloc discipline and posed a serious threat to the very core of the Soviet power sphere. The essence of the West German-Rumanian deal was the agreement to disagree on certain basic aspects of the German question, without regarding these differences as an unsurmountable obstacle. Thus Chancellor Kiesinger told the West German parliament that the agreement had in no way altered his government's right to speak for the whole German people, while a statement issued in Bucharest reiterated the Rumanian position on the existence of two German states and emphasized that their existence had to be recognized if European cooperation and a favorable political climate were to develop.

While the Rumanian Foreign Minister was still in West Germany after the formal announcement of the resumption of diplomatic relations, the East German press for the first time overtly and directly criticized a "fraternal" country for failing to safeguard European security. The party organ, *Neues Deutschland,* bluntly stated that the attitude of the Rumanian Foreign Minister was deplorable, because he was obviously not willing to reject the West Germans' presumptuous claim to represent the whole German people. The editorial also quoted the Bucharest declaration, which said that the interests of peace and security demanded that the West German rulers recognize the existence of two German states and renounce any claims to the revision of borders and to representing the whole of Germany. These demands were not, however, put as a precondition for the establishment of diplomatic relations with the Federal Republic, and the Rumanians could and did quote other paragraphs from the declaration in favor of normal relations and relaxation of tensions in Europe.

It is a matter of conjecture whether the attacks from East Berlin, followed by broadsides from Warsaw, which did not mention Rumania by name, were launched without the knowledge of or, as some observers speculated, even against the wishes of the Soviet leaders. The Rumanians immediately rejected the East German insinuations, which, "in contrast to the positive response evoked in international public opinion, distorted the meaning and character" of the agreement. "Is the author of the article perhaps unaware that the foreign policy of a socialist state is laid down by the party and the government of the country in question and that they have to account only to their people and nation?" a scathing editorial in *Scinteia* asked, and added, "The attempt of the newspaper [*Neues Deutschland*] to set itself up as a foreign political adviser to another state and to interfere in the internal affairs of another country do not serve the cause of friendship and collaboration between socialist countries; on the contrary they harm these relations."[42]

It became clear that the "go-it-alone" Rumanian initiative, significant though it was, would be less important in the long run than the effects that followed the cracking open of the whole façade of bloc solidarity. East Germany feared the specter of a rapid isolation from the rest of Eastern Europe, should the Rumanian example spark a chain reaction in Prague, Budapest, and Sofia who already counted West Germany one of their leading non-Communist trading partners. At the initiative of the East German and Polish leaders, a conference of the Warsaw Pact foreign ministers was hastily convened on February 8, 1967, in Warsaw. The Rumanians objected to East Berlin as meeting place and sent only a Deputy Foreign Minister. In a sense, the conference was an anti-climax since Rumania, ignoring East German pleas, threats, and warnings, had already presented its partners with a fait accompli. The communique about the "friendly exchange of views" in connection with the European situation failed to mention the German question at all.

To forestall the disruptive effects of the Rumanian move, East Germany swiftly concluded bilateral treaties with Poland and Czechoslovakia in the spring, followed a few months later by similar treaties with Hungary and Bulgaria. Almost simultaneously, the

Soviet Union renewed—well ahead of their dates of expiration—
friendship treaties with Bulgaria and Hungary.

The concerted efforts of the East Germans and Poles, seconded
by the Kremlin which remained outwardly in the background,
succeeded in frustrating further West German initiatives in the
sphere of Soviet influence. But the resumption of diplomatic ties
between Bonn and Belgrade in January 1968 (broken off unilaterally
by Bonn as a reprisal for Yugoslavia's recognition of East Germany in
1957), tremendously strengthened Rumania's moral position in regard to the recognition of West Germany. Rumania also reaped
international prestige and tangible benefits from its relations with
the Federal Republic, which is now its second largest trading partner after the Soviet Union. Trade exchanges in 1967 increased by 42
per cent. There was, however, a steadily growing Rumanian deficit,
which amounted to almost 180 million dollars in the 1963–66 period
and is estimated to have risen by a further 120 million dollars in
1967. The German government raised the limit on credits granted to
Rumania, and promised to provide new possibilities for larger Rumanian sales to West Germany. The agreements on economic and
scientific-technical cooperation, signed during the visit of Foreign
Minister Willy Brandt to Bucharest in the summer of 1967, were
also expected to contribute to the alleviation of the Rumanian
deficit.

But regardless of the short-term advantages, the real significance
of the establishment of diplomatic relations with Bonn lay in the
transition from an essentially defensive stance within the bloc to an
aggressively active and truly nationally motivated foreign policy,
which in turn transformed a "quarrel in the family" into a public
discord affecting crucial issues of the day.

A new major area of disagreement arose after the Arab-Israeli
war. Once again the Rumanian leadership correctly perceived the
underlying trends and showed a profound appreciation of the implications of new military technology and its effects upon international politics. Even during the period preceding the six-day war
the Rumanian mass media took a moderate line of non-interference,
in contrast to the other Communist countries.

The vindication of this policy constituted if not the most substantial certainly the most publicized victory of Rumania's independent course. When East European leaders, including Marshal
Tito, gathered in Moscow on June 9, 1967, Ceausescu and Maurer

refused to sign the joint statement condemning "Israeli aggression," and the Rumanian representatives stayed away altogether from the Budapest summit meeting one month later. Alone among the East European states Rumania continued to maintain diplomatic relations with Israel.

The Rumanian position, spelled out in a moderate and masterful speech by Premier Maurer at the UN General Assembly, was an act of remarkable audacity. But it tremendously enhanced Rumania's prestige in the world and aroused admiration at home.

To underline both the unity of the top leadership and popular backing for the country's flamboyantly independent course, a brilliantly managed special session of the Rumanian parliament, devoted exclusively to questions of foreign policy, was convened July 24–26. In the presence of many foreign journalists, lured to Bucharest after meaningful hints had been dropped by Rumanian diplomats in virtually every European capital, the debate, while admittedly staged, nevertheless reflected the general mood of a country proud and mesmerized by the world attention riveted on its deft diplomacy.

There were no sensations, let alone a dramatic break with the Warsaw Pact. Yet the session served notice to friend and foe that the "go-it-alone" moves on the Middle East conflict and the German question were facets of a coherent, considered, "principled and consequent" foreign policy, a policy that, in the words of Premier Maurer, was fashioned "by our own will and by no other considerations, be they of a geographic, economic, or military nature." In his speech, Ceausescu openly criticized Arab saber rattling: "We wish honestly to tell our Arab friends that we do not understand and do not share the position of those circles that speak in favor of the liquidation of the state of Israel. We do not wish to give advice to anybody, but the lessons of history show that no people can achieve their national and social aspirations against the right to existence of another people."

During subsequent months, Rumanian diplomacy performed the unique feat of dispatching high-level delegations to the Arab countries offering shipments of badly needed wheat as a gift and sending Foreign Trade Minister Ciora to Tel Aviv, the first East European official of ministerial rank ever to visit Israel. Intensified economic cooperation between the two countries had actually begun before the war when Israeli Finance Minister Shapir visited Bucharest in

April and signed a trade agreement providing for a substantial increase of from 5 million dollars in 1966 to 17 million dollars in 1967 and setting up of a mixed economic commission. During Ciora's return visit, a new trade protocol was signed for an increase to well over 30 million dollars per annum during the years 1968–70. A number of ambitious agreements covering the establishment of joint industrial enterprises in Rumania and direct air links were also concluded. In sum, Rumania cashed handsome dividends because its policy in the Middle East, as indeed everywhere else, was guided by calculated self-interest. An additional, secondary factor that influenced the country's pragmatic attitude toward the Middle East crisis was the presence of an estimated 300,000 people of Rumanian origin in Israel, which apparently contributes to the attraction of the country as a promising market for Rumanian products. As a small but significant gesture, Rumania's Chief Rabbi, Moses Rosen, at the end of 1967 paid an official visit to Israel bringing as a gift of the Rumanian government three thousand Torah scrolls.

To complete the act of delicate tightrope walking in the Middle East, Rumania's representative participated in the Belgrade meeting of the East European Deputy Premiers in early September and the Foreign Ministers' conference in mid-December in Warsaw, both devoted to Middle East problems. In startling contrast to the general line of the Soviet bloc, however, the communiques issued on both occasions avoided the condemnation of Israel as an "aggressor" and were couched in moderate words. This was the price of Rumanian participation; and the Rumanians remained reluctant to endorse any formal commitment of economic or military aid to the Arab countries.

The spectacular gains in Rumania's international standing were reflected in the audience granted by President Johnson to Premier Maurer in late June and the unanimous election of Foreign Minister Manescu as President of the UN General Assembly in the autumn, the first representative of a Communist country to attain this position.

Strengthened in their determination to carry forward their self-assertive foreign policy, the Rumanians expressed firm and detailed opposition to the Soviet-American sponsored project of a nuclear non-proliferation draft treaty, which, as Ceausescu and other leaders stressed, without built-in safeguards, "would only sanction the division of the world into nuclear and non-nuclear states." The

Rumanian objections and demands centered on the access of the non-nuclear countries to the peaceful use of nuclear power; the granting of adequate security guarantees by the big powers; the application of equal controls to nuclear and non-nuclear states; assurances that the control mechanism would not hamstring research and operations for peaceful use of nuclear energy; and precise obligations for the nuclear powers to undertake definite disarmament measures. In sum, Rumania insisted—and its position was strikingly similar to that of West Germany, India, Sweden, Brazil, and Japan—that the big powers had no right to impose nuclear disarmament on their own terms.

In accord with the Rumanian thesis about the increasingly active role of the "small and medium states" in world politics, the representative of the Bucharest government in the eighteen-member disarmament commission at Geneva several times submitted a series of important amendments to the draft treaty. Though the Soviet and American cosponsors of the treaty revised the original draft to meet the objections of the nuclear "have-nots," the Rumanian delegate along with the other opponents of the move insisted that further amendments were necessary. These objections were upheld at the summit meeting of the Warsaw Pact in Sofia (March 6–7, 1968) almost twenty months after the previous conference.

It was at this meeting that the Rumanian leaders for the first time abstained from signing a formal Warsaw Pact document. The statement supporting the non-proliferation treaty was issued by only six of the seven participating delegations, an obstruction without parallel in the thirteen-year history of the pact. The Rumanian delegation did sign the declaration condemning the "criminal actions of the American imperialists" against North Vietnam, but this only helped to accentuate the fact that, aside from Vietnam, Rumania had followed a "special" line on almost every major international issue. The omission from the official communique of such crucial problems as those of European security and Germany made clear how deep the divergences were.*

The show of disunity at the Warsaw Pact summit meeting followed by only one week the Rumanian delegation's spectacular walkout from the conference of sixty-six Communist parties held in Budapest. The Rumanian Communists had held all along to their position of

---

* After the Soviet Union and the United States jointly tabled some minor amendments, Rumania eventually in mid-1968 also signed the non-proliferation treaty.

non-alignment and strict neutrality in the Moscow-Peking conflict. When, eighteen months after the rump conference of eighteen parties in Moscow in March 1965 (which the Rumanians did not attend), the Soviet leaders and their associates launched a new campaign for a full-dress world Communist conference on the pattern of the 1960 meeting, the Rumanian leaders cautioned time and again that they should "undertake absolutely nothing that could add new elements of tension, absolutely nothing that would lead to a worsening of the relations between the Communist and Workers' parties."[43] In April 1967 the Rumanian party along with the Yugoslav and several non-ruling parties refused to participate at the Karlovy Vary meeting of European Communist parties because it did not agree with the "character, procedure, and purpose" of the conference.

It therefore came as a surprise when the Central Committee of the Rumanian party decided to send a delegation to the international consultative meeting held between February 26 and March 5, 1968 in Budapest. As the Rumanians had refused to sign the call issued the previous autumn by the eighteen members of the erstwhile preparatory commission of the 1960 meeting, the acceptance of the Hungarian invitation seemed to indicate a mellowing of the Rumanian stance. Yet the catalogue of conditions attached to the decision to participate revealed the profoundly subversive character of the tactics publicly proclaimed by the party leadership: the Budapest meeting should have a purely consultative character as a forum for the exchange of views and not make decisions about the place and time of the world conference; all parties should participate in "thorough" preparations for the conference, including at least one further consultative meeting; and, most important, the consultative meeting and the international conference to follow it should not "in any way" discuss or criticize the internal or international policy of any fraternal party, present or absent at the conference.[44]

The Albanian party organ in a scathing commentary on the "revisionist gathering" (though without naming "the revisionists who pose as autonomous") aptly summed up the real meaning of the Rumanian stance: "These ideas [non-interference, full autonomy of each party] not only surpass the revisionist ideas of Togliatti's polycentrism, but suggest that each party should become a center in itself. In other words, this means allowing not only one or two interpretations of our revolutionary theory, but tens if not hundreds."[45]

From the very beginning it was obvious that an acceptance of these conditions would have made even a "discussion of the concrete problems of the struggle against imperialism" impossible, since these very issues lay at the heart of the Sino-Soviet conflict. On the third day of the meeting, after the Syrian delegate directly attacked the Rumanian party's Middle East policy, the Rumanian delegation staged a dramatic walkout. The next day, March 1, a Central Committee plenum in Bucharest approved the walkout.

Whether the Rumanians came to Budapest prepared to state their case and then depart in dramatic style, or whether the Russians, working through their Syrian friend, deliberately drove them out is still not clear. In any case, the rupture impressively underlined the fact that, despite the arithmetic majority Moscow had mustered for the Budapest meeting, exactly half the ruling parties (those of China, Albania, North Vietnam, North Korea, Yugoslavia, Cuba, and Rumania) were, for different reasons, absent from the most important international Communist gathering held in eight years.

Thus by the spring of 1968, Rumania's insistence on absolute equality and full freedom of action had led to a series of more or less spectacular clashes in both interstate and interparty relations with Moscow.

There is no doubt that Khrushchev's successors also sought to pressure Rumania—albeit in a less heavy-handed way. In a series of speeches and statements, particularly following February 1967, the Rumanian leaders pleaded and warned that "differences of opinion should not be carried to the extreme of influencing economic relations."[46] At the December 1967 national party conference, Ceausescu for the first time mentioned that "long-term trade agreements are sometimes not strictly implemented, which affects economic collaboration adversely and hampers long-term economic planning." Shortly afterward, a communique issued about the visit of a high-level Rumanian delegation to Moscow mentioned that an exchange of views had also taken place with regard to "the fulfillment of previous agreements." According to sources in Bucharest, the controversies arose over Soviet failure to deliver raw materials (primarily iron ore and coke) contracted under long-term trade agreements, and also to purchase the originally agreed volume of oil-extraction and electrical equipment as well as chemical products from Rumania.

The Soviet share of Rumanian foreign trade shrank from 42 per cent in 1964 to less than 27 per cent in 1967, and the over-all share of the Comecon partners, including Russia, from 72 per cent in 1960 to less than 50 per cent in 1967.

Barring a ruinous intervention, it will be virtually impossible for the Soviet Union to whip the Rumanians back into line. The Russians' best response to the increasingly dangerous challenge appears to be to work for a higher degree of cohesion among a smaller number of the ruling parties, and thus to isolate Rumania. Paralleling to some extent the relationship between France and NATO, Rumania's formal presence in the Warsaw Pact and Comecon is no longer regarded as an obstacle to closer cooperation within the "inner core" of the Soviet power sphere. Rumanian leaders were significantly not invited to the hastily convoked summit meeting of the six other Warsaw Pact countries held in Dresden on March 23, 1968.

There is, however, an Achilles heel to the buoyant Rumanian nationalism—the status and role of Rumania's large Hungarian minority. Rumania is today a far more homogeneous country than it was before World War II; the proportion of ethnic Rumanians (always according to the official figures) has risen from 72 to almost 88 per cent of the 19.1 million population. The second largest, Germans (that is, the descendants of the Saxon and Swabian settlers from the Middle Ages), number just under 400,000, while ten other nationalities, including Serbs, Ukrainians, Bulgarians, amount to less than 2 per cent of the population. But for historical, political, emotional, and numerical reasons, the compact Hungarian minority associated with another, neighboring, country is another matter.

We have seen in Chapter II the roots of the old and bitter quarrels between Hungary and Rumania over Transylvania. After the Rumanians succeeded in regaining Northern Transylvania in 1945 and the Communists seized power in both countries, a good start was made to heal the wounds of the recent past and to accord not only verbal but truly equal rights and opportunities to the minority. The Rumanian Constitution of 1952 provided for the establishment of a Hungarian autonomous region where the Hungarians accounted for 78 per cent of the 700,000 population.

The Hungarian uprising in 1956 and its manifold repercussions, however, made the regime in Bucharest aware of the danger that Transylvania might become an opposition stronghold in both a national and a political sense. The elimination of the "alien elements" in the top Rumanian leadership also contributed to a gradual reap-

praisal of the Hungarian question. The shift toward a policy of
assimilation became evident in July 1959 when the Hungarian
Bolyai university in Cluj, the principal city in Transylvania, was
merged with the Rumanian Babes university. This measure, which
aroused a mixture of fear and resentment among the Hungarians,
was the beginning of the gradual process of introducing Rumanian
as the exclusive language of education, the law courts, and public
services. The second blow fell in 1960, when the autonomous area
was renamed "Mures-Hungarian autonomous region" and, through
an administrative reorganization, the proportion of Hungarians was
reduced from 78 to 62 per cent of the population. Finally, in the
course of the sweeping 1967 administrative reform, the autonomous
region was completely abolished and replaced by three newly set
up counties. It was, however, stressed that the full equality of the
nationalities and the use of their mother tongues would, as before, be
ensured in the state administration and in educational and cultural
institutions.

There is no overt discrimination against the minorities. Officials
produce impressive figures to show that the nationalities are
adequately represented in the legislative organs from top to bottom,
that their spokesmen sit in the policy-making party bodies, that
there are large-circulation newspapers and periodicals published in
Hungarian, German, and Serb. Nevertheless there is a curious duality
in much of the life in Transylvania between appearance and reality.
Read the official handouts and the Hungarian-language papers
(generally a verbatim copy of the Rumanian newspapers), and you
are in a country where all forms of national discrimination have
been stamped out, and the 1.6 million Hungarians,[47] the Germans,
and the other minorities are working hand in hand in the interests
of their common fatherland. Talk to the people in the cities and
the picturesque villages, and you have crossed the border into a land
where racial animosities and dissatisfactions still smolder.

The fundamental cause of the trouble appears to lie not so much
in particular grievances as in reciprocal suspicion. Many Rumanians
feel inferior to and mistrustful of the Hungarians. Educated Hungarians still often regard themselves as socially superior to Rumanians. There are nevertheless many mixed marriages, and in their
public statements the leading Rumanian officials repeatedly stress
the full equality of all citizens without regard to ethnic origin.
Ceausescu has visited the Hungarian regions several times, and at

the party conference in December 1967 Deputy Premier Janos Fazekas, an ethnic Hungarian, was promoted to full membership in the Executive Committee.

Yet for all the official efforts, one detects over a series of visits a deterioration of the atmosphere in Transylvania. This is partly due to the dynamics of the "Rominia Romanilor" ("Rumania first") line, which has propelled the nation as such into the center of all political pronouncements. It is difficult to judge whether the influx of so many Rumanians into areas and urban centers that were previously overwhelmingly Hungarian and the transfer of ethnic Hungarian experts to relatively distant locations in Moldavia and Wallachia are merely the natural population shifts that accompany rapid industrialization, or whether they also represent a deliberate, politically motivated policy. The important point is that many Hungarians *feel* that political motives play a part and, rightly or wrongly, discern a covert threat posed to their national identity. The fact that the key positions (for instance, even that of First Party Secretary in the former Hungarian autonomous region) are generally held by Rumanians hardly allays apprehension. It would be unfair, however, to lend credence to the complaints privately voiced by Hungarian chauvinists in both Transylvania and Budapest that the Hungarians have been deprived of their right to exist as a distinct nationality with individual traditions. The existence of Hungarian theaters and even of an opera alongside a Rumanian sister institution in Cluj prove the contrary. But it is equally evident that the Rumanians, who are now said to comprise 65 per cent of Transylvania's population (as against 53 per cent in 1910), are by and large the governing class.

What makes the entire problem even more delicate is Rumania's relationship with Hungary proper. Visitors to Eastern Europe are often surprised that Communist regimes born in the same period and with so many common features, facing the same problems of economic and social evolution, should have so few ties. When there is, however, a large minority in one country associated with a neighboring country, it is inevitable that mutual dissatisfaction over isolation should be diverted into national channels. Irksome controls on travel outside Rumania affect both ordinary Rumanians and the Hungarian minority. Yet in the case of the ethnic Hungarians in Transylvania the difficulties in obtaining permits to travel to Hungary proper cannot be explained by the habitual pretext of foreign exchange difficulties. Although almost every Hungarian family has relatives on the other side of the border, the over-all number of tourists (including ethnic Rumanians) traveling to Hungary was only 70,000 in 1966 and 1967. A mere 15,000 people from the regions of Cluj and the formerly autonomous area made trips to Hungary in 1966—out of a total of 700,000 Hungarians in these regions.[48] By comparison, the number of visitors between Hungary and Czechoslovakia in both directions is almost ten times greater, although the Hungarian minority in Slovakia is less than one-third of that in Rumania. The same is true of the half-million Hungarians in Yugoslavia.

The contrast between the fate of Hungarians living in Rumania and those in the two other Communist countries is repeatedly stressed in private by Hungarian officials. Other complaints concern the absence of newspapers, magazines, and novels from Hungary proper in Transylvania (as distinct from the output by ethnic Hungarian writers residing in Transylvania itself and translations from the Rumanian). On several trips to Transylvania, I found it easier to buy "bourgeois" French or West German newspapers than Communist publications from Budapest. The so-called cultural exchange between the two neighboring countries, meager as it is, has been channeled to the capital and not to the regions inhabited by the Hungarian minority. The few guest performances of Budapest theaters or book exhibitions are almost always held in Bucharest and rarely in the centers where most Hungarians live.

Having said this, one must point to the political background. In addition to a legacy of chauvinism, particularly on the Hungarian side, and the well-founded Rumanian suspicion that many Hungarians still cannot accept the frontier settlement as lasting, there are major political differences between the two Communist regimes. These, the only non-Slav nations in Eastern Europe, harbor an equally intense resentment against the Russians. But in contrast to the Rumanian drive for independence, the Kadar regime in Budapest has been a staunch supporter of Soviet policies and a vociferous critic of "nationalist deviations" in the Communist movement. This is not surprising considering the shaky legitimacy of the group put into power by the Red Army in November 1956 and the continued presence of four Soviet divisions in Hungary. But there is also a striking difference in the degree of internal liberalization in Hungary, where the popular uprising, despite its failure, forced the ruling party to grant a greater scope for dissent, and Rumania where the slow progress toward more freedom has been controlled all along from above.

On his official visit to Rumania in February 1958, Kadar reiterated in several speeches that Hungary had no territorial claims against its fraternal neighbor. Nevertheless the relationship since then has been subjected to growing strains and stresses, not over the status of the Hungarian minority, but because of the Rumanian defiance of Moscow. The new emphasis on Rumanian national traditions in history has also sparked debates between Rumanian and Hungarian historians about the character of the 1848 revolution and the conditions under which Greater Rumania was created in 1918—a friction that for the time being involves only historians and social scientists.

Yet the fact that such a prudent politician as Kadar in mid-1966 referred to the "diktat of Versailles and Trianon, imposed by the imperialists, which amputated Hungary's territory" constituted a veiled warning to the leadership in Bucharest. Both sides have several times recognized the inviolability of European frontiers, most recently in the 1966 Bucharest declaration. This has not, however, hindered the Rumanians from making oblique references to the fate of Bessarabia. There is no doubt that the existence of a large Hungarian minority in Rumania provides the regime in Budapest—and thus indirectly the Soviet leadership—with a powerful potential lever of pressure should Rumania's course pose a direct threat to Soviet national interests. In this sense, there is an interrelationship between such relatively distant but equally disputed regions as Bessarabia (and Bukovina) and Transylvania. On the first issue the Rumanian stance is offensive; on the second, defensive. But any rekindling of deep-rooted Hungarian nationalism could be a fatal experiment for the Hungarian Communists, whose regime already crumbled once from anti-Soviet nationalism. This is the main reason why the Hungarian leadership, which is opposed primarily to Rumania's general independent line and not to its specific repercussions on the status of the Hungarian minority, would be most reluctant, even with Soviet prodding, to resort to the double-edged weapon of abetting nationalistic resentments.

A review of the Rumanian revolution would be incomplete without a brief look at its impact on the domestic scene. Touring the country, the visitor is left with the overwhelming impression of an industrial boom. Consider, for example the city of Jassy, the cradle of Rumanian culture and science near the Soviet border, which has also become the symbol of new Rumania. Once one of the most backward areas in this part of the world, Jassy today surprises the visitor with its new rows of apartment buildings, often done with great taste, and its modern "industrial zone." The medieval monasteries and quaint old districts are beginning to be overshadowed by the new Jassy. During the past few years, a number of projects— a metallurgical plant, textile and food processing factories, and a plastic plant—have been completed. A new thermal power plant, a synthetic fiber factory and a host of other smaller plants will be opened in the near future. Machinery and equipment are assembled from an astonishingly wide variety of sources: West German, British, Swiss, Belgian, and Italian companies, and from Czech and Soviet enterprises.

On the road from Moldavia to Transylvania, the visitor reaches Turgu Neamt, a small town whose dilapidated houses and stores could well belong to the last century. Yet, only thirty miles farther on, he arrives at its sister city, Peatra Neamt, where most of the old houses have been pulled down and replaced by ten-story apartments with colorful façades. The same striking contrasts can be encountered in every part of the country from the Moldavian plains to the high rolling land of Transylvania, from the Black Sea coast to the poor regions of Dobruja.

The gap between Rumania and the more developed East European countries has undoubtedly been narrowed. The rise in production between 1965 and 1967, for example, was two and a half times higher than the entire industrial output before the war. Power, engineering, electronics, and petro-chemicals are regarded as the decisive sectors, and almost 80 per cent of the industrial investments during the current Five Year Plan have been earmarked for these branches and for steel. Steel output jumped from less than 300,000 tons in 1938 to 4 million tons in 1967, and with the completion of the first phase of the huge Galati steel plant is scheduled to reach 6.3 million tons by 1970. Power production was up from the prewar 1,100 million kWh to almost 25,000 million kWh in 1967 and should reach 34,000 million kWh in 1970. New industries have been created almost out of nothing, and the proportion of the labor force engaged in industry has doubled to over 19 per cent compared to prewar figures.

Nevertheless, peasants still account for more than 61 per cent of the population. Their rickety horse-drawn carts and the cows, goats, pigs, sheep, and water buffaloes herded by ragged peasants on horseback or on foot along the asphalt highways are still more representative of Rumanian traffic than the trucks, official limousines, and private cars. Looking at the crowds of peasants in white homespun shirts with black jackets and hats who fill the beautiful monasteries in Moldavia on Sundays, it struck me how little on the human level had really changed in the villages. It was all strangely like the rural Rumania I had encountered twenty-five years ago. There are still obvious signs of poverty; how could it be otherwise in a country where, before the war, the value of technical investments in agriculture was half that in Bulgaria and fifteen times smaller than Germany's.

Three consecutive bumper harvests in 1965–67 appreciably improved the supply situation, but a great deal remains to be done, as responsible officials now frankly admit. Since the end of 1966, when Ceausescu first publicly castigated the glaring weaknesses behind the industrial-boom façade, the atmosphere of self-satisfied optimism has changed dramatically. Among the numerous telling comparisons cited by Ceausescu and the press were candid admissions that productivity is still two to three times lower than in Western Germany, France, and Italy, while production costs are nearly double those in advanced countries. A Rumanian farmer produces food for only three persons, his German counterpart, for twenty. The per capita value of exports in 1966 was only half that of Bulgaria's and a fifth of Britain's or West Germany's.[49]

Thus for all its solid achievements, this rich country is still by and large a laggard in the European industrial league. The aim of the economic "spring-cleaning," which began in late 1967, is to maintain the rapid pace of industrialization and the utilization of the rich resources—but at a lower price in terms of waste and in a more rational fashion. The first cautious steps toward meaningful incentives—the replacement of administrative command by economic levers, a more realistic price structure, and investment financing through banks rather than the Budget—will gradually be implemented. By 1970 the economy as a whole should be working under the new system, but even then Rumania will lag far behind Yugoslavia in enterprise autonomy, workers' participation in decision-making, and the influence of the market forces in general.

The very success of Rumania's "economic miracle" may be one of the main reasons for the caution in testing new patterns and methods of economic management. The country's economic development, particularly in view of the large untapped labor reserves, is not yet sufficiently far advanced to have encountered the acute difficulties and harbingers of the structural crisis that is plaguing more developed industrial Communist countries, like, for example, Czechoslovakia. There are also overriding political considerations against daring economic experiments, which would involve unpredictable risks. At a crucial juncture in Rumania's relations with the Soviet Union, the leadership is clearly averse to anything that would rock the boat and conceivably weaken the domestic cohesion of state and party. Searching for a national consensus, the party is slowly and cautiously charting a course of internal reform. This is particularly evident in its conscious bid for the support of the increasing army of engineers and technicians valued more for their skill than for their party book. Class lineage too is becoming less important; what matters now is to find the best man for the job. Though the leadership attempts to combine a measure of economic reform with even tighter supervision and control of the party, it is difficult to believe that the economic reorganization once started will not eventually go beyond present limits, enhancing still further the influence of the "technocrats."

Except for the higher echelons of the bureaucracy and the managerial class, most Rumanians are, however, still primarily involved in the dreary struggle to achieve the ordinary, to get to work in overcrowded buses and trams, to search for something on the side to supplement the monthly pay check. Even after the latest pay increases, average earnings in 1967 were just over 1,200 lei and almost 40 per cent of the labor force received less than 1,000 lei. (At the tourist rate of exchange one dollar equals 18 lei; the official rate is one to six.) A man's suit of cheap to medium cloth costs 900 to 2,000 lei; a shirt is priced at 100 to 130 lei; a jersey dress 500 to 700; a wool pullover up to 700. With refrigerators costing between 3,900 and 7,000, washing machines 1,500 to 2,500, and television sets from 4,300 to 5,500, consumer durables are still widely recognized as something of a luxury.

When I once asked a woman translator about the reaction to the latest Ceausescu speech, she shrugged, "All this talk—speeches, meetings, interpretations. Who really cares, except a handful of us? All this talk has nothing to do with life." Beyond everything else, people who have known bleakness and overregulated grayness for so long are tired.

Measured in their own terms, however, living conditions have clearly improved during the past two or three years. Shops and self-service stores are better stocked with food and consumer goods. But the most visible changes are in road traffic. In the spring of 1964, the streets of Bucharest, once regarded by Rumanians as the "little Paris of the Balkans," were empty except for official cars—obsolete Russian-made black limousines with drawn curtains speeding through the red lights. With the Ceausescu era, the "leading comrades" have switched to Rolls-Royces and Jaguars, expensive Mercedes and Ford models, with the size of the model reflecting the official rank of the owner. Only low-level bureaucrats now drive Russian makes.

The uninhibited display of luxury by the Rumanian Communist "upper class" has no parallel in any other East European country. The hundreds of official cars that fill the enormous open space between the former royal palace and Communist party headquarters whenever congresses are held have become year by year more opulent. Ceausescu and his associates live in private houses, which in comfort, luxury, and amenities compare favorably with those in the fashionable suburbs of Los Angeles or Dallas. Rumania has no tradition of social egalitarianism; in the past it was ruled by the most corrupt privileged group in Europe. If, therefore, a member of the party Presidium today lives in a house built by the rich Bibescu family, most Rumanians regard it as completely natural. Easy-going tolerance tinged with cynicism is more in accord with Rumanian tradition and character than the sense of social discipline and group loyalty so noticeable among Slav peoples, particularly the Bulgarians.

Thus the ruling elite's Western orientation in cars and clothing, far from arousing spite and hatred, appears to confirm many Rumanians' hope that widening contacts with the West will ultimately yield tangible results, not only in the form of new factories but also in everyday life. The decision to build a car factory at an estimated cost of 75 million dollars with an annual capacity of 50,000 Renaults (characteristically called *Dacis!*) indicates the Rumanian leaders' willingness to meet popular aspirations for a more affluent life. Even today one frequently meets the happy owners of the 30,000 or so French and Italian cars that have been imported during the past three years. The number of imported cars was a mere 1,300 in 1961, rising to 8,000 in 1964. By 1966 the figure had doubled to 16,000. Though a small Fiat or Renault costs the equivalent of fifty months' wages for an average employee, there is a keen demand for cars. A Rumanian with money in his pocket, rather than save or build, will give first preference to a car.

The second major amnesty in December 1967, the curbs on the arbitrary use of police powers, and the tighter control over the activities of the dreaded secret police are important signs of the regime's more relaxed and confident attitude. It is worth recalling that a few years ago even the purchase or sale of a typewriter had to be reported to the police. The changes, which are evident in every walk of life, are neither the results of a battle by rebellious intellectuals or students, nor by-products of an abortive revolt as in Hungary, but due solely to initiative and guidance from above. Intellectuals and young people are no longer afraid to talk to foreigners. A Western journalist can travel wherever he wishes, perhaps not always unshadowed, but certainly undisturbed.

Even the frequent visitor to the country is struck by very noticeable changes in the psychological climate of Rumanian intellectual life. A strong undercurrent of optimism pervades conversations. Writers, sculptors, painters, and actors breathe more freely. The crust of ice is slowly but perceptibly melting. The "rehabilitation" of such great and long blacklisted figures of the past as the sculptor, Brancusi, the historian, Iorga, the poet, Blaga, and many others of lesser caliber, together with the respect paid to the cultural heritage have paved the way for a more liberal approach to the creative arts. Whether Ceausescu's promise, "We leave it to the man of letters and art to decide how to write, how to paint, how to compose, and how to find the most suitable forms" will be limited purely to styles and techniques remains to be seen. As in everything else, the rulers' pragmatic approach rather than ideological postulates are likely to define the given limits of dissent. Seeing the frequent exhibitions of abstract paintings and graphics, one gets the impression that whatever contributes to national prestige, and particularly to the nation's image abroad, is permissible so long as it does not impair the absolute power of the party.

As in Yugoslavia and Bulgaria, tourism is becoming a booming industry and an important factor in promoting wider contacts with the West. The number of foreign visitors has jumped from 30,000 to almost 700,000 during the last six years, and 1.2 million are expected to visit the country by 1970. It is still, however, difficult for Rumanians to make private trips to the West. "There is more hope now, but we are getting older, you know," a famous woman painter, who regards Paris as her second home, remarked with a sad smile. How is one to judge a meeting in Vienna in the autumn of 1967 with Rumania's foremost philosopher, who for the first time since the war was allowed to travel with his family to the non-Communist world? As a ray of hope, or as the measure of isolation? The Rumanian leaders have not yet faced up to the crucial test of allowing more freedom of movement. No foreign currency shortage can explain away the sad fact that out of a country with 19.5 million inhabitants, including almost 400,000 ethnic Germans, only 2,000 persons, including several hundred emigrants, received exit permits to Germany in 1967. Despite the introduction of organized group tours to Italy and Austria in 1967–68, Rumania is still a country of one-way tourism.

Nevertheless, for all the limitations and the authoritarian character of the system, if one tests the standards against those of Rumania a few years earlier, there have been important changes, as yet little appreciated abroad, in the progress toward a freer regime. More important still, the policy of national consensus is bound to prompt a policy showing more concern for popular sentiments. Having branched out on their own in a hostile environment, the Rumanian leaders must now base their power increasingly on the support of the people. One should not forget that after 1948 Yugoslavia for a relatively long period pursued unyieldingly rigid policies at home.

Will the curious Rumanian regime, now freed of the stigma of being a Soviet satellite, eventually go the tortuous but hopeful way of Yugoslavia from nationalism and successful defiance of Soviet power to a meaningful domestic liberalization? One might be tempted to say that this could not happen—had there not been so many startling and previously "unthinkable" changes during the past few years.

AFTERWORD

The air in the Balkans, as indeed in Eastern Europe as a whole, is electric with a sense of change. The rigid patterns of the Cold War period are breaking up and there is a more open game of political maneuvers. National assertiveness, the Sino-Soviet dispute, the increasing autonomy of the non-ruling Communist parties and the climate of reduced tensions have combined to create a wholly new situation. Despite the professed adherence of the ruling groups in Belgrade and Tirana, in Sofia and Bucharest to the belief that "the Communist idea" is bound, in the end, to triumph everywhere, the entire postwar political experience of these four countries shows that nationalism transcends ideology when the two are in conflict. The dramatic, at times even frenzied, revival of national feelings and antagonisms is undoubtedly the most momentous change in Balkan politics since the Communist seizure of power. Basic factors —historic, political, economic, ethnic, cultural, sentimental—that affect national interests go deeper than current regimes or doctrines.

It is easier to conclude that nationalism has re-emerged as the central underlying theme of political life than to gauge the full effects of the nationalistic trends upon political alignments in the area and to place the changes in the wider context of European and Communist politics. As we have seen, nationalism, that enormously powerful force, plays a complex and ambiguous role in the processes of change. In the case of nations that are fighting for their right not to be ruled by an outside great power or by a "majority nation" within the same state, the stirrings of national sentiments cannot possibly be identified with reactionary causes. Here, nationalism is an ally of democracy and decentralization. But it would be equally dangerous to express only uncritical praise for the nationalistic trends in the smaller East European states because they offer an opportunity to wean the vassals from the Soviet hegemonial center. The forces unleashed by national emotions can create crisis situations both between neighbors and within multinational states that may be carried beyond rational control.

Thus the arrows point in several directions. It is important to distinguish between movement and fluidity on the one hand and qualitative changes in power relationships on the other. The single, most important change in the balance of power has been the gradual but effective reduction of postwar Soviet domination over the core of the Balkan Peninsula to one important but isolated stronghold, Bulgaria. Whatever internal crises may occur in Yugoslavia or Albania, we can safely discard the idea that either of them will ever accept a satellite relationship to the Soviet Union. It is also highly unlikely that the process of emancipation can be completely reversed in Rumania. One should not lose sight of the important fact that the southern flank of Stalin's erstwhile empire has been eroded by Communist revolts without foreign intervention or any fundamental change in the social system of the states involved. The successful assertion of national claims against Soviet domination was considerably more than the self-defense of small states against rule by a hegemonial center or a disagreement among national states. As pointed out earlier, the significance of the Soviet-Yugoslav conflict in 1948 or, under different conditions, of Albania's defection and Rumania's bid for autonomy lay precisely in the fact that the Soviet Union was not just a traditional nation-state but the directing center of an empire and a church, of an international movement and what was purported to be a universally binding revolutionary creed.

This is the chief reason why Balkan nationalism, deliberately manipulated or exploited by the ruling Communist elite, has represented and does represent such a serious political danger to Moscow. Though the Marxist-Leninist concept of world revolution has profoundly changed, it cannot be said that other aspects of the official ideology have lost their operational effects upon Soviet policy. The examples of Yugoslavia, Albania, and Rumania, combined with the Chinese defiance of the Kremlin, have destroyed the sacred dogma that communism implies unconditional support of the Soviet Union. The epochal significance of the Sino-Soviet split is a large subject about which much has been written. It is also clear, albeit often overlooked, that the disrupting influences radiating from the Balkans have been an important contributory cause to the growing stresses and tensions in the international Communist movement and within the inner core of the Soviet sphere of influence. At the very least, the rise of Balkan nationalism has limited Soviet freedom of action, encouraged a greater degree of independence in other East European states, changed the character of intrabloc relations and thus had more bearing on European politics than the area's military potential and economic resources would warrant.

The cumulative effects of the changes have begun to transform the Balkans, once a solid bulwark of Soviet influence into something like a power vacuum. It is important to remember, however, that, in contrast to Central Europe, the nationalist ferment and the changing alignments in the south have not involved major security interests of the Soviet Union. This has been shown by the Soviet acceptance or toleration of the new situation in relations with three of the four Communist-ruled Balkan states. The reasons for Moscow's sober assessment of the fluidity in the area appear to be twofold.

First, the revolution in military technologies, transport, and communication has deeply changed the traditional geopolitical concept of vital interests in areas relatively near the borders of a great power. "Distance bears no simple relation either to interests or military strength."[1] This is not to say that the Soviet Union does not regard the wider Balkan area as a most sensitive spot, or that Russia does not remain the great power most intimately interested in the region. What the Soviet attitude suggests is that the criterion for what *is* essential has changed.

Secondly, the keystone of traditional Soviet diplomacy is the consideration that, regardless of the given degree of Russian control, a power vacuum in the Balkans should not be filled by dangerous outsiders. In contrast to the 1930s, there is little likelihood of great challengers emerging and creating genuine difficulties for the Russians. Yugoslavia's example has shown that Communist leaders can challenge Moscow and accept extensive, even military aid from "imperialists" without becoming subject to their dictates. In economic terms, the four Balkan countries are of only marginal importance to the Soviet Union. Soviet foreign trade per inhabitant in the late sixties was only 70 dollars (compared for example to 640 dollars for Western Germany and 1,170 dollars for Switzerland). Furthermore, the combined share of all four countries in the Soviet foreign trade total was merely 15.3 per cent, that is, less than the East German stake alone.

A further important field of query and doubts relates to the other aspects of Balkan nationalism—the animosities, claims, and grievances in relations between the states of the region and among national groups within one state. How do these contradictory processes affect their relations with one another, with the Soviet Union and the West? The movement toward autonomy and the decline in Soviet influence have also released emotions and aspirations that may strengthen the very forces against which the Balkan nations have been struggling. The postwar period of uniformity enforced by Soviet hegemony seemed to have restrained, some thought even to have eliminated, the many forms of petty nationalism of neighbor nations. But both Soviet domination and Communist ideology, devised to mollify nationalist tendencies, have intensified them.

If the Communist leaders are treading more and more openly in the footsteps of their nationalist predecessors, will this not lead to a return of the Soviet influence, as it were, by the back door? In manipulating nationalism for their own purposes, the Communist regimes have certainly raised the specter of old rivalries and even territorial feuds. There is not the slightest doubt that this aspect of nationalism also offers an obviously useful leverage to Soviet policies. Mutual animosities fed by such tangled issues as disputed Macedonia or Transylvania can be exploited by imaginative and unscrupulous Soviet policies to weaken united resistance in the Balkans and Eastern Europe against outside pressures. When Soviet Foreign Minister Gromyko visited Sofia at the height of renewed Bulgarian-Yugoslav controversies over Macedonia in February 1968, suspicions were immediately aroused—not only in Belgrade and Skopje—that the sudden bursts of what the Yugoslavs called "expansionist dreams" had been if not sponsored then encouraged by Moscow.

Events and public statements have so far failed to confirm the fears about Moscow's deliberately fanning the flames of discord in this sensitive area. Should the increasingly close Yugoslav-Rumanian cooperation assume a threatening aspect for the Russians, they may well resort in due course to the ancient device of divide and rule. But it is easy to exaggerate the Soviet capacity to control events and to stir up nationalist sentiments. The contradictions that have always plagued the use of nationalist motivation by the Communists with regard to the West and the Third World are also very much alive within the Soviet sphere. In his last public speech at the Nineteenth Congress of the Soviet Communist Party in 1952, Stalin appealed to the Western delegates "to raise the banner of national independence and carry it forward, if . . . you wish to become the leading force of the nation."

But the same nationalism within the Soviet power sphere as expressed then by Tito's Yugoslavia was decried, and with good reason, as a mortal danger. If there is one common feature in the developments in the Communist camp over the past decade or so, it is surely the fact that more and more ruling Communist parties are raising "the banner of national independence and national sovereignty" to gain popular support and to defy Soviet hegemony.

The opinion that "nationalism not only inspires but also fragments East European opposition to the Russians and helps the Soviet leaders in maintaining their predominance in the region"[2] may be correct. But, also for the Russians, the issue of nationalism remains as ever a dangerous two-edged sword. Covert encouragement, let alone open backing of certain nationalist claims in the Balkans or elsewhere would probably involve more risks than opportunities. The Soviet Union as a multinational empire is beset with grave and potentially explosive national problems of its own. To seek to arouse national sentiments as an instrument to bring smaller Communist states more in line—and this at a time when nationalism is increasingly described as "the main danger threatening the unity, defensive might, and ideological force of the Communist movement"[3]—would be playing with fire.

Will the pattern of diversity in the Balkans then lead to a cluster of separate autarkic national states, ruled by Communist but nationalistic elites, no longer subject to the hegemony of any great power, but constantly exposed to the dynamics of a suicidal uncontrolled petty nationalistic strife? We should neither ignore nor overrate the danger of a return to the interwar patterns of the old Balkan conflicts. There have always been two main but contradictory currents in Balkan politics, toward conflict and cooperation. The roots of bitter frictions persist but it would be unwise to overlook the movement for regional cooperation without Soviet participation. The improvement of relations between Yugoslavia, Rumania, and Bulgaria on the one hand and Greece and Turkey, the two non-Communist, semi-Balkan Mediterranean states allied to the West on the other, both reflected and promoted the easing of Cold War tensions. Albania embroiled in a bitter dispute with both of her land neighbors remains for the time being a significant exception. But the climate of reduced tensions, the frequent exchange of high-level visits, and particularly the common stake in tourism have imparted a new impetus to closer cooperation. Since the mid-sixties there have been numerous Balkan conferences on tourism and science, music festivals, and sport events (almost always including Greek and Turkish participants). Though the military coup in Greece has to some extent arrested the promising trend toward a limited but real cooperation, the self-interest of all the states of the wider Balkan region in bilateral and multilateral projects is bound to make itself felt. Powerful economic and technical forces are softening the ideological barriers and pushing the ruling bureaucracies toward regional cooperation.

Is "regionalism" a meaningful alternative to divisive nationalism and to Communist—or utopian—universalism? Historical experience has shown the economic advantages for these small and backward national units when they belonged to a much wider supranational grouping. But we have seen how the Soviet attempt at the integration of the East European countries into a large economic entity not only failed to retard but actually stimulated the revival of defensive nationalism. Interwar cooperation even without the danger of outside domination yielded only modest results in setting up various Balkan-wide institutions for commerce or tobacco marketing. The benefits to be reaped from being welded to a large market are evident, but it would be dangerous to draw from this economic fact conclusions about political behavior. "If economic considerations were the determining factor in such matters, nationalism would not exist, because it is inherently an economic absurdity."[4]

The idea of a union of the South Slavs and even of all Balkan peoples was in the center of various schemes in the thirties and in the early postwar period. Only a Balkan Federation of Yugoslavia, Bulgaria, Albania, and Rumania and involving Greece could cut through the Gordian knot of such tangled issues as Macedonia or Kosovo. But all unifying impulses have failed at a very early stage. The last major abortive attempt by Tito and Dimitrov to build a Communist empire in the Balkans aroused justified suspicions, not only in Moscow but also in Albania and Bulgaria, the two countries most intimately affected. The Balkan Pact of Yugoslavia, Greece, and Turkey signed in 1954 was a joint product of the Tito-Stalin conflict and the Cold War. And even this military alliance soon became a dead letter under the twin impact of the

Yugoslav-Soviet reconciliation and the outbreak of the Cyprus dispute. The network of conflicting and common interests has always extended far beyond the deceptively simple demarcation lines of the Cold War partition in Southeast Europe.

In the light of past experiences and present trends, the grand design of a Balkan Federation or even of a customs union seems as unrealistic in the seventies as it was in the thirties or late forties. Neighborhood in international relations, as Jacob Viner has emphasized, has never guaranteed neighborly feelings and has often prevented them. This is particularly true of the young nations in the Balkans which have hardly ever known a sufficiently long breathing spell, free from outside intervention, to be concerned with their own destiny. In the wake of waning military and ideological ties to Cold War alliances, fundamental factors are at work for the reassertion of the traditional multistate system in this part of the world. Whatever the merits or flaws of the ambitious blueprints for a new pattern of relations in a united Europe, we should look at present realities and the foreseeable future. Would it not be better to face the facts and not pretend that they are otherwise? There is no probability of the national state withering away or being absorbed into an institutional form of supranational cooperation. We must therefore take as starting point the reality—the existence of states as autonomous centers of decisions in the Balkans—and not what may or may not be desirable.

It does not, however, follow that the process of national reaffirmation must necessarily lead to crisis situations or an uncontrolled anarchy. There is already a broadening cooperation for specific and limited purposes such as the giant Yugoslav-Rumanian hydroelectric complex on the Danube, a Rumanian-Bulgarian scheme for a similar Danubian power project, the building of interstate highways, river regulation, and so forth. The fact that even such archenemies as Albania and Yugoslavia are jointly organizing excursions to the Adriatic coast shows that "tourism in today's Europe can be a greater revolutionary force than Marxism."[5]

The revival of nationalism has not stimulated any kind of parochial isolation from the great forces of our time. On the contrary, these countries—as indeed so often in the past—once again look westward for economic ties and cultural inspiration. It is the West and not the Soviet Union that can provide capital, advanced technology, know-how, consumer goods and possibilities for the absorption of surplus labor. It has become almost banal to say that the transformations in Eastern Europe offer a great opportunity to the Western nations to prepare the ground for an acceptable European settlement. The opening up of Eastern Europe to Western influences (but to a degree varying considerably from country to country!) appears to have acquired a momentum of its own, and there are almost daily reports about comings and goings between East and West.

Yet the over-all balance sheet of East-West contacts in the sixties in terms of substance rather than diplomatic niceties has been disappointing. There is a widening gap between high-sounding statements stirring expectations in the East and actual policies that by and large fail to yield tangible benefits. American policy-makers have been faced for some time with the basic dilemma of how to pursue a détente with the Soviet Union without jeopardizing the security and unity of the West. Most policy statements of the Johnson administration have had a globalist ring with hopes and fears hinging almost exclusively on the Soviet Union and scant, if any attention paid to the smaller East European countries. Failing to perceive the long-term significance of the process of differentiation within the Soviet bloc, American policy toward Eastern Europe has been static, operating with concepts that no longer correspond to the changing realities. In view of the nationalist and political ferment in the East, the United States has wavered between euphoria and disappointment without imparting any meaningful impulses toward the much publicized "bridge-building." Western European countries, primarily France, Italy, and more recently West Germany have undertaken numerous useful initiatives though the volume of contacts has been combined with a lack of coordination and political consciousness.

What George Kennan noted almost twenty-five years ago is if possible even more valid today: "For the smaller countries of Eastern and Central Europe, the issue is not one of communism or capitalism. It is one of the independence of national life or of domination by a big power which has never shown itself adept at making any permanent compromises with rival power groups."[6] In this sense any active Western policy toward these countries is bound to be intrinsically anti-Soviet for it lessens the dependence of the partners on the Soviet hegemonial center and promotes national individualism.

It has not been the purpose of this book to discuss the place of Eastern Europe or the Balkans with regard to the various blueprints for a European settlement. One may, however, venture the remark that a European system based on the reduction of American influence in the West but without a corresponding change in the Soviet presence in Central and Eastern Europe would be an absurd proposition. However long the process might take, it is a fundamental Western interest to encourage the trends that strengthen the ties with Eastern Europe and effectively weaken Soviet control.

A pragmatic and sophisticated Western policy must take into account both the scope and the limits of the possibilities in this area. The examples of Yugoslavia and Rumania show that the West does not and can not create new situations, it merely responds to them. On both occasions, the basic change took place before and independent of any Western involvement. Past American policy toward Yugoslavia, especially between 1949 and 1955, was a prime example of an imaginative use of aid extended to a totalitarian regime without strings or pressure. Even then the American involvement was not perhaps decisive, but it helped to protect Yugoslavia's independence and to encourage changes that brought considerable benefits to the people and to the West. At the height of the Cold War, the answer to a conflict situation was relatively simple.

But as Professor Kennan has pointed out, "There is today no such thing as 'communism' in the sense that there was in 1947; there are only a number of national regimes which cloak themselves in the verbal trappings of radical Marxism and follow domestic policies influenced to one degree or another by Marxist concepts."[7] The very complexities of the new situation create novel problems to which there are no easy or straightforward answers. No one would dream of devising universally applicable political recipes for Sweden and Italy, Belgium and Germany. Yet there is still a persistent propensity for an approach in "bloc" terms or in the framework of a mechanical "regionalism." The pitfalls of this simplistic attitude are as evident in the Balkans as in the wider area of Eastern Europe.

Thus the single, most important precondition for an active Western policy is to take account of the special situation in each country, to use a selective approach, and to aim at limited goals. The extension of a World Bank loan to Rumania, the involvement of Western investors in joint projects in Yugoslavia, or the granting of tariff concessions to Bulgarian tomato exporters are considerably more important than the visits of dignitaries, which yield mainly statements about the virtues of peace and cooperation of states with different social systems. In short, less rhetoric and more action is needed.

This is not a question of aid, but primarily of access to Western markets. Yugoslavia is a case in point. Though it belongs to the OECD (Organization for Economic Cooperation and Development) and GATT (General Agreement on Tariffs and Trade), the two important international economic organizations, and is the Communist country that has developed the closest relations with the West, the sharpening tariff discrimination of the EEC (European Economic Community, or Common Market) has badly hit its exports. Over one-quarter of the Yugoslav exports go to the EEC, with farm products accounting for 40 per cent of the total. But for beef worth 1,000 dollars the Yugoslav exporters have to pay 800 dollars in duties, levies, and taxes. No wonder that the country's deficit in trade with the Common Market jumped fourfold to 285 million dollars between 1966 and 1967. Yet despite several years of informal soundings and preliminary talks, at the time of this writing formal negotiations on some kind of institutional arrangements have not even started.

The progress toward economic integration in the West poses a serious threat to the ability of the East European exporters of mainly farm products to acquire the hard currencies with which they can purchase badly needed capital goods. To proclaim the desire to "Europeanize" the small Communist states with their historic ties to the West, yet at the same time to bar access to their biggest potential markets is hardly the best way to create a new Europe.

The lack of understanding of the enormous changes that have taken place in the Communist camp is painfully evident in the policy of boycott and isolation still preferred by the majority of the U. S. Congress, as shown by the denial of most-favored-nation treatment for the exports of most East European countries. It was indicative of the strength of manipulated pressures that in 1965 a leading American company was forced to withdraw from delivering a complete rubber plant to Rumania. At a time when Western European exporters, helped by government-backed loans, compete for the expanding Eastern market, American business is still hamstrung by Cold War restrictions that do not punish "communism" but harm its own interests.

There is no doubt that the Balkan states like their northern neighbors will remain single-party dictatorships for a long time to come. But increased East-West contacts and meaningful initiatives can only encourage domestic liberalization and economic progress, changes that are beneficial to the people and to the long-term interests of the West. Such organizations as the OECD, the International Monetary Fund, the EEC, and the European Free Trade Association provide possibilities for forging institutional links. Nevertheless we should not exaggerate the significance of and the real possibilities for multilateral ventures. What matters most at this stage is to deal in a flexible and practical way with the concrete problems faced by states, which regardless of official ideology can be drawn closer to the Western community. In short, the West has to show rather than promise the benefits to be reaped from moving cautiously and gradually toward independence.

Profound national and social transformations whose outlines may not become clear for some time are taking place in the Communist countries. The progress toward more complex industrial societies, the pressures for decentralization, the increasing weight of pragmatic technocrats instead of political bureaucrats and the emergence of a European-minded younger generation, the future elite, are forces that deeply influence the direction in which the national revival will in fact be moving. But no one can draw summary and oversimplified conclusions. Who can say where the "national path to socialism" will lead ten or twenty years from now? The return to the traditional diversity of national states has created problems, opportunities and risks almost as novel and as formidable as those that were produced in the upheavals of World War II. The outlook is for more movement and more fluidity with consequences that are likely to go far beyond the Balkan borders. Any Western policy that ignores these forces of momentum and fails to take into account the potential influence of the changes in the Balkans will be negatively affected in the pursuit of a new Europe.

POSTSCRIPT AFTER THE CZECH TRAGEDY

It had been my intention to leave this book untouched while it was passing through all its publishing stages. As it goes from galley into page proof in the autumn of 1968, however, profound changes have taken place within the power sphere of the Soviet Union. Changes so important and so far-reaching that—without altering any part of this study—I have to add to my concluding remarks a brief account and analysis of the impact of the Czech tragedy upon the situation in the Balkans.

In a sense, the invasion of Czechoslovakia by the Soviet Union and its four vassals gave a dramatic answer to what I described in the first chapter of this study as *the* key question: "Will the forced or voluntary toleration of autonomy save what is essential to Soviet interests or will it rather accelerate the process of disintegration?" The Russians did not intervene in Czechoslovakia to reestablish a strategic status quo, a military balance. They intervened because of their fear that a toleration of Czechoslovakia's search for meaningful reforms and external autonomy would ultimately erode what remained of Stalin's postwar empire and endanger the position of the ruling bureaucracy in the Soviet Union itself.

Faced with an agonizing choice between two evils—passivity or intervention—both involving great risks, the Soviet leaders (or at any rate the temporarily triumphant faction in the struggle for power at the top) opted for the latter. This decision was not a "tragic error" or an "accidental mistake" but as the Central Committee of the Yugoslav party correctly noted "rather the consequence of stubborn efforts to solve contradictions within socialism by use of force." Worse still, in its efforts to justify the aggression against Czechoslovakia the Soviet leadership has come forward with the ominous doctrine of legalizing the "right of intervention" on behalf of the "higher interests" of socialism. As *Borba* put it, "it is enough for a group of countries to conclude that socialism in a country is 'endangered' to intervene for the sake of higher interests, irrespective of what that country's leaders say."

The occupation of Czechoslovakia and the Soviet theory of "limited sovereignty," "quiet counterrevolution," and the "higher interests of socialism" appear to mark a new "general line," a qualitative change in Soviet foreign policy. One can truly speak of a "decisive historical moment," of a "new era" in the relations between the socialist countries and with regard to the future of socialism in the world. The neo-Stalinist restoration in the Soviet Union under the slogan of "calm and order" has logically led to a return to Stalin's concept of a "geographical socialism" (that is, true socialism exists only where there are Soviet soldiers present). Whatever may yet happen in Czechoslovakia, the military intervention has annulled the entire process that began with the Belgrade Declaration in May 1955 on the separate roads to socialism and gained new impetus after the Twentieth Soviet Party Congress and the Soviet government's statement of October 30, 1956, on relations between socialist states.

The Kremlin in 1968 went further than Stalin was willing to go two decades earlier against the rebels in Belgrade. But the balance of forces in the world Communist movement is basically different from the situation in 1948 and the aftermath of the crushing of the Hungarian revolution in 1956. In contrast to Hungary, where the Nagy government had passed the point of no return by leaving the Warsaw Pact and acquiescing in the restoration of a multiparty system, the vanguard of the Czechoslovak resistance to Soviet pressures was the official leadership of the ruling Communist party, which repeatedly reaffirmed its loyalty to the commitments of the Warsaw Pact. While the Soviet intervention in Hungary was approved by all major Communist parties and grudgingly sanctioned even by Belgrade, the attack on Czechoslovakia lacked even a semblance of "socialist legality" and forced the Soviet party, for the first time since the October Revolution, into a hopelessly isolated minority position in the world movement.

In a sense, the Russians hesitated too long and acted too late. Aside from the factional battles in the top leadership, the form and timing if not the substance of the intervention were to no small degree influenced by the emergence of Yugoslavia and Rumania as increasingly vocal and active allies of reformist Czechoslovakia. The more the Russians and their four vassals increased the pressure on Prague, the stronger became the warnings issued by the Yugoslav and Rumanian leaders, who knew better than anyone else that their independence also was at stake. The coordinated Yugoslav-Rumanian campaign (Tito and Ceausescu met three times publicly and at least once secretly between February and August 1968) had a two-fold effect on the Kremlin.

On the one hand, it temporarily restrained the most extreme "hawks," already subjected to the impassioned pleas of the large Italian and French Communist parties. On the other hand, however —and this proved decisive—the nightmare of a new "Little Entente," if not in name then in fact, began to haunt Soviet policy-makers. The ill-fated Bratislava Declaration signed by Czechoslovakia and the would-be invaders was followed by the triumphal visits of Marshal Tito (August 9–10) and Ceausescu (August 15–17) to Prague. The spread of the contagious disease of nationalism from the Balkans to the "northern tier" and the erstwhile "iron triangle" of the Warsaw Pact raised the specter of a further fragmentation of Moscow's postwar empire. Three days after Ceausescu's visit and the signing of a new Czech-Rumanian friendship treaty, the Russians struck.

The invasion—a military success and a political disaster for Moscow—immediately propelled Yugoslavia and Rumania into the foreground of tensions. Both countries sharply condemned the "flagrant violation of national sovereignty," rejected the Soviet explanations as "unjustifiable and unacceptable," and expressed full solidarity with the victim of the Soviet aggression. The fact that five Czech ministers, including Deputy Premier Ota Sik, happened to have been on vacation in Yugoslavia when the invasion took place unexpectedly strengthened the bargaining position of Belgrade and Bucharest and indirectly that of the Czech leaders. The declarations of the Czech ministers in Belgrade, their treatment as the only legal representatives of the Czechoslovak government, and Sik's flight to Bucharest where he was demonstratively received by Ceausescu implied a barely veiled warning to Moscow: the setting up of a government-in-exile harbored and supported by one or several Communist-ruled countries. This threat coupled with Yugoslavia's initiative at the United Nations Security Council debate on Czechoslovakia was the single most important external factor that, together with the magnificent popular resistance in the country, thwarted the Russian attempt to install a puppet regime.

After the invasion of Czechoslovakia, Yugoslavia as the twin symbol of nationalism and "revisionism" has naturally become the number one target of Soviet attacks. The relations between Belgrade and Moscow have become worse than at any time since the death of Stalin. As Foreign Minister Marko Nikezic put it, "The aggression against Czechoslovakia is not the end of a struggle but rather its beginning." The chief purpose of the concerted anti-Yugoslav campaign waged primarily by Moscow, Warsaw, and Sofia is to intimidate and isolate these fearless opponents of Soviet hegemony. As ever, the Russians are not averse to fanning the flames of old territorial discords. Thus the Yugoslavs with good reason regard the patriotic campaign in Bulgaria, particularly with respect to past and present Macedonia, as a deliberate Soviet attempt to put pressure on Yugoslavia. At the same time, the Russians also view the national question as a useful leverage to remind the Yugoslavs of their internal weaknesses.

The Soviet leaders are, however, making the same miscalculation that Stalin did twenty years earlier. In times of grave external dangers, there is an instinctive revival of common Yugoslav nationalism which, without solving the basic problems, nevertheless supersedes the petty strife between nations and republics. In this sense, the Soviet campaign against Yugoslavia is counterproductive since it more than anything else helps to reforge unity and to strengthen rather than weaken the awareness of common destiny.

The renewed open split between Belgrade and Moscow put a final end to the hopes, nurtured by Tito even after Khrushchev's fall, that a close cooperation, based on genuine equality, would be possible with Moscow. The silence of Nasser, Indira Gandhi, and other great friends after the Czech tragedy and the threats against nonaligned Yugoslavia punctured the myth of the solidarity of the "nonaligned countries." They, like great powers, do not have permanent friends or permanent enemies. As Lord Palmerston noted more than a century earlier, they have permanent interests.

Regardless of what form possible Soviet pressures might take, the repercussions of the Czech tragedy will have a major and lasting influence on Yugoslavia's external and domestic policies. Paradoxical as it may sound today, the reckless Soviet behavior may prove to be a blessing in disguise if it helps to erase wishful thinking about a basic change in Soviet expansionist aims and to keep the country more aloof from alignments serving no conceivable national interest. Internally, the new conflict with Moscow is bound to strengthen the positions of those who are pressing for further daring measures of political liberalization.

Rumania's position after the dramatic shift in Moscow from grudging tolerance of dissent to the Stalinist concept of Soviet primacy is much more insecure. At one point in late August the provocation of Rumania's public and sharp censuring of the invasion of Czechoslovakia appeared great enough and unforgivable enough to bring immediate retaliation from the Soviet neighbor. It is possible, as some maintain, that Ceausescu in his passionate speech at a mass meeting on the morning of the invasion and the Rumanian leadership in its quick, sharply worded resolutions "overreacted." In view of the Rumanian flair for prudence and timing, it is more likely that they feared action by an unpredictable Soviet leadership and wanted to give notice of their determination to fight if attacked. Following the so-called Soviet-Czechoslovak "Moscow agreement" (more correctly, *diktat*), the Rumanian leaders toned down their propaganda and scrupulously avoided any action that might further antagonize the Kremlin.

Nevertheless Soviet-Rumanian relations were on the verge of an open rupture, particularly after Chinese Premier Chou En-lai chose the reception at the Rumanian Embassy in Peking on August 23, the national day, to offer help to Rumania "which was also threatened" and to condemn the invasion of Czechoslovakia "as a treacherous attack of Fascist type launched by the Soviet revisionists." For the first time since Rumania's go-it-alone policy began, the policy was publicly attacked by Soviet, Polish, Hungarian, and Bulgarian mass media. But in contrast to the end of July when the Rumanians sent and published a protest note to Poland because of some relatively mild allusions to Rumanian separatism, *Scinteia* now refused to engage in polemics.

Despite their tactical retreat and declarations of loyalty to the Warsaw Pact, the Rumanians are deeply concerned about future Soviet intentions. It was at their prompting that President Johnson issued the long-overdue warning to Moscow against "unleashing the dogs of war" in Eastern Europe. A Soviet policy that treats spheres of influence as spheres of absolute domination poses a serious threat to Rumania's independent course. The Soviet offensive to tighten control over Eastern Europe involves new attempts to push forward military and economic integration. A resolution of the Bucharest parliament gave a covert answer to the persistent Soviet demands that Rumania as a member of the Warsaw Pact should allow the entry of allied troops to hold joint maneuvers on Rumanian territory. Within forty-eight hours of the invasion of Czechoslovakia, the Rumanian parliament solemnly declared that a decision regarding the stationing of foreign troops was a "matter exclusively within the jurisdiction of this supreme elected body."

Having an almost 1,500-mile-long common border with three potentially hostile neighbors (Russia, Hungary, and Bulgaria) and a virtually indefensible 150-mile coastline on the Black Sea, Rumania's only hope lies in deft maneuvering and internal unity. It was a deliberate gesture when at the height of the Czech crisis Ceausescu and his associates paid a series of visits to the areas with large Hungarian minorities in Transylvania. Barring a direct intervention, the Russians cannot force the Rumanians to turn back the clock. It is more likely that they will appear to yield temporarily in order to survive and to save what is essential to national interests.

In the psychological warfare against both Rumania and Yugoslavia, neighboring Bulgaria was allotted a key role. Though seemingly an isolated outpost of Soviet influence, Bulgaria also serves as a launching pad for an offensive Soviet strategy. Though not even a neighbor of Czechoslovakia, Bulgaria participated in the invasion. Much more important than the presence of token Bulgarian units in Prague and Slovakia, however, was the staging of army maneuvers between August 26 and September 6 in the vicinity of the borders with Rumania and Yugoslavia. The timing and place of the maneuvers and the reported participation of Soviet units constituted an unmistakable warning to the two heretical neighbors. As always in the periods of heightening international tensions, the Bulgarian regime launched a "vigilance" campaign and the security police arrested several spies. As Bulgaria is bound to remain the principal Soviet instrument to whip up tensions in the Balkan area, the immediate outlook for the continuation of a more activist external policy and of a course of internal reform is not very promising.

Finally, the Czech crisis has had interesting and important repercussions in Albania whose leaders were the first to castigate both "the Soviet revisionist aggressors" and the "Czechoslovak revisionist capitulationists." But the Albanian response went far beyond words. "As the Warsaw Treaty has been turned from a peace treaty into a war pact, from a defense treaty against imperialist aggression into a pact of aggression against the socialist countries," the Albanian parliament on September 13 unanimously voted to annul the country's membership in the Warsaw Pact. More important still, the lengthy statement made by Premier Shehu for the first time in thirteen years did not contain a single word about the Yugoslav "revisionist traitors." Instead, it proclaimed a "foreign policy of peace and good neighborliness."

The Czech crisis shook Tirana as it shook Belgrade. Both had seen the specter of further reckless Soviet blows against all the "troublemakers" in the Balkans. For all their tributes paid to "the best and most faithful friend, the great 700-million-strong People's China," the Albanian leaders know that their country's fate is inextricably linked with the independence of neighboring Yugoslavia and Greece. As an ironic by-product of the Soviet intervention in Prague, the two archenemies in the Balkans have been brought closer than ever before to the point of a mutually tolerable "coexistence" because they share a common fear and face a common adversary. The normalization may not go far or remain durable, and it certainly will not eliminate the roots of the national and ideological friction. But at this crucial juncture in Balkan history, it does contribute to the safety of both sides.

I do not end this study at any decisive stage in the agony of Czechoslovakia or in the new dangerous fluidity in the Balkans. What is certain, however, is that the Balkans have once again become a tension-ridden storm center. After the occupation of Czechoslovakia, they are more than ever the heart of the national challenge to Soviet domination. The unpredictability of Soviet behavior has injected a new element of permanent tension into the entire area. There is no guarantee whatsoever that the men in the Kremlin, aware of their superior force and the disunity of the West, fighting for power and driven by fear over the future, will not tomorrow or the day after tomorrow invade another country.

Tanks can slow down, but they cannot stop the historic process of decolonization and national emancipation. This indeed is the chief lesson past and recent Balkan history holds for the epigones of Stalin.

NOTES

I. COMMONPLACES, MYTHS, AND REALITIES

1. V. Dedijer, *Tito*, p. 306.
2. H. F. Armstrong, *Tito and Goliath*, pp. 263 and 277.
3. See R. V. Burks, "Rumäniens nationale Abweichung," *Osteuropa*, May–June 1966.
4. Hans J. Morgenthau, "Alternatives for Change," *Problems of Communism*, Sept.–Oct. 1966.
5. Raymond Aron, "The Impact of Marxism in the Twentieth Century," in *Marxism in the Modern World*, ed. M. M. Drachkovitch, pp. 1–46.
6. J. L. Talmon, *The Unique and the Universal*, p. 13.
7. *Ibid.*, pp. 13 and 21.
8. J. Wszelaki, *Communist Economic Strategy: The Role of East Central Europe* (Washington, D.C., 1959), pp. 68–77. See also for postwar economic exploitation, N. Spulber, *The Economics of Communist Eastern Europe*, and Z. K. Brzezinski, *The Soviet Bloc*, pp. 124–28.
9. H. Mendershausen, *Terms of Trade between the Soviet Union and Smaller Communist Countries, 1955–1957*, Rand Corporation, California, January 1959; reprinted in *The Review of Economics*, May 1959. See also by the same author, *The Terms of Soviet-Satellite Trade: A Broadened Analysis*, Rand Corporation, December 1959, and J. Wszelaki, "Economic Development in East Central Europe," *Orbis*, University of Pennsylvania, Winter 1961. For the changes in Soviet attitudes see W. Winston, "The Soviet Satellites—Economic Liability?" *Problems of Communism*, Jan.–Feb. 1958.
10. Dedijer, p. 263.
11. *Pravda*, Moscow, March 27, 1959.
12. G. F. Kennan's lecture in July 1965 at the Europa-Gespräch in Vienna. German text in *Europa Gespräch* (Vienna, 1965), pp. 16–33.
13. For the "global" views see particularly Z. K. Brzezinski's *Alternative to Partition*, New York, 1965, and his "American Globalism," *Survey*, January 1966, and "Framework of East-West Reconciliation," *Foreign Affairs*, New York, January 1968. For the opposite view, identical with the present author's, see e.g. Victor Meier, "Changing Realities in Eastern Europe," *Problems of Communism*, July–August 1967, and "Nationalismus in Osteuropa," *Der Monat*, Berlin, June 1967.
14. R. Lowenthal, "The Rise and Decline of International Communism," *Problems of Communism*, March–April 1963. See also by the same author "The Prospects for Pluralistic Communism," in *Marxism in the Modern World*, pp. 225–74.
15. Raymond Aron, "On Polycentrism," *Survey*, January 1966.

II. THE LAND, THE PEOPLE, THE INTRUDERS

1. Hugh Seton-Watson, *Eastern Europe between the Wars, 1919–1941,* pp. 146–51.
2. *Ibid.,* pp. 21–22.
3. R. L. Wolff, *The Balkans in Our Time,* p. 19.
4. R. W. Seton-Watson, *A History of the Roumanians,* p. 192.
5. *Ibid.,* pp. 383–84.
6. *Ibid.,* p. 457.
7. Wolff, p. 36.
8. J. Tomasevich, *Peasants, Politics and Economic Change in Yugoslavia,* p. 109.
9. R. W. Seton-Watson, p. 80.
10. Wolff, p. 87.
11. Quoted in R. W. Seton-Watson, p. 240.
12. H. Neubacher, *Sonderauftrag Südost, 1940–1945.*
13. N. Spulber, *The State and Economic Development in Eastern Europe,* p. 68.
14. *Ibid.,* p. 26.
15. *Ibid.,* p. 74.
16. Bernard Shaw, *Arms and the Man,* in *Plays, Pleasant and Unpleasant* (London, 1908), p. 74.
17. L. B. Namier, *Facing East,* London, 1947.
18. Tomasevich, p. 246, about the "Balkan version of bourgeoisie" in interwar Yugoslavia. The same estimate is probably true with regard to Bulgaria.

III. YUGOSLAVIA

1. Bertram D. Wolfe, "Leninism," in *Marxism in the Modern World,* ed. Drachkovitch, p. 87.
2. Armstrong, p. 31.
3. See e.g. J. B. Hoptner, *Yugoslavia in the Crisis, 1934–1941,* which argues that the regency's foreign policy—including the signing of the Tripartite Pact—was "the best possible" in the adverse circumstances.
4. F. Borkenau, *Der europäische Kommunismus,* p. 325.
5. Hoptner, p. 288; Neubacher, pp. 128–29.
6. Neubacher, p. 31.
7. *Ibid.,* pp. 146–49.
8. F. Maclean, *Disputed Barricade,* p. 267. See also Neubacher, pp. 165–75.
9. S. Clissold, "Occupation and Resistance," in *A Short History of Yugoslavia,* p. 215. See also his *Whirlwind.*
10. R. V. Burks, *The Dynamics of Communism in Eastern Europe,* p. 124.
11. *Ibid.,* p. 130.
12. Wolfe, p. 11; Brzezinski, p. 3.

13. I. Avakumovic, *History of the Communist Party of Yugoslavia*, I, 42–46; for membership figures, p. 185.

14. Burks, p. 129. For Comintern's pro-Bulgarian line, see also pp. 109–15; J. Rothschild, *The Communist Party of Bulgaria*, pp. 223–58; E. Barker, *Macedonia*, pp. 45–77; and Avakumovic, I, 68–85.

15. Avakumovic, I, 129. Number of victims revealed in *Politika*, Belgrade, October 7, 1961.

16. *Ibid.*, p. 141. See also pp. 159–73.

17. Maclean, p. 127. See also Armstrong, pp. 22–25, and Borkenau, pp. 322–31.

18. *Vjesnik u Srijedu*, Zagreb, August 2, 1967. For the role and strength of the Partisans, see Maclean, pp. 131–297; V. Dedijer, *Dnevnik*, I, II, III, Belgrade, 1945–50; Davidson, *Partisan Picture;* and Tito's *Report to the Fifth Congress of the Communist Party of Yugoslavia*, Belgrade, 1948.

19. Burks, pp. 21 and 52. See also Rankovic's *Report to the Sixth Congress of the Communist Party of Yugoslavia*, Belgrade, 1953.

20. Wolfe, p. 89.

21. *The Soviet-Yugoslav Controversy, 1948–1958*, eds. R. Bass and E. Marbury, p. 15.

22. Borkenau, p. 476.

23. Mosha Pijade, *About the Legend that the Yugoslav Uprising Owed Its Existence to Soviet Assistance* (London, 1950), p. 11.

24. Dedijer, *Tito*, p. 209.

25. E. Kardelj, "On People's Democracy in Yugoslavia," *Komunist*, Belgrade, July 1949.

26. Borkenau, p. 370.

27. Dedijer, *Tito*, p. 303.

28. M. Djilas, *Conversations with Stalin*, pp. 34–37.

29. *Ibid.*, pp. 154–66; Dedijer, *Tito*, pp. 304–29.

30. J. C. Campbell, *Tito's Separate Road*, p. 28.

31. *Borba*, Belgrade, October 1, 1967.

32. *Borba*, November 1, 1967.

33. A. Ulam, "On Titoism" in *Marxism in the Modern World* (Stanford, 1966), p. 151.

34. Clissold, *Short History*, p. 7.

35. R. Bicanic, "Economics of Socialism in a Developed Country," *Foreign Affairs* (July 1966), p. 635.

36. S. Pejovich, *The Market-Planned Economy of Yugoslavia*, pp. 55–57.

37. *Borba*, June 19, 1961.

38. Campbell, pp. 45 and 171.

39. *The Economic Reform in Yugoslavia*, in *Socialist Thought and Practice*, Special Issue, Statisticki Godisnjak JFRS, Belgrade, 1967. *Vjesnik u Srijedu*, Zagreb, November 8, 1967.

40. Tomasevich, pp. 316–21.

41. *Borba*, March 2, May 15, and September 7, 1967.

42. *Komunist*, Belgrade, October 21, 1965.

43. For investments in 1947–59 see G. W. Hoffman and F. W. Neal,

Yugoslavia and the New Communism, pp. 508–9. See also OECD survey for Yugoslavia (August 1966).

44. *Politika,* Belgrade, October 11, 1967.

45. Branko Horvat in *Gledista,* Belgrade, March 1967. See also Bakaric's speech reported in *Vjesnik u Srijedu,* October 26, 1967, and *Komunist,* October 19, 1967.

46. A. de Tocqueville, *The Old Regime and the French Revolution,* pp. 176–77.

47. *Borba,* October 10, 1964.

48. Mihajlo Markovic, "Socialism and Self-Government," *Praxis,* I, 2–3 (Zagreb 1965), 178–95.

49. G. Grossman, "Economic Reform: A Balance Sheet," *Problems of Communism,* Nov.–Dec. 1966.

50. Kardelj interview with *Ekonomska Politika,* Belgrade, November 27, 1965.

51. Kardelj speech at the plenary meeting of the Central Committee of the League of Communists of Slovenia in Ljubljana; text published in *Komunist,* October 6, 1966.

52. Crvenkovski's speech in Zagreb, reported in *Borba,* October 23, 1966. See also his article in *Komunist,* November 24, 1966.

53. Sixth Congress of the Communist Party of Yugoslavia, Belgrade, 1953.

54. Dedijer, *Tito,* p. 248.

55. *Komunist,* Jan.–Feb. 1954.

56. *NIN,* Belgrade, October 15, 1967. For the membership figures see *Komunist,* May 25, 1967, and *Borba,* July 3, 1967.

57. *Vjesnik,* March 19, 1967.

58. Lenin, *Collected Works* (Sochineniya), 4th ed. (Moscow, 1941–52) VI, 223.

59. V. Cvjeticanin, "Some Theoretical-Practical Aspects of Bureaucracy," *Praxis,* Jan.–Feb. 1967.

60. *Theses on the Development and Reorganization of the League of Communists of Yugoslavia (LCY)* adopted by the Central Committee on July 1, 1967. English text in special issue of *Socialist Thought and Practice,* Belgrade, 1967.

61. *Politika,* December 23, 1965.

62. *Socijalizam,* Belgrade, July–August 1965. See also *Borba,* November 2, 1965.

63. *Komunist,* October 11, 1967. Also J. Majarovic, "The Communists and the Political Decisions of Self-Managers," *Socijalizam,* January 1967.

64. J. K. Galbraith, *The New Industrial State,* New York, 1967.

65. Prof. R. Tomovic in *Komunist,* September 21, 1967. *Borba,* December 5, 1965.

66. For figures about qualifications, see S. Bijelic, member of Central Committee, in *Vjesnik u Srijedu,* February 15, 1967. For unemployment statistics, *Komunist,* July 20, 1967.

67. M. Mandic in *NIN,* October 29, 1967. For disparities between regions and industries in average wage levels and narrow spread of differentials in incomes between categories of skills, see OECD *Economic Survey for Yugoslavia*

(Organization for Economic Cooperation and Development, Paris, May 1965), pp. 34–39.

68. *Encyclopedia Moderna*, Belgrade, Jan.–Feb. 1967.

69. *Borba*, January 24, 1967. See also *Komunist*, March 1, 1965.

70. Cvjeticanin.

71. Tito's talk with members of the Committee for Electronics, Automation, and Nuclear Energy published in *Borba*, Dec. 31, 1965–Jan. 1–2, 1966. See also *Borba*, October 9, 1965. On refineries see *Vjesnik u Srijedu*, August 22, 1967, and *Ekonomska Politika*, August 26, 1967.

72. C. Zalar, *Yugoslav Communism: A Critical Study*, Washington, 1961. Quoted in V. Meier, "Der Soldat und die Kompagnie: Die politischen Probleme der jugoslawischen Kommunisten seit 1958," *Osteuropa*, 7–8 (July–August 1963), 462.

73. For assets see speech by the then Premier P. Stambolic reported in *Borba*, February 10, 1967; for investment returns, *Vjesnik u Srijedu*, February 21, 1964.

74. Author's calculations on the basis of figures in Statistical Yearbook, Belgrade, 1967.

75. Bicanic, p. 644.

76. *Borba*, Dec. 31, 1965–Jan. 1–2, 1966.

77. *Ekonomska Politika*, October 27, 1967.

78. Tomasevich, pp. 240–42. R. Bicanic, *Ekonomska podloga Hrvatskog Pitanja* (The Economic Basis of the Croat Question) (Zagreb, 1938), pp. 70–77. See also for 1917–20 I. J. Lederer, *Yugoslavia at the Paris Peace Conference*, particularly pp. 3–78.

79. *Vjesnik*, April 4, 1966, and October 10, 1964.

80. For details see *Borba*, July 2–3, 1966, and December 10, 1966. A considerable amount of information was given to me by well-informed and reliable persons in Belgrade, Zagreb, and Ljubljana, including one member of the Central Committee of the Yugoslav party (LCY) and several members of the Central Committees of the republican parties in Croatia and Slovenia.

81. Bicanic, *Economics of Socialism*, p. 646.

82. *Borba*, March 28, 1965.

83. *Komunist*, March 2, 1967. *Borba*, September 14, 1966.

84. *Borba*, April 20 and 28, 1967.

85. Bicanic, *Economics of Socialism*, p. 643.

86. *Borba*, July 2–3, and October 6, 1966 and personal information (see fn. 80).

87. For Crevenkovski, see *Komunist*, November 24, 1966; for Tomovic, *Komunist*, September 11, 1967.

88. Tito's speech reported in *Borba*, March 23, 1967.

89. For Tripalo, see *Vjesnik*, December 11, 1966; for Crvenkovski, *Borba*, October 23, 1966, and November 1, 1967. See also interview with J. Djordjevic, president of legal commission of parliament, in *Vecerni Novosti*, Belgrade, July 16, 1967. For Todorovic on the increasing autonomy of the republican party bodies, see *Komunist*, October 26, 1967.

90. Crvenkovski's speech in Zagreb reported in *Borba*, October 23, 1966.

IV. ALBANIA

1. *Zeri i Popullit*, Tirana, September 15 and 30, 1967; quoted in Radio Free Europe Research Report, October 11, 1967.

2. L. Thalloczy, *Illyrisch-albanische Forschungen*, II, 85, quoted in R. Schwanke, "Bildung von Nation und Staat in Albanien" (Formation of Nation and State in Albania), *Österreichische Osthefte*, 6 (Vienna, 1961), 453–62.

3. Wolff, p. 92.

4. Gianni Amadeo, *L'Albania dall' independenza all unione con l'Italia* (Milano, 1940), p. 147. Cited in Schwanke.

5. Wolff, p. 29.

6. *Ibid.*, p. 141.

7. S. Skendi, *The Political Evolution of Albania*, New York, 1954.

8. "Wissentschaftlicher Dienst Südosteuropa," Munich, Sept.–Oct. 1957. See also Avakumovic, I, 107–8. For the early party history, see W. E. Griffith, *Albania and the Sino-Soviet Rift*, pp. 9–20; S. Skendi, *Albania;* "History of the Albanian Communist Party," *News from Behind the Iron Curtain*, New York, Nov. 1955–Jan. 1956; Borkenau, pp. 371–82; Burks, pp. 143–49; and V. Dedijer, *Jogoslovensko-Albanski Odnosi, 1938–1949* (Yugoslav-Albanian Relations), Belgrade, 1949.

9. Neubacher, pp. 105–18.

10. J. Amery, *Sons of the Eagle.*

11. *Ibid.*, p. 334; for the previous quotes, pp. 322–26.

12. B. Page, D. Leitch, and P. Knightley, *The Philby Conspiracy* (New York, 1968), pp. 193–203.

13. For details see Griffith, pp. 13–17; *Yugoslav White Book*, Belgrade, 1961; and Dedijer, *Jogoslovensko-Albanski Odnosi.*

14. Djilas, pp. 120–33.

15. Griffith, p. 175. For leadership statistics see Skendi, *Albania*, and Burks.

16. Djilas, p. 131.

17. Burks, pp. 147–48.

18. Plaku's statement in *Borba*, May 23, 1961. See also Griffith, pp. 22–25.

19. Griffith, p. 22.

20. *Ibid.*, p. 12.

21. *Ibid.*, pp. 168–72.

22. Quoted in Griffith, p. 55.

23. Dragutin Solajic, "Obvious Facts," *Borba*, March 19, 20, 21 and 22, 1961.

24. Hoxha's *Report to the Fifth Congress of the Party of Labor of Albania*, English text, Tirana, 1966.

25. *Ibid.*

26. Quoted in Radio Free Europe Situation Report, October 9, 1967.

27. See for Yugoslav gestures *Politika*, October 5 and 7, 1967; *Borba*, October 26, 1967; *Komunist*, November 2, 1967; and *Vjesnik*, November 6,

1967. For Albanian rejection see speech by Politburo member H. Kapo on November 7, 1967 and editorial in *Zeri i Popullit*, November 16, 1967.

28. Quoted in *Borba*, November 8, 1967.

V. BULGARIA

1. Wolff, p. 387.
2. C. E. Black, "Bulgaria in Historical Perspective," in *Bulgaria*, ed. L. A. D. Dellin, p. 12.
3. Rothschild, p. 75.
4. Black, p. 9.
5. H. Seton-Watson, p. 255.
6. Rothschild, pp. 8 and 302.
7. *Ibid.*, pp. 302–3.
8. L. Trotsky, *In den Balkanländern*, quoted in Rothschild, p. 2.
9. Quoted by T. Tchitchovsky, *The Socialist Movement in Bulgaria* (London, 1931), p. 15.
10. Rothschild, p. 122. See also J. Swire, *Bulgarian Conspiracy*.
11. Rothschild, p. 132.
12. *Ibid.*, pp. 300–3.
13. Black, p. 22.
14. See Dellin, pp. 115–18; E. Barker, *Truce in the Balkans*, pp. 41–45. For figures on trials in text see Armstrong, p. 219; Dellin, p. 110; Barker, pp. 46–48.
15. Barker, *Truce in the Balkans*, p. 78. For details of Communist takeover see Barker, pp. 73–81 and 92–99; Dellin, pp. 122–24; Hugh Seton-Watson, *The East European Revolution*, pp. 211–19.
16. Djilas, p. 167.
17. For political evaluation, see J. F. Brown, *The New Eastern Europe*, pp. 12–14; R. V. Burks, "Die Auswirkungen des sowjetisch-chinesischen Konflikts auf die kommunistischen Parteien in Südosteuropa" (The Impact of the Sino-Soviet Conflict on the Communist parties in Southeast Europe), *Osteuropa*, 6 (June 1965), 398–403. For economic targets, see B. A. Christoff, "The Bulgarian Leap Forward," *Problems of Communism*, Sept.–Oct. 1959, and J. Kalo, "The Bulgarian Economy," *Survey*, December 1961.
18. *Narodna Mladezh*, Sofia, June 19, 1967.
19. Zhivkov's speech and concluding remarks at the Ninth Congress of the Communist Party of Bulgaria, November 14–16, 1966, trans. by Foreign Languages Press, Sofia, 1966. Speech by Deputy Defense Minister Transky and the secretary of the youth organization quoted in Radio Free Europe report, *Bulgarian Youth: A Serious Concern for the Party*, November 24, 1967.
20. *Borba*, February 9, 1967.
21. *Istoricheski Pregled*, Sofia, Nov.–Dec. 1966.
22. *Istoricheski Pregled*, Sept.–Oct. 1965. Since this chapter was written the Bulgarian-Yugoslav controversy reached a new peak in January–March 1968 in connection with the ninetieth anniversary of the San Stefano Treaty and Bulgaria's liberation. Articles alluding to Macedonia as "a land with a predomi-

nantly Bulgarian population" appeared in the Bulgarian party organ *Rabotnichesko Delo* on December 21, 1967, and January 12, 1968, and in numerous other papers. The Yugoslavs reacted sharply: see *Nova Makedonia,* Skopje, December 30, 1967; *Vjesnik,* Zagreb, January 10, 1968; *Politika,* Belgrade, January 14, 1968; and for political statements by Yugoslav leaders, *Borba,* January 31 and February 3, 1968. The Yugoslav government officially protested on January 27, 1968, and the Bulgarians handed a verbal note to the Yugoslav Ambassador in Sofia on February 2, 1968.

23. Black, p. 25.

24. *Politika,* February 16, 1967.

25. *Novo Vreme,* Sofia, February 1967.

26. *Novo Vreme,* May 1965.

27. *Trud,* Sofia, October 25, 1967.

VI. RUMANIA

1. R. W. Seton-Watson, *A History of the Roumanians,* p. viii.

2. *Ibid.,* pp. 192–200.

3. N. Iorga, *Geschichte des rumänischen Volkes* (History of the Rumanian People) (Gotha, 1905), II, 216.

4. R. W. Seton-Watson, *A History of the Roumanians,* p. 462.

5. Spulber, *The State and Economic Development in Eastern Europe,* p. 111.

6. *Ibid.,* pp. 99–115.

7. See J. W. Brügel, "Das sowjetische Ultimatum an Rumänien" (The Soviet Ultimatum to Rumania), *Vierteljahrshefte für Zeitgeschichte,* Stuttgart, October 1965; also, A. Hillgruber, *Hitler, König Karol, und Marschall Antonescu;* G. Gafencu, *Prelude to the Russian Campaign; and Documents of German Foreign Policy, 1918–1945,* Series D, Vol. X.

8. For dispute, see *Politika,* Belgrade, December 17, 1962, which quotes *The Annals of the Historical Institute of the Rumanian Workers' Party;* also Gheorghiu-Dej's speech at the Central Committee plenum on December 7, 1961, in *Scinteia,* Bucharest (and in Agerpress, Bucharest, English supplement). For Soviet acceptance of new Rumanian version, see E. D. Karpeshenko, "The Victory of Socialism in the People's Republic of Rumania," *Novaya i Noveishaya Istoriya,* 2, Moscow, 1963. For the gradual enlargement of the Rumanian claims, see Gheorghiu-Dej's speech on August 24, 1964, reported in *Scinteia,* and Ceausescu's speech marking the party's forty-fifth anniversary on May 8, 1966. For the role of "patriotic generals and court circles," see Maurer's speech marking the twentieth anniversary of the proclamation of the republic reported in *Scinteia,* December 30, 1967. For details of the 20th anniversary of one coup see Barker, *Truce in the Balkans,* pp. 129–33; G. Ionescu, *Communism in Rumania, 1944–1962,* pp. 71–86; and Hugh Seton-Watson, *The East European Revolution,* pp. 87–90.

9. Barker, *Truce in the Balkans,* p. 159.

10. See *Romania,* ed. S. A. Fischer-Galati, pp. 14 and 35–39. Ceausescu's

speech at the national party conference, December 6–8, 1967—English text published by Agerpress, December 1967.

11. Winston Churchill, *Triumph and Tragedy,* pp. 198–227. See also Wolff, pp. 248–67.

12. Brown, p. 202.

13. Quoted in Ionescu, p. 59. See also Brügel, p. 405.

14. Ionescu, p. 106; Barker, *Truce in the Balkans,* p. 136; and Wolff, pp. 282–83.

15. Fischer-Galati, p. 13.

16. Mosha Pijade, quoted by Armstrong, p. 177.

17. See Wolff, pp. 344–46; Spulber, *The Economics of Communist Eastern Europe,* pp. 207–23; Brzezinski, *The Soviet Bloc,* pp. 35–40.

18. See V. Winston, "Eastern Europe—Economic Liability?" *Problems of Communism,* Jan.–Feb. 1958.

19. See J. M. Montias, "Background and Origins of the Rumanian Dispute with COMECON," *Soviet Studies* (Oxford, Oct. 1964), 125–51; *Survey of Europe,* UN Economic Commission for Europe, 1957, 1960, and J. Smilek, "Coordination of the Economic Development of the CMEA [Comecon] Member States," *Hospodarske Noviny,* Prague, July 22, 1966. A study by a Soviet economist, J. Belayev, in *Voprosi Ekonomiki,* 7/1967, Moscow, claims that the per capita industrial production in Rumania, taking the Soviet figure=100, was 31 in 1950 and 48 in 1965. With regard to the national income per capita, taking Poland=100, he claims that the comparative figure for Rumania in 1950 was 48 but rose to 82 in 1965. In engineering output per capita, taking Czechoslovakia=100, Rumania reached only 10 in 1950 and 22 in 1965.

20. See speeches by Gheorghiu-Dej and Petre Borila at the December 1961 Central Committee plenum, *Scinteia,* December 7 and 13, 1961.

21. Ceausescu's speech at the 1961 plenum, published in *Scinteia,* December 13, 1961. See also R. V. Burks, "Rumäniens nationale Abweichung" *Osteuropa,* May–June 1966.

22. *Ibid.*

23. Ceausescu's 1961 plenum speech.

24. Burks, "Rumäniens nationale Abweichung."

25. Smilek. See also *Politika,* Belgrade, May 22, 1966.

26. For details of Galati controversy see J. F. Brown, "Rumania Steps Out of Line," *Survey,* October 1963.

27. Private information from Rumanian sources.

28. *Scinteia,* March 8, 1963.

29. *Politika,* April 9, 1963. See also G. Gross, "Report on Rumania," *Problems of Communism,* Jan.–Feb. 1966. Also private information of author.

30. Burks, "Rumäniens nationale Abweichung."

31. See fn. 8.

32. Chinese letter of June 14, 1964, in *Peking Review,* June 1963.

33. *Scinteia,* February 11, 1964. See also Brown, *The New Eastern Europe,* pp. 66–67.

34. *Pravda,* Moscow, September 2, 1964.

35. Quoted in Radio Free Europe Situation Reports, December 23, 1964 and March 12, 1965.

36. The Congress was called the Ninth rather than the Fourth because the party, having changed its name back to Communist party, now counted all eight previous congresses, both those before and after the Communist takeover.

37. Ceausescu's report to the Ninth Congress; full English translation, *Meridian*, Bucharest, 1965. For later figures see V. Trofin's speech at party conference in December 1967, cited in *Scinteia*, December 9, 1967.

38. *Scinteia*, May 7, 1967.

39. *Politika*, Belgrade, May 21, 1966. For various versions of Rumanian half-denials, see *Le Monde*, Paris, May 19–20, *The Times*, London, May 19, and the *New York Times*, May 19, 1966.

40. For Ceausescu's speech see *Scinteia*, June 19, 1967. News of Jakubovsky's appointment released by MTI, the official Hungarian news agency on June 19 and subsequently revoked the same day. Congratulations of East German Defense Minister carried by ADN, East Berlin, on July 2, but official announcement of the appointment was delayed until July 7, 1967.

41. July 24–26, 1967. Published in *Scinteia*, July 25–27; English translation in Agerpress supplement, July 1967.

42. *Scinteia*, February 4 and 10, 1967. For East German attacks, see "authorized statement" carried by ADN and published in *Neues Deutschland*, East Berlin, on February 2, and editorial on February 3, 1967.

43. See, e.g. in *Scinteia*, Nov. 16, 1966, Ceausescu's speech at Bulgarian Party Congress, November 14–19, 1966; *Scinteia* editorial, February 28, 1967; and Ceausescu's article, May 7, 1967, in *Scinteia*.

44. See Central Committee resolution of February 14, 1968, Ceausescu's speech on February 17, *Scinteia* editorial, February 27, and Niculescu-Mizil's speech at the international Communist conference in Budapest, February 29, 1968.

45. *Zeri i Popullit*, Tirana, March 15, 1968.

46. See *Scinteia*, February 18, 1967, and the speeches made by Ceausescu, Maurer, and Niculescu-Mizil at Parliament's session, in *Scinteia*, July 25–27, 1967.

47. According to the census of March 15, 1966, as reported in *Scinteia*, September 19, 1966, there were 1,602,604 Hungarians in Rumania. This figure compares with 1,587,675 Hungarians in 1956. Note that ten years should have brought a considerable increase in population yet these official figures show a mere increase of 1 per cent. During the same period the number of ethnic Rumanians, however, is claimed to have risen by 12 per cent, that is, ten times as fast as that of the Hungarians, and this despite the complaints about the halving of the natural population growth between 1956 and 1966. As a result, the proportion of Hungarians is alleged to have fallen from 9.1 to 8.4 per cent of the total population. The curious discrepancy between Rumanian and Hungarian population trends indicate the dynamics of Rumanianization and the growing tendency among Hungarians in Transylvania and elsewhere to declare themselves for professional and opportunistic reasons as ethnic Rumanians.

48. See Michel Tatu's series in *Le Monde*, November 11, 12–13, and 14, 1967. Over-all tourism figures based on the Hungarian Statistical Yearbook, 1966–67, since the Rumanians do not publish detailed statistics. Also, information collected by the author during three trips to Transylvania.

49. Figures quoted by Ceausescu at Bucharest party conference in *Scinteia*, December 22, 1966. See also speeches by Ceausescu and Verdetz at foreign trade conference, in *Scinteia*, February 23–24, 1967. Figures for farmers from *Scinteia*, November 22, 1967. See also *Probleme Economice*, Bucharest, September 1967.

V. AFTERWORD

1. Albert Wohlstetter, "Illusions of Distance," *Foreign Affairs* (January 1968), p. 244.

2. Brzezinski, *Alternative to Partition*, p. 35.

3. *Nowe Drogi*, Warsaw, February 1968. See also on growing Soviet concern, Brezhnev's speech at the Moscow party conference and Suslov's statement reported in *Pravda* on March 30 and May 5, 1968, respectively.

4. Richard Pipes, "Solving the Nationality Problem," *Problems of Communism* (Sept.–Oct. 1967), p. 129.

5. Campbell, p. 168.

6. G. F. Kennan, *Memoirs, 1925–1950*, p. 118.

7. *Ibid.*, p. 367.

BIBLIOGRAPHY

The material in this book for the most recent period is based mainly on the newspapers, documents, and collections of speeches published by the four Communist Balkan governments. A considerable part of the information was collected during the author's frequent trips to the area. Western journals specifically devoted to Communist or East European affairs such as *Problems of Communism* (Washington), *East Europe* (New York), *Survey* (London), and *Osteuropa* (Stuttgart) as well as the regular background and situation reports issued by the Research Department of Radio Free Europe (Munich) have been often consulted. References to specific articles are given in the footnotes.

What follows is not a systematic bibliography, still less a full list of sources consulted in the preparation of this book. It is a selection of the works in Western languages that have been most useful to me and that would assist readers who wish to pursue some aspect of the subject more thoroughly than I have been able to do. The list also includes works already cited directly in the footnotes.

HISTORY, BACKGROUND, GENERAL WORKS

Barker, E., *Macedonia: Its Place in Balkan Power Politics*, London, 1950.
—— *Truce in the Balkans*, London, 1948.
Borkenau, F., *Der europäische Kommunismus*, Bern, 1952. In English translation: *European Communism*, London, 1953.
Brailsford, H. N., *Macedonia: Its Races and Their Future*, London, 1906.
Brown, J. F., *The New Eastern Europe: The Khrushchev Era and After*, New York, 1966.
Brzezinski, Z. K., *The Soviet Bloc*, New York, 1961.
Burks, R. V., *The Dynamics of Communism in Eastern Europe*, Princeton, 1961.
Churchill, Winston, *Triumph and Tragedy*, Vol. VI of *The Second World War*, London, 1954.

Djilas, M., *Anatomy of a Moral*, London, 1959.

—— *Conversations with Stalin*, New York, 1962.

—— *The New Class: An Analysis of the Communist System*, New York, 1957.

Drachkovitch, M. M. (ed.), *Marxism in the Modern World*, Stanford, 1966.

Griffith, W. E., *The Sino-Soviet Rift*, London, 1964.

Jelavich, C., *Tsarist Russia and Balkan Nationalism*, Berkeley, 1958.

—— and B. (eds.), *The Balkans in Transition . . . since the 18th Century*, Berkeley, 1963.

Kann, R. A., *The Multinational Empire: Nationalism and National Reform in the Habsburg Monarchy, 1848–1918*, New York, 1950.

Kaser, M., *Comecon: Integration Problems of the Planned Economies*, London, 1965.

Kennan, G. F., *Memoirs, 1925–1950*, New York, 1967.

Lowenthal, R., *Chruschtschow und der Weltkommunismus*, Stuttgart, 1963. In English translation: *World Communism: The Disintegration of a Secular Faith*, New York, 1964.

Lukacs, J. A., *The Great Powers and Eastern Europe*, New York, 1953.

Macartney, C. A., *Hungary and Her Successors: The Treaty of Trianon and Its Consequences, 1919–1937*, London, 1937.

—— and A. W. Palmer, *Independent Eastern Europe: A History*, London, 1962.

Mitrany, D., *Marx Against the Peasant*, Chapel Hill, 1952.

Neubacher, H., *Sonderauftrag Südost, 1940–1945*, Göttingen, 1957.

Pryor, F. L., *The Communist Foreign Trade System*, Cambridge, Mass., 1963.

Seton-Watson, Hugh, *Eastern Europe between the Wars, 1918–1941*, New York, 1945.

—— *The East European Revolution*, New York, 1951.

Shulman, M. D., *Stalin's Foreign Policy Reappraised*, Cambridge, Mass., 1963.

Skilling, H. G., *The Governments of Communist East Europe*, New York, 1966.

Spulber, N., *The Economics of Communist Eastern Europe*, Cambridge, Mass., 1957.

—— *The State and Economic Development in Eastern Europe*, New York, 1966.

Stavrianos, L. S., *The Balkans since 1453*, New York, 1958.

Suranyi-Unger, T., *Studien zum Wirtschaftswachstum Südosteuropas*, Stuttgart, 1964.

Talmon, J. L., *The Origins of Totalitarian Democracy*, New York, 1961.

—— *The Unique and the Universal*, London, 1965.

Taylor, A. J. P., *The Habsburg Monarchy, 1809–1918*, London, 1948.
—— *The Origins of the Second World War*, London, 1961.
Wolff, R. L., *The Balkans in Our Time*, Cambridge, Mass., 1956.
Zagoria, D. S., *The Sino-Soviet Conflict, 1956–1961*, Princeton, 1962.
Zinner, P. E. (ed.), *National Communism and Popular Revolt in Eastern Europe*, New York, 1956.

INDIVIDUAL COUNTRIES

YUGOSLAVIA

Armstrong, H. F., *Tito and Goliath*, London, 1951.
Avakumovic, I., *History of the Communist Party of Yugoslavia*, Vol. I, Aberdeen, 1964.
Bass, R., and E. Marbury (eds.), *The Soviet-Yugoslav Controversy, 1948–1958: A Documentary Record*, New York, 1959.
Bilandzic, D., *Management of Yugoslav Economy, 1945–1966*, Belgrade, 1967.
Byrnes, R. F. (ed.), *Yugoslavia under the Communists*, New York, 1957.
Campbell, J. C., *Tito's Separate Road: America and Yugoslavia in World Politics*, New York, 1967.
Clissold, S., *Whirlwind: An Account of Marshal Tito's Rise to Power*, London, 1949.
—— (ed.), *A Short History of Yugoslavia*, London, 1966.
Davidson, B., *Partisan Picture*, Bedford, England, 1946.
Dedijer, V., *Tito*, New York, 1953.
Djilas, M., *Land without Justice*, New York, 1958.
Halperin, E., *Der siegreiche Ketzer*, Cologne, 1957. In English translation: *The Triumphant Heretic: Tito's Struggle against Stalin*, London, 1958.
Hoffman, G. W. and F. W. Neal, *Yugoslavia and the New Communism*, New York, 1962.
Hoptner, J. B., *Yugoslavia in the Crisis, 1934–1941*, New York, 1962.
Kerner, R. J. (ed.), *Yugoslavia*, Berkeley, 1949.
Lederer, I. J., *Yugoslavia at the Paris Peace Conference: A Study in Frontiermaking*, New Haven, 1963.
McClellan, W. D., *Svetozar Markovic and the Origins of Balkan Socialism*, Princeton, 1964.
Maclean, F., *Disputed Barricade: The Life and Times of Josip Broz-Tito*, London, 1957.
—— *Eastern Approaches*, London, 1949.
Markert, W. (ed.), *Jugoslawien*, Cologne, 1954.
Pejovich, S., *The Market-Planned Economy of Yugoslavia*, Minneapolis, 1966.

Seton-Watson, R. W., *The Southern Slav Question and the Habsburg Monarchy*, London, 1911.

Temperley, H. W. V., *History of Serbia*, London, 1917.

Tomasevich, J., *Peasants, Politics and Economic Change in Yugoslavia*, Stanford, 1955.

Ulam, A., *Titoism and the Cominform*, Cambridge, Mass., 1952.

ALBANIA

Amery, J., *Sons of the Eagle: A Study in Guerilla War*, London, 1948.

Griffith, W. E., *Albania and the Sino-Soviet Rift*, Cambridge, Mass., 1963.

Hamm, H., *Rebellen gegen Moskau*, Cologne, 1962.

Newman, B., *Albanian Back-Door*, London, 1936.

Skendi, S. (ed.), *Albania*, New York, 1956.

Swire, J., *Albania: The Rise of a Kingdom*, New York, 1930.

Thalloczy, L. von (ed.), *Illyrisch-Albanische Forschungen*, Munich, 1916.

BULGARIA

Black, C. E., *The Establishment of Constitutional Government in Bulgaria*, Princeton, 1943.

Dellin, L. A. D. (ed.), *Bulgaria*, New York, 1957.

Hajek, A., *Bulgarian unter der Türkenherrschaft*, Stuttgart, 1925.

Hemreich, E. C., *The Diplomacy of the Balkan Wars*, London, 1937.

Logio, G. C., *Bulgaria: Past and Present*, Manchester, England, 1936.

Rothschild, J., *The Communist Party of Bulgaria: Origins and Development, 1883–1936*, New York, 1959.

Swire, J., *Bulgarian Conspiracy*, London, 1939.

RUMANIA

Fischer-Galati, S. A. (ed.), *Romania*, New York, 1957.

Floyd, D., *Rumania: Russia's Dissident Ally*, New York, 1965.

Gafencu, G., *Prelude to the Russian Campaign*, London, 1951.

Hillgruber, A., *Hitler, König Carol, und Marschall Antonescu*, Wiesbaden, 1954.

Ionescu, G., *Communism in Rumania, 1944–1962*, London, 1964.

Mitrany, D., *The Land and the Peasant in Rumania: The War and Agrarian Reform (1917–21)*, London, 1930.

Patrascanu, L., *Sous trois dictatures*, Paris, 1946.

Roberts, H. L., *Rumania: Political Problems of an Agrarian State*, New Haven, 1951.

Seton-Watson, R. W., *A History of the Roumanians: From Roman Times to the Completion of Unity*, Cambridge, 1934.

INDEX

Abadzhiev, Ivan, 239 n
Abakumov, V. S., 192
Adrianople, 27
Adriatic Sea, 25, 27, 28, 33, 115, 145, 175, 176, 179
Aegean Sea, 25, 33, 34, 45
Afro-Asian countries, 205, 256
Agrarian Union (Bulgaria), 214, 215, 216, 219–21
Agriculture, 46, 47 (see also specific aspects, e.g., Collectivization; Land); Albania, 199–200, Bulgaria, 212, 222–27, 253, 254, 258; Rumania, 290, 299, 320; Yugoslavia, 80–82, 86–87, 101, 102, 106, 109–14
Aid, economic. See Credits (and aid); specific agencies, aspects, countries, projects
Ajtic, Predrag, 160
Alba Iulia, 271
"Albanci," 204
Albania, 174–205 (see also specific individuals, locations); army, 188, 201; and China, 5, 22, 174, 194, 195–201, 203, 205; "cultural revolution," 200–1; "defection" of, 2, 5, 11, 21–22; economy, 11–12, 179, 181, 188 ff., 196–201, 202; history, land, and people, 27–50 passim, 174–205; nationalism, 17–18, 175 ff., 198–205, 351, 354–60; and Rumania, 194, 198, 302, 304, 312, 313, 315, 327–28, 337, 338; and Soviet Union, 2, 5, 11–12, 17–18, 21–22, 174–75, 182, 186, 187–201, 202, 205, 351, 354–60, 366–67; territorial disputes, 175–79; and Yugoslavia, 61, 79, 83–86, 158–59, 170, 175–83 ff., 197–204
Alexander, King of Yugoslavia, 49, 59, 151, 153, 154
Alexander I, Tsar of Russia, 268, 269
Alexander II, Tsar of Russia, 209, 211

Alexander of Battenberg, Prince, 211
Alps, 25, 29, 62, 64
Aluminum plants, 145–46
Amery, Julian, 185–86
Anderson, Mrs. Eugene, 231
Anev, General, 236–37
Anti-Fascist Council for the National Liberation of Yugoslavia (AVNOJ), 78
Anti-Semitism, 7, 45, 274, 276–77, 280, 289, 312
Antonescu, Ion, 276–77, 312
Apostol, Gheorghe, 282, 290, 317, 323, 324
Apponyi, Geraldine, Countess, 181
Arabs, 168, 333–35. See also Middle East crisis
Aristocracy, destruction of, 37
Armies. See Red Army; specific battles, countries, wars
Arms and the Man (Shaw), 47
Aron, Raymond, 1
Artisans, 99, 102, 114–15, 259
Aurelian, Emperor, 28
Austria, 17, 60, 169, 170, 269–72; and Albania, 177; and Balkans, 23–24, 26, 27, 30, 35, 39, 40–46 passim, 50; economy, 102–3
Austria-Hungary. See Austria; Hungary
Autonomy, 85, 139, 148–49, 352–60, 361. See also Democracy; Enterprise autonomy; Nationalism; specific aspects, countries

Bakaric, Vladimir, 51, 100, 119, 143, 149, 151, 156–57, 167, 170, 190
"Balkan," definition of, 25
Balkan Federation, 37, 67, 182, 190, 216, 221, 355
Balkan Mountains, 25, 26–27, 28, 31, 32, 33, 35, 64
Balkan Pact (1934), 273, 275; (1954), 355–56

Balkan Wars (1912–13), 36, 46, 177, 209, 210, 214, 270, 275
Balli Kombatar, 184, 185
Baltic, Milutin, 105
Banat, the, 18
Banks and banking, 89, 90, 99, 134, 135, 136, 138, 146
Bar, 141, 145
Barthov, Jean Louis, 59
Bashev, Ivan, 245, 246, 247, 250, 251
Belgrade, 12, 15, 16, 23, 24, 33, 36, 42, 57–58, 72, 75, 79, 141, 145, 150, 157, 161; economy, 116, 118; terrorist bombings in, 171 n
Belgrade-Bar railroad, 141, 145
Belishova, Liri, 188, 189, 194, 197
Berghianu, Maxim, 321
Beria, L., 192
Berlin, blockade of, 82; Congress of, 27–28, 35–36, 176, 209
Bernstein, Eduard, 7–8
Bessarabia, 2, 11, 17, 18, 268–78 passim, 281, 288, 314–15, 343
Bicanic, Rudolf, 159
Bilandzic, Dusan, 51–52, 95
Birladeanu, Alexandru, 300, 321, 323
Bismarck, Otto, Prince von, 28
Black Sea, 25, 27, 32, 33, 241, 268, 296
Blagoev, Dimitar, 211, 213–14, 215
Blood feuds, Albania, 180
Blum, Leon, 67
Bodnaras, Emil, 282–83, 288, 306, 321, 323, 324
Bogomils, 39
Books. See Literature (writers)
Borba (Belgrade newspaper), 90, 116, 135, 136, 155, 247, 248, 361
Borila, Petre, 282, 306, 319
Boris, King of Bulgaria, 49, 212
Borkenau, Franz, 77, 82
Bosna River, 27
Bosnia, 37–41, 46, 64–65, 76, 106, 154, 157–58, 167; economy, 100, 143, 146
Bosnia-Herzegovina, 39, 46, 60–61, 64, 137, 147–48, 157–58
Bosnian Church, 39
Bosporus, Straits of, 26
Botev, Khristo, 211
Bourgeoisie, 48, 72, 73, 74. See also specific countries
Bratianu, Ionel, 272
Bratianu family, 272

Bratislava Declaration, 363
Brezhnev, L., 52, 315, 325–26
Brioni, 162, 164
Bucharest, 24, 194, 262, 266, 279, 342, 347; Declaration (1966), 343; Treaty of (1812), 269
Budapest, 271, 342; Communist parties conference in, 336–38; Rumania and, 271
"Bugging" of telephones, 161–63
Bukovina, 11, 24, 267, 270, 275, 276, 278
Bulatovic, Major, 193
Bulgaria, 6, 10, 17, 18, 206–61; army, 211, 212, 214, 229, 234–40, 243, 244; assassinations, 212, 216, 218; and Czech invasion, 366; economy, 11–12, 212, 213, 219, 222, 223 ff., 248–61; land, history, and people, 25, 27, 30–37, 40–49, 209–61; nationalism, 2, 6, 10–12, 22, 209, 213 ff., 234 ff., 240, 243–61, 351, 353–60, 364, 366; officers' plot, 234–40, 244; and Rumania, 210, 223, 246, 250, 270, 271, 274, 275, 286, 311, 330, 332–33; and Soviet Union, 2, 6, 11–12, 22, 206–61 passim, 351, 353–60, 364, 366; and Yugoslavia, 58, 61, 67, 80, 83–84, 85
Bulgarian Writers' Association, 31
Bulgars (Mongol tribe), 32
Bureaucrats (bureaucracy), 6, 8, 15, 48, 95, 99, 100, 121–40, 163. See also specific aspects, countries
Burgas, 252, 253
Byzantine influence, 30, 32–33

Capitalism, 6, 7, 20, 22, 46, 89–100, 109–19. See also Enterprise autonomy; Private enterprise; specific aspects, countries
Carinthia, 82
Carol I, King of Rumania, 269, 270
Carol II, King of Rumania, 49, 274, 276
Carpathian Mountains, 28, 33
Cars, 75, 102, 103, 104, 107, 112, 142, 260, 347–48
Caterers, 114–15, 117
Catholic Church. See Orthodox Church; Roman Catholic Church
Catholic People's Party (Slovenia), 42

Ceausescu, Nicolae, 246, 267–68, 272, 273, 276, 280–82, 330, 338, 346, 348; and Czech invasion, 365, 366; and Middle East, 333–34; rise of, 292, 316–26; and Tito, 363

Censorship (and suppression), 54, 124, 327. See also News management; Purges

Centralism (centralization-decentralization), 5 ff., 15, 51, 55, 66, 88, 92–100, 108–72 passim. See also specific aspects, countries

Chamberlain, Neville, 44

Chamber of Nationalities, Yugoslovia, 169

Chervenkov, Vulko, 192, 218, 220, 222–26, 227, 228, 229, 233

Chetniks, 62–65, 76–77, 78

China, and Albania, 5, 22, 174, 194, 195–201, 203; and Bulgaria, 205, 226, 227, 228, 236, 237, 246; and Rumania, 295, 299, 301–9, 312, 313, 314, 315, 326–28, 336, 365; and Soviet Union (see Sino-Soviet conflict); and Yugoslavia, 52–54

Chisinevschi, Iosif, 291–92

Chou En-lai, 196, 327–28, 365

Church(es), 38–43. See also specific religions

Churchill, Winston S., 44, 58, 79, 278–79

Ciano, Count, 181

Ciora (Rumanian Foreign Trade Minister), 334–35

Civil War in France (Marx), 94

Class(es), concept of, 14. See also specific aspects, classes

Cluj, 24–25, 340, 341, 342

Coburgs, 45

Cold War, 9, 44, 350–60 passim

Collectivization, in Bulgaria, 223, 226–27, 254, 258; in Rumania, 290, 299; in Yugoslavia, 80–82, 86–87, 110–14, 156

Comecon, 22, 174, 252, 296–302, 323, 330, 339

Cominform, 82, 85, 86, 226, 312

Comintern, 66, 67, 70, 72, 73, 77, 88, 182, 214–17, 276, 280–81, 325

Common Market (EEC), 359, 360

Communes, 55, 98, 99, 100, 113, 116, 123, 139

Conference of the League of Communists, 165 n

Constantinescu, Miron, 291–92, 316, 323

Constantinople. See Istanbul (Constantinople)

Cooperatives, 111–12

Corruption, 38, 49, 150, 163, 212, 272

Cosic, Dobrica, 16, 171 n

Council of Federation, Yugoslavia, 168, 169

Council of Producers, Yugoslavia, 99

Craftsmen, 259. See also Artisans

Credits (and aid), 11–12, 145, 196, 199–200, 253, 255, 286, 333. See also specific agencies, aspects, countries, projects

Crimean War, 269

Croatia (Croats), 14–15, 17, 24, 29–30, 38–45 passim, 57–68 passim, 71, 81, 150–72 passim; and economy, 102, 103, 105, 113, 114, 116, 140 ff.; Peasants' Party, 59

Croat-Serbian language, 30–31, 39, 187

Crvenkovski, Krste, 124, 142–43, 165, 170, 246

Cuba, 199, 228, 229, 305

Cusa, Jan Alexander, Prince, 267, 269

Cvetkovic, Dragisa, 57

Cyprus, 356

Cyril (missionary), 30

Cyrillic alphabet, 30

Czechoslovakia, 6, 11, 15–16, 43, 44; "Moscow Agreement," 365; nationalism, 363–67; Rumania and, 272, 307, 332, 342, 363; Soviet invasion of (1968), 22 n, 361–67

Dacians, 28, 29, 40, 262–63

Dalmatia, 26–27, 29, 30, 43, 45, 59, 60–61, 64–65

Danube River, 23, 24, 25, 27, 141, 268, 269, 310, 312, 356; basin, 25, 27, 29, 37

Danube-Tisza canal, 141

Dapcevic-Kucar, Savka, 51, 157

Dardanelles, 26

Davidov, Professor, 255

Decebalus, King, 262–63

Dedijer, Vladimir, 73

Dedinje, 161

Democracy (democratization), 6, 7, 9, 14, 15, 37, 47, 49 (see also Autonomy; specific aspects, countries);

Democracy (cont'd)
Yugoslavia and, 56, 124, 125, 128, 130, 132, 134, 137, 159, 163–72
De-Stalinization. See under Stalin (Joseph) and Stalinism
Deva, Veli, 158
Diljas, Milovan, 8, 14, 54, 67, 71, 72, 82, 94, 127–29; and Albania, 187–88, 189–90; and Bulgaria, 221–22; purge of, 125, 127–29; and Stalinism, 127–29
Dimitrov, G. M., 220, 221
Dimitrov, George, 67, 84, 207–9, 217, 218, 221, 222, 228
Dinaric Alps, 62, 64
Diocletian (Roman emperor), 28
Disraeli, Benjamin, 35
Djordjevic, J., 372
Dobrogeanu-Gherea, Alexander, 280
Dobrogeanu-Gherea, Constantine, 280, 318
Dobruja, 18, 209, 210, 269, 270, 275–76
Doncea, Constantin, 282, 316
Draghici, Alexander, 290, 319, 321, 323, 324
Dragoicheva, Mrs. Tsola, 258
Dresden, Warsaw Pact meeting (1968) in, 339
Dubcek, Alexander, 16
Durres (Durazzo), 177
Dushan, Stephen (Tsar of Serbia), 33–34
Dylan, Bob, 130
Dzhagarov, Georgi, 31, 240, 248

Eastern Rumelia, 35
East Germany, 6, 11, 13, 250–51, 286, 299, 303, 307, 329, 331–34
East Prussia, 11
Economy (economic factors; economic reforms), 6–15 passim, 21, 22, 44–47, 358–60, 365. See also specific agencies, aspects, countries, people, programs
Eden, Anthony, 278
Education (schools), 48, 102, 130, 135, 136–38, 187, 188, 232, 256–57. See also Illiteracy; specific countries
EEC, 359, 360
Egypt, 38
Ekonomska Politika, 147

Elections, 48, 54, 66, 80, 97, 137, 164, 221
Electricity (electric power), 90. See also Power plants and projects
Electric Power Community, 90
Elite, ruling, 47–49, 121, 130, 131 ff., 154, 165. See also specific classes, countries, people
Emigration, 106–7
Employment (unemployment), 52, 105–7, 109, 116, 135, 312
Engels, Friedrich, 94, 314–15
Enterprise autonomy, 96 ff., 119, 122–39 passim. See also Capitalism; Private enterprise; specific aspects, countries
Esad Pasha, 177, 178, 187
Exports and imports, 47, 112, 113, 114, 224, 359. See also Foreign trade; specific countries

Factories, 89, 93, 100, 135, 136, 138
Farms and farming. See Agriculture
Fascism, 41, 47, 48, 59–61, 73, 78, 181. See also Iron Guard; Italy; Nazism; World War II; specific countries
Fatherland Front, 207, 219–21
Fazekas, Janos, 241
Federal Executive Council, Yugoslavia, 166
Ferdinand of Coburg, Prince, 211
Five Year Plans, Albania, 196, 199–200; Bulgaria, 226, Yugoslavia, 81, 87, 141, 145
Foreign Policy of Hitlerite Germany (Ushakov), 277
Foreign trade, 224, 249. See also Exports and imports; specific aspects; countries
Foris, Stefan, 283, 323
"41 Club," 57–65, 73
France and the French, 43; and Albania, 177, 178, 183; and Bulgaria, 250; and Rumania, 43, 67, 270, 272, 274; and Yugoslavia, 51–52, 67, 82
Francis Ferdinand, Archduke, 39
Frank ("Frankovici"), 59, 68
Fundo, Lazar, 182, 183

Galati steel plant, 297–98, 306, 344
Galbraith, J. K., 90, 95, 134
Gandhi, Indira, 364

GATT (General Agreement on Tariffs and Trade), 359

Gega, Liri, 193

Gegs, Albanian, 180, 182, 184, 185

General Motors, 75, 88

Georgescu, Teohari, 282, 288, 289, 325

Georgiev, Assen, 231, 238

Germany and the Germans, 11, 26, 41, 43, 45, 47, 49 (see also East Germany; West Germany; specific individuals); and Albania, 181, 183, 185–86; and Bulgaria, 210, 220; partition of, 19, 22 (see also East Germany; West Germany); and Rumania, 269–70, 273, 274–78, 279; as Rumanian minority, 339, 340; and Yugoslavia, 57–64, 72–73, 79, 183, 185–86; and World War II, 26, 41, 45, 47, 49, 57–64, 72–73, 79, 210, 220, 273, 274–78, 279 (see also Nazism; World War II)

Gheorghiu-Dej, Gheorghe, 272, 282–83, 287–315, 323, 324; death of, 293

Giorgiev, Kimon, 220

Gladstone, William E., Lord, 35

Glas Koncila, 41

Gligoroy, Kiro, 108–9, 167

GNP. See Gross National Product (GNP)

Gomulka, Wladyslaw, 2, 4, 234

Gorkic, Milan (Cizinsky), 69–70, 71

Gosnjak, Ivan, 156, 161, 169

Grandfather (code name), 73, 78

Great Britain and the British, 35, 44, (see also specific events, individuals); and Albania, 182, 184, 185–86; and Bulgaria, 221; and Rumania, 278–79; and Yugoslavia, 58, 63, 78, 79, 82

Grechko, Marshal, 329

Greece and the Greeks, 82, 84, 354–55, 367; and Albania, 17, 18, 84, 175–76, 177–78, 179, 181, 190, 202, 354–55; and Balkan history, 25, 27, 34, 35, 36, 37–38, 40, 44; and Bulgaria, 210, 223, 230–31, 245, 246, 251; and Rumania, 265–66, 273, 354–55; and Yugoslavia, 82, 84, 367

Greek Orthodox Church. See Orthodox Church

Grigorov, Mitko, 229, 257

Grivita railroad strike, 282, 316

Gromyko, Andrei A., 353

Gross National Product (GNP), 101, 122. See also National income; Production (productivity); specific countries

Groza, Petru, 284, 292

Gypsies, 35

Habsburg (Hapsburg) monarchy, 17, 37, 60; and Rumania, 37, 266, 267, 270

Hajduks, 26

Hallstein doctrine, 331

Handicrafts and trades, 259

Heath, Donald, 231

Hebrang, Andrija, 81

Herta, 275

Hitler, Adolf, 45, 58, 60–61, 181, 185 (see also Nazism); and Rumania, 273, 274–78

Hohenzollern-Sigmaringen, 45

Holy Roman Empire, 29

Horvat, Branko, 135

Houses (housing), 259, 344

Hoxha, Enver, 5, 174–75, 183, 184–88, 190, 191, 192–97, 198, 199, 200

Humor, monastery, 267–68

Hungary and the Hungarians, 17–18, 24, 29, 30, 37, 40–45, 58 (see also Austria); and Albania, 192–93; and Revolution (1956), 1–4, 11, 13, 292, 339, 362; and Rumania, 17, 270–78 passim, 286, 291, 332–33, 337, 339–43, 366; and Yugoslavia, 59, 61, 79, 80, 84, 85, 159

Ideology, 4, 6; and nationalism, 9–20 ff.

Illiteracy, 40, 135, 137–38, 179

"Illyrian movement," 59, 64

Illyrians, 28, 29, 41, 43, 59, 64, 175

Imports. See Exports and imports

Income. See National income; Wages (earnings; salaries)

Indo-European language, 28

Industry (industrialization), 46, 47, 356 (see also specific industries, programs); Albania, 191, 193, 199, 200; Bulgaria, 219, 223–24, 251–61; Rumania, 272, 285–86, 295–306, 318, 344–48; Yugoslavia, 81, 86–87, 90, 101, 141 ff.

Inflation, 256

"Informal groups," 134, 135, 138

"Informbirovci," 86

Intellectuals (intelligentsia), 7, 8–9, 14, 15, 48; Albania, 182–83; Bulgaria, 230, 240–41, 248, 257–58, 260; Rumania, 348

Intelligentsia. *See* Intellectuals (intelligentsia)

Investment(s), and investment projects, 110, 123, 139, 140–51, 169, 251, 254–55, 286, 296, 345. *See also* specific countries, projects

Ionita (Rumanian Defense Minister), 330

Iron Curtain, 25

Iron Gates project, 27, 141, 312–13

Iron Guard (Rumania), 49, 274, 276, 287–88

Islamism. *See* Muslims

Israel, 333–35. *See also* Middle East crisis

Istanbul (Constantinople), 25, 27, 30, 33, 37–38, 39

Italy and the Italians, 45, 47, 57–65 *passim*, 73, 82, 177–79, 181, 184, 187, 201. *See also* specific events, individuals

Ivan Assen II, 33

Izvestia, 311

Jajce, 78

Jakova, Tuk, 191, 192

Jakubovsky, General, 329–30, 377

Japan, 57

Jassy, 344; Museul Unirii, 267

Jazavac (Zagreb restaurant), 57

Jelic, Bora, 166

Jews, 35, 42, 61 (*see also* Anti-Semitism; Israel); in Rumania, 270, 272, 273, 280, 281, 282, 289

Johnson, Lyndon B., 335, 357, 365

Juvenile delinquency, 7

Kadar, Janos, 4, 233, 234, 342–43

Kafka, Franz, 7

Kapo, Hysni, 194, 196, 374

Karavelov, Liuben, 211

Kardelj, Edward, 71, 80, 82, 83, 94, 148, 161–62, 168, 169, 190, 315; on bureaucratic centralism, 123; and Stalin, 190; and succession to Tito, 154–56; and Tito, 71, 80, 83, 94, 154–56, 161–62, 168, 169

Karlovy Vary meeting, 337

Karst, 64

Kastrioti, George (Skandenberg), 38, 175, 180

Katz (Cass), Otto, 280

Kavcic, Stane, 133–34

Kelmendi, Ali, 182, 183

Kennan, George, 357, 358

Khrushchev, Nikita S., 13, 18; and Albania, 174, 191, 192, 193–98; and Bulgaria, 206–7, 224–25, 226, 228, 232, 234; fall of, 198, 206, 234, 245, 311; and Rumania, 292, 293, 297–311; and Stalin, 6; and Yugoslavia, 55, 152

Kidric, Boris, 94

Kiesinger, Kurt, 331

Kodaly, Zoltán, 15

Kolak, Rudi, 166, 167

Kolakowski, Leszek, 8

Kolarov, Vasil, 67, 215–16, 217, 221, 222

Komitadjis (armed raiders), 35

Koncar, Rade, 71

Korca, 183, 187

Korea, 82, 87, 199

Korfu, island of, 178

Korosec, Anton, 42

Kosmet. *See* Kosovo-Metohija (Kosmet)

Kosovo-Metohija (Kosmet), 183–84, 187, 203–4

Kosovo region, 18, 34, 61, 68, 83, 137, 144, 145, 158, 159, 176, 179, 180, 183

Kostov, Traicho, 217–19, 221, 222, 223, 231

Kragujevac, 64

Krajger, Boris, 166

Kraljevo, 63

Krastev, Tsolo, 236–37

Kremikovtsi iron and steel works, 252

Kresimir Peter, 30

Kruja, 38

Krum, Khan, 33

Kufrin, Milka, 146

Kunin, Petko, 222

Kupi, Abbas, 184, 185

Land (land reform), 47, 48, 80, 87, 109–14, 118, 212, 223, 227, 258. *See also* Agriculture

Language(s), 149, 158, 167, 170; Albania, 28, 176, 180; Bulgaria,

Language(s) (cont'd)
212; Croat-Serbian (Serbo-Croatian), 29, 30–31, 39; Greek, 40; Macedonia, 31; Rumania, 40; Slovene, 29
Lazar, Prince, 34
League of Communists, 124, 126, 127, 130, 133, 137, 172
League of Nations, 178
Lenin (N.) and Leninism, 52, 56, 74, 80, 94, 113, 209, 214, 296, 298 (see also Marxism-Leninism); and nationalism, 11
Leskosek, Franz, 71
Literacy, 46. See also Illiteracy
Literature (writers), 7, 31, 40, 230, 240, 241. See also Censorship; Intellectuals (intelligentsia); Newspapers; specific countries, individuals, works
Little Entente, 272–73
Litvinov, Maxim, 273
Living standards (living conditions) (see also Wages; specific items, e.g., Cars; Houses); in Albania, 200; in Bulgaria, 224, 233, 248–49, 254, 258–59, 260; in Rumania, 347–49; in Yugoslavia, 103–7, 146–47
Ljubljana, 16, 24, 42, 103
Loans, 11–12. See also Credits (and aid)
London, Treaty of, 36, 177
Luca, Vasile, 282, 287, 289, 312, 324
Lukic, Vojin, 160, 161, 162
Lupescu, Magda, 274
Lushnja, 178

Macedonia, and Albania, 176, 183; and Bulgaria, 18, 31–37 passim, 209, 210, 212, 213, 218, 220, 223, 246–48, 353, 364; and Greece, 17, 18; history, land, and people, 15, 17, 18, 26–27, 31–37 passim, 44, 45, 46, 49; and Yugoslavia, 15, 18, 61, 66, 67, 68, 83, 106, 124, 135, 137, 140–44, 147–48, 167–72 passim, 353, 364
Macek, Ivan, 57
Maclean, Fitzroy, 72
Macmillan, Harold, 194–95
Maleshova, Sejfulla, 182, 189
Malinovsky, Marshal, 329

Management, and economy, Bulgaria, 256–57
Maniu, Iliu, 274, 277
Mao Tse-tung, and Albania, 198, 205; and Rumania, 304, 314
Maraseti, 270
Marcuse, Herbert, 8
Marin, Gheorghe Gaston, 298, 311–12
Maritsa River, 27
Marjanovic, Jovan, 171 n
"Market socialism," Yugoslavia, 122 ff.
Markovic, Mihajlo, 121, 137
Markovic, Sima, 67
Marmora, Sea of, 26
Martince (cooperative farm), 111–12
Marx, Karl, 7, 8, 94 (see also Marxism-Leninism); Notes on Rumania, 314
Marxism-Leninism, 5–8 passim, 12, 14, 18, 91, 94, 198, 203, 351, 358. See also Lenin (N.) and Leninism
Mates, Leo, 107–8
Maurer, Ion Gheorghe, background and description of, 292–93; as Premier of Rumania, 292–93, 303, 304, 311, 312, 317, 321, 323, 334; and rescue of Gheorghiu-Dej, 283
May Day, 75
Mehmet Ali, 38
Methodius (missionary), 30
Michael, King of Rumania, 2, 274, 276, 277–78, 283, 284
Middle East (Arab-Israeli) crisis, 168, 239 n; Rumania and, 22, 328, 333–35, 338; Tito and, 168
Mihailov, Ivan, 234
Mihajlov, Mihajlo, 54, 159
Mihajlovic, Draza, 62–64, 76–77, 78
Mijatovic, Cvijetin, 161
Mikoyan, A. I., 194
Military Frontier, 24
Military League (Bulgaria), 219
Milutinovic, I., 71
Mincev, Nikola, 142, 246
Minic, Milos, 152
Minorities (minority problems), 17–20, 21, 34–35, 42, 339–41, 366. See also Territorial disputes; specific people, places
Miskovic, Milan, 161–62
Moghioros, A., 319
Mohacs, battle of, 37

Moldavia, 2, 37, 40, 266–68, 270, 275, 341, 345
Moldovita, monastery, 267–68
Molotov, V. M., 189
Monarchists, Yugoslavia, 79, 80
Monarchs, hereditary, 49
Montenegro, and Albania, 176, 177; economy of, 100, 137, 144, 145, 146; history, land, and people, 26–27, 31, 35, 36, 42, 46, 61; and Yugoslavia, 31, 61, 64, 66, 71, 72, 121, 127, 159, 166, 167
Morava River, 27
Morava Valley, 62
Moscow Declaration (1960), 196, 329
Mountaineers, 64, 131
Mountains, Balkan, 25, 26–27, 28, 31, 33, 35, 64
Mugosa, Dusan, 183
Mukje agreement, 184, 187
Mures-Hungarian autonomous region, 340
Muslims, 24, 38–40, 42, 62; Albania and, 35, 175, 176, 180, 182–83, 184, 201; Bosnia and, 38–40, 61, 65, 154, 157; with Yugoslav Partisans, 65
Mussolini, Benito, 60, 178–79, 181, 275

Nagy, Imre, 67
Namier, Lewis B., quoted, 23, 47–48
Napoleon I, 30
Napoleon III, 43
Nasser, G., 364
National Democratic Front, Rumania, 277, 284
National income, average, 47, 56, 142, 144, 146, 147, 253, 296. See also Production (productivity); Wages (earnings; salaries); specific countries
Nationalism, 1–22, 35–50, 350–60, 363–66 (see also specific aspects, countries, individuals, people, places); different meanings of, 18–19
National Liberals, Rumania, 274, 277
National Liberation Council (NLC), 184, 185–86
National Liberation Movement (NLM), 184
National Peasants, Rumania, 274, 277

NATO, 326
Nazism (Nazis), 26, 41, 45, 47, 49, 57–64, 274–78. See also Germany: and World War II; Hitler, Adolf
Nemanjid dynasty, 33, 34
Nendori (Albanian literary monthly), 201
Neretva River, 27
Neubacher, H., 45, 185
Neues Deutschland, 331, 332
New Belgrade, 23, 141
News management, xiii, 307–8. See also Censorship
Newspapers (news media), xiii, 9, 307–8, 342 (see also Censorship; specific periodicals); freedom of press, 9
New Times, 265
Niculescu-Mizil, Paul, 321
Nikezic, Marko, 364
Niksic, 145
Nis, Serbia, 89
Noli, Fan, 180, 182
North Atlantic Treaty Organization, 326
Northern Epirus, 18, 176, 179, 202
North Korea, 199
North Vietnam, 198–99, 325, 328–29, 336
Notes on Rumanians (Marx), 314
Novotny, Antonin, 16
Nreu, Dali, 193
Nuclear disarmament, 335–36

Obradovic, Dositej, 40
OECD, 359, 360
Ohrid, 33
Oil production, 138–39, 200
Organov, Nikolai, 206, 238
Orthodox Church, 24, 30, 31, 37–38, 39, 40–43, 60, 170, 180, 202, 212
Ottoman Empire. See Turkey and the Turks
Overpopulation, 106. See also Population statistics

Paisi, Father, 40
Pan-Slavism, 42
Paris, Treaty of (1856), 269
Partisans, Albania, 50, 182, 183, 184–86, 192; Bulgaria, 218, 220, 233, 236, 237, 238; Yugoslavia, 24, 39, 45, 50, 51, 61–65, 72–80, 131, 166, 182

Pasic, Najdan, 100, 150

Passports, 9, 118

Patrascanu, Lucretiu, 283, 289–90, 323–24

Pauker, Ana, 1, 282–83, 287–89, 291, 293–94, 312, 324

Pauker, Marcel, 282

Paul, Prince (regent of Yugoslavia), 49, 57–58

Pavelic (Poglavnik), Ante, 59–61, 64

Pavlov, Todor, 258

Pay (earnings; salaries). See Wages (earnings; salaries)

Peasants (peasant class), 37, 43, 47, 48–49; Bosnia, 37; Bulgaria, 48–49, 212, 213, 215, 221, 258–59; Rumania, 37, 44, 48, 269, 270, 274, 281, 290, 296, 345; Serbia, 48; Yugoslavia, 54, 62, 64, 74, 80, 87, 109–14, 117, 129, 131, 135

Peatra Neamt, 344

Pec, 176

People's Front, Yugoslavia, 126

People's Liberation Army, Yugoslavia, 73

Peter, King of Yugoslavia, 58, 78

Petkov, Nikola, 221

Petroleum products, 138–39, 200

Phanariots, 37–38, 40, 265–66, 272

Philby, "Kim," 186

Pijade, Mosha, 69, 77

Pindus Mountains, 35

Pirin Macedonia, 223, 247–48

Pius XII, Pope, 41

Plaku, Panjut, 191

Plevna, Battle of, 269

Pliska, 32

Pliva, 104–5

Plowmen's Front, Rumania, 284

Pogled, Bulgarian newspaper, 242

Poland, 1, 2, 4, 11, 12, 37, 80, 81 (see also specific individuals); and Albania, 192–93; "Polish October," 1, 2, 4, 11; and Rumania, 266, 267, 332–33

Politburo, Albania, 197; Bulgaria, 206, 224, 226, 257–58; Rumania (later called Standing Presidium), 290–94, 306, 317, 319–24; Soviet Union, 206. See also specific members

Politika, Belgrade newspaper, 133

Polycentrism, 2 ff., 132, 337

Popov, Ivan, 257

Popovic, Blagoje, 89

Popovic, Koca, 72, 160–61, 169

Popovic, Miladin, 183

Popovic, Milentije, 167

Popovic, Vladimir, 169

Population statistics, Albania, 199; Bulgaria, 34, 210, 213, 259; Rumania, 271, 275, 276, 278, 318, 339, 340, 341; Serbs, 34; Slavs, 34; Yugoslavia, 56, 106, 130, 141–42, 144, 157, 158, 159

Power plants and projects, 90, 141, 252, 344. See also specific plants, projects

Prague, 16, 366. See also Czechoslovakia

Pravda, 84, 192, 193, 222, 277, 314, 330

Praxis (Zagreb bimonthly), 8

Presidium (see also Politburo), Yugoslavia, 165, 166, 168

Preslav, 32; Golden Church, 32

Press, freedom of, 9. See also Censorship; Newspapers

Prices, 11; Bulgaria, 255, 259; Rumania, 346; Yugoslavia, 103–5, 112, 122, 135–36, 138

Printing plants, 144

Pristina, 68

Private enterprise (private entrepreneurship; private sector), 109–19, 131–39 passim, 259. See also Capitalism; Enterprise autonomy; specific aspects, countries

Prizren, 176; League of, 27, 176

Problems of Peace and Socialism, international Communist monthly, 257, 304, 310

Production (productivity), 90, 136–37, 138, 141–47 ff., 252, 254, 255, 256, 344, 345. See also Gross National Product; Industry (industrialization); National income, average

Protestants, 42

Protest literature, 7

Purges (see also specific individuals); in Albania, 190, 193, 196–97; in Bulgaria, 217–21, 222–23, 228–30, 231, 238–40; in Rumania, 280, 281, 282, 287–96 passim, 316, 323–24; in Yugoslavia, 15, 16, 52, 74–75, 80–81, 141, 160–64, 171

Rabotnichesko Delo, Bulgarian party organ, 217, 218

Radescu, Nicolae, 283–84
Radio Free Europe, 250
Radomir rebellion, 214
Railroads, 46, 141, 145, 155, 282; strikes (Rumania), 282
Rakosi, M., 192
Rakovsky, Christian, 280
Rankovic, Alexander, 71, 139, 151–56 passim, 158, 160–64; and collectivization, 80–81; fall of, 15, 16, 52, 141, 162–63, 167, 169, 171, 203; and Serbian hegemony, 15, 16, 60 154–56, 158, 167; and Tito, 15, 125, 151–52, 154–56, 169, 203
Rares, Petru, 267, 304
Red Army, 2, 12, 13, 79, 220 (see also World War II; specific individuals, places); and Czech invasion (1968), 362, 366; and Rumania, 277–78, 279, 282, 284, 290, 329, 342
Reform, The (Yugoslavia), 104–16, 125, 129, 133, 138, 140 ff., 159 ff., 160, 169–72
Regionalism, 355. See also specific aspects, individuals, places
Reichstag fire trial, 207, 217
Religion, 38–43. See also specific religions
Revisionism (revisionists), 5, 7–8, 14, 175, 197–98, 201–3, 210, 363–64. See also specific aspects, countries, individuals
Ribar, Lola, 72
Roman Catholic Church, 14, 29, 30, 39, 40–43
Roman empire (Rome and the Romans), 28, 29, 262–63
Rosen, Moses, 335
Rumania, 262–349; and Albania, 194, 198, 302, 304, 312, 313, 315, 327–28, 337, 338; army, 276–79, 329–30; and Bulgaria, 210, 223, 246, 250, 270, 271, 274, 275, 286, 311, 330, 332–33; and China, 295, 299, 301–9, 312–15, 326–28, 336; Constitution (1952), 339; and Czech invasion, 353, 362, 365–66; "Declaration of Independence," 209–10; economy, 1, 265, 270–72, 285–88, 295–300 ff., 338–39, 344–49; history, land, and people, 2–3, 6, 9–10, 17–19, 24, 25, 28–30, 35–49 passim, 58, 67, 80, 84, 262 ff., 343;

nationalism, 3, 9–10, 17, 40, 263 ff., 309–10, 339 ff., 351–60, 362, 363; and Soviet Union, 1–3, 6, 7, 11–12, 17, 22, 263–349 passim, 351–60, 362, 363, 365–66; and territorial disputes, 266 ff., 339–44
Russia. See Soviet Union
Russo-Turkish War (1877–78), 269
Ruthenia, 11

St. Vitus (Vidovdan), feast day of, 34
Sakazov, Yanko, 211
Salaries. See Wages (earnings; salaries)
Salonika, 27, 34
Samuel, Tsar of Bulgaria, 33, 34
San Stefano, Treaty of, 35–36, 209
Sarajevo, 158
Sartre, Jean-Paul, 8
Sasseno, 177
Sava River, 23–24, 25
Schools. See Education (schools)
Scinteia, Rumanian publication, 332, 365
Securitate (Rumanian secret police), 288, 307, 319, 324, 348
Sejko, Rear Admiral, 195
Serbia and the Serbs, and Albania, 175–76, 177–78; and Bulgaria, 212; and Croatia, 17, 24; economy, 111, 113, 114, 116, 141 ff., 150–72 passim; history, land, and people, 15, 16, 17, 24, 27, 29–47 passim; and Hungary, 17, 24; Patriarchate, 33–34; and Yugoslavia, 15, 16, 57–65, 66, 67, 77, 81, 121, 125, 140, 141, 150–72
Serbo-Croatian language, 30–31, 39, 187
Serfs (serfdom), 37, 39. See also Peasants (peasant class)
Seton-Watson, R. W., 263–65
Shapir (Israeli Finance Minister, 1967), 334–35
Shaw, George Bernard, 47
Shegalin (Soviet Ambassador to Rumania, 1964), 308
Shehu, Mehmet, 174, 189, 191–92, 193–95, 196, 327, 367
Shkodra, 28
Shkumbini River, 180
Shquiptai, 204
Sibenik, 146

Sigurimi (Albania security police), 200

Sik, Ota, 363

Simeon I, Tsar of Bulgaria, 33, 34, 35

Simic (Communist Party Secretary, Yugoslavia, 1964), 160

Simovic, General, 58

Sino-Soviet conflict, 2, 13, 22, 30, 152, 350; Albania and, 22, 194, 195–201, 205; Rumania and, 22, 194, 295, 298, 299, 301–9, 314, 326–28, 336, 338; Yugoslavia and, 152

Sixtus VI, Pope, 267

Skandenberg. See Kastrioti, George

Skendi, Stavro, 181

SKOJ (Young Communist League, Yugoslavia), 72

Skopje, 34, 36, 141–43, 247, 248

Slansky, Rudolf, 289

Slaveikov, Pencho, 240

Slavo-Macedonians, 17

Slavonia, 59, 60

Slavs, 29–31, 34, 39–43. See also South Slavs; specific countries, places

Slovakia and the Slovaks, 15–16, 366

Slovenia and the Slovenes, 14–16, 24–25, 29, 30, 40–46 passim, 60, 61, 65, 66, 71, 150–72 passim; Catholic People's Party, 42; economy, 102, 103, 114, 133, 135, 137, 143 ff.

Smederevo, 89

Social Democrats, Bulgaria, 219

Social Democrats, Rumania, 277, 280, 283, 284

Social Democrats, Yugoslavia, 49, 65–66

Socialist Alliance of Serbia, 140

Socialist Alliance of the Working People of Yugoslavia, 126, 141

Socialist market economy, 91

"Socialist patriotism," 241, 243, 261

Social Science Institute, Belgrade, 120–21

Sofia, 31, 36, 67, 75, 207–9, 214, 216, 226, 230, 234, 241, 259

Sombar, 116

South Slavs, 29, 57, 59, 60, 66, 144, 151, 355; federation, 36

Soviet-East European mixed companies, 11

Soviet Union, 1–22, 35–50 passim, 66–101 passim, 174–205 passim, 206–61 passim, 263–349 passim,

350–67 passim; and Balkan communism, economy, history (see specific aspects, countries, events, individuals); and Balkan nationalism, 1–22, 350–67 (see also specific aspects, countries, events, individuals); and China (see Sino-Soviet conflict); Russo-Turkish War (1877–78), 269; and United States, 19–20, 325, 328–29, 335–36, 357–60, 365 (see also Cold War)

Sovroms, 285–86

Spahiu, Bedru, 191, 192

Spain, civil war in, 70, 72, 191

Spiljak, Mike, 166

Spiru, Nako, 188–89

Split, 28, 153

Sporazum (The Agreement), 57

Stalin (Joseph) and Stalinism, and Albania, 189–90, 192; and Balkan nationalism, 11, 354 (see also specific aspects, countries, events, individuals); and Bulgaria, 6, 209, 218, 222, 223, 225–26, 228, 230, 232, 251; death of, 127; de-Stalinization campaigns, 6, 15, 218, 291, 293, 298, 315 (see also specific aspects, countries, individuals); indictment of, 2; and Rumania, 6, 278–79, 283–90 passim, 312; and Tito (see under Tito); and World War II, 44; and Yugoslavia, 4, 51, 70–71, 74–87 passim, 94, 96, 98, 101, 110, 127–29, 189–90, 193, 195

Stambolic, Petar, 153, 162, 168, 171 n

Stamboliski, Alexander, 212, 214, 215, 219

Stambolov, Stefan, 211

Standards of living. See Living standards

Stanovnik, Janez, 104

Starcevic, Ante, 59

State and Revolution (Lenin), 94

Steel production, 138, 145, 147, 252–53, 297–98, 344

Stefanov, Boris, 222, 281

Stefanovic, Svetislav, 160, 161–63

Stephen the Great, Prince of Moldavia, 7, 267

Stepinac, Archbishop, 41

Stoica, Chivu, 282, 311, 323, 324, 330; as Rumanian Premier and President, 290, 317, 321, 322; replaced as Premier, 292

Stone, Miss, 44
Strikes, 52, 89, 90, 134, 282
Strossmayer, Bishop, 40–41, 156
Suceava, 267
Suslov, Mikhail, 238, 304, 307
Svabic, Mihajlo, 141
Syria, 338

Talmon, J. L., 10
Tanjug, Yugoslav news agency, 326
Targu Jiu, 282, 283
Taxes (taxation), 105, 116, 144
"Technostructure," 134
Teheran Conference, 78
Teng Hsiao-p'ing, 315
Terpeshev, Dobri, 218, 219
Territorial disputes, 10, 11, 17–20 (see also Minorities; specific locations, people); Albania and, 17–18, 175–81, 190–91; Bulgaria and, 17–18, 209 ff.; Rumania and, 11, 17–18, 266 ff., 339–44; Soviet Union and, 11, 17; Yugoslavia and, 17–18
Third World, 125
Thrace, 25, 28, 36, 209, 210, 220, 248
Tirana, 180, 182, 186, 187, 189, 192, 193; Palace of Culture, 195; Treaty of, 181
Tirnovo, 33, 35, 37, 244; Constitution, 33, 211
Tirnovo Constitution, 33, 211
Tito (Josip Broz), 1, 8, 14, 15, 16, 68 ff., 149, 152–53, 154, 156, 161–69 passim; background and biography of, 68–75; and break with Soviet Union (World War II era), 76–81 ff.; and Bulgaria, 218, 222, 223, 226, 228, 246–47; and economy, 93, 114–15, 120, 139; and Partisans, 62, 63, 76 ff. (see also Partisans; Yugoslavia); and role of Communist Party in Yugoslavia, 120, 121, 124–25, 126, 132, 139; and Rumania, 1, 287, 311, 312, 313, 326, 363, 364; and Stalin (Stalinism), 4–5, 76, 94, 96, 98, 101, 110, 189–90, 193, 195, 287, 355
Titograd, 145
Titulescu, Nicolae, 272, 273, 274
Tobacco crops and marketing, 222, 250, 253, 355
Tocqueville, Alexis de, 118, 230
Todorov, Stanko, 229

Todorov-Gorunia, Ivan, 236–37
Todorovic, Mijalko, 124, 166
Togliatti, and polycentrism, 337
Tomovic, Rajko, 165
Tosks, 180, 181–82, 184, 191, 197
Tourism (tourists), 355; Albania and, 204; Bulgaria and, 241, 242, 248–49, 259; Rumania and, 341–42, 348–49; Yugoslavia and, 101, 106, 107, 115–16, 118, 146
Tractors, 113, 117
Trajan, Emperor, 28, 40, 263
Transnistria, 276
Transylvania, 17–18, 267, 270–76 passim, 284, 291, 366; Hungarian and Rumanian quarrel over, 24, 25, 28–29, 40, 270–76 passim, 278, 284, 291, 339–43, 366
Travel, freedom of, 8–9, 118, 341–42, 348. See also Tourism (tourists)
Trianon, Treaty of, 271
Trieste, 82
Tripalo, Mika, 14, 140–41, 157
Tripartite Pact (Germany, Italy, and Japan), 57–58
Trofin, V., 377
Trotsky, Leon, 76, 213
Trucks, 112, 113, 251
Tsankov, Georgi, 229
Turgu Neamt, 344
Turkey and the Turks, 17, 24–46 passim, 50, 58, 63, 354–55; and Albania, 5, 175, 176–77, 197; and Balkan history, 17, 24–46 passim, 50, 58, 63; and Bulgaria, 35, 37, 209, 211, 212, 223, 245–46, 251, 354–55; and Rumania, 37–38, 265–73 passim, 354–55; and Yugoslavia, 58, 63, 354–55

UDBA (Yugoslavia secret police), 81, 85, 86, 125, 135, 151, 155–64, 169, 203
Ukraine, 1, 275, 311
Ulbricht, Walter, 13, 299, 303
Ulcinj, 176
UN. See United Nations
Unemployment (employment), 52, 105–7, 109, 116, 135, 213
UNESCO, 240
Uniate Church (Rumania), 40, 42
Union Bank of Belgrade, 89
United Nations, 312, 334, 363; UNESCO, 240; UNRRA, 188

United States, 2–3, 44–45, 325, 328–29, 336; and Albania, 178; and Balkan nationalism, 2–3, 19–20, 357–60 (*see also* specific Balkan countries); and Bulgaria, 218, 221, 223, 231, 241, 242, 250; and Rumania, 325, 328–29, 335–36; and Soviet Union, 19–20, 325, 328–29, 335–36, 357–60, 365 (*see also* Cold War); State Department, 2, 20; Voice of America, 242, 250; and Yugoslavia, 52, 54, 77, 87, 101, 358

United VMRO, 68
UNRRA, 188
Uravnilovka, 136–37
Urbanization, 102, 105–6
Usbek, 1
Ushakov (Soviet historian), 277
Ustashe, 41, 45, 59–62, 65, 68

Valenje, 147
Valev, E. B., 310–11
Vallona (Vlora), 177, 196
Vardar River, 27; Valley, 34
Varna, 32, 242, 253
Velchev, Damyan, 215, 219–20, 229
Venice, 30
Verdetz, Ilie, 321, 323, 378
Versailles peace conference, 177–78
Veselinov, Jovan, 162, 168
Veterans' Federation, Yugoslavia, 134, 135
Veteran's League, Yugoslavia, 73
Viata Economica, Bucharest weekly, 311
Vidakovic, Bosko, 160
Vienna, 181. See *also* Austria
Vienna Award, 275–76, 277, 278
Vietnam. See North Vietnam
Visas, 118
Vjesnik u Srijedu (Zagreb newspaper), 117, 130, 146
Vlachs (Wallachs), 28, 29, 33, 35
Vladimirescu, Tudor, 265–66
Vlahov, Dimitri, 68
Vlahovic, Veljko, 166, 167, 169
Vlora (Vallona), 177, 196
VMRO (Internal Macedonian Revolutionary Organization), 36, 68, 212
Vodnik, Valentin, 40
Voice of America, 242, 250
Vojvodina, 18, 59, 60, 61, 158

Voronet, monastery, 267–68
Vrachev, Ivan, 239
Vratsa, 216, 236, 239
Vukmanovic-Tempo, S., 72, 168, 169, 184
Vukovar Congress (1920), 66
Vutov, Petar, 207
Vyshinsky, Andrei, 283–84

Wages (earnings; salaries), Albania, 200, 201; Bulgaria, 254–55, 260; Yugoslavia, 89, 97, 103–5, 107, 112, 116–17, 119, 122, 134, 135–57
Wallachia, 37, 40, 266–67, 341
Wallachs (Vlachs), 28, 29, 33, 35
Warsaw, 8. See *also* Poland
Warsaw Pact Treaty, 22, 174, 195, 362, 363, 365, 366–67; Albania and, 366–67; Bucharest Declaration (1966), 331–32; Dresden meeting, 339; Political Consultative Committee, 325, 338; Rumania and, 299, 315, 325–34, 336, 339, 366; Supreme United Command, 329–30
West Germany (German Federal Republic), 11, 246, 249, 251, 325, 331–34
Wheat, 195, 254
Wied, Wilhelm zu, Prince, 177
Wilson, Woodrow, 178
Wolfe, Bertram D., 74
Workers' Councils, Yugoslavia, 55, 89, 90, 93, 94, 96–100, 122, 132, 134, 139
Workers' and Peasants' Bloc, Rumania, 281
World Bank, 115, 359
World War I, 17, 39, 44, 46, 177–78, 209, 210, 214, 270–71. See *also* specific countries, individuals, locations
World War II, 17, 21, 39, 44–50, 57–65 (*see also* Partisans; specific aspects, individuals, locations, participants); Albania and, 49–50, 182–86; Bosnia and, 39; Bulgaria and, 209, 210, 220–21; Rumania and, 49, 270–71, 274–79; and territorial disputes (*see* specific disputants, locations); Yugoslavia and, 45, 49–50, 57–65, 72–73, 76–80, 182, 183–84, 186

Writers. *See* Literature (writers)
Writers' Union, 240

Xenopol, A. D., 28, 318
Xoxe, Koci, 183, 187, 188–90, 191, 192

Yalta Conference, 80, 283
Youth (students; young people), 7, 233, 242–43
Ypsilanti (Greek rebel leader), 266
Yugoslav (South Slav) Academy of Science and Art, 40–41
Yugoslavia, 51–172 (*see also* Tito; specific republics); and Albania, 177, 178, 179, 181, 182, 183 ff., 197 ff., 202–4, 367; army, 15, 73, 85, 161–63, 168, 169, 172 (*see also* Partisans; Yugoslavia); and Bulgaria, 210, 212, 220–28 *passim*, 236, 246–49, 256; centralization (and decentralization) in, 5, 51, 55, 66, 88, 92–100, 108–72 *passim*; Communism (Communist Party) in, 5, 8, 14–15, 16, 21, 54, 66–75 ff., 91 ff., 119–72 *passim*; economy, 51–55, 75, 81 ff., 89–119, 120–39 ff.; "41 Club," 57–65, 73; history, land, and people, 14, 17–18, 23–24, 25, 27, 30–32, 37, 39–50 *passim*, 56 ff., 150 ff. (*see also* specific locations, people); leadership, 55, 57–65, 73, 88 (*see also* specific individuals); and nationalism, 9–10, 14, 17–18, 51, 59–65 ff., 76 ff., 140 ff., 151–72 *passim*, 351–64 *passim;* Partisans (*see* Partisans, Yugoslavia); and revisionism, 8, 9; Rumania and, 272–73, 312, 313, 326, 332–33, 336, 342, 353, 362–63; and Soviet Union, 1, 2, 4–5, 8, 12, 21, 52, 66–75, 76 ff., 100, 101, 120, 145, 152, 168, 351–66 *passim;* and World War II, 45, 49–50, 57–65, 72–73, 76–80, 182, 183–84, 186
Yugoslav Investment Bank, 146
Yugoslavism, 57, 59, 60
Yugov, Anton, 218–19, 225, 227, 228–29

Zagreb, 16, 39, 40–41, 57, 59, 60, 69, 72, 89, 105, 140, 146, 147, 157
Zemun, 23–24
Zhdanov, A., 82, 83
Zhikov, Todor, 206, 207, 209, 224, 226–39 *passim*, 243, 245–46, 247, 250, 255–58; described, 235
"Zhikov theses," 226–27
Zog I, King of Albania (and Zogists), 49, 178, 180–81, 184, 185
Zogu, Bey Ahmed. *See* Zog I, King of Albania (and Zogists)
Zujovic, Sreten, 81
Zveno group, 219–20

CZECHOSLOVAKIA

AUSTRIA

DANUBE RIVER

Vienna

Budapest

DATE DUE

Ljubljana

SLOVENIA Zagreb

ISTRIA

CROATIA

Y U G O S L A V I A

VOJVODINA

S E R B I A

Belgrade

BOSNIA &
HERZEGOVINA

DALMATIA

Sarajevo

MONTENEGRO

Titograd

KOSOVO-
METOHIJA
(Kosmet)

Adriatic Sea

ITALY

ALBANIA

Skopj

MACEDON

Tirana

G R